TEAM PLAYER

A Sports Romance Anthology

ADRIANA LOCKE CHARLEIGH ROSE ELLA FOX
EMMA SCOTT KATE STEWART KENNEDY RYAN
L.J. SHEN MANDI BECK MEGHAN QUINN
ROCHELLE PAIGE SARA NEY

Welcome to the team!

Hot jocks. We love them all.

Sexy baseball players. Intense footballers. Sweaty MMA fighters, and sizzling hockey hotties. Score!'

The good news? Eleven bestselling authors have gathered to give you a set of stories focused on the men we love most—sports heroes. We bet you'll love this thick ... book.

The bad news? The men in these novellas don't actually exist.

*This anthology does not contain calories, just eleven original, never-before-seen stories by the following authors: Adriana Locke, Mandi Beck, Charleigh Rose, Kennedy Ryan, LJ Shen, Meghan Quinn, Rochelle Paige, Ella Fox, Kate Stewart, Emma Scott, and Sara Ney. We aren't responsible for melted devices.

SIN BIN

#7 will take you to heaven!
Mandi Beck

To Ran, you're always my loudest, rowdiest, most supportive fan. I love you.

"You miss one-hundred percent of the shots you never take—"
Wayne Gretzky

Prologue

JASON

IT TOOK ALL OF A MINUTE FOR ME TO KNOW, WITHOUT A DOUBT, THAT I was going to have Stella Cruz naked and screaming my name in the near future. I didn't care that she was a student. No, that's a lie. I cared. I just didn't let it stop me. There was something about her that called to me on a level I wasn't used to. And that was without her saying a word. I felt the pull as she silently watched me from across the Treatment room.

Those dark eyes following as Levi and I moved around the space. At first, I thought she was watching him, but nah, Stella Cruz isn't interested in what Levi is offering to every girl on campus. The way her gaze traveled over me when she thought I wasn't looking tells me she's wicked interested in what I might be able to offer her. I can guarantee it's more than any of these pricks at FU can give her. I've got ten years on these guys. That's a whole lot of pussy. I've learned a lot along the way and have done things with, and to, women that would make a frat boy blush.

The thought of what it might take to make *her* blush makes me hard. Right now as she sits there in her sports bra and spandex, legs swinging, her skin the color of coffee with the perfect amount of cream. I can't wait to see what color that pretty skin turns when I have her underneath me. Just please let her fine ass be legal, because if she is, I'm going to show her that I can score *off* the ice as well as I can on it.

Chapter One

STELLA

THIS PITCHING CLINIC IS TURNING MY ARM TO JELL-O. I WALK INTO THE therapy room in my sports bra and yoga pants and head over to the table, hopping up to wait for the team's doctor. As I wait, I roll my shoulder. It's tender but nothing major. I'm going into my Senior year, gotta make it last just one more season.

The noise around me increases into excited chatter. This is a common space for the Fulton University athletes. With only one area for all of us, whether we need just a soak in an ice bath, a stretch, or more extensive therapy, this is the place for everyone. Being coed, the things that go on in this one area of the Athletic Department are legit insanity. I've seen break ups and makeups, hook ups and fights. All you have to do is wait and you won't be disappointed.

Like right now. Levi Sexton, the captain of the hockey team, is walking through with who I'm guessing is not a student from here or anywhere else the way the guys are acting. The other girls in the room must have picked up on it because there is way too much hair fluffing and tata readjusting going on right now for him to just be another student. He's hot. That's no lie, but I have no time for anything more than a hook up and that isn't gonna happen. I'm on track to graduate early and ain't no man alive worth messing with that. I've got plans and they don't include this guy or anyone else.

Before I can talk myself out of my vow of celibacy the department's doctor comes over.

"Stella, how's the arm?" He's straightforward. Literally, the worst bedside manner of any doctor on the planet, but he's good and that's all that matters. After my shoulder injury Sophomore year, I'm careful and do exactly what he tells me to.

"Good, Dr. Grayson. Little sore, but I'm training hard."

He just nods, makes some notes in the chart, ignoring the noise around him. "Let's get it rubbed out and iced."

"Sounds good. "

"I'll see who has time. Sit tight, one of the therapists will be right over."

I thank him but he's already moving on to go get one of the three physical therapists always on. "Nice to see you again, Dr. Grayson." I mumble.

I'm just about to pop my earbuds in when Levi and his friend come back out of the weight room. I don't even have to look, I can tell by the shift in the air. I'm probably the only girl on the softball team that hasn't hooked up with Levi. Hell maybe on campus. They don't call him "Sexy" Sexton for nothing.

I watch in appreciation as the two men make their way toward me. His friend is wearing a Chicago hockey hat, I recognize it as the same one Levi wears all the time, his jeans and Henley might as well be a suit in this room. It's kind of nice to see a guy in something other than sweats, not that that's not hot as hell. This is just a different hot. Adult hot. The way is mouth is set, I can't tell if he's a pissed or in pain. Levi catches me watching them and winks. All I can do is shrug. I have no shame. That man just got the eye fucking of his life and he doesn't even know it.

When they don't stop until they're next to me, I can feel my pulse start to race. Damn it. I'm not the kind of girl who gets a racing heart over a guy.

"Hey Cruz. How've you been? I haven't seen you around much."

"Sexy." I greet. After catching me checking out his friend, I do my best to ignore his knowing smirk. "I've been taking a few extra classes. Not much time for anything other than studying and ball."

I can feel the warmth of his friends gaze roaming over my not nearly covered enough body without even seeing him do it. I'm not sure if I'm brave enough to look at him, the way my body is reacting to his nearness. He makes the decision for me when he clears his throat.

"Oh, my bad. Stella Cruz, this is Jason Dagger. Jason, Stella. She's the Fire's starting pitcher. Chick's a beast." Levi says, his voice dropped to an exaggerated octave, making me laugh.

Jason offers his hand. The rational side of my brain is screaming for me to not touch him, while the rest of me is urging me to touch all of him. Or let him touch all of me. Slowly I slip my hand into his and will myself not to close my eyes at the contact. There's something about this man that has me acting a fool. He oozes confidence in a way that's just as cocky as Levi, but more controlled. I feel a little zing of excitement rip through me. Damn.

"Stella." I detect the hint of Boston in his tone. "Nice to meet you."

"Jason."

When I take the hand he offers, he smiles at me with what looks like expectation, but I'm not sure what he's expecting. My brow raised in question, I wait for him to enlighten me. When he doesn't, I drop his hand. He looks a little surprised when I pull my hand from his.

My guess is he's not used to women *not* throwing themselves at him. I can't blame them. I kinda want to throw myself at him. But it has nothing to do with who he may be, because I honestly don't know, and everything to do with how he looks, the way he carries himself and the reaction my body is having to him. Like someone flipped a switch on my girl bits. They're all lit up for Jason Dagger.

"Shoulder acting up again?" Levi asks, allowing me to swing my attention his way.

"Little bit. Nothing a little massage won't fix. This is my last year on the mound, I'll survive until graduation."

Out of the corner of my eye I see Jason smile, if you can call it that, at something I said. Curious, I look over at him but that hint of a smirk is already gone and he has that pissed off in pain look again. Maybe he is in pain.

Doing some digging I ask Levi, "What are you guys doing down here?"

"We had to come down and talk to Coach Kiehn about some ice time. Figured we'd hit the weights a little too." Levi says, glancing around the room, probably looking for whatever chick he's gonna let come back to his place with him. The guy gets more ass than a subway seat. It's incredible really. "You going to the award dinner tonight?"

"Yep. Your dad will have my ass if I'm not there." Levi's dad is my coach and the man doesn't play when it comes to his team and his rules.

"Be right back you guys. I gotta go see a chick about...something." Levi laughs when I roll my eyes at his lame ass attempt to hide the fact he's penciling in a hook up. I don't even think he heard what I said.

"Is Charlie still a PT here?" Jason asks the moment Levi walks away, startling me.

"He is."

"Have him rub you down. He's the best."

"Oh, you went to school here?"

"It's been awhile, but yeah."

"So, are you a coach now or what?" I ask, curious. I half expect him not to answer.

"Not a hockey fan, huh?" A sexy smirk slides over his full lips.

"Nope. I mean I like hockey, try to go to as many FU games as I can."

"How about NHL games?" His stance widens like he's getting comfortable, settling in for a chat.

"I've been to a few. My brother is a Bruins fan."

"Your brother has okay taste. How does he feel about Chicago?"

"About the same as most people who aren't them do."

A quiet laugh fills the space between us, "Can't even argue with that."

I can't help but smile at his amusement. "So, I take it you're a Chicago fan?" I feel like I'm missing something. Before I can ask any more questions, Charlie the therapist with the magic hands comes over.

"Dagger, that you? How you been man?"

The two shake hands and do that man hug thing. "Can't complain, Charlie."

"Sure can't. I saw that game the other night. I had my money on you boys to win the Cup this season. Bought me a new TV with the money I won." Charlie beams like a proud uncle and finally all the pieces fall into place.

Jason Dagger plays for the NHL and here I was worried that I would have to shut him down. I'm a college student and he just won the Stanley Cup. Hell would freeze over before we hooked up.

Chapter Two

JASON

"You're a brave man betting on Chicago around here, man."

"I kept it on the down low, don't worry." Charlie winks at me then turns to Stella.

She's leaned back, her palms flat on the table behind her, tits high and round, stomach taut. Her legs are so long they seem to go on forever. The thought of offering to be the one to rub her down swirling around in my mind.

"Doc Grayson said you need that shoulder worked on. You pushing it? I told you not to push it." He scolds as he rubs his hands together to warm them.

"Same ol' ballbuster, I see." I chuckle.

"He's always yelling at my ass." Stella says as she grimaces at his prodding of her shoulder.

"Well, try listening." Charlie responds. I can tell he has a soft spot for her.

I'm not sure why I'm still standing here, watching him massage her neck and shoulder while her head lolls to the side, a look of pleasure-pain creasing her forehead and softening the features of her face. Now that I know that she is in fact legal, I don't feel nearly as bad about checking her out and envisioning her spread out on my bed.

"What are you doing in town?" Charlie breaks into my less than pure thoughts.

My eyes meet Stella's to find her watching me watch her. A look of hunger in her eyes. Fuck me. I cannot be messing around with some twenty- year-old college kid. I know I said I didn't care but fuck. She keeps looking at me like that though and it will be hard to say no.

"I'm here to check in on Levi and to give out an award at the dinner tonight." I answer, gaze still locked with Stella's.

"He's a good kid. Bit of a player, but then again so were you. And look how well you turned out." Charlie says, laughing.

He pushes Stella so that she's laying flat on her stomach. Her ass might as well have a bullseye on it, my attention is drawn to it immediately. I fuck around with some of the hottest chicks out there. Models, cross fit addicts, yoga instructors, the list goes on and on but not a single one of them come close to Stella's smokin' body. When she lets out a moan I know I have to get the fuck out of there.

"Charlie, it was good seeing you, man. Stella, I'll see you tonight." It sounded just like the promise it is.

OVER THE RIM of my glass I watch Stella as she laughs at something one of her teammates says. Not a single one of them has drawn my attention away from her. And they've tried.

Her hair is straight now instead of in the waves earlier. She's traded in her sports bra and spandex for a sheer red dress. Just like the spandex, it clings to every single one of her long lines, dips and curves, her toned thighs bared by the short skirt. Watching her and waiting for this thing to wrap up might kill me. The only plus about this long ass banquet is that it's giving me time to figure out how I'mgoing to convince Stella that we should be fucking.

Sooner rather than later. I haven't been able to think of much else after leaving her face down, ass up in the treatment room. Not something I'm used to. I don't think about women. I think about hockey.

I fuck women and then they leave. That's how I like it. But somehow, in a matter of seconds, Stella got under my skin. Maybe it's because she doesn't give a shit about who I am. Even after she found out I was a pro athlete. I'm not sure when that started to matter but her not caring and treating me any differently made me want to reward her. With my cock.

They're just about to start handing out the rest of the awards when I feel someone's gaze on me. I glance around, and lock eyes with Stella. Her smile is slow and sexy and screaming "fuck me" and I want nothing more. I tip my head toward the door as discreetly as I can and watch to see if she bites. After watching her all damn night I'm ready.

I'm hoping it won't take me too long to get her naked because I have no patience for a game of cat and mouse tonight. I want to be balls deep in Fulton University's star pitcher regardless that she's ten years younger than me or because of it. I'm just hoping that she's game. I can't remember a time I was ever shot down, I don't want today to be the first.

"Excuse me." I say to the table as I stand to leave. I've already done my part tonight so they won't miss me.

I glance over again at Stella's table, she's still talking to her friends even as she watches me leave the dining room. Making my way through the room, I keep my interactions brief and I'm grateful when one of the coaches takes the podium making talking impossible. Once out the double doors, I lean against the wall in a darkened corner and wait to see if Stella follows.

I unwrap a piece of gum and watch the doors, it only takes about a minute before she's sliding through them. Slowly she walks my way, her long legs eating up the space between us. As soon as she reaches me I take her hand and lead her further down the hall away from prying eyes. Spinning her so she's against the wall, I lean into her. In her heels she's only slightly shorter than I am. Knowing that she's not this little delicate flower is so sexy. "You know why I called you out here right, Stella?" I whisper in her ear, loving the smell of her skin and hair, the heat of her body where it presses against mine like an inferno.

"I hope so."

It's music to my fucking ears. I'm no stranger to one night stands. This feels quick even for me but I can't stop it. Don't want to. Won't stop unless she says to. With that in mind and her hand in mine, I start walking and don't stop until we hit the side door to the arena.

"You taking me ice skating? Gotta be honest, that's not what I thought you had in mind." She teases.

"I'm taking you, but not skating." I wink at her over my shoulder.

"Are we supposed to be in here?" Her voice is dropped to a whisper once we enter the cold, dark rink.

"Coach gave me keys so that I could have ice time whenever I needed it."

"And you need ice time now?" Stella asks confused.

For a change it's not ice I need. It's this girl and it's fucking with my head because I'm not sure exactly why. Leading her through the arena, the only lights coming from the exit signs and the glare of them off the ice, her soft hand tucked in mine, her other wrapped around my bicep as we pick our way between the aisles.

"I need...something." Why did I bring her here? Is my plan to bend her over the boards? I didn't think about it, I just went where I knew we weren't going to be interrupted. Not sure if she has roommates and not wanting to drive all the way to my place, I brought her to my most favorite place on campus.

"I've never been in here when there wasn't a game or something going on. It seems so...naughty." Her voice is still pitched low like someone might overhear her, even the giggle that slips out into the quiet around us.

"You trying to get me to put you in the Sin Bin, baby?"

"What's a Sin Bin? Is that where they put you when you're being bad? The penalty box?"

"Wanna find out?" If I remember correctly, there's a bench in the penalty box here. A bench I'm going to decorate with her lithe body, long hair and that pretty red dress. With Stella snug against my back, I step onto the visitor's bench and then turn to help her over, catching a flash of red panties in the process. Unable to stop myself, I palm her ass and pull her into me. I've been controlled this whole time but the sight of those sheer panties, the same sheer material as her dress sleeves and the bare pussy underneath them and I'm done for.

Stella looks up at me from under a hooded gaze and the heat in those inky eyes is all the invitation I need. My lips cover hers, my tongue demanding entrance as I fill my hands with her ass, fingers gliding underneath her skirt and along the crease where her long legs meet her cheeks.

I'm certain the goose bumps covering her flesh has nothing to do with the temperature in here and everything to do with my hands on her. I'm thrilled to fuck that I'm not the only one feeling this...whatever it is. Moving us onto the ice, I bring her flush against me to keep her steady and then maneuver us into the penalty box. I'd fuck her right on the ice if thought I could manage it in dress shoes. In skates it wouldn't be a problem. But since I'm not taking the time to lace up, the Sin Bin would do.

As soon as we get in the box, I close the door and lean back against it. Stella follows, allowing no room between us as she meets my tongue thrust for thrust, nipping at my lip and pulling a growl from low in my throat. I know I should slow this down, but I'm almost desperate to be inside her. When she grips my cock through my dress pants, I know that she wants it as badly as I do. Which does nothing to convince me to dial it down a notch.

Hating to let go of her, I do just long enough to drag her dress up around her waist. I need to feel her, get at what she's hiding underneath the tiny red scrap of material that's been driving me crazy all night. When my hands slide over the soft skin I grab a handful, digging my fingers into the plump flesh. She melts into me with a sigh on her lips.

"I'm not sure what you did to me, Stella. But all I've been able to think about since the moment I saw you is fucking you. You put some kind of spell on me. Had to because I don't need anyone. I need to fuck you. I know I shouldn't. Know better, just don't fucking care."

With a smile against my lips, she starts unbuttoning my dress shirt. "I feel it too. I'm about to break a six- month vow of celibacy because you looked my way. Don't make me regret it, Dagger."

I can't wait to get her sassy mouth wrapped around my cock. I shuffle forward, forcing her back until the backs of her legs hit the bench. Stella sits and looks up at me questioningly, hungrily. Slowly, I work my belt free, my eyes on her as she watches my hands. Slipping the button through the hole, the hiss of the zipper loud in the quiet in the arena.

With one hand, I reach into my boxer briefs and pull out my cock, the other hand tangled in her hair. Stella raises her eyes to hold mine as I paint her lips with the tip of my cock, the precum that had gathered leaving a glistening trail on her plump, plum colored mouth, her pink tongue following the path I've left behind, chasing after my length.

Gently, I squeeze her face between my thumb and index finger until she opens, allowing me to slip past her lips and into the wet warmth of her mouth.

Not stopping until I hit the back of her throat before pulling out and doing it again, all the while her gaze never leaves mine.

"Not so sassy now, huh, Stella?" I grit out as I press further into her mouth.

When she swallows around me, a low moan working up her throat to vibrate against my over sensitized head, I think I may have spoken to soon. My head falls back on my shoulders as the sensations of her hot tongue, flicking over my cock as the cold air from the arena cools my skin with every slide of her lips. If they're teaching students how to give stellar blow jobs at FU, Stella is earning herself several fucking degrees in it. Not wanting to miss watching her I shake off the fog just as she palms my balls, stroking and tugging as she lets my cock choke her.

Fingers shaking slightly, I slide them into the neckline of her dress, working it down and under her tits, bared to me, berry colored nipples hardened and pointing at as if they're begging for my attention. When I pinch one nipple, then the other, she slows over my cock, a little shiver sliding up her spine.

"You like that, Stell?" I murmur doing it again as I step even closer, straddling her on the bench, my knees bracketing her hips.

She releases my cock with a pop, her lips wet and shining in the dim light. "Not yet, Stella. This mouth is too perfect." I tell her as I press her head down on me until I'm sheathed in her warmth again, holding her there when her lips are at my base. "Fucking, fuck." I hiss as I slide back out. I've had a lot of head in my life. A lot of fucking head. But this girl and her mouth are fucking magic.

Her pussy is going to be the death of me, I know it. My hands cupping her tits, I bring them together around my length watching as she swipes a tongue over the head of my cock as it slides through the satiny soft valley. Every pass over my cock causes her to lick over the rounded tops of her tits, making me impossibly harder. Painfully so.

Knowing I'm not going to last much longer if I let her keep this up, a thread of control holding it all together, I pull out of her grasp and yank my arms out of my shirt before pulling her to her feet and taking her seat on the bench. Feet planted wide, I hand her the condom and watch as she rolls it over me.

"So hard." Stella says reverently. "I'm going to feel it tomorrow." She grins at me, a sexy, wicked, smile that screams "fuck me."

"You're gonna feel it right now. Tomorrow. Next fucking week if I have my way." I growl, yanking her closer and shoving her dress up further so it sits around her waist. Her scent wraps around me. Citrus, Stella and arousal, that good pussy smell. The kind that you want to wear all over you. A reminder of how it got on you.

"You like these?" I ask softly, running my fingers over her panties, tiny strings and rhinestones holding them together. She wore these with fucking in mind. She nods that she does. Pulling them up, I watch transfixed as they wedge into her slit, her lips hugging around the red material. "Mmmmm. Stella. Your pussy is so fucking pretty. You ever see a pretty pussy before?" I ask, not taking my eyes from her center. Just plucking the now wet panties from her and pulling them back up, rubbing them back and forth through her slickness and over her clit. Her legs tremble, her hips arching toward me, pointing at me in a silent plea.

Since she likes these, I force myself not to rip the delicate fabric as I slide them down her legs, stuffing them in my pocket when she steps out of the damp scrap of red lace.

"Have you?" I ask again. "Because I have and this may be the prettiest pussy I've ever seen."

That's no lie. Completely smooth but for one thin strip that I trace with the back of my index finger before sliding it into her, slowly adding another before lowering my head to nip at her clit. Stella's hands fly to my head, clutching at the long strands of my hair, gasping in pleasure. Careful not to let her lose her balance I tug at her leg, placing her heeled foot on the bench next to me, opening her up and allowing me a better view and easier access.

"So pretty." I murmur taking my time to appreciate the sight before me, watching as my fingers slide in and out of her, disappearing into the vice-like tightness of her pussy.

"Jason," escapes from her lips.

My name sounds good all breathy like that. Twisting my fingers and watching as the pleasure takes over her features, my breathing starts coming faster, same as hers. Just when I can feel her tightening and pulsing around my fingers, her grasp on me becoming almost painful, I pull my fingers from her and hook her around the waist so she's straddling me.

No longer able to wait, I push into her slowly giving her time to adjust to my size. Stella said she hasn't fucked anyone in months, I don't want to hurt her so that she's too sore for when I take her back to my place. Once she's settled on my lap, long legs dangling behind me, soft tits crushed to the hard planes of my chest, my cock nestled inside of her to the hilt I grip her nape, tangling my fingers in the hair there and tug.

Back arched, her nipples look like perfectly ripened blackberries. My mouth falls to her neck, biting and licking at her throat and that spot that runs to her shoulder, making her shudder as I rock into her in a steady rhythm. Not getting the traction I need, I swivel us so that I'm the one straddling the bench and lay her flat. Her hands go over her head to grip the sides of the wooden seat, stretching her out in front of me like a sacrifice. Still inside her, I grab her hips and thrust, rocking the entire bench with the force.

Her eyes flutter closed, her mouth falls open. I do it again. Every thrust has me hitting bottom. Stella's tits bounce with every one of those thrusts. Sighs and moans echoing around us in the enormous arena, it's all too much and not nearly e-fucking-nough.

The slight tremble I can feel in her legs draped over my thighs is nearly my undoing. Bending at the waist, I catch her mouth, my tongue dancing against hers as I slide in and out of her. Each time pulling out farther than the last time and driving harder. She stops kissing me to pant words incoherently into my mouth. I stop moving to lavish attention on her tits, taking each pebbled nipple into my mouth and suck until she's squirming against my cock, driving me out of my mind.

"Fuck my pretty pussy. Beat it up so you can kiss it better." Stella moans as she rolls her hips in a figure eight, chasing the orgasm she's so close to.

"I'll kiss it better. I promise." And I will. Right after I tear it up. Gripping the bench just above her head, I drive punishingly into the tightest pussy I've ever had wrapped around me until I see stars and I hear the roar of my blood in my ears mingled with Stella screaming my name loud enough to be heard on the other side of campus.

As our breathing evens out, Stella's head tucked into my neck, I shake my head. She definitely put a spell on me. Still inside her and already I'm thinking of what I want to do to her once I get her into a bed.

"I know I should know better and that this shouldn't have happened, but I don't even care right now. All I know is once won't be enough." I lean back to look down at her. Dark hair draped over my arms, her eyes pools of ink, lit with satisfaction wearing nothing but a smug, content smile. She's fucking stunning. I'm hardening even as I'm still inside her.

"What are you doing this weekend, Stella?

"You." She answers soft and sure.

"Good answer."

Chapter Three

JASON

Six months later...

My leg bounces as the plane bumps across the tarmac in a rough landing. I'm on edge and this flight didn't help in the least. It's good to be home even if I have shit to do while I'm here. Back to check in on the team's golden boy, being on top of the list. Since I'm the assistant captain and what they call a veteran player, I've been playing with Chicago for ten years now, it's part of my job to also mentor one of our incoming new guys.

Every year I have at minimum, one draft pick out of Fulton University to babysit since it's where I went and Boston is my hometown. At least it allows me to come home a couple times a year to see the family. This trip is perfect with Christmas being in a few days. Two birds, one stone. Then get back to Chi-town and back on the ice.

The flight attendant comes over the PA and announces that we've arrived in Boston and that the temperature is a chilly twenty degrees. Fuck. It's not any warmer here than it was in Chicago. I really need to think about splitting my time between Chicago and someplace tropical. There's only so much cold a man can take, even if I do live my life on the ice.

I unbuckle and stand, careful not to bump my head on the bins. As I wait for them to let us off, I catch the pretty attendant giving me one last look over. She spent the entire flight catering to my every need. If I wasn't so sore from last night's game I might have let her cater to another *need* of mine. Maybe. Probably not though. She's not my type.

Hell, lately nobody is. Still, a slow grin steals across my face as I make my way past her and she discretely brushes her chest against my arm slipping something into the palm of my hand. I'm guessing it's her number. Not slowing to check, I shove the scrap of paper in the pocket of my jeans until I can toss it. I'm not here for that. Normally, I would be all over that but not this trip.

My sister offered to pick me up from the airport but I turned her down insisting on taking a cab to my place. I needed the down time to relax before being surrounded by the whole family. There would be plenty of time for that in the coming week. It's the longest break I've had mid- season. The NHL doesn't stop for the holidays typically. By some freakish stroke of luck, our team has a seven-day blackout while they do some work on our stadium and practice facility. That it came at Christmas time is truly a miracle. This will be the first Christmas that I've been home in the ten years I've played in the NHL, unless we were in town playing Boston.

Bypassing luggage, one nice thing about maintaining a house here, and heading straight for the curb and the lineup of taxis, I pull my beanie out of my back pocket and pull it low on my forehead doing my best not to make eye contact with anyone. It's not the norm for me to be recognized, but hockey is a big deal here in Boston and this is my hometown. So it has been known to happen from time to time.

I'm almost in the clear when the guy putting people in cabs recognizes me and asks for my autograph which then draws the attention of other people, most of whom probably still don't know who I am, but don't want to miss out on the possibility of meeting someone who may or may not be famous. For ten minutes in the freezing ass cold, I smile and sign autographs.

The only one I didn't mind was a kid, Jake, about ten or so, who came over reciting stats and telling me he's going to play for FU when he's older just like I did. Him I liked and made sure to take extra time with, even getting an email address from his mom so I could send him some stuff. He reminded me of myself when I was that age. With a two finger wave, I climb into the waiting cab and give him my address and we head out to the harbor and home.

We pull up in front of my building on Commercial Wharf and I can't help but smile. I love Chicago, but this is home. After paying the cabbie, I slide out of the backseat, the crisp winter air swirls around bringing with it the smell of the harbor.

"Hey, hey, hey! It's the man with the plan. Welcome home!" The doorman, old enough to be my grandfather, greets.

"What does that even mean, Harry?" I chuckle, taking the hand he holds out for a firm shake.

"You know, the plan." The old guy is looking at me with an expectant look, waiting for me to get it.

"Whatever you say, old man. You'll send my mail up?"

"You got it, kid. You need anything else? You got food up there?" Harry is more than the doorman here. He's a little bit of everything. Concierge, locksmith, handyman. Hell, I've even had him go on a beer run a time or two.

"Nah, should be good. Thank you, sir." I give him a mock salute and walk into the lobby and out of the cold. As I wait for the elevator, my phone buzzes in my pocket. I pull it out and grin, "Hey, ma."

"You home, sweetie?"

"Yeah, just got here. I need a shower and a nap, maybe a massage before I head your way though."

"It was a rough game last night, huh? That Slejek kid hit you hard."

I can't help but chuckle. The "Slejek kid" is a six foot four goon. My ma has always been my biggest fan and the one to drag my ass all over the damn country to freeze her ass of in one rink or another. "Yeah he did. Few times."

"I saw. Dad wasn't real happy about it. Said he always was a dirty player."

The elevator opens on my floor as I listen to her go on.

"It happens. I gave it back to him though."

"You sure did, sweetie." She says, pride in her voice. Only a true hockey mom would be proud of her son for knocking a player on his ass.

"Okay, ma. I'll be by in a couple hours. I promise."

"We'll be here. Your sisters are coming for dinner to see you."

"Sounds good. Bye."

Shortest conversation I think I've ever had with the woman. Letting myself in and tossing my stuff onto the counter, I make my way over to the floor to ceiling windows to take in the view of the harbor, park and the city. All right there. My eyes drift to the hot tub and I can't help but think about the last time I was in it and what I was doing.

"What if the neighbors look out their windows? They'll see us."

"Let em' watch, Stella."

I scrub a hand over my face willing the thought away. After our last run, in I can guarantee there won't be a repeat of that performance. No matter how often I think about it and her. She got under my skin in four days. How?

With a groan I walk to my bedroom, stripping along the way to wash off the plane ride. I'll hit the shower then head over to the Fulton University campus to talk to coach and Levi and maybe even get that massage from one of the Athletic Departments techs. It won't have the happy ending calling Shelly, the masseuse from the service I use in town, but it will do the trick.

I tell myself that I can't decide if I want Stella to be there or not. I know the truth, though. It's the reason I take an extra couple minutes to get ready. Like the spray of cologne and the washed hair is going to make her happier to see me somehow. Can't blame a guy for trying I guess.

"DAGGER! What's up, man? I didn't know you were coming this week." Levi says standing from the bench extending his hand for me to take. The kid is stand up. He's hell on the ice and he's great off it. I look forward to playing with him next season. He'll be a great addition to the team.

"That's the point, Sexton. If I give you a warning, you'll be ready and I can't you getting into any shit." I tell him slapping him on the back.

"Ha! Only thing you'll ever catch me in is pussy." Levi says, grinning.

"Nothing wrong with that." Shrugging, I look around the empty locker room. "Where is everyone?"

"Mostly home for Christmas. I was just running drills with the few guys who haven't left yet." As the captain of the team, it's his job to make sure nobody gets lazy. "About to go pick my dad up from the airport, you wanna ride?"

"Nah, I'm gonna go see coach really quick before I head out to Cambridge to see the fam. Where's your dad?"

"Connecticut working on getting a pitcher. He's got two prospects he's looking at." Levi says as he stuffs his gear in his locker.

"A pitcher? What about Stella?" I try to act casual, nobody knows about Stella and I spending that weekend together. Especially not Levi.

"Out for the season."

"The whole season?" What the hell?

"Yup." I'm staring at the top of his head as he ties his shoes, wanting to shake the information from him. It's like pulling fucking teeth.

"Why?" My tone is clipped in frustration. Levi must pick up on it. He looks up at me puzzled.

"She's knocked up. Big ol' belly. It's kinda hot."

His grin grates my nerves even as I try to let what he said sink in. Stella is pregnant. Stella. Is. Pregnant.

"She drop out?" I manage to ask.

"Nah, she's working in the treatment room to keep part of her scholarship and then someone said that she was also working at Ruma." Ruma was an upscale restaurant, there were a few of them around the states.

"She's working pregnant? Where the fuck is her boyfriend?" I can't hide my disgust. This is not the trip home I was expecting. I thought I'd let Stella be pissed at me and I'd convince her to get over it and then lock her in my apartment again for the next few days.

"No boyfriend. In fact, in all the time I've known her I don't think she's ever had a boyfriend. Girl that fine should never be alone." He tries to joke. When I don't laugh he clears his throat. "Anyway, no boyfriend and she won't say shit about who her baby daddy is."

All of a sudden, my whole body goes solid with tension. Vertebrae by vertebrae, ice dances up my spine trying to do the math in my head but not being able to quiet the roar in my ears long enough.

Doing my best to swallow so I can speak I manage to croak out, "How pregnant is she?"

"I don't know bro. Pregnant, pregnant." Levi holds his hands in front of his stomach to indicate how far her belly is. Son of a bitch. "Shit. I'm gonna be late. My dad will kill me."

"Go on. I'm going to see if Charlie has time for a massage." I lie. I need to go find Stella.

"Maybe Cruz is down there. Ask for her. All the guys do. Perverts love a pregnant chick rubbing on them." He shakes his head and laughs. "Like any of them wants any part of that."

The muscle in my jaws begins ticking at the thought of those fuckers making her work them over while she's pregnant. Or at all. I do my best to play along though

"Maybe. Get out of here. I'll catch up with you later."

Levi gives me a high five and then jogs out of the locker room leaving me alone to try to get my thoughts straight.

Fuck. Is Stella pregnant with my kid? Fuck.

Chapter Four

JASON

AFTER GOING DOWN TO THE TREATMENT ROOM AND FINDING NO STELLA, I called my ma and told her I was going to be late. There was no way I was driving to Cambridge without answers. I don't even have Stella's number and when I stopped at the apartment on campus I remembered dropping her off at they said she didn't live there anymore so Ruma it is.

I'm furious and I don't even know why. It's probably not even my kid. I mean she's in college. I can't be the only guy she was fucking. She said I was but isn't that what all chicks say? Whipping my truck into the full parking lot, I curse under my breath. Of course, it's fucking busy. A couple deep breaths later, I'm getting out of the car and walking through the doors into the dimly lit restaurant. Fucking hell.

"Hi, welcome to Ruma." The bubbly hostess greets.

"Is Stella Cruz working?" Her smile slips at my question and her eyes narrow.

"Stella's shift is just about to end" She looks at her watch, "in about five minutes."

"Great. Can you seat me in her section?"

"No."

I blink, confused. "Didn't you say she was here?"

"Yes."

"Okay, then I'd like a table in her section." I'm starting to get aggravated with this one.

"Do you have a reservation?" The once cordial hostess asks smugly. What is with this chick?

"No, I don't."

"Then I can't seat you in the dining room. You can have a seat in the bar though."

"Is Stella in the bar?"

"No."

Okay. I'm done with her shit. "Listen. I want to sit down and I want Stella to be my server. It's not a difficult or even unheard of fucking request."

Her eyes widen at the flare of my temper. Then narrow back to slits. "Oh look, her shift is over." She gestures with a flourish to the bar area, "shall I seat you in our lounge?"

She knows god damn well she can't. Not sure what I did to piss her off, I storm out the front door before I start cursing at her again. Days like this I wish I didn't have to watch the way I acted in public because I would love nothing more than to go in there and flip a couple tables I'm so frustrated. I should call the fucking manager and have her fired.

At my car, I turn to walk back in there when I hear her. Stella is walking out the front door with two other servers, laughing at something the guy said. Levi wasn't kidding, she's pregnant as fuck and it's hot. Even in her black pants and white dress shirt I can see the swell of her belly.

"Stella." She stops in her tracks whipping her head in my direction. Much like the hostess her eyes narrow into thin slits.

"What are you doing here?" She's not happy to see me.

"Holy shit man! You're Jason Dagger." The guy that was making Stella laugh says excitedly. "Holy shit! Can I get your autograph? Oh my god, the guys aren't going to believe this. Can we get a picture?"

He never lets me answer, just keeps rattling off questions as he pulls a pen and paper from his book all while juggling his phone. Figuring it will be faster just to get it over with, I pose for the picture and sign his paper with a hasty scribble, the whole time keeping my eyes on Stella.

"Oh man, thank you! This is awesome." He finally notices that I haven't said anything and that I have Stella in my sights. "Sorry. I'll let you guys do whatever. Stella, do you need me to wait to give you a ride?" Before she can answer, I make the decision for her.

"I'll take her."

"Like hell." She responds.

"Stella."

"You can go ahead, Eric. I'll catch a bus or an Uber." He looks uncertain so she reassures him again. We both watch him walk to his car before speaking.

"What are you doing here, Jason?"

"Looking for you." She looks tired. Beautiful. But tired, which pisses me off.

"Well, you found me. Can I go now?"

"We need to talk."

"I have nothing to say." She says stubbornly.

"Is the baby mine?" Go big or go home right? No bullshitting around with her.

"Oh, nooowww you want to talk, huh?" She drags out, taunting me.

"God damned right I want to talk, Stella. You're clearly pregnant. I want to know if the baby is mine."

I say it through clenched teeth, not liking that we're doing this in public and doing my best to keep myself in check. Half of me is feeling sheer terror, we were careful, every time. The other half of me is elated. The thought of being a father exciting. How fucked up is that?

"Why do you care, Jason? You sure didn't care about anything I had to say when I came to see you a couple months ago." Stella says, hand fisted on her rounded out hip

I treated her like shit that day and regretted it ever since. I don't know why I cared so much about anyone finding out. Especially the guys. The league would definitely not be thrilled, but my boys wouldn't have given a shit. Hell, they'd probably be jealous. The only twenty-year-olds that we have a shot of banging are Puck Bunnies and Stella wasn't even close.

"Is that what you came to tell me that day?"

"Wouldn't you like to know." She bites out, pulling her scarf around her neck to ward of the cold air around us.

I think back to that day and try to do the math. It was my turn to have the Cup and I came home with it. And then Stella showed up at my door and I acted a fucking fool.

THE GUYS ARE POSING with the Cup and snapping pictures when the doorbell rings. I put my bottle of beer down and go to answer, it's gotta be our takeout.

"Coming!" I call, although I'm sure the delivery guy can't hear me over the noise in my apartment. Throwing the door open, I can feel the smile fall from my face as if it were melting off. Stella stands in front of me holding up two brown paper bags of food. Quickly, I close the door behind me, snuffing out the sound of the raucous laughter from my friends.

"Caught the delivery boy in the lobby, and told him I'd bring it up. Hope you don't mind, I gave him a tip and signed the slip for you." She shrugs.

"Stella, what are you doing here? You can't be here like this. I mean, we're not...like that." I bite out with a little less tact than I probably should have.

Lowering her arms so that the food dangles at her sides, she tilts her head and looks at me like she's just seeing me for the first time, and maybe she is. I mean, we fucked around a few times and had a whole lot of fun. The weekend we spent together was probably one of the best times I've had in way too long. I was able to just be me. No bullshit. We laid around and talked and just hung out. And fucked. A lot. but...she's a college student.

I don't need some stage five clinger hanging around. I can't even call her a puck bunny because she didn't know who I was until I told her and up until now I hadn't heard from her once. Not that she had a way of getting a hold of me.

Regardless, I need to shut her down right here and now before she goes and gets attached or some shit. And definitely before any of the guys find out. I'll never live it down.

Never mind that, I would love to take her inside and let her do all kinds of things to me, if only she weren't a twenty-year-old kid. Not that she looks like a kid. There's nothing childlike about Stella Cruz. She's all woman. With her dark wavy hair, long lean lines, rounded hips and eyes so dark they look like pools of black ink.

She interrupts my wayward thoughts and I can tell by her tone that it's about to go down.

"Ahhhh, I get it. Your friends are here and you don't want them to know you messed around with some chick from FU is that it?"

"Stell- "

"No, I get it. I'm good enough to fuck all over your fancy apartment but we wouldn't want anyone to know you were slummin' it."

"It's not slummin', Stella, you're fucking 20." I hiss. "A student for fucks sake. You know what they would say about me in the league if they knew that while I was checking on their draft pick, I went ahead and fell into some college-aged pussy?"

There's that Dagger temper that always gets me in trouble on the ice coming out to play. I'm pretty sure it was the "slummin' it" dig. Like because she's from Lynn and not Cambridge or because I'm a pro athlete, I don't want to be seen with her. Fuck that. It's her damn age that I'm worried about.

"Yeah, Jason, twemty. Way past legal, you asshole. You act like I'm some sixteen-year-old little girl. In case you haven't noticed, I'm a fucking adult."

Oh, I noticed. I noticed a lot. But still there's a ten-year age gap that is way too wide to be acceptable.

Her voice raised in anger she goes on, "You didn't seem to mind my age when I was going down on you. Or when you had my spread across your kitchen counter, and especially not when we fucked in the hot tub on your balcony."

I really don't need these visuals right now. The last thing I need is to get hard over this girl and her sassy ass mouth and attitude. But just thinking about the way her perky tits bobbed on the water in time with her bobbing on my cock...

"Keep your voice down, Stella. And watch your damn mouth." I take hold of her elbow and guide her further down the hall and away from my door. She jerks her arm free and thrusts the food bags at me.

"Don't tell to watch my mouth." She grinds out between clenched teeth.

Never in my life have I felt the urge to lay someone across my lap and paddle their ass until this moment. I'm gonna blame it on the way her ripped jeans cling to her thighs and the dip of her hip or the way I can tell she doesn't have a bra on under the cropped shirt she's wearing. Yeah. I need to get her the hell out of here.

"So, what, you came here looking for an encore? Another dip in the hot tub, maybe a neighbor will catch us this time?" I ask stepping closer, forcing her to back up even as I continue forward.

"In your dreams" her eyes narrow into slits.

"Maybe." I smirk. "Most definitely in yours if you're here right?"

With a fingertip I trace the shell of her ear and let it trail down her neck to the spot I know drives her crazy. "You come back for more, Stell? Four days wasn't enough? Or maybe...maybe you need a little more to go back and tell your friends about?"

Stella swats my hand away and pushes against my chest.

"Don't flatter yourself, Dagger. You weren't that good."

I laugh at her blatant lie.

"I had scratches down my back that tell me I was."

"Whatever you have to tell yourself. Have a nice life." Stella says as she storms away not even bothering with the elevator and instead taking the stairs.

"IS IT, STELL?" Thinking back on that day has me softening my tone.

"Would you believe me if I said yes?" She asks with just the tiniest hint of a wobble underneath all that bravado.

"Yes." I don't know who is more surprised by that, me or her. But it never crossed my mind to doubt her. I may not have known Stella for long, but I feel like in those few days I got to know more than her body. I got to know her character and who she is in the hours we spent naked in my bed and if she says the baby is mine, then it is.

Chapter Five

STELLA

I MUST HAVE MISHEARD HIM. THINK IT HAS TO BE THE SHOCK OF SEEING him standing in the parking lot. How did he even know to look for me here?

"Just like that? I say it's yours and you believe me?" I question in shock.

"Yes, Stella. Just like that." He replies.

"You're not as smart as I thought then. Too many hits to the head probably."

"Might be."

"What if I'm lying? Just trying to pin a baby on you so I can cash out." Shaking my head at him, a part of me wants to smack some sense into him. The other part is so relieved I can barely breathe.

"Are you?"

This is not the Jason Dagger I know. Granted I don't know him that well, but still. The Jason I spent time with ran hot. Almost like he had too much passion or pent up...something, simmering just under his skin. Testosterone most likely.

"No. Of course not. But I could be."

"No, I don't think you could." His tone is low, trusting.

Too damn trusting. Doesn't he have an agent to warn him about this kind of thing? Why am I so upset that he believes me? I should be happy. Relieved. But here I am aggravated with him. Hormones, man.

"Can we go someplace and talk? Its cold out here."

"You're used to being on the ice." He's right though, it's cold as hell and my feet hurt and my back is screaming. I would give anything to sit down and get off my feet.

"But you aren't." Jason points out, surprising me yet again with his compassion. "We can go to your place if you want."

"You don't want to talk in my dorm. There's less privacy there than in the middle of the dining room." I jerk a thumb over my shoulder at the restaurant.

"You're in a dorm?" He asks confused.

"Yeah." I didn't elaborate. I wasn't embarrassed to tell him that I couldn't afford my apartment and tuition since I only have a partial scholarship now. I just didn't want him to think that I was working him over for money.

"Okay. We can go to my place then."

It's clear that he's not going to let this go. The sooner I answer all of his questions, although I don't know what he wants to know, I can go to bed. I have a nine o'clock class tomorrow morning.

"Fine. I have to swing by my place and change though because the smell of food on me makes me sick."

I walk past him to his truck hoping to god that I can manage to get into it without any help.

"That's fine. Do you need help getting in?"

His question is met with a glare over the bed of his shiny midnight blue truck. Lifting his hands in surrender, he presses the button to unlock the doors, coming over to my side to open mine for me.

"I have it. I'm already pregnant, you can save the chivalry for someone who isn't carrying your baby." I snap.

God, I don't want to be a bitch, I don't. I just can't seem to help it.

"I'll give you that one, Stella because I treated you like shit the last time I saw you. Go ahead and get it out of your system now so that we can talk about what we're going to do like adults. I'm not the bad guy. In fact, I'm doing my best to be a good fucking guy here. Let me."

The frustrated look pinching his face is understandable. As much as I don't want to admit it, he's right. He's going out of his way to make this easy on me, but I'm still bitter and hurt over the way he treated me when I went to see him. Without apologizing or saying a word to him, I step back and allow him to open the door for me.

"Thank you." It nearly killed me to be gracious. My petty is strong. My Abuelita would be ashamed. Just that little reminder hurts my heart. With a sigh, I watch him through the window, saying out loud in the empty cab of the truck.

"Fine Abuela, I'll try to be more kind."

SITTING on the couch in Jason's apartment, my backpack at my feet with the assignment I still have to do before tomorrow's class and a paper I have to begin, I lean back in the buttery leather couch and look at the twinkling lights on the harbor below. It's so pretty. So peaceful and relaxing. Too relaxing.

"You falling asleep on me, Stella?" Jason asks startling me awake. I'm not even sure when my eyes slid closed.

"Sorry. It's been a long day." I groan as I shift into a less comfortable position.

"Are you doing too much?" His eyes roam over me, the concern evident on his face.

"I feel okay. The baby is healthy. I'll survive."

"So, you have seen a doctor?"

"Jason. I'm six months pregnant. Of course I have." I laugh at him.

"Six months." He shakes his head and rubs a hand over his jaw. "We were so careful. How the hell did this happen?"

I asked the same exact question.

"No clue. But before you ask, and I get pissed, there's no way this baby isn't yours. I hadn't slept with anyone in months, six to be exact, before that weekend."

He's already proven that he's too trusting and believes me without any real proof, but I didn't want him to start questioning me now.

"I remember you saying so." Jason hands me a bottle of water. "I feel like I should have more questions, but I can't think of a single one now that I have you here. Truthfully, I expected your stubborn ass to fight me more." He laughs.

"Thought about it. Figured you'd just keep showing up, though."

"Damn right I would." A smile kicks up the corner of his mouth and I have to will myself not to stare. I hadn't forgotten how hot Jason Dagger was, I just didn't want to be reminded.

"Yeah well, this isn't something you can just kiss better." I say before I realize that those were the exact words I used on him the first time we had sex and then he used on me the second, third and fourth time. Obviously, he remembers too if the devilish gleam in his eyes and the wicked grin is anything to go by.

"I can try."

We're not going there. Not today or ever. Not that this baby isn't a blessing but not gonna lie, he or she has thrown a wrench in my plans in a big way.

"Yeah, no. You're kissing it and making it better have landed me in enough trouble, Dagger. Thanks, though."

"Trouble isn't always a bad thing. I mean, sometimes trouble can be so damn good."

Jason grins at me as he hands me a bottle of water. Is he fucking with me right now? Is this a line? I narrow my eyes and try to figure it out but I'm too tired and my brain won't work. In fact, my brain is screaming for me to do whatever he wants if it means going to bed and sleeping.

Although I'm certain that sleep is not what would happen. We spent four days in his bed and on his terrace, and the kitchen and shower and every other surface he could pin me to and I don't remember doing a whole lot of sleeping.

"So, what do you want to talk about exactly?" I have to keep him on track otherwise I'll try to convince him to get naked. Pregnancy hormones are no joke.

"Well first, are you hungry? I can order Chinese from Wu's." A man who knows his way to my heart. "Singapore Mei Fun, extra spicy, no shrimp, right?"

The fact that he remembers what I ordered that weekend blows my mind. Who is this guy?

"How do you remember that?"

He just shrugs and winks before turning back to the kitchen to order. "I have to make a couple phone calls too, I'll be right back."

While he does that I pull out my text book and notes and try to concentrate on the assignment I know I won't get finished. How can I when Jason is being all...perfect. I think I hate it.

No, I just don't know what to do with it. This wasn't the reaction I expected. Freshman year my roommate got pregnant, her boyfriend offered her money for an abortion and dumped her. Not that I was expecting that from Jason, but I honestly didn't expect this either. I think I thought he would deny it, say I was looking for a handout or tell me again, "We're not like that." He's got me confused as hell right now.

I'M HIGHLIGHTING passages for my paper when he comes back in the room bringing the sexy scent that is all Jason. It's a mixture of cold fresh air, like the ice he spends so much time on clinging to him, and leather. I close my stuff when he sits across from me on the bog leather love seat.

"You done in January? Or do you have another semester?" He asks, twisting the top on his bottle of water and drinking.

"Technically, I can finish in January but I need the student loans to help carry me until I can nail down a job. Since I'll have a newborn soon, I'm going to take a few online classes and work on my Masters. This way I can be home with the baby and still get some help from student loans."

I've planned this all out. I'm working now to put money away for a small one-bedroom apartment since the baby and I can't live on campus. Between my partial scholarship and my student loans nearly all my schooling is covered, thankfully. It's not ideal, but I have a few feelers out on some really great job and coaching prospects.

I see a muscle ticking away in his jaw. He looks like a bomb ready to detonate.

"How much are you getting in student loans?"

I don't understand the anger in his tone.

"About five thousand a semester, I think. My scholarship is still covering a majority and I picked up a grant for multiracial women this semester."

"Damn it, Stella. Why didn't you come ask me for help? If you're carrying my kid, You. Are. My. Responsibility. Too." He bites out, pushing to his feet he starts to pace. "You're working your ass off in school, two jobs. You need to be resting. Not rubbing guys down for some bullshit scholarship."

Okay. He's pissed. But so am I.

"Umm...first of all, I'm not *rubbing guys down.* I'm working in the treatment room as part of my scholarship as well as one of my classes."

"Yeah, and they're getting off on the hot pregnant chick working them over. I don't like it." Jason crosses his arms over his chest and glares my way.

What the hell?

"Okay, well you don't get a say. So— "

"That's my kid. I get a say." He interrupts.

"You can dial it back, caveman. As of an hour ago, you had no idea this baby even existed so you don't get to just come in and start making demands. Let me remind you *yet* again, I am an adult. Legal. On my own for awhile now. I don't need you or anyone else telling me what to do or how to do it."

As gracefully as I can I get to my feet so that we're both standing now, sitting made me feel as if I was at a disadvantage and I needed him to hear what I'm saying.

"I'm doing the very best I can for *my* child and I plan to continue to do so. If you'd like to be in this baby's life, then that's great, fantastic, but that doesn't mean you get to start dictating what I do."

I'm standing in front of him now, my fingernails poking at his rock solid chest. Certain that there's steam billowing from my ears, I'm just about to pack up my stuff and get out of there when Jason grabs me by the nape and pulls me into him, causing me to stumble. He steadies me with his mouth slanting over mine, devouring my lips and swallowing my half assed attempt at refusal. The minute his tongue slides against mine, I'm a goner.

I can blame it on the pregnancy hormones all I want, truth is Jason Dagger has something, some crazy pull on me that I can't deny. Couldn't do it the first time I met him, can't do it now. I'm headed for heartbreak, I know it because there's no way a man like him could ever want more than *this,* from a girl like me.

Chapter Six

JASON

SHOULD I BE KISSING STELLA CRUZ RIGHT NOW? NO. NO, I SHOULD NOT be but there was no way I couldn't. She stood there, handing me my ass, poking me in the chest with her hair up in a messy bun, big black glasses swallowing up her face, comfy sweats and a T-shirt that said Jolly AF.

How could I not kiss her? I couldn't explain the pull I felt to her all those months ago and I can't explain it now, but the fact that she's carrying my kid makes that pull magnified by about a fucking million. I want to tuck her under my arm, roll her in bubble wrap and let nothing and no one hurt her.

That's a problem for me. I don't do relationships and I don't do chivalrous shit but this girl is pushing all my buttons, making me want to do things I don't normally do. Just when I'm trying to decide how far to take this, the doorbell rings making her jump back.

"Easy, Stell. It's just the Chinese." I grin, taking a second to admire the way she looks with her lips bruised from my kiss, her belly swollen with my baby and her glasses slightly askew. Fuck me I'm dead. Before I can grab her up again, the delivery guy rings the bell again. "Go sit on the couch, I'll bring it in."

After paying the guy and kicking the door closed, I walk back to where Stella sits on the floor Indian style, gazing at the tree and lights my sister came and put up for me. The lights from the harbor and the decorated boats and slips like glittering diamonds from up here.

"Your tree is so pretty. I always put up a little Charlie Brown tree or something in my room. I love this time of the year, used to love decorating the tree and making cookies but since my abuela passed away..." She trails off, the sadness evident in her voice.

"I'm sorry, Stella. I wish I could have met her." And I do. Stella told me stories about what it was like growing up with her grandmother after her parents died. The way she stepped up to take care of Stella and her brother.

"She would have liked you." She tells me, smiling, as she removes containers from the bag.

"You think so?" Sitting next to her on the floor I stretch my legs underneath the table.

"Yup. Abuelita had a thing for handsome guys, especially successful ones. I think she always hoped some successful man would show up on his white horse and save me from ending up like her."

"Like Pretty Woman?"

Stella snorts out a laugh. "Yeah, except without the prostitution."

I can't help but chuckle at that. "Probably."

"Jason, who the hell is going to eat all of this? Are you expecting company?"

Looking around the table at all the food I shrug, "I was hungry when I called. Plus, it's season, I burn a lot of calories." I say defensively.

"Not this many." She sasses.

Chopsticks in hand, she starts digging into her container, moaning around a mouth full of the spicy smelling noodles.

"This is so good. I haven't had Wu's since the last time with you." Stella says, dipping back in for another bite.

"It's the best. I think I must have eaten there three times a week when I was in school here."

"I don't blame you. You probably miss it when you're back in Chicago."

"I do, but there are some amazing places to get Chinese. Especially in China Town."

"Yum. A whole little town with Chinese food. I would love that."

The look on her face is pure bliss. It makes me happy that I can make her this content with something so simple.

"So, what do you wanna be when you grow up, Stell?"

"A teacher and a coach."

I snort out a laugh. "You can't be a teacher."

"Ummm..why the hell not?" She demands.

"Because you're too damn hot. I think there's a law or something about it."

"Oh my god. Shut up." Her laugh is infectious; I can't help myself from joining in.

"It's true! Those poor boys wouldn't stand a chance."

"Well, that's the plan. I already have a couple prospects. All of them know about the baby and are super understanding and accommodating."

My fork stops mid bite as I think about what she just said. I hate that she is going to be alone but how the hell was I going to convince her she should come to Chicago. Did I even want that?

"Where at? Here?" I ask, avoiding the things I really want to say.

"Couple places, Florida, here in Mass, and even Chicago." Her chopsticks make a clacking sound as she works them into her mouth like a pro.

"They're all for high schools which excites me because that's serious softball. I don't want that part of my life to be over yet. Probably not ever really." She admits.

"I can understand that. I don't know what I would do without hockey." I love that we have something like that we can connect on. Sports are a way of life not everyone can understand.

"You ever think about what you'll do when hockey is over?" She asks, genuinely curious.

"I don't like to think about that day." I admit, laughing self-consciously. I don't have too many years left in hockey, it's tough on your body. A decade is what I'm hoping for.

Full, I push my containers away and stretch out, my arm resting on the seat cushion that Stella leans against. I can feel the heat she's throwing and move my arm closer so that it's touching her now. If she notices, she doesn't say anything, just continues to eat happily giving me the chance to watch her. The way her glasses slide down and she scrunches her nose up to try to lift them back into place. Her smooth, soft skin the color of caramel. Full lips that bring me back to the vision of her on her knees in the penalty box, that mouth on my cock. Biting back a groan, I drop my napkin in my lap to try to hid the growing hard on.

"What does your brother think about the baby?" I ask, knowing that it will matter to her. He's all she has left, her grandmother passed away last year. She told me that weekend we spent together that her parents died when she was little, a car accident. Her and her brother, Carlo went to live with her grandmother in a tiny apartment in Lynn and that's where they stayed until he went off to the Marine's and she got a scholarship to FU.

"He's disappointed in me, but excited to be an uncle." I can tell by her tone that it bothers her.

"I'm sorry."

I'm not sorry that she's pregnant. Actually, actually the more I think about it, the more excited I am. I am sorry that her brother is disappointed in her. Makes me want to throw the gloves with his ass though. He has to know how upset that would make her.

"Don't be. Carlo will get over it." Stella leans back releasing a long breath. "Oh my god that was good. This baby can't get enough of the spicy food."

She pats her belly and smiles at me. Without thinking I reach out and place a hand over her rounded belly. She's so slender it looks like she swallowed a basketball. She tenses for a moment, then covers my hand with her own and drags it over to the side a bit.

"He was just rolling over here, maybe you'll get to feel it. It's wild." Her eyes shine brightly with a happiness that literally makes her glow.

"He? Is the baby a boy?" I ask excitedly.

"Oh, I don't know. I just get tired of calling it *it* all the time."

I nod in understanding. The baby already seems like so much more than "it" to me, so I get it. "Will you find out the sex?"

"I want to. The student insurance is mediocre at best and they only cover one ultrasound so I've been saving it just in case something happens."

My teeth clack together in irritation. She's carrying my baby. Mine. Multi-million dollar a year contract holding NHL player Jason Dagger and she's going to student aid for health care. If I lose my cool with her over this she's going to give me hell.

Stella is proud and independent and not impressed by my money or the fact that I'm a pro athlete. This one fucking instance I wish she were, though.

"Will you do me a favor and see if they can schedule you for an ultrasound while I'm here. I'll pay for another one if you end up needing it." I say, treading carefully.

I can see her thinking about it before nodding, "I can try. I think they're gone during the holidays. I swear I'm the only one on campus or taking any classes during this break."

Glad that it went easier than I thought, I relax again. I need to figure out a way for her to allow me to pay for this shit. The thought that her and my kid aren't getting the best care makes me want to break shit. Funny how easily I've accepted all of this. I'll probably freak the fuck out later, but right now I just want to take some of the pressure and responsibility from her.

And stop wishing I could lay her down and strip her naked. I'm not sure I'll ever quit that one though. Gathering the food containers to bring in the kitchen, stopping her when she gets up to help,

"No way, woman. You've just got off work. Sit and chill. I'll get this."

I need the minute to think about how I'm going to convince her to take money from me. I probably have a better chance of fucking her and as tempting as that sounds, I know it won't help me right now. Well, it'll help me but it won't help our situation.

"Okay, I've fed you so that you're not hungry and we can talk." I tease.

Stella groans, "I'm gonna hate this aren't I?"

"We gotta talk about things, Stella. I'm only here for a few days, my schedule is gonna get nuts as soon as I get back."

"I know. I know." She slips from the floor and settles on the couch, tucking her legs underneath her. "Well, you know that I don't want your money. Of course I won't stop you from seeing the baby, but that's stuff we'll have to work out after I have her."

"I know you don't want my money but whether you like it or not, you're going to get it. I mean, I have to pay child support."

She's about to argue with me when I go and sit beside her.

"No, Stell. I know that you're proud and independent and used to doing things on your own, but so am I. What kind of man would I be to not take care of my kid? You asking me to be a deadbeat dad? I'm just as proud as you are.

I'm going to provide for my child. I'll call my lawyer tomorrow and have paperwork drawn up and see how to go about coming up with a fair amount for you."

"Your lawyer? You have a lawyer? I can't even wrap my mind around that." She shakes her head and I can see that I'm losing her.

"I have to have one for my contracts and the team's legal obligations and stuff. It's not like I just have a lawyer to follow me around for shits and giggles."

"I don't want money from you. People are gonna talk so much shit. I'm not a gold digger, Jason."

"I know that. If you were a gold digger, I wouldn't be finding about this baby when you're just a couple months from giving birth, fighting with you to take my damn money."

Never in my fucking life did I think I would be saying shit like that to a woman. I take a deep breath and go for the kill.

"I also want the baby to have my last name." Her eyes fly to mine, wide in surprise, then filled with tears. Oh shit.

"You do?" Voice cracking, she watches me like she's expecting me to take it back.

"Absolutely. No kid of mine is gonna walk this Earth without my name." I tell her adamantly.

"Who are you?" She asks bewildered.

"Tell you the truth, I have no fucking clue. I'm scaring myself a little." We both burst into laughing, the heavy moment lightening with the sound in an instant.

"Can we be done with all this adulting now? I'm exhausted." She admits, flopping back into the soft cushions looking sleepy.

"You want to crash here? You can sleep with me in my big king size bed, I'll even rub your...back" I finish with a waggle of my eyebrows.

"Not gonna happen, Dagger."

"Can't blame a guy for trying."

Chapter Seven

STELLA

After waiting a damn eternity for the elevator, I say screw it and head for the stairs. The exercise will be good for me and the baby. At least that's what I tell myself before starting the trek up the eleventy million stairs. Last time I took them I wasn't nearly as pregnant and going down is a whole lot easier than going up.

Finally reaching the top, I head toward Jason's place pretending like I'm not winded and then when I'm unable to lie about that, convincing myself that the only reason I am winded is because of the stairs and nothing to do with seeing him again. We weren't supposed to see each other 'til tomorrow, but I left my book here last night and I need it for my paper. I knock on the door and will my breathing and heart rate to get their shit together. I'm just about to knock again when the door flies open and a beautiful, and surprised woman stands there gaping at me.

Shit. Didn't take him long did it? Ignoring the crushing feeling I have no right to feel, I stand a little straighter. Determined to not allow her to see how much this just hurt me. With a fake smile, I push on.

"Sorry to bother you, is Jason here?"

The woman's mouth opens and closes three times, I know because I counted, before she says

"Yes. Yeah. He's in the shower though." She pauses, looking me over from head to toe before going on, "Do you want to come in?"

Her tone is dripping with uncertainty and curiosity. Clearly, she has a close relationship with him if she's answering his door and he's in the shower. Plus, it's not even noon yet. Did she spend the night? Come just after I left? That hurts even more after the talk we had.

"I just need to grab a book I left here last night."

"Last night? You were here last night?" The woman asks confused and even more curious than before.

Before I can answer, I hear Jason from somewhere inside the apartment "Joey, I love you and all but—Stella?"

I can see him over her shoulder. Standing in the middle of his living room, a towel knotted low on his hips, water dropping onto his shoulders and chest from his mop of wet hair. The sun from the floor to ceiling windows casting him in a god-like glow. Why does he have to be so damn hot?

Jason moves forward so that he's standing directly behind the woman he called Joey now, looking at me with concern.

"Is everything okay? The baby?"

I nod, not able to talk past the lump in my throat when Joey barks out a laugh.

"Ooooohhh you're in so much trouble. I'm telling Ma." She sing songs gleefully.

"Shut up, brat. Let Stella in. Cruz, this is my sister Joey. Joey this is Stella Cruz my—" he stalls, not sure what to say when Joey pipes in

"Your baby mama?"

She's practically bouncing on her toes she's so excited. I'm not sure if it's at the prospect of being an aunt or getting Jason in trouble. I'm too embarrassed by my reaction to her being there to look too closely, but I'm guessing it's more to do with ratting him out.

Jason shoves her gently out of the way> "Come in, Stell. Ignore my little sister. She's a pain in the ass," he says good-naturedly.

"Hey! I am not! Okay, I kind of am." Joey laughs. "Nice to meet you, Stella," she says, still eyeballing me and my wicked pregnant state.

"Hi." I wave awkwardly. "I'm sorry to just show up, I just need my book. I must have left it last night and I have to try to start on this paper before I go to work."

"Come in. And you can show up here whenever, Stella."

I give him a look that screams 'are you fucking kidding me?' that he catches and has the decency to look remorseful.

"Yeah, not my best moment, okay?"

"No. No, it wasn't." I'm not sure I'll let him live that one down anytime soon. Or ever.

"I'm sorry, I don't mean to be nosey— "

"Yes, you do." Jason cuts in.

She sticks her tongue out at him reminding me so much of myself and Carlo.

"Anyway, as I was saying, I don't mean to be nosey but how old are you and are you pregnant with my brother's baby?" Right to the point she is.

Opening my mouth to answer Jason interjects, "She's old enough and you'll hear all about it *after* mom does. Speaking of which, I was just going to call you. I told my ma we would come for lunch."

"You what? Your mom? Why?" I stammer.

"Well, because I told her I had someone she had to meet and since I'm only here for a couple days..." I'm aware of Joey watching this whole thing go down like a spectator at a tennis match.

"I can't, I have to work."

"Call in."

"Can't do that. I won't be able to work for much longer."

"I will pay you what you would have made." He says a little exasperated.

"Don't do that. Don't throw your money at me like that. Remember this isn't Pretty Woman. I don't need a pimp or a sugar daddy or whatever." I tell him, pissed that he would even suggest that.

"I was going for Knight in shining armor, but pimp works." Jason says, grinning from ear to ear. "Take the night off. Please. I promise you, you will not miss the money. My lawyer—"

I raise my hand to stop him not willing to discuss this in front of his sister.

"Okay, okay." He lifts his palms in surrender. "But seriously."

He gives me the puppy dog eyes and I can't deny him. How could anyone say no to those baby blues? God, I hope the baby doesn't have those eyes. He or she will be spoiled rotten if they do.

"Fine. I'll go."

"Oh, this is gonna be good." Joey murmurs.

AN HOUR later I'm walking into Jason's parent's house in Cambridge, palms sweating, legs a little unsteady as he takes my jacket from my shoulders.

He leans into me and whispers in my ear, "Don't worry, Stella. They're going to love you and be excited about this baby. Just as excited as I am."

He presses a kiss to my temple that I want to lean into. Wonder about. Ask him what it means. If he's really excited about the baby and why in the hell he believes me. But there's not time. A woman in her mid-fifties comes into the hallway wearing a Chicago hockey shirt and a pair of black leggings. Here we go.

"There's my favorite hockey player." She says excitedly pulling him into a tight hug. "How are you, baby? Still sore from the game?"

"Nah, I'm okay, ma."

"Good. Bastard." She says ferociously. Just like a mama bear. I saw the game; I may have called the guy who hit him a bastard myself.

"Ma, this is Stella Cruz. Stella, Carly Dagger." When she turns to me her eyes widen, almost to the point I think they might fall right out of her damn head before she catches herself.

Holding my hand out to hers I force my lips to stretch into a wobbly smile. "Mrs. Dagger."

She takes my hand, eyes on my belly then to Jason and back to me. "Please, call me Carly. My mother in law was Mrs. Dagger and she was not a nice woman." I laugh nervously.

Jason interrupts the awkward moment, "Whose all here?"

"Just you guys and your dad. Your sisters won't be here until tomorrow night."

"Perfect, I don't want to overwhelm, Stella."

He places a reassuring hand on the small of my back. I've never been so grateful for such a simple touch. I feel on the verge of a panic attack. I've never been a part of a large family and for the last little while it's just been me since Carlo has been deployed and Abuelita passed away. I'm ready to jump out of my skin until his warm palm through my thin sweater anchors me. Calms me. What in the world is happening to me?

"Let's go into the family room. I think your dad is watching a game. We can probably tear him away from it." She laughs.

"Stella, can I get you anything to drink?"

"No. I'm fine thank you." If I even attempt to drink anything right now, I'll choke.

With Jason's hand guiding me, I follow his mother into the room. A man, I presume his father, looks up from the TV. His eyes land on his son and then on me and he says "Well, that took a lot longer than I expected. I assumed I'd be a grandpa before you graduated high school the way you carried on." The room erupts into laughter, I even find myself giggling.

"Whatever old man." The men embrace and then Mr. Dagger turns to me.

"And who is this pretty girl?" His eyes are the same color blue as Jason's and smiling right along with the rest of him. He's like a young Santa Claus if that makes any sense. He just looks...jolly.

"Dad, this is Stella Cruz. Stella, my dad, Johnathan."

I hold out my hand to him and he waves it away, "Bring it in for the real thing, sweet pea. If you're gonna make me a grandpa, we can't be strangers." His dad scoops me into a gentle, yet warm hug. "Welcome to the family, Stella. We've been waiting for you." He says quietly, so only I can hear. That simple statement had tears pricking at my eyes. Family. I forgot how much I've missed being a part of one.

"Johnathan, let the poor girl go so I can get a look at her." Carly Dagger says swatting at his arm. He releases me and steps back, bringing Jason with him to gather him into a back thumping hug and murmured words.

There are tears in her eyes now as well, no judgment or distrust and just like that, all of the tension leaves my body. These people are inherently good and kind just like their son and my child would be a part of this. Of them. The peace I feel at that is overwhelming. I was determined to do this on my own.

To be the only family this baby would ever need and now the fact that I don't have to be, that he or she would have the Daggers with their big hearts and open arms, is more than I could have ever hoped or imagined. I look over at Jason who is smiling at something his dad is saying to him and realize that even though we may not know each other well, we're not even in a real relationship, and yet I wouldn't choose anyone else to be this baby's father.

Chapter Eight

JASON

CHRISTMAS EVE IS A BIG DEAL IN MY FAMILY. MY PARENTS ARE OVER THE moon about having us all together for the holiday this year and even more excited that they convinced Stella to come. The thought of her spending it alone in her dorm while her roommates were with their families was a little more than any of us could deal with. Even my sister Joey insisted she come.

Introducing her to my parents and sister and telling them she was having the first Dagger grand baby was easier and more emotional than I ever imagined. I know that my parents have some questions but they were so damn excited we decided all of that could wait. My ma gave Stella the third degree about her doctor's appointments, morning sickness, stretch marks and all kinds of shit I never even thought to ask.

I have a couple hours before I have to go pick her up, so I'm meeting Levi on the ice since I'm supposed to be spending time with him while I'm here too. Pulling open the doors on the arena, I'm immediately brought back to that night here with Stella. Probably the hottest sex of my life. Maybe because it was her. Or because it was in here. But it's something I'll never forget.

"What's up, bro! I was about to give up on you."

"Sorry, man. This trip has been nuts. Between the holidays and family." I toss my bag down and pull out my skates.

"Heard you showed up at Cruz's job looking for her." He leans on his stick, watching me lace up.

"Oh yeah? Who said that?" I'm betting it was that Eric kid who had me signing shit.

"Eric Andes. Said you were waiting in the parking lot for her when she came out of work."

"And?" Levi is a good guy, but I'm not about to just tell him all my business.

"And is the baby yours?" His gaze on me is steady as he stands on the ice waiting for my answer.

"If it is?"

"If it is what do you plan to do about it? Cruz is good people. She's a hard worker and has had a shit time the last couple of years. You fuck her over and maybe I have to tell them I need a different mentor. One who doesn't go around knocking up college chicks and then leaving them high and dry."

The little shit says in a tone that tells me he means every word. Good. I'm glad that Stella has people protecting her. She doesn't need protection though. Especially from me.

Standing, I step onto the ice and bump his shoulder. "You can take it easy tiger, I'm not going anywhere. Stella doesn't need you to protect her from me."

"I'm glad to hear it. I like you, but I'd still drop your ass if you weren't doing right by her."

"Is that right? You wanna go, Rookie?" I ask playfully, putting my fists up and skating around him in a circle.

"Don't make me hurt you, old man." He laughs skating off in the opposite direction. "Try to keep up, I've learned a few things since the last time you were here." Levi calls out, his voice echoing in the empty arena.

Grabbing my stick, I follow after him. Cocky prick, reminds me of myself when I was his age. Probably why I like him so much and didn't beat his ass for questioning me about Stella.

"HEY, Stell. I'm out front, what's your dorm number?" I ask, juggling my phone as I climb out of the truck. The cold air cutting through me as the wind whips around, blowing snow in every direction. Fucking frigid ass state.

"Just stay there, I'll come down."

"It's slippery out, we got a fuck ton of snow. Let me come get you."

"I'll be fine." She huffs.

I know it won't do any good to argue with her, so I go to the door of the building and wait for her to come out. Stubborn ass woman. She bursts through the door about a minute later and all I can do is stare.

She's stunning. Literally. Her hair is down and wicked wavy, which I've decided is my favorite. Her lips are painted a sexy Christmassy red, the snow already gathering on her lashes and cheeks adding to her festive look. From the moment I laid eyes on her, I thought Stella was hot as hell but she's more than that.

Even in Christmas pajamas that look a lot like a onesie. I wonder if there's a butt flap on them? The thought makes me smile. A laugh slips out when I think back to telling her. I've never seen someone get so excited about being able to wear pajamas.

"Do I have to dress up because I don't fit in a single thing other than sweats right now."

"Nope. Family tradition, my ma insists we all wear Christmas pajamas."

"Oh my god, really? That's so amazing. I just fell in love with your mother."

"Where's your coat, Stella?"

"Let's not talk about my coat and how it doesn't fit over my belly." She all but growls.

"You're gonna get sick."

"No, I'm not. That's not how you get sick. You get sick from germs."

"Smart ass." I slip my coat from my shoulders and put it on her. Even six months pregnant, she swims in it.

Two steps from the door and she slips on a patch of ice. Catching her easily, I narrow my eyes at her.

"You're lucky I'm more stubborn than you are. Had I not come to the door you would have busted your ass and hurt yourself."

"But I didn't." She says smiling sweetly as she hooks her arm through mine.

I help her into the truck and crank the heat. "You ready?"

"As I'll ever be." She looks nervous.

"What's wrong?" Reversing and maneuvering through the snowy parking lot, I glance over to see her gnawing on her bottom lip.

"What if they don't like me? I mean your parents and Joey were wicked sweet but your other sisters..."

"I'll kick their asses." I say simply with a shrug of my shoulders. That gets a laugh out of her.

"Really, Jase. I mean, there's a lot of them. The odds are not in my favor."

Not sure is she notices the little nickname but I did. Maybe I'm winning the battle after all. She seems more comfortable with me and the thought of having me around.

"Stella, it'll be fine."

Truthfully, it should be. The only one who will not just accept Stella and the baby without some kind of proof is my oldest sister Johnanne. She's a ball-buster. That's actually putting it nicely. She's a bitch. But she's our bitch and we love her. I don't tell Stella that though, she's nervous enough. I already had a talk with my ma about my oldest sister.

"Okay, tell me their names again."

"There's Johnanne, she's the oldest and a lawyer recently married. Then Jordan, Joey and Jessie. Jordan is a teacher and also married, Joey is still in school for nursing and Jessie owns a bakery."

I give her the cliff notes version.

"I love how you guys are all J's. Should we name the baby with a J name?" The question is asked so nonchalantly and yet it means so much to me that she's willing to carry on our tradition and that she's asking my opinion.

"My ma would love that. We don't have to, though."

"Your sister's names, are those nicknames or?"

"Nope. My dad was sure he would have all boys and would only come up with boy's names so my ma went with it. Johnanne was supposed to be a junior. When she was born and obviously not a junior the old man convinced my ma to still use his name, she compromised by adding the Anne." I tell her.

"That's so cute though. Poor guy gets one son and he's stuck with you." Stella teases, biting her lip to hold back her laugh.

"Hey now. They broke the mold with me, baby."

"They broke something." She snorts out a laugh.

I'm glad that she's loosening up and smiling freely now. I don't want her to worry because honestly, I won't stand for anyone giving her shit, not even my sisters.

We pull into the driveway behind my sister's Tahoe. Everyone is here. I look over at Stella and she's looking nervous again, eyeing the full drive. I slide my hand underneath her hair, cupping the back of her neck and tugging lightly until she looks my way. My eyes fall to her full lips then up to her eyes, nearly black in the dark interior of the truck. Without saying a word, I tug again until we're meeting over the center console, mouths a breadth away, our eyes touching over every inch of the others face before locking.

"I'm going to kiss you right now Stella. Here, when it's just you and I, because I want to. Not because you're pregnant with my kid, but because you're fucking beautiful and I want you more than I've ever wanted another woman. And I gotta tell you, that scares me. The way you fit so well in my life, with my family, scares me. But it also feeds this need for you."

"It scares me too." She whispers before her eyes flutter closed in invitation.

Not wanting to waste time talking anymore, I tilt her chin and slant my lips over hers, biting at the plump bottom lip until she opens to me, allowing me to slide my tongue along the seam of her full mouth. Her hand snakes into my hair, holding me to her, begging me without using words to keep kissing her. I pull away to rain kisses along her jaw and down her neck causing her to purr like a contented cat.

I only meant to kiss her to ease her nerves. Once she looked my way though, something shifted. This all just feels so damn right. She feels right. I've never even had a serious relationship and yet I'm ready to start a family with this woman, ten years younger than me. A woman some might say I barely know, but I do. I know her character and to me that's everything. Without caring that those same people are going to talk. With total and complete trust, I'm doing this thing with Stella Cruz. All I have to do is convince her, right after I kiss the ever loving shit out of her.

We finally break apart both a little dazed. "You ready?"

"I am now." Stella says, a sexy smile slipping over her face.

Chapter Nine

JASON

"WHERE MY HO'S AT?" I CALL OUT AS I USHER STELLA INTO THE HOUSE.

My ma comes from the family room, a smile brighter than her Christmas tree lighting up her face. "There you two are. I was worried you wouldn't make it." She takes the bags from us so I can help Stella off with my jacket. "Oh my word, how cute are you in those jammies?" Ma says laughing. "May I?" She asks Stella, hand stretched toward her belly.

"Oh yes! Thank you for asking though. People are crazy." Stella shakes her head in disgust. "Perfect strangers will walk up to me and rub my belly. It's especially bad at the restaurant I work at. I think maybe because they're eye level with it when I'm standing next to the table."

"People are nuts. When I was pregnant with one of the girls, Jonathan had a shirt made for me that said 'You touch my belly I'll touch yours.' It slowed some folks down."

The whole time my ma is talking my eyes are glued to Stella's ass and the flap on her pajama's that I was wondering about earlier. That flap shouldn't be sexy. Shouldn't have me thinking all the filthy ways I can get at her by just unfastening those two little buttons. Damn it, this is going to be the longest night of my life. Okay, maybe not my life, but it's gonna be fucking long.

"Everyone here?" I ask, planting a kiss on my mother's head although she's preoccupied with Stella's baby bump.

"Yes, they're all here." Her head shoots up, "Oh! I felt a kick."

"All day he's been extra feisty." Stella laughs. Not wanting to miss this, I place a hand on the other side of her belly from my ma and wait but get nothing.

"What is everyone doing in here?" Demands my oldest sister.

"Hey, there big sis." I greet, scooping her up in a bear hug.

"Put me down you goon." Johnanne demands, laughing. Placing her on her feet, I'm just about to introduce her to Stella when she blurts. "Oh my god, nobody told me she was a minor! A little heads up would have been nice."

She turns to me. "You do have a lawyer right?"

And this is what I was afraid of. There was no way in hell Johnanne was gonna let this be easy. She's an attorney, this whole thing screams red flag to her.

"Johnanne." My ma says in a warning tone.

"What ma? He's not just anybody. He has got to protect himself. Jason doesn't have the luxury to just go with the flow. He's worth a lot of money and a perfect target. No offense, I'm sure you're a nice girl." My sister says to Stella, flippantly.

Thirty seconds and I've had enough. "That's enough Johnanne." I bite out before she says another word. Next to me Stella has tensed, my mother's hands falling from her stomach.

"Jaso— "

"No." I interrupt, my tone leaving no room for argument. "I—

"Jase." Stella says, a hand on my arm. "It's okay."

"It's not okay, Stella." My frustration is rising. I knew Johnanne was going to have something to say but I expected her to wait to speak to me in private.

"It is. Your sister's concerned and she should be." Stella turns to my sister. "I'm glad that you have some sense because he doesn't."

She smiles over at me and winks. "Just so you know, I'm not a minor, I'm twenty, so no lawsuit for Jason there. And I don't want your brother's money. In fact, before I take a dime from him for anything I will be insisting on a paternity test. Not for me, because I know the truth, but for his protection. There are too many crazies out there who would jump at the opportunity to pin a baby on a pro athlete."

"But not you?" Johnanne asks curiously.

"I'm not trying to pin anything on anyone. As of a couple days ago, I was content to raise this baby on my own even if I had to work four jobs to do it. Hell, I'm still prepared to do just that. After meeting your parents and sister, I would love for them to be a part of this little one's life even if your brother isn't. I don't have much family left, only my brother actually, who is deployed more often than not, and family is as important to me as it is to all of you." Stella's voice waivers with emotion.

Stepping behind her I pull her into my chest to assure her that I'm here for, I'm in her corner. She has nothing to prove. No one to convince. Mine is the only opinion that matters and right here, right now, I think Stella is a mother-fucking queen. At twenty, she's more poised and confident than any woman I've ever dated put together.

I can feel her inhale deeply before going on. "So again. I don't want money from you brother, I just want a family for my baby."

"It's true, she doesn't. The dumb ass tried to be all cool guy and pay her to take off from work the other day and she about beat his ass." Joey says from the doorway, drawing our attention. "She's savage."

We all break out into laughter, the heaviness in the room dissolving. Leave it to Joey. I need to buy her better Christmas present for her coming to the rescue.

"Well, now that that's out of the way, come in and meet the rest of the family, Stella. I promise none of them will give you the third degree, they probably all voted for Johnanne to be the bad guy and are just waiting for her stamp of approval." My mom says, her smile back in place.

She's probably right too.

AS PROMISED the rest of the family was on their best behavior. Stella even managed to win over Johnanne, who was sitting next to her on the couch laughing at something Stella is saying, gesturing wildly. In her cute jammies, her face animated and my sisters around her, hanging on her every word you would never know that she hasn't always been a part of our family.

All night I've watched her. Put my hands on her, innocent touches, inhaled her scent, smiled when she laughed, laughed when she snorted at something my brother-in-law said, and the whole time I was dreaming about all the ways I was going to make her mine tonight. The places I would strip her bare and make her shake from pleasure. Scream my name until her voice went hoarse.

Over pecan pie and coffee when everyone was talking about my sister's new boyfriend, I was envisioning bending Stella over my ottoman and fucking her while she wore her Christmas pajama's, her hair a wicked tangle of curls for me to hold onto. I'm pretty sure I'm going to hell for having such impure thoughts while sitting at my mother's dinner table. At least I'll have fun getting there.And Stella is partly to blame. Constantly looking at me with those fuck me eyes of hers. Just begging me with heated looks over the rim of her glass, as she liked whipped cream from her spoon. All night. Torturing me without a care.

I PLUCK Stella from her new fans, laughing when they complain about me taking her away.

"I love you guys too." I tease.

Making the rounds and wishing everyone a Merry Christmas, we make it out the door as fast as I can without being rude.

"You in a hurry?" Stella asks.

"I'm in a hurry to get you naked." I admit. When she doesn't shoot me down I pick up the pace.

WE MAKE it back to my place in record time. Stella goes and turns on the Christmas tree lights and puts the presents under there from my parent's place as I start the fire and put on some Christmas music.

"I love Christmas music." She says, humming along with Nat King Cole.

"I love Christmas onesies with back flaps that drive me wild all night." I flash a wolfish grin, the kind that leaves no doubt what I'm thinking.

"There is nothing sexy about Christmas onesies. Especially when you're pregnant." Stella laughs as she continues situating stuff under the tree.

"Oh, I beg to differ. I think they're all kinds of sexy...on you. Especially when you're pregnant."

Straightening she turns to face me, the light from the fire dancing over her skin, casting her in flickering shadows.

"Get over here, Stella." I order, my voice gritty with lust for her.

She comes to stand in front of me, red flames from the fire reflecting in the inky wells of her eyes. Gently taking her shoulders in my hand, I turn her to face the tree, dropping to my knees behind her. My gaze settles on the flap that has been drawing my attention all night. I make work of first on button and then the next, letting the material fall open to reveal my own personal gift.

Two perfectly rounded ass cheeks with the thinnest bit of candy cane striped cotton nestled in between them. When I place a kiss to one then the other cheek before landing an open handed slap on them. Stella's hands fist at her sides as a moan slips from her lips.

Reaching behind me, I drag the ottoman over and place it in front of her. "On your hands and knees, Stell."

She looks at me over her shoulder before doing what I asked.

"Good girl," I praise as I hook a finger into the top of her panties and drag it over the globes, pink with my hand print, just far enough that I can get at her. I take hold of her ass and spread her open, the pink of her pussy glistening with her need.

"So fucking pretty." I murmur before putting my mouth on her, making her rock forward. My tongue working through her slit, hands tugging on her hips to bring her closer, I suck and nip and kiss her better. I pull away from her just long enough to tug my sweater over my head before burying my face back in her pussy from behind, kneading her ass and loving the weight of it in my hands. When her legs start to tremble and she pushes back against my face, I nuzzle my nose through her wetness to clamp down on her clit making her scream my name over the crooning sounds of Christmas music.

With my mouth I pull every last bit of the orgasm from her, waiting until she stops her rocking and only the soft mewls of contentment fill the room around us.

"You okay, baby?" I ask, as I yank at the button on my jeans, getting them off and kicking them to the side.

"Mmmm, better than okay. You're a freak." Stella says with a soft laugh, resting her head on her folded arms.

"You like it."

"I really do." I can hear the smile in her voice.

With her ass in the air, just poking through the open flap of her pajama's the happy penguins dancing around it, I place a knee on the ottoman beside her, reaching into the opening, and my hand through the slick arousal. She moans in pleasure, a sound that mingles with my own as I slick her wetness over the head of my cock and down my shaft, coating myself with her before I bury myself so far into her pussy she'll feel me there every time she moves tomorrow.

"You ready, Stella?"

I wait, watching my cock at her opening as I slide it back and forth through her lips, up in between her cheeks and back again. When she hisses out a yes, I rock my hips into her, the warmth of her pussy swallowing me, making me groan.

"You're so fucking tight." I praise, pumping in and out, her rounded hips filling my hands. With every thrust her breath comes in a whoosh, my name following the breathy escape.

"Jason. God, Jason. I needed this. I needed you to fuck me. Didn't want anyone to touch me but you."

I hear her murmur and something snaps inside me. Something virile, and savage. With a barely tamed control, I tangle my hand in her hair pulling her head back until I can see into her eyes. Using my hold on her as leverage, I growl in her ear as I pound into her.

"Mine. You're mine, Stella. This pussy is fucking mine. Nobody else's, Mine." M

y orgasm hits me hard and we ride the wave together as she spasms around my cock. I feather kisses down the side of her neck, licking at the corner of her mouth. When she turns her head to meet my kisses I tell her again so that she can hear me, feel me.

"Mine."

Chapter Ten

STELLA

My eyes flutter open, the lights from the Christmas tree and the flicker of the fire casting the room in a warm glow. Jason's arm around my waist, hand splayed against my belly. His hand light against my much darker skin making a beautiful contrast.

Under his hand, the baby rolls and shimmies to his own little beat, or maybe to the cadence of my heart beat. Lord knows it's strong enough laying here in the warmth and safety of Jason's arms. Doing my best to hold back a sigh, I think of all the ways he made love to me last night. All the things we did together, the whispered words and promises. What did it all mean? What did I want it to mean? Did he mean it?

"Come to Chicago with me, Stella."

He sounded sincere. I pretended to be asleep so that I didn't have to answer. So he wouldn't know just how much I wanted that. Jason stirs behind me.

"You awake, baby?" He presses a kiss into my hair.

"Yeah, the baby woke me."

I feel him tense behind me. He lifts his head.

"Everything okay?" Moving his hand just the slightest bit I press his palm into my belly, right where the baby is pushing against me.

"You feel that?"

"Is that the baby?"

The excitement and wonder in his voice is palpable. It makes my heart soar. That he finds as much joy in this baby as I do is more than I could have ever hoped for.

"Yep. Dancing up a storm in there today." I giggle softly.

"Wow. Does it hurt?" He asks, concerned.

"No. Well not always. Sometimes it's uncomfortable but I don't mind."

And I don't. It's a reminder that there's a life inside of me. That my body is housing a tiny little human, part me and part Jason. This baby may not have been created out of love, but he or she is already so loved beyond measure. Shifting so that he can feel the baby at a different angle, I groan.

"What's the matter? You okay?"

"Yeah, I'm just sore."

"From the baby kicking?"

"No. From you, you sex fiend."

He erupts in laughter. "Because I slipped the kitten past the mitten?" He teases.

"What does that even mean?"

"Or because I lit the lamp? A little slappy where mama keeps the peanut butter? Put the biscuit in the basket."

I turn to glare at him, but I can't his face is lit up like the damn Christmas tree he's so pleased with himself.

"It's like you're speaking a different language.You know that, right?"

"That's hockey lingo, Stella. That all means I scored big." He chuckles. "You better learn all this because it's a second language and the kid is gonna speak it."

"What if we have a girl?"

"So. Girls play hockey."

"They also play softball."

"Only if they're smokin' hot." He tweaks my nose before a somber look steals over his face. "I know you heard me last night, Stell."

Shit. My eyes fall from his. I don't know what to say. I don't want to say no but I don't know how to say yes either.

"Come to Chicago. You don't even have to move in with me if you don't want to. I can find you an apartment in my building or close by." He implores.

"And what happens when the team finds out?"

"Stell. I was being stupid before. You're right, you're an adult. They'll probably give me a fucking high five and ask me how I landed a twenty-year-old rocket." Jason teases, trying to reassure me that my age isn't an issue with him anymore.

"Jason, I can't just up and leave everything I have here to follow you around like a lost puppy." I huff, ducking out from under his arm and slipping his sweater over my head. It's the first thing I find on the floor.

"What would you be leaving behind, Stell? You're almost finished with school, you said yourself that your plan was to do your classes online next semester. You can do that from anywhere. Do it from Chicago." He says earnestly.

I walk over to the tree to give myself a bit of space. "You won't even be there, Jason." I argue lamely. I just can't give in on this. If I do, I become exactly what Johnanne accused me of being.

"I'll be there enough. More than I'll be here, that's for fucking sure." He stands. "I'm not asking you to marry me, I'm not forcing you to move in with me, I'm just asking for the chance to take care of you and my kid. I can't stand the thought of you being here and me being there not knowing what's going on with you. I can't, Stell."

"If it weren't for the baby we wouldn't even be standing here having this discussion right now, Jason."

That truth hurts more than it should.

"Maybe, maybe not. But we'll never know. I'm not sorry you're pregnant. I'm just sorry I treated you the way I did when you came to tell me." He says sincerely.

"Me too." I say softly. "When do you have to leave?"

"Tonight." Coming up behind me he wraps his arms around me, settling his big hands on my belly. "Come with me."

My heart is at war with my head. I cannot be *that* girl. It would be so damn easy. "I can't."

"Can't, or won't?" He asks, dropping his arms from around me, bitterness lacing his voice.

"Both." I admit shakily.

TWO WEEKS. That's how long Jason has been gone. Seems like an eternity. Funny how in such a short time I got used to having him around. We talk on the phone almost every day, exchange texts and emails. I sent him an ultrasound picture just this morning. I've even seen his ma and sister Joey a few times. They insist on checking on me constantly. I'm sure Jason put them up to it.

Pulling open the door of the student union, I head back to the financial aid office. It's the last day for the loan deposits and mine still hasn't gone into my account. I have until tonight to pay for my classes or they won't save me a spot. Just as I'm walking in my counselor pops her head of her office.

"Hey girly! I was just about to email you, I have some great news for you. I'm about to go into a meeting, though. Can I call you later?"

"Sure. I have the night off, I'll be around."

She waves and disappears down the hall. Karin has been my counselor since my Freshman year here at FU and my biggest support. She's been the one helping me with my resume and putting feelers out for a job after I graduate.

When I reach the financial aid office, I knock softly to get Harriet's attention. She's one of the three ladies I work with in the department and my favorite.

"Stella, come on in sweetie."

"Hi Harriet. I was just looking at my account so that I can pay for my classes and noticed that the depot didn't go in."

"Well, let's just take a look. I've been on vacation and I swear everything is falling apart."

She clicks her tongue like a mother hen. "Clearly they need me to keep this place running smoothly." Smiling at me over the rim of her glasses she goes back to her monitor. "Huh. Well that's strange."

"What? What's strange." I ask, panic rising. If I don't get this loan money, I'll have to dip into my saving for classes and books. I need the savings for the apartment though.

Harriet swings her monitor my way so that I can see what she's looking at.

"Says here that your classes are paid for and your loans have all been paid off."

She sounds as stunned as I am. I don't have to ask who did this, I know who, I just wasn't expecting it. With tears spilling down my cheeks I stand, mumbling about having to go and walk out of her office before I embarrass myself even more. Reaching for my phone I fumble with it, trying three times to call Jason. He picks up on the third ring.

"Your ears must've been ringing, I was just talking about you, Stella. How you feeling?"

"Did you pay off my student loans?" I manage to get out past the lump in my throat.

"Shit. Stell, don't be mad. Please. If it makes you feel any better, I paid of Joey's too." He says, trying to keep me from getting mad at him.

Mad at him for lifting a burden from my shoulders that keeps me up nights more often than I like to admit.

"I-I'm not mad. Thank you. So much. I know that's not enough but I don't know what else to say." My voice cracks as I start crying even harder.

"You don't have to say anything, baby. Please don't cry." Jason pleads, his voice soothing even as far away as he is.

I don't know how I allowed it, but I've gone ahead and fallen in love with Jason Dagger. Hell, who am I kidding, I didn't allow anything, I never even stood a chance against this man and his big ass heart and capacity to care for those around him.

"Stella, you there?"

"Yes." I sniffle.

"Good. Listen, practice is starting, I gotta get on the ice but I'll call you later okay?"

"Okay."

"Big game tomorrow, I'm playing your boys." He reminds me.

"You're my boy." I tell him.

"Yeah I am. Bye, Stell."

"Bye, Jase."

Chapter Eleven

JASON

Hand over my heart as the National Anthem plays around me, the crowd drowning out the words with their applause and cheering, I try to think about the game but instead I'm worried about Stella. She never answered the phone last night or my texts this morning. It's not like her. I called my ma to check on her but didn't hear back from her before the game so now here I stand, shifting in my skates on the ice, getting ready to play the number two team in the league thinking about my pregnant not quite girlfriend instead of the game I'm about to play.

The anthem ends in a flourish and we skate off the blue line and head for the bench. As I pass the Sin Bin I come to a stop, ice spraying out around me. There, in one of the designated seats they use for contest winners, is Stella beaming at me through the plexiglass. She's wearing a red shirt with a number seven emblazoned on it along with the words 'Future Hockey Player' and an arrow pointing at her belly.

"What are you doing here?" I yell to be heard over the crowd. She just shrugs and points at me. The whistle blows and my name is called by the guys on the team. With one last glance at Stella, I skate off. As much as I hate leaving her, I have a game to play. Not that I'm going to be able to keep my head in the game.

As I get into position and wait for the puck drop, I glance once more at Stella over my shoulder. She waves excitedly and sits in her seat to watch.

"Who's the pregnant chick? She's a rocket!" one of the Boston players says, making eyes at Stella. "I heard pregnant pussy is the best. Maybe I'll show her how a real man scores. Eh, Dagger?"

Before he even finishes his sentence my vision has gone red. I throw my stick down and drop my gloves, shaking my hands free and swing before the fucker even sees it coming. I swing and connect two more times before he grabs a hold of my sweater and tries pulling it over my head.

"Wanna talk shit about my woman, Fleddy, you fuck?" I demand as I swing again.

Whistles blow and players are yelling around us, getting in their own scuffles now. When I get him on the ice the refs pull me off him, my teammates encircling me to keep Fleddy from coming at me now that the refs have blown the whistle on the fight. One of the linesman takes my arm and leads me to the penalty box where Stella is standing, pressed against the glass, her face a mask of worry. Stepping into the box and ignoring the seat the linesman points me to I open the little door that separates me from Stella.

"How are you here?" I yell, ignoring everyone around me blowing whistles and shouting at me.

"Levi called in some favors." She says, eyes roaming my face I can feel bleeding from my fight with Fleddy. "Are you okay? You're bleeding."

"I'm fine."

"Dagger, what the fuck are you doing?" Taner, my captain yells and bangs on the glass. My ass is gonna get on so much trouble. But once I saw Stella I didn't really care.

"Better tell me what you're doing here before you get me kicked out of here." I shout near her ear.

"I got the job, here in Chicago!" Stella yells excitedly. "So I was wondering if you wanted a couple roommates?" She bites her lip and looks at me, eyes big and hopeful, face flushed from all the excitement.

"Yeah?" I ask in shock. Never in a million years did I think she would give in. I know that she said she's here because she got the job, but I'm what really brought her here. She doesn't have to say it for me to know.

"Yeah!"

"What if I want more than a roommate?" My eyes search her face, looking for the answers that I need.

I get my answers when she launches herself into my arms, tears streaming down her face, as she kisses me, her tears mingling with my sweat. The crowd explodes in cat calls and cheers, drowning out everything else. I pull back to look down into her face and kiss her one last time before putting her back on her feet. My teammates are all beating their sticks against the boards in applause reminding me of where the hell I am.

The ref comes over a look of absolute bemusement on his face, "Can we play the game now, Dagger?"

With a wink at Stella, I plop down on the bench in the penalty box. "Yeah, I'm good."

"You sure?" He asks bewildered.

Turning my head, eyes locked with Stella's I nod, my lips sliding into a wicked grin when she blows me a kiss. "I'm sure."

The End

Thank you for reading!

Thanks so much for reading Sin Bin! If you enjoyed Stella and Jason's story, make sure you pick up the next standalone in the Fulton University Hockey series. Levi's story, Sweater Weather comes out this winter. You can add it to your TBR now!

http://bit.ly/2zeisuCSweaterWeather

About the Author

Mandi Beck has been an avid reader all of her life. A deep love for books always had her jotting down little stories on napkins, notebooks, and her hand. As an adult she was further submerged into the book world through book clubs and the epicness of social media. It was then that she graduated to writing her stories on her phone and then finally on a proper computer.

A nursing student, mother to two rambunctious and somewhat rotten boys, and stepmom to two great girls away at college, she shares her time with her husband in Chicago where she was born and raised. Mandi is a diehard hockey fan and blames the Blackhawks when her deadlines are not met.

Also By Mandi

STONED

A Wrecked Novel-

Amazon US: My Book

Amazon UK: My Book

Amazon AU: My Book

Amazon CA: My Book

Rhythm:

Wrecked novella 1.5

LoveHurts

Caged Love Series Book One

Amazon US: http://amzn.to/1uh4bKd

Amazon UK: http://amzn.to/1sUgoDK

Amazon AU:http://bit.ly/1KUKs8b

Love Burns

Caged Love Series Book Two

Amazon US: http://amzn.to/1JjgqGG

Amazon UK: http://amzn.to/1JjxoGt

Amazon AU: http://bit.ly/1F9J16u

TWISTED

An Imperfect Love Kindle World story

Amazon: http://bit.ly/2ved6xCTwisted

Find Mandi

Places to find MANDI on the internet

- FACEBOOK PAGE: www.facebook.com/authormandibeck
- TWITTER- https://twitter.com/authormandibeck
- WEBSITE- http://www.authormandibeck.com/ (sign up for my Newsletter and order signed paperbacks)
- INSTAGRAM http://instagram.com/authormandibeck/
- FACEBOOK READER GROUP (MANDI BECK'S BOOKS): https://www.facebook.com/groups/1023028511060131/
- YOUTUBE CHANNEL:http://bit.ly/2osZ78sYouTube

OUT OF FORMATION

Star cheerleader Elena Murray has had a crush on Colin Findlay for most of her life. She was sure he had no interest in her— right up until the night came when they couldn't keep their hands off each other, but an unexpected development followed by a misunderstanding brought her hopes for a relationship with him to an end.

For more than two months Elena thought there was no chance she and Colin would ever find a way to be together.

And then he turned up at her university as the new head coach for the football team.

Chapter One

Elena

My backpack is in the process of sliding down my arm when Becky Hillstrom—of the acclaimed *Virginia* Hillstroms, she frequently brags— starts one of her infamous inquisitions. Her firing off questions is in no way surprising since we jokingly refer to her as The Interviewer because she never stops.

"How was your uniform fitting? Did you get that body butter I told you about with the shimmer, the one that doesn't smell like alcohol? And last but not least, tell me you took the time to read Julia's email."

I nod as I set my bag on the floor and slide into my seat.

"Which one is a yes?" she asks.

I let out a little laugh as I unzip my bag to pull out my iPad, a notebook, and a pen, all of which I set out on the desk.

"Most of the above," I answer. "The fitting went well—no gains since last year, which means I didn't get any crap from Mandy. The body butter is as good as you said it would be, I'm so excited I finally found one that complements my apricot and honey body wash. As far as Julia's email goes, I got it on my way here but didn't even have time to skim it. Feel like breaking it down for me or should I start reading?"

The way Becky's face lights up tells me that whatever the email says, it's exciting and she cannot wait to fill me in. Her expression suggests it's either significant team news or unbelievably juicy gossip.

When she dramatically leans closer to my desk, I'm sure there's gossip involved. "I freaking knew you wouldn't have read it! Honey, prepare yourself because I am about to give you some knowledge."

I snort out a laugh and nod my head. "Hit me," I joke. No doubt this is gossip based, but I'm betting it's nothing too good seeing as how this is the first day of our senior year in college. There hasn't been time for anything exciting to happen with our group since a lot of people only arrived back in town over the last few days.

Since I spent the majority of the last eight weeks camped out on the couch at home trying to get over a broken heart, I've been pretty oblivious. Not anymore, though. As of today, I've officially pulled my head out of my ass, and I am going to get back into the swing of things. No more sad sack me. From now on, it's all going to be positive.

"Coach Adams got fired. F-I-R-E-D *fired*," Becky announces dramatically.

My brows shoot up as I take in the information. Coach Adams has been the head coach of the Tigers for the last thirty years. In this town, he is to football as God is to earth. There's a freaking *statue* of him out in the front quad for goodness sake, and each year theres a parade in his honor after the last game of the season. In the three seasons I've been a cheerleader for the university I've never heard anything less than reverential about him, which honestly has always struck me as a bit weird. Personally, Ive always found him a bit pompous and a lot stiff, but that's just me.

Football is a serious money maker here. Having a Division I football team and an award-winning cheerleading squad is a big deal at the university, and Coach Adams's high profile got the football team and the cheer squad a lot of money for equipment and travel. Whether he's the warmest guy in the world or not, he's like a religion in this town and on this campus. I can't imagine the athletic department without him at the helm.

The more I think it over, the easier it is to conclude that Becky is wrong. There's no way Coach Adams is gone. I'm pretty confident he could run around the quad naked, and no one would say a word.

"Wait a minute," I say, my tone dripping with suspicion. "You're pulling my leg, right?"

Becky shakes her head. "No," she whispers emphatically. "He had an affair with a student last year and then dumped them during the summer. Apparently, it wasn't the first time he's slept with a student—but it was the first time the student he dumped had pictures and video to share with the administration. It was also the first time Coach Adams was dumb enough to have had an affair with someone who comes from a family full of major donors to the university. Even though technically the student is now an alumnus, it's provable that the affair took place over the course of their senior year."

It's the juiciest thing to happen at our school since ever. I'm shocked but also endlessly curious about who Coach Adams had an affair with. *"Shut. Up,"* I whisper-squeak. "Does anyone know who the student was?"

When Becky's eyes light up as she grins like a Cheshire Cat I can tell she's been waiting for this very question. "That shitty little ass-grabber, Michael. *Freaking*. Simmons."

Swear, my eyes bulge out of my head for like four seconds. Maybe even five. My brain rejects her assertion in the most definitive of ways. Michael Simmons was one of the biggest douchebags on campus. He graduated last year, but for the three years he was on campus when I was, he managed to hit on or have sex with every girl I know. "There's no way—"

"Bible, this is the truth," Becky assures me. "I thought everything you're thinking right now when I found out. Captain of the football team, future president, Mr. Never-Without-a-Girl-on-His-Arm and voted Most Likely to Have Five Wives is at least bi, if not gay. To say he hid it well is an understatement."

"How is *no one* talking about this on Facebook or Snapchat? Both are like gossip central to this school," I point out.

"It's because the whole thing is just starting to leak out now. By later tonight, social media and the entire campus will be on fire with gossip since we'll all be getting read the riot act this afternoon. A lot of this was covered in Julia's email, which you really should have read on general principle alone considering she's your coach," she says dryly.

I give a sheepish shrug because it's not like I can argue the point. She's right.

"Anyway," Becky continues, "the staff found out in waves. Julia was told to be on campus two weeks ago for an official meeting of the athletic department. She said she knew right away that calling her in before the school year even started meant something was up, and she wasn't wrong. Once she and the other team coaches had the info, they were sworn to secrecy. Some of what I know didn't get covered in the email, but since shes my cousin, I leaned on her until she gave up what she could."

Becky's eyes sparkle with excitement as she shifts in her seat, her hands sliding over the bright orange surface of her desk. "The bottom line is that we only know about it now because they've canceled all practices today for a mandatory meeting where the dean will be reading the entire athletic department the riot act. Anyone involved in sports here at the college has to attend. They're going to lay the law down about personal relationships with the coaching staff."

I flip my hair over my shoulder as I roll my eyes. "Michael Simmons may have dabbled in some ancient ass but come on," I say dismissively. "Not one of the rest of us is even a little bit attracted to any of the coaching staff. They're all *old*. The college has absolutely *nothing* to worry about."

Becky nods in agreement. "I know," she whispers dramatically. "Like any of us care about geezers who blow up balls all day."

I haven't held on to my virginity to lose it to a random coach—not that I'm saying being a virgin right now makes me smart. In fact, quite the opposite. I've held onto it because I'm an idiot who has spent far too many years focused on one person—the very one who wants no part of my virginity. I've done my best to like other people, including guys here at college that I tried dating but that quickly went nowhere. All of the binge-drinking around campus (and closet steroid use with the athletes) isn't attractive to me at all. Don't even get me started on how many of them don't know how to do laundry. There's a smell in the boy's dorms and apartments that is stomach turning, so staying away from them hasn't been a problem.

Meanwhile, whenever my friends talk about my virginal state, I lie and tell them that I'm holding out for a business type. It's a lie. I have—*um, had, dammit! Why does my brain not understand that it's time to use past tense when thinking of him*— a major crush on a man who is the epitome of the athletic type, and no one else has ever measured up to him in my eyes. Not even close. After the events that went down two months ago, I've decided I need to move on. The harsh insinuation that I'm too young to know what I want was a tough pill to swallow—one that's still giving me indigestion.

No, I need to focus. And right now, I've decided the best thing to do is to set my sights set on what happens after graduation because once I'm out of college, I'll be meeting and interacting with different men. Surely it will be easier to find someone, right? In a perfect world, Monday through Friday my man will wear a suit, and on Saturdays, he'll wear nothing at all because we'll be busy rolling around in his bed. Sundays will be casual—maybe khaki pants and a button-down that is most *definitely* not sexy jeans that perfectly emphasize a ridiculously sexy ass or a T-shirt that shows off an unbelievably perfect upper body. Certainly not a chiseled jaw with a perpetual five o'clock shadow, perfectly kissable lips and coppery chocolate colored eyes that make me weak in the knees.

Andddd I'm now thinking of *him* again. Dammit!

Picturing that body and those see-through-everything eyes, even for a few seconds, makes my heart beat funny in my chest. I do my best to push those thoughts away. I need not to focus on him anymore. When will that get easier? I'm so lost in my thoughts that I startle when Becky taps my shoulder.

Following the finger she's pointed to the front of the room, I realize our professor is writing something on the board. Shaking off my dreams of a perfect future, I open my blank notebook and uncap my pen to take notes as the first class of my senior year gets underway.

Chapter Two

Elena

Now

I had to run all the way across campus to make this meeting on time. I'm not even sure how I managed it, but somehow I did. A quick glance around the gym shows that the bleachers are almost full of cheerleaders, football, baseball, soccer, and basketball players. I breathe a sigh of relief when I see that none of the coaching staff are in place yet, which means I'm not going to get yelled at for being tardy. I spot my best friend waving at me from the very front row of the bleachers in the section where the cheer squad is sitting. I hurry across the shiny wooden floor and take the seat he saved me next to him, stretching my legs out in front of me dramatically as I lean into his side. Yes, my best friend is a guy. No, he isn't gay. No, we don't like each other. There's zero sexual tension, and there has never been.

Miles is the yin to my yang. In addition to being the best friend a person could ask for, he's also my cheer partner and has been since we were thirteen years old. I love the camaraderie of the cheer squad in general, but Miles is my person. The two of us are considered to be a big deal in cheerleading circles, which is why we were offered full scholarships to a dozen schools. We narrowed it down to two universities with Division I teams, one Miles wanted and the one I'd had my heart set on from the start. There were two reasons I wanted to come here. First, it's less than twenty minutes from Nanny and Pop's house. Second, it's *his* alma mater and I idolized him. What can I say—my reasoning on the second thing seemed solid at the time.

In the end, Miles let me choose, which is why we're here, under an hour away from where we went to high school. The university Miles wanted to go to is clear across the country. Especially after the events of this summer, I know we made the right decision in coming here.

On every level, this school has been good to us both academically and physically. In the three years we've been here, we've helped the cheer squad earn half a dozen state and national championships, and for the last three years running we've taken first place in every one of the coed partner stunt competitions.

The trust I have in Miles—as the person who tosses me into the air only to catch me—literally—within the palm of one hand is immeasurable. I've met dozens of fly girls over the years who *could* be amazing but are instead stuck at being "good" because their partners aren't rock solid. That isn't the case with me. In all honesty, Miles is the more talented of the two of us. It takes incredible strength and stamina to throw a one hundred and twenty-five-pound five-foot five-inch girl for hours and hours every day, but he does it without complaint. I enjoy cheerleading, and I always have, but at the end of the day, the reason I've taken it as far as I have is entirely down to Miles.

I grin as he playfully jabs at my side with his elbow so that I don't do something crazy like fall asleep on him, something I've been known to do. The joke on the squad is that I'm borderline narcoleptic. I frequently fall asleep while waiting for the team to assemble and I also tend to nod off at the picnic tables on the quad. What can I say? I like sleep. A lot.

"Are you cooking chicken breasts tonight or am I on my own for dinner?" Miles asks.

After our freshman year when we both lived in dorms, we moved in together into an off-campus townhome his parents rent for him on a month-to-month basis. His family refuses to allow me to pay rent or any of the bills, despite my protests. I make up for it by keeping the house stocked with food and by doing all of the cooking. It's the perfect arrangement for all of us.

I yawn and stretch my arms as I sit up straight. "Don't be a dope, of course I'm cooking. I forgot my afternoon snack, which means I haven't eaten since lunch. Two tablespoons of peanut butter, an apple and a cup of cottage cheese weren't enough to fill me up. You don't know how badly I wish there were a way to automate the chicken breasts dropping onto our George Foreman grill about eight minutes before we get home. I'm that hungry."

Miles narrows his eyes as he shakes his head. "You know how important the afternoon snacks are," he scolds. "You're off by about two hundred calories for the day because of that. I should've checked your backpack this morning before you left the house."

I shrug, not in the least bit concerned. "Cut me some slack, *Dad*," I say dryly. "I was in a rush this morning and forgot. The first day of school and all, ya know? I solemnly swear that I'll do better tomorrow."

"See that you do," he says firmly. "I'm the one throwing you around all afternoon, and when you're hangry, you turn into a major bitch."

I snort out a laugh as I give him the finger. It's not like I can argue—he's one hundred percent right. I get cranky as hell when I'm starving, and during our official season, I'm hungry almost all of the time because my diet is so strict. I have to keep my weight steady and my core strength on point, which doesn't give me much wiggle room at all. There are no off days for flyers—there can't be. If I gain five pounds, that's five extra pounds that Miles has to balance when he's tossing and catching me. Cheerleading is a far more brutally regimented sport than most people realize.

Since Miles and I spent a fair amount of our free time today texting each other about the gossip with the football team, I'm able to launch directly into questioning if he's heard anything about who will be replacing Coach Adams.

"Just wait until I tell you what's up! I just found out before I sat down—I can't believe you don't know yet. First of all, this has been going on for quite a while. I gotta think the school got lucky that it all blew just after the semester officially ended because it meant the football season was over and they could keep it quiet. They've spent the weeks since it all hit the fan scrambling to find a new coach. The football team was told about this last week, at which time they were warned that if they valued their scholarships, they would need to keep their mouths shut until the announcement could be made. They'd originally offered the coaching job to Mr. Peters, but since he didn't want to move from the assistant coach position, they went outside and found someone else."

I nod as he finishes talking. "Interestingggg," I drawl. "Any word on the new guy?"

Miles leans in closer with a look of clear excitement on his face. "It's your... um..." his brow furrows as he pauses. After a second of thinking he makes a dismissive motion with his hand. "Doesn't matter I guess. I just never know what to call him, so I guess we need to work on that. Anyway, it's none other than Colin Findlay! Makes sense they went with an alum. Gotta say though if the dean was looking for a way to ward off sexual crushing on coaches, he just failed miserably. I think you might be the only person here who'll be immune to him."

My smile feels frozen in place, my stomach is buzzing like I just arrived at the top of a roller coaster and my mouth seems to have become a damn desert. I let out a fake sounding laugh because I know I have to react to Miles's words, but it's the best I've got.

As far as Miles knows, Colin Findlay is merely a part of my extended family. That's a very simplistic description of how we're connected, but it's the one I normally go with. I know Colin because his grandparents were such a huge part of my life. Miles has no clue that I've had feelings for Colin since forever, and I would like to keep it that way especially since he's asked me a million times who my first crush was, and I've always said I can't remember.

That is one big ass lie because a girl never ever forgets her first crush. That's doubly true when the crush in question is Colin Findlay. I just never wanted to talk about it because I knew it would get me a ton of side eye and jokes about me wanting someone so far out of my league. Colin is ten years older than I am, after all.

I swallow nervously as my heart skips a beat. Jesus. Of all the colleges in the world, he's taking a job at mine? And why freaking now of all the times?

The Findlays came into my life when my mother—I use the term loosely—rented the guesthouse on the back of his grandparents' property. She was there from the time she divorced my dad when I was six until she went off to find herself shortly before I started seventh grade.

During those years unless there was a game, Colin would show up at his grandparents' house every Sunday to hang out during the afternoon and then have dinner with them. Since the majority of my time was spent in Nanny and Pop's house, I got to spend a lot of time swooning over Colin up close and personal. Of course, there was nothing real to it back then—he's ten years older than me and even as a kid I was smart enough to know that little girls in pigtails doing cartwheels on the lawn were hardly going to light up his heart. It didn't matter though because he was always, always nice to me. As a child I idolized him, but around the time I was fifteen, my feelings started to morph into something a lot deeper than that.

Colin has always been gorgeous and he could've been a giant, entitled prick who blew off the annoying little girl who trailed after him and hung on his every word but he never did. Instead, he was kind and engaging, and he never made me feel worthless, something I'd needed back then since my mother spent the years between divorcing my dad and marrying husband number two "finding herself." I suspect the reality is that what she was actually doing was trying to figure out a way to make me disappear. Her lack of interest in me and the endless caravan of boyfriends strolling in and out of her life had been difficult.

The one good thing about living with her during those years had been the Findlays. Nanny and Pop, as they'd instructed me to call them, were the grandparents every child wishes they had. On the alternating weekend that I wasn't visiting my father, my mom found one reason or another to dump me on Nanny and Pop, and they never hesitated to take me. They were my constants during those years, and I'd missed them desperately when I'd moved forty minutes away to live with my dad.

Fortunately, my dad had been good about allowing me to maintain a relationship with them. He was smart enough to know that cutting off the people I considered to be my grandparents would've gone over like a lead balloon. I'd visited the Findlays every other weekend for at least one night; they were always in the bleachers for my cheerleading competitions—even the ones that were out of state—and they attended both my junior and senior high graduations. They were two of the most important people in my life until nine weeks ago when they passed away within hours of one another.

It was a nightmare, something I'm still struggling to deal with. Nanny passed first, very suddenly in her sleep. The tone of Pop's voice when he called that morning to tell me she was gone is something I'll never forget. If heartbreak were a sound, it was his the way he spoke when he said she was gone. I raced out of my house and drove like the wind to get to Pop so that I could be by his side when the funeral home came to take Nanny away. Colin arrived less than an hour after me, and his parents showed up about ten minutes after that. We all stood together and prayed as the hearse took Nanny away.

I flash back to that day a lot, looking for a moment where maybe there was a clue that Pop was about to die too, but there's nothing. He was heartbroken and sad, but he didn't seem ill. It was the first—and obviously last— time I ever saw him cry. About two hours later Colin's dad, Carson, picked up soup and sandwiches for lunch and the five of us ate it at the table together. After we finished eating, the men had gone to the funeral home, and I'd stayed behind with Colin's mom because she wasn't getting around well.

As bad as the day had been it only got worse when Colin and his dad walked back into the house two-and-a-half hours later, without Pop. In a voice thick with emotion Colin had been the one to tell his mother and me that Pop had died. We hadn't believed him until he and Carson explained how it happened.

After they'd finished agreeing on all the arrangements, the funeral director had left the room to give his secretary the obituary so she could call the paper. Colin and Carson told us that about a minute or so after the director left the room, Pop, in the middle of nodding his head at something one of them had said, abruptly stood and smiled. "It's time for me to go," he'd said before he hugged his son and then his grandson. "I love you all. Kiss my girls for me."

They understood he'd meant Colin's mom and me, but were confused about why he was talking like he couldn't do that himself. Then he held out his arms as he took three steps across the room like he was going to hug someone.

"My Gracie," he'd said.

Colin and his dad were understandably confused about why Pop was talking to his wife like she was there. They never got to ask what was going on since the next thing they knew, Pop crumbled to the ground, dead. He was just there and gone from one minute to the next. Colin performed CPR, and the paramedics were there within minutes, but it was too late.

Losing two of the most significant influences in all of our lives rocked our worlds, to say the least. Because of that, I'll never be sure if what happened in the days that followed was just a moment of insanity brought on by grief. The only thing I can say about that is it didn't end well.

Before the drama between us, Colin was the person I fantasized would be my husband someday. Some might say that it was nothing more than a case of hero worship or even wave it off as some form of weird attraction because he was once a big deal in sports. He'd been drafted about four seconds after he graduated from this university and was then in the NFL for three years before a torn ACL sidelined him for good. He took two years off after that and then went back to school one state over to earn his MBA. After graduation, he took a job there on the coaching team. Granted, coming here isn't a big move—it's only about a two-hour drive—but it is a big surprise. Why he's picked up his life and moved here is a mystery—one I'll likely never get an answer to, considering the way things stand.

Realizing that Miles is staring at me because he's expecting a response, I shrug and toss my hair over my right shoulder in a disaffected way. "That's, uh, great," I offer weakly. "It'll be... nice to see him and say hi," I lie. "How's the team about all of this? Excited?"

Miles shrugs. "They're kind of all over the place from what I'm hearing. Coach Adams was like fucking royalty here—they all looked up to him. To find out that he was cheating on his wife with a student didn't sit well. I mean, it's a Division I team, and no one wants to fuck with success. It's a big old mess."

"I wonder why Colin took the job," I say, thinking out loud. "I didn't know he'd even thought of coming... um, home."

Miles is only half listening to me because he's suddenly busy eye-fucking Stella, one of the female soccer players who just sat down across the way on the bleachers. "It's possible that he's going back," Miles says in a distracted sounding voice. "It's a trial contract—the school is understandably wary about committing to anything in the wake of what Adams did—so right now it's only for one season. I'm sure he'll tell you all about this at some point. I'm surprised he didn't call to tell you this. I guess there hasn't been time. Dude's been single for a long time—maybe he finally found a serious girlfriend."

Miles has no idea how those two throw-away sentences just sliced at me, and I do my best not to let it show on my face but the truth is that inside I feel like I just got kicked in the gut. I don't know what I'll do if Colin is dating since the very idea makes me ill. The last serious girlfriend he had, Amy, was in the picture from around the time I was sixteen to sometime before Christmas about two years later. He hasn't brought anyone else home for any family events since Amy, and Nanny and Pop had both commented that he was holding off on dating until it felt real. If he's dating again now, that's not good.

Forcing myself not to think about the possibility of him having found the future Mrs. Findlay in the weeks we haven't spoken, I focus on the other issue—the fact that he didn't call or write to tell me he was coming. Granted, I'm the one who didn't take his calls for several weeks but this is big news. You'd think he'd have found a way to let me know. At the very least he should've had Sam or Lolo—his two best friends—call to give me a heads up.

I'm a mess and staying in this seat is costing me. Apparently I have acting skill I never knew about. Taking a deep breath I try to pump the brakes on the million scenarios that are going through my head right now. Colin is here. At my school. And Miles is right too in pointing out that he didn't bother to call, text or email any heads up.

My thoughts come to a screeching halt as my skin breaks out into goosebumps and I get a tingling feeling in my stomach. Turning my head to the left, I'm not surprised to see the Adonis I've had a crush on since I was just a kid walking into the gym with a group of other coaches as well as the president of the university and two of the deans.

The amount of nervousness I'm feeling right now is on a whole other level. My palms are clammy enough that I have to wipe my hands nervously against my jeans, never taking my eyes off of Colin as he makes his way to the center of the court.

I've never been so glad to be dressed well in my life. I put a little extra effort into my appearance this morning since it's the first day of school for this year and I started the day with that whole new year new me, mantra. My short sleeved aqua colored dolman top shows off my tan, my white skinny jeans make my legs look long and lean, and the teal colored Converse I'm wearing make the outfit cute and day appropriate. I even took the time to barrel curl my hair this morning, so it's down and styled in beachy waves. I'd be dying of shame right now had I been foolish enough to schlep my butt in here in sweats and one of my team T-shirts.

I fiddle with my small gold hoop earrings—a gift from the Findlays for my thirteenth birthday— as I watch Colin talking to someone from the athletic department I don't recognize. I can't take my eyes off of him, but he hasn't so much as looked in this direction. I'm somehow crushed that I felt a change in energy within the gymnasium as soon as he entered, yet he doesn't notice me sitting here, not fifteen feet from where he's standing. He *knows* I'm a cheerleader here. That he doesn't appear to have even the slightest bit of curiosity about whether I'm in the gym is horrifying, all things considered.

The butthurt grows when he never looks my way at any point during the meeting. Not when the president and the dean take turns speaking, not when the head coaches each take a minute to assure everyone that all rules will be followed, and not when he himself is introduced to say a few words. It's as if my portion of the bleachers don't even exist, and that stings. Whatever connection I believed we had was nothing more than temporary idiocy. As the university president speaks, I force my gaze away from Colin, determined to ignore his very presence on earth.

"In closing, I want to reiterate that this is very, very serious. If any of the rules about student/staff behavior are violated, the staff member will be dismissed *immediately* and the student will face expulsion. There is no middle ground on this. Be mindful of these rules when the normal athletic schedule resumes tomorrow, and everything will be fine. Break them and you'll feel the consequences immediately."

I've never heard Rothstein speak so firmly about anything. Normally he's an uptight but fairly affable type of man. Not today. Clearly, this whole thing with Coach Adams was a game changer. Pun intended. But right now I care about none of that because I'm too busy being salty about Colin's complete and utter obliviousness to my presence on this earth, even though I am one hundred percent certain he knows I go here since I told him myself.

"...feeling some Italian dressing as the marinade for your chicken tonight. You cool with that?"

Shit. I've been so focused on my anger for the last few minutes that I forgot where I am. Shaking it off, I look up and find Miles staring down at me expectantly.

"Uh, yeah, sure," I agree as I hastily stand and grab my peach colored wristlet from the bleacher. "Italian dressing it is. I'm also going to make some broccoli and a baked potato for us to split so if you'd take charge of throwing together a salad, that'd be tops. Maybe after dinner, we can watch an episode of *Modern Family*."

Miles throws an arm around my shoulders and pulls me into his side before dropping a kiss on the top of my head. "No can do tonight, baby girl. After dinner I'm going to Stella's to *study*," he jokes, only loud enough for me to hear.

Leaning in closer to him, I look up and give him puppy dog eyes as I push my lip out and pretend to pout. "Should I worry? I've heard if you use it too much *it falls off*," I joke.

Miles tosses his head back and laughs, which draws the attention of pretty much every girl within fifty feet. Since we were thirteen years old, Miles has always been one of the most popular and most sought-after guys I've ever known. He gets more ass than Lazy Boy, but somehow he doesn't have a man-whore reputation. I suspect this is because he's kind, funny, and doesn't treat girls like dog shit to make them do his bidding.

I'm not blind—he's a smoking hot twenty-one-year-old version of Alexander Skarsgård. Blond haired, blue eyed, six feet tall, muscles for days, clear skin, perfect teeth, a sexy jawline *and* a sense of humor. On top of all that he's rich as hell, drives a Mercedes and has impeccable manners. People often suspiciously ask us how he and I have never hooked up. Our answers are the same—we're like siblings. I understand that he's attractive, but I have absolutely no interest in him, and I know he feels the same way about me.

"You're a nut," he jokes. "You wanna stop and say hi to Colin—"

"No!" I squeak. "I mean, not now. I'm sure I'll see him later. I'm so hungry right now I could eat your arm. No time to chat. He looks busy anyway."

Miles chuckles and nods as he guides us toward the exit. I breathe an inward sigh of relief that he bought my excuse. As far as Miles is concerned, Colin isn't on my radar—nor has he ever been. I mean to keep him oblivious to the reality. If he knew how I really felt—and what's gone on—he'd be grilling me on the daily.

As we make our way to the double doors that lead to the hall, I get the strongest sensation of being watched. I refrain from turning back for as long as I can, but just as we get to the doors curiosity gets the better of me, and I look over my shoulder.

My mouth goes dry as I stumble, eyes wide as I realize that the person looking at me is Colin. Standing with his arms crossed over his chest he's watching me with narrowed eyes. Even from this far away I can see that his jaw is clenched. I barely have time to blink before Miles is tugging me through the doors, but I keep looking back over my shoulder at Colin until the large silver door closes behind me, cutting off my view.

Judging by the anger on his face, I'm guessing seeing me was not a highlight of his day. Great—this is just what I need. It's bad enough that I've never gotten over him. Having to now live in the same town as him is going to be hard—and his obvious displeasure with seeing me is going to make it worse.

After parting ways with Miles in the parking lot, I head for my white Honda Accord Coupe. As I get in and buckle my seatbelt, my cell phone chimes to alert me to a text. Lifting it out of my purse I lift it up to see who it's from. My eyes widen when I see Colin's name on the screen.

Colin: **House. 7pm. Tonight.**

Well, shit.

Chapter Three

Elena

Nine Weeks Ago

It's so foreign to be here in Nanny and Pop's kitchen without them around. How can it be that they're both just... gone? I bite my lower lip to keep it from trembling as I finish towel drying the large chafing dish. Earlier this afternoon it held the mountain of chicken cutlets the caterers dropped off when we got back from the cemetery. After setting the plate on the area of countertop I've designated for dry dishes, I turn and pick up the final clean platter from the dish drainer and start swiping across the glazed surface with the dishtowel. A hint of a smile plays on my lips as I conjure up an image of Nanny telling me to let the darn things drip-dry. Naturally, thinking of her gets me emotional. Setting the platter and the towel down, I rub my hands over my face.

I startle when I hear a noise from behind me. Spinning around, I see Colin. His black suit jacket is gone, his gray tie is loose, and his white dress shirt has one button undone. His left shoulder is propped against the door jam, and his right hand is comfortably in his pocket like he's been in that position for a while.

Although Colin looks tired—or tuckered out, as Pop used to say—it does nothing to diminish how attractive he is.

His gentle smile causes my mouth to go dry. "I told you not to worry about any of this until tomorrow. Why am I not surprised that you didn't listen?"

I can feel a faint blush spreading across my cheeks as I run a hand over the smoothness of the updo I spent a hell of a lot of time perfecting this morning. "I tried but I just couldn't... Nanny always said that dirty dishes left overnight become the next day's science experiment."

He smiles then, the first one I've seen since the day started. No one ever warns you about just how emotionally draining funerals are.

"She pulled that on me too," he chuckles. "I grew up convinced dirty dishes were the first step to damnation. You know it was just her way of teaching us all to be tidy, right? Science experiments on dishes take more time than a night on the counter."

I gesture toward the window over the sink that looks out to the guesthouse I once called home. "Since my mom was a slob I know exactly how long it takes for the science experiment to happen," I sigh. "Without your grandmother to guide me, I'm fairly certain I'd have wound up just like my mother."

He takes his hand from his pocket and lifts it to the back of his neck and begins to rub at it. "She was a mess," he agrees. "Pop told me if it weren't for you, they'd have booted her out within the first three months."

My brows go up as I lean back against the counter, bracing my hands on the coolness of the granite as I stare at him. "They knew that early on she was like that?"

Colin snorts as he nods. "Couldn't have missed it. Hell, even I knew, and I only caught glimpses. My grandparents..." his voice cracks on the word.

I watch the way his throat moves as he swallows and looks away. He closes his eyes for a second or two, the silence stretching between us before he looks back at me. "They both adored you," he says. "A mess in a house they didn't live in was a small price to pay to have you here where they could see you nearly every day."

My hand goes to my mouth, and I do my best to cover a choked sob as the enormity of his statement hits me. I thought I couldn't love them any more than I did a minute ago, but I was wrong. I'd give anything right now to hug Nanny and Pop one more time and tell them how much they mean to me. Colin crosses the room to me and puts his arms around me as I try my hardest to hold back my tears.

I've cried more in the last few days than I have in the last ten years. Consequently, I've also had Colin hug me more than at any other point in my life. It's the most pleasant kind of torture, to be held by the man who has long been the object of my affection. The comfort he's offered me in the days since his grandparents passed has been invaluable. I'd be lying if I didn't admit that in addition to the safety and security I find in his arms, I'm also having one of my lifelong dreams fulfilled.

My four-inch heels give me enough height that I'm only three inches shorter than his six-foot-two-inch frame. This allows me to tuck my head under his chin as I take a few measured breaths to get myself back together before I finally feel strong enough to stand up straight. His arms loosen, but he doesn't let me go. When I look up, I find him looking down at me. There's an expression on his face that makes me feel weak in the knees. I nervously run my tongue along my lower lip only to forget how to breathe when his eyes drop to my mouth and his nostrils flare. Holy crap—is Colin attracted to me?

"Leni," he says huskily. "I wanted to wait—"

The sound of a throat clearing interrupts the moment. Colin's arms drop as he steps away from me to turn toward the kitchen door. Leaning to the left, I see one of the crew from the party rental place that provided the outdoor seating for the luncheon.

"We've got the tent, tables, and chairs loaded into the truck, Mr. Findlay. I just need you to initial here, and we'll be out of your way."

"Right, sure," Colin coughs.

His tone is slightly harried, and I can see the tension in his frame as he walks to the door and accepts the tablet the man is holding out to him. He initials quickly with his finger before he looks back over his shoulder at me with an expression I can't possibly decipher.

"I'm going to walk him to the door and then head upstairs to shower, okay?"

He waits for me to nod before he turns and walks away. Watching him retreat, I can't help thinking about him in the shower—and the fact that we're now alone in the house. For the last four nights, his parents were here as well, but they left directly after the luncheon today since his mom—Mariana—has her four-week post-op checkup tomorrow from her recent knee replacement.

This means that for the first time in my life I'm sharing space with Colin and no one else is around. My room—the one Nanny and Pop decreed was mine within months of my meeting them— is two doors down from Colin's, the large hall bath the only thing separating our rooms.

After wiping down the kitchen counters and folding the kitchen towel over the handle of the dishwasher, I head upstairs. As I walk past the exterior wall of the bath that Colin and I share, I hear the water running through the pipes. The sound makes me think of him in there, naked, and I feel hot and flushed. I quicken my steps and fling the door to my room open, hurrying inside before closing the door softly behind me. I roll my eyes at myself as I meet my reflection in the full-length mirror on the back of the door. You'd think I just went through some Mission: Impossible obstacle course to get up here.

Laughing at my idiocy, I kick off my heels, pull the pins out of my updo and toss them onto my dresser before heading straight for my bed and dropping backward onto it, arms out wide. Across the room, the door to the Jack and Jill bath Colin and I share is firmly closed. In all the years I've stayed here, we've never had a bathroom run-in, not that I haven't fantasized about it. When we're in the house at the same time we know to knock twice on the door before opening it, and the system has always worked.

Rolling my head from side to side on the bed, I inhale the clothesline-fresh scent of my crisp white bedding. For a second or two it's like nothing has changed and Nanny just had them hanging out in the yard, but then the reality hits all over again. Nanny and Pop are really gone now. The thought of them immediately causes a lump in my throat. Sitting up, I scoot myself back on my bed and settle into a comfy spot so that I can rest my head on a pillow and look around at the one place I've ever felt utterly secure in. Here,

I've always known I was loved. Here, I've had no question about my importance.

I love my dad, but a part of me will always be hurt that he spent so long pretending that my mom was parenting. On the other hand, if he'd been more pro-active I wouldn't have had this. And this has been my everything, at least until now. I'm trying my best not to focus on what it will be like not to have this bedroom anymore. The room itself hasn't changed since the year I was eight when the four of us painted it a pale lime green that I'd been obsessed with. I can still remember the way Colin's eyes went wide as he took the lid off the can and saw the color for the first time.

Looking back over his shoulder at me, he smiles. He's always handsome, but his smiles make it over-the-top. "No pink for you, I see," he teases.

I scrunch my nose as I set my hands on my hips. "Pink is for babies, Colin. Lime green is for big girls. ***Cool*** *big girls."*

He chuckles as he pours some of the paint into the paint tray Pop set up on the tarp covering the plush cream-colored carpet. "I can't argue with that logic, Little Bird," he jokes. "After all, you are the coolest."

Obviously, he wasn't attracted to me when I was a child, and that didn't change when I was a teenager. For about five seconds during our summer vacation two years ago I'd thought he was looking at me differently, but later I dismissed that as being wishful thinking. Today, down in the kitchen, there was palpable sexual tension between us and I don't know what to think about it. I mean, what's the deal? Should I be dying of embarrassment because he was about to rebuff me— or was he feeling the attraction as strongly as I was? Of course, I wish for the second, but with my luck, he was just about ready to walk on hot coals to get away from me.

I haven't slept well because I've been too keyed up about the sudden loss of Nanny and Pop. The last few days were a flurry of activity to get ready for the funeral. Colin's mom and I spent the first two days I was here creating photo memory boards to display at the funeral home. Then yesterday Colin, his parents and I all worked together to make some of the food for the luncheon. A lot of things we had been able to order from the caterers but before Pop passed he'd mentioned that he wanted to make some of Nanny's favorite dishes. We'd gone all out to whip up several of both their favorite dishes.

Colin and his dad spending five hours out in the yard grilling chicken and ribs while his mom and I whipped up Nanny's favorite blueberry tarts, cherry cheesecake bites, and a five-layer honey-coconut cake. Now that the funeral is over it's like the exhaustion of it all is hitting me in one giant wave. I can't stop yawning, and my eyes keep drifting shut. I love sleep more than most people do, but this kind of tired is on a whole other level.

Forcing myself not to nod off just yet, I stand up and take off my dress, bra, and thigh high stockings. Too tired to hang any of it up or go to the hamper in my closet I drop it in a pile on the floor before I grab the fluffy coral colored throw at the end of my bed. After getting back into a comfortable position on my bed, I pull the throw over me so that I can take a short nap to recharge my battery.

Chapter Four

Colin

Nine Weeks Ago

I like to believe I'm a decent guy, but right now I'm questioning just how accurate that is. The reason for this is the five-foot-five-inch chestnut-haired beauty who's fast asleep on the bed I'm standing next to. For the record, my intentions coming in here were above board. It's been three hours since I saw Leni in the kitchen and it's well past time for dinner. I texted and called her cell multiple times and then spent a solid minute knocking. When I got no response to any of that, I started to panic. Granted she sleeps at every available opportunity but usually she's easier to wake up. I'm sure the fact that my nerves are still stretched taut after losing Nanny and Pop on the same day played into my panic as well. A series of worst-case scenarios had been playing on a loop in my head as I'd opened the door with the intention of making sure everything was okay. It was supposed to be quick—just a check-in. And then I saw her, and something other than my brain took over.

The bright throw she's got over her may have started out covering her entirely, but right now the top of it is resting just above her belly button, which means she's completely exposed on top. I've been standing here for a good two minutes now fucking transfixed by her unbelievably sexy tits—firm and perky with dusty rose-colored nipples that I'm dying to taste. Then there's her beautiful as fuck face. Poets could write volumes about her lush lips, but I'm no scribe, so all I can say is that Angelina Jolie needs to be jealous of Leni's mouth. I've spent the last few days jerking off to it multiple times a day because of this girl. Hell, I've spent the two years since the family vacation we took the summer after her freshman year of college getting off thinking about her. I come the hardest when I imagine her lips stretched around my cock as I come into that hot little mouth. Jesus *fuck* I want that.

To get myself under control, I look away from her, then swallow back a groan when my gaze drops to the floor, and I see black silk stockings and a sexy black bra there. I'm so hard right now I can barely fucking think straight, and my dick is all but chanting her name. If I weren't wearing fitted boxer briefs under my black sweatpants, my cock would be tenting out like Pinocchio's nose. The impulse to wake this sleeping beauty up with a kiss is almost impossibly strong.

Closing my eyes, I fist my hands and breathe deeply, nearly losing what little resistance I have as her delicate apricot and honey scent permeates my senses—the same smell that almost had me breaking down and fucking her on the kitchen floor just a few hours ago. I breathe through my mouth and start counting backward from one hundred. By the time I get to eighty-two, I'm in a better place. Cracking my eyes open just enough to be able to see, I quickly grab the blanket and position it over her so she's covered and then tuck it around her. Stepping back, I clear my throat and watch her for a reaction. Nothing. I shake my head in wonder at just how out she is and then reach out to nudge on her shoulder.

"Time to wake up, Little Bird."

The little moan she lets out blows my control to smithereens, and it only gets worse when she licks her lips. I can't decide if the universe is trying to reward or torture me right now. She mumbles unintelligibly when I shake her shoulder again. When she cracks open her eyes and smiles dreamily, I forget to breathe for a second or two.

"Mmm, Colin," she says, her voice husky with sleep.

I damn near fall to the fucking floor. Yeah. This isn't a reward. I'm officially being tortured.

"You have to get up, baby," I croak in a voice that sounds like I just spent fifteen hours in the desert without water. And fuck my life, I just called her baby out loud. I normally save that shit for when I imagine pumping into her tight little cunt. The thin cracks in my resistance are quickly becoming a fucking chasm.

She blinks a few times and yawns sweetly as she goes to sit up. My hand shoots out lightning fast and settles on her shoulder to keep her in place. As soon as I touch her, her eyes go wide. Ah. *Now* she's awake.

"Pretty sure you're naked under there," I say before I take my hand away.

"I—what? How do you know?"

The expression of confusion on her face shouldn't be sexy, but it is. I shrug as though I'm unaffected as I very fucking reluctantly take two steps back. "I don't know for sure, but your clothes are on the floor, so..." I trail off, letting the implication hang in the air.

"Oh," she murmurs. "Oops."

I swallow thickly as I look away, doing my best not to focus on how badly I want to fuck her through the mattress. "I came in to make sure you were okay," I explain. "I haven't seen you in three hours, and you weren't answering your cell or your bedroom door."

She blushes and bites her lip, a visual I immediately file in my spank bank. "Wow," she says in a breathless sounding voice. "I passed out."

"It's understandable since on a normal day you could sleep anywhere. Today was far more emotionally exhausting than normal. I fell asleep after my shower for about an hour."

I don't mention that in addition to being emotionally wiped out I'd also been wholly spent after I jerked off and came twice in the shower in response to holding her in my arms earlier. The feel of those sweet little tits pressed against my chest was like a hit of pure lust. Thinking of the way she felt in my arms isn't helping me calm down. I know that if I don't get the hell out of this room immediately, I'm going to need to take care of business again. It's a wonder my palms aren't callused and my dick isn't chafing at this point.

"I'm going to go heat up dinner for us so that we can eat something before we go to Benny's to meet Lolo and Sam."

"Ah," she says with a smile. "Thank you for waking me. I'd have been really upset if I slept through SamLo time. I'll be down in a few."

I nod as I take another step back. "Any particular requests from the leftovers?"

She considers for a few seconds. "A piece of barbeque chicken, a cup of Spanish rice and some of the Caesar salad, dressing on the side."

"No macaroni and cheese?"

Elena loves macaroni and cheese, and Lolo made the world's best for the funeral luncheon.

"Can't do it," Elena says with a disappointed sounding sigh. "When we go to the bar with Lolo and Sam I'm going to treat myself to a drink or two. The calories add up. I can't get off course going into this last season."

I hate when she deprives herself of food that she loves. I don't know why it bothers me since it's not as though she starves herself—she's got curves and she's strong and sexy as fuck—but it does. It's admirable that she's so hardcore about maintaining an exact weight because of cheerleading, but sometimes I'd like to see her eat without worrying about it.

"I'm going to whip up our plates while you get ready for our SamLo time," I say as I turn and head for the door. After leaving, I close it behind me and let out a deep breath, silently giving thanks that I survived having a nearly naked Elena within touching distance. Lolo and Sam would tell me that my self-control is beyond stupid at this point, but I disagree. As much as I value their opinions, they're wrong about trying to push me toward Elena before she graduates.

Lolo (short for Lauren) and her wife Sam (short for Samantha) have been my best friends since further back than my memory even goes, which is to say we were hanging out in our cribs together. We grew up in the same neighborhood, so we've always been a trio. For years people would joke that I'd end up with one or the other, but I've known since at least ninth grade that they were going to wind up together—even during the hard times when they were both trying to pretend they weren't gay. As my longest and dearest friends, there aren't any secrets between us. Not because we haven't each *tried* to be secretive about a thing or two, but because we see through each other. This means they are *well* aware of my Elena obsession. I'd been fairly certain they'd tell me I was insane once they figured it out, but that didn't happen. Instead, they're both supportive of it. Whether because they both adore her or because they're sappy-ass romantics at heart, I don't know.

Elena is a one-in-a-million-girl, the kind people search for and never find. She's gorgeous, compassionate, kind, smart and she makes me laugh like no one else. The future I want has her in it—at the very center of it—and there's nothing I won't do to make that happen. The plan—and I'm trying to stick to it —is to wait until Elena graduates college before I make my play for her. I've been damn firm about that until this afternoon in the kitchen when I almost buckled. Without a doubt, I know that the second we see Lolo and Sam at the bar their Colin-radar is going to ping like crazy. I already know I'll be forced to explain just how close I came to caving in today before the end of the night.

College was where I sowed my wild oats, and I know it was a fundamental transition for me between being eighteen and being a fully functional adult. Trying to tie Leni down would've meant depriving her of the experience, and as much as it has killed me, I believe she needed that. I also didn't think getting into what would primarily be a long-distance relationship with her would've been right. I'd have burned with jealousy sitting in my apartment one state over while she spent her days with frat boys. No, the right thing to do is to let her enjoy all of that without having to worry about a thirty-something boyfriend.

I've come this far—it won't be much longer now. Only one more school year separates me from making my play for her. The way I feel about her isn't small or temporary—if she'll have me I mean to make this permanent. Less than a year now, I remind myself. As I head down the stairs to the kitchen I chant *I think I can; I think I can* in my head.

For the first time in the two years since I realized how deeply I feel for her, I'm not sure I believe that chant anymore. My once iron will is cracking by the hour.

Chapter Five

Elena

Now

My stomach is in knots as I pull down the drive at Nanny and Pop's house and park my car next to Colin's black Jeep Grand Cherokee Trailhawk. This is the first time I've been to the house since the day things blew up and I left in a huff, which also means it's the first time I've been here since the days following the funeral. The emotion of knowing that Nanny and Pop won't be inside is colliding with the anxiety of having to see Colin again and both are making me feel less prepared to deal with this.

Gathering up my courage, I turn off my car, get out and inhale. The scent of Nanny's heirloom roses soothes my soul enough that I'm able to feel a bit calmer. I can do this. Hell, I have to do this because it isn't like I can avoid him forever. We own a home together, after all.

NIGHT After The Funeral

"Yummy," I groan as I set the sugared lemon I sucked after taking a lemon drop shot down on a bar napkin.

"Good stuff, right?"

I grin and give Lolo the thumbs up. "Delicious," I answer. "In fact, I might even have another."

"You should slow your roll so you don't wind up praying to the porcelain god later."

Lolo, Sam, and I all burst out laughing at the same moment.

"In the last two hours I've nursed one beer and now I've taken one shot. I'm not anywhere near drunken puke status," I assure him.

"Funny that you haven't had a peep to say about the two beers I've had or the three fingers of Glenorangie in my glass right now," Sam points out.

Colin looks abashed for a fraction of a second before he grins and makes a dismissive gesture. "I'm fairly certain that Irish whiskey runs through your veins," he jokes. "We all know you could drink at least half this bar under the table without breaking a sweat."

Sam raises her glass in a mock toast. "Factual," she concedes before taking a sip. "Doesn't change the fact that a beer and a shot aren't going to put your Little Bird down, though."

Colin coined the nickname Little Bird for me during the first year I lived on the Findlay property. He'd started calling me that because I used to swing on the elaborate wooden swing set the Findlays had installed in the yard for me for hours on end. He used to joke that I spent more time in the air than on the ground—something that became even funnier when I took up cheerleading and became a fly girl.

Sam and Colin have some kind of weird stare-off for a few seconds before he inclines his head at her in concession.

It's not like he can really deny it since it's very noticeable that Colin is protective of me—more so in the last few years than ever. For some reason he seems to worry more now than he did at any point in time before.

"Who's up for a game of pool?" he asks.

I'm up and off my bar stool in a blink. "Me! I'm breaking."

The three of them laugh in unison. "Of course you are!" Lolo snorts. "We don't call you the ball breaker for nothing."

I shrug as we begin walking back to the game room that holds four pool tables, six pinball machines and three dartboards. On the weekend, the bar is jam-packed but since it's a weeknight we're able to go right to an empty table.

We pair off as we always do—Team SamLo and Team ColEna. We're evenly matched and we all play the same way because Pop is the one who taught us how right at his prized mahogany pool table in the basement.

The way we do it is that after the first round the top two players on either team play each other. Colin and I win the first round but since he sank more balls, he's facing off against Sam. After taking a seat at one of the pub tables against the wall, Lolo and I place an order with the waitress for two more lemon drop shots. After the waitress goes to the bar to put in our order, Lolo turns her attention to me.

"Are you ready for tomorrow?"

I scrunch up my nose in confusion. "What's tomorrow?"

"Will reading," she reminds me.

I nod. "Oh, yeah. I was more worried about getting through today. Honestly, I was surprised when Sam's dad said I was included in it at all."

She frowns as she traces her index finger in an infinity pattern on the tabletop. "It's always hard, even when you know what to expect. After my father died and everything was said and done, the thing that hit me the hardest was the will reading. It made it final for me—more than the funeral, even. I'm not sure why."

"I can see that," I say as the waitress slides our two shots onto the table. After paying her, we quickly clink shot glasses before downing the deliciously cold shot and sucking on the sugar-covered lemon wedges to finish the drink off. For the next few minutes, we sit and cheer on Colin and Sam as they blow through their lightning round of pool. When it's all over, Sam is the victor. They high-five before they start going about the re-setting of the table. Once they hang the sticks back in place on the wall, they stand huddled together to talk instead of coming directly to the pub table Lolo and I are at. As the minutes pass without them coming back, I turn to Lolo for a read on the situation. "It looks like they're discussing world peace."

She snorts and watches them for about two seconds before she shrugs. "They're wrapping it up now," she declares.

I see no signs that they're anywhere near finished but damn if she isn't right since they're headed back this way. The three of them read each other so well it's a little like dealing with triplets who have groupthink.

Lolo and I stand from our seats and grab our purses as they walk our way. Although Colin and I have nothing on our agendas, Sam and Lolo both need to work in the morning and it's after midnight now. Even though I took a three-hour nap, I feel exhausted. The last lemon drop shot has me feeling languid, so I'm mostly quiet as we walk to the parking lot. After exchanging hugs with the girls, Colin and I settle into his car. I love being in the car alone with Colin, especially at night when it's like being in a little cocoon. His Dave Matthews Band playlist is on and right now "Satellite" is playing through the speakers. I yawn as I lean back against the headrest.

"Sometimes I wonder if you'd be able to sleep around the clock if no one woke you up," he says.

"Maybe," I chuckle as my eyes drift shut.

The sound of his car door closing wakes me up a few minutes later. I have just enough time to take my seatbelt off before Colin opens the door for me. "Thought I might have to carry you in," he says.

His husky voice causes an immediate surge of desire to race through my body. Anxious to hide my stiffening nipples I lean forward and grab my purse. Since my bra isn't padded and I'm wearing a fitted off-the-shoulder emperor blue top, I know damn well that they're visible. I clutch my purse to my chest as I step out of his car. The second I put my foot down, I realize my error. Because I didn't look down, I didn't notice where Colin's feet were. The hands I'm clutching my purse with immediately go wide as my foot goes out from under me and I try to balance myself as I start to fall. Colin grabs me and keeps me from going down entirely, but I can already feel my ankle swelling.

My purse is now down on the asphalt but I couldn't care less because my ankle is throbbing. I know this feeling well since I've sprained my ankles cheerleading half a dozen times over the years. The good news is that I've got a few ankle braces upstairs in my room here, so at least there's that. Clutching at Colin's shirt, I look up at him.

"I dropped my purse and I think I sprained my ankle. I'll need to lean on you to make it into the house."

"The hell you will," he growls.

Before I can ask what the heck that means, he's swinging me up into his arms. I startle when he tilts me back and says, "Grab the purse, Little Bird."

Once I reach out my free arm and grab my purse, he closes the car door with his foot and strides toward the side door. This is the one door that Nanny and Pop allowed him to install an electronic door lock. They'd both chosen to eschew the keypad in favor of a traditional key but Colin and I both favor entering the code. When we get to the door, I quickly press the buttons to unlock it. Inside the house, he takes me directly to the living room before setting me down on the couch.

"First let's get your shoes. Then you can elevate it and I'll go make an ice pack," he says as he helps me into a comfortable position. My shoes are easy to remove since I'm wearing a simple pair of slip on leather sandals. Tossing the shoes to the side, Colin crouches down to check out my foot. I hold in a shiver when his hand wraps around my lower leg just above my ankle. Lifting up gently, he looks at the ankle. I've got on a pair of black jean shorts and the warmth of his palm against my skin feels electric.

"It's definitely swollen," he says quietly. "Are you certain it's just a sprain? We can head to Urgent Care to have this checked out."

I shake my head. "It's definitely a sprain. Sadly I know the feeling well. After I ice it for twenty minutes, if you can take me upstairs so I can pull out one of the ankle braces I keep here. I never wear them to bed but if I'm awake, I can use it for a few minutes."

He nods as he grabs two of the decorative pillows on the couch and uses them to elevate my foot. "I'm going to go grab the ice. Do you want me to bring you back anything else?"

"Two ibuprofen would be great."

He returns two minutes later with the ice pack, the pain relievers and a bottle of water, which he opens before handing it to me. I make quick work of swallowing the ibuprofen as he carefully places the ice pack on my swollen ankle.

"So you're an old hand at sprains?" he asks as he sits down on the wooden coffee table. The way he's chosen to sit allows him to keep the ice pack in place. I'm selfishly enjoying the way he's taking care of me.

"It's kind of an occupational hazard. It's one of the reasons I'm okay with the upcoming season being my last. It takes a toll in a lot of ways but for me, the biggest issue has been my ankles. You'd know better than anyone how hard any sport is on the body," I point out.

He lets out a dry laugh as he nods. "So true. I loved football, but I'm not sure I'd have played professionally if I'd known going in that I'd be tearing my ACL. Even though I had surgery, I'll need to be careful with it for the rest of my life. There's a reason pro-ballers get such big paychecks. Between the back, knees, ankle, tendon, and head injuries, most players aren't lucky enough to rock a fifteen-year career like Tom Brady."

"Do you miss it?"

Colin shrugs as he moves the ice pack a bit to the right. "Not as much as I might have had I not wound up coaching. I still love the game—it's just in a different way now."

"Do you plan to stay where you are?"

"Coaching jobs in Division I teams aren't a dime a dozen. Right now I'm there but if something else came up..."

I swallow and look away, a flutter of panic in my chest as I consider what it would feel like if he moved across the country. I've tried not to focus on it, but I'd be lying if I said I'm not scared about what the loss of Nanny and Pop will mean about our future. Will I still see Colin or will we fade out of each other's lives? I don't want to lose him, ever.

"Hey," he says softly as he sets his free hand down on my leg. "Where'd you go?"

I sniffle and try to regain my composure as I swipe my fingers under my eyes. "It's just me being a crybaby," I answer. "I was just wondering how often I'll get to see you now, especially if you took a job thousands of miles away. I'm... scared. It feels like my whole world is crumbling around me."

"Hey, hey," he says soothingly as he gets off the table and crouches down next to me so we're face to face. "I'm not going anywhere, Little Bird. If anything, in two or three years you'll be sick of just how much you see me."

"Never," I answer, my voice trembling.

When he leans in close and pulls me into his arms, I think my whole world stops turning for a second. I sigh in contentment as I wrap my arms around him and return his hug. Somehow he maneuvers around so that he's sitting on the couch with me in his lap—all without disturbing my ice pack.

Being held by Colin is like relaxation in a bottle. I yawn as my eyes flutter shut. I smile as I breathe in the smell that's so distinctly Colin—Calvin Klein One cologne mixed with his natural scent. There's nothing more comforting.

Colin's chest rumbles beneath my ear when he says, "You're tired."

I nod and snuggle in closer as he shifts forward. "Grab the ice pack and hold on," he says. I grab the top of the pack and hold on as he stands with me still in his arms. I'd pay really good money to do this every day of my life. I don't want this to end at all. Now more than ever I need this feeling.

He carries me up the stairs and down the hall like I weigh nothing. My heart pounds at top speed as I try to form words. I know that what I'm about to ask is nuts and perhaps even selfish but I can't not ask.

"I don't want to be alone yet," I blurt anxiously. "Would it be okay for me to chill out in your room with you on the bed and watch some TV until the ice melts?"

Did I mention that the ice pack is insulated and thus will take forever to melt? Although I can't see his face, I couldn't miss the way he gulps. "Of course," he says after a beat. "Anything you need."

When he strides into his room and sets me down on his bed, I just about combust. How many years have I wanted to be in Colin's bed? I idolized him as a child, crushed on him as a tween-ager, and then I developed stronger feelings around the time I was fifteen. They've only grown as time has gone on.

He's gentle with me so as not to jostle my ankle as he uses one of his pillows to elevate my foot before he comes around to the other side of the bed and sits down with his back against the headboard. Picking up the remote from the bedside table he turns the television on before handing it off to me.

"You choose. Whatever you're in the mood for is good with me," he says.

I raise a brow at him as I accept the control. "You sure about this?" I ask in a teasing tone. "We both know I'm going to take you right from a Sports Center rerun to Nick at Nite."

"S'all good," he chuckles as I turn the TV on and do exactly what I said I would. The Fresh Prince is on, which is one of my favorites. I settle into Colin's side with a smile, enjoying the fact that his bed is a queen size. This means there's really no room for us to be separated. I can't contain my giant ass grin when he lifts his arm and wraps it around my shoulders, bringing me in closer to him. I don't think I've ever been this comfortable in my life.

Chapter Six

Elena

Nine Weeks Ago

I feel like I'm in a daze as Colin pulls the car up to the curb and jumps out to get me from the bench I'm on just outside of the offices where Nanny and Pop's will was just read. He's tried to carry me around all day, but for the most part, all I need is an assist to get around. The swelling on my ankle was about eighty percent gone this morning, which is good. Right now I'm so gob-smacked that I'm a little tempted to ask him to carry me over to the car. I won't, but the desire is there.

He watches me carefully as he covers the distance from the car to me. He's been monitoring me closely ever since the reading of the will. Right now I can't say I blame him. I use him for support as I stand, letting out a deep breath as we begin the short walk to his car. After helping me into the passenger seat and buckling me in, Colin shuts my door and walks around the car. Sliding into the driver's seat, he looks over at me.

"You okay?"

"I don't really know," I say softly. "I never, ever expected them to leave me anything at all, much less half of the house."

"They loved you," he says, "and that house is your home. You love it as much as they did—as much as I do. I have no doubt that's why they left it to both of us."

I nod as I bite my lip and look away. I'm touched and emotional about the whole thing, but I'm also scared to death.

"What's upsetting you about this, Little Bird?" he asks, his voice full of concern.

Focusing on the dashboard, I reach out and brush away a speck of dust.

"Do you think your parents will be angry when you tell them what the will said?" I blurt, finally giving voice to what's stressing me out.

"What?" he asks in a tone of complete surprise. "No, Leni. Absolutely not."

Reaching out he softly grips my chin and turns me to face him. "They already know, honey. My dad is the one who told me what to expect, and they aren't angry at all. It makes sense to them, too. Dad already has a house of his own. He and my mom got all of the cash assets my grandparents left behind. Things worked out the way Nanny and Pop wanted, and there's nothing wrong with that at all."

I breathe out a long, relieved breath as I lean back against the headrest. "You have no idea what a relief that is. Losing any of you—"

"Never," he vows. "I really wish you wouldn't worry about this, Little Bird. None of us are going anywhere."

Words seem so inadequate right now. All I can think to say is, "Thank you."

Reaching out, Colin takes my hand in his and laces our fingers together. I do my best to keep any surprise from my face as he brings our hands to his lips and kisses the back of mine. "There's nothing to thank me for," he says quietly. "I need you just as much as you need me, Leni. Don't ever forget that."

I hate to admit that in a lot of relationships in my life it's always been hard for me to truly let go and trust in actual permanence. Granted my dad is in my life now, but he wasn't super-reliable during the first years after the divorce. I view his commitment to me as something he feels he *has* to do as opposed to something he *wants* to do. But with Colin, I have faith. If he says he'll be there, he will be.

When he places our entwined hands back on my leg and doesn't move to sever the connection, I look out the window to hide my smile. The way he has been here for me these last few days is nothing short of perfection. I spent the entire night in his bed last night and woke up this morning snuggled against him, and he never made me feel weird about it. Instead, I felt warm, protected, content and completely at home. I also felt desired—but I'm almost afraid to believe that's the case. But right now looking down at our hands, I think I might be right.

COLIN HASN'T LEFT my side at all today and to say that I am enjoying this is a vast understatement of facts. After a dinner consisting of more leftover funeral food—a really delicious baked chicken casserole and a tossed salad—we're now setting up camp in the living room to binge watch *Stranger Things*. We've both been dying to dive into it since people are constantly raving about it so now is the perfect time to give it a try.

He sets me up on the couch first and then uses pillows to elevate my foot on the coffee table. Twisted ankles are a common enough occurrence for me that I barely feel it (and the brace I'm wearing is a huge help), but I'm not about to turn down the TLC from Colin. After turning off the lights and cuing up the show, he settles in next to me—close, but not as close as I want him. I make it through almost the entire first episode before I work up the courage to scoot in closer. He doesn't hesitate to lift his arm so that I can settle into the nook of his arm. Setting my head against his chest, I grin as my heart melts.

As episode two starts he begins running his hand up and down my arm. Immediately the tension in the room rises exponentially, and I'm more and more certain I'm not the only one who feels it as each second passes. Taking a breath for courage, I snuggle in closer as I set my hand down on his jean-clad thigh. He freezes for half a second before he turns his head and looks at me. Because my head is on him, we're now super close to one another—close enough for me to feel his breath as it skates across my lips.

I shiver at the way his coppery brown eyes flash in the dim light. "Leni," he groans. "Do you know what you're doing?"

I'm nervous about taking such a massive leap of faith, but I'm doing it anyway. Taking a deep breath, I climb into his lap, careful to keep from hitting my ankle. "Yes," I say, my voice firm and clear. I'm scared I've gone too far until his hands grip my waist and the heat of his palms warms my skin through the loose cotton of the spaghetti strap dress I've got on.

"Fuck, baby," he rasps.

Goosebumps break out over my entire body when I see the desire in his eyes. I clench my thighs and bite my lip as I lean in closer, anxious to take the next step. I've dreamt of kissing Colin for years and right now I'm inches away from having that dream become a reality.

"Give me that sexy little mouth," he orders as he uses his hold on my waist to bring my lower body in snug against his.

Jesus, he's hard—and it's all for *me*. My clit throbs and my sex clenches as I slowly lean forward, the hem of my dress raising as I do. His eyes are hooded as he watches me getting closer and closer. Just before I reach his lips, he raises his hands from their position at my waist and takes my face between his hands, halting my movements. I clench again, loving the way he takes control.

One of our phones buzzes on the table behind me but neither of us looks. Ignoring the buzz, he guides me in close enough to kiss me, but stops just short. I open my lips to say something—probably to beg—but I lose all my words when he uses his hands to tilt my head before he begins tracing my lower lip with his tongue. The sensation is so erotically charged I can feel my temperature rising. Unable to stop myself I open my lips and touch my tongue to his. He lets out a harsh groan and bucks beneath me, his hard cock rubbing against my sex through his jeans and my underwear. I whimper as he deepens the kiss, holding me tightly as he does.

I've been kissed before but never, ever like this. This feels like a claiming—a declaration of ownership and I'm absolutely not complaining about that. Lost in the sensation, I hold onto his shoulders as I lean in as close as I can. My nipples harden as I shamelessly rub myself against his chest, moaning as he tears his mouth away.

His breath is as ragged as my own, the sound of both filling the room. Somewhere in the background *Stranger Things* is still going, but all I can think about is Colin.

"Need to touch you," he rasps.

"Yes," I agree without hesitation. "Please."

He drops his hands from my face to my shoulders, toying with the soft thin straps of my dress.

"This dress might not survive," he says.

I bite my lip and let out a husky sound as I grind down on his cock.

"I don't care about the dress."

It's like pouring lighter fluid onto a fire. His hands drop from my shoulders to the hem of the dress. "Lift up," he orders.

The way he takes control is making me crazy. My clit is throbbing, and my nipples have never been harder. Balancing on my knees, I lift my bottom, holding still as he raises the hem to my waist. "Sit and raise your arms."

I do as instructed, shivering as he whips the dress over my head allowing the cold air to brush over my skin. His eyes flash fire as the dress drops, and he realizes that I'm naked from the waist up since there was a sports bra built into the cotton dress. My breasts are a small B cup, but my worry that he might be disappointed is quickly forgotten when he slides his hands up my torso and stops when he reaches them. The combination of his hands on my skin and the look of raw desire on his face as he stares at my tits throws my already aroused body into overdrive.

"Perfection," he growls as his hands move around to my back. I shiver as he begins sliding them ever so slowly down my spine. When he reaches the top of my underwear, he moves a bit faster, gripping my ass in his hands. "Put your hands on my knees and arch your back."

When I comply, he leans forward and licks my right nipple. The heat of his tongue against the stiffened peak is everything. Needing a better grip, I let go of his knees and transfer my hands to his shoulders one hand at a time. He groans as I rock back and forth against him, the friction of his hard length beneath his jeans hitting me just right. It feels like my body is on fire internally as he divides his time between my breasts, licking, sucking, and gently nibbling each one. Every scrape of his jaw against my sensitive skin is like a thousand points of pure sensation.

I groan when he lifts his head and looks up at me. "Kiss me," he says.

When our lips fuse, the kiss is one hundred percent carnal, so perfect it takes my breath away. There's an intensity to this that goes so far beyond anything I ever imagined—and believe me, I've spent hours dreaming about what this moment might feel like if it ever happened. I'm grinding on him faster, the need inside of me so acute that all I can focus on is the pleasure. I tear my mouth from his and let out a tortured sound when he traces his fingers over the top of my simple pink cotton bikini panties. When he slides beneath the elastic, I damn near forget how to function. I watch his face as he focuses on the sight of his hand touching my skin beneath the cotton and nothing has ever looked sexier.

"Fuck, Little Bird," he groans, "you're so wet."

My breath leaves me in a whoosh when his middle finger starts rubbing circles against my clit. "Colin, so good," I whimper.

"I knew it'd be fucking perfect to hear you calling out my name. Only thing that's going to make this any better is getting to taste this little pussy," he murmurs.

I squeak in surprise as he stands up, spins around and lays me down on the couch. Grabbing the sides of my panties he drags them off of me in one fluid motion, leaving me completely exposed to his gaze.

"So motherfucking perfect and sexy," he says as he gets onto the couch between my legs. Raising my right leg, he sets my ankle up on the back of the couch so that it's elevated. Once he's satisfied with my comfort, he slides his hands beneath my ass and raises me up. I barely have time to blink before his mouth is on me.

It's almost embarrassing how loud I'm being as he works me over with his tongue, but judging by the way he's watching me with heated eyes as he does it, I know he's enjoying every second. The feel of his stubble against my sensitive inner thighs is incredible.

"Oh Jesus," I gasp as his tongue swirls faster. Reaching down, I thread my fingers through his hair, holding on as he sucks my clit into his mouth.

"Colin!" I cry, my body beginning to tremble as he applies more pressure. "Yes! Now!"

The orgasm hits me hard, the magic of it racing through my veins as he slows down and moves his tongue from the very tip of my clit but doesn't stop licking me. I let out a gasp when he slides his finger against my opening, slowing circling it. Lifting his head, he grins devilishly as he slowly starts pushing inside.

"You'll like this next one even better," he promises, "but the one after that where you come all over my dick will be your fav—"

His sudden stop confuses me. Looking down, I see him staring up at me wide-eyed.

"What is it?" I ask.

"You're a virgin," he whispers.

Right at that moment, I realize I'm feeling his finger against the evidence of that very thing. I nod and cock my head. "Does it matter?"

His eyes bulge out almost comically. "*Does it matter?*" he asks incredulously. "Leni, this isn't at all what—"

The sound of the kitchen door opening stops everything on a dime. "Since you didn't text back with your order we got you hot fudge sundaes," Lolo calls.

"Stay in the kitchen!" Colin yells.

Scrambling off the couch, I grab my dress and underwear and race for the stairs, ignoring the twinge of my ankle.

Somehow he gets rid of Sam and Lolo without me seeing them. I wonder what they thought when he called out for them to stay in the kitchen, but assume I'll never know. When he knocks on my bedroom door and says we need to talk my stomach plummets.

Everything he says after that is nothing but a series of words that tell me one thing—he thinks being with me would be a mistake.

Chapter Seven

Elena

Now

As I turn to walk around my car to go to head to the house, Colin opens the side door. I swallow thickly as his gaze connects with mine as I cross the driveway and then brush past him at the side door, which he holds open for me. I wrinkle my nose as I smell something unfamiliar to the house hanging in the air but then forget all about it as Colin continues to hold my gaze as he closes the door behind him.

"I was afraid you wouldn't come. I'm glad you're not avoiding me anymore."

My pulse speeds up as I spin on my heels and cross my arms over my chest.

"You think *I've* been avoiding *you*?" I ask, my tone one of clear disbelief. "That's rich, all things considered. You're the one who said I needed to focus on myself and finish out college—all while I begged you to reconsider. Then you disappeared into thin air and stopped calling or writing."

He sighs and leans back against the door.

"Don't twist things around, Little Bird. I called you *every day* for three weeks, and you didn't answer the damn phone even once. I let up because I could see you were angry and needed time to stew."

"You're damn right I was angry. You made it seem like my being a... a virgin," I continue after a pause, "somehow made me defective. You have no clue how humiliating that was. Yeah, you called but after the way things shook down, you should've realized why I wasn't answering. I was embarrassed. And what? Now you're just—" I gesture to the room around me "—here?"

"Yes, I'm here. I'm *home*," he stresses. "But to be perfectly blunt, today hasn't gone the way I'd hoped, and I've spent the hours since you left the gym wondering if I'm too damn late. Is there something you want to tell me, Leni?

I don't know what the hell that means, and I'm too agitated to decipher it.

"Too late for what?" I snap. "You didn't even see me in the gym today! I might as well have been invisible, and I wasn't even fifteen feet from you. Not once did I see you looking through the crowd for me even though you had to know I was there. Do you have any idea how badly that hurt?"

Putting his hand up to the back of his neck, he rubs at it as if he's stressed. "Of course I knew you were there, Leni. I always know where you are, even if you think I don't. You have no idea how fucking difficult it was not to look your way today, but it had to be done. If I want to keep this job—and keep us in the position of living in this house full time—I needed to keep to my end of the agreement, which was something I was hoping to discuss with you. Meanwhile none of that really fucking matters right now after what I saw in the gym this afternoon."

I'm so confused I must look like Britney Spears judging the X Factor, and it's surprising that there are not little birds circling my head. "What did you see in the gym this afternoon?"

Colin frowns as he drops his hand from behind his neck. "Miles was all fucking over you, Leni. It didn't take a rocket scientist to figure out that you've transitioned from just friends to—" he grimaces as he looks away "—Lovers," he finishes a second later.

Did I say I was confused a second ago? Back then I was only slightly off-kilter. Now I'm stunned.

This big lug is so exasperating! After admitting to actively ignoring me in the gym, he pulls this craziness out of his ass?

"Miles is my best *friend*," I remind him. "Always has been and always will be. He is not now, nor will he ever be, anything other than that. It'd be like you sleeping with Sam or Lolo. We're no more and no less affectionate than you are with them. There's nothing sexual between the three of you and nothing sexual with Miles and me. He's like a brother—"

I get no further because in the blink of an eye he's covered the space between us. With one arm he pulls me against his chest. His free hand traces the curve of my face as he leans in close and covers my mouth with his. If I live to be one hundred and nine, I'll never get over the way it feels to be kissed by Colin Findlay because he owns me with each and every one.

My senses are overloaded with Colin—the taste, the feeling of his muscular body beneath my fingers, the scent that I'm insanely addicted to. I haven't seen him in weeks, but there's absolutely no discomfort. Being in his arms is where I feel most at home.

I shiver as he threads his fingers through my hair just above the nape of my neck, the gesture proprietary, and oh-so-him. I grumble as he lifts his lips from mine, unwilling to break the connection. Taking control, I reach up, grab his chin and pull him back in to extend the kiss. His warm chuckle tells me that he has no problem with my forcing the issue.

Suddenly we're moving. It's my turn to laugh when I feel the counter behind me. Gripping my waist, he lifts me up and sits me on the edge before pulling his lips away again. Raising his hands, he cups either side of my face and looks at me.

"God, I fucking missed you. These past two months have been torture, baby. If you ever spend so much as two minutes avoiding me again, I'm going to lose my shit."

I can't help narrowing my eyes. "You're the one who told me we were making a mistake," I remind him.

"How you took it is not at all what I meant to say," he growls. "You make it sound like I said I didn't want to be with you and *nothing* could be further from the truth."

"Well, that's what I heard," I admit. "To me, every word out of your mouth sounded an awful lot like someone who wanted to get as far away from me as possible."

"What I was trying to say back then—apparently poorly—was that I didn't think it was fair to *you* to start a long distance relationship. You kept your virginity for a reason, and I didn't want to do anything to take away from how monumental that is. Making love and then being separated from you wasn't okay with me. You're young and in college and I'm—"

I raise my hand between us and slap it over his mouth. "I swear if you say old I'm going to pitch a fit. The argument was ridiculous then, and I guarantee it'll be the one thing in this room that hasn't aged well if you say it again."

He chuckles before nipping at my palm playfully so that I'll remove my hand. "What I'm saying is that I want a lot from you, Leni. I needed you to have the option to wait, especially once I knew you were a virgin. Me living two hours away and you dealing with college douchebags hitting on you all the time wasn't how I wanted us to start our relationship."

My eyes go wide at his use of the *R*-word.

"Relationship?" I ask with an endless well of hope in my tone.

"You see me here right now?" he asks.

I nod.

"I came home for you because I'm in love with you. Relationship is way too fucking tame a way to describe what I want us to share."

A huge smile breaks out on my face as I lean in closer. "I love you, too," I murmur.

As his lips cover mine, I don't think I've ever been happier—until a dose of reality slaps me upside the head. Tearing my mouth from his, I grimace.

"But what about the university? They made it very clear today that if anyone gets caught, shit will hit the fan. I don't want you to lose your job!"

"They can't catch us doing what they already know about," he says dryly.

I cock my head and wrinkle my brown in confusion. "What?"

"As soon as you ghosted out of here like a thief in the night I knew I needed to do whatever it took to move here permanently. I might've said it wrong, but the thought behind my words was right. Long distance relationships are hard, and I didn't want that for us. Two days after you left, I heard about Coach Adams from Sam's dad. Mr. Lewis is tight with President Rothstein, so he didn't hesitate to sit in as a consultant on some of the legal aspects of the separation between the university and the coach. He put my name forward as a candidate and Rothstein and Dean Pritchard were immediately interested because I'm alumni."

He's ever so gently rubbing his hands up and down my sides as he speaks which is making it just a bit difficult to follow along.

"I stretched the truth a little during my interview and told the dean that you and I have been together for a long time. I kept to the truth when I told him it's so serious that we own a home together."

My eyes go wide with surprise. "You did?"

"I knew it was the only way to get them on board. They needed to be aware that we aren't having some tawdry affair, and that settled it for them. If you were anything other than a senior, or if I were your teacher or coach, it would've been a harder sell. In the end, they made the exception because the cache of having a former member of the NFL who also happens to be an alum was too damn perfect for them to pass up. Rothstein asks that we keep it respectful and not flaunt the relationship on campus, but otherwise we're good to go."

I can't contain the shit-eating grin that is spreading across my face. Colin moved here for me—for us. Holy shit there's an *us* now. This is happening. We've said the words. We're in love, and now we're together.

"So we'll get to see each other a lot now that you're home," I say happily.

"Hope so," he says with a strangled laugh, "since I'm thinking we'll be living together."

Holy crap. He's really, really serious about this. No hesitation at all.

"Really?" I squeak, the excitement I'm feeling very apparent in my tone.

"Yes, really. When you love someone you want them with you all of the time. That's how I feel for you, Leni. Our future starts now. In fact, I have something to show you."

Lifting me from the counter, he carries me through the kitchen and the living room and then up the stairs. The scent I noticed when I first walked in gets stronger as he goes up the stairs. I've only ever smelled something like this in a new home. I open my mouth to ask him what it is only to lose the train of thought entirely as he crests the top of the stairs and I see the hall which has been freshly painted. The carpet is gone, replaced by beautiful espresso hardwood floor. The biggest shock is that where once there were two doors on the left side of the hall—one for his bedroom and one for mine—there's now a set of double doors in the middle, where the wall for the bathroom used to be.

"What did you do?" I whisper.

He laughs as he comes to a stop in front of the double doors. "I made us a home, Little Bird. I knew neither of us was going to want to move into Nanny and Pop's room—so I had some work done. This is our master and I turned what was their giant room into two smaller rooms. It worked out to be an even swap, space wise."

When he turns the handle to our bedroom—holy shit, Colin and I have a bedroom—my jaw drops. It's absolutely positively perfect. The espresso floors are accented with a giant area rug that sits under a black four post king-sized bed covered in the most gorgeous duvet set. The furniture and the linens are just some of the things I've been coveting at Pottery Barn for the last year. I sniffle at the same time I laugh because this tells me Lolo and Sam helped decorate. They know how much I love Pottery barn because I spent weeks shopping with them when they redid their house last year.

"It's perfect," I murmur, my voice thick with emotion. "You did all this in eight weeks?"

He snickers as he carries me through the room to a large barn-style door on the wall. When he slides it to the left, I find myself looking into the world's most stunning bathroom.

"Not eight weeks, baby. It was five from beginning to end up here. They'll be here next week to run the hardwood all throughout the downstairs as well but all the furniture and décor down there is on you. I think Lolo and Sam were ready to fucking strangle me having to guide me through it up here."

I giggle as he sets me down in the middle of the bath. Running to the glass shower wall, I let out a long sigh of contentment as I open the large door in the center. The massive bathtub takes up a large portion of the right side, but the entire left is dominated by showerheads on the ceiling and the walls. There's a long bench and tons of insets for shampoo, conditioner and body wash. This couldn't be more perfect. For years I've dreamt of having a separate wet room, and now, I have one. Looking over my shoulder at Colin who has been assessing my reaction, I wiggle my eyebrows. "Get ready to spend a *ton* of time in here," I tease.

"I've *been* ready," he answers huskily.

I walk out of the wet room directly into his arms, hugging him tightly. Standing on my tiptoes, I rain kisses on his face. "You did really, really good."

Chapter Eight

Elena

Now

"You keep doing that, and we won't make it into the closet," he says huskily.

I'm all for clothes but if I'm picking up what he's putting down correctly I really, really want not to make it into the closet right now.

"I'll take door number two," I say cheekily. "Show me. It's fine with me if we don't make it into the closet until much, much later."

Colin laughs, grips me by the waist and lifts me up and off of my feet in one fluid movement. I laugh and wrap my legs around his torso as he carries me into the bedroom. Into our bedroom. As much as a part of me is screaming 'pinch yourself bitch, this can't be real life'—I know down to my marrow that nothing has ever been more real. I've never been more grounded in reality even though my feet feel like they'll never touch the ground again.

We both laugh when he rips the comforter down before dramatically plopping me on our bed so that I bounce a little. "Mm," I grin. "Comfy. I think I'm going to love this bed."

Coming to the edge of the bed he stands between my legs before placing his hand behind my neck as he grins down at me. "I think you're going to love the things we do in this bed even more," he says. The promise in his voice makes my nipples hard.

"Kiss me," I say, just loud enough for him to be able to hear.

"Always," he answers before swooping in and doing just that.

Again, the way this man kisses is a form of art. I lose myself in it completely, many minutes passing as we learn each other all over again. Kissing Colin is like coming home and walking through fire. When he lifts his head and breaks the kiss, I'm breathing like someone who just ran a 5k. I start to pout but quickly stop when he tugs at the hem of my shirt before he starts pulling it up. Raising my arms up, I let out a happy sound when he pulls it over my head before tossing it toward the end of the bed. Crouching down, he pulls off my Converse and my ankle socks before standing.

His eyes blaze with unchecked desire as he takes in my periwinkle pushup bra. "You're so gorgeous," he groans. "Did you know that ever since the summer we went to the beach at the end of your freshman year I've been fucking obsessed with you?"

Approximately eight trillion butterflies take flight in my stomach. "Really?"

He looks into my eyes as he nods. "You're without compare, Leni. One day you were just as you'd always been. The next, you were everything. It scared the ever-loving fuck out of me at first because of the age difference. Now I just love you too much to care," he admits as he traces circles over my stomach with his right index finger.

I lift my hand to reach out and cover his. "I love you too. So, so much."

The rest of my clothes and then his are peeled away layer by layer between soul deep kisses that mean more than any words ever could. When I get my first look at Colin naked, I lose my breath. Clothed he's spectacular. Naked, he's a god. If I were an artist, I'd paint pictures or chisel his likeness out of marble. When he spreads my legs and starts trailing kisses down my naked body, I feel combustible. The first time he did this I didn't know what to expect. Now that I know how good his mouth feels on me, I can hardly wait to retake the ride.

The first swipe of his tongue against my center has me arching my back and crying out his name. "Fucking love the taste of you," he growls as he slowly pushes a finger inside. A few minutes later he adds another. I feel stretched and full with just the two fingers, but I know that in a few minutes I'll be feeling a hell of a lot more than that.

He's playing with me now—getting me to the point where I'm about to come before he backs off and leaves me wanting more and I'm so turned on it hurts. By the fifth time he does it, I'm ready to explode.

"Please," I beg on a keening wail. "Make me come."

I hear him groan as he swirls his tongue over my clit faster, applying the perfect amount of pressure. My body races toward ecstasy as I chant, "Don't stop, don't stop, don't you dare stop."

When he comes up over me without letting me come, I let out a harsh sound. "Please, please," I beg.

Settling between my legs, he rubs his cock back and forth against my clit. "You want to come, Leni?"

I nod, the movement frantic. "Yes," I whimper.

He stops the back and forth movement to grip his cock and place it at my entrance. Feeling him there, knowing he's about to be inside me is heady stuff. I grasp his shoulders and look into his eyes as he slowly moves forward. My eyes go wide as I feel him making his way in.

"Start making circles on your clit," he rasps.

My hand is a little shaky as I reach between us to do it. All of his work has left me slippery and desperate for release, which means I'm more focused on that than the impending pain.

"Elena," he groans as he sinks deeper. "Fuck, Leni."

I move my fingers faster, clenching around him as he moves his hands to my waist. "Now," he growls.

When he surges forward, I lose my breath for a second or two before I gasp for air. Keeping one hand on my hip, he slides the other between us and takes over rubbing my clit. With my hands free, I grip his back and hold on as he starts rocking in and out. The feeling of him so deep and so full inside of me is like nothing I ever could have anticipated.

Soon the bed is rocking beneath us as he picks up speed, his fingers and his cock working together to make me insane. "Colin," I gasp as he pumps deeper and harder. "Oh, fuuuck," I whimper. "Like that. Right thereeeeee!"

The way it feels to come with him inside of me is indescribably good, but it gets even better when he yells my name and finds his release. The heat of his cum is so intense that it makes my orgasm stronger.

"Fucking so good," he groans as he jerks inside of me.

When it's over, he stays inside me for another minute or two, kissing along my neck and murmuring about how much he loves me before pulling out. The feeling of losing him is not my favorite. Lying down at my side he pulls me into his arms and kisses me softly.

"That was the best I've ever felt," he says. "Fucking loved coming inside you, Leni. Know I'm putting it all out there, but I have to tell you, I can't wait to fill you up when you aren't on birth control."

My eyes widen in surprise. "You want to have a baby?"

"Yeah," he answers with a grin. "About four seconds after you graduate I'm going to start begging you to let me knock you up. Fuck," he laughs. "Even thinking of you pregnant is making me hard again."

My smile has to be big enough to be visible from space. "Kids," I murmur.

"The whole nine yards, baby. We're going all the way."

Yes. Yes, we are.

Chapter Nine

Elena

Now

I get three steps inside the front door before I hear an exaggerated cough. Looking toward the couch, I'm not surprised to find Miles lounging on it.

"Lucy, you've got some 'splainin to do."

"Um, what do you mean?"

"Don't play dumb. My antenna went up the second I got the text from you at ten last night letting me know you were spending the night at the house. That you're prancing in here just after dawn wearing a hoodie that's for someone much, much taller than you—someone with a penis I'm guessing—is a dead giveaway."

So much for sneaking in and avoiding this conversation until later after I've loaded up on coffee. Colin and I were up off and on all night, touching, talking... and making love two more times. I've never been happier but I'm exhausted, and I admit that I'm anxious about having this conversation with Miles. If he's mad about my misleading him for so long, I don't know what I'll do. Letting out a long sigh, I brace for the coming inquisition.

"Well—"

"And what stands out for me about this deviation from your normal pattern of behavior," he continues, completely ignoring my attempt to speak, "is that Colin's home. Well, that and the fact that the hoodie you're wearing is from his previous university. Anything you want to say about that?"

The jig. Is. Up. Without hesitating another second, I haul ass across the room and plop down on the couch next to Miles.

"Don't be mad," I say pleadingly.

He shakes his head, tosses an arm over my shoulders and kicks his feet up on the coffee table. "I'm not mad, I'm relieved. You have any idea how many times over the years I've tried to get you to admit you were crushin' on Findlay? Probably hundreds. I'll give you credit—you played it so cool that I started to doubt what I'd been able to see with my own eyes. Doubted it so much that I was half convinced you were secretly in love with me and just couldn't say it. Talk about a fuckin' nightmare, E. I love you to death, but I couldn't lay pipe in you."

I shudder and make a gagging noise as I slap my hand down on his leg. "Love you *sooo* much it's borderline ridiculous— but if your p ever even tried to come near my v, I'd die. Incest is not best. I don't even care that technically we're not related—you're the only brother I'll ever have. And also the only one I'll ever want, too," I throw in for good measure.

He throws his head back and laughs. "Kiss ass. I'll forgive you on one condition."

I'm no fool. His conditions are always crap, and I know it. "How much is it going to cost me?" I ask suspiciously.

"It's free. My laundry hampers are overflowing, and they've got your name all over them."

I love Miles, but my God is it annoying how much he hates doing his wash. He's got four giant hampers in his closet—the fact that he's saying they're overflowing means there's like six hampers worth of laundry. Total pain in the ass but if it gets him to forgive me for being a tool, I'll drag it to the house now that I have a laundry room and have it all finished in less than two hours.

"Just confirming— once I do the laundry you'll forgive me for being a dummy?"

"If that laundry is clean, folded and put away, I'll write the whole thing off. But from now on, no more secrets. Ever."

"None," I vow.

Miles holds out his free hand, pinky extended. Lifting my right hand, I chuckle as we pinky swear.

"Now I'm going to put it to the test," he announces. "You still a virgin?"

My face feels hotter than a bottle of fresh hot sauce. "Nope."

"Heh." He laughs. "Guess I'm going to have to start calling you teacher fucker."

"Hey! He's not a teacher."

"Semantics," he retorts. "He's off limits as hell, and if you get caught, he's losing his job."

"You're wrong about that."

"How?"

I spend the next ten minutes filling him in on everything that's gone down, pinching myself from time-to-time as I realize that this is all happening.

ELENA
Six Weeks Later

"BABY, did you move my lucky hat? I put it here on the counter before I left for work this morning. I need it for game day tomorrow, but now it's gone."

I chuckle as I peek my head out our bedroom door to yell down to the kitchen. "It's up here. Come get it."

Hearing his footsteps on the stairs, I race across the room and jump up onto our bed, positioning myself, so I'm sitting right at the edge facing the door. Naked—save for the hat on my head.

"Trying to steal my—"

His words fade away when he sees me. I giggle when his giant smile morphs into a predatory look. "Fucking look at you," he growls as he crosses the room to me.

I hold out my hand, halting his movements. "Get naked and wait for further instruction, Coach."

"You taking charge today?"

I grin and wiggle my brows. "I so am."

He groans before he quickly divests himself of his shoes, socks, team shirt, black athletic pants and gray boxer briefs. As always, he takes my breath away. Naked Colin might be my very favorite thing in the world.

"What now?"

I crook my finger at him in a come-hither motion. When he reaches the bed, I motion for him to stop before I reach behind me and grab a pillow. Climbing off the bed I walk around to stand in front of him before I drop the pillow on the floor and get down on my knees. He watches me through hooded eyes, his expression reverential as he takes off the hat I'm wearing and tosses it over his shoulder.

"Seems like I'll be needing hair grip," he growls.

I lick my lips slowly as I stare into his eyes and slowly begin running my hands up his thighs. "Looks that way," I agree.

When I reach his upper thighs, I gently scratch my nails down a few inches before repeating the maneuver on the way back up. Just when I'm back where I started I lick my tongue over his swollen head to collect the pre-cum at the tip. His cock jerks against my tongue as a gravelly sound escapes his throat. His gaze is trained on my tongue as I trace circles over the tip. "Fuuuuck," he groans.

Opening my mouth I slide forward, taking in a few inches of his thick length. His hands thread through my hair as he swallows thickly. "Baby. God. Fuck."

Wrapping my left hand around the base of his shaft, I twist it up and around in time with the up and down motion of my head. With my right hand, I scratch my nails against his skin. The inside of his ankle, the sensitive spot just above his knee, the top of his inner thigh and then his pubic bone all make him crazy, as evidenced by the way his breath is coming in gasps and his fingers are tight in my hair.

"Oh God," he gasps as I take him deeper, sticking out my tongue and breathing through my nose so that he can hit the back of my throat. I start moving faster, watching as his eyes turn to liquid fire. Seeing how much he loves this gets me so, so wet. Needing to touch myself, I stop scratching at his skin and slide my hand between my thighs. I shiver as I rub my clit while he fucks my face, moaning as sensation races through my body.

"Stop! Stop," he growls as he pulls himself out of my mouth.

Lifting me up from the pillow he spins me so that I'm facing the bed. "Hold on," he orders.

I shiver as I grip the comforter. He wraps his left arm around my waist at the same time he rubs his cock against my opening. "So goddamn hot," he groans. "So fucking wet. I can't wait to feel this all over my dick."

"Colin," I gasp as he slowly surges forward.

"Love watching your tight little cunt taking my cock," he says in a gravelly voice. "Looks so fucking good wrapped around me, baby."

"Oh God," I cry as he pulls out and then slams back in, deep.

Settling his hands at my waist, he starts pushing and pulling me back and forth. The slap-slap-slap of skin on skin fills the room as he fucks me harder and faster.

Letting go of my right hip, he brings his hand between my legs and starts rubbing my clit. It's so good I can barely breathe. Arching my back, I scream out his name as I feel the first flutters of my orgasm starting. Knowing I'm there, he focuses on what he calls my sweet spot. "Colin," I moan. "I'm coming. Oh fuck, I'm coming!"

As my pussy clenches around him, I feel him jerking inside of me. "Baby, fuck," he yells.

The heat of his cum inside me makes me shiver and moan louder as my orgasm crashes through my body. He fucks like a goddamn machine when he comes, burying everything he has to give deep, deep inside of me. When it's over, he pulls out, turns me around and puts me up on the bed before he gets on next to me, takes me into his arms and starts kissing me.

After several minutes of making out, he raises his head and smiles down at me. "That was one hell of a welcome home, baby. Have I told you lately how much I fucking love you?"

I grin as I run my hands over his cheek scruff. "It's been at least an hour since the last time you said it."

He laughs as he drops another soft kiss on my lips.

"Love you, Leni."

Wrapping my arms around him, I snuggle his chest and smile. "Love you, too."

Epilogue

Elena

Five Months Later

"Sometimes I still find it hard to believe you moved out one day after school started and left me home alone," Miles sighs.

Looking across the island to where he's seated, I shrug and continue slicing the yellow squash, zucchini, and baby carrots I'm about to put into my vegetable steamer. When I finish cutting the last vegetable, I gesture toward him with the tip of knife and smirk.

"I moved out, but it's hardly accurate to say I left you all alone considering you live out in the guest house Monday through Thursday nights," I point out. "You get all the home-cooked meals and reminders to study to keep you on track and then Friday through Sunday you get to act like a fool without me giving you the stink eye. It's perfect for both of us—me in particular since I no longer have to hear *the ohhhhh, Milesssss* chorus," I mimic in a breathy voice, "nine zillion times each week through your bedroom wall. The last five months have been *phenomenal* without that making my eardrums bleed at regular intervals," I joke.

He rolls his eyes and waves away my complaint. "I see what you're saying, but I'll always be a little salty that you never confirmed he was your jam until five minutes before you announced you were moving out."

For the most part, he's joking, but he takes some pleasure in giving me shit for being a secret keeper. "First of all, I did eleven loads of laundry for you that afternoon. Second, I feel like this is why you're the yin to my yang," I say sweetly as I turn the steamer on. "You've always over shared, and I was too embarrassed to admit being in love with an older man I thought I had no chance with."

"Really?" My favorite voice laughs as he walks in the side door. "I think we both know it was *me* who never stood a chance, Little Bird."

Colin and Miles greet each other by way of the traditional bro lifted chin gesture before my man makes his way directly to me like a heat-seeking missile.

"Missed you," he says after kissing me stupid.

I smile as I rub my fingers over his sexy stubble. "It's only been four hours since I saw you in your office," I remind him.

His shit-eating grin makes me blush. Although we've never flaunted our relationship, we've made good use of his private office many, many times.

The sound of fake gagging from the counter makes us both laugh. "That's my cue to leave," Miles says. "Text me when dinner's ready."

After the door closes behind Miles, Colin pulls me in for a real kiss. We put the next half hour to good use up in our bedroom, just the way I like it.

COLIN

Two Years Later

"LOOK, GRACIE—DADDY'S HOME!"

I will never, ever tire of hearing my wife's voice or the sound of our eleven-month-old daughter calling out, "Da-dee, da-dee," happily as she sees me come around the corner into the living room. Gracie is sitting on Elena's lap, smiling and waving to welcome me home from work. Pulling my phone from my pocket, I slide my finger across the screen and pull up the camera. I take a few pictures— by this I mean somewhere in the neighborhood of ten, which is par for the course anytime I start taking photos, which is often. There's no possible way I can ever take enough pictures of these beauties.

Setting the phone on the end table, I crouch down in front of Elena and open my arms, laughing as Gracie throws herself into them. My daughter is so much like her mother; fearless in the way she takes every leap always knowing someone will catch her before she can hit the ground. I've had to let go of giving her Uncle Miles shit for tossing her around the air because it makes her too happy for me to be a dick about. It's not like he doesn't have a stellar track record of keeping my girls from being hurt.

When I married Elena two days after her college graduation, I never imagined I could love her more than I did right then. I was wrong. Having Gracie—a part of both of us—has only brought us closer together. After accepting and returning a dozen sloppy baby kisses, I lean forward and kiss Elena's growing belly before arching my neck up to kiss her. The slide of her tongue against mine is the perfect welcome home. Any motherfucker who tells you that they don't find their wife sexy as fuck during pregnancy is a douchebag. Elena is always gorgeous—always—but Christ is it hot watching her body go through the stages of pregnancy. It's absolutely the reason behind her being six months pregnant when Gracie isn't a year old yet. If I have my way, Elena will be knocked up again sometime next year—and then one more for good measure a year or so after that. We're both only children, but we both agree that we want our own family to be bigger than that.

Our kiss comes to an end when our daughter's tiny baby fingers poke at our faces. We break apart laughing and Gracie giggles along with us as I stand and then sit down next to Leni. With our daughter comfortably settled on my lap, I turn to face my wife.

"How's Connor doing?" I ask as I run my free hand over her belly.

The feel of our son kicking from inside her stomach never gets old. I was mesmerized by it the entire time Grace was in there, and that is equally true with Connor.

"Any thought we had about him being like Pop since he's named after him is quickly fading away," she jokes as she sets her hand down over mine. The sparkle of her engagement and wedding rings a visual reminder of some of the happiest days of my life. "This kid is a kicker—just like his dad. I won't be surprised if he's born wearing a team jersey."

I can't help my laugh. "Like father, like son. Guess that means we're in for it."

Leni smiles as she leans into me and sets her head on my shoulder. "I wouldn't have it any other way."

Neither would I. Our home is filled with love and through our children, the legacy of my grandparents and the love they had for me and, more importantly, for this beautiful and amazing woman that I am so fucking lucky to call mine, lives on.

The End

Books by Ella Fox

The Hart Family Series

Broken Hart
Shattered Hart
Loving Hart
Unbroken Hart
Missing Hart
Finding Hart

The Renegade Saints (Rockstar Romance) Series

Picture Perfect
Twist of Fate
Between Us
Something to Believe In

The Catch Series

Catch my Fall
Catch and Release

The Enamorado (In Love) Series

I Don't
I Want

Standalone Books

Consequences of Deception
All That's Left to Hold Onto
Strictly Temporary

YARD SALE

Dear Reader,

Yard Sale is a complete standalone, but if you've read ***Bad Habit,*** you'll run into the characters we know and love from Cactus Heights and River's Edge.

Yard Sale is a quick, fun, dirty read about what happens when a good(ish) girl has a one-night stand with a professional snowboarder. Hope you enjoy the ride!

Xoxo,

Charleigh Rose

Yard Sale definition

Yard Sale

When a skier or snowboarder eats it on the slopes and loses all of their gear. If a skier loses his skies, poles, hat, goggles, and anything else, shout "YARD SALE" from the ski lift above him.

Chapter One

Cam

5 MONTHS AGO…

Eat.

Sleep.

Ride.

Fuck.

Repeat.

That's life. My *glorious* fucking life. At least, it is during snowboarding season. In the summer, I trade my snowboard for a skateboard. It helps retain that muscle memory and core strength while improving my skills that carry over onto the mountain. I may have started off as a skater, but my drug of choice will always be that snow-white powder. And not the kind that goes up your nose.

I'm still high on the perfect fucking season, even though it's August. I spent the entire winter touring and snagged myself another gold medal in the X Games for landing a quadruple underflip. The very first person in history to pull off that type of trick, making it my third medal total. I've been back home in River's Edge for the past three months, living it up, taking advantage of my celebrity status with the local females, until the season starts again.

"So," I drawl, taking a swig of my beer in the crowded waterfront bar. "When's that pretty redhead coming back to visit?"

"She's off-limits," Briar reminds me. *Again.* Briar is my friend, Asher Kelley's girl. I don't know exactly what went down, except that Asher left for a while, and when he came back, he had acquired a girlfriend. It was about damn time. He was a grumpy fucker without her. Well, he's still a grumpy fuck, but he smiles now. Sometimes.

I don't even want her friend. I mean, I wouldn't throw her out of bed, but truthfully, I just like to tease Briar. Especially about that time she got it on with Kelley in the Jacuzzi when she thought none of us noticed. Spoiler alert: we did.

"That's a shame. I bet she likes hot tubs just as much as—"

"Don't even say it," she warns, holding up a palm. I can't blame her for not wanting me anywhere near her friend. She knows how I am with women. It's not that I'm a *bad* guy. I love women. I love the way they smell. I love the way they sound when they're writhing beneath me. Love how they feel pressed against me. I respect them. I've never been anything but honest when it comes to my intentions. We have our fun, and then go our separate ways. No strings. No attachments. At twenty-six, I'm too young, and this world is too big to be settling down this soon. I'm in my prime, professionally speaking, and I want to milk it to the very last drop.

My brother, Cordell, laughs, and even our broody friend Dare cracks a smile, probably remembering that night. I can tell that I'm testing Asher's patience by the way he works his jaw, not to mention the death glare he's sending my way. He knows I'd never break the bro code, but it doesn't mean he likes to hear other guys joke about seeing his girl get fucked.

I avert my gaze and take another drink to hide my amusement just as the door to the bar opens and in walks a gorgeous brunette. She hesitates in the doorway for a minute, and I can't look away. Tiny waist, toned, tan legs. Perky tits. Long, dark hair falling in waves to her waist. Her black and white striped dress—that looks more like a slightly oversized T-shirt—hangs off one sun-kissed shoulder. As if she can sense me watching her, our eyes lock for a long moment before she breaks the connection. She adjusts her dress where it slipped down her shoulder and heads toward the bar.

I slam my empty bottle onto the table and stand, zeroed in on the way her ass seems to stretch the stripes in her dress as she makes her way toward the bar.

"Here we fucking go," Dare says, recognizing the determined look on my face.

"Don't wait up," I say, flashing them a grin before making my way to the bar. Shoving my way through the masses, I manage to squeeze in next to her. I look down at her—she's shorter than I thought, maybe five feet four—and wait for her to acknowledge me. She doesn't.

"Can I buy you a drink?" I finally ask, and I almost roll my eyes at myself. I couldn't come up with anything better than that?

"A little cliché, don't you think?" she deadpans, still not looking my way.

"I prefer straightforward. You look like a girl who can appreciate that."

She finally looks up at me, her big, brown, doe eyes glossy and red, like she's been crying. I instantly feel like a dick for hitting on a crying chick. But, she doesn't seem sad. She seems irritated, maybe even angry. She bites down on her lower lip, assessing, before she seemingly comes to a conclusion.

"I'll have a Blue Moon. With an orange," she adds.

I give her a nod and flag down the bartender, my friend Ephraim, telling him I want two Blue Moons, *with oranges*, and return my attention back to the girl next to me.

"Camden Hess. You can call me Cam," I say, holding out a hand. She ignores it. She doesn't seem to recognize my name. *Maybe she's not from around here.*

"Mollie Mabey," she offers after a beat. *Mollie Mabey*. I like it. It suits her.

"Where are you from?"

"San Fran. You?"

"Here."

She nods, not knowing what else to say, and looks down at the bar top.

"You okay?" I ask, unsure of what to make of this quiet little thing next to me. Usually, I don't have to work so hard for a girl's attention. She looks back up at me with a tiny twitch of her berry-colored lips. Our beers arrive, and she takes the orange, sucking it between those lips, before squeezing it into her glass and dropping it inside. Juice from the orange trails down her chin, and I use my thumb to swipe it away, before sucking it off. She tries to hide it, but I hear the small hitch in her breath. The slight widening of her dark-amber eyes.

"Can I kiss you, Mollie Mabey?"

I've caught her off guard, like I knew I would. Her eyes dart to mine, and at first, I think she's going to turn me down and maybe knee me in the balls for good measure. Instead, she licks her bottom lip, and her gaze drops down to my mouth.

Ding, ding, ding, we have a winner.

I decide to capitalize on the moment, curling a palm around the back of her slender neck, my fingers lacing through the thick strands of her hair. It should be weird that I'm touching a complete stranger so intimately in such a public place, but being bold and brash has always worked for me. Chicks dig that shit. I feel her pulse thumping a mile a minute, and I make my move, lowering my mouth to hers.

But, instead of feeling those soft, warm lips pressed against mine, I feel the complete opposite. Ice fucking cold. And hard. My eyes open in confusion to find her glass wedged between us. I raise an eyebrow. *Cockblocked by a cup. That's a first.*

"I don't kiss on the first date," she says, with an edge to her voice. I hear my brother's hyena laugh above all the raucous, and I flip him off, without even bothering to look in his direction.

"Good thing this isn't a date."

"You don't even know me."

"Even better," I quip, not missing a beat. At that, she laughs.

"I'll make you a bet," she relents, with a devious glint in her eye.

"I'm listening," I say, folding my arms across my chest. I'm suspicious, but I'm listening.

"Give me your beer," she starts, with a nod toward the counter. "I bet I can down both glasses before you can take two shots. As long as you give me a head start," she adds. "The only rule is that we can't touch each other's drinks. If you win, I'll kiss you."

"And if you win?" I ask out of pure curiosity. There's no fucking way this tiny ass little girl can out-drink me. Especially when all I have to drink is two measly shots to her full glasses of beer.

"If I win, I'm going to walk out of this bar, and you're going to let me."

"That's it?" I scoff. "Not even streaking or jumping into the lake naked?"

"Nah," she says easily, lifting a shoulder. "I'm easy."

"Somehow, I doubt that," I say, and I can't deny that the blush creeping up her neck turns me on.

"Ephraim!" I shout. "Give me two shots of Johnny Walker."

Mollie bites her lip to hide her smile as Ephraim sets the two shot glasses down in front of us.

"Ladies first," I say, giving her the head start she requested. She brings the pilsner glass to her lips and tips the contents into her mouth, while looking me dead in the eye. Impressively, she downs the entire thing in about fifteen seconds, and I have to fight the urge to adjust the growing bulge in my pants. She's better than I would have guessed, but there's still no way I won't beat that time.

Giving her a cocky grin, I toss back the shot like it's nothing. She smirks right back, but before I can grab the other, she flips her empty glass upside down, effectively trapping mine inside. Shooting her a confused look, I go to lift the glass, but she stops me.

"Ah, ah, ah," she tsks. "Remember the rule? We can't touch each other's glass."

"You've got to be fucking kidding me."

Mollie takes her sweet time drinking the second glass, *my* glass, knowing I can't do fuck to win now. *She fucking played me.*

"Thanks for the drinks, *Cam*," she says, wiping the corner of her lips with the tip of her finger.

"Okay." I nod. "I see you, little trickster."

And then she's walking away from me.

She walks away from *me*.

Before I even realize I'm doing so, I'm prowling after her. Prowling might not be the best description—more like scurrying. Like a lost fucking puppy. Who is this chick, and why do I need her to want me?

Chapter Two

Mollie

I'M the picture of cool, calm, and collected as I saunter away from Camden Hess. As if I didn't just break up with my fake boyfriend and lose my job in the same weekend. As if the sight of this cocky, tattooed bad boy didn't set my insides on fire despite those things. He's gorgeous. And intimidating. And, I can only assume, a player. He's everything I don't need in a boyfriend, but he's exactly what I need tonight.

My parents roped me into coming up for a family trip before summer is over. Of course, Tucker was supposed to come with me. But when I got the news that the magazine I've been working for since before I graduated college was no longer going to publish a print edition—therefore, leaving me jobless—I came home lost and upset, not to mention recovering from a gnarly bout of strep throat. Imagine my surprise when I found Tucker cozied up to another woman on our couch. His assistant, no less. How cliché, right? It didn't matter that we weren't *really* together. We hadn't ever talked about hooking up with people and how that fits in with our...*unique* situation. He wasn't straightforward with me. Needless to say, he was no longer invited.

Telling my parents that we "broke up" would open the door to questions I don't want to answer, so I spilled my guts to my friend, Sutton, who lives in River's Edge. We met when we were kids on the bunny slope and stayed in touch ever since. We planned to get day drunk and find some gorgeous locals to get my mind off real life. Turns out, Rum Runners and boating don't mesh well with Sutton, so she's laid up at home. I hung around until she kicked me out and then went back to our cabin until my parents and brothers started with their barrage of questions. I'm twenty-two. I don't have to explain myself. But, I don't feel like rehashing the ugly details just yet.

If I'm being honest, I'm embarrassed—about losing my job *and* Tucker—even though I know neither one was my fault. They're not a reflection of me. Our relationship wasn't really a relationship so much as an understanding between two people. I wasn't in love with Tuck, so it's not like I'm heartbroken. Not in that way, anyway. He was more like my best friend than a boyfriend, so the betrayal still stung. It almost made it worse, somehow.

When Tucker first confessed his feelings for me, I didn't know how I felt, but I didn't think it was the way he wanted. We gave dating a try. We were best friends and spent all of our time together, anyway, so what did I have to lose? *Our friendship, that's what.* I figured out pretty quickly that it wasn't what I wanted. It wasn't fair to Tuck, either, to be with someone who, in the words of Cher Horowitz, "wasn't majorly, totally, butt-crazy in love with him".

Problem was, Tucker's dad took our relationship as a sign of maturity and told him that if he kept moving in the right direction, he'd give Tuck more responsibility at Hastings Architecture, and eventually, he'd think about making him partner. Tucker has always been wild, if not a little rebellious, but design and construction is one of the few things he does take seriously. So, I told him we should keep up the charade for a while at least.

And it worked. Tucker has clients of his own now, and he couldn't be happier. Eventually, I think we both just became too comfortable. Dependent, even. We slept together, but it wasn't anything more than scratching an itch. I didn't have the time or desire to date anyone, and something tells me that Tuck was hoping I'd catch some feelings of the romantic variety, so we kept it up longer than necessary.

So, while I still feel cheated on and betrayed by my not-boyfriend, I also feel strangely...*relieved.* And for the first time in forever, I wanted to hook up with someone. Someone who just wanted a night of fun followed by an ass slap and a *good game* afterward. Someone who made me *feel good* for just an hour. And I found the perfect candidate. It should have been a no-brainer. Except, somewhere between the cabin and the bar, the self-doubt snuck in. I got into my own head and started second-guessing my skills as an art director. My skills in the bedroom. Pretty much everything. I blame the quiet. Silence always turns into fears and overthinking for me. The fact that I chose that moment to check my texts from Tucker didn't help matters. He said he was sorry, that he loved me, and begged me to call him. I didn't.

By the time I walked inside, I wanted to drink away my sorrows instead of finding a sexy stranger to spend the night with. It's too bad, because Cam looked like he knew his way around a woman's body. He was arrogant, but weirdly charming, and truthfully, I wouldn't mind being another notch in his bedpost.

I make my way out into the fresh air as I push open the heavy door. It slams behind me, shutting the music and chaos inside. It's cooler than I anticipated, given the fact that it's August. I visit River's Edge a couple of times a year, at least, but it's usually during winter. I haven't been during the summer since I was a kid. My flip-flops crunch against the dirt and pine needles as I head toward the water that lies mere feet from the bar. I nearly trip over a pinecone the size of my head. *What are these things, bionic? They're huge.* I don't get more than three steps before the door swings open behind me.

"You said I had to let you leave, but, you didn't say anything about not following you."

I spin around and pin him with an impassive stare as I walk backwards.

"I can be tricky, too," he says, wiggling his brows. I shake my head and turn back for the water. I sit down, the rough sand cold against my thighs. I slip my flip-flops off and bury my toes in the wet sand. I'm surprised when Camden lowers himself to sit next to me. He's fully clothed in a white V-neck and black jeans, but he doesn't seem to mind. He props his elbows on his knees and stares out at the lake, unspeaking. I use the opportunity to take him in. His dirty blond hair underneath his backward hat, the tattoos on his arms and the ones that cover his throat. The light stubble on his jaw. He looks vaguely familiar, but I know I don't know him. I'd never forget meeting someone like him.

"Are you just going to stare at me all night? It's kind of creepy," Camden says, interrupting my perusal.

"You're the one who followed me and sat down next to me without an invitation. If anyone's winning the *creepy contest*, it's you." The corner of his lip lifts in an almost-smile.

"Touché."

"Why did you, anyway?"

"What, follow you?"

I nod.

"I'm a sore loser, I guess." He shrugs, and I burst out laughing. *Well, at least he's honest.*

"She laughs," he says, flashing his perfect teeth in a Cheshire grin. "Does that earn me a kiss?"

"You're not going to quit, are you?"

"Quitting isn't in my vocabulary."

"Somehow, I don't think a guy like you is only interested in a *kiss*," I deadpan.

"Would you rather fuck instead?" he asks with a straight face, and I realize that he is dead serious. My mouth clamps shut, and I feel my face heat. He has zero filter. I doubt there's a single thought he's had that hasn't been spoken aloud.

Camden chuckles at my reaction and leans close to my ear.

"Does that word make you nervous?" he rasps, his lips brushing the shell of my ear over my hair. "Because I want to *fuck* you, Mollie Mabey."

My core clenches at his dirty, blunt words, and he tucks a lock of hair behind my ear. Our eyes lock, and it's not humor in his eyes that I see, but heat. My arms tingle with goose bumps and I shiver, but it's not from the cold.

I shouldn't do this. I don't even know this guy. Even though my initial plan was to have a one-night stand, I figured I'd at least spend more than ten minutes with the guy. But I *want* this. *God, do I want it.* And I'm going to take it. I'm going to take everything this gorgeous, egotistical stranger can give me in spades.

I catch Camden off guard when I swing a leg over his and straddle his lap. His hands immediately find my ass, and I feel his hardness between my thighs. His tongue darts out to wet his bottom lip, and when I lean in, that's all the permission he needs.

One of his tattooed hands fists my hair, and the other presses against my lower back. My hands cup both sides of his scruffy face as our mouths crash together. No longer playful, but hungry. Frantic. Desperate. His tongue tastes like oranges, and I moan when it slides against mine. The hand on my back slides under my dress and up my back, coming to rest between my shoulder blades.

Maybe it's the fact that it feels wrong to be like this with a man I don't know that's turning me on, or maybe it's just *him,* but I've never felt so much from a kiss before. I'm completely consumed, and I feel like I'm burning from the inside out. The hand on my upper back snakes around my side and comes to rest flat on my ribs, and his thumb grazes the underside of my breast. Everything inside of me ignites at his touch, and I pull back from his kiss on a gasp.

"Is this okay?" he asks, his voice thick and gravelly.

"Do whatever you want with me," I whisper. And I want him to. I want more of this feeling, and I'll chase it until the very last drop. His thumb brushes my nipple, and I shudder. Cam groans and circles it some more, applying more pressure this time, causing me to arch into his touch. Shoving my dress up to expose my braless chest, he cups both of my breasts before leaning in to suck a nipple into his mouth. I grind into his lap, uncaring of the fact that all that separates us from a crowded bar is a few sparse trees.

"You want more?" Cam asks.

"I want everything."

"Then, we need to go to my place," he says, reluctantly letting my dress fall back into place. "As much as I want you to sit on my dick—right here and now—beach sex is overrated. You don't want sand where the sun don't shine. Besides," he says, curving one hand over my ass, not stopping until he's sliding his fingers over my panty-covered crotch, "if we do this, it's not going to be quick. You're going to let me take my time with you."

His words do little to break through my lust-induced trance. Here I am ready to give it up to a guy I met five minutes ago, right out here in the open, and now he's asking to take me home. I know I should stop and think about this. To, I don't know, take a picture of his license and send it to Sutton or something. But, tonight isn't about making rational decisions. Tonight, I'm going to throw caution to the wind, because *nothing* about Camden Hess screams safe.

His eyebrows pull together, creating a crease between them as his icy blues search my browns, waiting for my answer. His fingers squeeze the tops of my thighs, as if he's trying to keep them from straying, and I say the word that could quite possibly result in the best sex of my life.

"Okay."

AFTER SCOOPING me up and throwing me over one shoulder, Cam prowled straight to his house—which happened to be right around the corner from The Edge—without another word. His entire demeanor changed after I agreed to go with him. He went from fun, witty stranger to scary, sexy stranger, and I was both terrified and intrigued. He strode through his house, and hanging upside down, I could only make out a brown leather couch before we were in his room. The door was slammed shut, and then I was slammed against it. I dropped my wristlet to the floor and wrapped my legs around his waist as he sucked and kissed and licked at my skin.

Now, we're both panting, desperate for more, and he swings around, walking us to his bed. He drops me into a pile of gray and black bedding before bracing himself above me, his hands planted on the bed on either side of my head. I spread my legs, welcoming him between them, and I smooth my hands up his back, dragging his T-shirt along the way. He pulls back to rip it off, and then he's right back where he was.

"Do you have a condom?" I have one in my abandoned wristlet over by the door, but I'm betting a guy like him comes equipped with an entire arsenal of them. He smirks at me, and I get the feeling that I've said something stupid. Isn't that how these things go? Some quick kissing and fumbling around in the dark before getting down to business? He's already surpassed my expectations.

"We're nowhere near that part yet. I told you, I'm going to take my time doing whatever the fuck I want, and you're going to let me, aren't you?"

I don't let people tell me what to do. I'm not a doormat. But in this bed, with this man, I'm more than happy to comply.

Taking my silence as confirmation, he slides down my body, bunching my dress up as he goes. He hooks a finger into the sides of my black panties and drags them down my legs, before tossing them behind him. The nerves hit me, being exposed like this, and I clamp my knees together. It's not that I'm a virgin—far from it—but I've only been with Tuck in the past year. It feels foreign to be with another man, let alone one that does more to my body with a single look than anyone I've ever been with before.

"No," he says simply, but firmly, lifting his head to look me in the eye. His pale blue eyes seem to glow, even in the dark. "Spread your legs for me, Mollie."

I do, slowly, but his eyes stay trained on mine. He parts me with one finger, sliding through my wetness, and I suck in a breath at the sensation. He circles my clit a few times before plunging that finger inside me. Finally, he breaks eye contact to watch his finger slipping in and out of me.

"Look at you. So pink and wet and tight."

His words cause me to clench against him once more, and his teeth dig into his lip as he slides down to get a closer look.

"Lift your knees," he orders, and I comply, completely mindless with pleasure. "Now hold your legs up with your hands," he instructs. "Good girl. Just like that."

My legs are spread obscenely wide. This angle has him reaching a spot that has me panting and causes a moan to slip free. His unoccupied hand glides up my stomach and rests in the center of my heaving chest.

"You're beautiful, Mollie Mabey."

My eyes are closed and my head back—unable to focus on anything but the sensations coursing through my body—when I feel Cam's hot breath between my legs half a second before his tongue is there. He doesn't clumsily poke around, nor does he attack me with sloppy, overeager kisses. No. Cam is slow. Intentional. He knows exactly what he's doing. He drags the flat of his tongue through my slit, applying more pressure once he gets to my clit, and then repeats the process again. He adds another finger into the mix, and this slow torture is almost more than I can take. I squeeze my legs together, rocking against his face as his firm strokes turn into sucking.

Just when I think I'm going to explode, he pulls his fingers from me and rips my legs apart. Wet, tattooed fingers grip the insides of my thighs and hold me open for him. My hands fly to his Jax Teller-esque hair and he growls into me. Cam moves his hands, and before I know what's happening, he's pushing my legs backwards and sliding his tongue even further south, to where no one else has ever been.

I jerk away at the sensation. It's not that it doesn't feel good—because holy Jesus, it does—but the fact that I'm completely caught off guard, if not a little embarrassed to have his tongue there. Cam doesn't allow for shame or discomfort, though, because in response, he flips me onto my side, so my knees are almost touching and angles his head underneath me to devour me that way. I bury my face in the pillow, balling his gray sheets in my fist as I forget inhibitions and take everything he's willing to give me.

A thick finger is shoved inside me as his tongue continues its assault on my other hole.

"*Oh, fuuuck,*" I whine, low and keening.

He moves his mouth back to my clit, and then he's slowly inserting another finger, but this time, he slides it into my ass. I freeze, locking up as he works his way in, little by little. It's wet enough not to hurt, but it still takes a minute to adjust to the burning fullness.

"Relax," Cam soothes before nipping at the bundle of nerves. Slowly, the discomfort turns to pleasure—full-blown fucking pleasure—and my legs go slack. It's all I can do to lie there as he works my body better than I knew possible. He pumps harder, the knuckles of his other fingers pounding into me, bruising the sensitive flesh, but it feels too good to care.

I'm writhing against him and his scruff scratches against my delicate skin, but I welcome the discomfort. I feel that familiar tightening that tells me I'm close. His choreographed movements don't miss a beat. Tongue, teeth, and fingers all work together to send me over the edge, leaving me a shaking and shuttering mess beneath him.

Cam crawls up my body before brushing sweaty hair from my cheek once I start to come back down to earth. Sleepy, sexed-up eyes meet his for a beat, and then he stands, dropping his pants. Even his muscular legs are full of ink. He's fucking magnificent. He saunters over to the open bathroom connected to his room, his glorious ass on display without an ounce of shyness, and looks at me in the mirror as he washes his hands.

"*Now*, we're ready for a condom," he says with a cocky smirk.

It's going to be a fun night.

Cam

Good golly, Miss Mollie. She's turning out to be more fun than I anticipated. I pegged her as a missionary-only kind of girl who wouldn't let my tongue anywhere besides her mouth. I've never been happier to have been wrong.

Now I see it—that curiosity, that dark side hidden beneath the surface. She's innocent, that much is clear, but she isn't a prude. She's untapped talent. A goddamn needle in a haystack. And tonight, I just happened to be the lucky bastard who found it.

I walk back to my bed, condom in hand, making a mental game plan of where I want to start. I didn't get near enough time with those puffy nipples that are just barely a shade darker than her olive skin, but I can't get enough of that pussy. I lick my lips as I climb into bed next to her, about to dip back between those creamy thighs, but she surprises me again by straddling my lap.

Mollie snatches the condom out of my hand and I twirl a lock of her long, brown hair around my finger as she carefully rips the top open with her teeth. She looks at me from beneath dark lashes, and suddenly, I feel like the one who's being seduced here.

Just to get the upper hand, I tweak her nipple with my thumb and forefinger, and she gives a little yelp. I lean forward to lick away the sting at the same time she reaches between us and starts to roll the condom down my length.

Fuck, her hand feels good on my dick. She works me up and down for a minute before planting her hands on my shoulders and sinking down onto me.

"Goddamn," I groan at the same time she whimpers, feeling her tight heat swallow me whole. I fight the urge to thrust upward and grip her hips instead while she adjusts to my size. She finds her rhythm soon, and her confidence follows. Mollie rises on her knees, until just the tip is inside her, and then she slams herself back down. I want to close my eyes to think of something else —*anything* else—to keep from blowing my load, but willingly missing out on this fine ass female learning and exploring and grinding on me, using me for her pleasure, is a sin punishable by death.

Mollie tangles her fingers in my sweaty hair as she moves her hips faster. Her eyes are shut, mouth parted, and I've never seen anything hotter in my life. I find myself wishing for half a second that she were local, so we could make this a weekly ritual. Daily, even. Hourly.

Mollie circles her hips and I palm her ass cheeks, keeping her pressed close. Her breathing is ragged, her movements jerky, like she's about to come again, and that's when I take over. I practically throw her off me, and when she squeals, I push on her shoulder blades to get my point across. She takes the hint and presses her chest into my sheets and lifts her ass in the air.

"Fuck me, you're perfect," I rasp, lining myself up with her entrance before sliding into her. I smooth my palms up and down her back as I start to move inside her. Mollie shudders, and I know she's enjoying this just as much as I am.

"Rub your pussy," I instruct, and she obeys instantly.

"Oh God," she moans, pressing her face into the sheets. I feel her fingers move from her clit to where we're connected, and she spreads them apart, sliding on either side of my cock.

"Fuck yeah. Keep doing that."

Timid fingers creep back even further to cup my balls, gently rolling them in her hand, and that's when I snap. I curl my body over hers, nipping and biting her spine as I rut into her like a fucking animal. Mollie arches her ass against me, taking my punishing thrusts. Pulling back, I watch myself disappearing inside her, her pink heat hugging my cock, unwilling to let go. Her asshole is on display, and I suck on my thumb before bringing it to that little hole, pressing and rubbing, but not penetrating. Half of her face is smashed into the bed, and she gasps as she presses backwards onto my thumb, spreading her legs even wider.

"You like it when I play with your ass?" I ask, my voice ragged.

"Yes," she breathes, and this time, there's not a trace of self-consciousness. It's pure, unadulterated lust that drives us both in this moment. The all-consuming kind of sexual chemistry that doesn't come along every day.

"Do you want more?"

"Please," she begs, looking back at me over her shoulder with desperate eyes and puffy lips. That word coming from that mouth is my undoing. I press my thumb inside the tight ring and reach around to rub her clit with the other hand. I'm about to blow, and I'm going to make sure she's coming with me.

Mollie screams and clenches around me, and I can only assume her limbs gave out from the way she collapses to the bed. I fuck her through her orgasm, gripping her curvy hip with one hand while my thumb continues to work her hole. I feel the familiar tingle in my balls a second before I start to come, long and hard.

Before I'm even finished, my bedroom door opens, and an inebriated Cordell stumbles into my room. Mollie is oblivious, eyes closed, still catching her breath, so I try to discreetly wave him away with a look that says *I will fucking kill you in your sleep if you don't walk away right now.* But he doesn't see my warning, because his eyes are fixed on Mollie's ass.

"Get the fuck out!" I bark, and both of them jump at the sound of my voice. Mollie yelps and lunges for the blanket, but it's still stuck underneath us. I cover her body with mine, trying to preserve some modicum of modesty. Cord looks at me like he doesn't even recognize me. He's watched me with girls before. He's probably wondering what makes tonight any different.

"I heard screaming," he says lamely, with an annoying smirk plastered to his mug.

"We're fine. Leave. *Now.*"

Cord shrugs a shoulder before turning to leave.

"Fuck, sorry about that," I say. I press a kiss to her nipple before lifting myself off her to take care of the condom. Except, when I look down, there is no condom. *The fuck?* I dig around in the sheet, thinking it must have slipped off after I pulled out, but it's nowhere to be found.

"What is it?" Mollie asks, her eyebrows tugged together in concern.

"I can't find the condom."

"What? What do you mean you *can't find it*?" she asks, her voice rising in pitch.

"Relax, it's here somewhere."

I turn on the lamp next to my bed, and we both scour the sheets, the floor, under the bed...and it's just *gone*. There's only one place left to check.

"Mollie," I say, and her head snaps up from the side of the bed.

"What? Did you find it?"

"No, but I think I know where it is. Don't freak out," I warn.

"Where?" she asks skeptically and stands, her naked body on display.

"Inside you."

"Nope." She shakes her head. "No. Nuh-uh. There's no way."

I pin her with a blank stare, waiting for her to come to the same realization. It has to be.

"Don't you think I'd feel it if it was?"

"Lie down. Let me check."

She hesitates before lying on her back, bent knees clamped shut. I lie on my stomach in front of them and gently pull her knees apart.

"I was just up close and personal with your pussy, baby. Relax, it's no big deal."

"This date just went from one-night stand to OB-GYN appointment," she mutters, covering her eyes with the back of her hand.

I chuckle, as my palms skate along the insides of her thighs, pushing them open. I spread her lips with my thumbs, but I can't see anything. She squirms when I hook two fingers inside her, and a little moan slips free. I feel my dick getting hard again already, and my hips automatically grind into the mattress on their own accord.

I'm just about to see how she feels about round two when I touch rubber. I fish it out and hold it up between two fingers.

"All right, Miss Mabey. The procedure went well. I didn't run into any complications. You may expect some mild discomfort, but it's nothing that some Tylenol won't fix. Come back in a week and I'll examine you again. You know, just to make sure we got everything."

Mollie giggles, and I dispose of the condom.

"Are you...okay?" I ask, not knowing how to broach the subject of what just happened.

"What do you mean?" she asks, perplexed.

"I mean, are you on birth control, or do I need to run and get you some Plan B?"

"Oh," she says, shifting uncomfortably. "I'm on the pill. And I'm clean, obviously," she tacks on at the end.

"Me, too," I assure her.

"Can you grab my dress?" she asks, after an awkward beat of silence.

"Why?"

"*Soooo*, I can leave?" It comes out as a question.

"You're leaving?"

"I mean, I just figured..." she trails off.

"You just figured, what? That our time is up? Because we still have about," I check the alarm clock on my nightstand, "seven more hours until the sun comes up." And there's a lot I can do to her in seven whole hours.

"Seven hours, huh?" she asks, blush creeping up her neck.

"And lucky for you, only about seven more minutes until I can go again."

"Hmm," she says thoughtfully, tapping a finger against her chin. "Hooking up with a stranger once is totally acceptable. But twice? I think we at least need to know some basic facts about each other."

"Is that so?" I ask, raising a brow.

"It's a rule," she insists.

"Well, you've got seven minutes to get to know me," I say, lying down next to her with my hands crossed behind my head.

"What do you do?" she asks.

"I snowboard."

"No, like, for a living," she clarifies.

"I snowboard. Professionally."

"Oh," she says, sounding shocked. She scans my room, as if looking for clues. She won't find anything but a few of my sponsors' stickers, unless she opens my closet.

"Why were you upset earlier?" I ask. "Boyfriend issues? *Daddy* issues?"

Mollie huffs out a humorless laugh. "Sort of. I guess you could say I just got out of a complicated relationship right before I came here."

"Ah, so I'm the rebound," I guess. Mollie shrugs and gives me an apologetic smile.

"Maybe?"

"I hate it when beautiful women use my body to get over their boyfriends. You should be ashamed of yourself," I say, reaching over to grab her by the waist and pulling her on top of me. My cock nestles between her wet pussy lips, and she slides back and forth on top of me.

"So ashamed," Mollie says, feigning innocence.

"Is it working?" I ask, flexing my hips upward. "Are you over him yet?"

"Almost," she breathes, as my hands reach up to palm her perky tits.

"I guess we'll just have to try again," I say, and then she angles her hips just right to take me inside her.

"Just one more time."

Chapter Three

MOLLIE

Now...

"You're coming. You haven't missed a Christmas here since we were seven," Sutton's voice blares from the speaker of my phone.

"She's right," Tucker agrees, tossing random items into the open suitcase on my bed next to me. "River's Edge at Christmas is your favorite part of the year."

After I got back from our trip, I finally decided to hear Tucker out. His reasoning didn't excuse the fact that he wasn't honest with me. But...it made sense. He said he wanted to be with someone who *actually* wanted him for once. Of course, I felt bad. But I still don't think he went about it the right way, even if it did force us to reevaluate.

"I can't," I start, and my hand automatically finds my rounded stomach. "He doesn't know."

"Well, then merry fucking Christmas to him, because you *need* to tell him, Mollie."

I know I do. And I will. I don't have Cam's number, but I found his Facebook page. I've drafted up the message at least ninety-two times, I just can't bring myself to hit *send*. I mean, what do I even say? *Hey, remember me? You gave me the best eight hours of my life, then I called an Uber before you woke up and we never spoke again. Oh, by the way, I'm pregnant with your baby. Happy holidays!*

"Mollie, it's December," Sutton says, stating the obvious.

"I got knocked up, not a lobotomy. I know what month it is." Both she and Tucker laugh.

"Which *means*," she sings, "Cam isn't even here."

"What? Why?"

"He's almost never here in the winter. Why do you think you haven't ever seen him around before? He's always on some tour. But especially now. He'll be preparing for Aspen."

"Aspen?"

"The X Games! You know, because he's a professional snowboarder? Do you know him at all?"

"Apparently not!" I don't know anything about snowboarders and their schedules. I knew Cam was pro, but I guess I didn't realize he was on that level.

"Well, then you have nothing to worry about. But you do need to tell him. The sooner, the better," Tucker chimes in, like the annoying voice of reason he is.

"I have time," I insist. I never planned to keep it from him. I could never let Cam go on living his life, not knowing he brought a child into this world. I just needed a while to wrap my brain around it. To make a plan. For the first month or so, I was terrified. Well, I still am, but now, I'm starting to get excited.

"You have, like, five months."

Five months. I physically feel my face drain of color. Five months is nothing. Tucker must see the panic spreading through me like wildfire in my expression, because he drops to his knees in front of me, taking my hands in his.

"It's okay. *You're* okay. Breathe."

I nod, trying my best to take in air.

"We're going to River's Edge, just like every year. We're going to get hot chocolate wasted and watch all the *Die Hard* movies, and you're going to love every second of it. Agreed?"

"Even the last one?"

"Even the last one," he agrees. "Even though it was trash. I'll never deny your fixation with Jai Courtney."

"You're a real pal."

"The best."

"Yeah, except for that time he *cheated on you*," Sutton yells through the line, around what sounds like a mouthful of chips. "Am I the only one who remembers that minor detail?"

"I'm hanging up on you now," I say, rolling my eyes. "I'll see you next week."

I hang up the phone and reluctantly finish packing what Tucker started.

"We're telling our families the truth," Tuck surprises me by saying. "After the holidays," he clarifies. "About not being together, about the baby, all of it."

"Tuck—" I start, but he cuts me off.

"It's time, Mollie. I shouldn't have let it go on for this long."

Once I finally told my parents about being pregnant when I started showing last month, they naturally assumed it was Tuck's baby. We asked them not to tell his parents, that Tucker wanted to tell them on his own. That way they wouldn't be planning for a grandchild that isn't even theirs.

I know he's right. This thing between us has snowballed out of control, and right now, with this baby coming, there's no better time for a fresh, clean start. We'll tell our families we aren't together, and then I'll tell Camden Hess he's going to be a father.

After the holidays. After.

I STOMP the snow off my tan and black Sorel boots before stepping inside The Pines ski resort. I scan the grandiose building with the wood flooring and rock walls. The circular, metal candle chandelier that hangs above a sitting area next to the stone fireplace. It's only half past five, but the sun is already down, and there are clusters of tourists in snowsuits that have just come off the mountain in every corner.

"Have you ever stayed here before?" Tucker asks, lugging both of our suitcases behind him. Since I've been pregnant, it's like he thinks I'm incapable of lifting a finger. It's annoyingly endearing.

"Nope. Craig and Andrew want to snowboard, and apparently, the cabin is too far away." My brothers complained about how long it took to get to The Pines from the cabin we rented on the outskirts of River's Edge last year, so my parents booked us rooms here for the first few days.

"It's nice," he says, making his way to the front desk, the wheels of our suitcases echoing off the walls.

"That's an understatement," I say, tightening the messy ponytail on top of my head. My hair is so thick now that I don't even attempt to tame it. *Must be the prenatals.*

"What are *we* going to do?"

"What do you mean?"

"I mean, you can't snowboard pregnant." Tuck pauses. "Wait, can you?" he asks, second-guessing his initial assumption.

"No." I laugh. "Well, I guess you could," I amend, "but I don't want to risk it."

"Does this mean getting drunk is out of the question?" he teases, gesturing to the hotel bar on the other side of the lobby. I roll my eyes and follow his gaze, about to give him some sarcastic response, but the smile falls from my face.

"Mollie? What's up?" Tuck asks, his eyebrows scrunched together as he searches the bar for whatever caused my shift in behavior. I'm frozen for half a second, looking at Camden as he poses for a photo with a group of girls. He doesn't smile, though. He looks like he'd rather be anywhere but here. As soon as they're done, he leaves them with barely a nod of acknowledgment. If it wasn't for the tattoos on his throat that I can make out from here, I might not think it was him.

The Cam I knew, albeit for five minutes, was happy and funny and brighter than the sun. This guy looks miserable. I'm lost in my thoughts, and I don't realize I'm staring until it's too late. He pauses his stride, and as if he senses me, his eyes lock in on mine. I whip around, pulling my dark green vest closed. I'm wearing a loose black long-sleeved shirt and black skinny yoga pants—mostly because it's the only thing that fits comfortably anymore—but right now, I'm thankful that I picked something that would camouflage my stomach.

"Can we get the room key?" I ask out of the corner of my mouth while trying to covertly hide the side of my face with my ponytail. Tuck looks concerned, but he acts quickly, approaching the front desk, and then he's handing me the little envelope with the plastic room key inside. Tuck ushers me toward the elevator with a hand on my lower back.

"Our suitcases—"

"They're going to bring them up. I told them you weren't feeling well, and we needed to hurry."

I nod, thankful for his quick thinking.

We're almost to the elevators when I give in to the urge to look back, and I immediately wish I hadn't. He's standing in the middle of the lobby, staring straight at me. His arms are crossed, and the look on his face is something between perplexed and mildly irritated.

Can he tell I'm pregnant? Why is he looking at me like that? I'm surprised he even recognizes me, to be honest. How many girls have come before and after me? But unless he likes to have angry staring contests with strangers, he definitely recognizes me.

The elevator dings, signaling its arrival, and I turn my attention back to it. Tucker guides me inside and hits the button for the eighth floor.

"Wanna tell me what just happened?" he asks with an expectant look.

"I saw him."

"Like, *him* him?"

I nod, pacing the elevator. Why is he here? Sutton swore he'd be gone. I suddenly feel hot—*really* hot—and not in a good way. My stomach tangles with nerves.

"I thought he was in Aspen," Tuck says, confused.

"Yeah, well, he's not," I snap. I don't mean to, but I feel like I'm on the verge of throwing up, and I haven't done that since starting my second trimester. The elevator doors slide open, and Tucker leads the way. We walk in silence, Tucker knowing that it's best to let me work through things on my own and calm myself down before he tries to talk to me.

Once we're in our room, I sit on one of the queen beds with the wooden posts, while Tucker snatches the remote off the dresser and flips through the guide. A few minutes pass, and there's a knock on the door. My head snaps over to Tucker.

"Relax," he says, knowing exactly what I'm thinking. "It's our suitcases. Remember?"

Oh. *Duh.*

A middle-aged man in a polo that sports The Pines' logo wheels our luggage in. Tucker tips him as I dig through my bag, searching for my phone. I shoot off a text to Sutton, telling her that I'm going to kick her ass, and then I check my family group chat.

Mom: Dinner at the Pine Top buffet. 6PM. Top floor. Dress nice.

Craig: But I really wanted to wear my new crop top.

Andrew: New phone. Who dis?

Craig: My milkshake brings all the boys to the yard.

Mom: You're both idiots.

Mom: Where's Mollie?

Craig: Probably being pregnant somewhere.

Mom: Funny.

Despite my impending meltdown, I laugh and let them know we'll be there. I freshen up in the bathroom and fluff my ponytail, but I don't change my outfit. When I come out, Tucker is standing outside the door, looking down at his phone while he waits for me. He gives me a reassuring smile, and then we're on our way to the buffet.

Dinner proves to be a good distraction, between my brothers' antics and the plethora of delicious food. Everyone makes plans to get up early tomorrow—my brothers snowboarding and my parents skiing. I decide to do some shopping in the outdoor mall right next to the resort.

We kiss and hug our goodbyes, and then Tuck and I are heading back to our room. We're in separate beds, something I insisted on a couple of months ago. We haven't had sex since I hooked up with Cam, but even sleeping in the same bed feels wrong now. It blurs the line, and right now, boundaries are our friend. It would be easy to crawl into his bed, into his arms, and accept the comfort my best friend has to offer me, but I know I shouldn't. It would be selfish, knowing he still harbors feelings for me on some level.

"Molls?" Tucker asks after a few minutes, his voice low and sleepy.

"Yeah?"

"It'll be all right."

I smile in the dark.

"Thanks, Tuck."

Chapter Four

Cam

"Wake up, shitbag. It's time to teach the privileged," Cord says, throwing my snow boots at me. I double over in bed, clutching my stomach as the boots narrowly avoid my nuts.

"Fuck off," I grumble, pulling the pillow over my head. I stretch and feel a pang in my knee that reminds me exactly why I'm in this position in the first place—not that I need reminding. I think about that day twenty-four seven and what I could've done differently.

I didn't even hurt myself snowboarding, for fuck's sake. I was on my skateboard, trying to smith grind down a rail when I unexpectedly locked into another trick. My weight was distributed for the smith, leaving me no chance to bail. And that's how I tore my ACL, also known as every athlete's worst fucking nightmare.

I had surgery a few months ago, and instead of doing everything in my power to heal, I was on a downward spiral from hell. I never wore my brace, never went to physical therapy, and if I did leave my house, it was to get belligerent, and most times, ended up thrown in the drunk tank for bar fights. If that wasn't enough, all my sponsors dropped my ass like a sack of potatoes. I don't blame them, though—they were sick of my shit. I couldn't compete, and I wasn't taking recovery seriously. I was a PR manager's worst nightmare.

I had my wake-up call when Cordell bailed on Aspen because he was afraid to leave me alone. Me—a grown-ass man—couldn't even be left alone. That's a whole new level of fucked up, even for me. I didn't care about messing my own life up, but I didn't want to drag my brother down with me.

Slowly, I stopped getting black-out drunk, started going to physical therapy, and last month, I took a job as an instructor for the resort's ski school. I'm able to ride, but I'm nowhere near ready for the X Games. So, for now, I'll put in time at the gym and kick it on the bunny slopes, teaching a bunch of six to eight-year-olds to ski and snowboard.

Most days, I'm okay with how my life has changed. I wish I would have kept my ass off that skateboard, but it could be worse. Surprisingly enough, working with the mini assholes has done wonders for my outlook and my mood in general. But yesterday was just one of those days where I felt like a failure and like I lost my shot at my dream career.

Then, I saw her. Mollie Mabey. The girl I hooked up with right before my injury. She was looking fine, too. But then, she noticed me and acted like she had no clue who I was. Maybe it had something to do with the fact that her boyfriend was with her. Did she think I was going to make a scene because we had one night together? Fuck if I know. I was already in a sour-ass mood, and her looking at me like I was the person she made the mistake of slumming it up with over summer vacay did nothing to help my mood.

I could have my pick of any girl on this mountain when I was in my prime. And she was *embarrassed* of me? Fuck that. Hell, I can still have my pick. Chicks love athletes, and an injured one? Even better. They have this innate instinct to nurture and nurse them back to health. That shit is in their DNA.

I look up at my ceiling and see the time glowing in blue from my alarm clock projector. Eight thirty-eight. I have twenty-two minutes to get dressed and be on the mountain. I scrub my hands down my face, trying to shake off the sleep, and make a mental note to shave. I let myself get a little burlier than I usually am.

I throw on my snow pants and jacket with The Pines' logo, grab my board, goggles, hat, and gloves, and head out the door. I throw my board onto the roof rack of my cobalt blue WRX, and then I'm off. Once I park in the resort's garage, I grab my shit and make my way toward the lift. This is my favorite part. The ride up the mountain. The crisp, quiet air. The calm before the storm.

Once I'm at the top, I round up the hula-hoops and tip connectors for the kids' skis and trudge through the snow.

"Camden!" a tiny voice squeals, and I turn just in time to see Emersyn barreling toward me. She tackles me at the knees, and we both go down. Good thing we have fresh powder today, or that would've been a bitch for my tailbone. I chuckle, righting the beanie that shifted during the fall, and she uses her mitten-covered hands to push the blonde hair from her face. Red cheeks and a toothless smile beam up at me.

Emersyn may be seven, but I can already tell that she's going to be a lifelong snowboarder. When she first came to me, I made her start with skiing. Kids usually do better learning that way first. She was a natural, so I spoke to her parents about getting her a snowboard. The kid fucking loves it. And I know she's going places. Which is why I agreed when her parents asked if I could give her private lessons.

"What's up, Mini Shredder?" I ask, grabbing her under the armpits and propping her on her feet.

"Nuffin'." She shrugs. "Can we try the box today?" she asks, clapping her hands together.

"*Nooo*," I drawl. "We're going to work on carving and getting your pops nice and clean with the other kids. We'll do some tricks during your private lessons. Deal?"

"Deal," she grumbles.

Most of the kids in my class have pretty solid skills. At the beginning, I had to weed out the kids who didn't truly want to be there. Usually, the parents threw them into it so they could snap a few photos and brag about it on social media. Those kids weren't ready, and I had to explain to the parents that pushing it now would result in fear that could potentially ruin boarding or skiing for the rest of their lives. Now, I'm left with a good group of kids who have a genuine love of the mountain and desire to learn.

The rest of my group has gathered by the cones I have set up, and we make our way over to start the class. I help Emersyn trek through the snow by guiding her by her hood. The kid is a beast on a snowboard. But walking on two feet? Not so much. Especially when snow boots are involved.

"All right, dudes and dudettes, get your helmets on. Let's hit some drills, and then we'll move on to some new skills."

I LIFT my goggles off my eyes and onto my forehead over my beanie and slide into the lift. On the way down, I realize that my knee doesn't feel as stiff as it usually does by the end of the day. That's got to be a good sign.

My phone buzzes in my pocket once my service kicks back in, and I see texts from Dare inviting me over for dinner. Which really means Briar forced him to invite me because she's worried. But I shoot a text back letting them know I'll be there, because Briar feeds me. I'll never turn down a home-cooked meal, even if the main ingredient is pity.

Once I'm at the bottom, I decide to head straight to my car instead of stopping for a beer at the resort's bar. I'm walking through the outdoor shopping center toward the parking lot when I see her. Mollie. She's sitting on the Blues Brothers bench—which is exactly what it sounds like; a bench with the Blues Brothers statues at both ends—next to the outdoor ice-skating rink. The skating rink sits right in the middle of The Pines, surrounded by the actual resort, the lifts, and all the stores and restaurants.

Mollie sits there, watching the ice skaters, drinking something that appears to be hot. This time she has on a grey beanie with a tan pompom on top, those tight, black things that girls try to pass off as pants—not that I'm complaining—and a white coat over a flannel shirt. Before I can talk myself out of it, I'm heading right for her.

"Well, if it isn't Mollie Mabey," I say, causing her to jump. Her big, brown eyes shoot up to mine, and she looks like a deer caught in headlights.

"Camden," she says, seeming nervous or unsure as she crosses one leg over the other. An image pops into my head of me between those thighs, eating that perfect pussy, and if she wasn't here with her boyfriend, I might ask her for a repeat. I still might, boyfriend or not.

"So, you do remember me," I say, even though her reaction last night made that more than clear.

"Sorry about last night," she says. "I just wasn't expecting to see you."

Her response strikes me as odd. Maybe if she was a stage five clinger who wanted to make our one-night stand into something serious, it might make sense. But she never once tried to contact me afterward. We both knew the deal.

"What are you doing?" I ask, giving her an out. She doesn't have to explain herself.

"My family's up there," she says, gesturing toward the gondola in the distance. "I was just walking around the shops, waiting for everyone to be done."

"Why didn't you go up?"

"I suck at snowboarding," she admits. "Plus, I wasn't feeling well earlier."

I want to ask where her boyfriend is. If he went up without her. But I don't.

"Come with me," I say, surprising her. She starts to shake her head, but I grab her dainty hand, pulling her up from the bench. She shivers and zips her jacket, wrapping her arms around her middle. It's not even that cold now, but I guess it might be for someone who isn't used to River's Edge's winters.

"I really can't. They'll be done soon, soooo..." she trails off, looking toward the lift.

"Bullshit. You've been down here all day. You deserve to do *something* while you're here. Give me one second. Okay?"

She looks like she's going to say no. Indecision wars in her eyes. But she surprises me by nodding yes.

"Wait here," I instruct.

"Okay..." she says suspiciously.

"I'll be right back."

I turn around and jog toward the kiosk a few feet away and buy her a lift ticket before running back in her direction.

"Come on," I say, tugging on her hand. She lets me guide her to the gondola, her tiny, freezing palm in mine. We hand our tickets to the lift operator.

"Mind holding onto my board for a few?" I ask him. I don't want to lug it around. He agrees. He's seen me around, so he knows I work here, if the black and forest green snowsuit with The Pines' logo wasn't enough to tip him off.

"Thanks, man," I say, helping Mollie into the lift. She sits on the opposite side of me and rests her oversized purse on her lap. When the lift jerks, she startles and gives a little yelp. I chuckle, putting my hand on her knee.

"You're safe. There's nothing to be afraid of in here."

Mollie swallows thickly, and after giving me a searching look, she turns her gaze to the mountains.

"This is my favorite part, you know. It's so quiet and peaceful," she says with a small smile, echoing my thoughts from earlier.

I clear my throat. "Like the calm before the storm," I mutter.

"Exactly!"

Once we're at the top, I hop out first and extend my hand to help her down.

"This way," I say, and she follows. I lead her to the lookout deck. You can see the whole lake from here. People pay just for this view.

"Oh my God," she breathes, taking it all in. The crystal blue lake that reflects like a mirror, the snow-covered mountaintops in the distance. "It's beautiful."

"Beautiful doesn't even fucking begin to describe it," I say, but I'm not looking at the lake. The pink in Mollie's cheeks deepens. I like making her blush. I want to make that whole body blush, again and again.

"Why did you bring me here?" she asks, doubt lacing her tone.

I could give her some bullshit line, but if I remember correctly, Mollie is the type of girl who appreciates straightforwardness.

"You looked sad." I shrugged. "I guess I wanted to fix it. Also, your ass looks fucking phenomenal, and I wouldn't mind spending time with it again. I mean you. *You* again. And also your ass."

She looks up at me with tears swimming in those brown eyes. *Okay, I guess she didn't appreciate the honesty...*

"Whoa, my bad, Mollie. Don't cry."

"No," she says, waving me off. "That was just really sweet."

That's not exactly the word I'd use to describe it, but I'm not going to argue. I notice a little smudge of brown on the corner of her berry-colored lips, and without thinking, I lean in and slowly slide my thumb across it. Mollie's breath hitches, as I pull it back and suck it off my thumb.

"Mmm. Hot chocolate."

Mollie bites her lip, and in a bold move, I lean forward again to lick it straight from the source. Her mouth parts, and I take the opportunity to suck her bottom lip into my mouth. Her palms come up to my chest, but instead of pushing me away, she grips my jacket. I take that as permission to slip my tongue inside, sliding it against hers.

"Cam!" a familiar voice shouts. I break away from Mollie with a groan and look over to see Emersyn with her parents and two older people. She holds up a finger, letting them know she'll be right back, and runs over to us.

"Long time no see, Mini Shredder." *Who shall from now on be mentally referred to as Mini Cockblock.*

"My mom and dad wanted to show my grandparents the lookout," she says, rolling her eyes.

I laugh at her attitude and ruffle her wind-knotted hair. "Tough break," I say sarcastically.

"I know, right? Is this your *girrrrrlfriend*?" Em sings.

"No," I say, clearing my throat and scratching at the back of my neck. "Emersyn, this is my friend, Mollie. Mollie, this is one of my kids."

Mollie's wide eyes dart to mine, and I realize how that sounded.

"One of my *students*," I'm quick to amend. "I teach at the ski school."

"His *best* student," Emersyn clarifies, tucking her hair behind her ear.

"You cocky little—" I start, but then I turn to Mollie. "She's right, though. You'll be seeing this kid on TV someday soon. Mark my words."

Emersyn preens like a goddamn peacock and Mollie laughs at her antics, but her eyes are still glassy.

"I really have to go," she says, hooking a thumb behind her. "But it was nice to meet you!" she tells Emersyn. Turning back to me, she adds, "Thank you for this."

She doesn't even give me a chance to respond before she's walking back toward the lift. I take a minute to talk to Em, letting her know I'd see her in a couple of days for her private lesson before I decide to head back down myself.

Welp. That was a fat fail. At least I have dinner to look forward to.

Chapter Five

Mollie

That was, quite possibly, the most embarrassing moment of my life. I cried after someone complimented my ass. It wasn't just that Cam was being sweet about wanting to cheer me up. It was a combination of things. The view. Seeing him interact with Emersyn. And knowing that I have to share my secret soon, when part of me likes having this little pinecone all to myself. Worrying about his reaction. All of it.

If I'm not crying, I'm horny, hence letting him *kiss me*. What was I thinking? That's all pregnancy is for me at this point—crying over nothing and fantasizing about everything. I feel like I have exactly zero control over my emotions or hormones, and that's the most frustrating part.

This morning, Tuck planned to keep me company, but my brothers wanted him to go boarding. He was reluctant, but I told him he should go. I'm not his girlfriend. It's time for us to act like it. After I took the lift back down, I didn't wait for anyone. I decided to go back to my room and get ready for tonight. Besides, I needed a minute to clear my head after running into Cam for the second time in as many days. Small towns suck.

Sutton and I have plans, so I showered and then grabbed a quick bite to eat with Tuck. Now, I'm staring at my suitcase, debating what to wear. I'm not sure what we're doing, but I think she said something about going to her friend's house. Since I don't think we're going to be out in public, I decide to wear a cute gray formfitting wrap dress that does nothing to hide my growing stomach and my taupe-y suede over-the-knee boots. I throw on a gray scarf and an oversized cardigan, grab my purse, and head down to the lobby, hoping I'm not unlucky enough to run into Camden Hess for a third time. Sutton's waiting for me in her SUV outside the revolving doors, and I rush toward the passenger door, already feeling the bitter cold seeping into my bones. Sutton squeals when I open the door, hugging me over the middle console.

"I fucking missed you!" she yells into my ear. "And look at you!" She pulls back, pushing my cardigan out of the way to get a better look. "I knew. I just fucking knew it," she says, shaking her head.

"What?" I ask defensively.

"I knew you'd be the cutest pregnant bitch alive. You're all tummy, and even that is tiny."

"I'm only like twenty weeks. You'll have to roll me around soon."

"Doubtful," she says, pulling out of the parking lot.

"So, where are we going again?"

"I asked my friend Briar to hang out earlier. She's sort of new in town, but she's good people. You'll like her. She invited us to hang out at her friend's house."

"Like, a party?" I ask. "Because I don't want to be the pregnant chick at the party."

"No." Sutton laughs, "They're just hanging out. Probably playing some pool and some snowskate."

"What the hell is snowskate?"

"Like skateboarding...in the snow."

"So, snowboarding?"

"Huh," Sutton says, looking contemplative. "I never thought of that. They're different somehow." She shrugs. "Anyway, Briar is gorgeous and the most genuine chick I know—besides you," she adds belatedly. "And her fiancé? Jesus Christ, that guy is probably the hottest guy I've ever seen in real life. I mean, I'm a little afraid of him, but he's fun to look at."

"You're a mess." I laugh.

"Says the pregnant girl in denial," she slings back, rolling her eyes.

"Shut up! I am not in denial. I'm very aware that I'm going to be in charge of a human life in just a couple of months."

"And you're going to rock it, so get that panicked look off your face. This is a good thing, Mollie. The *best* thing, even if you can't see it now."

My stupid pregnancy hormones strike again, and it's all I can do to nod without bursting into tears. I've been working temp jobs since being laid off, while looking for other career opportunities. I still live with my best friend-slash-fake boyfriend. The baby's father doesn't even *know*. I feel like a failure of a mom and my kid hasn't even been born.

I turn up the radio to avoid talking about this particular subject, and "Closer" by The Chainsmokers blares from the speakers. We're driving for longer than I expected, past the city limits. There aren't any streetlights out here, and the roads are long and windy.

"Are you sure you're not actually taking me somewhere to kill me?" I ask, only half-joking.

"I'm just following the directions she gave me. I've never been out this far."

We drive for a more miles on the edge of the lake, the road becoming increasingly narrow, and the sky darker. The snow is really starting to come down now, and the streets are covered in white. Finally, we pull up to a dark brown cabin. It's covered in snow, and there are three guys with what appears to be skateboards without the wheels and one tiny blonde girl bundled up, standing in the front yard.

The blonde, whom I assume is Briar, waves as we walk up the icy driveway.

"Be careful," she says, gesturing to the ground. "It's super slippery."

Sutton and Briar hug, and when they pull apart, Briar beams at me. "I'm Briar," she says, holding out a hand. I take it and introduce myself.

"This is Asher," she says, tugging him over by his arm. *Damn.* Sutton is right. He's nice to look at, but intimidating as hell. He gives me a nod, squeezes Briar's ass, and kisses the top of her head before he jumps onto his skateboard without wheels and slides down the little hill in the yard.

"This is Adrian, who's basically my brother," she says, pointing to a guy who smiles suggestively at me, his deep dimples on display. "My actual brother is...away," she says cryptically. "And this is Dare. He's grumpy, but he's harmless."

Tall and tattooed grunts at me in response. He looks vaguely familiar. They're all gorgeous, but Dare is like the leader of the beautiful, and even more threatening than Asher. I think it's a rule that you must be ridiculously attractive to hang out with this crowd.

"We should go inside before the ladies get cold," Adrian says.

"We're fine," Sutton insists.

"Not you. I mean these assholes," he says, flicking his chin toward Dare and Asher.

"Where did Tweedledee and Tweedledum go?" Asher asks, as if suddenly noticing someone is missing, as we walk inside.

"They'll be right back," Dare says, holding the door open for us.

Inside, it's sort of bare—which is to be expected for a guy's house. What I don't expect is how beautiful it is. Tall, wooden beams and vaulted ceilings. Floor-to-ceiling windows. A pool table sits in the middle of an open room off to the side of the kitchen, and there are two rustic brown couches that sit in front of a somewhat formidable fireplace made from stone.

Sutton takes off her coat, revealing a cream color off-the-shoulder sweater and skinny black jeans, and Briar tells her to hang it on the hook by the door. I follow suit, hanging my cardigan and scarf next to hers.

Sutton's hands are immediately on my belly. "I can't even handle it, Molls. This is amazing."

"You're pregnant?" Briar asks, extending her hand, but she snatches it back before she makes contact. "Can I feel? I mean, is that weird?" I laugh and assure her that I don't mind.

I know a lot of pregnant women hate their stomachs being touched—I've been on enough online baby forums to know that's generally a no-no—but I'm not one of those women. I think it's sweet. Ask me again when a stranger tries it, though, and I might answer differently.

I don't even see how it happens, but Adrian's on his knees in front of me in a flash, adding his hand to the mix. I've got three sets of hands on my body—two of them belonging to strangers. *This is the most action I've had in months.*

"How far along are you?" Briar asks. "If Sutton didn't start rubbing you like a Magic 8 Ball, I wouldn't have even known. You're tiny."

"Like twenty weeks. Now is when I'll really start packing on the pounds, or so I hear." It feels good to talk to people about this who don't know me or my situation. They're just genuinely curious and excited. Babies have a way of doing that to people.

Briar is the first to step back, and Sutton is next. Adrian lingers, gripping my bump like a basketball.

"I'm weirdly aroused right now, I'm not gonna lie."

The room goes dead silent, everyone looking to each other, each expression a variation of *did he really just say that?*

"What?" Adrian asks, looking around, genuinely confused.

I'm the first one to break, unable to keep the full-on belly laugh inside. Dare snorts out a laugh, and like a domino effect, everyone else follows.

Just then, I hear the front door open. It happens in slow-motion, the way I turn my head toward the sound, only to see a tattooed hand dropping a set of keys and said keys clanging to the hardwood floor. The way the smile melts off my face, and the way that happy, carefree feeling morphs into horror.

Because it's Cam at the door, staring right at my pregnant stomach, and Adrian's hands that are all over it.

"Who's the pregnant chick?" a guy who looks a lot like Cam says from behind his shoulder as he chews on what appears to be a breadstick. I realize now that he's his brother, and he was at the bar that night. That must be why Dare looked familiar to me.

"What the fuck are you doing here?" Cam barks, his eyes hard in a way that I've never seen from him before.

"I'm sorry," I say softly. "I was going to tell you."

Once again, the room is quiet, everyone seemingly confused—not excluding myself—but knowing something significant is going down.

"*Okay,*" Briar drawls, yanking a baffled Adrian up by the back of his hoodie. "This is our cue to leave."

The guy behind Cam moves around him, with a pizza box in one arm, and everyone makes their way up the stairs, except Sutton, who hangs back for a minute.

"I didn't know," she says, sincerity dripping from every word, her eyes begging me to believe her. "I swear."

"It's okay," I tell her, because this moment has been a long time coming. It might be a bit more dramatic than I'd have liked it to be, but it needs to happen nonetheless.

Once we're left alone, Cam kicks the door closed behind him and walks to the fridge, helping himself to a beer. Weirdly, I wonder how close of friends he is with these people. Obviously comfortable enough to walk in without knocking and raid Dare's fridge. *What are the odds? And why me?*

"I wanted to tell you," I say again, not having any idea where to start.

"I don't think there's anything to say, really," he says with a shrug.

My eyebrows cinch together in confusion. "Can you let me explain?"

"What is there to explain? You let me kiss you when you're *pregnant*. Now, I'm not the fucking moral police, but that seems a little fucked up to kiss another man when you're pregnant, even for me. I'm sure your boyfriend super appreciates it."

What? Is that what he thinks? That it's Tucker's*?*

"Cam—" I try again, but he interrupts me.

"And not only did you hide it from me, but then I walk in to find my friend's hands all over you. Just how many guys have you let have a piece of that pie, Mollie Mabey?"

I can't begin to explain the anger that ripples through me in waves. In the short time I've spent with him, I've seen fun, cocky Cam, I've seen moody, guarded Cam, but I've never seen this *mean* side before.

"You don't know what the *fuck* you're talking about," I seethe, walking past him to grab my sweater and stuff off the hook. "Sutton!" I yell. "I'll be in the car."

Chapter Six

CAM

Mollie storms out of the house, slamming the door behind her. *Unfucking-believable*. How did I not notice it before? I think back to the few times I ran into her, and she always had a jacket or a loose shirt to camouflage her stomach. I think about how she always seemed to position her purse in front of her, and how she reacted the way she did in the lobby.

But why? Why did she care what I thought?

Mollie's friend comes barreling down the stairs after her and stops in front of me.

"You and Mollie hooked up like four months ago, right?"

I nod my confirmation, as a sinking feeling hits my gut.

"Weird, because she's four months pregnant," she says, sarcasm dripping from every word. "Do the math, asshole. It's yours."

I stand here, feeling the color drain from my face. And then she's shoving past me, too, shoulder checking me on her way out.

Fuck. Fuck. *Fuck*. The condom. It slipped off inside her, but she said she was on birth control. I remember asking, specifically. And she's just now telling me? How long would she have waited if I hadn't found out inadvertently? We never exchanged numbers, but she knows my name. She clearly knows my fucking friends. Tracking me down would be a no-brainer. Would she have told me at all? Would I ever know that I fathered a child? Is this even my kid? So many thoughts bombard me at once, and I drop down onto the bottom step, holding my head in my hands.

I hear someone coming down the stairs a moment later, and then Cord plops down next to me.

"Was she telling the truth?" he asks, probably having eavesdropped on the whole thing.

I blow out a breath, scrubbing a hand over my stubble. "I think so," I admit. I can't be sure, and I barely know the girl, but my gut tells me she wouldn't lie about something like that.

"Then, what the fuck are you doing? Go," Cordell says, jerking his chin toward the front door. *Fuck*. He's right. At the very least, we need to talk.

"You good?" I ask as I stand.

"I'll get a ride back. I might even crash here tonight."

I give him a nod, retrieve my forgotten keys from the floor, and then I'm hauling ass through the snow back to The Pines.

AFTER ASKING MY FRIEND, who happened to be working the front desk, which room Mollie was in, I dart over to the elevator, not wanting to miss it—it's the kind that you don't see for ten minutes once it's gone—and my snow-slick boots slip against the hardwood flooring. I flail for a second, but I end up being able to catch my balance. The elevator went up without me, though, so I do what any normal person would do.

I take the stairs.

I fly up all eight flights of stairs, taking two or three at a time. I walk in the direction of her room number, the plush beige carpet muffling my footsteps—a stark contrast to the urgency I'm feeling inside. I raise my fist to knock, not having any idea how she's going to react to me showing up uninvited. Either way, I'm not going anywhere until she gives me some answers.

Mollie opens the door, her doe eyes red from crying, and it makes the brown appear almost orange. Her wet eyelashes cling together, and her nose is red. Her heart-shaped mouth parts in shock, and I brace my right arm on the doorframe, leaning in closer.

"I'm going to be a dad?" I ask her, surprised to have to speak around the lump in my throat.

She nods, her bottom lip trembling, trying to hold back the tears. In this moment, I don't care that she lied to me, that she kept it from me, or anything else. I don't care about her fuck bag of a boyfriend. All I care about is this woman in front of me that is beautiful and carrying my child and *mine*.

Sliding my hand behind her neck, I crash my mouth to hers. She stumbles back, the hotel door hitting the wall, but I have her. I push her against the wall, and when her mouth parts on a gasp, I slide my tongue into her mouth. She tastes like peppermint and hot chocolate. I bring both hands to cup her face, angling her head to devour her to the best of my abilities.

Mollie pulls back, panting. "Cam," she whispers. "Tucker is here."

Keeping my hands on her face, I slowly angle my head to the right, and sure enough, Tucker is standing there, and he sheepishly lifts his hand in an awkward, limp wave.

"Well, Fucker, you can leave now."

"It's *Tucker*, and you know it. Don't talk to him like that," Mollie snaps with bite in her tone that I've never heard before. "He's been there for me through everything. He's taken me to every single doctor appointment, and he's held my hair while I puked for six weeks straight. He's not my boyfriend, and he's not your enemy. In fact, he's essentially your unborn child's uncle, so don't fuck up your first choice as a father."

"It's not like you gave me that opportunity!" I yell, letting my temper get the best of me. "Don't you think I would've loved to be the one to do that stuff for you? Do you think I'm happy about missing doctor appointments? No. But I'm trying not to hold that against you, Mollie, because the truth is, we didn't know each other. Hell, we still don't. But I'm not going to act like I'm happy that some other guy is over here playing daddy."

"Tuck?" she asks, sniffling.

"You okay, Molls?" he asks, stepping forward, and I have to hand it to him. He doesn't cower. If he's intimidated, he doesn't show it. He's ready to protect Mollie, even if it means pissing me off. And I respect that. Reluctantly.

"I'm fine." She nods, but her eyes are still on me. "Can you give us a minute?"

"Sure," he says, swiping a room key off the dresser. "I'll go to your brothers' room. Call me if you need anything."

"Thank you. I will."

I eye him until he's out the door, and then Mollie pushes past me to sit on the bed. She's even more beautiful pregnant—her belly swollen with my kid and her lips swollen from my kiss.

"I'm sorry for snapping," I say honestly. "Can we just start from the beginning? How did this happen?"

Mollie takes a deep breath, tucking her dark brown hair behind her ear.

"As you know, we had what I like to refer to as Condomgate. But, I thought we were fine. I was on birth control," she says, corroborating my memory of how things went down, and I nod for her to continue. "Well, then my period was late. And sometimes that happens, so I didn't freak out right away. But then it never came. I made an appointment, and when my doctor told me I was pregnant, I flat-out called her a liar." She laughs, but it lacks humor, and then swipes her thumb under her eye to wipe away a tear. "I told her the situation, and she asked if I had been on any antibiotics. And that's when it hit me. I was just getting over strep throat when we met, and I was still taking antibiotics."

"And?" I ask, not sure how that fits into anything.

"And, antibiotics can interfere with birth control."

I scratch the back of my neck and take a seat on the bed opposite from her, our knees almost touching.

"I wanted to tell you. So many times. But I was scared. I didn't handle it well myself, so I couldn't expect you to react well. I looked you up online and started writing to you several times, but nothing sounded right. How do you tell someone you hooked up with for one night that they're tied to you forever? Or the next eighteen years, at the very least."

"That all makes sense, but why did you continue to hide it from me after I saw you in the lobby?"

"Sutton told me you'd be in Aspen for the X Games, and then *boom*, there you were. I panicked. I wasn't ready. I mean, how many women try to trap men? Especially professional athletes? Would you have even believed me?"

"I would have," I say, and I realize it's the truth. "We only had one night together, but I know you well enough to know that's not your style."

"I should've given you the benefit of the doubt."

"And Tucker?" I ask, not completely sure where he fits into all of this.

"We dated...sort of. It's mostly a show for his dad. He wants Tucker to be more responsible in *other* areas of his life before he gives him more responsibility at his firm. That doesn't mean that we didn't sleep together—we did. But we haven't been together in that way since before I met you. I just don't feel that way about him."

Well, I guess that's a relief, besides the part where they ever slept together. We're both silent for a minute, not knowing what else to say.

"So, what does this mean for us?" I ask the only question I have left.

"What do you mean, *us*?"

"I *mean*, are you gonna be my girl, Mollie Mabey?"

"Your girl?" She laughs. "I don't know, Cam. You live here. I live in San Fran. We don't even know each other."

"So, let's get to know each other so we can stop fucking using that excuse. Listen, I've been with a lot of women. And I mean *a lot*," I stress, but Mollie arches a brow and holds up her hand to stop me.

"I get it."

"Anyway," I say and then clear my throat. "The point is, we had chemistry right off the bat. You're the one girl I didn't want to leave the next morning. And when I saw you in the lobby, my gut reaction was to be glad that you were back. And the more time I spend with you, the more I fucking *want* you."

I put my palm on her exposed knee, rubbing in small circles.

"Give us a chance," I say, my voice thick with lust at one touch of her smooth skin. At one look at the way her dress has ridden up her thighs and the way it hugs her rounded middle.

"How?" she whispers.

"I don't know. I'll come down on weekends and court your ass. Hard."

Mollie laughs, and I decide that I want to hear more of that. No more tears.

"You'd do that?" she asks doubtfully. "Because I have to stay there. My doctor is there. My insurance is about to lapse. I have to find a real fucking job," she says, rolling her eyes, listing things off on her fingers.

"I'll probably try to convince you to come live with me in River's Edge every chance I get," I warn. "But yes, I will. And, I'll add you to my insurance."

My palm skates up her thighs, and I pause when it lands right below her belly.

"Can I touch you?" I ask, tilting my head to meet her gaze. She nods wordlessly, and her breath hitches when I make contact. It's firmer than I expected—a perfect little baby belly. It's surreal, knowing something that came from me is inside her, that my hands are touching the result of our night full of fun and fucking. I don't know what kind of man it makes me to be turned on by the thought of putting a baby inside her, but that's exactly what's happening.

"You know one good part about being pregnant?" I ask, my hand dipping between her thighs, rubbing her pussy through her clothes.

"What?" she asks, already breathless.

"I can come inside you, all I want." And fuck, I want to. Need to. All night long, as long as she'll let me.

"I don't know if that's such a good idea," she says, but her eyes are closed in ecstasy, and she rocks into my touch.

"I think it's the best idea I've ever had," I counter, "and I think you want it, too."

Mollie spreads her legs further apart, giving me better access.

"Is that a yes?" I slip my hand beneath her underwear, sliding it through her already wet lips. "Your pussy seems to think so."

Mollie

How did we get here? Twenty minutes ago, I was crying about Cam and how he treated me, and now, his hand is between my thighs as he tells me that he wants to be with me. My heart says *be careful*, my head says *impossible*, but my body...my body is screaming at me to let Cam show it magic again. Because that night with him *was* pure magic.

I know we should take it slow, but what's the point? I'm pregnant. The damage is done. If I'm going to sleep with someone, it might as well be the father of my unborn child.

Cam sees the moment I decide, and he gently lays me down on the bed. My pulse is jumping in my neck, my heartbeat erratic. Cam takes two fingers and drags them from my collarbone to my cleavage before sliding one side of my wrap dress open, exposing one of my breasts through thin, black lace. Cam lifts that, too, then swirls his thumb around the puckered tip.

My nipples are extremely sensitive lately, and I arch my back into his touch, wanting more.

"You like that?" he asks, uncovering the other one. Using both hands, he massages my nipples with just his thumbs, and I swear on my life, I'll come like this if he keeps it up.

"These are puffier than I remember," he remarks before dipping his head to take one into his mouth. "Fucking beautiful."

Cam sucks on me, and my body jerks at the sensation, feeling it straight down to my core.

"Keep doing that," I insist, holding the back of his head to my chest. His hands slide under my back and he holds me to him, feasting on me like I'm his last meal. He alternates between each breast, sucking and nipping and biting, and it isn't long before I'm threatening to implode in his arms.

"Cam, I think—"

"You think you can come like this?" he asks, reading my mind. I nod frantically, not wanting him to stop for even a second. I reach for my clit, but he slaps my hand away.

"No cheating," he says firmly before going back to work. He tweaks one nipple while he gives the other long, fat swipes of his tongue, and soon, the stimulation gets to be too much. My legs lock up, my core tightens, and my body breaks out into pinpricks as I come, long and hard, shaking, even after it's over.

"That was the sexiest fucking thing I've ever seen," Cam says, laying me flat again and then pulling my dress and panties off. My limbs are listless, my eyes heavy. I feel drugged and sated. Heavy, but somehow weightless.

Cam moves down my body, peppering open-mouthed kisses on my belly before dipping lower. He pushes my knees back and wastes no time diving between them.

"I missed this pussy," he mumbles into me. There is no slow buildup. I'm thrust right back into ecstasy. My nipples tighten as he flicks at my clit with his tongue, and then he sucks it into his mouth. I gasp, my back rising from the bed, and he pulls back abruptly.

"I need to be inside you. I can't wait anymore."

Cam pulls off his hoodie and shirt in one swift move, then he shoves his jeans down his muscular thighs. He lowers his beautiful, colorfully inked body to mine, and then his huge thick cock is nudging against me, seeking entrance.

"Open up for me, Mollie," he grunts, wedging his way inside. Cam grips my knees and pushes them to my chest as he starts to slide in and out. I watch the way the muscles in his arms flex and the way the veins strain in his neck as he controls my movements with his hands now on my hips. It's different this time. Everything is hypersensitive. I can't usually come from penetration alone, but I just orgasmed from nothing but him touching my nipples, so anything is possible.

His thrusts go from agonizingly slow to quick and powerful, and I have to drop my legs open, letting them fall on either side of him.

"I can hear how wet you are," he grits out, and his eyes follow the sound, locking on to where we're joined. He stares at my belly, and I start to feel self-conscious about it as his movements slow. But then, he smooths his big palms up my stomach, rubbing it reverently with wonder in his eyes.

"I can't hold back," he says, regret lacing his tone. "I have to come."

I can't find words, so I nod, the desperation in my eyes telling him that I'm there, too. He lowers himself onto his forearms, his ragged breaths heating my neck. He nuzzles into me, and I feel his scruff scrape against my neck, shoulder, and collarbone as he ruts into me. Our sex-slick skin slides against each other, and I cling to his muscular back, digging my nails in for leverage.

When my orgasm hits, it's more powerful than the one before it—more powerful than *any* before it. Like no one's ever been this deep inside me. Literally, and maybe even figuratively. It's almost painful how hard I come, and I seem to endlessly clench and contract around him.

"Fuck yeah, Mollie. Milk it out of me."

And then I feel him spilling into me as he shudders and jerks. He pulsates inside me, and he doesn't make a move to pull away. He's dead, sweaty weight on top of me. I'm trapped underneath two hundred pounds of tattooed flesh and muscle, but I've never felt safer in my life. Cam shifts his weight slightly, as if he could hurt the baby somehow, and I suddenly feel like crying. *Again.*

Cam pulls back to look at me. He brings his palm to the side of my head and strokes my eyebrow with his thumb. The crease between his eyes deepens, as he notices my glassy eyes, yet again, but he doesn't say a word. Because I think he knows that it isn't necessarily a sad cry. And maybe—just maybe—he's feeling something similar.

"Are we having a boy or a girl?" Cam asks, breaking the silence.

"I don't know," I admit. "My anatomy scan is next week. They check the heart, brain, spine, and other stuff, too."

"What are you hoping for?"

"Healthy," I say, lifting a shoulder. "That'd be nice." I spent the first few weeks wishing that the test was somehow wrong. Then, at my first ultrasound, I fell in love and felt my first taste of mother's guilt for ever wishing him or her away. I went from hoping it wasn't true to being scared to death that something will happen that will take this baby away from me, such as a miscarriage or a defect that's incompatible with life. Funny how that works.

Cam's quiet, probably not having considered the fact that something could go wrong, and I feel guilty for ever putting the thought into his head.

"I've been calling him or her Pinecone," I admit, hoping to distract him from the way his thoughts must be going.

"Pinecone, huh?" The corner of his lip twitches into an almost-smile.

"Yes, Pinecone. This town is full of 'em."

"Pinecone," he says again, rolling the word around on his tongue. "I can dig it. Have you thought of actual names?"

"I like unisex names," I say, but then I realize that he has a say now, too. I'm not used to having to share these kinds of decisions. "I mean, if you're okay with that. Do you have any ideas?"

"Considering the fact that I found out about two hours ago?" He chuckles. "Not a one. But I'll think on it."

He finally rolls off me, his semi-hard length sliding from my body, and I feel his absence like a missing limb. I don't like what that means. I don't want to need anyone, especially not so soon. I consider myself to be a realist. I know the odds are stacked against us. And the fact that I'm tied to him for the foreseeable future makes it an even trickier situation. I don't want to do something that will negatively affect this little pinecone's life.

"Your parents must think I'm such a fucking punk." He sighs, sliding his hands through his dark blond hair.

"Well..." I trail off, not knowing how to tell him that they think Tucker is the father.

"*What?*" Cam asks, rolling on his side to face me. I pull the sheet over me and roll toward him.

"They don't really...know you exist?" It comes out sheepish, like a question more than a statement.

"What do you mean?" His nostrils flare, probably having an inkling to where this is going.

"They think Tucker is my boyfriend, so, naturally..."

"Oh, yeah, *naturally*," Cam says, every word packed with sarcasm.

"Don't," I warn. I don't want this to turn into a Tucker-bashing session. "He doesn't want to take your place, Cam. It was his idea to come clean to our families after the holidays."

He reels in his temper, blowing out a breath.

"I just hate that I didn't know. You didn't have to do this alone, Mollie."

"I know, and I'm sorry. I'll always regret not telling you. But, since you're here, and you know now," I start, taking a fortifying breath, "what do you think of telling them tomorrow night at dinner?"

Hopeful blue eyes lock onto mine. "Are you sure?"

"Yeah," I say, and I *am* sure. "The sooner, the better, right?"

"I concur. And the sooner I bury my cock back inside you the better, too," he says, pulling me on top of him. "Show me what you got, Mama."

Chapter Seven

CAM

After sending Tucker away when he came knocking a couple of hours later, I stayed the night with Mollie. I practically slept *inside* her all night, if you want to get technical. Her family checked out of The Pines earlier, so I helped her pack before she took her things to their usual cabin. It's Christmas Eve, and we usually spend it with Dare since our parents retired and moved to Arizona to get out of the cold. I told Cordell where I'd be instead, and surprisingly, I didn't even catch shit for it. Mollie invited him along, but I want to do this alone.

Before I can knock, Mollie opens the door, pulling me inside, out of the cold.

"Merry Christmas Eve." She smiles, and she looks extra happy, considering the conversation we're about to have.

"Who spiked your eggnog?" I tease.

"I'm just *relieved*. Regardless of how everyone reacts, it's going to be such a huge weight off my chest."

"I can imagine."

Mollie leads me through the stereotypical River's Edge vacation rental. The walls are always either green or tan, and the décor is almost always bears or pinecones. This one opted for bears. And there is *always* a bearskin rug. This place is no exception. Mollie leads me through the house and to the kitchen, where everyone sits at the impressive dinner table that's packed with food.

"Everyone, this is my friend, Camden. Camden, this is my mom, Sarah, my dad, Nick, and my brothers, Craig and Andrew. You know Tucker."

Mollie's mom smiles warmly at me; her dad gives me a wary look, assessing, but he gives a polite wave. Tucker appears to be mildly peeved about my presence. I give myself a mental reminder not to fuck my chances with Mollie by beating his ass.

"Dude, you're friends with Camden *Hess*?" one of Mollie's brothers—don't ask me which one—asks, disbelief written all over his face.

"Nice to meet you, man," I say, bending over to shake his hand from where he sits.

"What does that mean?" Mollie's mom asks, a confused smile plastered to her face.

"It means Mollie's been holding out on us," the other brother says.

"He's a professional snowboarder," Mollie clarifies, rolling her eyes. "I met him when we were here over summer."

"And yet, we're just now finding out about it," one of them says. I still don't know which is which, but I'm going to go with Andrew.

"I didn't even know who he *was* then!" Mollie exclaims.

"You know what they say," he says. "Excuses are like assholes—"

"That's enough, Andrew," their mom warns. *The one with the dark hair is Andrew. Light hair is Craig. Got it.*

"All right, all right, leave the guy alone," Mollie's dad says. "Can we eat now, or are we still waiting for someone else to join us? The Prince of Wales, perhaps?"

"Let's eat," her mom says, shaking her head. "Camden, please, have a seat."

"Yes, ma'am," I say, rubbing my palms together. "This looks delicious. Thank you for having me."

"We're glad to have you," Sarah insists, and Mollie gives me a secret smile. Maybe this won't be so bad.

DINNER WAS OFFICIALLY A SUCCESS. To her family's credit, no one made any shitty, passive-aggressive remarks about my tattoos or asked me thirty-seven questions about each one. After we were all stuffed to the brim, I helped Mollie and her brothers clear the table before they all sat back down to play games. When Mollie said they wanted to play games, I pictured fucking Monopoly. Nope. Craig busted out Cards Against Humanity.

After we sat through an awkward five minutes of Andrew trying to explain *bukkake* to his confused, slightly horrified mother, Mollie squeezed my knee and motioned for me to follow her. And that's how we ended up heavy petting in the downstairs bathroom.

"I can't help it," Mollie says, playfully nipping at my lip. "I'm always horny now." She lifts her dark green dress, revealing her smooth pussy, and grabs my wrist, pulling it toward her.

"No underwear?"

"It gets in the way," she says, and then she drops her head against my shoulder as I push two fingers inside her.

"Lift your leg," I instruct. "Let me see that pretty pussy."

She complies with a moan, leaning her palms against the sink behind her before bringing her right heel to rest on the edge. This position puts everything on display for me, from her tight cunt that's swallowing my fingers, to her rounded belly, to her perfect, swollen tits.

Unable to resist, even though I know her entire family is out there, I drop to my knees and bury my face between her legs. I tug her clit between my teeth as I continue finger fucking her. Another moan, this one a little too loud, and I know I need to make this quick. I pull my fingers from her, ignoring her whine of protest, and smear her wetness to the tight ring of her ass.

"I'm going to fuck this ass one day," I tell her quietly. "But for now, I'm going to use my fingers. I remember how much you liked it."

"Yes," she breathes, and then my mouth is on her again. I slide my middle finger inside her asshole, and she jerks against my face. Anchoring her thigh to the sink with my free hand, I suck her clit into my mouth, batting at it with my tongue. I work my finger in and out of her as her breathing becomes erratic, and then her foot slips off the ledge and her thighs squeeze me, keeping me in place as she comes apart.

"Jesus, fuck," I say as her thighs continue to shake. "You're beautiful."

Mollie pulls me up and kisses my face that smells of her. I pull her dress back down as she wraps her arms around my neck. I lift her by her hips and plop her back onto the counter. Her legs lock around my waist, and I'm about to say *fuck the consequences* and take my dick out when the door opens and Mollie's mom walks in.

Fuck.

"Mollie!" she gasps, and I whip around to face her, making sure to shield Mollie's body in case anything is still hanging out.

"What, did you find another spid—dear God! My eyes!" Andrew yells, attracting the attention of everyone in a ten-mile radius.

"Mom! Get out!" Mollie snaps.

"You have two minutes to get your lie together and get out here." She slams the door, and Mollie jumps off the counter.

"Oh my God, oh my God, oh my God," Mollie rambles, her bare feet pacing the tiles of the bathroom floor.

"Relax," I tell her. "We need to look at the positives here."

"*Positives?!*" she shrieks. "There aren't any positives in this situation."

"Well, I wasn't eating your pussy like dessert, for one thing. She could've come a couple of minutes earlier and got an eyeful. Plus, we were planning to tell them, anyway. That's one way to do it."

"Oh my God," she says again. "This is real. This is happening."

"It is, so buckle up, Buttercup, and let's go tell them the truth."

Mollie takes a fortifying breath and opens the door to face the music.

Chapter Eight

Mollie

Six sets of eyes are on me, each with varying degrees of horror plastered to them.

"What were you *thinking*, Mollie?" my mom asks, throwing her hands up.

"I'm sorry. We shouldn't have done that," I say.

"Ya think?" my dad says, as if I just informed him that murder is bad.

"Why aren't you upset about this?" Craig says to Tucker, who looks like he wants to melt into the wall and disappear.

"I, uh..." Tucker trails off, not knowing what to say. "Molls?"

I don't know how to do this, so I decide ripping the Band-Aid off is the best way to go about it.

"I'm not with Tucker," I admit, and no one looks surprised except for my parents.

"We never really were," Tuck chimes in. "I'm sorry. I love you guys like family, and we didn't mean to lie to you. This whole thing just kind of got out of control. My dad thought we were together, and he started giving me clients at work, talked about making me a partner at Hastings. And then it just kept getting harder to come clean."

"That doesn't make any sense, Tucker. Why lie to us?"

"I didn't want you to slip up around my parents."

"This is bullshit. I'm going to bed. Merry Christmas, you're all crazy," my dad says, before heading upstairs.

"Wait, Dad," I say, before the courage leaves me completely. "There's one more thing."

"Jesus Christ, Mollie. Are you trying to kill your old man?"

"Tucker isn't the father. Cam is."

My dad throws his hands up as if to say *of course, he is,* and then he's upstairs, hiding from the crazy.

"You guys just assumed—" I start, but my mom cuts me off.

"Because we thought he was your *boyfriend*!"

"I know, I know. I don't know what to say, besides I'm sorry."

We go around and around again, until all of us are yawning and seeing through half-closed eyelids. Mom grills Cam, but Andrew and Craig are pretty much just hyped that they're essentially going to be related to him now. Tucker is the first to bow out. He offers to leave, but my mom insists he stay here. He's still family.

I can tell she isn't comfortable with Cam being here, but honestly, I'm not comfortable being without him right now. I only have a few more days in River's Edge, and I want to get to know him as much as I can. To soak him in and drown in him. So I decide to stay with Cam, leaving her with a promise to come home first thing in the morning, being Christmas and all.

Once we're back at his house, I'm too tired to function, which is unfortunate for the case of blue balls he's been nursing since the bathroom incident. Cam curls up behind me in his bed, wrapping an arm around me. We talk about everything. He explains his injury to me and how he ended up teaching at the ski school. How he went off the rails for a bit. I tell him my fears about being a parent, and he tells me we simply need a plan. That he isn't going anywhere, no matter what.

His hand ghosts across my bare belly in a rhythmic, soothing manner. Just as we're drifting to sleep, I feel it. It starts with the familiar flutters, but then it turns into more of a roll and then a sharp jab.

"Holy shit, was that—"

"The baby kicked," I say, exhausted but excited, and then I press his hand against the right spot.

"I like you, Mollie, but I already love this baby," he says, his voice thick with sleep.

"Me, too."

Epilogue

MOLLIE

Aspen, one year and one month later...

"Dada!" eight-month-old River babbles from my Ergobaby carrier. Cam picked her name, and when he suggested it, I instantly fell in love.

"Yes, I know, baby girl," I say, bouncing in place, trying to keep her happy. "I want Dada, too."

I'm a nervous wreck. I've seen Cam compete before, but this is his comeback. His chance to win back his King of the Mountain status and snag another medal. He's going to attempt some trick—that I won't even try to remember the name of—that's never been landed in an event before.

"Craig" I shout over the mass of spectators and family members watching next to us. "FaceTime Emersyn. She'll kill me if I forget."

He nods, taking my phone and letting her watch via video chat. Cam is still Emersyn's coach, and someday soon, she's going to be better than him. He knows it, and I know it.

Once I left River's Edge, I realized I didn't really have a good enough reason to stay in San Francisco. Cam kept his word, attending every doctor appointment and coming down almost every weekend, all the while I made plans to relocate to River's Edge. I illustrate children's books now, and I can pretty much work anywhere, plus I get to put my art degree to work—just not in the way I thought.

By the time I was nine months pregnant, we were living together. My parents still think we're batshit, and maybe we are. But that's what happens when you're in love. Love doesn't wait until you have your shit together. It just happens, and you have to decide how badly you want it. I'm majorly, totally, butt-crazy in love with Cam and River, and I wouldn't change one moment of this crazy road we took to get to this moment here and now.

I hear Cam's name over the speaker, but the blood is rushing through my ears, making it impossible to hear what they're saying. Before I can ask one of my brothers, I see Cam. I see him flying down the mountain, and when he hits that jump and is launched into the air, I fight the urge to cover my eyes with my hands.

I count his flips, the moment seemingly in slow-motion, though it's actually probably only about four seconds.

One...two...three...four...five.

"And he lands it, ladies and gentlemen! Camden Hess is breaking records here in Aspen again, and I think it's safe to say, the King is back."

Cam slides down the hill, cutting through the snow, coming to a stop directly in front of us. He rips his helmet and goggles off and kisses River before smashing his lips to mine.

"You did it, baby!" I squeal, so unbelievably happy for him. I know he's missed it. Being Emersyn's coach and dragging River on a mini snowboard around the living room floor just isn't the same.

"Hey, Mollie Mabey!" he shouts over the chaos. "What are you doing for the rest of your life?" He holds out his hand, and Andrew reaches over to drop a little box into Cam's palm before he goes down on one knee.

"Oh my God," I gasp, completely taken aback. Cam pulls my hand away from my shocked expression and slides the ring on.

"You know, when a snowboarder or skier goes down hard, and their gear goes flying everywhere, and they're completely laid out? We have a name for that. It's called a Yard Sale, and baby, you're my fucking yard sale. Dare and Cordell called it from the start. You knocked me on my ass, and I was never the same again. And I never want to be, because this life with you and River is more than I will ever deserve. Will you marry me?"

"Yes!" I scream, and River mimics the sound, throwing a little mitten-covered fist up. "I love you," I mouth, as the crowd bursts into applause. My eyes fill with tears—I'm starting to think I'll be an emotional sap for the rest of my life at this point—and Cam leans over the barrier, giving me a kiss far too indecent for public. But I let him, because he's my yard sale, too.

"I love you, Mollie Mabey," he says against my mouth.

"I am majorly, totally, *butt-crazy in love* with you, Camden Hess."

The End

Other books from Charleigh Rose

Check out *Bad Habit*, my forbidden, brother's best friend romance for FREE with Kindle Unlimited!

BRIAR

I was infatuated with Asher Kelley the moment he came tumbling through my brother's window five years ago.

Even bruised and bloodied, he was the most beautiful boy I'd ever seen.

We couldn't ever be together.

I was too young, and he was too untouchable.

He was too troubled, and I was too naive.

But the heart is rebellious, and mine decided it didn't care about any of those things.

As I got older, harmless flirting turned to stolen moments in dark corners.

Until one day, he was gone without a trace.

Now, three years later, he's back.

Callous and cruel.

He's my brother's best friend. My parents' worst nightmare.

I should hate him.

But like a Bad Habit, I can't quit him.

ASHER

I was drawn to Briar Vale from the first time she looked up at me with stars in her big, blue eyes.

She was just a kid, nothing but elbows and knees, but she was the most beautiful creature I'd ever seen.

We could never be together.

I was too old and she was too off limits.

She was too good and I was too fucked up.

Eventually, the temptation became too much to resist.

I risked everything for a kiss and she betrayed me.

Three years have passed and I'm forced to see her again, but now she's all grown up.

She's my best friend's baby sister. My downfall.

I hate her for what she did.

But she's always been my drug of choice.

***Misbehaved*, an edgy, student/teacher romance is also FREE with Kindle Unlimited!**

Remington Stringer has never been like most girls. She's outspoken, brazen and wants nothing more than to escape the Nevadan hell hole that she calls home.

On the brink of eighteen, with a deceased mother and a well-meaning, yet absent father, she is forced to fend for herself. The only person she's ever had to depend on is her borderline obsessive stepbrother, Ryan. But, what used to be her anchor is quickly becoming a loose cannon.

When Remi gets the opportunity to attend the best private school in the state during her senior year of high school, she jumps at the chance. Then she meets Mr. James. Ornery, aloof, and totally irresistible.

Most girls would swoon in secrecy.

Most girls would doodle his name with hearts in their notebook.

But Remi Stringer has never been like most girls.

SLAPPED INTO LOVE

This hot hockey player is skilled on and off the ice...

Ryan Forrester hasn't been able to get a particular blonde off his mind. She disappeared on him after a one-night stand, and didn't turn up again until a team practice a couple months later.

But this sexy speedskater is going to make him even better...

Tamara Antonov was hired to help Ryan's team get faster on the ice, but she knows first-hand the kind of moves he has off it. She didn't expect to see him again. Now that she has, things are about to get hot enough to melt the rink.

Slapped Into Love can be read as a standalone. Each book in the *Bachelorette Party* series features a different couple.

Chapter One

Ryan

PRACTICING OUR SLAP SHOTS WAS MY FAVORITE PART OF PRACTICE. IT wasn't just because it was fun to show off a bit since I had the best slap shot on the team. This drill was one of the last ones, which meant we were almost done. Jason Campbell, my defensive line mate, set up on the top of the circle opposite from where I was. Our friend, and my neighbor at the apartment complex where I lived, Alec Rourke, setup at center ice on the blue line while his line mate moved past me to the bottom of the circle. Alec didn't wait long before he fired a pass to Jason, who cycled it to me for a one timer that sailed straight into the net.

Snagging a puck, Jason passed it to Alec. When his shot went high and slammed into the boards, I flashed him a cocky grin. "Shut it, Forrester. We all know you're the king of the slap shot," he growled.

"Only because he keeps calling himself that," Jason laughed, sending the puck Alec's line mate had passed to him my way.

Raising my stick, I pivoted my hips and put some extra force into my already powerful shot. My aim didn't suffer for it, and the puck crashed into the back of the net. "What can I say?" I shrugged my shoulders. "When you've got it, flaunt it. Right?"

"I thought flaunting it was puck bunny territory?" Jason asked.

"Ask Ryan, he'd know," Alec replied.

Their gazes turned my way. "Like I'm the puck bunny expert? Alec would know just as well as me," I snapped. "Better even, since I've been staying away from them."

"Oh, yeah? Since when?" Alec snorted.

Coach sent a glare our way, and we started cycling the puck for slap shots again. It didn't stop Jason from sticking his nose in my business, though. "Now that you mention it, I guess you have been flying solo lately. I hadn't noticed it before because I've had my own stuff going on with Cee-Cee. What's up with that? Did I miss something?"

"Just a mystery woman who ruined puck bunnies for me forever," I mumbled, wincing at the memory of how shitty I'd felt when I woke up alone after the last time I'd hooked up with someone. Just the memory of her gave me a semi, while being near any other woman since then had my dick shriveling and my balls trying to creep back up into my body. Not that I was going to share shit like that with the guys. Some things were better left unspoken.

The blowing of a well-timed whistle dragged their attention away from me and the story I wanted to keep to myself. "Bring it in, guys!" Coach hollered.

We skated to center ice and took a knee in front of him. As I dropped down, my muscles protested. Hockey seasons were long, and at that moment I swore I felt every minute we'd spent on the ice.

"I've got good news and better news for you guys. Which do you want first?" our coach asked, his lips tilting up in a smirk.

I didn't trust that look.

Or his tone of voice.

And definitely not the gleam in his eye.

He was happy about something, and Coach was never happy. Not during season, anyway. Win or lose, he was always serious. I had a feeling that we weren't going to agree with his classification of the news he had. Some of it was going to be bad—at least from our point of view.

"Good!" about half the team yelled out.

"Better!" the other half hollered.

"Neither," I mumbled under my breath, earning me an elbow in the ribs from Jason.

Coach rubbed his hands together in excitement, and I jerked my head in his direction as I turned to glare at my line mate. "Just wait for it," I hissed at him.

"I guess I'll start with the good news since it makes more sense to do it that way anyway," Coach chuckled. "The data guys in the office were doing some number crunching, and our playoff chances are looking better and better each week. They said we have a ninety-eight percent chance of securing our spot. As long as you guys keep playing the way you have been lately—which you damn well better do—we can clinch it by the end of this weekend."

Jason nudged me. "See, it's good news. Stop being such a suspicious bastard."

"And there's something better than that?" our team captain asked. We all wanted the championship cup badly, but none more than him. It was his last season before retirement, and for him nothing would beat going out on top.

"The better news is that I've secured a power skating coach who'll make the most of the month we have until the start of the playoffs to improve your speed on the ice. Starting today."

Tired groans echoed around the rink. We'd just finished a grueling practice, and I was beyond ready to hit the locker room and take a shower. "Told you so," I muttered.

Jason shrugged. "Don't be a dick. It's not like this is the end of the world. We'll do some extra skating drills; so what?"

Coach held up his hand, putting a stop to all of our grumbling and side conversations. "I don't want to hear it, guys. Every single team in this league is looking for little things to make themselves better, and I've found us someone who can give us that. At the level of game play we'll be facing in the playoffs, even a one percent improvement on your speed can make the difference between winning and losing. So suck it up and do what needs to be done to help us get to the championship."

"You heard Coach," our captain called out. "I used to do power skating camps back in my youth hockey league, and they helped make me the player I am today."

Several guys nodded in agreement, including Jason. "He's right, man."

"Yeah," I sighed, as I tried to shake off my exhaustion and get ready to skate hard. "I know."

At our coach's signal, I shuffled to my feet along with everyone else. "Do a few laps," he ordered. "She should be here soon."

"She?" The question echoed around the rink, voiced by several of the guys including me.

"Yes, *she*," Coach responded, stressing the second word. "And I don't want any bullshit about it because we're damn lucky to have gotten her to fit these sessions with us into her training schedule."

"Training schedule? What is she, a figure skater? I bet I could out-skate any figure skater any day of the week," one of the rookies snorted.

"You heard Coach; shut it!" our captain chastised. "Besides which, you're being a dipshit since some of the best power skating coaches are figure skaters."

"They are," Coach agreed. "And there's nothing wrong with that because there's a lot that a figure skater could teach you guys about using the edges on your blades. But Miss Antonov isn't a figure skater. She's a speed skater. The best one in the country. Hell, make that the world since she's got the Olympic gold medals to prove it. She's coming straight here from a big win at the World Single Distance Championships this weekend." He turned his attention to the rookie who'd mouthed off. "And you can mouth off all you want, but she'd beat you in a race without even breaking a sweat."

The rookie nodded jerkily and skated off to lap around the rink.

"Coach sure told him," I laughed. "Can you imagine how embarrassing it'd be to get beat by a girl on the ice? We're professional hockey players, for fuck's sake."

Jason's gaze darted over my shoulder, and his eyes widened in surprise. I started to turn my head to look behind me, but it was a good thing that I didn't do it quickly or else the smack I took across the back of my helmet would have landed on my jaw. Even though my visor only protected my eyes and nose, the hit wasn't hard enough to hurt. But it would have been a blow to my ego to take a slap to the face in front of the whole team. Especially from the stunning blonde with dark brown eyes that'd delivered it. The one who'd rocked my world after an away game in Anaheim and then disappeared before the sun came up the next morning. The sight of her accomplished something no other woman had been able to do for months—she made my cock hard as steel.

It was uncomfortable as fuck to stand there with my dick pressing against the confines of my cup, but it was worth it to know that I was able to get it up again. And it was all thanks to the beauty who was glaring at me like she'd like nothing more than to shove her skate up my ass.

Fuck me and my big mouth. Or not fuck, considering I'd probably screwed my chances to ever have her in my bed again.

Chapter Two

Tamara

"Sorry," I mumbled, glaring at the last guy on Earth I'd expected to see again. I didn't bother to try to sound like I really meant it. Because I didn't. Not really. I might have felt slightly bad about hitting him except that I was sure he barely felt it through his helmet. And he'd earned it with the sexist comment he'd made, even if he hadn't known that I was going to overhear what he'd said. At least I could take comfort in the knowledge that I'd been right to bail on him after our one-night stand, even though I'd been second-guessing myself ever since because it'd been so fucking good between us.

If I hadn't been so tired, I probably would have been able to resist the urge to hit him. But after a long trip to Norway for the ISU Speed Skating World Cup and an expected sixteen hours of travel time to get home that somehow turned into thirty-one because of delayed flights at both of my layovers in Copenhagen and Heathrow, I wasn't in the mood to take crap from anybody. Not even if it was a guy who knew my body intimately and was sexy enough to look hot when he was dressed in full hockey gear and wearing a helmet with a partial visor.

Skating away from him, I joined their coach at center ice. He nodded at me, seemingly unconcerned that I'd just hit one of his players on the back of his helmet. Then again, this was hockey so I was sure he'd seen worse during a practice before.

The guys who were doing laps around the ice skated over to us. "Since there seems to be some skepticism about my ability to teach you guys anything about skating, how about we settle this on the ice?" I let my gaze skim over the team before it landed on Ryan. "You up for the challenge?"

The confident grin he flashed me was incredibly annoying, but it also sent goosebumps up my arms that had nothing to do with the temperature of the rink. "Sure. I'm up for whatever you want to throw my way."

The guy he'd been mouthing off to when I'd skated onto the ice whacked him in the shin with his stick, and I offered him a grateful smile before turning my attention back to the mouthy, sexy player who deserved to be taken down a peg. I was just the woman to do it too.

Skating closer to the boards, I stopped at the nearest blue line and pointed at the spot next to me. "C'mon, then. One lap around the rink's perimeter. First one of us to cross the blue line wins."

He didn't hesitate to take me up on the challenge, handing his stick, gloves, and helmet off to the teammate standing closest to him. His dark hair was sweaty and sticking up in places, but it didn't take away from his good looks. Not with the way his hazel eyes gleamed and the cocky tilt to his full lips surrounded by a closely trimmed mustache and beard. My heart started to beat faster, and it had nothing to do with the race we were about to begin. No, it was due to my reaction to him—a completely unwanted one since all indications pointed towards him being totally wrong for me no matter how good he was in bed. I dealt with enough cocky bastards professionally. I didn't need to add one to my personal life.

"Ready?" he asked when he situated himself next to me.

"You'd better believe it," I quipped, dragging my gaze away from his and focusing on the team's coach. "Can you do the countdown for us and judge who wins? Not that there'll be much doubt since I plan to beat him by a big enough margin that it'll be obvious to everyone which one of us is faster—and better equipped to run power skating drills for the team."

"I sure can," the coach chuckled.

"Too bad I don't have my phone with me. I could take a photo to commemorate the day a woman made Ryan eat his words after he made an ass out of himself," one of the players added, winking at me.

Based on the low growl in his throat and the glare he gave the guy; Ryan didn't appreciate what his teammate had to say as much as I had. Then he bent his legs, positioning his skates so he could push off quickly, and nodded at his coach to let him know he was ready.

Crouching low, I nodded as well and then aimed all of my focus forward. I shut off all thoughts except for the skate ahead of me, tensing as I heard the coach call out, "Three."

I took a deep breath. "Two."

And another. "One."

I burst forward on a sharp exhale as soon as he yelled, "Go!"

Legs pumping as hard as I could go, arms swinging in unison, I powered ahead. Ryan was in my peripheral vision past the red line at center ice, crossing over the other blue line, and circling around it again. If it'd been a short sprint, he might have been able to beat me. But he started to edge back the tiniest bit as we crossed the center line again. And as we round the curve behind the net, I pushed myself even harder to reach the place where we'd started so I'd get there well ahead of him. I dug deep on the last few strides, and it was worth it because I crossed the blue line a couple of seconds ahead of Ryan.

"Miss Antonov wins!" the coach yelled. "And that's why I hired her, boys. There's a lot that you can learn from her, so head to the center of the ice and get ready to skate your asses off."

"It's Tamara, please," I panted. "Miss Antonov makes me want to look over my shoulder for my mom."

"Shit, you're fast," Ryan huffed.

"And I've got the gold medals to show for it." I winked at him before turning to face the rest of the team. "Now that I've given all of you a demonstration of how fast I can skate, how about you do the same for me? Line up at the blue line"—I jerked a thumb over my shoulder—"show me what you've got."

When he didn't move, I turned to Ryan and lifted an eyebrow. "You'd better get moving before your teammates leave you in their snow."

"But I already showed you how fast I am on my skates."

"Fast?" the teammate who had Ryan's equipment laughed. He kicked the gloves towards us before skating over and handing the stick and helmet to Ryan. "Did you miss the part where she kicked your ass?"

I beamed a smile his way, nodding. "Exactly."

"She beat me, but not by that much," Ryan grumbled, earning him a glare from me that had him backpedaling. "I'm not saying you didn't win. You did. I'm just saying that—"

I held up my hand, and his friend jabbed him in the side with an elbow. "Dude, shut up. You're just making it worse."

"Exactly," I agreed. "Mouthing off earned you the race against me. You can consider it a warm-up since I'm not going to reward you for your bad behavior by letting you skip out on the team skate."

His teammate laughed and skated towards the blue line. Ryan shook his head, but he turned to follow after his friend without any further complaint. When he stopped to toss his helmet, gloves, and stick onto the bench, I decided to cut him a little bit of slack. "But I have another reason for wanting you to skate with the rest of your team. It'll allow me to focus on their stride while also being able to judge how fast they are, based on how they measure up to you."

He flashed me a smug grin over his shoulder. "A few of the forwards might be faster than me on the ice, but I can assure you that none of them measure up to me off it—something you're damn well aware of already."

"Alrighty then," I grumbled to myself as my cheeks heated. Shaking it off, I skated to the other side of the ice and positioned myself behind the net. "Ready?" After getting a bunch of nods, I pulled a whistle out of my pocket and hung it around my neck. Lifting it to my lips, I blew and the guys sprung forward in a race to where I stood. I repeated the process several times, until I felt like I had a decent handle on who the fastest skaters on the team were. And damn if Ryan wasn't right—four of the forwards beat him consistently, but he was the fastest of the defensive players for all but one of the races.

"Good job, guys," I offered as I moved from behind the net to stand in front of them. I raised my voice to make sure it carried to everyone, and took the time to scan the line and make eye contact with each and every player. "You're pro hockey players, and you wouldn't have made it here if you couldn't skate. You know it." I paused to glance at Ryan, and he offered me an apologetic smile. "Your coach knows it, and I know it. Nobody is saying that you're bad skaters, but I can make you faster."

"How can you do that?" one of the centers asked.

"That's a great question. I'm glad you asked," I complimented him. "As a speed skater, I know things that can help you to be more efficient on the ice because that's what I've been trained to do since I first stepped on the ice when I was two years old. The more efficient you are, the easier it is to go faster and the less tired you'll be."

Ryan stunned me by chiming in with a supportive comment. "We're also less likely to get hurt if we aren't tired, and that's more important than ever since we can't afford to lose anyone right before the playoffs."

It sounded like I'd convinced the cocky defenseman that a girl had something to teach pro hockey players, but it remained to be seen if he could prove to me that he wasn't the ass he seemed to be with his earlier comments. For some reason—one that I refused to admit had anything to do with how sexy he was and the way he'd made by body feel during our one night together months ago—I found myself hoping he'd manage to do it.

Chapter Three

Ryan

BY THE TIME TAMARA FINISHED RUNNING US THROUGH DRILLS, I WAS dripping with sweat and beyond exhausted. She'd worked us hard in a short amount of time, focusing on getting us to skate with more knee bend and developing more power by pushing to the side.

"The things I'm working on with you may seem like small changes, but I get that they're also difficult adjustments to make since you've been skating one way for your entire lives and now I'm trying to make you do it differently. With how comfortable you all are on the ice, I know it's almost like telling you to walk differently."

"It really is," Alec agreed, earning him a smile from her that had me glaring at him. If it'd been Jason, I wouldn't have cared as much since he was happy with Cee-Cee. But Alec was as single as I was and if anyone as going to be in Tamara's good graces, I wanted it to be me.

"With you running the drills, I'm sure we'll figure it out," I assured her.

"Uh huh," she hummed, giving me a doubtful look before smiling at the rest of the team. "That's all for now, guys. As long as your coach doesn't need you for anything else, you're free to go and I'll see you again tomorrow."

Coach gestured at the door leading to the locker rooms, and my teammates took that as their cue that practice was done. While they headed to the bench to grab their equipment, I skated towards Tamara. Coach shook his head as he passed me and mumbled, "Good luck with that. You dug yourself a deep hole there, Forrester."

He was right, but in my defense we mouthed off to each other on the ice all the time. We didn't mean anything bad with the jabs we took at each other; not really. And I'd intended for mine to be aimed at my rookie teammate. Not Tamara. I just needed to make her understand that.

"Look, Tamara—"

"Do you call your coach by his first name?" she asked, cutting me off.

"Sometimes."

"Just because you've seen me naked doesn't mean it's okay..." She paused and looked at me with confusion clear in her wide brown eyes. "Wait. You do?"

"Yeah." I glided a couple of inches closer to her. "I'm not calling you Tamara as a sign of disrespect."

"Are you sure about that?" she asked with a hint of challenge in her tone.

Coach had definitely been right to offer me luck. I was starting to wonder if the hole I'd managed to dig for myself was too deep for me to get my way back out of it. It figured my fucking mouth would screw over my chances with the woman who'd killed my ability to get a boner for anyone else.

I was willing to admit that I'd been an idiot who hadn't bothered to look much beyond a woman's appearance when it came to who I slept with. I hadn't been interested in anything more than a night or two of fun, and they never bothered to get to know me beyond the fact that I was a pro hockey player, so it seemed like a fair trade. But after seeing for myself how having Cee-Cee in his life had made Jason both a happier man and a better hockey player and the way I couldn't get Tamara out of my head, I'd started to rethink my view on relationships. Only it hadn't done me much good when I'd had no idea how to find Tamara since I hadn't even known her last name.

If only I'd pulled my head out of my ass back in Anaheim and treated her like more than a one-night stand. She was worth way more than a night or two of my time, and that was before I knew she was an accomplished athlete in her own right. A hot as hell one who was as comfortable on the ice as I was. And she wasn't willing to take shit from anyone, including me. For a guy who was used to women agreeing with just about anything and everything I said, no matter how ridiculous, it was a nice change of pace. Except for the part where she was pissed at me and didn't care that I knew it.

"Yes, I'm positive." Her stance relaxed a little. "It fits you perfectly. A beautiful name for a gorgeous woman."

"Really? Do you really think I'm going to fall for your lines again?" she sputtered, shaking her head. "I'm your power skating coach; not some woman you're trying to pick up in a club. Again."

"Shit," I muttered to myself as she skated away. She was already through the door leading to the visitor's locker room before I started to follow. I cursed myself for being too slow. And for managing to fuck up with her yet again.

Chasing her into the locker room she was using would be an even dumber move, so I grabbed my stuff off the bench and headed into mine instead. After I set my stick against the wall, I shoved my helmet and gloves onto the top shelf, snagged a cold bottle of water off the table in the middle of room, and dropped down onto the bench. I stared down at my skates for a moment before I bent over to unlace them.

"How'd it go?" Jason asked quietly from his spot next to me. Not that it did any good because the guys were worse than a bunch of bored high school students when it came to gossip.

"How did what go?" Alec asked from my other side, his gaze shifting between Jason and me as he undid his shin guards. "Wait. Are you really going to try to go there with her even after the shit she heard you say?"

"Are we even allowed to go there? I mean, technically she's one of our coaches. There's got to be a rule against it, right? Not that she isn't worth breaking a few rules. She's hot as fuck," one of the forwards chimed in from the other side of the locker room.

"Shut the fuck up about her," I growled.

"Shit. She's not another one of those chicks that you guys don't even want us to look at, is she? Like Alec was with that PT who ended up getting engaged to his brother?" our starting goalie asked.

"Or her best friend, the hot redhead Campbell's dating?" the backup goalie added.

"Wait. We can call dibs on chicks?" one of the rookies asked.

"The only thing you can call dibs on is your jock strap, at least until after you've paid your dues just like the rest of us had to do," Alec answered before he turned his attention back to me again. "But the question remains, are you claiming her?"

Considering how pissed I'd been when Tamara had given him even a hint of her approval, the answer was obvious. "Yeah, I am."

"Dude, you don't have a chance in hell with her," he chuckled. "But at least you don't have to worry about one of us stealing her away from you. We'll be too busy watching you go down in flames to hit on her ourselves."

"Fuck off," I muttered as I stripped out of the rest of my gear and headed for the showers. I cleaned up and got dressed in less time than usual for me since the guys kept on giving me a hard time about Tamara. Nothing they said crossed the line since it was all aimed at making fun of me and how she wasn't going to look at me as anything more than another skater on the ice while she ran us through drills. Little did they know I'd been inside her and planned to remind her how good it'd been between us before.

As I was putting on my jacket, Jason came up next to me and grabbed my shoulder. "Don't let them get in your head."

"What if they're right?"

He squeezed his hand tight before dropping it. "It's not like you to be uncertain around women. You're usually so confident, you're basically cocky."

"Yeah, well, being cocky is only going to do more harm than good when it comes to Tamara," I sighed.

"Stop feeling sorry for yourself. Now's not the time for it. Not if you want to get the girl. Learn from me and all the months I missed with Cee-Cee, man. Go after her. Now," Jason urged.

I hadn't missed as much time with Tamara as Jason had with Cee-Cee, but it'd been enough for me to know good advice when I heard it. "Fuck," I groaned. "You're right."

I raced out of the locker room and pounded on the door down the hall. When she didn't answer, I pushed the door open and groaned when I saw that the lights were all off. Turning swiftly, I raced down the corridor to the exit that led to the secured parking lot for the players in back of the arena. I was just in time to see an unfamiliar car drive past with Tamara behind the wheel. "That woman is too damn good at disappearing acts. It looks like I'm going to need to get faster off the ice as well as on it if I want to catch up to her."

Chapter Four

Tamara

When I spotted Ryan as he shoved open the rink door, I was doubly glad that I'd been able to get out of there as quickly as I had. Coach had slowed me down a little bit to give me directions and keys to the apartment the team had lined up for me. Between having a place to stay and a rental car to get around without having to depend on public transportation or an Uber, it was almost like being home. Except for the hot-as-heck hockey player, who'd been haunting my dreams for months, staring at the back of my car as I'd pulled out of the lot.

After the way I'd shot him down on the ice, I hadn't expected him to try anything again. I was familiar with guys like that—athletes who thought they were God's gift to every woman they met. They weren't used to women saying no, especially one who'd foolishly said yes before, so it sometimes came as a shock. But their interest quickly waned since there always seemed to be a never-ending supply of other women to take your place if you weren't interested. I'd spent most of my life in rinks surrounded by them; which was probably why my mother continually complained to me about my lack of a dating life. The guys I met weren't boyfriend material so I usually wasn't interested enough to give them a chance...except for that one time with Ryan. But then I'd freaked out when I woke up because one-night stands weren't my style, and I wasn't sure how to act around him after the night we'd spent together. And that was before I'd known he was a professional hockey player.

My brain knew that Ryan was no different than other guys who played off the ice just as hard as on it, but damn if my body would listen. When my gaze locked with his in my rearview mirror, my stomach clenched in a way that reminded me of how I felt before a race. I was filled with those excited nerves at the anticipation of what was about to happen; which was ridiculous in this situation since nothing beyond what'd already happened was going to develop between Ryan Forrester and me except for a professional relationship on the ice.

It wasn't like I was even going to see him outside of the power skating sessions I ran at the rink. Something that was probably for the best because it meant I had a good eighteen hours before I had to face him again—plenty of time to get over my reaction to seeing him again. Or at least that was the pep talk I gave myself as I stopped at the nearest grocery store and grabbed enough stuff to tide me over for a couple of days until I had the energy to do a full shop.

By the time I made it to the apartment complex, I was almost ready to drop from exhaustion. Jet lagged wasn't strong enough to describe how I felt. Between the time difference, arriving a day late and having to head straight to the rink, running the power skating session with the guys, and the shock of seeing Ryan again; my body was running on empty. I needed a hot meal followed by about a dozen hours of sleep, but I was going to have to settle for a huge sandwich and a solid eight in bed.

"Maybe I'll have time to stop somewhere for breakfast on the way to the arena in the morning," I mumbled to myself as I hefted the two grocery bags, my suitcase, and carry-on out of the trunk of the rental car. I tried to knock it back down with the arm holding the groceries, but the damn thing wouldn't cooperate. "Shit."

I bent down to set them on the ground, and when I popped back up a male hand was shutting the trunk for me. I wasn't ashamed to admit that I was startled enough to yelp before I dug in my purse for the mace my mom insisted I carry whenever I was traveling. It was gripped in my hand, still in my purse, when I recognized the voice of the man telling me to calm down. My head jerked up and met familiar hazel eyes.

Ryan held his hands up in a non-threatening gesture. "Fuck, I'm sorry for scaring you. I was getting ready to head over to the building"—he dropped his hands and jerked his chin in the direction of a silver Porsche SUV parked a few spots down from my rental—"and saw you struggling, so I figured I'd come over and help."

"What're you doing here?" I asked him suspiciously. "Did you ask your coach how to find me? Because if so, you shouldn't have bothered. We don't have anything we need to talk about off the ice, and I'll see you at the arena tomorrow."

"I'm guessing Coach didn't tell you?" he chuckled, the raspy sound sending shivers through me even though it couldn't mean good things for me.

"Tell me what?"

"A bunch of the guys live here."

"Including you?"

"Yup." His lips tilted up in a small grin.

I wanted to bang my head against the car for jumping to the wrong conclusion, and then sharing it with him. "Sorry about that. I shouldn't have assumed that you followed me here." It went without saying that a guy like him didn't need to chase down a woman, especially ones he'd already slept with before.

"No worries. It's not like I can be angry with you after how I managed to keep shoving my foot in my mouth in front of you earlier today. Right?" His hazel eyes twinkled with humor as his grin turned into a full-fledged smile. "And I'd be lying if I said I'm not thrilled as fuck that you're going to be my neighbor since it'll make it harder for you to stick to that whole spiel about how we'll only see each other on the ice."

My cheeks filled with heat, and I shifted my carry-on strap on my shoulder because I wasn't sure how to respond. Things were a lot more complicated now that I knew he wasn't just a player I'd see on the ice during power skating sessions. He was an insanely hot guy I was still attracted to who I was bound to bump into off of it as well. One who was apparently going to use every opportunity he got—both on and off the ice—to flirt with me.

"Here, let me help you with that," he offered, grabbing the handle of my rolling suitcase and lifting the grocery bags off the ground.

"Thank you." I had years of my mom jamming manners into my head to blame for instinctively offering him my gratitude when a big part of me wanted to yank my stuff out of his grasp and run for my apartment. Wherever it was. Jackass Ryan was easy—okay, fairly possible—to resist. Polite Ryan? Not so much.

"Which unit are you in?" he asked

I told him the number his Coach had given me and walked next to him as he led me to the building nearest us.

"If they got you an apartment, does that mean that your contract with the team is long-term? Coach didn't mention how long you'd be with us when he told everyone about you."

"Probably because you guys were too busy whining about the idea of having a girl teach you how to skate," I joked...sort of.

"I'm sure you're right," he agreed as he unlocked the door to the building and held it open for me. "And I'm sorry for my part in it."

"Thanks." And there went my mom's deeply ingrained manners again. "And yeah, I'll be here until the end of the season, however far into the playoffs you make it."

He nodded as he pressed the button to call the elevator. "It's a good thing they set you up with an apartment here. It's a popular location for those of us without families to worry about because it's an easy drive to the arena and there's a great workout room a lot of us use during the off-season. Plus, most of the units have a Jacuzzi tub in addition to a walk-in shower."

We stepped onto the elevator, and I let out a little involuntary moan at the thought of a hot bath in a Jacuzzi tub with the jets going at full power. The doors closed behind us, shutting me in with Ryan. His heated gaze dropped to my lips, and the elevator suddenly seemed much smaller than it really was.

Chapter Five

Ryan

FUCK, I WANTED TO HEAR THAT WHIMPER SHE MADE AGAIN.

Repeatedly.

While naked.

In my bed.

Not fully clothed in this damn elevator while she was thinking about the fucking Jacuzzi tub in her place that was bound to be an exact match for mine. A tub I wasn't going to be able to look at without picturing her in it. Just thinking about it made me hard as fuck. I adjusted myself when the doors opened before I followed her off the elevator.

"Which way?" she asked, with a glance over her shoulder towards me.

If it'd been a split second earlier, she would have busted me with my hand on my cock. It would have been another strike against me—one I didn't need if I wanted the chance to ever see her naked again. Schooling my face into an expression that I hoped was at least semi-innocent, I jerked my head to the left. "Your unit isn't too far down. This one's mine."

I released the handle of her suitcase and rapped my knuckles against my door with a smile on my face. It'd be virtually impossible for her to avoid me from such a close distance. But as I snagged the handle and moved past the apartment between hers and mine, my good humor quickly vanished. "And there's a fireman in between us," I grumbled. A single fireman. Hell, at least three quarters of the complex was filled with single guys. Firemen, cops, hockey players...this place had 'em all. Something that I'd never minded; not until Tamara moved in.

"A fireman, huh?" she echoed with a gleam in her brown eyes as she unlocked the door to her unit. "That'll come in handy if I have any incidents in the kitchen, so I don't end up burning the whole place down."

I peered into the grocery bags I was carrying for her and found the basics—a bunch of cartons of Greek yogurt, sandwich fixings, protein bars, almonds, granola, cherries, beef jerky, coffee, water, and sports drinks. "Doesn't look like there's anything dangerous in here."

She flipped on the lights as she walked inside the apartment. It was fully furnished; an option I hadn't even known they offered. After she dropped her carry-on and purse onto the couch, Tamara turned around and reached for the groceries. I reluctantly let her take them from me, rolling her suitcase next to the coffee table before following her to the kitchen area. I leaned against the counter while she unloaded her items and put everything away except for the sandwich stuff.

"Is that what you're having for dinner?"

"Yup. It's been a long day." Her gaze drifted over my shoulder at the door, and I had a feeling that she was about to ask me to leave—something I didn't want to do.

"Which makes a healthy dinner even more important." I shook my head slowly and made an exaggerated tsking noise, hoping to distract her from wanting me to go. "I'm sure you know better than to skimp on meals, what with your gold medals and all."

"Of course I do." She rolled her eyes and huffed. "But I spent thirty-one hours traveling due to delays and didn't make it into town last night like I'd planned. I don't have the energy to do a big shopping trip and cook dinner. Or to deal with you."

"Could you find the energy if it meant I was going to feed you a hot, nutritious meal in fifteen minutes flat?" I pointed at the package of sliced, deli turkey. "Dealing with me has to at least be worth not eating that for dinner, right?"

"Hmmm." She tilted her head to the side and tapped her finger against her cheek like my question required deep thought.

"C'mon, I owe you after I was such an ass earlier. Let me pay you back in food." But only because we weren't in a place where I could do so in orgasms. I'd forgo dinner to feast on her pussy without a second thought, even if I was starving. That's how badly I wanted another taste of her.

"I guess I could eat a real meal if I didn't have to cook it myself."

She didn't sound too sure about her answer, so I didn't give her time to think about it. I scooped up the deli meat, tomatoes, lettuce, cheese, and mustard and tossed them into the fridge. Then I tugged on her hand and led her out the door and down the hall to my apartment. As I flipped the light switch on the wall, I sighed in relief when I remembered that the cleaners had come today while I was at the rink. Maybe my luck had shifted from shitty to good when it came to Tamara.

"Grab a seat and get comfortable while I wow you with my cooking skills." I waved towards the two bar stools at the kitchen counter while I walked past them to grab ingredients from the fridge.

"I'm not too sure about the wow-ing part, but comfortable sounds good to me."

I turned and quirked a brow at her. "Is that doubt I hear in your voice?"

"It could be." She propped an elbow on the counter and rested her cheek on her palm. "Or it might just be sheer exhaustion."

"This is where my secret weapon comes into play." I pulled my George Foreman grill from the cabinet, set it down, and plugged it in. "Dinner will be ready in less than ten minutes."

"You're a cheat. That's not cooking. It's not even grilling. Did you have to turn in your man card when you bought that thing?" she laughed.

"Hey! I can grill with the best of 'em. Charcoal or gas," I grumbled. "But I don't always have the time. At least this way, I can eat right during season without having to order out all the time."

"You might have a point there," she conceded as she aimed a smile my way. Finally. I didn't even mind that it'd come at the expense of her making fun of me. "I'd say that I should get one except my mom would spot it in an instant, and then I'd never hear the end of her lectures on cooking things the right way."

I oiled down the grill and placed boneless, skinless chicken breasts on it after sprinkling them with seasoned salt and garlic. "Your mom sounds like a handful. The apple didn't fall too far from that tree, did it?"

"Since she's awesome, I'll take that as a compliment."

I measured equal amounts of instant brown rice and water into a dish, covered it, and placed it in the microwave. Then I pulled out my cutting board and sliced a zucchini and squash to put into the steamer. "You mentioned that you were two when you started to skate. Is she the one who got you on the ice?"

"Yeah." Her tired eyes light up. "If it was possible to learn how to skate before walking, she would have tried it with me."

"She's that into skating?" My parents were supportive, but they hadn't cared which sport I played growing up as long as I was doing something. They'd just wanted me busy enough to stay out of trouble. It'd been a stroke of luck when I stumbled across hockey and fell in love with it.

"She has the Olympic gold medals to prove it, too."

I hadn't been expecting that answer. "For speed skating?"

"Yup. It's kind of a crazy story because she grew up in Russia, well it was part of the Soviet Union back then. She earned some of her medals playing for them, but when she was at her third Olympics in Calgary in 1988, she defected to the States with the help of one of the coaches from the US team."

"Like Sergei Fedorov?" I asked, thinking of the hockey star who'd defected a couple of years later during the Goodwill Games. "He ended up returning to Russia and playing for a team there after his career with the NHL was over. Has your mom been able to go back, too?"

"No, but it's not that she couldn't have. It's more because there isn't anything left for her there," she answered with a shake of her head. "My grandparents died before she left, and she was an only child. She wasn't close to anyone in her extended family since she spent most of her time training from a young age."

"It sounds like you have that in common with her as well if she had you on skates when you were two."

"Yeah, but it was more than worth it since I went to my first Olympics when I was only seventeen."

I did a quick tally in my head and figured her to be twenty-four, a year younger than me. What she'd accomplished was damn impressive, and I wanted to slap myself upside the head for not putting the time in to get to know her back when we first met. But I damn well wasn't going to waste the second chance I'd been given. "Did you get your work ethic from her, too?" I asked while I piled food onto our plates.

"Yup. I had the best damn coach money didn't have to buy—my mom."

I went to set the plates on the higher part of the counter where she was seated, but then I rethought that decision. "Let's eat in the living room."

"Are you sure?"

Hell yeah, I was. It meant I'd be on the couch next to her instead of on separate stools at the counter, and getting closer to her was my goal.

Chapter Six

Tamara

My eyes snapped open when a loud banging noise filtered into my dream. I traveled often enough that I was used to waking up in strange beds, but they weren't normally decorated in masculine colors. And they definitely didn't smell like the specific cologne a certain sexy hockey player wore. A scent that'd invaded my dreams more times than I wanted to admit over the past few months. "Shit! What the hell did I do?"

I jackknifed off the mattress, and the thick, navy blue comforter that had been covering me fell to the floor. I was relieved to see I was still wearing my clothes from the night before since I didn't have any memory of how I'd ended up in Ryan's bed this time around...and because I heard male voices coming from the living room. I would have preferred to wait out whoever it was out there with Ryan instead of having a witness to my walk of shame, but a quick glance at my phone confirmed that I couldn't afford the delay.

"Here goes nothing," I sighed, pushing open the bedroom door and walking down the short hallway to the living room. I inwardly cringed when I recognized Ryan's guest as one of his teammates, Alec Rourke. When his blue eyes landed on me and lit up with humor, any hope I had of avoiding gossip at the rink flew out the window.

"Well, hello there," he drawled. "It's suddenly clear why Ryan's spent the last couple of minutes trying to shove me out his door with promises of a ride to the rink if I'd just give him a little time to get ready first. Since he's never had a problem with me hanging around, I should have known he was trying to hide something from me."

"Shut it, Alec," Ryan growled.

"C'mon now, you can't expect me not to react when Tamara was the last person I expected to see in your place this morning. How in the hell did the two of you manage to hook up last night?"

"We didn't hook up!" I yelped. And it was the truth...this time around.

"Nothing happened," Ryan backed me up, waving towards the couch. A pillow was at one end, and a blanket was bunched up opposite of it. "Coach set her up in the apartment a couple of doors down, and we bumped into each other in the parking lot. I made her dinner, and then her jet lag caught up with her and she passed out on the couch about two seconds after she finished eating."

"If that's the case, how'd she end up in your bed?"

As frustrated as I was with Alec's nosiness, at least it saved me from having to ask questions to which I should already have the answers. Especially ones that caused a super cute blush to stain Ryan's cheeks.

"None of your damn business."

"But—"

"The only way you're getting a ride to the rink from me is if you disappear for at least fifteen minutes. Now."

Alec's eyes, gleaming with humor, darted between the two of us. "Do speed skaters like it fast in—"

Ryan slapped a hand over his mouth and pushed him towards the door.

"I'll call you when I'm ready to go," he told Alec, right before he shoved him through the door and slammed it in his face.

"Shit, I'm sorry about that. His ankle is bothering him, and since it's his right he didn't want to drive to the rink in case it hurts more after practice," he explained.

"It's not your fault. I'm the one who should be apologizing since I passed out on you like that." But there was still part of the story that I definitely wanted to understand. "You didn't say; how did I end up in your bed?"

His cheeks went ruddy again. "I tried to wake you up, but you were out cold. So I carried you in there and set myself up on the couch."

"You carried my stuff to my apartment, made me dinner, and let me sleep in your bed while you took the couch?"

"Yeah," he confirmed. "I made double my normal amount of coffee, too. Just in case you wanted some."

I walked over to him and held my hand out. "Hello, I'm Tamara Antonov. Olympic speed skater and power skating coach. It's nice to meet you."

His low chuckle rang in my ears, and humor filled his gorgeous eyes as he slid his palm against mine. "I take it this means I'm forgiven for being a jackass yesterday."

"Absolutely. You more than earned a clean slate as far as I'm concerned. Let's start over?"

His hand tightened around mine and he tugged me closer. "Fuck no.

There's no way in hell I'm ever going to agree to a deal that requires me to pretend that the night we spent together didn't happen." I gulped as he acknowledged the elephant in the room; one I'd managed to avoid the night before. "If you want to avoid talking about it for now, I'll agree to that but only because I don't want to make you uncomfortable."

Putting off that conversation as long as I could worked for me. "If you give me that cup of coffee you mentioned, then you've got a deal."

"You could get me to agree to almost anything if it meant you'd give me another shot." My breath caught in my throat when he lowered his head and briefly brushed his lips across my cheek. I'd thought for sure he was going to aim for my mouth, and if I was being honest with myself I'd admit that I was a little disappointed he hadn't. But also damn impressed—even more so when he went into the kitchen, poured a mug of coffee, and handed it to me without asking if I take anything in it. "How'd you know I take it black?"

"It seemed like it was a safe assumption since there wasn't any milk or sugar in with your groceries," he answered.

"Aren't you an observant one?" I snickered.

"When it comes to you, count on it." His hazel eyes burned into mine with an intensity that had the laughter drying up in my throat.

I wasn't sure how I wanted to respond, so I avoided it by lifting my mug and taking a sip of coffee. "Damn, that's good."

"Anytime you want a cup, you know where to find me," he offered.

"What brand do you use?"

He flashed me a sly smile. "I'd tell you my secret, but then I'd have to find a new excuse to get you to come over and see me."

I gulped down most of the coffee and set my mug on the counter. Then I sidled closer to him. "I'm not going to turn down meals or coffee that's a thousand times better than what I could make for myself, but I have a feeling you're not going to need any tricks to make that happen." I rose up on my toes and brushed a kiss against his cheek the same way he'd done mine earlier. "But right now, we've both got somewhere else to be. You'd better get ready since Alec is waiting for you, and I've got to run so I'm not late for my morning training session."

"It can't be easy to train for the Olympics while working."

I shrugged as I headed towards his door. "It's pretty standard for Olympic athletes to have jobs. Well, except for the pros like the hockey players. If only speed skating paid as well."

"Hey! I work damn hard for my paycheck." I looked over my shoulder and quirked an eyebrow at him, smiling when he had the good sense to grimace. "Shit. That made it sound like you don't when I know damn well that you work hard, too. I'm lucky to make good money doing something I love."

"And I'm lucky your team is willing to pay me to turn you guys into the fastest skaters you can be."

It wasn't until the door was shutting behind me that he responded, "I'm lucky for that, too, and it has nothing to do with my skating."

Hearing that, I would have walked right back inside if we both didn't have other places where we had to be. Instead, I forced myself to head down the hallway and slumped against my door in the privacy of my apartment. "I might be lucky, but I have a feeling I'm also in trouble."

Chapter Seven

Ryan

"WHERE'S YOUR NEW GIRLFRIEND?" ALEC ASKED AS WE LACED UP OUR skates in the locker room. We'd been at the arena for a couple of hours already, but we'd spent most of that time with the trainers. It's how most of the players usually started their day since we all dealt with injuries throughout the season. They'd treated Alec's ankle and determined he was okay to skate on it today, but they wanted him to go a little easy on it so he'd be okay for our home game tomorrow night.

"She's not my girlfriend, asshat." Not that it wasn't what I was aiming for with her, which was a completely new experience for me.

"Hey, wait. What'd we miss? Yesterday she could barely stand to be on the same ice with you, and now Rourke is calling her your girlfriend?" one of the rookies asked.

"It's none of your damn business," I growled.

"Ooohhh...he sounds super sensitive about the whole thing. Something definitely happened," our starting goalie laughed. "It's a good thing your slap shot's on point since that's the only scoring you're going to do around here."

"I don't know; when I stopped by this morning, they looked awfully—"

I grabbed one of my elbow pads and tossed it at his face to shut him up. "Like I said; it's nobody's business but mine and Tamara's."

I tuned the guys out and focused on getting ready. If I let them get to me, the razzing would only get worse. It's just how things were.

Jason waited until we were walking through the tunnel out to the ice to ask, "Something happened, right?"

"Yeah."

He tapped my stick with his. "That's all you're going to give me? You know I'm not going to give you shit. Hell, I'm the one who told you to go after her in the first place!"

"Coach set her up with a place in my apartment complex; two doors down from me." I flashed him a satisfied smirk as I yanked the rink door open.

"Nice. Although I'm guessing there's more to the story based on your shit-eating grin," he drawled, skating past me onto the ice.

"Maybe. Maybe not."

"That's a definite yes." He shook his head and glided towards the bench to set his water bottle on the wall.

I scanned the rink, looking for any sign of Tamara and frowning when I didn't spot her anywhere. "Hey, Coach!" I called out. "Is Tamara sticking around after her training to watch our practice before she does her session with us?"

"I have no idea what you're talking about, Forrester. She isn't scheduled to be here until Noon, for her power skating drills with the team."

I skated over to where he stood. "What about her training? The Olympics are only eleven months away. She can't take the months she's coaching us off from her training; not if she wants to make the US team again."

"When we were negotiating the contract with her, she was specific about not being able to do morning sessions because it's when she prefers to train." He shrugged. "But she didn't say anything about what rink she was going to be using."

I looked around the ice like Tamara would magically appear before me. "She's not skating here in the mornings?"

"Nope."

"Where's she skating then?"

"Like I said. She didn't say. Is there a specific reason you're hell-bent on finding her?" His eyes narrowed as he considered me, and he held up a hand when I opened my mouth to answer him. "Forget I asked. Just don't fuck things up to the extent that we lose our power skating coach."

"I can't fuck things up if I don't know where she is."

"She'll be here in a couple of hours," he reminded me. This time, it was me who narrowed their eyes, making him sigh. "I think there are a couple of local rinks that have speed skating clubs who set up short tracks. Maybe she reached out to one of them and asked if she could use their ice. It'd be a great opportunity for them to see her in action and learn how to improve their own skating. If they're smart, it could even increase awareness and help build their numbers."

"We have a whole sheet of ice right here that nobody uses in the mornings while we're all with the trainers," I reminded him.

"And your point is what exactly?"

"Some of those advantages you described for the local speed skating club apply to us too," I explained. "I bet the public relations team would love the opportunity to get some reporters in here and talk about how we're using an

Olympic speed skater from the women's team to help improve our speed while gearing up for the playoffs."

"Aren't you the same guy who pissed her off enough to earn himself a slap upside the head and a challenge on the ice that he lost?"

"Yup." I grinned at him.

"And now you're her biggest advocate. Young guys and their dicks," he chuckled, shaking his head. "Do me a favor and don't let yours get you into trouble until after we've earned ourselves a championship cup."

"I won't." My dick was finally pointing me in the direction of the right woman. I had no intention of messing things up with her.

"If you can get the PR team on board—which we both know you'll be able to do since Jason's girlfriend will love the idea of helping you impress a woman —and facilities management is okay with the extra work they'd need to do to clear the ice between her training and our practice, then it's fine by me if she uses it on days we don't have a home game."

"Consider it a done deal, starting tomorrow." I wasn't going to take no for an answer, not when it was within my power to make Tamara's stay in Chicago easier on her. It wasn't just because I wanted back in her pants, either. It bugged me that she had to go hunting for ice when we had an empty sheet of it here that she could use and nobody thought to offer it to her. She was an Olympian, for fuck's sake. She deserved some goddamn respect as a fellow athlete.

"It's a good thing you've got the skills on the ice to back up that cockiness, Forrester. Or else I wouldn't put up with your shit."

I skated away, determined to remind him why I was worth the bother. I turned in one of my best practices in a long time, and still had energy to spare during the power skating session with Tamara. It was one of those days when everything went my way, and I even ended up beating two of our fastest forwards in a couple of the races. I felt on top of the world when I headed upstairs to talk to Cee-Cee.

"Hey, Ryan," she greeted me when I rapped my knuckles against her open office door.

"You got a minute?" I asked, flashing her a charming grin.

"Sure," she laughed. "Just remember I'm still new around here. Don't make me regret it or else I'll have to sic Jason on you."

I dropped down onto the chair in front of her desk, chuckling. "He might be your boyfriend, but he's my line mate. He wouldn't hurt me." She rolled her green eyes and smiled confidently. "Okay, he'd hurt me for you. But not too badly when we're in a race for the playoffs."

"You're probably right," she sighed. "So what can I help you with?"

"Coach hired an Olympic speed skater to run power skating drills for the team."

"And that means something to me because...?"

"She's in training for 2018 in PyeongChang, and I'm trying to swing it so she can use our ice to do it."

"She is?" Cee-Cee squealed, clasping her hands together. "That would be amazing! Is she open to the idea of doing interviews? I could easily line some up, and it'd be both to her benefit and the team's since good press means more butts in seats."

"I'm pretty sure I can talk her into some interviews if it means she gets to skate here since the arena is so close to her apartment."

"Wonderful! I'll get to work on it as soon as she gives me the green light."

"Plan on it being soon," I told her as I stood. "Thanks."

"Hold it. Not so fast there, buddy." Her green eyes narrowed. "Anything else you want to tell me about the woman you're running around doing favors for? Like when you guys met, and if she has anything to do with the way you've been avoiding all the puck bunnies who throw themselves at you?"

"As our publicist has drilled into our heads, I'll have to go with 'no comment,'" I answered.

"Well played," she laughed.

Cee-Cee's excitement about publicizing Tamara's role with the team added to my good mood. A quick conversation with the Zamboni driver, and I had his agreement to clear the ice after Tamara was done with it each day.

What I didn't have was any way to reach Tamara to share the good news. I hadn't asked for her phone number before she left my place that morning. I figured I'd be able to easily find her since I'd see her at the rink, but she hadn't been there until right before our power skating session and then she'd left again before I had the chance to talk to her about my plan to get her ice time at the arena.

It shouldn't have been a big deal since her apartment was so close to mine, but she hadn't answered her door any of the times I'd walked down to knock on it. I'd been home for a few hours already and had basically been walking the hallway hoping to bump into her the entire time. Like a damn stalker.

"Desperate times and all that bullshit," I muttered to myself as I pulled my door open, for what felt like the thousandth time, and almost collided with her in the hall.

Chapter Eight

Tamara

"Oomph!"

Strong arms wrapped around me, and the citrusy smell of Ryan's cologne filled my nostrils as my nose bumped into his sweater. I'd spent the day reminding myself of all the reasons why it was smart to keep my distance from him—my raging hormones whenever he was close being at the top of that list—after it had only taken one evening and morning with him to convince me that I probably shouldn't have bailed on him the night we slept together...and that was after he'd been a complete ass at the rink.

Ryan was hell on my willpower, so it figured that I'd bump into him as soon as I came back to my apartment. It barely took any effort on his part to get me to do things completely out of my character. Like the urge I had right then to yank him even closer and kiss the hell out of him.

Taking one last breath of his scent deep into my lungs, I forced myself to take a step backwards instead. He was dressed in dark blue jeans and a forest green cable-knit sweater that brought out the green in his hazel eyes. A lock of his dark hair hung over his forehead, and his mustache and beard looked freshly trimmed.

He looked deliciously perfect, while I was a disheveled mess after my strength training session at the gym since I hadn't bothered to do anything more than brush my wet hair after I took a quick shower. Damn his sexy ass for catching me like this when he had the upper hand.

"I'm glad I caught you," he murmured. "There's something I need to talk to you about."

"Umm, okay."

His door was still open, and he tugged me through it into his apartment before I could suggest we go over to my place instead. Not that it mattered where we were; what was important was that we were alone. Again. And there was a bedroom just down the hall.

"What's up?" I blurted in an effort to shove any thoughts of what we could do on his mattress out of my head.

"Come sit down with me." He pulled on my hand and led me to his couch, settling us next to each other on the cushions.

I was getting the feeling that he had something serious to discuss with me, and my stomach started to tie into knots. "What's going on?" An idea popped in my head, and that nervous feeling took a turn to nausea. I yanked my hand out of his hold. "Do you have a girlfriend?"

"No! Shit, Tamara. There's nothing wrong," he assured me. "And I sure as fuck don't have a girlfriend."

"Oh."

He wrapped his hand around mine again and smirked at me. "Correct me if I'm wrong, but it sounded like it'd bother you if I did."

"Maybe."

His smirk turned into a full-out grin, and his eyes filled with humor.

"Oh, stop," I sighed. "It doesn't necessarily mean anything more than I wouldn't want to come between another woman and her man. And with our history..." My cheeks filled with heat as I realized I'd just brought up the very topic I'd hoped to avoid.

His hand tightened and he shifted closer. "I didn't have one back then, either."

"Good."

"About that night—" he started.

"I don't do one-night stands," I interrupted. I wasn't sure I was ready to hear what he had to say about what happened between us, but I definitely wanted to get that out in the open. "I'd had a shitty day the night I met you and you were...well, you." I waved my free hand at him. "You're too sexy for my own damn good, but then I woke up the next morning and had no idea how to handle the whole thing."

"So you ran," he murmured.

"Yeah."

His thumb swept across my palm. "But it wasn't because of anything I did wrong?"

"No, it wasn't you. It was just me and my awkwardness."

"I can't say that I've never done the one-night stand thing before you." My heart dropped, but it soared again with his next words. "But I can tell you that I haven't been with anyone else since that night with you."

"Nobody?" I gasped.

"You're a tough act to follow, Tamara."

"Wow," I breathed. It'd been months since that night. Not for one second had I ever thought to even hope he'd spent all that time alone—like I had.

"See, that right there is why I haven't been able to get you out of my mind. Only you could pull off that irresistible mixture of adorable and so damn gorgeous at the same time."

My hand trembled in his hold, and his compliment made me blush. "I'm not the irresistible one in this duo."

He tilted my chin up with his finger. "I've got a solution for that."

"Oh, yeah?" I murmured.

"Yeah," he echoed softly, his head bending towards mine. "Stop trying to resist me and go with it. Give this a chance."

"This?" I whispered against his lips.

"Us, Tamara. Fate gave us a second chance, and I'd like to use it to see where this thing between us goes."

I needed a little more clarification before I did something I'd regret later. "'This thing' as in a possible relationship?"

"Definitely a relationship, baby. Now that I've found you again, I'm not going to settle for anything else. I've gotta make sure you don't have reason to run again."

Running was the last thing on my mind as he claimed my mouth in a passionate kiss. Fisting his hands in my hair, he held my head in place while his tongue tangled with mine. Just like it had so many months before, his kiss set my body aflame. By the time he lifted his head, I could barely catch my breath.

"You have no idea how relieved I am that you said yes." He rubbed his nose against mine in a gesture that should have been cute but instead had me shivering at how intimate it felt.

"As if I have the willpower to say no to you."

"Is that another yes?" His hand wrapped around my back and pressed us close together, my pebbled nipples brushing against his chest.

"Yes to what?"

His cheek slid against mine, and he whispered his answer into my ear, "To letting me have you again. It's been too long since I felt your tight pussy wrapped around my cock. I need you so damn bad."

My walls clenched at the reminder of our night together, my body screaming for me to agree. So I did. "Yes."

We tumbled back onto the couch cushions, ripping at each other's clothes—just like we had in his hotel bed the night we met. His mouth devoured mine, and I dragged his sweater over his head. Then I went after the snap and zipper on his jeans while he stripped me out of my long-sleeved shirt and bra. His hips lifted up to let me drag his jeans and boxers down his legs while he whipped my workout pants and underwear off my body.

With his body levered over mine, I trailed my fingers over his chest and down his abs, wrapping my hand around his cock as his mouth claimed mine again. "Fuck that feels good, baby," he groaned, his hips rocking and pressing his hard-on deeper into my palm. "Too damn good since it's been so long."

He trailed his mouth down my chest to my breasts, nibbling and sucking on one while his hand kneaded the other. I kept working his cock while he switched back and forth between my breasts until I couldn't take it anymore.

"Please."

"Not until I make you come with my mouth. I miss the taste of you." He kissed his way lower. "And I'm not going to last long once I get inside you."

He slid off the couch, going to his knees on the floor and settling my legs over his shoulders. The muscles in his arms flexed as he cupped my ass and lifted me towards his mouth. With his hazel eyes locked on mine, he lowered his head and swiped his tongue through my wetness.

"Ryan," I gasped, my fists pushing against the couch cushions while I lifted my hips higher.

He took that move for the encouragement it was and devoured me. Sucking. Licking. Fucking me with his tongue as he built the need within me. And when he slid two fingers inside me, I flew apart. He ate me through my orgasm and then crawled onto the couch with me, wrapping my legs around his waist and positioning his cock at my entrance.

"Fuck," he bit out. "I don't have a condom."

"None?" I gasped.

"I told you," he growled. "There hasn't been anyone since you, so I haven't needed 'em."

"I'm on the pill." His hips jerked forward at my admission.

"Are you saying I can take you bare?" His head dropped against my forehead, his eyes blazing into mine. "Fuck, please let that be what you're telling me."

It was way too soon for promises, but he'd called what he wanted a relationship and wanted to forgo condoms and there was only one way that was going to happen. "If I'm going to trust you with my safety, you have to promise me there won't be anyone else."

"I swear it, Tamara," he hissed out, rocking his hips forward and inching inside me. "I have no desire to be with anyone else. You cast some sort of spell on my cock and it only wants you."

"I guess that makes it mine, huh?" I laughed.

He pushed forward slowly, inch by inch until he was buried to the hilt. "Just so long as you know your pussy is mine, too."

I nodded jerkily, and he pumped his hips. He thrust in and out of me hard, pinning my hips to the cushions with his hands to hold me in place. It didn't take long for another orgasm to build in me.

"So close," I panted.

He swiveled his hips and ground against my clit, sending me over the edge. With my pussy clenching down on his cock, he planted himself deep and exploded inside me. As we both tried to catch our breath, he wrapped me into a tight embrace and rolled onto his back. Lying in his arms and basking in the afterglow of my orgasms, I felt like I could run a marathon even though I was still jet lagged and had a double workout day, with sessions both on and off the ice, plus power skating drills with the team. Sex with Ryan did wonders for my stamina.

Chapter Nine

Ryan

WATCHING MY GIRLFRIEND ON THE ICE NEVER GOT OLD. HELL, NEITHER did calling her my girlfriend. Not even after a month of dating her. I got the same kick out of thinking of her that way as I did saying it aloud to the guys and rubbing in their faces how wrong they'd been about my chances with her.

The morning after we got together again, we'd headed to the rink to set up a short track on the ice so she could use it for her morning training—after she'd sucked me off to show her appreciation for me getting permission for her to use the team's rink. And then I'd gone down on her to return the favor, which led to us finally fucking in my bed...and almost being late to the arena because I'd been thoroughly enjoying having a girlfriend.

It wasn't the last time we barely made it to the rink in time because we could barely tear ourselves away from each other. This morning was no different.

"Judging by that shit eating grin on your face, things are still going well for you and Tamara," Jason murmured as he joined me where I leaned with my elbows on the low wall in front of the bench.

"They sure as hell are," I admitted, my grin only getting bigger.

"A whole month," he chuckled. "I never thought I'd see the day where you'd be with the same woman for more than a night or two."

"Look at her out there." We both turned and watched Tamara move on the ice. She was almost a blur as she skated past us, bending so low her hand brushed the ice as she took a turn around the short track I'd helped her set up a month earlier.

"I still can't believe they let you mark the ice up." Jason shook his head.

I glanced down at the dark purple spots in the ice which were already barely visible. "You should have seen the look on the facilities manager's face when I told him we'd need to drill the ice and pour colored water into it."

"It probably matched most of ours as we watched you desecrate the ice for a woman."

"Like you wouldn't have done the same damn thing if Cee-Cee asked you," I grumbled as I bumped my elbow against his.

"There's no denying that I'd do just about anything my woman asked of me," he agreed. "But you'd only been with her for a night before you started acting as crazy as me. That's got to be a record of some kind."

"Ahem," I coughed.

"Dude. I was right there"—he pointed to the far end of the ice—"when you met her. I saw it with my own damn eyes when you shoved that big foot of yours in your mouth and almost lost any chance in hell of getting in there with her. Are you telling me it was all an act and you guys already knew each other?"

"No, that was real. I was too damn close to fucking it all up with her." I glanced over my shoulder to make sure nobody was behind us listening in. "It just wasn't the first time we met."

"What the hell? When did you meet her? What happened? And why didn't you ever say anything about her?" he fired off his questions.

"About four months ago, when we were in Anaheim for a game. I met her in a club, one thing led to another, but she disappeared in the morning and I didn't know how to track her down," I rattled off before punching him in the shoulder. "And it's not like you can give me shit for keeping my mouth shut about my mystery woman when you did the same damn thing with Cee-Cee."

"Yeah, and you guys ran your mouths off about it for-fucking-ever once you found out about her," he reminded me.

"Exactly," I chuckled. "Why do you think I never planned to say anything? I learned from your example."

"Only you did better than me and channeled your frustration into the game. We'll owe it to her in more ways than one if we win the cup."

I dragged my attention away from Tamara and turned to look at Jason. "You think so?"

"Yeah, she's made all of us better players."

"She sure as fuck has," I agreed, my gaze sliding back to her on the ice. "And with the help of Cee-Cee's magic, Tamara has brought more fans to the games, too."

Jason stepped back and dropped down onto the bench. "I don't think even Cee-Cee guessed the national media was going to be so fascinated by the story."

"I don't know; I wouldn't put much past your woman. She's damn good at her job."

"Mmm-hmm," he hummed, his attention on the ice. "We're lucky men when it comes to our women. Only we're not the only ones who know it."

My gaze scanned the ice and landed on the guy holding a stopwatch in the center. He was tall, with wavy, sandy-blond hair and green eyes. His dark-blue athletic pants were just snug enough to show how muscular his legs were, and his light-blue Cavaliers shirt with matching, unzipped hoodie were stretched taut across his biceps.

"Fucking Mike," I growled. I normally got along well with the team's trainer but ever since he'd volunteered to lend Tamara a hand with timing her laps, he'd been on my last nerve. I didn't begrudge her the help; not when I knew she needed it. I just wished it didn't come from a guy who checked out her ass every opportunity he got.

"He's persistent; you've got to give him that," Alec chuckled as he stepped into the bench area.

"And fearless," Jason added. "Since he knows how much it pisses Ryan off when he flirts with Tamara right in front of him."

"You've got to give props to a guy who's seen Ryan demolish players on the ice and still isn't intimidated enough to back off his woman."

I glared at Alec over my shoulder. "You might want to watch your ass during practice or else I might decide to work out some of my anger on you."

"Cut Alec some slack," Jason suggested. "He doesn't get it because he doesn't have a woman of his own."

"The day I get that riled up over some chick is the day hell freezes over."

Jason and I burst out in laughter at Alec's declaration, and we were still at it when Tamara skated over to us with Mike following right behind her.

"What's so funny?" she asked.

"Just Alec being totally clueless," I responded, pulling her close and dropping a quick, hard kiss on her lips. When I lifted my head, I locked gazes with Mike and flashed him a satisfied grin as I reached down to palm the ass he'd been eyeing all morning when she stepped into the bench area. He just shook his head and scooted past us with a head nod to the guys.

"We'd better finish getting ready." Jason tugged on Alec's arm, and they left us alone on the bench.

"I'm going to miss hanging out with you guys while the Zamboni clears the ice between my training session and your practice," Tamara sighed.

"I'm sorry you have to switch rinks."

She waved off my concern. "I was lucky to be able to stay here as long as I did. But with the playoffs starting this weekend, I totally get it. The ice needs to be pristine for those games so nobody can complain when you kick their ass and knock them out of the running."

"Damn straight." I tugged her close. "There's one good thing about you switching to another rink."

"What?" Shocked brown eyes flew up to search my face.

"I won't have to watch that asshole try to flirt with you right in front of me."

"Mike isn't that bad," she laughed. "He mostly does it to get a rise out of you."

"Mostly isn't good enough," I growled, claiming her lips again. "The guy needs to get it through his thick skull that you're mine. No flirting allowed. Not for any reason."

Concerned brown eyes scanned my face. "You know you don't have anything to be worried about, right? There's only one guy I'm interested in, and that's you."

"I know," I sighed. "It's the only reason I haven't settled the matter with my fists."

"If I can refrain from getting into a cat fight with any of the puck bunnies, you can keep your hands in your hockey gloves where they belong, slugger," she laughed.

"A cat fight, huh?" I waggled my brows at her.

She brushed her lips against mine, and whispered, "Cat fights are out of the question. But if you score me some goals during the playoffs, I might let you have just about anything else you can think of."

I hadn't needed the extra motivation to play my best during playoffs, but I sure as shit wasn't going to turn down Tamara's offer.

Chapter Ten

Tamara

ALTHOUGH I'D TRAINED PLENTY OF PLAYERS, I'D NEVER BEEN ONE TO watch hockey games. Not unless I was pulling tapes to analyze how the players skated so I could use the information during power skating drills. It had always been too difficult for me to turn off that part of my brain and just enjoy the game for what it was.

Having my boyfriend on the ice had changed that for me, though. Especially during the last month of playoff games, when I was too nervous to do anything but sit in the edge of my seat and pray that they pulled off another win so they didn't get knocked out of the running for the championship.

"C'mon, get the puck out of there, Ryan. C'mon," I chanted.

The opposing team was cycling the puck in our defensive end, and I had a bad feeling it wasn't going to go well for us. The longer the puck stayed on our end of the ice, the more likely it was that they'd be able to score a goal against us.

"Shit." I winced when Ryan slammed a player into the boards. I thought for sure that the ref was going to call him for a penalty, and I breathed a sigh of relief when I didn't hear a whistle. But that feeling was short-lived when the other team got a shot off and the puck went flying past the goalie and into the net.

"Dammit," I groaned.

Cee-Cee reached out and grabbed my hand, both of us looking up at the score board. With that goal, the Cavaliers were down by two with only three minutes left on the clock. Ryan and Jason skated back to the bench, while Alec and his line mate took their place in the defensive positions for the puck drop.

"Jason's going to be so pissed at himself for not clearing the zone on that one," Cee-Cee grumbled.

"Ryan isn't going to be any happier."

Cee-Cee and I had gotten to know each other well over the past couple of months, both professionally and personally. Some of the press she'd gotten for the team had bled over to me, and she'd also managed to snag me a sponsor for the Olympics next year. Between the money they'd committed to, what I'd earned with my win at the World Single Distance Championships, and the money I was earning from the Cavaliers, I was in a position where I didn't have to worry about earning enough to make it to South Korea in February.

"I should have grabbed an extra beer when I had the chance," I groaned. "I swear the game clock is running in slow motion."

Cee-Cee's hand clenched mine harder. "You don't have room to complain too much. At least you had a few, right? This was not the night to stick to ginger ale. Alcohol would have helped with the stress."

I gulped down the last of my beer. "It hasn't done me much good."

She released my hand to rub her belly. "I feel like I'm going to throw up."

I tore my gaze away from the ice to look at her. "Wait a second. Why aren't you drinking?"

"Umm," she stuttered.

"They've been in close games before, and you've never mentioned anything about feeling sick to your stomach."

"Well," she drawled, her gaze sliding to the ice and back to me. "Can we pretend like you didn't notice?"

"Pretend? Ohhhh," I breathed as realization dawned. "Yes, that's totally fine."

I grabbed her hand and squeezed it, letting her know I got what she was saying and I was excited for her even though she hadn't confirmed my suspicion.

"Win or lose, I can't wait any longer," she mumbled. "I put it off as long as I could because I didn't want to do anything to mess with Jason's head when it needs to be in the game. But I really want it to be something for just the two of us to share for a little while."

I nodded. "I think you made the right call. If you're talking about what I think you're talking about"—I tilted my head in her direction and offered her a gentle smile—"then it will be wonderful news to help ease the sting of what's almost definitely going to be a loss."

"I'm not confirming or denying anything, but I hope so," she whispered.

"I know so," I assured her. "It's obvious to anyone who sees the two of you together for even a minute; that man loves you."

Her lips tilted up in a dreamy smile, and she twisted her engagement ring around her finger. "I love him, too."

"Trust me, your love for him is also obvious."

"And I'm totally fine with that." She grinned at me, shaking her head. "Because only love has the power to keep me in a relationship with a professional athlete. It's so damn difficult sometimes, between the grueling schedule, road trips, and puck bunnies."

"Tell me about it," I snorted. "Just imagine how much harder it is when you're both athletes with conflicting schedules."

She slumped back in her seat. "I don't know how you two manage to juggle all that you do."

"Very carefully," I murmured.

"Will you be able to stay in Chicago after the season is over?"

"The sponsor you lined up for me makes it a possibility, but Ryan and I haven't had the chance to talk about it yet." There was a big gap between dating exclusively and changing your entire life for a relationship, and I wasn't sure if we'd reached the point where it made sense for me to make my move to Chicago permanent. The only thing I knew for sure was that I wasn't excited by the idea of a long distance relationship.

"Well, if I get a vote, mine is for you to move here."

A buzzer went off, and we both turned our attention back to the ice. The clock had only run down another minute, and the score was still the same. We'd missed a penalty against the other team while we chatted, and our guys were back on the ice again for a power play.

We were quickly pulled into the action as the seconds ticked down. The Cavaliers moved the puck from their defensive zone, past both of the blue lines, and cycled it around the net. One of the opposing team's defenders got lucky and intercepted a pass between the forwards, but Jason stepped up and stole the puck back. He sent it across the ice to Ryan with a hard pass, and I jumped to my feet.

"C'mon, Ryan!" I screamed. "Use that slap shot of yours and score a goal!"

As though he'd heard what I'd yelled, his stick went up and then he pivoted forward and nailed the hell out of the puck. It went flying towards the net, sailing just over the goalie's outstretched glove to crash into the back of the net. Cee-Cee and I jumped to our feet and hugged each other.

"He really is the slap shot king!" Cee-Cee cried.

"Hell yeah, he is."

We stayed on our feet, along with the rest of the crowd, and watched as the ref dropped the puck. Our center got his stick on it first, and sent it back to Ryan. He cycled it to Jason, who sent it up to the right wing. The forward got a shot off, but the goalie deflected it and as it bounced towards our center's stick the buzzer sounded.

"Damn," I groaned.

"I'm not sure if it's better or worse to lose in such a close game."

I thought about how it felt when I raced. "In some ways, it's worse because you know you were so close to that win."

"Yeah, that makes sense," Cee-Cee sighed as she dropped back down in her seat, tugging on my hand until I sat down too. "Okay, now that we talked about all my shit and have plenty of time to wait for the guys, how're things going for you and Ryan?"

I fanned myself with my hand, my cheeks heating. "Considering what I promised him if he scored during the playoffs...things are about to get wild."

Chapter Eleven

Ryan

LOSING IN THE REGULAR SEASON SUCKED. GETTING KNOCKED OUT OF THE playoffs during our division finals at an away game by only one goal was even worse. The only positive thing to come from tonight's game was the goal I managed to score at the end of it—and the offer Tamara had made me a month earlier. One I was looking forward to cashing in on tonight.

"Tamara?" I called, walking into our room. We'd gotten the girls an Uber to the hotel since we had to ride back with the team. Cee-Cee was waiting for Jason in the lobby, but Tamara was nowhere to be found. She wasn't answering my texts, and Cee-Cee's answer when I asked had been to burst into a fit of giggles and tell me to look for her in our room.

Since I could see the bathroom light from under the door, I headed that way. I made it about halfway across the room when it swung open, and I froze in my spot. Tamara was standing in the doorway, wearing a Cavaliers home game jersey and a pair of white thigh-high stockings. My cock was rock hard at the sight.

"Fuck, you're beautiful," I growled as I stalked towards her.

"I hope you don't mind that I borrowed your jersey." She pivoted on a heel and my gaze locked on my name spread across her back. My cock hardened further at the sight.

"I don't mind at all," I promised. "In fact, you look so damn sexy I think we need a rule that you walk around wearing my name on some part of your body every single day."

She spun back around laughing, and I pulled her against my chest. "Hmm, that'd be hard to do without starting a whole line of Forrester gear. Jackets, shirts, shorts...underwear."

My hand slid between us to reach under the jersey and cup her pussy. "I like the sound of my name right over this, marking it as mine."

"Except nobody but you would ever see them," she pointed out.

"But I'd know they were there," I rasped as I lifted the jersey over her head, giving me an eyeful of all the beauty she was hiding underneath it. Those high, slightly rounded tits that fit perfectly in my hands. Her pink, pebbled nipples were practically begging for my touch, so I lowered my head and sucked one of them into my mouth.

"Ryan," she gasped. Her hands clenched my shoulders, and her head fell back while she thrust her tits higher.

Releasing her nipple with a pop, I wrapped my arms around her lower back and lifted her off the floor. She circled her legs around my hips and held on tight as she lowered her head to brush her lips over mine. I felt the heat of her pussy was hot as it pressed against my abs. I was beyond grateful that we were only steps away from a bed, or else I would have been searching for the nearest hard surface instead of dropping her down on the edge of the mattress.

Desperate for the taste of her, I dropped to my knees and wedged myself between her legs. There was a tiny scrap of light blue lace covering her pussy, and I ripped it from her body, leaving her in only the matching thigh-high stockings.

"You owe me a new pair," she moaned as I dove down to bury my head between her legs. Her legs widened, and she fell back against the mattress, her fingers clenching the sheets.

I ate at her pussy, plunging my tongue inside her and licking up all her juices. Her cries rang in my ears as her hips began to jerk, and I thrust two fingers in her core. Her wet heat tightened around them, and I flicked my tongue back and forth against her clit until her body tightened up and she screamed my name.

"Ryan! Fuck!"

I licked her through her orgasm but the second it was done, I tore my mouth from her pussy and ripped my clothes from my body. Shoving her further up the mattress, I climbed on top of her and kissed along her jaw as I lined up my throbbing cock with her wet heat.

"I need to feel your tight pussy gripping my cock, baby," I rasped.

"Need you inside me, now," she panted, her hips wriggling until I slid an inch deep.

I anchored my arms under her knees and forced them as wide as they'd go. "You ready for me?"

"So ready."

"Good," I bit out as I slowly pushed inside. I fought the urge to ram inside her, hoping the slow slide would help me gain control. Instead, it did the opposite, pushing me closer to the edge. "You feel so damn good."

"Fuck," she groaned. "You're going to torture me if you keep going so slow. I need more."

"Don't you worry, baby. I'll give you everything you need," I assured her as I lowered my head to her tits and took one of her hard nipples in my mouth. Her walls clenched around me when I bit down on it, and I chuckled against her skin. "You like that, huh?"

"Yes," she hissed, her hands coming to my head to press my mouth against her skin.

"Then I'd better make sure to get this one, too." I kissed my way to the other side and gave it the same attention. She cried out as I sucked hard, my cheeks hollowing out before I rolled her nipple between my teeth. She whined in protest when I let her nipple go with a pop.

"Don't stop," she pleaded.

"Need your mouth, baby," I whispered against her lips before I kissed her fiercely.

Our tongues tangled together as my hips bucked against hers. Building up speed, my cock shuttled in and out of her heat. Her core gripped me tight, not wanting to let me go each time I pulled out, and making me fight for it when I powered back inside. Tightening my grip on her legs, right at the bare skin above her thigh-high stockings, I shoved them wider and lifted up on my knees to hammer into her.

"Fuck yes, baby. Come for me. Now."

Her walls clamped down on me as she screamed my name, her hands coming up to grab my ass and pull me even deeper while she pulsed around me. I only managed one more thrust, and then I buried my cock deep inside her pussy as I came. Jets of come burst from my body, spilling out of her and onto the sheets. When I was done, my body felt like it was wrung dry. I reluctantly pulled out and collapsed on the mattress next to her. We were both panting, our bodies covered with a light sheen of sweat.

"You're sleeping in the wet spot," she giggled, rolling into my side.

"Who said anything about sleeping?"

She leaned up on an elbow and smiled down at me. "No rest for the wicked?"

"If so, you must've been a naughty girl because I plan on keeping you up all night."

She laughed and reached over to grab the phone off the nightstand. "I'd better order us some dinner then. We'll need it to keep up our energy."

"I could eat," I answered, trailing my fingertips up her stockings.

She slapped my hand away. "Food and a shower first. Then we'll see if you still have enough energy left over to go for another round."

I slid my palm around the base of her skull and pulled her close to claim her lips. When I was done, I rolled off the mattress and padded to the bathroom. "Challenge accepted, baby. I'll hop in the shower now so I'm ready to eat as soon as room service gets here. And then you'd better be ready for me."

"Promises, promises," she giggled.

Three hours later, those promises were fulfilled and she didn't have the energy left to laugh.

"Damn, I totally forgot that you were supposed to get whatever you wanted since you scored a goal," she murmured.

I shifted her in my arms to look down at her sleepy face, lids half closed as though she could barely keep them open. Dropping a kiss against her cheek, I whispered, "You didn't need to remember, baby. You already gave me exactly what I wanted."

"I did? Was it lots and lots of hot hotel room sex?"

"No, it was you, Tamara. Just you."

She fell asleep with a smile on her lips, and as I held her tight I promised myself I'd figure out a way to ensure it was a sight I got to see for the rest of my life.

Chapter Twelve

Tamara

THE PAST TWO WEEKS WITH RYAN HAD BEEN BOTH AMAZING AND frustrating. Since his season was over, his schedule was wide open. But mine? Not so much. I had less than seven months until the Olympic trials in Utah, and my mom was putting pressure on me to move out there early for training. I'd sidestepped the issue a couple of times, but she wasn't going to let me avoid it much longer. Just that morning, she forwarded information for an apartment complex and two different rental houses within a few miles of the arena in Utah.

I needed to figure out where I wanted to live, and fast. It wasn't a decision I could make by myself, though. Not when Ryan factored into it so much. I wasn't a shy person normally, but I was having a difficult time bringing the topic up to Ryan. I only had the apartment the Cavaliers had rented for me for one more week, so I needed to pull up my big girl panties and ask Ryan if he wanted me to stay. But that had to wait until he came back from his trip to Vegas.

Rolling over on my bed, I yanked a pillow over my head and screamed into it. "I'm such an idiot. Why the hell didn't I just go with him?"

Jason and Cee-Cee had decided to get married there. It wasn't a normal elopement, though. They were getting married in a fancy hotel Jason's mom had lined up for them, and a big group of their friends and family were all going to be there. Ryan had wanted me to come with him as his date, and Cee-Cee had also called to make sure I was more than welcome to join them.

The timing was worse than shit for me since I had two friends from the US Speed Skating team in town for the week so we could train together. I couldn't exactly bail on them after I'd extended the invitation. They thought it was cool as hell that we'd been able to set up the short track on the Cavaliers' rink. And they'd given me a hard time for dating one of the players since I'd always been adamant about not hooking up with athletes because they were conceited jerks.

"I miss my conceited jerk," I mumbled as I turned over again.

My friends had left that morning, and Ryan wasn't due back until the next afternoon. The wedding had been this morning, and other than a quick phone call from Ryan after the ceremony I hadn't heard from him again. "The big jerk is having fun in Vegas and probably doesn't even miss me, while I'm alone here wondering what's next for our relationship."

I jerked upright, clutching the sheets to my chest when I thought I heard a noise in the living room. I sat stock-still, straining to listen in case I was imagining things. But then I heard it again, and I quietly slid off the mattress on the side away from the bedroom door and grabbed my phone off the nightstand. I hit the nine and one button, and as I was getting ready to press the one again my door swung open and I heard a familiar male voice whisper, "You awake, baby?"

"You scared the shit out of me!" I yelled, jumping to my feet.

"Fuck, sorry." He rounded the bed and pulled me into his arms. "I didn't mean to scare you."

"It's okay. I should have at least guessed that it could have been you since you're the only person other than me who has a key, instead of freaking out and assuming it was a robber." I tilted my head back to peer into his face. His hazel eyes were bloodshot, his hair was mussed, and his beard was extra scruffy. But he still looked sexy enough to melt my panties. "What're doing back? I thought your flight wasn't until tomorrow."

"It was, but I changed it." His hold on me tightened.

"Why? Are you okay?"

"I missed you." I felt his lips press against the top of my head. "I'm fantastic, now that I've got you in my arms."

"Missed you, too," I murmured against his chest.

We stood there, holding each other tight without saying anything else for several minutes. "C'mon, get out of your clothes and come to bed."

I stepped away, fixing the sheets and blankets while he stripped down to his boxers. He climbed in first, piling my pillows behind his back. When I crawled in next to him, he settled me against his chest and tangled our legs together.

"How was the trip?"

"Surprising," he chuckled, his chest vibrating underneath my cheek.

"It sounds like there's a story behind that." I traced a heart shape with my fingertip on his abs. "Give me the details." I gently yanked on his hair at his chest. "Or else."

"Ouch." He wrapped his hand around mine. "You don't have to torture me to get me to talk."

"Then spill it, Forrester."

"Let's see," he drawled. "Cee-Cee and Jason ducked out of their co-wed bachelorette party early because she's knocked up and needed her rest."

"Yes!" I cried, tilting my head back to look up at him and flashing him a big smile. "My guess was right. I'm so happy for them."

"How'd you know? Nobody else did."

"I didn't *know* know. But when we were in Pittsburg for your last playoff game, she wasn't feeling great and I put one plus one together and came up with a possible pregnancy."

"Smartypants," he teased, slipping inside my pajama pants to palm my ass. His hazel eyes darkened when he encountered bare skin instead of panties.

"Focus, babe. The old saying about stuff that happens in Vegas doesn't hold true when you go there without me. I need the rest of the gossip before you're getting lucky."

"Fine, but you're getting the Cliff Notes version," he grumbled. "Alec wanted to hit the Strip when Jason and Cee-Cee called it a night. Josie and Andrew bailed, too. So I was stuck hitting some clubs with Alec."

"Stuck," I snorted.

"Yes, stuck," he echoed. "Because it just made me miss you even more. I wasn't in the mood to drink or party, so I headed back to the hotel early and ended up missing all the excitement."

I propped my chin on his chest and made my very best puppy dog eyes at him. "What kind of trouble did Alec get into? Was he arrested? Did you have to bail him out of jail so he didn't miss the wedding?"

"Nope, he made the wedding alright." He paused for dramatic effect. "Two of them."

I jolted up, my jaw dropping while I stared at him. "Whose else got married?"

"Alec."

"Shut up!" I shrieked as I bounced on the mattress. "You're pulling my leg, aren't you?"

"I wish I was," he sighed. "Had I known that Alec was going to have such a wild night that it ended with him marrying some chick he'd just met, I would have sucked it up and stayed with him to at least try to be the voice of reason. But I didn't know, so I got to meet his new wife at Jason and Cee-Cee's wedding instead."

"Whoa," I breathed. "Now I wish I'd kicked my friends out a day early and met up with you guys instead. I can't believe I missed all that."

"In a way, I'm glad you weren't able to make it."

I hadn't been expecting our playful conversation to head in that direction, and I slumped over in disbelief. My hurt must have shown in my expression because Ryan gathered me close. "It's not that I wouldn't have loved to hang out with you in Vegas, baby. I would. More than anything."

"Then why in the world were you happy I wasn't there?"

"Because it opened my eyes to how much I missed you." He pulled me onto his lap. "The only other times we've been in different cities since we started dating was for road trips when you weren't able to make it. I missed you during those, too. But this was different because I wasn't distracted by hockey. It was just me with my friends, feeling like I'd left a part of me back home."

The hurt was washed away, replaced by fierce joy. "And I'm the missing part of you?"

"You are."

"Because you love me?" I whispered.

"Yes."

A huge grin spread across my face. "Could you maybe tell me instead of just saying yes?"

"Only if you say it back."

"Together on three?"

"Sure," he chuckled.

"Three."

I took a deep breath. "Two."

And another. "One."

I tossed myself into his arms as we shared in unison, "I love you."

This countdown wasn't a race, but we both came out winners in the end.

Epilogue

Ryan

I NEVER THOUGHT I'D BE HAPPY TO BREAK A BONE, BUT DAMN IF I WASN'T thrilled with the timing of my broken right hand. It put me on the injured reserve list, with an estimated four-week recovery period, smack dab in the middle of the winter Olympics. I would have been pissed, except it meant that I could hop a plane to South Korea to surprise Tamara.

Finding a flight had been more difficult than I anticipated, and it pushed back my arrival until the morning of her five-hundred-meter race. I hated that I missed her win the gold medal in the thousand meter four days earlier, but I'd had a game in Minnesota that night and watched it on television after I got home. The time difference had made it hard for us to Skype each other, but we'd sent what felt like a million texts back and forth since she left more than three weeks ago. It had been the longest time we'd spent apart, and my bed felt empty without her. The whole apartment did since I'd quickly grown used to sharing space with her since she moved in with me the day after I came home from Vegas after Jason and Cee-Cee's wedding.

"Ryan!"

I searched the crowd in front of the arena and spotted Tamara's mom, Tatiana. She was waving at me frantically, and I hurried towards her.

"Hurry," she urged me forward after a swift hug. "I haven't told her you're here. I did not want to distract her before the race since we couldn't be sure you would arrive before it started. But I know she will want you there when she comes off the ice."

Tatiana's words were hard to follow because her accent was thicker than usual, something I'd noticed happened when her emotions ran high since I'd had the chance to get to know her well when she moved to Chicago to help with Tamara's training.

How Tatiana got her hands on a ticket for me, I'd never know because her lips were sealed. But I would be forever grateful because we made it inside and down near the ice just as Tamara's race began. I got to watch her skate faster than I'd ever seen her go before—and faster than any of the other skaters there. She earned another gold medal, and this time I was there to cheer her on as she took the top place on the podium.

Later that night, I settled her on the edge of the mattress in the privacy of our hotel room. She was still dressed in her Team USA uniform, with two gold medals hanging from her neck, when I got down on one knee in front of her.

I pulled a two-karat diamond engagement ring in a gold setting out of my pocket and held it up for her to see. "I was thinking, as long as you're adding more gold to your collection, maybe you'd like to wear this too."

"Oh my God," she cried, tears leaking from her beautiful brown eyes.

"You're going to have to help me out here, baby. Is that a yes?"

"Yes!" she shouted, scooting off the bed to fall into my arms. I slid the ring onto her finger and admired how it looked there for a moment before claiming her lips in a brutal kiss that quickly led to a naked celebration of her win and our engagement...thirteen months to the day since our first night together. Lucky number thirteen, just like my jersey.

CURIOUS ABOUT JASON and Cee-Cee's story? You can read all about them in Checked Into Love. Or start out with the first Bachelorette Party series story, Sucked Into Love. Also, Alec's story is available for pre-order...Married Into Love.

WANT UPDATES ON NEW RELEASES, giveaways, and exclusive content? Sign up for my newsletter!

Also by Rochelle Paige

BLYTHE COLLEGE SERIES

Push the Envelope

Hit the Wall

Summer Nights (novella duo)

Outside the Box

Winter Wedding (novella)

BACHELORETTE PARTY SERIES

Sucked Into Love

Mixed Into Love

Checked Into Love

CRISIS SERIES

Identity Crisis

Protection Crisis

FATED MATES (BLACK RIVER PACK & McMAHON CLAN)

Crying Wolf

Shoot for the Moon

Thrown to the Wolves

Bear the Consequences

Bear It All

Bear the Burden

Ask for the Moon

BODY & SOUL SERIES

Bare Your Soul

Save Your Soul

Sell Your Soul

Feed Your Soul

STANDALONES

Star Pupil

About the Author

I absolutely adore reading—always have and always will. When I was growing up, my friends used to tease me when I would trail after them, trying to read and walk at the same time. If I have downtime, odds are you will find me reading or writing.

I am the mother of two wonderful sons who have inspired me to chase my dream of being an author. I want them to learn from me that you can live your dream as long as you are willing to work for it.

Connect with me online:

www.rochellepaige.com

BACK IN THE GAME

Chapter One

CALDER

"No, daddy, like this." Shea repositions the tiara on my head. "You can't wear it sideways like that, you have to show off your jewels."

"Showing off daddy's jewels could get him in trouble. That's called indecent exposure, sweetie."

"Huh?" Shea's head tilts to the side, a pull in her brow.

"Never mind." I clear my throat and take a look at myself in the reflection of my car window.

Tiara . . . check.

Showing off the jewels (tiara jewels, that is) . . . check.

Pink scarf wrapped around at nipple height and tied like a bow . . . check.

Purple sparkly fairy wings strapped around my bulky shoulders . . . check.

Looks like I'm ready for lunch with my daughter. Let's just pray there aren't any super fans in the area, because I'm a walking Instagram story right about now. Although . . .

I squat down next to my daughter and pull out my phone. Opening up the Instagram app, I go to my stories and turn the camera so it's facing me.

"Want to do a story with me, Shea?"

"Yeah!" She claps vigorously.

I press record and bring Shea closer to my side. "Off to lunch with this beautiful girl today. Fairy wings and tiara are on, I'm dad-ing hard right now. Blow a kiss." She blows a kiss right before I stop recording.

"What is dad-ing hard?" She asks, twirling around in her pink, sparkly tutu.

"Eh, don't worry about it." I share my story and pocket my phone. "Grab daddy's hand. We have some food to eat."

I open the door to the restaurant for my little girl and usher her in, unfazed by the looks I'm getting. This isn't the first time I'm dressed as Wanda the Fairy. Yup, I have a name and everything. I would do pretty much anything for Shea, not just because she's my daughter and I love her more than anything, but because she hasn't had the easiest life. Her mom, who we won't speak of much, took off after one month of being Shea's mom. She now lives in France, where she travels with her violinist boyfriend. We were never going to be a couple, ever—that shipped sailed after our one-night stand—so I'm not hurt about her being with someone else, but what makes me want to choke some sense into the woman is the way she totally abandoned her daughter. Especially since I play professional hockey for a living, and my schedule is demanding and hectic. It would have been nice to have her mom available to help out. Thankfully, my brother and his wife are there for me when I'm out of town.

"Wanda, what a treat to see you today," Eduardo, the owner of Noodles and Donuts, greets me with a giant grin on his face. "And Little Miss Shea, looking beautiful as ever."

"Thank you kind sir." Shea curtseys then does a spin in her tutu. Kind sir . . . I shake my head, she must have picked that up from my brother.

"Would you like your usual table?"

"And two pink donuts," Shea adds, holding up two fingers.

Eduardo tips her chin. "Coming right up, sweetheart." He nods to the back of the restaurant. "You can go and take a seat. Coffee?"

"Please, and a Thai peanut chicken bowl for me, extra veggies."

"Coming right up."

We walk to the back of the restaurant and to the table that sits under the window, overlooking a tiny garden. Shea takes no time in hopping up on her seat and placing her elbows on the windowsill, looking out over the vegetation.

"One, two, three, four, six."

"Five sweetie, don't forget five, remember, that's how old you are, you don't want to skip it."

"Daddy," she gives me a "look." "I said five in my head."

"Ohh, okay, but when you're counting let's refrain from saying numbers in your head."

"But it's not fun like that, daaaaad," she drawls out.

"My mistake," I mumble.

Glancing around the restaurant, I'm surprised to see there aren't a lot of diners today. Noodles and Donuts is a popular little hole in the wall in Philadelphia. It's the perfect spot for something sweet and savory. What else do you really need besides noodles and donuts?

Well, plenty of things, but Shea loves it here, so it's our special place.

"Eleven tomatoes, can you believe it dad? Eleven!"

"Wow, eleven, that's crazy."

"I KNOW!" She giggles and shakes her head. "Eleven tomatoes is definitely crazy."

"The craziest." My phone buzzes in my pocket, but I ignore it. Most likely it's either my coach or my agent, and I'm less than interested in talking to both of them right now, especially since it's my day off from an arduous road trip and we are coming down to the end of the season with playoffs looming over us. I just want to focus on my girl.

"Two pink donuts for the prettiest girl I know," Eduardo says, holding out a plate.

Shea goes to reach for her donuts but I snag the plate away before she can shove the whole thing in her mouth. She has a goal in life, a ridiculous goal mind you, to shove an entire donut in her mouth. She watched my brother do it once and now any chance she gets, she tries. Thanks, Chuck.

My leg bouncing, I really have to go to the bathroom, I point my finger at Shea and say, "Listen here you fairy princess, we are not shoving the entire donut in your mouth, and you will have a bowl of my veggies as well before you can even think about that second donut, got it?"

"But daddy, how am I going to fit a donut in my mouth if I don't practice?"

Sighing, I eye Eduardo, who's chuckling to himself. "Can you watch her for a second while I go to the bathroom?"

"No problem, man. But if she shoves a donut in her mouth, that's her business."

I stand, my height five inches taller than Eduardo. "Don't let her shove the damn thing in her mouth, break her off a piece. Come on, be the adult."

"But she's so cute."

Yeah, she's cute, which makes it so much more difficult. I make my way to the bathroom while I pull my phone from my pocket.

Voicemail from Greg, yup, my agent wants something and I'm not in the mood to find out what it is. I love my job, being able to play hockey for a living, feeling the scrape of the ice beneath my blades and making money doing it, there is nothing greater than that, but I'm more of a homebody when it comes to the outside responsibilities that come along with the job. I just want to skate around, play the game, slam some guys into a wall, and collect my paycheck. The promotions, and marketing, and appearances, yeah I could do without those. Don't get me wrong, six years ago during my rookie season when I was maybe a little too wild, hence the child I have, I had a damn good time, but now I'm a little older, a little wiser, and a little more banged up. Maybe a little boring.

When I reach the bathroom, I quickly take care of business, wash my hands, and take a look at myself in the mirror.

Fuck am I a pretty little lady.

Wanda, sparkling from glitter, pretty in pink, and shiny jewels for days. Even though I wouldn't trade this life for anything, I kind of feel like I'm in a rut. Like I should go put on some nineties mom jeans, perm my hair, and start jogging around with a fanny pack.

I can't remember the last time I went on a date, or even had a woman around. I don't fuck around on road trips, and I don't bring girls home because of Shea. So to say it's been a while is an understatement. Maybe that's the reason why I've been extra aggressive on the ice recently.

Sighing, I take one last look at myself, and exit the bathroom, just as my phone rings in my pocket again. Jesus, Greg.

Reaching into my pocket, I pull out the phone and see Chuck's idiotic face displayed on the screen.

What does he want?

I'm about to answer the phone when I'm bumped to the side by a slim shoulder. I really must be off my game, because I lose my balance and fall into the wall, knocking down a picture frame. Before it can hit the ground, I spin to catch it just in time as I hear someone from behind grunt.

When I turn to see who so easily pushed my six-foot-three stature to the side, I'm greeted by a woman maybe five inches shorter than me, her blonde hair curled and bouncing at her shoulders while her bangs pull my attention to her deep blue eyes. Her hand is cupping her cheek as she looks me up and down, humor lighting up in her features.

"Oh shit, are you okay?" I ask, even though I was the one who flew into the wall.

"I think so." She pulls her hand away and checks her palm then pats her face again. "This is the first time I've been bitch slapped by a fairy wing before, so I'm trying to see if you left any of your pretty fairy dust on me. I've never been tested to see if I'm allergic."

A slow, lazy smile spreads across my face. "I heard getting tested is an intense process where they dangle fairy wings over your face and every thirty seconds they lower the wings and give you butterfly kisses."

She tilts her head to the side, studying me intently. "From your knowledge of butterfly kisses, your obvious dress-up game, and the tiara that seems to fit you perfectly, I'm going to guess you either have a daughter, or are the best, most invested uncle or big brother on this planet."

"Daughter," I laugh. "She's five and I don't get to spend a lot of time with her, so when I do, I go all out."

"I can see that." The twinkle in her eyes that sparkles when she looks at me does something funny to my stomach, something I haven't felt in a while. "If it matters, I have to say, you're quite fetching in a tiara. It's very becoming of you."

"Do you really think so?" I pretend to primp my buzzed hair.

"Oh it's so you."

"Thank you." I rearrange the picture back on the wall and then hold out my hand. "Calder, also known as Wanda, the fairy princess."

Chuckling, she takes my hand in hers and says, "Rachel, also known as . . .hell, I don't have a fairy name, and now feel like I'm missing out."

"All the cool kids have fairy names."

"Apparently." She crosses her arms over her chest and looks me up and down. "You know, it takes a very confident man to strut around in your outfit."

"Confident or desperate to put a smile on his daughter's face."

"I think both." She eyes my hand and says, "From the lack of ring, I'm going to say there is no wife?"

"You're assuming right." Is she about to . . . ask me out? I don't think I've ever had a girl ask me out before. I've had women throw themselves at me because I'm a professional hockey player, but from what I can detect from Rachel, she for one doesn't recognize me and two, doesn't seem like the kind of girl who just throws herself at men.

"And there is no husband in the picture either?"

Laughing out loud, I shake my head. "Definitely no husband. Straight and single."

"Hmm." Her hand plays at the base of her neck as I await her next move. "Well, Calder, it was a pleasure meeting you. Don't forget to polish your tiara, a foggy headpiece is an ugly headpiece." She taps me on the shoulder and starts to walk away, leaving me in a wave of what the fuck.

"Hey, hold up." I jog after her and when she turns toward me, I'm hit with an unsettling yearning. For the first time in a long time, I actually want to spend some time with a woman, with her wit, with those beautiful eyes. Clearing my throat, I ask, "By any chance, would you be willing to go out on a date with Wanda?"

Shit, why did I say Wanda? The guys would just about roast me right now if they were hearing this conversation.

"Wanda?" She raises a questioning brow in my direction. Yeah, she doesn't want to go out with Wanda. I don't blame her.

Shucking the tiara and undoing my nipple covering, I tuck them in my back pocket and try to look like the masculine defender I am on the ice. Speaking in a deeper voice than normal, I repeat, "Would you like to go on a date with me? You know, since you asked about my relationship status and all."

Eyeing me up and down, the wheels spinning in her head, she says, "You know, I've never picked up a fairy princess outside of the men's bathroom before . . ."

Why do I feel like this is a moment that will forever be engrained in my memory, the day I tried to ask a girl out wearing a tiara and fucking fairy wings?

"Is that a bad thing?" I stick my hands in my front pockets and try to flex my arms at the same time, showing off my triceps. Yes, I've sunken to that level. I have to display any ounce of my masculinity I have.

Her lips twist to the side, it's evident she's trying to hold back a smile. "I think for a lot of women it is, but for me, I find it intriguing."

"Sooo . . . is that a yes?" I wait on bated breath for her answer.

"You know, Calder, I think it is."

A large smile spreads across my lips as I pull my phone out of my pocket, unlock it, and hand it to her. "Put your phone number in there and I'll call you tonight, how does that sound?"

"Call, huh? That's very old fashioned of you. I'm so used to a text, a call might be a little intimidating."

I shrug. "Old fashioned isn't a bad thing, just means under all this glittery dust and pink bedazzles, there's a real gentleman waiting to take you out."

She finishes typing her information into my phone. "A real charmer. My, my, my, I might just have scored myself a real winner outside the bathrooms of a donut and noodle joint. No one will ever believe me."

"Especially if you tell them the man you scored got your attention by bitch slapping you with his fairy wings."

She chuckles and shakes her head in disbelief. "You are so incredibly right. I might just have to make up a story. Maybe something like I met you outside the library, where I tripped and fell and you caught me and my books before we wound up diving head first into oncoming traffic. A hero, that's how I could describe you. A true, spur-of-the-moment, meant-to-be-there kind of hero."

I pull on the elastic of my fairy wings and snap it against my chest. "That's what I am, a true hero."

"I believe it." Her eyes soften. "You probably are to that little girl of yours." Patting my arm, she says, "I look forward to your call tonight. Until then, have fun with your daughter and don't eat too many donuts. I love a good set of abs."

Leaving with a brush to my arm from her fingertips, I call out, "A donut isn't going to change these abs, I can promise you that."

Walking backwards, she says, "We'll just have to see."

Well damn.

Commence countdown until Shea goes to sleep.

Chapter Two

CALDER

"Do I wear something nice?"

"What? Why would you wear something nice?" Hayden, my best friend and teammate asks. He's a rookie this season and even though I'm older than him and have more experience, we've quickly bonded through the season and now he's the guy I go to for everything.

"I don't know. It just seems like something I should do. I took a shower, so I smell good."

"Dude," Hayden deadpans on the phone. "It's a phone call. It's not an actual date, you're just going to be talking to her, it's not like you're going to be dry humping on your kitchen counter while she licks your Adam's apple."

"Have you had someone lick your Adam's apple lately? Why is that something you would say?"

Frustration comes through the line as he sighs. "I'm trying to help you here, man. There is no need to get dressed in anything nice, just make sure your dick isn't hanging out, because to me that seems a little inappropriate."

"Why is that inappropriate?"

"I don't know, you just met girl, talking on the phone with your dick out almost seems like something a pervert would do. Like she's telling you about her day and you're over there on the other end, legs spread on the couch, your nuts snuggling against the fabric, and your cock bobbing up and down, just doesn't seem right man."

Naked phone talk with someone I barely know does seem odd, not that I planned on being naked for the conversation, but from the "pretty" picture

Hayden just painted for me, I'm one hundred percent sure I won't be dangling my balls against the couch while talking to her.

"Yeah, I'll be sure to just put some sweats on." I sigh and run a hand over my face. "Why am I so goddamn nervous? It's a phone call. It's not like I'm going on an actual date with her tonight."

"Maybe it's because you haven't been interested in anyone for a really long time, someone you actually want to take out on a date."

"For good reason," I answer, thinking about Shea and all of my reasoning for putting my personal life on hold.

"She is old enough to understand that you're going to go on dates, that shouldn't be an issue anymore."

"I don't want her to become attached. Her mom has already made things tough on me, bringing a possible date into the mix will make it that much harder. Plus, our schedule is fucking insane, how am I really going to date someone when I'm barely home? And who the hell knows if this girl wants to be in the spotlight? Because you know the minute the media catches wind that I'm taking someone out, they're going to be all over her. I signed up for that kind of life but she didn't. I should really just call her and tell her never mind, or hell, maybe I just don't call her at all. Not get her hopes up, because you and I both know this is going to be a very bad idea."

I take a deep breath just as Hayden says, "Are you done?"

"This is a bad idea." I continue. "Besides the fact that I have no idea what to wear for a phone call anymore, I don't know what I was thinking trying to pick someone up while I was wearing a bedazzled tiara." I slouch on my couch and cover my eyes with my hand, trying to relieve the tension I can feel forming in my head. "What if she just felt pity for me? You know, look at the poor man dressed up like a lady, calling himself Wanda and flapping his fairy wings for attention. Maybe she was throwing me a bone."

"Dude—"

"And Hayden, she was hot. No not just hot, but beautiful. So fucking beautiful and she had a quick tongue on her, good sense of humor. And her body, tits for days man."

"Calder—"

"And who wants someone with a daughter? We're young, she probably has better things to do than be some pseudo-mom for my daughter, especially when I'm out of town all the time. And who's to say they'll get along? They might hate each other, and then what? I like this girl but can't go out with her because what happens if Rachel says she likes Paw Patrol more than Sophia the First? That's just asking for a living nightmare."

"Will you shut the fuck up," Hayden yells into the phone. "Fuck, man." His tone and agitation are evident from the huff of breath he takes before saying, "It's a phone call, that's it. You're not marrying this girl, she's not moving in with you, and she doesn't have to meet Shea any time soon. If you liked this girl, just take it one step at a time. I know you're a planner and you have a daughter to think about, but there is no need to do any worrying when you're just going to make a phone call. Take the first step man and worry about the rest later."

"I don't know." I drag my hand down my face. "Am I ready for this? Rachel, she's not a girl you take home for a night, you know? She's more than that. I haven't really dated since Shea was born, I haven't had time between her and hockey."

"And you're a lonely mother fucker who watches 90 Day Fiancé at night once his daughter is asleep. It's time, man."

He's right, I'm too invested in Antonio and Nikki's lives.

"You know I'm right, I can tell by the silence that you know I'm right, don't be shy, just come out and say it. Say Hayden, even though you're younger than me and are a rookie with one hell of a slap shot, you know more about life than I do."

Now he's stretching it.

"Pushing it with that slap shot stuff. I've seen better."

"Ha, okay man. Seriously though, stop coming up with excuses and just call her, alright? I can help you sort out the bullshit later, just go on the date and see where it goes."

Even though I'm apprehensive and careful of my personal life and the decisions that affect it, I can't help but think about Rachel and what it would be like to take her out on a date. I really want to see what makes her tick, why she would stop to talk to a guy in fairy wings and a tiara.

"Okay." I take a deep breath. "I'm going to get off the phone now and just call her before I tell myself not to bother."

"You know, you're really losing that alpha card you like to slap down in the locker room. If only the guys knew about this conversation . . . that and the tiara."

"And if you want me to continue to bring my mom's homemade brownies to the stadium for your eating, then you'd better keep your damn mouth shut." The threat rings truer to my personality than the indecisive man I've been over the last few minutes.

"Don't take my brownies . . . you animal." He chuckles at the exaggeration. "Your secret is safe with me."

"Damn right it is."

I say my goodbyes and hang up. Keeping my phone in my hand, I scroll to Rachel's name in my contact list and stare at it, willing the universe to telepathically send me an opening remark full of swagger that will make Rachel all fucking swoony and needy to go out with me.

But I get nothing. I'm drawing a blank.

Maybe it will just come to me . . .

Before I can lose the courage, I press dial and put the phone on speaker do I don't have to hold it up to my ear.

The phone rings three times before she picks up. "Hello?"

My breath catches in my throat and my voice comes out as more of a squeak than the voice of a manly hockey player with a set of abs that would put any body builder to shame.

"Hey." Clearing my throat, I try again. "Hey Rachel." There, that's better.

"Is this Wanda?" She asks in a teasing tone, a tone that puts me at ease.

"Why in fact it is. Were you impatiently anticipating my phone call?"

"On the edge of my seat." There is a teasing lilt in her voice. "So tell me," Her voice drops to a low, sexy tone, "What are you wearing?"

"Asking what I'm wearing already? Seems a bit forward, don't you think?"

"Never."

Laughing, I look down at my red, faded sweatpants and say, "Do you really want to know? I kind of expected to start this conversation out a little bit differently."

"I wouldn't have asked if I didn't want to know. Don't get shy on me now, Calder."

Chuckling, I answer with a hint of "seduction" in my voice, because I have to make sweatpants sound sexy somehow. "I'm wearing what I would describe as a sensual red sweatpant, a little racy, with no shirt, and no socks . . . eat your heart out."

She's silent for a second before she asks, "You didn't dress up for this phone call? I wore my blue sequined ball gown with white, glittery tulle, and you show up in a pair of ratty old sweatpants. What's that about?"

Even though I know she's kidding, I still feel a bout of sweat form on the back of my neck. I knew I should have worn something nice, like jeans and a button up . . . although, that seems pretty dumb to dress up for a phone call, now that I really think about it.

"Blue glittery ball gown with tulle, huh? Does that dress come with a pumpkin carriage as well?"

"Are you calling me Cinderella?"

"Well, I mean you have the blonde hair and the ball gown, just need to prepare myself in case you decide to run out on our date at the stroke of midnight."

"Oh no need to worry about that," she deadpans. "I never stay out past nine-thirty."

"Really?" That seems odd.

"No," she laughs. "But on school nights I call it an early night because I need my sleep when my days call for wrangling children. It's exhausting."

"Wrangling up Shea is exhausting, I can't imagine multiple kids. Does that mean you're a teacher?"

"I am. Kindergarten. Want to show me how you can count to fifteen and then backwards? I'll give you a scratch-and-sniff sticker if you nail it."

Chuckling, I start to relax. Talking to Rachel seems almost too easy.

"Scratch and sniff, huh? That's one hell of a prize."

"Root beer is the favorite amongst the kids which I have low stock in, so don't even try to ask for one."

"Wouldn't dream of it." I pause for a second before asking. "So about that date?"

"Yeah, about that . . ."

"When are you available?" I think over my schedule and cringe to myself when I recall all the nights I DON'T have off. This is going to be difficult.

"You tell me . . . Calder Weiss." Oh shit, she knows who I am.

"Do some Googling when you got home?"

"Talked to my dad actually. Told him I met a guy outside the toilet and he was wearing a tiara and his name was Calder. I said you were positively irresistible."

"Hell, you told your dad that?"

"Of course. I tell him everything. But in the midst of me describing the beauty that was your fairy wings and how they bitch slapped me, he interrupted me and asked for your name again. When I told him, he asked if your last name was Weiss and I told him I had no clue, which then spurred him to send me a text message with a picture attached and guess what? The picture was you."

"Imagine that." I chuckle.

"I asked him how he knew who you were, and can you believe he went on and told me you're some professional hockey player with a knack for ramming full-grown men into walls with what seems like zero effort?"

"Oh believe me, there is effort involved. They're not as light as they seem."

"Shocking." She laughs. "So, you're kind of a big deal in the sports world. Now that I think about it, before we went on winter break, I saw some kids wearing Brawlers jerseys with Weiss on the back."

I smile to myself. Knowing I'm a role model for little kids will never get old, it's why I try to conduct myself in the best way possible, especially when it comes to my daughter. Setting a good example is one of my top priorities, besides taking care of Shea.

"I wouldn't say big deal, but if you're looking for an autograph, don't think I'm just going to hand you one, you're going to have to earn it."

"Oh yeah?" There is humor and intrigue in her voice. "And how do you expect me to earn that precious autograph of yours?"

"I have a night off this Friday, go out with me."

"Mmm . . . I like how forward that was." She pauses and I hold my breath. "I think I can move things around so I can go out with you."

"Yeah? You can clear your schedule for me? I feel honored."

"As you should." God, I like her. "Okay, so text me the details and if you really like me, don't wear those ratty sweatpants on our date."

"Wouldn't dream of it."

"Good, see you Friday." Her voice drips with promise.

"See you Friday, Rachel. Have a good night."

I hang up and rub my fingers up the side of my jaw while staring at the wall in front of me that's covered in pictures of Shea from birth up until now. Frolicking in meadows, jumping in puddles, sitting in buckets, all personal photos I'd taken of my little girl. There's a bright, beautiful smile on her little, cherub face, a light in her eyes that would make any father proud. I've done well raising her, I'm not ashamed to say that, especially given the challenges of my job and schedule. I've pulled in every resource I had available to me and spent countless hours making sure Shea has a normal life, despite being raised by a single parent.

I'm tired, I'm spent, and I'm lonely.

Shea is thriving. She's kind, and sweet, and so goddamn funny—I created that. I've given her everything in me, the last five years of my life belonged to her and the Brawlers. I think it's about time I give some time back to me. I think it's time to do something for myself.

Snagging my computer from under the couch—not the best storage place, I know—I start searching for date ideas for Friday. If there is one thing I know, it's that I want to impress Rachel, and since I'm out of practice, I'm going to need a little Google magic to help myself out.

Chapter Three

CALDER

Rachel: Have you ever been slapped in the back of the knees with a hockey stick?
Calder: No, but the hamstrings, calves, and ass, yes.
Rachel: Did the ass slap hurt? I would think it would actually feel more kinky than painful. If I was slapped by the blade of a hockey stick, I would probably welcome another one < - - too much?
Calder: LOL. Never too much. I appreciate your honesty. Question, did you have to look up the term blade?
Rachel: Are you stalking my internet search history? If so, please ignore the searches on there for resale value of Beanie Babies.
Calder: I heard the tie-dye rooster is going for a thousand dollars.
Rachel: Seriously???
Calder: No.
Rachel: You bastard! The date is off!
Calder: No it's not, there's no way you can get out of it now. You've committed, there's no turning back.
Rachel: Damn it. You're right, there's no possible way I could stand you up . . .
Calder: Don't even think about it. You already gave me your address. If I have to, I will camp out on your lawn until you come out for our date.
Rachel: Challenge accepted.

Rachel: Do you eat breakfast every morning? Are you one of those guys who eats half a dozen eggs, downs a rainbow sherbet flavored protein smoothie, and grabs a Power Bar on the way out to your gym session?
Calder: If I said you were almost one hundred percent accurate with that assessment, would you cancel our date on Friday?
Rachel: Yes.
Calder: Then nope, don't eat breakfast every day, but when I do, it's about a donut for each finger. I dangle them like rings and nibble away at them in the morning, just to feel whimsical.
Rachel: That's my kind of man.

Calder: Have you ever gone skydiving?
Rachel: No, have you?
Calder: No, but I think we might on our date.
Rachel: You're joking right? You're drunk right now and have lost your damn mind. Tell me you've lost it, that you are truly certifiable at this moment right now.
Calder: Sober as sober can be.
Rachel: The date is REALLY off now.
Calder: I thought you had some adventure in you, maybe I read you wrong.
Rachel: Oh don't get me wrong, there is adventure in me, but I like to keep it to a minimum. Jumping out of a plane with a guy I met outside a place where humans deposit their excrement doesn't scream "best idea."
Calder: Jumping out of planes with strangers is America's new favorite pastime.
Rachel: Lies! America's new favorite pastime is taking pictures of their food and letting it get cold until they get the exact shot they want. Cold fries is America's favorite pastime, not plane jumping with bitch-slapping fairy men. Nice try, Weiss.
Calder: So I'm assuming that's a no to the skydiving.
Rachel: That's a hard no.

Rachel: Are you taking me to one of those wine-and-paint places? You know, where you get drunk and accidentally paint a nude-colored, phallic-shaped tree rather than what the instructor is teaching you to paint?
Calder: I take it you've been to one of those places before?

Rachel: I have two penis trees hanging above my fireplace. I named them Rueben and Jerry.
Calder: Are they . . . lovers?
Rachel: Who? Rueben and Jerry? Are you insane? Of course they're not lovers, they're brothers. God, what is wrong with you? Is that what you're into, incestual dick paintings?
Calder: I can't believe I gave myself away and you figured it out. God, I love some good brother dick-on-dick action . . .
Rachel: Okay, our date is REALLY, TRULY off now.
Calder: That's what you keep saying, and yet you continue to talk to me.
Rachel: Consider it a sick fascination.

Calder: Thoughts on laser tag?
Rachel: Thoughts on spending Friday night alone?
Calder: Noted.

Rachel: How many times have you searched "Fun dates in Philly" on the internet this week?
Calder: About seven.
Rachel: Impressive, I would have guessed twice that amount.
Calder: I rounded down.
Rachel: How far did you round down?
Calder: Little less than half.
Rachel: That sounds about right. Are you having a hard time coming up with something?
Calder: The hardest. There aren't many places that seem suitable for your ball gown-wearing self, who needs to be home by nine-thirty or else you turn into a ragged chambermaid.
Rachel: Don't forget pumpkin carriage parking, it's important that's added into the mix.
Calder: Believe me, I've called two places already asking if they valet pumpkins.
Rachel: Any luck?
Calder: No, but I have received a few numbers for psychologists.
Rachel: Can you pass those along? From the sound of it, I might need to talk to someone after this date. . .
Calder: As a parting gift Friday night, I will hand you a laminated card with their numbers.

Rachel: A man who laminates, now we're talking.

Calder: Hang up the ball gown and pull out your casual attire. I have our date planned and it doesn't require you to drown yourself in tulle.
Rachel: What about pearls?
Calder: No.
Rachel: Sweater set?
Calder: I would prefer something not so . . . stuck up.
Rachel: Let me guess, you're hoping for something along the lines of skinny jeans, tight shirt, heels, and a form-fitting leather jacket?
Calder: Now you're talking.
Rachel: Too bad for you I'm ironing my peasant dress as we speak in preparation for Friday. And if you're lucky, I might just don my bonnet.
Calder: Okay, I think it's my turn to cancel the date.
Rachel: DON'T YOU DARE!
Calder: I don't know . . . a bonnet?
Rachel: They're very fetching.
Calder: Yeah, I think I'm busy Friday night . . .

Rachel: (Rubs hands together) Are you ready for tonight?
Calder: I thought we cancelled.
Rachel: Please, if I can look past your fairy wings, you can look past my bonnet.
Calder: I guess that's fair. But for the record, I'm going to be sans tiara and wings tonight. Wanda will be nowhere near this date.
Rachel: But how on Earth am I supposed to recognize you then?
Calder: I'll be the guy in the navy-blue button up and dark jeans.
Rachel: Aw, you already picked out what you're going to wear.
Calder: After our phone call wardrobe mishap, I figured I better have an outfit picked out ahead of time, with a few backup options, just in case. I don't want to disappoint again.
Rachel: Smart man . . . oh shoot (snaps fingers) looks like my bonnet is still at the dry cleaners. What a shame.
Calder: Oh no, how can we possibly go on? < - - said with all the sarcasm I could possibly muster
Rachel: I can feel the disappointment from here. Alright, Wanda, I'll see you tonight. Can't wait. :)
Calder: Me neither.

Chapter Four

RACHEL

I TAKE ONE LAST LOOK IN THE MIRROR BEFORE I HEAD TO THE FRONT DOOR of my apartment. Hair is in place, makeup is on point, and my boobs look amazing. I'm wearing a high-cut shirt, but it's incredibly tight, perfectly framing my boobs under my snug leather jacket.

I'm nervous.

Yup, jittery, sweaty nervous. The worst kind.

I've been nervous since this morning when I was texting Calder. Knowing that I'm going out on a date with him tonight, with his charming sense of humor, it sets a ball of butterflies free in my stomach.

And it's not because he's a professional hockey player, or a celebrity, for that matter. I could care less about that.

No, I'm nervous because he seems like a larger-than-life man with enough confidence to rock me to my core. Hell, when I met him, he was dressed up like a fairy for his daughter, in public, completely and totally owning it while peeing into a urinal. If that doesn't scream confidence in his manhood, I don't know what does.

And what does confidence in one's manhood lead to? Oh I'll tell you . . . it leads to long, laborious, and mind-blowing nights in bed. Don't get me wrong, Calder attracted me with his sense of humor and unabashed humility, but that confidence, that confidence I see in his texts, yeah, that's what's causing me to shake in my heels.

Knock, knock.

He's getting impatient. But I don't feel ready.

I bite on my bottom lip and take a deep breath. "You can do this. Be charming, be flirtatious, and be you."

The pep talk feels foreign, since I really never do that, but for some reason, it has me puffing my chest forward and walking with a bit of a sway to my hips.

Opening the door, I plaster on a bright smile and cock my hip to the side, trying to put on a little bit of a show, but all the bravado I'd mustered up seconds ago quickly vanishes the minute I lay my eyes on Calder.

Standing before me, head tilted down, hand gripping the back of his neck, Calder is dressed in a navy-blue button up, sleeves rolled to his elbows, dark jeans—just like he said—and a panty-melting smile caressing those plush lips of his.

Oh hell.

I kind of wish Wanda had showed up.

"Hey there." He gives me a once over, that smile growing bigger with each passing glance.

Swallowing hard and gathering my wits, I say, "Hey." I shift on my feet, unsure of what to do next. Thankfully Calder is smoother than me.

He nods toward his car parked out front. "Ready? I don't want to be late."

"Sure." I snag my purse and start to walk out the door when Calder stops me.

"Uh, is that shirt stretchy?"

I glance down at my shirt and then back up at Calder. "Uh, what does it matter? Do you plan on stretching out my shirt?"

"Maybe a little. Does it stretch?"

Confused, I pull on the hem of it. "Yeah, I guess so."

"Good." He takes my hand and shuts my door behind me. "Let's go."

"Should I be concerned as to why you're asking about the stretch of my shirt?"

"Not even a little." Guiding me by the hand, he helps me into his black Range Rover and shuts my door. The seats are heated and immediately make me feel comfortable. New car smell still lingers, and I wonder how old his SUV must be. Can't be that old if he has a five-year-old. Believe me, I know all about five-year-olds and the smells they're able to create.

Calder hops in and roars the engine to life. He must have had my seat warmer on during his drive to pick me up. That's a thoughtful man right there. Take notes, ladies.

"Are you ready for this?"

"I'm not sure. I'm telling you right now, if you take me skydiving, I'm going to give you a swift kick to the nut sac."

He puts the car into drive and takes off down the road. "There won't be any extreme sporting tonight. We're going old school."

"Old school?"

He glances over at me and says, "Just you wait."

Zipping through the one-way streets of Philly, Calder drives with ease, one hand on the steering wheel, the other on the gear shift, looking powerful, sexy, and commanding. While he maneuvers his way to our destination, I take the time to really absorb him. His square jaw is freshly shaven, his dirty-blond hair smoothly shaven all the way down, the buzz cut looking incredibly attractive on him, and those eyelashes of his, criminal on a man. Not to mention the fullness of his lips . . . I wonder what they taste like?

"Are you a chocolate candy girl or a fruit candy girl?"

"Eh?" I ask, pulling myself away from his looks and into the conversation he's trying to have.

"Candy. Do you prefer chocolate base or a fruit-flavored base?"

"Oh. Hmm." I take a second to ponder his question. "Depends on my mood."

"What about tonight?" He switches his blinker on, looks over his shoulder, and pulls into a parking spot that's parallel to a CVS drugstore. "What is your mood telling you tonight?"

He puts the car in park, turns off the ignition, and faces me, the street lights casting an orange glow over us. "Tonight? I'm not sure. You're putting me on the spot. I don't even know what my choices are."

Shaking his head, he sighs and says, "Fine, come on."

He meets me around on my side of the car, helps me out, then locks up. We walk into the CVS and I'm seriously concerned about where this date is heading. If he starts buying blood-cleaning supplies and tarps, I'm out.

"CVS, wow, you sure know how to woo a woman," I joke, looking around the establishment, my eyes falling on the display of As Seen on TV products. Does that foot egg thing really work? You know, the thing that's supposed to get all the dead skin off your feet? It seems too good to be true.

"CVS is not our date, just the beginning."

"Are we getting supplies to kill someone? Because I don't think we went over our hard limits when it comes to dating. Unfortunately, murder is on the no-no list for me."

Not even sparing me a glance or a smile to let me know murder is OFF the table, he brings me to the candy aisle, where the bright colors of hundreds of candy bars stare back at me. This aisle is a child's dream and a parent's nightmare.

"Go ahead, pick out what you want."

"What?" I ask, looking at him. "Pick some candy?"

"Yeah. Whatever you want. Just know, we'll be having dinner, so don't get too much."

"And what's for dinner? Lucky Charms and milkshakes?"

He chuckles. "Yeah, that would be my daughter's dream dinner." He almost mutters the sentence halfway through, as if he's catching himself.

I press my hand against his arm. "You know, you can talk about her, right?"

"Yeah, I know." He lets out a long breath. "But I don't want to turn this night into a montage of everything adorable my daughter does because I could occupy your entire night about stories of Shea, and I really want this night to be about us, about something nostalgic I used to do before responsibilities and jobs, and being a dad came into my life."

"Sounds like a dream." I turn back to the candy. "Okay, so you have to give me some kind of information about where we're taking this candy. What I choose really depends on what we're going to do with it. I mean, are we playing fast and loose with this candy? Riding into the wind, candy bar in hand? Or are we taking it slow and easy, something where I can casually pop a few pieces into my mouth."

He nods in understanding. "Ah, I get you. You're very thoughtful when it comes to your candy."

"I have to be. I know I'm an adult and I can do whatever the hell I want, but it's not every day I get to dabble in the candy department."

"No?" He quirks an eyebrow at me.

I shake my head. "No, I have to keep up a great figure if I want to attract tiara-wearing fathers like yourself."

"If I wasn't so confident in my own skin, you'd be giving me a complex about my choice of headwear." Confident, oh believe me, I know.

Turning back toward the candy, I study it and ask, "So, what's the plan? You have to give me some kind of information."

"Fair enough." He sticks his hands in his back pockets and for the first time since I met him, he shows a small bit of insecurity, making him more relatable, more human, easier to breathe around.

Okay, maybe he's just as nervous as I am.

"I spent all week trying to come up with the perfect date for us. I looked into everything around the city, all the new fads and restaurants, and honestly, none of them seemed good enough. Hell, you wore a ball gown on our first phone call. How could I sit back and think you deserve a lesser date?"

"I am fancy." I primp my hair and give him a smirk.

"I figured, so I thought, why not play it completely old school?"

"I'm intrigued. What's old school to you?"

He reaches in his back pocket and pulls out two tickets. He holds them out to me and splays them with his fingers. In bold, black writing, right down the center, the tickets say "Die Hard."

Brow raised, I give him my best are-you-kidding look. "Die Hard?"

Chuckling to himself, he put the tickets back in his pocket. "Old-school dating, to me, is sneaking snacks into a movie and making out the entire time."

I snort and cover my mouth. Oh my God. "So when you say old-school dating, you don't mean old school as in 1950's gentlemanly actions, you mean . . . like high school dating."

"Is there anything better than high school dating?"

"A lot." I laugh, loving how his cheeks are starting to blush from his idea. "But I'm digging this. Still iffy about the make-out session, but we'll see where the night takes us." I turn back to the candy and start assessing what I want to grab. "Why Die Hard?"

Standing next to me, his shoulder brushing against mine, he says, "Seemed like the cheesiest thing to take you to, plus, I figured if I took you to the cheap theater that plays old movies, I have a higher chance of getting you to make out with me."

"How do you figure?"

"Because if you've seen the movie, it's not like you would be missing anything." Looking down at me, a boyish charm exuding from his smirk, he sheepishly asks, "Have you seen Die Hard?"

Crossing my arms over my chest, I hold my answer back for a few seconds, just to make him sweat a little. "Lucky for you and your endeavors to get me to make out with you, I have seen Die Hard."

Cutely, Calder does a small fist pump to the side, expressing his excitement over my answer.

"You know what's funny?"

"What?" he steps forward, his space invading mine, heating my body up to dangerous levels, like sweat levels. I don't want to be sweaty, not if he plans on making out with me, because I think you and I both know what happens during a make-out session: roaming hands. I love a good wayward hand that accidentally flicks a nipple, but what if I'm sweating and he grips the back of my neck, where it's all dewy? What an embarrassing nightmare that would be.

Trying to hide the affect he has on me, I answer, "You're a professional hockey player, very well known not just here in Philly, but around the country. Grown men would kill to have a make-out session with you—"

"That's weird."

"But true." He takes a second but then humorously nods. "So you have all these men who worship you, children who want to be you, and a giant bank account with over a million reasons as to why men, women, and children adore you so much."

"Your point?"

"Instead of taking me on a fancy date, you paid two dollars for a movie ticket and we're sneaking treats in so we don't have to pay for the up charge on movie theater goodies." I smile brightly at him. "I like that a lot."

"Yeah?" There is hope in his eyes.

"Yeah."

"So," he steps closer and grabs my hand with his. "Does this mean my chances of making out with you have grown exponentially?"

"I wouldn't say exponentially, but I would say you've gotten closer to at least a peck on the cheek."

"Damn." He grips his jaw and stares down at me. "I don't even have a peck yet? You're a tough crowd, but I'm willing to work for it."

"Good, because you're going to have to." I wink and start gathering candy.

Little does he know, he's not going to have to work that hard, because I don't think it's going to be possible to stay away from his lips for that long.

"IF YOU THINK I'm wearing that, you can think again."

"Come on, I can't wear it."

"You sure as hell can," I protest.

"Men don't get pregnant."

I look him up and down and say, "Men get beer bellies."

He looks down at his stomach and back up at me. "Sure, men get beer bellies, but star hockey players don't. I was on the cover of Men's Health, shirtless, sporting an eight pack last month. There is no way in hell I can walk in that theater with a beer belly."

How did I miss that issue of Men's Health? Note to self . . . subscribe!

"So when you were thinking old-school dating, you thought I would walk into the movie theater with a Styrofoam half circle under my shirt containing not a fetus, but a bag full of candy." Leaning forward in the car, I say, "You want me to give birth to chocolate in the movie theater."

Maybe a bit of an exaggeration, but never in my life have I ever seen this idea. And what's super cute—and it's weird that I think it's cute—is that when Calder told me about his idea, he was genuinely excited, as if we were about to pull a fast one.

From behind his seat, he brought forward a hollow Styrofoam half circle and held it out to me, giddy to see me pretend I'm pregnant so we can smuggle in all our treats. He said his brother and sister-in-law do it all the time.

I mean, it's a good idea . . .

"Is that why you wanted me to wear a stretchy shirt?"

"Maybe." His guilty look weirdly warms my heart.

Sighing, I stare down at the circle. "You're insane, you know that?"

"Insanely fun."

I chuckle. "God, this is ridiculous." I take the half moon, pour my twenty candy bars, Skittles, and Fun Dip in the shell and then stick it under my shirt. My shirt stretches around the little orb, and I'm relieved the only thing living inside my fake stomach is a toothache waiting to happen.

Laughing to himself, Calder asks, "Are you ready?"

"I'm going to get you back for this, you realize that, right? And your little make-out session is loooooong gone."

"We'll see about that." He exits the car and rounds the front where he opens my door. Holding out his hand, he helps me out. My hand instinctively goes to my fake belly, and I hold it in position.

I glance at my belly, not able to see my cute heels, and say, "Never in a million years did I think you would impregnate me on the first date."

As he closes the door, he starts laughing so hard, he starts coughing. I give him a few sturdy pats on his back, just to be nice, because honestly, what else do you do when someone chokes on their own saliva?

"Damn, I'm so good, I impregnated you without even taking your pants off."

We walk toward the older building that houses the cheap movie theater, Calder's hand on my back, his body especially close. "You know, I've heard of hot guys getting girls pregnant just from a picture on the internet, but I never thought it would happen in real life."

"Do you feel special?" His smile is so brilliant.

"Yeah," I rub my hands together. "Child support and the life of luxury here I come." I point my finger at him. "Don't you dare think I'm going to let you just walk away. You have responsibilities now, mister."

"Ahh, you're one of those girls, huh?"

"Better believe it."

Calder hands the guy at the front door our tickets that he picked up earlier in the day, then walks us into the lobby. There is red everywhere. Curtains, carpet, counters, tables, and chairs. Track lighting frames the baseboards and molding, and the concession stand worker is wearing an old hat and jacket like they used to wear back in the day. The poor kid.

There are two theaters. One is playing Happy Feet, and the other is playing Die Hard. The movies change every week to keep things fresh. Between the two movies for today, I'm glad he chose Diehard, because dancing penguins doesn't quite scream sexy. But Bruce Willis killing people, showing off his man-chest, now that's sexy!

When we reach the theater, I'm reminded how small the seating area is, and how tiny the screen is. I'm sure there are home theaters bigger than this place, but I'm kind of enjoying the intimacy. Calder picks a row with only two seats in the back. He takes the seat next to the wall and lifts the arm rest so there's nothing between us.

I see what he's doing, getting all snuggly.

Eyeing my "stomach" he says, "Are you ready to push?"

"Will you catch the baby?"

"Gladly," he chuckles.

Peeling my shirt up, I lift it over the "baby bump" and release the Styrofoam that Calder expertly catches by the dome so the candy is right side up and ready to be picked at. He sets the dome on the ground and says, "Look, the perfect bowl. It's useful in so many ways."

I have to give it to him, he's right. The damn thing is useful. I make a mental note to tell all my friends about this idea. Sorry movie theaters, maybe lower your concession stand prices and I won't have to be so stealth, with my fake baby bump.

"I hate how much I like this Styrofoam thing."

"Stick with me, babe, I have so much more to show you."

Oh damn, I hope he shows me with his tongue!

"DOES it sound like I'm ordering pizza?" Bruce Willis screams into a phone, making me chuckle.

I've worked my way through two candy bars; I kept it respectable, because I don't feel like gorging myself on the first date. Now the second date, I hold nothing back, but the first, I try to present myself in somewhat of a dignified manner.

Since the movie started, Calder has been very much to himself. He's kept to his side of his seat, leaning on the opposite arm rest, and he's been focused on the screen in front of him, not once giving me the idea that he remembers I'm on the date with him.

It's kind of weird actually, almost as if he's been all talk this entire time and when the moment is here, to make a move, he's choking. It's seriously odd.

What happened to the suave man with all the confidence? Right now, he looks like a guy who has never been on a date before, or someone who's so infatuated with Bruce Willis that—

Oh, hold on a second . . .

Calder shifts to the side, his shoulder brushing against mine now, his eyes still trained on the screen in front of us. From the corner of my eye, I watch as his hand slowly makes its way to the edge of his thigh, where my leg is brushing against his.

Is he going to make a move?

Wanting to make it easy on him, since he seems a little nervous despite his bravado from before, I move my hand close to his but keep it on my leg, not being too bold, just in case I'm looking too far into things.

Gunshots splash across the screen, Bruce Willis looking damn good in his white tank top, trying to defeat the Christmas Eve terrorists. The room lights up from the screen, giving me a quick view of Calder's hand moving even closer to mine.

When he said old school, he really meant old school didn't he? I don't think I've felt this kind of innocent anticipation since I was in high school and went on a date with Ricky Kingston, who took an hour to even look me in the eyes.

Holding my breath, I wait for his next move, and when his pinky reaches out and touches mine, an entire wave of euphoric heat shoots across my body. It's a pinky touch, just a pinky, but it offers so much promise of what's to come.

At first, he's hesitant, his pinky barely stroking my hand, but when I turn my hand over, wanting to clasp his, he doesn't initially take the offer.

Instead, he does something I wasn't expecting, something that has me squirming in my seat.

Carefully, almost feather like, he starts to brush his index finger over my palm, drawing lazy, slow circles, sending chills all the way up my arms and down my spine. It's a small movement, something that shouldn't have such a huge affect on me, but it does. Feeling his thick finger drag over my small palm has me thinking of all the other things he could do with that digit.

Now using all his fingers, he traces his fingertips up mine. His low-cut nails barely scraping along my skin, making the pads of his fingers feel so light, so unscathed, as if he doesn't hold a wooden stick in his hand for a living.

Up and down, up and down, his fingers sending me into a blissful state. I curve my hand around his, so my fingers touch the back of his, and that's when he clasps my hand and rubs his thumb along my skin, turning my hand over in his and resting our connection on my thigh.

He continues his slow, methodic movements, making the movie practically unwatchable because my mind is racing, wondering what he might do next.

Did he plan this? Did he do this little round about way of getting my attention on purpose? Is he slowly seducing me, turning me into a ball of putty?

If so, he's damn good at it. I mentally slow clap for him, because damn, I'm in all kinds of need for him.

Chapter Five

CALDER

I'M SO OUT OF MY FUCKING ELEMENT RIGHT NOW.

It's been five years since I've truly tried to impress a girl, truly cared enough to want to make her like me, and it's showing right now, because it's taken me a good portion of the movie to make my first move.

Hell, I've been all talk up to this point. Does she even know how nervous I am right now? How apprehensive I am about every move I make? I thought about taking her hand at the beginning of the movie but chickened out. I haven't paid attention to one second of this damn movie because I can't stop chastising myself for being a giant pussy where this woman is concerned.

Fuck, she's so cool, and witty, and funny. I've never met another woman like her, and the more I get to know her, the more I like her, making me fumble and act like a fucking teenage boy, hence the delay in hand holding. I might as well have yawned and stretched my arm over the back of her chair at the same time. That's the kind of "game" I have at this point. Completely pathetic.

When we had Shea and I became a single dad, the thought of jumping back into the dating scene never crossed my mind, not until I met Rachel, and now I'm kind of wishing I had a little bit of practice before meeting her, at least two other dates so I could fumble over someone other than Rachel.

Biting the side of my mouth, I try to decide what do to next. This hand holding thing is nice, but I feel like I need to step up my game, especially after seeing from the corner of my eye how much my little palm tracing affected her breath. It became slightly labored as her mouth parted open in an "O" shape.

Feeling the warmth of her thigh, I figure I should just go for it, jump right into stage two of whatever the hell you call this pre-pubescent perusal I'm doing. The back of my hand is against her leg, so I casually slip my fingers away from hers and turn my hand over, placing my palm over her skinny-jean-covered leg. I hold my breath, waiting for her reaction, waiting to see if she's going to slap me away, but she doesn't. Instead, she places her hand on top of mine, giving me reassurance that what I'm doing is okay.

Loving the way her hand is eclipsing mine, I start rubbing the inside of her thigh with my pinky and ring finger. Her hand grips mine tightly so I immediately stop, thinking I might have pushed too far, that's until her hand wanders over to my thigh—my upper thigh—where she rubs her palm up and down my jeans, just a few inches, but enough to have me squirming in my damn seat.

There are a few other couples in the theater, but they're all sitting in front of us, giving us all the privacy we need. Well, not all the privacy, but enough so they don't see the dance of wandering hands being conducted in the back row of the theater.

With every pass of her hand, it climbs higher and higher and closer to my crotch without actually touching me inappropriately, just enough to make me harder than a fucking stack of nails.

Fuck, I can't remember the last time a woman made me this hard in a matter of seconds, like fucking seconds. One pass up my thigh and my dick is knocking against the zipper of my jeans, looking for more attention.

I clear my throat and adjust myself in my seat, pushing down on my jeans because I'm really unsure of how to react. She adjusts as well, crossing her legs in my direction, her perfume wafting towards me, making me hazy with lust as John McClane shoots off his gun, acting like a total badass. It's a weird combination, being turned on while Bruce Willis does his thing, I just hope this doesn't turn into some Pavlov mind trick. If I start getting hard when I see Bruce Willis, I'm going to have a huge issue with that . . . no pun intended.

Hand still on my thigh, Rachel leans closer toward me so I take the opportunity to lift my arm up and around her shoulders. At first, I miss the contact of her thigh, but once she snuggles into my side, I couldn't care less about where my hand once was.

She feels so small up against me, so petite, and fragile, the complete opposite of her personality. She's bold and almost larger than life when you talk to her. I love the stark contradiction, it makes her that much more special.

And fuck does she smell good. Like honey and fresh mint, it's an addicting combination that has me taking deeper breaths to soak her all in.

She continues to rub her hand along my thigh and I continue to get harder and harder with each passing second. I'm biting my bottom lip to keep myself under control when she pulls on my shirt and looks up at me. I glance her way just in time to hear her say, "Thank you for taking me out tonight."

Smiling, I say, "Thank you for saying yes."

Her eyes go to my lips, just as her tongue peaks out and wets her mouth.

That's the universal sign, the open invitation for kissing, the one and only way besides saying it out loud to tell someone to kiss you.

I'm not so out of touch that I don't understand what she's asking, or the moves she's making. Does she sense my hesitation, my nerves? Can she tell I'm trying to figure this all out as I go? That I'm not as suave as I wished I was?

I sure as hell hope not.

Her eyes trained on me, the movie barely even noticed by both of us, I decide to take it to the next step, and if she wants to stop me she can, but from her signals, I'm thinking this is where this night is going.

With my hand that's not wrapped around her, I cup her cheek and inch her forward.

"Are you going to kiss me?" Her eyes search mine.

Wanting to be assertive, I don't answer her. Instead, I lower my lips and gently caress my mouth against hers. It's the lightest of touches, nothing overly sexual, just a general getting to know each other, gathering the lay of the land.

Soft and smooth, just what I thought she was going to be like, with a slight hint of urgency in the return of her kiss.

I pull away just as there is a huge explosion on the screen. I glance to see what's happening when Rachel turns my head back toward hers and presses her mouth against mine, taking me slightly by surprise, but I'm quickly put at ease once her lips start exploring mine.

Demanding but sweet.

She nibbles on my lower lip, parting my mouth open just enough for her tongue to touch mine. Fuck yes.

Wanting more, I turn in my chair so I'm facing her and grip her cheeks, locking her in place, giving her no wiggle room to retreat from me, and from the way she's leaning her entire body into mine, I'm going to assume she doesn't want wiggle room.

The way her eyes sparkle up at me, the way her lips part ever so slightly, and the tight grip she has on my shirt is a lethal combination that has me propelling forward, diving my lips into hers.

Instinctively, her lips part and my tongue finds hers, causing us both to quietly moan to ourselves. Mouths locked, tongues tangling, hands gripping, ready to wander, this is the old-school date I was hoping for.

There is something about making out with a girl, something so innocent about it, that has my balls tightening, begging for more.

I grab one of her thighs and drag my hand around her side to her ass, where I grip it tightly. Clad in jeans, and tight as fuck, I love the feel of her ass in my palm, how firm it is, but also soft. I squeeze tightly, sending her up and off her chair for a brief second.

I can feel her smile against my mouth, the humor a total turn on for me. She inches closer and I help her until she's straddling my lap.

Rachel is straddling my lap . . . in a movie theater, with Bruce Willis in the background.

Anyone could turn around and see the compromising position we're in, even possibly take pictures, but I couldn't care less at this moment. I can't remember the last time I did anything like this in public, and it's igniting an old flame inside of me, an adventurous flame, a throw-caution-to-the-wind kind of flame, a flame I would have kept burnt out, until Rachel came and set it on fire.

Her hands fall to my shoulders, my hands find her waist, and our lips meet in the middle as her core presses against my very aroused lap. Either she can't tell, or she doesn't care, because instead of making it known that she can feel just how turned on I am, her lips go back to work.

When I said I wanted a make-out session, I was hopeful at best, I didn't think it would actually happen, but now that it is happening, I tune everything around us out and focus on one thing and one thing alone: how perfect this feels, to have Rachel pressed against me, her lips branding mine.

I'm not sure this night can get any better.

RACHEL TOSSES THE STYROFOAM "BELLY" in the back seat and buckles up before turning toward me. When the movie ended and the lights came on, Rachel quickly scurried off my lap, leaving me harder than stone, and so damn turned on that I made her sit with me until I could calm myself enough to make the walk back to the car.

We haven't spoken a word to each other since we left the theater and now that we're in the car, it feels incredibly awkward that we haven't said anything to each other.

I grip the back of my neck and say, "So . . . you're a good kisser."

See that ladies and gentlemen? That's something someone who hasn't been on the dating scene for a while would say.

It seems so lame, so immature.

Chuckling, Rachel squeezes my arm. "You're pretty good yourself, and feeling how hard you were underneath me was a welcome little treat."

Oh fuck, she could feel me.

Swallowing as if my throat has compressed, I ask, "Yeah, you could feel that?"

"Hard not to when it was turning me on to no end." She bites her bottom lip. "You're big."

Cue the blush.

Fuck, guys should not blush, but for some reason, I fucking do. Thankfully it's dark enough in the car that she can't see how red I just got. I know I have a big cock and I've had women tell me I have a big cock before, but it was in the middle of fucking, so hearing the words spoken from someone else never truly affected me, not until now.

Awkwardly, I answer, "Uh, thank you."

"Like . . . really big, Calder."

I chuckle awkwardly. "Is that going to be a problem?"

"It might be, but that's not something we have to worry about just yet."

Damn, I wish it was.

Clearing my throat, I put my hands on the steering wheel and ask, "Are you hungry?"

"After our little make-out session back there, I would say so. What do you have in mind?"

"I have the perfect thing."

It doesn't take us very long to drive through the city—surprisingly—and the dating gods must love me, because I pull up to the restaurant and find a parking spot on the side of the street, only a block away. I was convinced we would be driving around for a bit, looking for a place to park.

"Is it weird that watching you parallel park is a turn on?" Rachel asks just as I turn off the vehicle.

"Um, maybe? That's the first someone has ever said that to me. Why is it a turn on?"

She gestures to my hands. "I don't know, but there's something about watching your forearms flex as you turn and reverse the car. You handle big machinery very well."

I'm tempted to give her a cheesy joke like, "I've been handling big machinery my entire life," but I refrain and hop out of the car. When I help Rachel out on her side, I catch another whiff of her scent, which just about knocks me back on the sidewalk of Philadelphia.

So fucking sweet.

So fucking addicting.

"I hope you like mac and cheese."

Rachel links her hand with mine, the gesture calming my racing heart. Why does it feel like she was made for me? Is that weird to think so early? There's just something about how she fits me so well, how when she was snuggled up against me in the theater, she was the perfect fit. And right now, holding her hand, it just feels so right it's almost startling.

"Mac and cheese is one of my top-five favorite meals, along with tacos, beef stroganoff, pot stickers, and burgers."

"Wow, you rattled those off pretty quickly."

Leaning into me, she says, "I'm going to let you in on a little secret, I like food and I'm not afraid to admit it. My dream job would be to travel the world and eat all the food while someone records all my yummy noises. Who wouldn't want to be paid to do that?"

"Someone with IBS?" I ask, no clue as to why. Believe it or not, I'm pretty sure IBS is on the list of things you don't talk about on a first date.

Standing tall, Rachel thinks about my suggestion. "I don't think you could be any more correct with that response. You're so right, IBS would ruin that job. Thankfully I don't have to worry about that. Next time I send in an audition tape for a traveling television show on Food Network, I will be sure to heavily emphasize that I do not have IBS. I'm sure that's a plus for them, not having someone run to the bathroom all the time, especially when filming."

Confused, I ask, "Have you auditioned before?"

"Just once," she answers, her fingers squeezing around mine. "I sent in an audition tape for Top Chef."

"Oh shit, really? You must be a really good cook."

"I'm not," she answers, "but I thought it would be fun to apply because if you never try, you'll never know what you can do."

"So that means you have at least some skills."

"Not even in the slightest. In my audition tape, I cut a potato with a butter knife. Not my finest moment, but oh hell, did I tear open that potato. By the end of my night in the kitchen, that potato was asking me what it could do to make my job easier."

I study her. "You really love exaggerating, don't you?"

"One of my favorite pastimes."

"Good to know." I chuckle and open the door for her, the smell of melted cheese consuming us. Damn that smells good. Not as good as Rachel, but pretty damn close. "Have you been here before?"

"Never, and now I'm hating myself for it because from what I can tell, this is my new Mecca." She releases my hand and goes straight to the counter, where she starts chatting with one of the employees. She's animated with her hand gestures and speaks with such enthusiasm . . . about mac and cheese. It's adorable.

Walking up behind her, I put my hand on her hip and listen to their conversation.

"Are we talking crispy bacon? It's got to be crispy if it's on top of mac and cheese."

"It's the crispiest, ma'am. I agree with you, soggy bacon is a travesty, especially when mixed with noodles and cheese."

"Amen." Rachel waves her hands in the air. "I'll take the BBQ Bacon Bowl then." Leaning her head back, she asks, "And what would you like, big guy?"

Big guy? Jesus.

"I would like the Crabby Mac Bowl please and two drinks." I pull out my wallet and hand the guy some money while Rachel snuggles in close to me.

"We're on our first date." Rachel coos up at me. "Can you tell?"

The cashier smiles up at us and when he looks me in the eyes, his mouth drops open and he starts to point. "You're . . . you're Calder Weiss. Oh man, your game last night, when you slammed Declan into the wall, stole the puck, and shot it down to Holmes for that goal, dude, I re-watched that at least five times in a row. He had no idea you were coming for him." He reaches his hand out. "Can I just shake your hand? Would that be alright? Just give me a sturdy shake."

Chuckling, I reach out and take the guy's hand. "Thanks for watching the games, man."

"I never miss one. Even when I'm working here at The Mart. We have the game going on in the back." He looks at me in disbelief, still holding onto my hand. "Man, this made my night. I'm so glad I work here now. Shit, I might start crying."

Casually slipping my hand from his and placing it on Rachel's lower back, I say, "No need to shed tears man. Hey, how about you give me your information on the receipt and I'll be sure to send you over some tickets."

"Are you fucking kidding me right now?"

Rachel giggles next to me. "No, it would be my pleasure."

The kid rips paper from the receipt printer, pulls the cap off a pen, and starts writing frantically. "Holy shit, holy shit, holy shit. Calder Weiss is going to give me tickets. I can't fucking believe this." Holding out the paper, he hands it to me then oddly bows, clasping his hands together. "Thank you. Holy shit, thank you. This made my year."

"It's no problem. I put the receipt in my wallet and give him a small salute. "I'm going to try to woo my date now, but have a good night."

"You too." The kid has tears welling up in his eyes and before he can set them free, I guide Rachel to a table and chairs, away from the potential crier. I like fans, I really enjoy them actually, but when they cry, that just makes me feel weird. I don't think anyone should be crying over me.

I pull out her chair for her but before she sits down, she places her hand on my arm and says, "That was super sweet of you, to send that guy tickets. You truly made his day."

"It was nothing." I try to shake off the compliment, because I just did what any other professional athlete would have done, or at least should have done.

"No, it was everything." Standing on her toes, she presses a kiss on my cheek and takes her seat.

Heat billows at the base of my stomach as I take a seat next to her, spreading my arm over the back of her chair, not really sure what to say. Thankfully, Rachel is talkative.

"So, since you're handing out tickets and everything . . ."

I laugh. "Would you like to go to a game?"

"I would love to. I've never been to a game before, so it would be really exciting."

"We have a home game tomorrow; do you want to go?" I hold my breath, wondering if that's too presumptuous, too quick, but when she smiles brightly and claps her hands in excitement, I think differently. She is genuinely excited.

"Oh I would love to. That would be so much fun."

"Do you want me to get a ticket for your dad, since he knew who I was?"

"Are you serious?" She presses her hand on my thigh and right about now, I would do anything she wanted just to keep it there.

"Yeah, of course. I'm assuming he would want to go."

"Are you kidding me? He would die. Oh my God, look at me, I'm being just like that guy back there."

"Nah, I think that guy was ready to kiss—"

Rachel leans over and presses her lips against mine, her hands gripping my shirt, her tongue pressing into my mouth. I grip the back of her neck, my fingers tangling with her hair while her tongue dances with mine in the most intimate way. Just like in the movie theater, I start to get hard, but before I can get comfortable with the way her mouth is moving across mine, she puts unwanted distance between us, her hand cupping my cheek, her eyes incredibly sincere as she says, "Thank you, Calder."

Clearing my throat, I twirl a piece of her blonde hair with my finger. "Of course. Hell, I'll get you all the tickets if that's the kind of thank you I get."

"Don't push your luck."

I hold my hands up. "I wouldn't dream of it." Chewing on the side of my cheek, I think for a second before saying, "You know, if you want, after the game we can go out, maybe grab a drink with my buddy, Hayden."

She raises a fucking cute eyebrow at me. "Are you asking me out on a second date, Calder Weiss?"

"I think I am. What would you say to that?"

She leans back in her chair, assessing me. "Let's see, you've been a gentleman all night, aside from the blatant ass grabs in the movie theater. You make me laugh, and are very handsome. You are a safe driver, which is important since you have a daughter, and you have a huge cock. Hmm . . ." she scratches her chin. "I think I'm going to say yes."

Laughing, I shake my head. "It's the big cock that got you, wasn't it?"

"Nope, it wasn't the big cock, that's just the cherry on top of the cake."

"Then what was it?"

She presses her lips together, giving my question some serious thought. "Honestly? It's the way you treat people. Your daughter, you dress up for her. The guy at the theater, you asked him how his night was going. The boy at the register back there, you're giving him free tickets. You're a genuinely sweet, kind, and giving man. It's a very attractive quality."

"Thank you." I look down at my hands.

"And that right there." She pokes my cheek. "The way you blush, it's hot. You're this confident, attractive man, but you can blush as red as a tomato in seconds. Some women like a cocky son of a bitch, not me, I like my men sensitive, sweet, and animals in bed. I know the first two are true, waiting to find out about the third." She wiggles her eyebrows.

This woman, she has me by the fucking balls, and quickly. It's scary how much I like her, and it's not just because she's smart, funny, and keeps me on my toes. It's the way she can easily pick out my best qualities, the qualities I take great pride in.

Leaning closer, I bring my hand to her hip and whisper in her ear while squeezing her. "I'll tell you right now, you will be more than pleasantly surprised by the third quality you're looking for." I bite down on her earlobe. "You can count on it."

"Oh sweet heavenly mother . . ."

Chapter Six

RACHEL

"THANK YOU FOR TONIGHT, I HAD A LOT OF FUN."

Calder squeezes my hand, his thumb still rubbing my skin, the feeling so comforting. "So did I, especially when you manhandled me in the movie theater and took advantage of me."

"Excuse me?" I put one of my hands on my hip. "Manhandled? Took advantage? You were the one begging to be made out with before we even got to the theater, I was just throwing you a bone."

He raises both eyebrows, his forehead creasing with surprise. "Throwing me a bone?" There is humor lighting up his voice. "Are you saying . . . you felt bad for me?"

I shrug, not committing to his statement and loving the way he's so easily joking around with me, how comfortable he feels. We've spent a few hours together, but it almost feels like we've known each other for years.

"I see." He releases my hand and steps away, pulling on the back of his neck while staring down at me. I'm about to take back my teasing when he pins me with one of the most consuming and sexy looks I've ever seen. Eyes dark, heady, full of lust. His body powerful, heaving, ready to pounce. His lips wet, desirable, addicting.

Stepping forward, in one motion, he pins me against the door of my apartment, his hand to my hip, the other one by my head. His gaze locks on mine, the air suffocating me with his scent. His chest is so close, his head mere inches away, his lips glistening and ready.

I'm aware that we've already made out, that we've explored each other's mouths all night, but right here, right now, this feels more intimate than anything we've done thus far.

"I don't like it when people take pity on me, Rachel." His voice is low, sultry, so freaking smooth. "I want a woman to want to kiss me, I don't want her throwing me a bone."

He knows I'm joking, there was so much humor in his voice a few seconds ago, but right now, it almost seems like he's trying to prove a point, and oh boy, am I going to let him.

"Not only do I want a woman to want me, but I want her to crave me, to want to breath the same air as me."

"You want them obsessed?"

He nods. "I want to consume them so I'm the only thing they can ever think about."

"That's pretty cocky of you, isn't it?"

He shakes his head. "No, because I know when I'm with someone who I really like, someone who makes me laugh and smile, and someone who challenges me . . . someone like you, I will feel that exact way about them. I'll be consumed by their scent, by their smile, by the way they gently take my hand in theirs. I'll crave to hear their voice, to make them laugh, to catch a quick glance in my direction. They will be the only person I think about, the only person I want to hear talk on the phone, and the only person I want to see at night."

I take in a deep breath, my lungs feeling shaky and my heart beating a mile a minute.

Calder's eyes burn a path down my shirt, back up my neck, to my face, where he gently licks his lips and leans forward, his mouth a centimeter from mine.

"I like you, Rachel, I like you a lot. You're someone I can get lost in, easily, without even trying." His lips skip my mouth and direct back again, where he whispers, "Have a good night. I'll see you tomorrow."

And with that, he pushes off my door and without a retreating glance, he takes off, hopping in his car and driving away.

My hands are pressed against the door behind me, granting me balance. My heart is nearly beating out of my chest while my lungs try to recover from the lack of oxygen inflating them.

On shaky legs, I make my way through my apartment and straight to my bathroom, where I grip onto the counter and look at myself in the mirror. There is a light smirk on my face, my eyes seem brighter, clearer, and there is a warm feeling inside my stomach—it's all fluttery and gooey and excited.

God, I like him.

Scratch that, I'm borderline infatuated with him.

And that whole speech back there? He's unlike any man I've ever met. One second he's wearing fairy wings and a tiara for his daughter, and the next he's handing out free hockey tickets to an unsuspecting fan, and then he's pushing me up against my apartment door, telling me all the things that make me swoon and swoon hard.

There's no denying it, I'm more than thrilled with my bladder, because if it wasn't for its inability to hold onto one more ounce of Coke Zero the other day, I never would have run into Calder.

This is life-changing, I can feel it. You know how you can sense when something is so right deep, down in your bones? That's what I'm feeling. This is so right.

Rachel: Are you still awake?
Calder: Yeah, staring at the ceiling. I feel like I can still smell your perfume on me.
Rachel: You didn't take a shower?
Calder: I did, I had to . . .
Rachel: What does that mean? (Gasp) Did you . . . pleasure yourself?
Calder: Isn't it a little early to be sexting?
Rachel: It's never too early to sext, and I'm not sure this qualifies as sexting, more of an informative text. So, did you wank off?
Calder: Didn't really have a choice. Do you not remember straddling my lap tonight? I swear to God, I can still feel you on top of me, barely rocking back and forth.
Rachel: It took all the energy in my body not to dry hump you right there while Bruce Willis saved the world.
Calder: You held back? That was you holding back? Damn, I can't imagine what you would be like full force.
Rachel: I very well might be too much for you.
Calder: I'll be the one who decides that.

Calder: Good morning, beautiful.
Rachel: Beautiful, is that your pet name for me? We've only been on one date and you're using pet names already?
Calder: Not a pet name, just a . . . uh . . . term of endearment?
Rachel: Oh okay then. Good morning, prickly penis.
Calder: Prickly penis? Uh, how is that a term of endearment?
Rachel: I have no idea, it's legit the first thing that came to mind.
Calder: Well that's concerning. Especially since you were pressed up against my penis last night. Did something sharp snag you?
Rachel: If something sharp sprouted from your penis last night and "snagged"

me, you can bet your beefy forearms I would have said something about it. I'm not one to be snagged by a penis and not say anything.
Calder: You're right, you definitely don't seem like someone to go quiet after being penis snagged.
Rachel: You get me. You so get me.

Calder: Tickets are being held at will call for you, under the name, prickly penis.
Rachel: They are not!
Calder: . . .
Rachel: Calder Weiss!
Calder: I thought that was our pet name for each other.
Rachel: *You're* prickly penis, I'm beautiful. How could you possibly get those two confused?
Calder: Hmm, my bad.
Rachel: Are the tickets really under prickly penis?
Calder: If they are, what will happen to me?
Rachel: I'll make your dick eat a cactus to ensure it really is prickly.
Calder: (Runs to will call)
Rachel: Smart choice, Mr. Weiss, smart choice.

Rachel: I just ate a protein bar. I never eat protein bars, but for some reason, I thought maybe if I eat a protein bar, in some cosmic way it will make you bigger and stronger for your game tonight.
Calder: You know, I picked up a car in the parking lot today and tried to understand where that incredible strength came from.
Rachel: It was me! You're welcome.
Calder: You very well might have to eat a protein bar for me every day now if it gives me those kinds of super-human strengths.
Rachel: But it was so chalky.
Calder: But it gave me car-lifting strength.
Rachel: (sigh) Fine, stick one in my mouth, maybe sucking on it will help.

Rachel: I know you're probably in game mode right now, but I wanted to say thank you for the tickets, my dad is in heaven right now, and good luck. Go kick some ass.

Calder: Thank you. Glad you got the tickets.
Rachel: Glad there was no prickly penis involved.
Calder: It was tempting, believe me it was tempting.
Rachel: I'm sure. Thank you again, I can't wait to see you after the game.
Calder: Counting down the minutes. Enjoy the game. See you in the family suite afterward.
Rachel: Pummel some ass!

CALDER SKATES ACROSS THE ICE, determination in his movements, and slams into the glass, his opponent being the cushion for his check. The sound of them both hitting the glass, followed by the roar of the crowd, sends shivers up and down my spine.

He's hot.

Yup, Calder Weiss is extremely hot on the ice.

And it's not just because I know the man outside of the rink and minus the giant pads on his body. His current hotness is distinctly superficial. There is nothing I can say to keep this from sounding superficial, but there is something about a grown man, playing a sport at the highest of levels, owning the game, taking charge, that turns me on so hard.

Like, I've been clenching my thighs this entire game because every time I look over at Calder, a long, deep yearning takes root inside of me. Oh, I want him, and I want him bad.

And the worst part about all of this is I can't even sit here with my shirt up and over my breasts, flashing Calder just for the hell of it. Do you know why? Because the frog-like man cheering next to me is my father. And how awkward is that, to tell your father how turned on you are by watching a grown-ass man play hockey? Pretty awkward.

"Wooohooo!" My dad fist pumps the air then shakes my shoulder for the hundredth time. "What a game, what a game!" He clasps his hands together and shakes them, almost as if he can't believe he's sitting in the stands right now.

The Brawlers, Calder's team, is up by three goals thanks to Calder's superior defense and their goalie's uncanny ability to do the splits every other shot made at him. I kind of want to yell, "We get it, you're flexible!"

"I'm glad you're having a good time, dad."

"And your boy, look at him go." He shakes his head. "I wouldn't want to be caught in an alley with him. He looks really big in person, is he? I've only seen him on television, but even from this vantage point, he looks like a destroyer."

If only my dad knew the kind of sensitive and caring man Calder really is.

But in real life, not on TV, Calder is huge. Larger than life, almost, with his broad shoulders, tapered waist, and long, thick legs only someone who's grown up skating back and forth on ice would develop.

"He's very large."

My dad slaps his hands together. "I knew it."

I hold back the roll of my eyes.

"And he's nice? He was nice to you last night? Treated you like a gentleman would?"

"Yes, dad." I smile to myself, loving how he's still protective. Balding and older than ever, my dad, despite his age, still has a little spark inside of him, and there is no doubt in my mind that if given the opportunity, my dad would kick butt for me if he had to. "Calder is super sweet and thoughtful."

"Not an asshole? You know all I hear about athletes is their penchant for having gaggles of women surrounding them. Is he a cheater?"

"No." I scrunch my brow together. Honestly, I don't know the true answer to that, but from what I gathered last night and through our texts, Calder is not the type of man who would cheat.

"Ohhhhhhh," the crowd erupts as Calder slams into another opponent, this time, with his right shoulder leading the way. They both fall to the ice, the puck sputtering away.

I keep my eyes trained on Calder and watch as he slowly gets up from the ice. He rotates his shoulder in small circles before his coach changes the line.

Concerned, I watch Calder speak with a trainer and try to stretch out his shoulder while spraying water all over his face, trying to cool down from the fifteen pounds of gear he has to wear. I think it weighs something like that, at least that's what Wikipedia told me, and you and I both know how reliable that is.

"Looks like Calder is hurt," my dad points out, standing on his toes, trying to get a better look.

"That was a pretty hard hit." I bite the side of my lip. Is he going to be okay? I sure as hell hope so, because I have plans for him. Wicked-hot plans that require him to be fully functioning.

Chapter Seven

CALDER

A HISS ESCAPES MY MOUTH AS I ATTEMPT TO PUT ON MY BUTTON-UP SHIRT. I'm fucking sore, sore as hell. And even though I sat in ice for twenty minutes, hating that I had to make Rachel and her dad wait, I'm still sore.

I sent a text to Rachel, letting her know I was getting some extra treatment after the game and that I'd sent someone to bring them to the friends and family suite until I was done. She texts back with a heart emoji. It was simple, yet made me feel so damn special.

We ended up winning the game by four goals. Hayden was on fire tonight, it was a memorable game for him, especially because he scored a hat trick. The first hat trick of his rookie season. There will be lots of celebrating tonight, that's for sure.

"You're going to O'Houlihans, right?" Hayden asks, tying his tie around his neck.

"Yup. I'm going to go pick up Rachel and her dad and meet you there. Grab us a booth in the back?"

"Not a problem. I'm going to say a quick hello to my family and then head on over. Want me to order you a beer?"

"Nah." I button up my shirt. "I'll wait to see what Rachel and her dad want."

"Sounds good." Hayden grips my good shoulder. "Everything okay, old man? That shoulder going to hold out?"

"Yeah, just a little sore, it should be okay with some more ice and ibuprofen."

"Okay, see you at the pub." Hayden takes off.

I take a few extra minutes, struggling with my shoulder, taking deep breaths with each movement. A few more ibuprofens, some Icy Hot, and rest, and I'll be better in no time.

Hurrying along, I grab my belongings and head out to the family suite, my nerves taking hold of me. My brother is being brother of the year right now and watching Shea for me, once again. When I asked him for the second night in a row, he wanted an explanation, so I had to tell him all about Rachel. His reaction was exactly what I expected: elation. He was so damn excited to hear that I was going out with someone that he even offered to keep Shea overnight. Now that's a good brother.

As I make my way through the hallways, employees and media congratulate me on the win. It was a team effort, that's for sure.

When I reach the family suite, I immediately spot Rachel—it's hard not to, with her bright blonde hair and gorgeously blue eyes. She's standing next to an older, bald gentleman with an impressive beer belly given how small his frame is. I'm going to assume he's her father, even though they look nothing alike. Straightening up, I push forward, butterflies lighting up inside me. It's been twenty-four hours since I've seen her, and it almost seems longer. Talk about infatuation at first sight.

When she spots me approaching, her face immediately lights up and for a brief moment, it almost looks like she's about to propel herself forward and throw herself into my arms, but she stops herself and instead clenches her hands at her side and bounces in place. It's a subtle bounce, but noticeable enough to make me grin like a damn fool.

Do I kiss her as a greeting? Do I just wave? Do I give her a hug? I have no idea, I don't want to be awkward in front of her dad. We've only been on one date, what's the protocol for that?

"Great game," Rachel says, reaching out to me and pulling me into a hug. My shoulder strains under her hug and I have to bite down on the inside of my cheek to keep from making any noise.

"Thank you." I give her an awkward pat and turn to her dad. "You must be Rachel's father."

"Staff Sergeant James Perry." He grips my hand tightly, showing me that even though he's sporting a cue ball of a head and a portly belly, he's still got a little bit of gusto in his grip.

"Mr. Perry, it's wonderful to meet you. I hope you enjoyed the game."

"Splendid game. You gave those boys some really good shots."

I grip my bad shoulder. "Yeah, did a little too much bruising, if you know what I mean."

"Can't run into a wall and think it's not going to hurt."

"Well said." I chuckle. "Have you been a Brawlers fan for a while?"

"Ever since I can remember." Mr. Perry looks around. "This has been a surreal night for me, so thank you." Facing me again, he becomes stern. "But don't think you're going to win me over with your fancy hockey team. You still have to treat my daughter well to gain my approval and respect."

"I wouldn't want it any other way, sir."

Mr. Perry nods his head in approval and then takes a look at his watch. "It's late, I best be heading home."

"Oh, I was going to take you and Rachel out for some drinks."

"I'll take a rain check if you don't mind. You two go have fun. But can I ask you to drive my daughter home safely?"

I glance in Rachel's direction and then level with her father. "You have my word, sir."

"Good man." Reaching out, he shakes my hand again then pats me on the shoulder, causing me to wince. "Have fun, kids."

Without a parting glance, he takes off, making his way through the crowd and almost running into a wall when he spots one of our forwards speaking with his family.

Pulling on my hand, Rachel grabs my attention. "Are you okay? You winced when my dad touched your shoulder."

"Just a little banged up, nothing you need to worry about." I take a look behind me to make sure her dad is gone before I grip Rachel at the waist and pull her in close. She wraps her arms around my neck and stands on her toes to press a kiss against my lips.

"Hey, there."

"Hey." That smile she garners from me reappears, spreading across my face.

"Can I tell you something?"

"Always," I answer, loving the way she fits so easily in my arms.

"Tonight, watching you out on the ice, I don't think I've ever seen anything so sexy. That was until you showed up in this suit."

"Yeah?" My eyebrow rises. "You like the suit?"

"It's super hot. Tailored so well to your body that I can still see your muscles, but it also has me begging for you to reveal just a tiny bit of skin."

"If you're lucky, maybe I will." I wink and link my hand with hers, leading her out of the building and straight to my car. It's time to get some drinks.

"HAYDEN, this is Rachel. Rachel, this is Hayden Holmes, our all-star rookie and a good friend of mine."

"Aw," Rachel coos. "Whenever I've been introduced to a guy's friends, there's always some ribbing involved, but you were very complimentary."

I shrug. Should I have thrown some kind of friendly barb in there? Maybe, but nothing really came to mind.

"He loves me too much—he's kind of infatuated with me, actually," Hayden says, shaking Rachel's hand and offering a seat in the booth across from him.

"See, that's what I was expecting." She takes a seat and I slide in next to her. Gripping my thigh, she says, "This guy though, he's just a giant sweetheart, isn't he?"

"A real teddy bear, that guy. Did he ever tell you about the first away trip we had? What he did for me?"

Where is Hayden going with this?

"No he didn't, what happened?"

Nothing, as I can recall, but I can't wait to hear what Hayden has to say.

Taking a sip of his beer, he swallows and says, "It's a scary thing, being a rookie on a professional hockey team. There is some light hazing, stupid shit like having to wear lady pajamas at night, real idiot things like that."

"Lady PJs? Did you wear some?" Rachel asks me.

"Lavender silk ones, one of the best nights of sleep I've ever had."

"I wore flannel, kind of wish I went with the silk," Hayden adds, causing Rachel to laugh. A waitress brings the drinks we'd ordered at the bar, handing both me and Rachel a Guinness. I'm kind of impressed with her drink choice.

She takes a sip, a bit of the foam sticking to her upper lip before she swipes it away with her tongue. "So, what happened your first night."

"Yeah, what happened?" I egg Hayden on and he leans back in his booth, a giant smile on his face.

Oh he's getting ready to tell one epic story, I can feel it.

"It was after the game, the guys decided to go out and celebrate our first on-the-road victory. Being a rookie and wanting to fit in, I relished in the ability to celebrate with my boys, especially since I'd scored one of the goals to help us win."

"Naturally," Rachel adds.

"Now when you think of hockey players celebrating, what do you think of?"

Oh shit, I know where he's going with this. "Eh, we don't have to tell this story."

Rachel turns to me, her eyes burning me with their gaze. "Oh, I'm pretty sure he does have to tell this story. Hayden, please proceed."

"Like I was saying," Hayden smiles at me over his beer. Shit, I lean back in the booth and put my arm around Rachel, and she snuggles into it. "What kind of celebration would you expect from a hockey team after a win?"

Rachel gestures around the pub. "Not to be stereotypical, but I would expect this, beers in some pub. Maybe a nacho platter split amongst two ravenous guys."

"Exactly, but not this night, instead we went to a place I least expected . . . FroYo."

"Huh?" she asks, a pinch in her brow.

"We went out and got frozen yogurt."

"Like . . . what teenage girls take pictures of on their Snapchat? What women burn calories for? Frozen yogurt?

"Yup," Hayden nods slowly, the opening of his beer resting on his lower lip. "Frozen yogurt, and the kind where you pay by the weight of your cup."

"The kind where you get to pick from a million toppings?" Rachel leans forward, really getting into the story."

"That exact kind of place."

"Well, that sounds delightful, what could be so wrong with that?"

Hayden shakes his head. "All the things, Rach, all the things." He takes another sip of his beer and sets it on the table. "Let me ask you this, have you ever wondered what it would taste like if you not only picked up the biggest cup, but filled it with every ice cream . . . and every topping?"

"Nooooo," she drags out."

Hayden presses his lips together and nods. "Yup. As a rookie, I didn't get to make my own FroYo cup, it was made for me and I had to sit there and eat it all. So you can understand how much we're talking about here, my cup alone cost over twenty dollars."

"Oh my god," she chuckles. "You had to eat that entire thing?"

"Yup and it was fucking nasty. You know how as a kid, you would fill up your soda cup with every flavor at the fountain machine and it would form this magical concoction that was so damn good, you went back for seconds and thirds?"

"Of course, I always topped mine off with orange soda."

"Smart girl," Hayden points at her. "Well this was the complete opposite. All the flavors combined was not only a diabetic coma, but it was fucking nasty, especially when the ice cream turned into soup." He shivers. "So fucking gross."

"So you ate it all, then what happened?"

"That's where your little friend comes into play." Hayden nods at me. "He was the one to help me back to my room, he was the one to get me water when I was puking in the hotel toilet, and he was the one who . . ." Hayden eyes me, his smile so damn cocky. He's waiting for me to stop him, but I don't, instead I let him expose me. "And he was the one who laid next to me in my bed, whispering into my ear that everything was going to be okay, and when I asked him to rub my belly, he did, for an hour. He just laid there, rubbing my sicky belly, which was what he called it."

"That's what my daughter calls it," I defend myself as Rachel laughs next to me.

"You rubbed his belly?" Rachel asks incredulously.

"He asked me to. What was I supposed to do? Let the man suffer? That's not fair. He's one of our top-scoring men. I wanted to make sure he was taken care of. I wasn't just going to leave him there with a sicky belly."

"Oh my god, this is too ridiculous."

"But sweet, right?" I ask, cringing.

Rachel presses her head against my good shoulder. "Really sweet."

"See, he's a softy at heart," Hayden says. "He spent the entire night with me. We watched old reruns of Seinfeld while he made sure I didn't throw up again. He also made me drink a lot of water to flush all the sugar out of my body." Hayden reaches over and grabs my hand. "We really bonded that night. He became my work husband."

Okay . . . too far.

I shake him off my hand. "Okay, settle down, dude."

"It's true. After he met you, Rachel, he called me, told me all about his encounter with you by the bathroom. We talked for hours about it while lying on our beds. Just gabbing away. He loves to gab."

"Yeah? Anything else he likes?"

"You know, I'm sitting right next to you, you can always just ask me," I say, tugging on Rachel's shoulder.

"No, I like Hayden's exaggerated, borderline-lie version better. It's more fun that way."

"She likes me, Weiss, you better watch out."

"I'm not worried." I sip on my beer, entirely too confident in the connection I have with Rachel. Plus, Hayden would never step in. If anything, it's all in good fun.

"He might be a teddy bear, but he's also a cocky bastard."

"I'm beginning to see that." Rachel pats my thigh with her hand. "And I'm liking it."

We spend the next hour telling stories about each other, doing that male ribbing Rachel was looking for, laughing our asses off, and sharing a plate of nachos—it was Rachel's idea.

For the first time in my life, I actually feel like the woman I like is a contender for my heart. She's smart, sweet, fucking sassy, and has no problem hanging out with my friends. She's unlike any woman I've ever met. She's so easygoing, so energetic, but not a pushover, not even close. She's someone I would consider taking home to Shea, someone I could see having a part in Shea's life, and if that's not equal parts terrifying and exhilarating at the same time, I don't know what is.

I barely know Rachel, but what I do know so far is that she makes me laugh, she keeps a smile on my face, and she has a way about her that makes me feel so fucking alive, it's addicting.

Chapter Eight

CALDER

"Hayden is so much fun."

"He's a good guy," I answer, pulling into Rachel's apartment complex.

"Is he seeing anyone?"

"Why the interest?" I ask, with a teasing tone.

"I need to keep my options open in case this doesn't work out between us. Now that I've been to my first hockey game, I think I might be addicted. I need to keep someone in my life who can continue to feed my addiction with free tickets. Hayden is hot, funny, and an amazing athlete. Total package, he's a good backup."

I put the car in park and turn toward her, my forearm resting on the steering wheel. "Sorry there babe, but if this doesn't work out, there will be no dating my teammates. It's bro code."

"No dating your teammates?" I shake my head, no. "Well that seems ridiculous. What if one of them is my soulmate? Are you really going to deny me of being with my soulmate?"

"Yup," I answer, not feeling bad about it at all.

I hop out of my car and open Rachel's door for her.

"Calder, are you not good at sharing?"

I clasp her hand with mine. "I can share things, I just don't share what's most valuable to me, that's all."

"Are you saying I'm MVP in your book?"

"Ahh come on, Rachel, that was a total cheeseball thing to say. You're better than that."

"I am." She pokes me in the side. "You must be having some kind of effect on me."

We reach her door and I prepare myself to say goodnight to this woman again, but when she pulls my hand closer to the door, unlocks it, and ushers me in, I'm guessing she has other plans.

Flipping on a light switch, the living room brightens revealing a very, very white apartment. Her couch is white, her furniture is white, and her walls are white. The only "color" in the apartment are a few grey accents. It's actually soothing.

"Nice place."

"Thank you. Make yourself at home, I'll be right back."

"Okay."

She takes off down the hall, leaving me to snoop. Not that I would, but the thought crosses my mind. It might be rude, but snooping is the best way to find out about someone you're getting to know . . . well besides asking them, of course. But there's something about revealing a bit of a mystery when you're snooping, not that I would know or anything.

I take a seat on her couch and check out her coffee table. Books and magazines. What is this girl reading? With my toe, causally I knock the stack down so they spread across the table. Let's see, what do we have here?

People Magazine—okay, she likes a little celebrity gossip, who doesn't? A book on leaves and covered bridges—that's odd. 101 crockpot recipes—crockpots are the shit. And . . . huh, will you look at that. I lean forward and pick up the magazine that's garnered my attention. Maxim, I thought only men read this.

"Find some reading to keep you busy?" Rachel asks, stepping into the room.

I turn to answer her when I'm greeted by Rachel wearing a loose, low-cut tank top without a bra and a pair of boy-butt underwear, that's it.

I swallow hard as she walks up to me, her hair loose and wavy around her shoulders, her bangs highlighting her brilliantly colored eyes. Fuck, she's so hot.

"Uh, I didn't think women read Maxim," I answer, unable to take my eyes off her.

She sits next to me, her legs kicked up under her butt, her body leaning toward mine, her shirt dipping extremely low, giving me one hell of a view.

"It's always fun to get inside a guy's mind. I like to know what they want, what they fantasize about. Every woman should read Maxim."

I push down on my thighs, trying to move my pants, but they seem to be growing exponentially smaller by the second.

"Yeah, the articles are good," I answer awkwardly, keeping my eyes trained forward, but not for long, because Rachel turns my head toward that devastating smile of hers.

"Why aren't you looking at me?" She tilts her head to the side, awaiting my answer.

Facing the music, knowing I'm going to lose control in two seconds, I turn toward her and let my body take over.

Placing my hand on her exposed thigh, I run it up to her hip where I grip her tightly, her breath hitching from my touch. My fingers graze the hem of her underwear, where they sneak underneath and gently push into her firm ass.

A low growl escapes me. "Do you always dress like this for your guests?"

From beneath her shirt, her nipples pucker, pressing hard against the fabric, making my cock swell to an uncomfortable state.

"Only the ones who I want to see me naked."

Fuck. Me.

Where did this woman come from and why was I so damn lucky to find her?

Removing my hand from her leg, I take my jacket off, yank on my tie, and undo a few of the buttons to my dress shirt, as well as my cuffs. She gives me a once over before I yank on her arm and pull her on top of my lap, my erection pressing against her right away.

"Oh yes," she whispers, grinding her hips gently, like it's involuntary, her hips can't help it.

Placing my hands on her hips, my thumbs finding their way under her shirt fabric, I say, "This shirt is revealing, you know that?"

"Mmm-hmm." She releases my tie from around my neck and starts to unbutton my shirt. "Well aware of how revealing this shirt is. I thought about wearing lingerie for you, but then went with the whole casual, yet sexy, look. Do you like?"

I move my hips so she can feel just how much I like her outfit. "I think you and I both know that I approve of the shirt."

"You're not upset about no lingerie?"

I chuckle and move my hands further up her shirt. "Rachel, I'm not that kind of guy. I'll take you any way I can get you."

"Good." She spreads my shirt, revealing my chest, and sits back on my lap. She sighs and dances her fingers across my pecs. "I knew you were going to be built, but abs, pecs, and big cock—you're killing me, Weiss."

Chuckling, I move my hands up even further, my thumbs grazing her flat stomach. "You think that's bad, what about you? You think you can just waltz in here, wearing this thin tank top, and no pants, and not make me want to fuck you on this couch?"

"It was my intention." She leans forward and presses her lips against mine, her hands moving up my neck until they grip my cheeks. She's slow at first, her lips tempting me, teasing me, moving across my lips with absolutely zero pressure. It's just a whisper of a kiss, a gentle reminder that she can easily hold the cards in this relationship, that she has the power to bring me to my knees, and that's exactly what's happening right now.

An ache builds at the base of my cock, her hips grinding down on me at a snail's pace. Beneath my thumbs, I feel her abs flex with each movement, from the way she's rocking back and forth, to the short breaths she's taking.

Needing more, I try to pry her mouth open with my tongue, but she doesn't budge, she continues to place small, short kisses along my lips, torturing me. Not wanting to wait any longer for more, I reach up with both hands and palm her breasts, her soft and full breasts. Just like I wanted, her mouth pops open and I slip my tongue inside while my thumbs graze her nipples.

She moans into my mouth and her body settles into mine, the tension between us easing as our tongues tango, tangling and twisting, our bodies warming up, our need for one another growing.

She releases my head from her grasp and moves her hands down my body, fingers grazing the light splattering of hair on my chest. She barely touches my nipples, giving them only a whisper of a touch, igniting a pulse in my cock, and then moves her wandering hands to the belt of my pants, where she scoots back on my lap and starts to undo my buckle and zipper.

The way her fingers brush against my stomach muscles and near my hardened length, I can feel my body start to tingle all over, the blood in my veins setting on fire, causing a light sheen of sweat to glisten my skin.

Squeezing harder, I focus on her nipples, pulling and pinching. Her head parts from mine as she leans back and moans from my touch. Reaching between us, she snags the hem of her shirt and pulls it over her head, dropping the thin fabric to the side.

I release her breasts and take her in as she arches her back, her nipples tight, her expression one of utter pleasure as she rocks back and forth on top of me.

Holy fuck she is so hot, with her blonde hair swaying across her dark pink nipples, and her stomach contracting with each slide over my throbbing, needy cock.

"Babe, I need you to take my pants off. I'm so fucking hard for you."

"Bedroom, now." Rachel hops off me, and pulls me up in a rush. She ushers me down a hallway to a dark room lit only by the moon.

Spinning around, she pushes me down on the bed, causing me to chuckle from her impatient force.

I watch in fascination as she pulls down my pants and removes my shoes and socks, leaving me in nothing but my boxer briefs, exposing my straining erection. Eyes glued to my crotch, her tongue wetting her lips, she removes her boy shorts and stands in front of me completely naked, confident in her skin.

I don't think I've ever seen anyone more beautiful than Rachel in this moment, and I've most definitely never wanted anyone more in my life.

"Condom, in my wallet," I stammer, unable to control the nerves coursing through me. I haven't been with a woman in a few months, I just hope I live up to Rachel's expectations.

She wastes no time in retrieving the condom from my pants and tearing it open. With heady eyes, Rachel approaches me, condom in hand, and pulls down on my boxer briefs, springing my cock free. Tossing my briefs to the side, she focuses on my straining cock, her eyes wide, impressed.

"Oh my God, Calder." Her fingers gently touch the wet tip, moving my pre-cum over the head. A hiss escapes me, my toes starting to grow numb just from that little connection. Shit, I don't want to know what's going to happen when I'm finally inside her. "You're so big." In one swift movement, she sucks my cock into her mouth and licks the tip, causing my hips to fly off the bed and my hands to clench the comforter beneath me.

"Fucking hell," I groan, her hot mouth so damn good on my dick. "Oh fuck." She grazes her teeth along my sensitive skin. My head flies back as Rachel plays with my balls at the same time she sucks me, hard, the sensation overwhelming. "Fuck, babe, fuck, you need to stop."

She lifts her mouth off me, slips the condom on and starts to straddle me, but before she can get comfortable, I flip her onto her back. Hovering over her, those beautiful eyes staring up at me, lust clouding them, I spread her legs and press the tip of my cock over her slit, making sure she's ready. And holy fuck is she.

Wanting to feel how wet she is, I replace my cock with my fingers and I slide right in. "Jesus Christ, Rachel, you're so goddamn wet."

"I've been turned on ever since you took the ice," she confesses, shifting underneath me, seeking my heat. "Watching you tonight, so powerful on your skates, so domineering, it was really hot, Calder. I couldn't wait to get you back here, to see how domineering you would be in the bedroom."

"Is that right?" I pin her hands to the bed, mine linking with hers, pushing into the mattress.

"Yes, all I wanted was this, to feel you, to have you buried deep inside of me.

"Fuck, that makes me so goddamn hard." I kiss her, fucking madly, my lips and tongue working in tandem as they move across her mouth, not begging, but taking, taking every last ounce of her she has to offer.

As my tongue fucks her mouth, my stance keeping her in place, I push my knee against her inner thigh, making sure she's spread as wide as possible before I sink myself inside of her. When my cock reaches its hilt, she gasps, her words of surprise caught against my tongue.

My shoulder is screaming with pain from the weight of holding my body up, but I don't fucking care, there is no way in hell I'm stopping now.

Taking a deep breath, her chest heaves and pants. "Oh God, Calder. You're . . . you're so big. So thick. I don't know . . ."

"I'll take it slow," I mumble, my control hanging on by a thread. She feels so good, so tight, so warm, so everything, like I belong here.

"I don't know if I can handle slow. I want you now, you're just so overwhelming . . . so thick." She moves her head to the side, her teeth biting down on her lip. "Take me, Calder, make me feel so good."

"I don't know how long I'll be able to go slow if you keep contracting around me like that." I groan, squeezing my eyes shut.

"I'm not . . . meaning . . . too." She moans even louder. "Oh God, Calder, I'm so close, just from you, just from your cock."

What a fucking turn on.

Willing myself to go slowly, I clench everything in my body and start to thrust into her, as slow as I can. My length gliding along her tight sheath, torturing me with every inch. My breath becomes labored, my toes start to curl, my legs going numb. Oh fuck I'm going to come, there is no denying it, there is no stopping it.

"Babe . . ."

"Harder, fuck me harder, Calder."

"Christ." My voice sounds so deep, so tortured that I almost don't recognize myself.

Giving up on my slow idea and capitulating to Rachel's demands, I let go of one of her hands and bring her legs over my shoulders, pressing into her until my thighs are slapping her ass over and over again. The sound is so erotic, so damn sexy.

"Yes, harder. Oh God, yes, Calder." She's so vocal, I love it. I love knowing how I make a woman feel, if I'm pleasing them or not, if they're on the cusp like Rachel is.

My impending orgasm looms over me, knocking at the base of my cock as my balls tighten up, a wave of pleasure shooting up my spine.

"Fuck," I grunt. "Fuck, I'm going to come, baby."

"Me too." Rachel bites down on her lip just as her pussy contracts around my dick, milking me so damn hard my vision goes black, the only sensation rocking through me is my throbbing cock, pulsating over and over again into Rachel. Spurt after spurt, I come, I come so fucking hard.

"Oh God," Rachel screams, her fingers digging into my skin, her beautiful tits bouncing as she finishes rocking back and forth on my cock, her movements slowing with each pass, slowly falling from the euphoric bliss we both experienced.

Holy shit, it's never been that good, ever. I've never come like that, as if I was about to black out from the pleasure, and there is only reason why: Rachel.

It's been two dates, two fucking dates and I already believe this woman was made for me, that she was brought to me for a reason. I can only hope she feels the same way.

"Oh Calder, oh hell." She drapes one of her arms over her eyes. "What just happened?"

"I don't know." I answer, peppering her face with soft, slow kisses.

"That was . . . incredible." She moves her arm and looks up at me. "Why did that feel so good?"

I shrug and kiss her lips. "Maybe because we were meant to meet each other."

Chapter Nine

CALDER

Rachel: Remember when you licked my nipples for ten minutes straight and I came? That was fun.
Calder: Babe, you can't text me stuff like that when I'm in the locker room with a bunch of guys, they'll think I have a boner for other reasons.
Rachel: Well . . . do you?
Calder: Yeah (deadpans) I just love staring at all the dicks and nut sacs in the locker room.
Rachel: That's disappointing for me, but yay for Hayden, you two would make a cute couple.
Calder: Why do you torture me like this?
Rachel: Because it's too much fun.

Calder: I miss you.
Rachel: This text made me smile. When do you get back to Philly? P.S. I miss you more.
Calder: Two more nights.
Rachel: Ugh, that seems like forever. Can't you just always have home games?
Calder: I fucking wish, then I would be able to fuck you before and after every game.
Rachel: Mmm . . . I love it when you say you like to fuck me.
Calder: Seriously, it's my favorite thing to do.

Rachel: So the blow-up doll Hayden keeps saying was your girlfriend before you met me, she's not your main squeeze anymore?
Calder: That isn't a real story. I don't have a blow-up doll. Fuck.
Rachel: Awfully defensive, for someone who "doesn't have a blow-up doll."
Calder: That's it, you and Hayden are no longer allowed to hang out together.
Rachel: Hey now, what about our little tripod?
Calder: The tripod is over.
Rachel: You savage!

Calder: Shea is with my brother and sister-in-law, are you coming over tonight? Please say yes, I miss you so goddamn much.
Rachel: I can't drive to your place fast enough. I need to be in your arms tonight. Will I be able to stay?
Calder: Yes, there is no way in hell you're going back to your place tonight. Fuck, I need you so damn bad.
Rachel: The feeling is mutual, Calder. These road trips are killer.
Calder: I know. Just a few more months and then it will be over.
Rachel: I like our late-night phone calls though, hearing your voice through the phone, it's one of my favorite things.
Calder: Personally, I like having FaceTime sex with you.
Rachel: How did I know you were going to say that?
Calder: Maybe because you rocked my world last night with your striptease. Fuck, I'm hard just thinking about it.
Rachel: I'm wet thinking about it too . . .
Calder: Get that beautiful ass over here, NOW! I want to fuck you against a wall, then in the bathtub, and most definitely eat you out on the kitchen counter.
Rachel: Your tongue, oh my God, Calder, it's magic.
Calder: I know, baby. Shit I'm hard thinking about that sweet pussy of yours. Hurry up.

Rachel: Have you ever thought about what life will be like after hockey for you?
Calder: Are you asking this because you didn't like the fight I got into tonight?
Rachel: You got punched in the face, Calder.
Calder: Well aware, baby. I have the headache to remind me. It's part of the game though.

Rachel: I don't like it. You're so handsome, I don't want fists flying at your face.
Calder: You're cute . . .
Rachel: Hmpf (folds arms) So . . . about life after hockey.
Calder: Not for a long time. You're going to have to get used to the fights.
Rachel: Orrrrrrr instead of fighting, you can do a thumb war. Those can be very riveting. Oooooo who's going to win? (twiddles fingers)
Calder: You want me to challenge a hockey player to a thumb war? Yeah, that's just asking to get my ass beat. I'm okay, babe, really.
Rachel: Really? Because it looked like he got you good.
Calder: He did, but don't worry, I'll get him next time.
Rachel: THERE WILL BE NO NEXT TIME! No more fighting.
Calder: You're cute.

Rachel: Question.
Calder: Possible answer, depends on what the question is.
Rachel: Now I don't want you to get upset that I'm asking you this through text, but I'm nervous, and you know what happens when I'm nervous, I clam up, and if I don't get this off my chest soon, I might combust.
Calder: Oh shit, now I'm nervous. What's up?
Rachel: Well, we've been dating for two months now.
Calder: Yeah, best fucking two months of my life.
Rachel: You're sweet, but I kind of want to know something.
Calder: If you don't spit it out I'm going to call you.
Rachel: Fine, why haven't you introduced me to your daughter yet?

I PAUSE, staring down at my phone, my heart rate picking up, my eyes reading her words on repetition. She wants to meet Shea? I knew this time was going to come, that they were going to have to meet at some point, but I never prepared myself for it.

There are so many factors that go into introducing your child to your significant other. She is so young, so impressionable, what if Rachel and I don't work out and Shea has already fallen in love with her? Then what?

And I know that would happen, that Shea would immediately take a liking to Rachel, it's hard not to—she has a contagious personality that puts you in a better mood no matter the circumstances. Shea would love Rachel right off the bat, and it terrifies me to wonder what I would do if Rachel and I break up. Shea already lost her mom, I couldn't stand for her to lose Rachel too.

Fuck, *I* can't stand to lose Rachel.

But meeting Shea? I don't know if I'm ready for that, I don't know if I'm ready for the impact Rachel would have on my daughter, the kind of love Rachel so easily exudes.

I can't risk it.

Biting my cheek, I read Rachel's question over again, trying to figure out what to say, how to break the news. Conflicted, I start to type out a response but erase it, several times. After the fourth time, I give up and pocket my phone, my stomach flipping on itself. Shea is not ready, I don't want to disappoint her again . . .

Chapter Ten

RACHEL

"JACE, I DON'T KNOW WHAT TO DO," I SAY, TALKING TO ONE OF MY BEST friends on the phone. I finally got in touch with him after playing phone tag. He plays shortstop for the Colorado Boulders and he's in the beginning of his season, making it almost impossible to touch base with him given all of the media, practices, and games he has to attend.

"He hasn't responded to you yet?" I've updated Jace briefly through text about my dating life, but this is the first time I've gotten to talk to him on the phone, and it's really nice to hear a friendly voice, since I haven't heard Calder's in two days.

"No, nothing. He's gone radio silent on me. I knew I shouldn't have pressured him. I should have let him introduce me to his daughter at his own pace."

"No, don't do that, Rachel. Don't make excuses for him. If he wasn't comfortable with you meeting his daughter, then he should have respectfully told you that."

Jace is right, if Calder was the kind of man I thought he was, he would have just been open and honest about his feelings, instead of running away, which really doesn't seem like him.

It makes me wonder . . .

"What if something happened to him? What if he got hurt and I can't get—"

"Pretty sure the dickhead is fine, at least he looks fine on TV, skating around the rink, warming up."

Oh, right.

"Then he's just an asshole."

"Seems like it."

I sigh, leaning back on the couch, looking up at the ceiling. "Ugh, what do I do, Jace?"

"Let me ask you this, do you like the guy, or do you *really* like him?"

Knowing this is the God's honest truth, I answer, "I really, really like him, borderline L-word status."

"Oh shit." Jace pauses and asks, "Are you okay, Rachel? I didn't know you liked him that much."

I bite on my lip, willing the tears away. Don't cry, DO NOT cry, it only makes Jace feel awkward and it will solve nothing.

Taking a deep breath, I answer, "I've been . . . better."

"Are you going to cry?"

"Maybe." I sniff.

"It's official, I'm going to kick his ass."

"He's bigger than you, Jace, if that's possible, and he fights other big guys for a living, when he's not pushing a puck around on the ice."

"But I have the best-friend rage."

"True." I laugh, letting silence fall between us.

Finally, Jace chimes in. "Just confront him. What will you lose? It's not like he's talking to you now. At least if you confront him, he'll have to give you a direct answer."

"But that's scary."

"Yeah, it is, but it's better than sitting around wondering. You deserve better than to be pushed to the side. Take what you want and go ask him in person. Be the assertive girl I know."

"And if he breaks up with me?"

"Then he's the biggest moron on the planet."

I really hope he's not the biggest moron on the planet, because I'm not sure my heart will be able to take it.

SHEA SHOULD BE at Calder's brother's house, she always is when Calder has a late game. After his game ended in a loss—good timing on my part—I waited two hours before heading over to his place, giving him time to settle in, and giving myself a little more time to gain some courage.

I'm not nervous to confront him, but I am worried about how he's going to react when he sees me on his doorstep. I don't want him to break up with me.

Please don't let him break up with me.

Taking one last deep breath, I knock on his grand door and shift on my feet while I wait for him to open it. It takes a few seconds before the locks are shifted and the door opens. Calder is wearing a pair of pajama pants and that's it, showing off his well-defined chest, muscular arms, and cut stomach, where I could count each and every ab with my tongue.

I've missed him so damn much, from his buzzed hair, to his soulful eyes, to the warmth of his arms. Seeing him like this, not feeling comfortable enough to dive into his embrace, makes me feel not only awkward, but also incredibly sad.

"Rachel," he says with surprise. "What are you doing here?"

Twisting my hands together, I try to steady my voice, not wanting to show how much he affects me. "I . . . I came to confront you." Not the most eloquent or the best way to ease into the topic, but there's something to be said for getting to the point.

He grips the door, his muscles straining under the tension I just laid in front of him. "Rachel—"

"No," I cut him off. "Please, don't lie to me, okay? Please don't give me some spiel about how you've been so busy, because that was never the case with us, you always made time for me. So the least you can do is tell me the truth."

Lowering his head, he stares at his feet for a few seconds before opening the door wider and welcoming me in. That's right . . . you jerk!

I take in my surroundings, his house feeling so much like home it hurts. When he turns toward me, door shut behind him, there is regret written all over his face, regret and pain. And even though I'm mad at him for shutting me out, I can't help but be drawn toward him.

Pressing my hand against his chest, his heat encompassing me, I ask, "What happened, Calder? Do you really not want me to meet your daughter that much? I can wait, I really can, but I just don't want to lose you."

He presses his hand against mine and twines our fingers together right before he pulls me into a hug, his chin resting on my head. I melt into his embrace, my eyes welling up with tears. It's been two days, two days of not talking to him, of wondering where we stand, of not being able to get lost in this man, and it's been torture.

I try to hold back the tears, I really do, but when he squeezes me, as if he never wants to let go, the floodgates open.

"Shh," he coos into my ear, hearing the silent sobs coming from me. "I'm so sorry, baby. Fuck, I'm sorry."

In the entryway, we hold each other, my heart slowly healing with each kiss he presses against my head and with every sorry he mutters under his breath, his voice filled with self-hatred.

He's regretful, it's evident in the way he's holding me. This gives me hope, just a glimmer of hope, but hope, nonetheless.

When my crying subsides and I gather myself, Calder brings me to his couch, where he pulls me onto his lap and holds onto me tightly.

"Rachel, I'm so fucking sorry. There really is no excuse, other than I was scared." He takes a deep breath, so I place my hand on his chest, trying to calm his racing heart. "Shea asks about her mom almost once a week, and it kills me having to tell her why her mom is no longer in her life, that she's never coming back. I fucking hate that her mom just up and left and I can't do anything about it. It's the reason why I've been super selective when it comes to bringing people into Shea's life, it's the reason why I went on a dating hiatus for so long —I didn't want to fall for someone and introduce them to Shea, just to have them leave her too.

My heart aches for Calder and Shea, and the pain they have to face on a daily basis because of someone's selfish needs.

"Calder, I had no idea, I'm sorry."

"Don't apologize, there is no need for you to. I'm the one who should be apologizing. Things just got really intense with us really quickly. I've never . . ." he holds his breath and then he says, "I've never truly loved someone like I've fallen in love with you, and that terrifies me, because what if you don't love me back? What if you don't get along with Shea? What if you decide to leave us, not only breaking my heart, but my little girl's heart, too? I don't think—"

"Stop." I gently place a kiss on his lips, lingering for a few seconds. "Calder, I love you. And every day we're together, I fall deeper in love with you." I tilt his chin so he's forced to look me in the eyes. "I'm not going anywhere. I have plans to stick with you for as long as you want me. And as for your daughter, as for Shea, I know that she's your world, and I will do anything to not only gain her love and respect, but to keep her safe."

Calder shakes his head in disbelief and squeezes me tightly against his chest. "Fuck, I love you so much. Thank you, baby."

"No need to thank me, just don't shut me out. You about destroyed me, Calder. I'm kind of addicted to you. I need you like I need air to breathe. I'm sticking around, I think it's time you get used to it."

Laughing, he answers, "That's a pretty easy thing to get used to."

"WHY AM I SO NERVOUS? She's five. I work with five-year-olds day in and day out. I shouldn't be this nervous."

Calder laughs next to me, the rumble from his chest easing me slightly. "Trust me, babe, she's going to adore you."

"I hope so." I adjust my shirt and watch as Calder's brother pulls up in the driveway of Calder's house. It takes all of a minute for Shea to pop out of the car and sprint to the house, right into her dad's arms.

And oh boy, is she the cutest little thing. She shares Calder's eyes, but everything else about her must be her mom. Wearing pink leggings, a pink sweater, and her hair in a messy bun on the top of her head, she is everything I expected.

"Daddy, you didn't win last night."

"I know, love bug, that's okay though."

"You'll get the next game." She gives her dad a little fist bump and it melts my heart. "Do you like my hair, daddy? Carissa helped me style it this morning. Don't I look so cool?"

Chuckling while Shea tosses her head from side to side, he says, "The absolute coolest." Standing tall, he continues to hold Shea's hand when he says, "Hey, I have someone I want you to meet."

Reaching out, Calder clasps my hand and says, "Shea, I want you to meet Rachel, my girlfriend."

My stomach flips as Shea looks me up and down, her once-over making me more nervous than any job interview I've ever had.

"Girlfriend?" Shea crinkles her nose. "Like, you guys kiss?"

Pressing his lips together for a second, holding back his laugh, Calder says, "Yes, love bug, we kiss."

"Huh." Leaning closer to me, Shea asks, "Is daddy a good kisser?"

I nearly lose it as I throw my head back and laugh, way too hard, letting all my nerves fly out of me.

Kneeling to her height, I look Shea in the eyes and say, "Your dad is a very good kisser."

Looking up at Calder, Shea gives him a tap to his flat stomach and says, "Good job, daddy." Then she turns toward me and holds out her hand, which I take without pause. "Do you want to see my stuffed animal collection? It's huge!"

Smiling, I answer, "I would love to."

And that right there, that's the moment I fell for not only Calder Weiss, but also his darling little girl. Calder was so worried about me going somewhere, but he has absolutely nothing to fear. There is no possible way I could leave, not with this little girl's hand gripping mine so tightly, and the look of absolute adoration beaming from Calder.

Nope, I'm here for good.

Epilogue

CALDER

"When is Uncle Hayden going to be here, daddy?"

"Right now," Hayden says, causing Shea to squeal loudly when he scares her from behind and picks her up. "Were you worried I wasn't going to come?" He spins her then sets her on his hip.

"You're late."

"I know, please forgive me."

Shea ridiculously sighs. "Fine, only this time, though."

"Thank god." A devilish smile appears over his face as he starts walking toward the pool, Shea understanding her fate in seconds.

"No, no, no," she laughs, squirming in his arms.

"Oh, it's going to happen little girl. Get ready, you're about to get wet." Like the "Uncle" that he is, he counts to three then tosses a bathing-suit-wearing Shea into the pool, who luckily already knows how to swim. Thanks to my brother.

I point my grilling spatula at him and say, "You realize you just started a war, right? And Rachel is ALWAYS on Shea's side. It's hell man."

Hayden grabs a beer from the cooler next to the grill and says, "Oh please, you fucking love it."

"I do."

Speaking of my girl, Rachel walks up to me, a plate of patties in her hand, a glittering ring on her finger, claiming her as mine, and a little belly poking out from under her tight-fitting shirt.

A month after Rachel met Shea, and after seeing their immediate connection, I wasted no time in proposing to Rachel. We wasted no time in getting pregnant, either. We have yet to get married, but we will do that in time, we're just trying to enjoy our little family right now.

And Rachel's hormones at the current moment, fuck, she has me bending her over at least twice a day, if not three times. If my dick makes it through this pregnancy, it will be an absolute miracle.

Although it will be worth it, because there is something to be said about seeing the woman you love carry your baby—it's such a beautiful sight. But what's even more beautiful is watching your daughter talk to your girl's belly every night, telling it stories.

Want to make me melt, just show me a video of that. I'm done.

"Hayden, we haven't seen you in a while." Rachel leans over and places a kiss on his cheek, before walking into my arms, where I gently squeeze her ass and press a tongue-filled kiss against her mouth. She moans quietly, making me hard in an instant. It's that easy with this woman.

"Maybe it's because this is all you two do, make people uncomfortable with your love."

"Oh don't be jealous, man, just because your girl wants something casual doesn't mean you need to hate on us long-term, committed couples.

With far too much interest, Rachel turns in my embrace, practically bouncing up and down. "You have a girl? When did this happen? Why haven't you told me?" She swats me on the stomach. "And you knew?"

"It's not serious, there was no need to tell you about Hayden's whoring ways."

"As a tripod, we tell each other everything. I told you about my sore nipples the other day."

Hayden lifts his beer at Rachel in salute. "Yeah, thanks for that text by the way. You know, we don't have to tell each other everything. It's okay to keep some things a secret."

"No secrets in a tripod. So who's this girl?"

Hayden shrugs, trying to act casual, but there's an underlying hurt in his eyes. "My good friend, Racer, introduced me to her this summer."

"Oh, tell me more."

Knowing Rachel is persistent, Hayden gives in without putting up much of a fight. "We met at a party. I didn't think much of it. She knows I play hockey and she's a nurse. Our schedules clash, especially during the season, so we decided to keep things casual, knowing there is an end to our summer fling."

"But you like her," Rachel cuts in before he can admit it himself.

Running his hand over his face, he nods. "Yeah, I like her."

"So what's the problem?"

Biting on his lip, Hayden glances in my direction and his entire demeanor turns sullen. "My, uh, agent called me today. I've been traded, man."

"What?"

Rachel gasps next to me. "You're kidding me."

"I wish I was. I've been traded to the LA Quakes. I leave in a few weeks."

Rachel and I both sit there, silent, unable to form words, just as Shea comes running up to Hayden, begging him to throw her in the pool again.

Kids are so weird.

Hayden obliges her demands then comes back to talk to us. "It sucks, really fucking bad since all my family and friends are here, but I know she's not going to want to do something long distance, especially since she's not willing to commit to something long-term when we're in the same city."

"Shit, man." Rachel squeezes me tightly, knowing this is a huge loss for me. "I don't know what to say."

Hayden shrugs and then says, "Just say you'll come visit me in LA, and for the love of God, take it easy on me when we're on the ice. I know how you crush men, I'm not quite ready to break a rib just yet."

Laughing, trying to take the bad news in stride, I say, "Well when you're ready, let me know, because I would love to blast you into the wall."

"I can't believe this. I can't believe you're leaving."

"I'll be back. I'll still have a home back east to visit you guys." He bites on his bottom lip. "Is it wrong that I'm more concerned about my relationship status than where I'm going to play hockey?"

Rachel shakes her head. "No, it's endearing actually. Means you care for this girl."

"I do, but I guess sometimes things don't work out. Who knows, maybe I'll meet someone in LA, someone I'm meant to be with, someone who wants to be with me."

We spend the rest of the evening reminiscing, celebrating Shea and her birthday, and playing with all the presents she got. She's so fucking spoiled, but hey, it just means she has so many people in her life who love her, including Rachel.

She went crazy getting Shea so many toys, some educational, and a lot of things they can do together, like a bead set, and a tie-dye T-shirt kit so they can have matching shirts. Fuck, that present made my heart ache with so much love for Rachel.

It's funny how I was so worried about Rachel and Shea. I should have known from the very beginning, from the moment I bitch slapped Rachel with my fairy wing and introduced myself as Wanda, that she was a keeper and would easily become the mom my little girl so deserves. I should have known that the girl with the blonde hair and bangs was going to sweep me off my goddamn feet and slip my world upside down in the best way possible.

Love always shows up in mysterious ways. Here's hoping Hayden can accidentally run into love as well.

THE END

Want to know what happens with Hayden? Don't worry, you won't have to wait long. THREE BLIND DATES comes out JANUARY 4th, 2018. Add it to your TBR - -> http://bit.ly/2zYoZuf And do you want to be ONE OF THE FIRSTS to find out about more release information and Hayden's story? Then click here - -> http://bit.ly/2ikhDI8

INTERESTED IN WHAT happens to Hayden? Check out the blurb to THREE BLIND DATES right here.

"Good Morning Malibu, it's another beautiful day on the west coast! I'm Noely Clark, your host, and I'm in the market for love..."

When the publicity team of the new local restaurant, Going in Blind, began their search for a hot, local celebrity to promote the wildly popular eatery, they couldn't have found a better person than me.

Outgoing? Check.

Single? Check.

Open to finding love? Check.

I signed up immediately.

A hopeless romantic with an exceedingly demanding schedule, I've found it impossible to find the man of my dreams—so Going in Blind seems too good to be true! That's until they start setting me up on dates—three very different, very attractive, very distinct blind dates—and only one thing is for certain . . .

I'm in big trouble.

"Good Morning Malibu,

I'm Noely Clark, and I have a choice to make.

The question is who will I choose: the suit, the rebel, or the jock?"

SWEEPING THE SERIES

Sweeping the Series

a romantic dramedy

Ren Makavoy is one season away from realizing his Major League dreams. Unfortunately, his bad-boy reputation off the field has landed him in hot water. Ren swears his days of drinking, brawling, and seducing starlets are over, but management sees fit to bring in PR to clean up his act. Determined to prove himself as a reputable catcher, his plans of playing along backfire when he comes face to face with the woman who shattered his heart.

She is the last hope of saving his reputation.

And things are about to get a hell of a lot hotter.

This sinfully sexy second-chance romantic dramedy is a stand-alone and spinoff of The Balls in Play Series. Join the rest of the gang from Anything but Minor and Major Love for one last season of love, laughter, and baseball.

Dedication

For my dear friend, Donna Cooksley Sanderson. You are my champion. Thank you for the gift of your friendship.

And for my best friend, Erica Ann Fischer. I love growing old with you.

Prologue

Once upon a pre-season . . .

Ren

"You look lonely."

"I'm good," she said as she looked up from the newspaper that partially covered her tan legs. It was the morning of the first game day of spring training; the sun had barely cracked the sky. I always got to the field before anyone else. It was a habit of mine and helped me prepare my mental game. I never expected company, and I'd watched her arrive hours too early for a regular fan. I had assumed she came with one of the players, but no one claimed to know her when they started trickling onto the field. She looked completely at ease as she ignored the bullshit and the banter that surrounded her when we began to warm up.

With minutes to spare before the stands started to fill, I let curiosity get the best of me and thanked Christ for that as soon as I got a better view of her. I pulled off my hat, ran my fingers through my hair, and flashed her my best smile. "Let's not fight the inevitable. I think it's pretty important we get to know each other for the good of the team."

Her shoulders stiffened. "In that case, you're wasting your time on the wrong girl."

The scorn in her voice gave me temporary pause. "Not a fan?"

"Of yours? I don't even know your name. But if I had to guess—" She crossed her legs playfully before she placed her hands at her sides, tilting her body my way.

I enjoyed the display, but I would have rather had that look back, the one of discovery we'd shared minutes earlier when I peeked over my shoulder and damned near got nailed with a dinger in the mask. She scrutinized me before she'd flashed me a breath-stealing smile.

She hid that smile as she looked up at me but kept the scrutiny front and center. "I would say you're a rookie. First year."

"You know damn well who I am," I chided. My name had been in the papers—including the one she had in her lap—for weeks. It wasn't every day a catcher got a contract the size of mine.

"You," she mused as her eyes trailed down my body. "Well, you're trouble with a number." I was dismissed. She gripped her paper and shook it out, determined to brush me off. Her words behind the wall of paper and ink between us confirmed as much. "I'm flattered, really, but I don't date ballplayers."

"Oh, well, then I fucking quit." I threw my glove. She chuckled dryly as she looked up wistfully through thick lashes. That look told me my chances were slim to none.

"If only it were that easy, right?"

She was like a mirage sitting in the stands with her raven black hair and vibrant brown eyes. I'd kept my neck craned for half of warm-up. Getting distracted by beautiful women while I was on the field had never been an issue, but I couldn't stop staring. I needed to look at her. I needed to have another hit of that smile.

"What do you have against baseball?" I asked, taking the seat next to her.

She wrinkled her nose. "Everything."

"You want to tell me what you're doing perched up like hot-shit hours before the first game? Unless—" I nodded over my shoulder "—you're here for someone?"

"I'm *definitely* not here for any player on that field."

"Ouch. You can't mean that. Baseball is America's sport. A national pastime. It's worthy of your attention."

She quirked a brow. "Are we still talking about baseball?"

"Maybe," I said, brushing my shoulder against hers. "Let me take you out tonight. I bet I can convince you we're both worthy of your attention."

"Absolutely not, Makavoy, but I'm flattered." She picked up her paper and resumed her reading, and I stuck a finger in the crease then lowered it.

"Ah, caught you in a lie. You do know my name, and if you play your cards right, I'll let you chant it as often as you like."

"That's disgusting. Never going to happen for us, Ren."

I bit my lip at my piss-poor choice of words. This girl wasn't even close to the type that line would work on. If she wasn't a fan, she damn sure wasn't a groupie. But she was a beautiful mystery that I wanted to solve.

"I'm not changing my mind," she sighed as she shot a wary glance my way. "It's not in the cards for us."

"Now there's an idea," I said, standing.

"Makavoy!"

Without turning in the direction of the field, I flipped the bird toward the shithead fuming at the mound then sank back into my conversation.

"You're wanted on the field, number two," she muttered.

"You know my number, too. Now I'm flattered," I teased, my lips twisting into a satisfied smile. I could see the barest hint of a blush beneath her sun-kissed complexion. She was a hard sell, but I knew just the trick. "Wait right here, okay?"

I hustled to the dugout, grabbing a stick of gum and my lucky deck of cards. I made my way back and sat next to her, my hip touching hers as she scanned her article, doing her best to seem indifferent.

She slowly shook her head. "You know, you're probably about ten seconds away from having your ass handed to you, and quite publicly."

Just as she predicted, my name was barked from the field. "Makavoy!"

"They can wait," I said dryly. I pulled my cards out and began to shuffle. She glanced over at the working of my hands before she pressed her full, glossy lips together. She was dressed in an old, faded series T-shirt—not a fan, my ass—and shorts, but the sight of her had my breath coming out ragged. I had the innate need to touch and taste, but more than that, I wanted to know what her laugh sounded like.

After a few minutes of shuffling my deck, I had her full attention.

Her face lit up as she watched me manipulate the cards. "Wow, that's—that's awesome."

I let out a dry laugh as I flicked the deck with precision; the cards flew toward her, and I caught them before they hit her in the chest.

Wide brown eyes scrutinized me. "Holy shit! How did you do that?"

I chuckled. "I'm one of the best defenders in the League, and this is what impresses you? They don't call me the 'Tin Man' for nothing."

Another wrinkle of a perfect nose and an eye roll. "For a second, I forgot you were a ballplayer."

I ignored her blasphemy against the greatest sport in history and sliced the deck in half with quick fingers before I thrust them in front of her.

"Pick a card out of either hand, and if I guess what you pull, we eat dinner tonight."

"Ren," she groaned. "I'm seriously not worth your trouble. Trust me."

"I'm pretty good at making calls." I lifted the cards up again, forcing her hand. She set her paper aside then locked eyes with me. Something raw tore through my chest at that moment and filled my throat. Intuition told me even if I had pulled that trick off over a dozen times, knew it inside and out, I'd be devastated if I fucked it up this time.

She pulled the card I purposefully but subtly thumbed toward her fingers before she held it up, curling it at the sides so that I couldn't see it.

"All right, now put it back in," I said, spreading the deck.

She pushed the card in carefully as we kept our eyes glued. For a moment in time, there was no outside noise, nothing to distract me, and nowhere in the world I'd rather be than sitting across from her.

Another second passed and then another as something inside told me this woman would change every-fucking-thing. Swept away by the feeling of her, I leaned in. Her lips parted, and I knew, without a doubt, she was feeling the same thing.

I traced her hairline down her cheek with a single finger as I spoke. "So, this is where you come in, huh?"

We were still caught in the moment when I heard my name growled at my back.

"Queen of hearts," I whispered.

Even with all the static between us, she didn't miss a beat. "But where's the card?"

"Do you like Italian?" I asked, pushing my cards back in the box.

"You didn't show my card, Makavoy," she said, pulling back, doing her best to hide her disappointment.

"I'll see you tonight," I assured, readjusting my hat with a wink.

"That was so lame," she protested as she lifted her paper, and the card fell into her lap.

"Oh my God," she whispered as she studied her card.

Appreciative and warm eyes glanced up at me before she rewarded me with her smile.

"That was awesome."

"Goddammit, Ren!" I knew that tone. And I was about to be publicly humiliated.

"Shit," I muttered as I glanced over my shoulder.

"Thought you were quitting," she reminded, her paper forgotten.

I grinned down at her. "You're really going to make me choose?"

"Never," she said without second thought. "Because I don't date ballplayers."

"I'll let you convince me of that over dinner. Oregano's, eight o'clock. And bring my card back to me, would you?"

"I won't be there," she insisted.

"I've had that deck since I was thirteen years old. I can't play a game without it, so I'm going to need that card back. You don't want to be responsible for ruining my career, do you?" Her silence had my smile stretching wide.

I wasn't a superstitious man. In fact, when I was young, I never believed in luck, so I decided to make my own. Over the years, I guess life got the memo because it started cooperating. Staring at that beautiful woman, whose name I didn't know, but whose smile had me practically kneeling before her, I knew luck and I were still in sync.

Sliding my hand in my glove, I kept my eyes locked on hers until I had no choice but to leave her there.

"I'll see you tonight."

Chapter One

THREE YEARS LATER

Ren

My throat burned with the bitter aftertaste of the woman wrapped around me. I didn't have to glance down at her to know that I had once again fucked up. If the non-stop buzzing of my phone wasn't already a sign, the state of my head was a further reminder.

The woman in my bed was one of Hollywood's elite, and she'd just slummed it with the "black tar" of baseball. I think that was what that prick journalist had labeled me. These days I couldn't keep up. It was one flying insult after another.

It didn't matter that I had earned the golden ticket to play for Denver. All that mattered was who I was fucking. And I was to blame. Still, the amount of attention I was getting was staggering.

Just to spite the tempting ass-lashing messages I had waiting for me on my buzzing phone, I knocked it away from the nightstand and grabbed another condom. Nothing felt better than sinking into warm, sleeping pussy. No conversation needed, no foreplay, and I knew she was still dripping from last night. I'd fucked Natasha six ways from Sunday, and I would do it again this morning before any words were uttered about expectations I wouldn't meet. Her blue eyes—wrong color—popped open as I buried my cock deep, thrusting her awake. Her swollen lips formed an 'O' as I kept our conversation nil and our fucking filthy. Her orgasm rolled through her within a few minutes, and I smirked down at her as she looked up at me in a daze.

I impressed her, but she depressed me. Just another woman willing to deal with the abominable bastard I'd become because she thought I had a pretty face.

"Ren," she moaned as I twisted my head, avoiding her morning breath and any connection she needed because it wasn't there.

We'd met at a party the night before, and we'd part this morning no closer than we were the second her eyes spoke to my cock and it answered. I had a "reputation" according to her, and that was all I heard about as I slid my fingers through her wet heat going a hundred miles an hour on the way back to my hotel.

She knew what to expect, and I didn't disappoint with the sex. I wouldn't be changing that reputation any time soon because every male in the country stripped their cock-skin to the sight of her on the big screen.

She wasn't a conquest; she was temporary warmth. Another night of blurry comfort. And she would get the respect that she deserved for it.

Ripping the condom off with a grunt, I fisted myself over her as she gazed up at me with surprise. It was easy to tell she'd never had quite as dirty as me, and her pupils dilated at the sight of herself soiled.

Too bad I opened that box for her because I couldn't satiate her appetite.

I was no longer hungry.

And so it went. We showered together. I faked the half-assed grin I flashed her during the breakfast I ordered. And I only found a breath of relief when she was safely on the other side of my hotel door.

Sitting on my borrowed bed, I finally answered my phone to avoid a knock on my door.

"Yeah?" I grunted out.

"Ren! I can't keep doing my job if you're going to act like a goddamned lunatic at every function and defile high-profile actresses."

"Then don't do it," I snapped before I popped the aspirin waiting in my palm and followed it with some water.

"What?" I heard Walter's voice deflate. He'd been in charge of my PR for the last six months. And that was the longest relationship I'd been in for years.

"Listen, I appreciate all you've done, but I just really don't give a fuck. I think it's time we parted ways." I hung up and killed the ringer before I checked my texts.

Andy: Natasha Arden. Are you fucking serious? Get out of your own way, asshole.

Then one from Rafe.

Rafe: Jesus Christ, you're a fucking idiot. This isn't high school man. Jake is going to cut your dick off.

Rafe was referring to our assistant coach. He'd handled enough of my headaches in the last year. I had no doubt when the incident after the party last night—my fist connecting with a reporter's face who didn't respect boundaries—hit the papers. I was going to be on paper-thin ice. I'd been warned far too many times to play dumb. In my defense, said reporter stuck his head inside the damn limo with his camera and scared Natasha. Still, whatever picture he took before I dented his teeth was sure to damn me with management and the public. Again. But I was the one who kept my private life separate from ball, while media and management were the ones who forced them together. It was still my fault because I'd started the circus my damn self a few years ago with a night similar to the one that I was currently paying for.

Playing for Denver had been my goal in the year I was a catcher for Atlanta, especially when the dream pitching team included Rafe Hembrey.

My mentor and old bullpen coach, Andy, had worked with Rafe in the Minors and helped me sharpen my calls when he coached me in Atlanta. Together, Rafe and I ruled the MLB. There was no denying it. Last year, we'd come close to winning the pennant. This year we would win. And we'd sweep the series. Regardless of my behavior, there was no way my club was parting with either of us. So, while a small part of me felt like a dick for telling Natasha I would call her, the eight-year-old kid in me who made up his mind he would win the World Series didn't flinch.

I flipped on SportsCenter just as a fist landed on my door. Despite my shitty attempt to handle my indiscretion, I knew exactly who it was.

I opened it to see the shit-eating grin of one Rafe "The Bullet" Hembrey. He pushed past my outstretched arm and surveyed the hotel room.

"I should kick your ass with training starting in two days. That's all we need is more press hounds interested in your cock instead of the team," he mused, glancing over at me. "You're looking sincerely remorseful," he said dryly.

I shrugged. "I did us a favor. No such thing as bad publicity."

"Hamlin is going to cut your dick off," he assured as he pulled an apple off the room service cart, shined it on his T-shirt and took a healthy bite.

"Save me the theatrics." I waved my hand in dismissal and grabbed my jacket.

"Where you off to now? Are you thinking you might take down a nun and impregnate her?"

"I've got shit to do."

"Look, man, I'm no stranger to pussy," he said, matter of fact. "I enjoy it. I eat it regularly as part of a healthy diet. But, said pussy is attached to my beautiful wife. I don't have to sniff around for it while I catch a drunk and disorderly or an assault charge. Choosing one pussy is not that bad, I assure you," he said, taking another bite of his apple.

"Look, I respect you, but this isn't necessary. I'm going to hire new PR."

"PR isn't the problem," Rafe said pointedly. "Seriously, Ren, you're getting kind of fucking old to be holding the rattle."

I squeezed my temple, willing the aspirin to kick in. "Not that I owe you a damn explanation or shitty reassurances," I said through gritted teeth, "but I'm over it. All of it."

Rafe glanced at my bed. "So, cold turkey? No more women?"

"Fuck no," I grinned, "Never. But I'm ready to focus on ball."

Rafe looked at me skeptically. "I don't know man. You seem so much smarter than this. I don't get why you're choosing this. It's not like you love the attention. You're no socialite. But it seems to me you want to make sure the bullseye is on your back. What gives?"

I let out a heavy sigh.

"Look, Ren, I'm not much of a fucking girlfriend to talk feelings with, but if something is going on, you can run it by me. I've had my fair share of shit storms."

I knew that to be the truth. Rafe had disowned his dad due to a stunt he pulled trying to strong-arm Rafe into a League team by taking bribes. Rafe's track record wasn't exactly clean, but he was nowhere near the target I was. His drama happened even before he threw his first pitch in the Minors. His reputation in the Majors was nothing less than stellar, despite his stance on backing me when my shit hit the fan.

I kept my mouth clamped as Rafe studied my packed suitcase and then me. I couldn't stand the slight amount of pity in his eyes.

"Right," he said, shoving his hands in his jeans. "You know you're always welcome over at my place? I mean, I know hanging out with my family might be weird for you at first, but I didn't see it as a future for myself until I met Alice. You'll get used to it."

I'd been to Rafe's little piece of paradise in Denver, met his beautiful wife and little girl. It wasn't weird for me. But it was fucking torture. Because what Rafe didn't know, what nobody knew, was that I had been a centimeter away from having that life a few years ago. Still, I didn't want him to think his invitation didn't matter. Rafe had become one of the only people I trusted. We were professionals on the field, but friends off of it. We fought like hell in the heat of the game at times and even got a little bloody once or twice, but it didn't mean shit. We were better teammates for it. No one fucked with our dynamic. He was a pitcher worthy of respect, and he had mine.

"I'll get to your house more when we get back to Denver."

Seeming satisfied, he picked my buzzing phone off the floor and handed it to me.

"Handle your shit. This is the year we're going to win it, and you know it." Rafe wasn't one to bust balls or make house calls, or in my case, hotel calls, but he had the same dream I had, and he didn't want anyone fucking it up.

I deadpanned, "I'm just as sure as you are."

Rafe eyed me carefully, a warning beneath his calm exterior.

"Don't fuck this up."

I ran my hands through my hair. "You didn't have to say shit."

He shrugged. "I'm just wondering which one of us you are going to listen to."

Irritation started to simmer. "Tell me how *who* I stick my dick in changes our game? Tell me why it changes any damn thing."

He tipped his chin toward the ceiling. "It shouldn't, but then again, you are a world class dickhead and well on your way to becoming a cliché."

"Thanks for the talk." Translation: Get the fuck out. Despite the fact he was one of the very few who I spent my time with, something was gnawing at me, and my patience was non-existent at this point. I didn't do lectures about self-conduct. There was only one god I answered to, and he reigned baseball.

Rafe read my posture. "See you at camp." He hit my shoulder with a friendly bump as he passed me.

I shoved my hands into my jeans with a smirk. "You aren't going to ask me how she was?"

"Hell no, I'm married to my daydream," he said as he closed the door behind him.

I grabbed my wallet and took the buzzing phone out of my pocket and threw it in my open suitcase. I had no issues with cooling my shit. In fact, last night had been the last hurrah of sorts. I had a series to win and over a hundred games to play to get there. For the next two days, I would pay penance for any misgivings that my game was a gift. Physically, I was ready, but my mental game had to be razor-edged, and that meant I had work to do.

Chapter Two

Erica

"I GOT YOUR STATEMENT. I'M LOOKING AT IT NOW," I ASSURED LARRY George, another politician who'd pulled a mid-life moron. An articulately put, yet apologetic stance was my goal when we spoke for the third time in the three hours since a photo leaked of him lip-locked with a busty brunette. A brunette ten years his junior who wasn't his beloved wife. Instead, I got self-indulgent garbage rolling out of his mouth. But it was my job to twist his mishap into something less than the scandal he had caused when he screwed his tennis coach.

"I just . . . I love her. I love my wife. I do," he pleaded.

"You don't have to sell it to me, Larry. I'm not your therapist. In fact, I highly recommend that becomes your next phone call. If I can add in the statement that you and Susan are going to counseling, it would probably be more favorable."

"How about no comment?"

"We've done that before," I reminded. "Accusations are flying. It's time to roll up our sleeves. I'll handle this; you handle Susan. If she talks, we're looking at a shit storm."

"I'm on it."

"Try to stay *off* of it," I said with ice in my voice. I knew Susan, and she loved her husband. Larry was a prick for publicly humiliating her, but he was my priority and client, not his wife. We hung up as I used the last half hour before my meeting to twist his philandering-ass story into something a little less scathing. He was guilty. And if I made it look questionable in any capacity, it was a win. Cleaning up the messes of scandalous politicians had never been my goal when I got into public relations, but it was par for the course. I wasn't in charge, and until that changed, I didn't have the ability to choose my clients.

My assistant, Rowe, buzzed my office. "Erica, Rob wants to see you." I picked up my phone, cringing at the thought of a meeting with my boss.

"What about?"

"I didn't ask," she piped as I looked out through the large window that separated us and saw she was browsing Gucci.

"I like the red," I said in monotone. The screen switched to email, and Rowe turned to look back at me with guilty eyes. *Busted.*

"Sorry, I have a date tonight."

"Good for you. I have a press release coming your way. Contact the usual troops."

Sinking into her chair, she regarded me cautiously. "You need to get out more, ya know?"

"What I need is this press release circulating within the half hour," I said sharply. Rowe sighed through the speaker. "Yes, *boss*."

"And have fun tonight."

I had been working us both weary, and I knew she deserved a break.

I pulled my blazer on and walked out of my office, curious as to why the owner of my PR firm wanted a one on one with me. It was atypical of him to give me the time of day. Rob Zellner was a force to be reckoned with. I respected him for representing some of the biggest names in sports, corporate, and Hollywood, but that's where it ended. He was a prick with a god complex. And though it was his job to make his clients seem warm and approachable, he was anything but either of those. I walked down the carpeted hall to his corner office and smiled at his receptionist, Diane, who managed a sunny disposition despite working beneath Rob's dark cloud.

"Is he free?"

She held up her hand and buzzed him before giving me a warm smile. "Go on in."

In the two years since I'd joined the firm, I'd only been nervous a few times with my boss. Once during my first interview for the job, and another when I'd screwed up royally and ran a press release without a client's permission. I stepped through the door of the black-shrouded office. Rob was one of *those* types who preferred that daylight didn't exist. He had blackout curtains drawn across his floor to ceiling windows, obstructing his view of the New York skyline. His more-salt-than-pepper hair was greased back, and judging by the number of empty coffee cups on his table, he hadn't left his office in a day.

"Sit down," he said as he brought a cup to his lips and tossed back more caffeine. At forty-six years old, Zellner ran a PR empire, and he had no intentions of stopping.

Taking a seat in one of his plush, leather wingback chairs, I looked around his office as he kept an even flow at his keyboard. He had a wife, who never visited the firm, but the photo on his desk suggested she was every bit of the Park Avenue Princess that candied his arm when the occasion called for it.

"Got something for you," he said gruffly before he lifted a paper and tossed it onto the far corner of his desk in front of me. "This paycheck comes from the MLB."

Keeping my disappointment contained, I piped up with false enthusiasm. "Team?"

"Player," he said pointedly, finally glancing my way.

"Player?" My stomach began to knot, and I knew the name before he spoke it.

"Catcher for Denver," he said, nodding toward the paper. "Makavoy."

Heart racing, I cringed as I looked down at the headline. Ren was making them often, and they were impossible to avoid. I inhaled a deep, silent breath and swallowed before I spoke. "I appreciate the fact that you know I'm capable of handling this. But there is a conflict of interest. I know this client. We were romantically involved."

A hint of surprise flicked over Rob's features before he sat back and examined me.

I knew what he was thinking. Compared to Ren's conquests, I looked nothing like the buffet of women he went through. Ren had acquired a new type. Or maybe I had never been his. I winced at the thought before I met the cold, gray eyes of Rob Zellner.

"I assure you," I uselessly pleaded. "This isn't a good fit. It was years ago, but this could get messy."

He remained wordless for several moments before jutting his chin out toward the paper in my hand. I looked down at Ren, whose smug grin graced the cover while his starlet waited in the back seat of the limo. I used to cry when he began making headlines. His seedy behavior had worn me to the point that it disgusted me.

"This is perfect," Rob said confidently. "Have you told anyone else about your involvement with him?"

"Only a few people knew we were dating. He was secretive."

Rob raised a brow. "Things have certainly changed."

"Yes, they have. Ren's a PR nightmare, and I have zero confidence he will listen to me. In fact, I'm positive he will be very resistant to this idea." A thought flickered through my mind. "Unless he requested me?"

"No," Rob said, clasping his hands, his posture slack in his seat. "Management called on this one. He's on a tightrope."

"Really?" I said, leaning forward ignoring the tinge of concern that threatened. For a moment, I briefly entertained the thought of taking him by surprise before I ruined his fun. But even that small amount of satisfaction couldn't sway me. I didn't want to see him. I couldn't face him. "Sir, I don't want to waste any more of your time. I'm sure you can find a better fit for him."Straightening the hem of my blazer, I stood.

"Sit down."

"Sir?"

He can't expect me to—

The cold, dead look in Rob's eyes cut me off mid-thought and told me that hell had, in fact, frozen over, and I was now living in my worst nightmare. All I needed now was Pennywise behind me, letting me know "They all float."

Reluctantly, I sat and tried to maintain my composure. Inside, I was boiling. Rob spoke on as if he hadn't just ruined my life.

"They are planning on a little tough love before Makavoy's training starts in a few days. And you'll be there to greet him. This is his wake-up call."

It was brief, my fear for Ren's career: the chance he might lose his dream because he was acting like an untouchable playboy.

I shrugged as the woman in me spoke out of turn. "He's made his bed."

Rob's piercing scowl was enough to make me retract that.

"And now it's time to clean the sheets," I offered with a lead tongue.

Rob kicked back, his leather seat bouncing with his weight. At that moment, I saw a whisper of a smile that indicated just how much he was enjoying my discomfort and the situation he was about to throw me in.

"You will leave tonight for Scottsdale, and you will rep him through the entire season."

"Sir, I have twelve priority clients—"

"Oh, yes," he deadpanned, "I forgot about the part where this is negotiable."

"I understand, Mr. Zellner, but—"

"Pass your clients out to the capable." He tapped a finger on his desk. "I don't have time to reminisce with you about your ex. He's gone through four reps, and he needs one to stick. You will be that rep. The commission alone is worth your sacrifice. Make no mistake that this job is a test of your abilities at this firm, Ms. Wild. The club is fed up with Makavoy. Be on that plane, play nice with him, and make him the new golden boy of Major League Baseball or I will redecorate your office."

"Understood, sir."

"This will be good for you," he said, dismissing me. "It's time to get your feet wet in sports." It took everything I had not to roll my eyes at the irony.

"Agreed," I conceded as I deflated before I stood with dread-filled limbs.

Zellner peeked over his screen, satisfied with my misery. "This could mean something for your future here. The opportunity is yours to make or break."

I was close to pulling a Jerry McGuire with a "Who's coming with me?" But unlike Jerry, I didn't even have one loyal client to get away with a stunt like that, not to mention the media connections. As long as my name was associated with Zellner Public Relations, I had the devotion of the press. Going at it alone would inevitably end my career. It was a laughable notion at the moment. "Thank you, sir."

I closed the door behind me, my entire frame rattling in trepidation. I was going to have to face Ren for the first time in two years, and not only that, babysit him. I sighed as Diane gave me a sympathetic smile before I walked defeated back down the hall, shut my door behind me and leaned against it before I finally let my anger take hold.

"FUCK!"

A sharp knock at my back seconds later had me jumping out of my skin.

Rowe pried the door open an inch against my weight. "You okay?" she asked in a whisper.

"Yes. I just like to scream fuck," I said dryly and pressed my ass against the door to shut it on her.

"Open this door," she snapped in a muffled order.

I opened it to face her. "Go away, Rowe. I can't talk right now, okay?"

"Do we still have jobs?" she asked as she weighed the look on my face.

"Yes," I said as I fought against threatening tears.

"How bad can it be?"

I stared at the paper clutched in my hand and Ren's smirk.

"The apocalypse."

Chapter Three

Erica

BASEBALL, THE BANE OF MY EXISTENCE FOR SO MANY REASONS. THE current one being I was about to be uprooted from my comfortable corner of the universe in New York to face the desert and my ex.

Rowe's mouth was still hanging open from my admission.

"You dated Ren Makavoy?!"

"Yes."

"And you didn't tell me?!" She was sitting on my bed in our shared loft next to my open suitcase as I began to pluck clothes from my closet.

"Yes," I answered softly. Shoulders slumped, I stared at the shirts in my hand.

This cannot be happening!

"We've been roommates for a year! How could you not tell me?!" The amount of hurt in her voice had my eyes drifting to her.

Rowe was a godsend after my first year alone in New York. I adored her, everything about her, from her sandy blond, sleek-cut bob to her ruby red pumps. Inside and out the woman had class, confidence, and she was exactly what I needed to pull me out of my slump. She was also inappropriate and crass at times, which only made me love her more. She was the sister I never had growing up in a house full of brothers. I'd wandered around New York my first thirteen months a zombie, and she helped to bring me back from the dead.

As if she could read my mind, she nodded. "Ren is why you wore yoga pants the first few months after I met you."

"I'd already been through the worst of it and I just wanted to forget about it. Move on and start a life here."

As far as living in New York went, I finally felt I had everything I needed. Leave it to Ren to screw me out of a comfortable place without him, even if it was temporary and unintentional on his part. Still, his shitty behavior is what landed us both in this situation. It was no real surprise the MLB reached out to the best PR firm in the country. It wasn't just a coincidence; it was also my shitty luck.

"Are you going to tell me what happened?" She sat patiently on the bed, her petite frame taking up only a quarter of it. She was manicured for her date but was making him wait for her in the lobby downstairs while seeing me off.

I tucked a few shirts in my suitcase and grabbed her hand before I sat down next to her.

"I've told you all about him. I just left out who he was."

"That's a pretty fucking *big* detail, Erica. Woman, he's the most beautiful man on the planet! Like the hottest guy I've ever seen in my life," she said, placing her hand on her chest. "I don't know how you handled that."

"His looks were never an issue for us. He used to hate being labeled a pretty boy," I said ironically. "I guess he's finally using it to his advantage."

"It all make's sense now," she said, piecing it together. "Why you hate watching baseball."

"He's one of the reasons, now. My mom is the other."

Rowe nodded. She knew enough to put the pieces together. "So exactly what happened between you two?"

"I didn't wait around to see," I said with a thickening throat. "I couldn't, Rowe."

"In a way, I get it," she said thoughtfully. "But, Ren Makavoy! Tell me he was as good as he looks."

"Better than anything you can imagine," I said softly.

"Do you regret it?" she asked carefully.

"For as long as it took for him to make his first headline." I closed my eyes as a bitter laugh escaped. "How could I regret it now?" The threatening lump dissolved as damning images of him surrounded by a sea of silicone tits flashed through my mind. "He turned into exactly what I was afraid of."

She looked at me with doe eyes and glossed lips. "Do you still have feelings for him?"

"Yes and no. He's ruined my opinion of him, right along with everyone else's. I know not all that's printed is the real story, but if *half* of its true, he's not the guy I knew. He got caught up in the celebrity of it all, I guess. There's nothing there to hold on to. I'm moving on," I said with a grin. "Thanks to you."

Rowe pursed her lips.

"What?"

"It's just that you haven't dated much this last year. Like, at all."

"I have," I defended weakly.

"Yeah, right," she deadpanned.

"I've been busy at the firm. You know that."

Rowe nodded. "Fine. Blame the firm." Before I had a chance to argue, she stood. "Erica, you can do this. I want you to call me every damn day."

"I know I can," I sighed. "I just don't want to."

She squeezed my shoulders as if she was prepping me for war. "Listen to me, woman. You can do this. You are the toughest bitch I know. Just be the annoying professional you are and get it done."

I groaned as I zipped my suitcase. "I have to trail him like a club wife all over the country. It's ironic, isn't it? This is exactly what I didn't want."

She stood and smoothed out her dress. "If there's one thing I know about you. Erica Wild, it's that you know how to play ball."

A sharp laugh escaped despite my mood. "That's the cheesiest pun I've ever heard in my life," I said with a smile.

"Give him hell, babe," she said before she pulled me into a hug. "And call me if you need backup."

JERKED awake as the wheels of the plane touched down, I mourned the last of my New York reality. Ten months of my life were about to revolve around baseball and Ren, and I didn't know which I dreaded more. It was like a jail sentence, or I was paying penance for leaving him, or both. City lights twinkled out of the dirty window and distracted me as the captain spoke about the time and temperature. I'd never been to Scottsdale and had no desire to. I hated the heat. It was a good thing the weather would be bearable for spring training.

I pulled my abused suitcase from the overhead compartment and hailed a cab to the hotel. To my surprise, the hotel was a small consolation. Zellner had his secretary arrange my stay, and if I had no other comfort, at least I could take solace in the posh surroundings of my temporary home.

My shoulders sagged in relief for the first time that day, until I heard a familiar laugh come from the bar just across the lobby. Ren was a room away. Momentarily stunned, I took a deep breath.

An older man greeted me at the front desk. "Welcome to Paradise Valley."

I bit my lip in an attempt to hold in my sarcastic reply. "Thanks," I said dryly.

"Wild, Erica, checking in."

The desk clerk eyed me. "Wild?"

"Yep," I popped out, avoiding eye contact as another laugh crashed into my chest and threatened to rattle me.

Don't look. You know if you look around that corner you will see him. You need a night of prep. Just. Don't. Look!

"They are making a little noise tonight," the clerk said with a chuckle. "They've calmed down a bit. Training starts in two days." The man, in his upper fifties, leaned over to me conspiratorially with wide eyes. "Baseball. Major Leagues."

I had no choice but to smile. "Ah, I see."

"They shouldn't be a problem for you," he assured me.

My smile still plastered, I spoke through my teeth. "From your lips to God's ears."

"I've got you in room 212, and the bellman will take up your bag."

"No need," I said as I took the keycard. "I'm all set."

"Enjoy your stay, Ms. Wild."

"Thank you."

The next laugh shattered my resolve. Using a rubber plant as camouflage, I peeked around the corner. I recognized Hembrey, the pitcher, first. He'd made a fast track from the Minors and pitched his way onto one of the best teams in the Majors. And standing opposite him with a beer in hand was Ren.

I fought for breath as I took in his tall, muscular frame in dark jeans that clung to his thick thighs and perfect ass. The T-shirt he modeled was unfit for the classy bar. Except it wasn't the clothes that made him stand out. It was the way he held himself.

He had a Denver cap on backward that hid his thick black hair. And I knew if he glanced my way, I'd be paralyzed where I stood, like the first time I saw him three years ago. No other man I'd ever met had the soul-stealing eyes of Ren Makavoy. And no man ever would. My pulse kicked up as I studied his profile made up of dark, thick lashes, high cheekbones, full lips, and a masculine jaw. He was a living dream.

And at one point in time, he had been mine and I his, and now we were total strangers. The man I knew wasn't a playboy. Sure, he was cocky to a point and assured of his talent. But off the field, he was a different kind of man. He dreamed of having a family, baseball, and little else. And though his dreams weren't very original, they were the dreams of a man who grew up with nothing. So, for Ren, that made them big. He was a closet nerd behind his perfect structure and sexy swagger. Ren had the perfect mathematical brain for ball, and that was one of the aces he carried up his sleeve. And I doubted any of the women he'd bedded in the last few years knew how excited he got when a new Transformer movie trailer came out. Or that he color-coded his closet. Or that he was a germaphobe and sanitized everything.

And every one of those quirks had me falling harder for him than I'd ever imagined possible. Even when I told him we wouldn't happen within the first ten minutes of meeting him. Even when I let him kiss me that night after he pulled his first card trick to get the date. Two years apart seemed like nothing as I gazed at him only feet away.

Aching to see his vivid, neon blue eyes, I watched him as a flood of precious moments filtered through my aching brain.

"What happened to you?" I murmured across the space between us.

As if he knew someone was watching him, he began to turn his head my way. Within seconds, I was safely on the elevator, chest heaving and throat on fire.

With the doors safely closed, I sank against the weight of the feelings that threatened to stir. I was nowhere near ready to face him. Ren was one of those men that physically stunned with his looks, paralyzing you before he devoured you. And when he struck, he did it with precision. Nerdy quirks aside, the man knew how to use it to his advantage.

I'd talked a fair game to Rowe, but I knew without any doubt my mental game had to be strong to face him head-on. My attraction to him went far deeper than his skin, always had, but the man's beauty was a tough thing to press past. It was no exaggeration that he was one of the best-looking men alive. And I had first-hand knowledge of what it felt like to have his full attention. I shivered at the memory of his mouth, fingers, and tongue.

Walking on Jell-O legs toward my room door, I cursed the weakness in me and pressed the key card in before I burst into my room and tried to catch my breath. An hour later, and after a very expensive mini bar raid, I felt the tension start to ease.

In less than twelve hours, I would have to face those eyes, but it didn't mean I had to rehash our past. I may have a weakness for the man, but I damned sure didn't have to show it, and any feelings I had left were for the former version of Ren.

I was in charge of fixing his reputation. It was a job. He was a job, no more. And I would handle it like I did everything else. Despite my earlier remark to Rowe, who was a safe world away, she was right. It was time to play ball.

Chapter Four

Ren

I'D BEEN SUMMONED TO ANOTHER MEETING ABOUT MY BEHAVIOR. MY LAST. I would be damned if I made the same mistakes this season. If there were a hand to shake or a baby to kiss, I would do it. I would become the baseball equivalent of an ass-kissing politician. It didn't matter that I hated being in the public eye, aside from ball. It was part of the program. They didn't call it "The Big Show" for nothing.

So, while I may have earned my reputation—lashing out at the douche bags who taunted me with their cameras while inadvertently slipping into the role of a womanizer—I knew it was time to clean it up.

This season I was determined to turn that around. I didn't have it in me to keep up the charade anymore. I was going mute. As silent as a church mouse. But as much as I hated admitting that to Jake, the assistant coach who had scheduled the meeting, I was hard pressed to try and stop the shit storm I was about to walk into.

"Jake, I've got it covered," I assured as we walked down the hall toward one of the conference rooms of the hotel.

"Don't bother pleading your case," he said, refusing to glance my way.

I blew out a slow breath of frustration and kept my pace just behind him. Resolved to deal with whatever shit they decided to dish out, I kept my mouth shut and followed him through the door. It was only when I saw the woman sitting at the head of the conference table that I faltered.

Jake looked back at me and nodded toward an empty chair. "Shut the door and take a seat, Makavoy."

But the sight in front of me—long, dark hair I could still feel dance over my skin, large round brown eyes, lashes for days, and perfect, plump lips—rendered that order impossible. Shock filtered through my system as I looked on at the only woman I ever loved. Cool as ice, she sat in her seat, her gaze locked on her tablet.

Jake cleared his throat, and I saw her reluctantly lift her eyes to meet mine. There was a beat of recognition, a flicker of the two us in them before her gaze moved back to the iPad in her hand.

I already knew her play.

I bit my lip to hide my smile and took a seat at the opposite end of the table. I felt the solid burn, the inescapable urge to feast on her. It had been too damn long.

Two years. Two fucking years I'd waited to set eyes on her again, and I was going to take my time. I let them drift from the table back to her. She was furiously typing out a text on her phone before she set it down to face me head-on. "Morning, gentlemen. Good to see you, Ren," she said evenly.

"Likewise, Erica," I mused as I soaked in her flawless face.

She looked sharp and completely unfazed. She'd been ready, but I was still reeling. Her hair was tied back in a sleek ponytail, and I clenched my fists at the urge to free it. She was every bit of the woman I remembered, but even more beautiful. Time had been kind to her and a motherfucker to me.

Jake took the seat next to her. "You two know each other?"

"We're well acquainted," she said sharply, dismissing the year we spent together.

But I wasn't about to let it go and leaned in Jake's direction. "Very well acquainted. We—"

"Baseball is a small world," Erica said, cutting me off and turning to Jake. "Shall we start?"

I kept my eyes on her as she handed her iPad to him. "This is what I propose."

Jake scanned it and nodded toward me. "Erica is with Zellner PR, New York. We got the call from Walter yesterday that you'd taken it upon yourself to relieve him of his position. She will be representing you throughout this season."

All amusement left my face. "You mean the team?"

"No, I mean *you*, Ren," he said pointedly. "Do you see the rest of the team in here? Whatever objections you have, I frankly don't want to fucking hear them."

I let out a chuckle. "Not even the fact that I gave this woman her first orgasm?"

Erica shook her head as if she was prepared for that, her demeanor unchanged. She gave me a stone gaze. "Ren, let's be adults. I'm here to help you."

Unable to resist, I raised my hand like a good boy.

"For Christ's sake," Jake said as he glared over at me. "Ren, this is my last time walking you to school. Either let this happen, or I'll make goddamn sure this season hurts. I'm over this shit. You aren't the only catcher in the League."

"Nope," I said confidently, crossing my arms, "but I'm the catcher you need."

Erica chose that moment to jump in and hand my ass to me.

"You snub your teammates. You're the only man in the League with an all-woman fan club. You've got zero respect from those you need it from. And you've lost millions of dollars in endorsements because of your indiscretions. So, you tell me, Ren, does Jake need to be explaining this to you? Does anyone? You want to be taken seriously as an athlete? I'll do my best to turn this around, but I need your full cooperation."

I could see it then, in her eyes, I repulsed her. She wasn't acting anything like the woman that left me shattered. She was shrewd, cold, yet so fucking beautiful. I hated the way she looked at me. I expected it, but it got under my skin. Still, I felt the bittersweet relief of just sharing space with her.

Cornered in a way I'd never imagined possible, but just as easily as I had done three years ago, I handed her my fate. Because I had no choice.

"All right then, Erica. Tell me," I said, steepling my fingers underneath my chin, "how do you plan on fixing me?" I couldn't resist sucking my bottom lip. Her eyes flared.

"There's no fixing you, Ren. It's all about perception, and before this season ends, we'll make them all believers."

I leaned forward, determined to keep her engaged. "Make them believe what, exactly?"

"That you're an athlete with a heart for and to play baseball. Because that's all you have left."

Touché, Ms. Wild, but you made it so ball was all I had left.

I kept that comment to myself. This had to be a pre-season gift from the god of baseball. Not only did I have her attention, I would have her all season. I'd had two years to think about why she left me so callously. Two years of a well-deserved explanation I had every intention of getting.

She stood and shook hands with Jake before she walked in my direction. I tilted my head back to get a good look at her but remained planted in the leather chair. All business, she pushed a printed schedule in front of me. It was impossible to ignore the hint of mint in her hair, the vanilla scent on her skin, or the curve of her hips in the skirt she wore. Her long locks slid over her shoulders like silk. Silk I used to wrap in my fist before I rode her into screaming my name.

"You'll be working double time during training. This is your itinerary preliminary to the season. You will be doing multiple interviews due to the public interest you've provoked to start the trek back into the good graces of the fans. I have prepared some questions, and we will go over the answers in the morning."

I didn't bother glancing at it as I studied her face, her eyes cast downward.

"My cell number is on the top. I'll be in touch."

Jake held the door open and closed it behind her with a "thank you" as she left. I unclenched my fists as he sat next to me. "She's your one chance at turning this circus into something respectable."

I held my palms out in surrender. "I agree."

Jake's brows drew, full of suspicion. "Don't get any fucking cute ideas."

"I'm out of them, Jake. Scouts honor," I said, folding the paper in half and sliding my fingers along it.

"I doubt the Scouts would let you in. Don't piss on her, Makavoy. Just let her do her job."

I had been a Scout, but he didn't need to know that. "Like I said, Jake, I've got this covered. I'm done with all the bullshit. You can tell them, or I'll tell them myself. Either way, I'm not for sale other than on the field. You might do well to remind them of that. My private life is just that: *private*."

"Your behavior off the field is a reflection on this team, Ren. You know that, and the fact that I must spend time away from what's important to help manage your shit is ridiculous. Your contract's up after the season. You might do well to remember that," he said, snuffing out the rest of the argument.

I'd gone too far, drawn too much negative attention to myself, to the team. My heart beat erratically in my chest as I thought of the repercussions of not signing for another season with Denver. I was throwing it all away.

But in a way, I felt rewarded by the sight of the woman who just walked out the door. But because of her, ball *was* all I had. And my heart, well, that belonged to ball now, too, because she'd handed it back to me with enough seam scars to never forget it.

Jake shut the door behind him as I absorbed Erica's words. It was evident she had washed her hands of me when she left for New York; her actions had said as much. I knew without a doubt she didn't want to have a thing to do with me in Arizona either. But before the season ended, I would make damn sure I got the satisfaction of an explanation.

It wasn't about revenge; it was about living with the feeling that, for all that time, I'd been wrong about her. And I fucking hated it. Opening the door, I shoved the paper into my pocket and paused when I saw her waiting for me on the other side of the hall.

The thrill of seeing her after so much time was cut short when she spoke to the floor between us.

"Ren," she said softly. "I'm asking you—no, I'm begging you, not to bring us or our past up again in front of anyone. I've worked so damn hard to get to where I am, and I don't want anything circulating."

"Ashamed of me?" I asked with a chuckle as I stood in the doorway, my arms on the frame. She may as well have shot me in the chest as she brought her dusky gaze to mine with a "Yes."

"Don't give it a second thought," I assured.

She closed her eyes as if it pained her to look at me. I was hoping that was the case as my gut churned. I kept my voice level despite the need to confront her, ignoring the fire brewing in my chest. "Tell me something. If you hate me so much, what are you doing here?"

She opened her eyes with steely resolve. "I have a job to do. I didn't come by choice. You have a job to do as well. So, can we at least just keep this civil?"

Ignoring her plea to keep the peace—though I had every intention of playing along with her tactics to better my image—I took a step forward, closing the space between us. I was enjoying her discomfort far too much to let her off the hook so easily.

"Suddenly you're worried about the state of our relationship? That's rich. You know, I haven't changed my number. A phone call would have been nice. 'Hey, Ren, how are you doing?' or something to that effect."

She shook her head. "I won't do it. I won't rehash our past."

"It's funny you say that," I said with a slow exhale, commanding her eyes.

She let out a breath of her own and threw her shoulders back, nothing but fight in her stance. "Oh?"

I nodded. "I think you're right."

Relief covered her features as she spoke. "You do? That's good because—"

"Yeah, it was a long time ago, Erica. There's no sense bringing up the past." But it was all I could see when I looked at her: a curious brown gaze, a beautiful smile the first time we locked eyes, my name whispered in prayer from her lips as she clutched me to her, her head thrown back the first time I fucked her, her tears the first time she told me she loved me, our late-night talks in the dark, naked and wasted on each other, the fit of her in my arms when she needed me, the feeling of her when I needed her, the sweet catch of her breath the first time I told her I loved her. It was all there, on replay and circulating in the air between us. I hadn't imagined her love for me. I knew it, and she did, too. And then it was gone, and so was she, like we never happened. No trace but the ache that I tried to kill with every swig of liquor, every thrust of my cock, or punch I threw. I'd acted out of hurt at first, and it had spiraled into something I never wanted. But the more I woke up and hated myself, the more the pattern grew. Staring at her, still fucking hurt, brought out anger I didn't realize I was still holding onto.

With Erica in Arizona, I wasn't sure I could handle letting that door swing open again. It was just a matter of a season before she walked away again, and this time I could keep myself from being ripped apart when she did it.

But I would have to keep my distance. Even as the thought crossed my mind, I took a step toward her.

She surveyed my face for any sign of a catch for my earnest cooperation. She knew me too well.

"Okay, then. That's—" she swallowed. "That's great, Ren. I just . . . want to get along and get you out of this mess."

I inched forward as she plastered herself to the wall. Her eyes dilated as I leaned in. Undeniably responsive. She always had been, and my cock twitched in recognition.

"I'm all yours, Wild. Do what you will."

Steadfast, she pushed at my chest before she crossed her arms defensively. "Don't come at me like that. Don't be a pig."

"I'm just being sincere, Erica," I taunted. "Maybe that's a foreign concept to you. To say something and mean it." I couldn't help it. It made me look like a whiny, jilted bitch, but then again, I'd never got the chance to state my grievances when she fled my apartment in Atlanta. She deserted me in the most cold-hearted fucking way imaginable.

She searched my eyes as the anger brewed. "What happened to you?"

"Me?" I taunted innocently, taking a step back before I forgot myself and did something fucking stupid. Because I was done with stupid. "Can't say much has changed."

"The headlines indicate otherwise."

"You know better than to believe everything you read," I said absently.

Arms still crossed, she raised a brow. "So, you're not the biggest douche bag in Major League Baseball?"

I clicked my tongue at her. "Not a nice way to start our friendship by insulting me."

Her shoulders slumped. "Sorry, you're right. I apologize."

Crowding her again, I dug in, my eyes masked. "For what exactly?"

She hesitated. "For insulting you."

"Oh, is that all?"

"Ren, I—"

"You left. I guess that's all I need to know," I said, giving her space back and shoving my hands in my pockets. I was burning hot and throwing cold. Space from her is exactly what I needed. "It's going to be a good season. Let's focus on that."

"I don't follow ball anymore."

"No?" I shrugged. "A traitor to all things, I guess."

Narrowing her eyes, she tilted her chin toward me. "Traitor? Hardly. I think I've done enough time."

"Jail sentence, huh?" I leaned in again, my arm above her head, my lips an inch from hers. I could feel the same vibrations between us. "So now it's my turn to ask. What happened to you?"

She opened her plump lips, and I placed my finger on them. "On second thought, I don't give a shit." Her eyes widened as I pushed off the wall and started to walk away. I spoke over my shoulder. "Let's not get this twisted; you work for *me* now until I say otherwise. My nights are my fucking own. Make me look good, but don't get in my way."

She was on my heels in an instant. "So that's how you're going to play this?"

I stopped, and she ran into my back with a thud. I stood with her breath on my neck and closed my eyes. "I'm not playing anything, Erica. I don't have an angle. I'm done making headlines for anything other than ball. But you can bet your sweet ass that I'm not yours to handle. It's my image you'll manage, not me.

"Ren, you just said—"

I turned to face her again, stifling the jilted bitch inside me to bring the brutal bastard forward. "It's about ball. I'll play along. Paint any picture you want, just remember you don't know a damn thing about me anymore. So, don't pretend to."

I was a few steps down the hall when she called after me. "Oh, I know you, Ren Makavoy! I'm betting there's a deck of cards in the front pocket of your jeans. Oh, and I'm positive you still take off your shirt and sanitize the toilet seat before you take a shit!"

Chapter Five

Erica

Not my finest moment. Not at all. Especially when Rafe Hembrey caught the ass-end of my outburst and began laughing hysterically at Ren's retreating back before he squinted his eyes at me curiously.

Rafe was a tall drink of water, and if I weren't so damn high from being in Ren's proximity, I would've appreciated the sight of him more. But it just so happened that Ren was the only man who had dazed me to the point of being manic, and it was only partially due to his beauty. It was what was between us, the connection that'd sent me into a head-first spiral. And it was still there because I was shaking.

Rafe spoke up as I glared at Ren's retreating back. "Don't worry, sweetheart. He's just a little hellbent on ruining himself. I'm sure it's nothing personal. You can do better."

"Thanks for the pep talk, but I'm not his latest conquest. I'm his new publicist."

"Oh, well then," he said, taking a step forward extending his hand. "Rafe Hembrey."

"I'm aware," I said, managing a sincere smile and shaking his hand.

He was a gentleman, unlike the jerk who just walked away from me. "Erica Wild. I'm a fan."

"Always nice to have those," he said with a panty-melting smile. Rafe was the opposite of Ren; he had a stellar reputation for being both a family man and an outstanding team player. He was the best pitcher in the League.

He had that cocky assurance thing going on, but he was as humble as a player could be. I was sure he didn't go walking around with Ren's newly-acquired God complex. Rafe simply was the best. So was Ren. He just wasn't good at being the best.

Thinking on my feet, I addressed Rafe. "I could use your help this season. We need him acting a little less like him and more like you. Do you have a minute?"

He ushered me out of the hall and into the lobby, where we both took a seat at one of the comfortable couches. Without looking back, Ren made his way out of the sliding glass doors of the hotel, full-on badass swagger in tow. I ignored the sting of his brush off. Because, in truth, I deserved it more than I cared to admit.

"I'm all for helping the sad bastard. I've been telling him for years he needs to wipe his nose."

I sighed as I leaned back on the couch. "Can I buy you a beer?"

"No thanks, I'm set," he said, leaning back in his own seat. "I've got meetings to get to."

"I won't take much of your time. I have sort of a game plan in mind for the season, and I was hoping I could run a few strategies by you."

He gave me a devilish grin. "If you're going to speak in sports metaphors, you get my full attention."

I shrugged. "When in Rome, right?"

"I'm open to any suggestions you have, but I should warn you now, he won't make it easy for you."

"I'm aware," I sighed. "We're sort of acquainted."

"Apparently, since you are aware of his bathroom habits," he said with a knowing smirk. "Being on the road with him is a nightmare. He's got serious issues. This one time—" he chuckled "—at the airport, I had to snatch off some freaky face mask he ordered on the internet because he was scaring children. Is he your ex?"

I bit my lip and nodded as I sank into the couch. That admission of our past relationship was solely on me and my outburst.

"We dated a few years ago."

"Interesting. And you're in PR." Rafe chewed on that a minute. "Bullseye," he whispered to himself.

"Pardon?"

Rafe moved forward bracing his clasped hands between his knees. "I just find it ironic that he hates the spotlight and he's been in it quite a bit lately."

"He's a different man than he was when we were together," I replied, trying to hide the disappointment in my voice. Still, I knew what I was getting into when I walked into the situation.

"That's just the thing though, Erica. Why is he so hellbent on making headlines?" He widened his eyes as he looked me over carefully.

It wasn't in the way a man appreciated a woman; it was as if he was trying to tell me—

"Wait," I asked incredulously. "You don't think that shit show was for *me*?"

Rafe shrugged. "Can you think of a better reason? How close were you?"

Close enough to have hurt us both so badly that there was no way to come back from it.

Even when I realized it was a mistake to leave.

Even when I realized it wasn't a mistake because of the womanizing pig he became. And still, I loved him anyway. Every minute of every day for years. But I finally got myself together, and I'd hoped the same for him.

"We were close. But if he thinks screwing everyone with two legs and acting like an idiot off the field is the way to go, he's mistaken."

"You're here," Rafe pointed out.

"It wasn't his doing," I said confidently.

Rafe slowly nodded as if he didn't believe a word I was saying.

"Do you really want to know this story?" I asked sheepishly.

Rafe nodded. "I've known that man two seasons and never once seen him with a woman more than a few hours. So, color me curious."

"We dated exclusively for a year and then things started to go in a direction . . . I didn't want." I kept my eyes low with my admission. "I left him while he was in spring training. We were living together at the time and I took a job in New York. I made sure he couldn't come after me because of ball."

Rafe paused. "Ouch."

"At the time, I thought I was doing the right thing, and when I realized I screwed up, it was too late."

Rafe leaned in. "What happened?"

"He made his first headline."

His first headline was being caught in the back of a limo with two well-known reality TV stars. *Naked* reality TV stars. Since then, he'd moved his way up to Oscar-winning actresses. And I'd lost every piece of myself to every word, every picture, and had no choice but to follow because it was my job. Realization dawned as Rafe cupped his chin. "So, he lashed out to hurt you. Looks like he got what he wanted."

I guffawed. "Hardly," I said, staring in the direction Ren left. But that was a lie. And maybe it was time to start telling the truth. Maybe I could finally try to explain it to Ren to make him understand why I left the way I did. He didn't deserve it, even if he had hurt me back just as badly.

I looked over to Rafe. "Yeah, he got what he wanted."

I couldn't believe the best pitcher in the MLB was talking to me about my failed relationship. But Ren had made it impossible to avoid. If Ren was still pissed at me for old hurts, he was dragging his reputation and his team down with him. Rafe and Ren were a team within the team, so if one was off, it threw them both off.

Rafe read my thoughts. "I need him sharp. This could do more harm than good."

"I need my job. My boss gave me an ultimatum. I worked extremely hard to get here. I had no idea which way that meeting would go."

"From the looks of it, it didn't go well."

I bit my lip and shook my head.

"I'm going to ask you a question that's none of my business."

"Okay," I said carefully.

"Is he alone in the way he feels?"

I swallowed and crossed my arms over my chest. "I can't be with him the way he is. And it's more complicated than that. So much more complicated."

Rafe picked at a piece of leather on the corner of the couch.

"Looks like we're fucked."

"Rafe, this is what I do. You keep his head in the game. And I'll keep his nose clean off the field."

"And what about your predicament?"

"Let me handle it," I assured, on shaky ground. "You have a series to claim."

Rafe gave me an award-winning smile. "Damn right I do."

"We need all hands on deck this season. He has no family, no real support system."

Rafe nodded. "I'm aware."

"If there's anything you can think of, I'll make it happen. You have anyone in mind who could help?"

A slow budding smile spread across Rafe's face. "Fuckin' A, I do."

Chapter Six

Ren

"YOU PLAN ON JOINING US IN WARM-UP, MAKAVOY?" HAMLIN CALLED AS I started another set of reps on the bench.

I had more than enough aggression to get out due to an early breakfast with Erica. We were staying in the same damned hotel and I didn't know how to feel about it. Before the meeting in the conference room, the last time I saw her, she was wrapped around me against my front door, clinging for life as I drove into her like a crazed man, desperate to make sure she knew she had me in both body and heart.

No matter how hard I baited her that morning, she stayed on topic, not straying from the plans she had for me.

"Are you fucking serious?" I said as I shoveled in the last bite of my wheat banana pancakes.

"There is nothing wrong with being a big brother, Ren. Except don't say fuck when you're around him." She kept her eyes on her tablet, while her long lashes danced along her cheekbones. Erica surpassed beautiful and was the most stunning woman I'd ever met. Her beauty was all natural. And it wasn't just her silky black hair, deep-set brown eyes, or smooth, olive skin. She had a glow about her, a deeply-nestled charisma that made her loveable before she even spoke a word. It was the first thing I noticed about her. It's what drew me to her. That and her sense of humor, which seemed to have vanished. The woman I knew had jokes; this woman had an agenda, and I hated it.

"It's the most obvious publicity stunt ever," I argued. "The media won't buy that I'm trying to be a positive role model."

She widened her eyes as she twisted her hair into a bun on top of her head.

"How about this novel idea. You actually try to make an effort to mentor a kid who needs your help."

She knew I hated her hair up when we were together. I ignored it as I also tried to ignore the sight of her perfect tits in a sports bra, flimsy T-shirt, and yoga pants. Fuck me, she looked perfect.

"Not a good move," I dismissed. "What's next?"

"It's happening. He'll be at the field tomorrow after school for an introduction. His name is Malcolm Bruce, and he's thirteen. You're his idol, and he's been in and out of foster care for years." Realization struck as I pushed my plate away and glared at her.

"What are you trying to do, dredge up the sympathy card?"

"I'm trying to remind you of where you came from," she said in a whisper. "You're a twenty-seven-year-old millionaire with the world at your fingertips. It wouldn't hurt him to see a future is possible no matter the circumstances he's in now."

"I'm a fucking lottery winner," I said. "This won't change anything for him."

"He's varsity potential and an all-around catcher at thirteen years old. So, I'm going to disagree with you on that," she said, popping a piece of melon ball into her mouth. "And you worked your way up to the MLB. You didn't win anything. You earned it."

I couldn't argue with her there. I'd spent a majority of my life working my way to the season I was about to play. And her compliment didn't go unnoticed, but I was too busy staring at her peaked nipples to acknowledge it.

"Stop staring at my chest. Jesus, Ren, you and Malcolm will probably get along famously with your maturity level."

"Hey, apparently your nipples are reminiscing with the way they're waving at me," I said with a shrug. Her olive complexion reddened. She used to beg me with the lips she was biting. I swiped my tongue over my lower lip, and she stared at me blankly before snapping back to focus.

"So, back to Malcolm. We'll see how it goes and then take it from there. We won't release anything until we're ready." I was shaking my head while she spoke. "I won't manipulate the media at the cost of hurting some kid's feelings."

She looked me over with lost, glossy eyes as if she had seen a ghost. "There may be some decency left in you, Ren. And it won't be manipulating if it's the truth. What exactly are you doing that is so important with your time? You can't make a little room for a kid who wants to believe life is better than being passed around like he's been for the last few years? Like you were?"

I was in three foster homes before I graduated high school, but I had no complaints. The families were friendly, but I didn't take part in any family-like activities. I didn't leave any of the homes as a favorite child. Only one family kept in touch and managed to come to a game. I remembered the day they visited me. They asked for money. I gave it to them and never let them back in. I didn't even blame them. I wasn't angry, but I was done pretending I was ever a part of any family. Because I wasn't. I didn't have one, but I eventually hoped for my own. Hoped with the woman who sat in front of me. I wanted to have as many kids as I could put in her. I wanted a house full of brown-eyed girls, and if we were lucky, a little slugger to teach ball to.

"Ren?" Erica looked over at me as I brushed the thoughts aside and wiped my hands free of crumbs. My anger slid back into place.

"Fine. Tomorrow." I pushed my chair back, and it slammed into the table behind me.

"Ren," she said in a whisper. "I'm sorry if this upsets you."

Her posture screamed coward, but her words rang sincerely. It didn't matter. No matter how relieved I was to just lay eyes on her the day before, or how much I wanted to understand why she left and forgive her, I couldn't. Not in that moment and maybe not ever. Because in all honesty, it hurt. She. Just. Fucking. Hurt. "Don't bother being sorry now, Erica," I said as I swiped my hat from the table and left her there.

"Makavoy!" Hamlin snapped, breaking me out of my pissed off bench press. How many reps had I done? Did it even fucking matter?

"Jesus, man, what are you doing pushing and without a spot? You're a toddler," Hamlin scolded as he pulled the bar up and set it on the rest.

Grabbing my gear, I followed him onto the field where he directed me.

"Go warm up with Hembrey and meet me back here for some mitt work. I have some things I want to go over."

"Aye, aye," I muttered as I paused my feet before I spoke at his retreating back. "Who's that with Hembrey?"

Hamlin was already gone as I took another step forward and my mood lifted when I saw the stance of the catcher. "No fucking way." I jogged over to see Rafe rocket a ball toward the man in my place behind home plate.

"Pracht, what in the hell are you doing here?" I asked like a giddy fucking school girl.

Andy stood and grinned at me behind his mask. "Sup, Tin Man? I heard you were having problems with your period. When are you assholes going to let me quit this game?"

He threw the ball back to Rafe and tossed my mitt at me before we clasped hands and bumped shoulders.

"It's you that's on the rag, isn't it? Now that you're all housebroken. How's the kid?"

"I had twins, idiot," Andy said with the shake of his head. "They are fine. You want to explain to me why this dipshit here decided that I needed to uproot my family this season to come babysit you?"

No matter how much he protested, I knew he was happy to be back on the field. It showed on his face, in his posture. It was in his blood.

"You probably booked a flight the minute you got the call," I said, sliding my hand into my glove. "Thanks for ruining my mitt with your fat-ass fingers."

"One of us has to use it properly," he barked. "You sure you want to stick your hand in that without wiping it down? I changed a few diapers before I got here."

I cringed at the thought, and Andy had a good laugh at my expense.

"I bet you still look at people who sneeze like they are terrorists," he joked as Rafe approached us from the mound.

"What's going on?" I asked between them. "Are we having a slumber party? Andy, I hate to be the one to break it to you, but your balls are gray and your knees are shit, so I know you aren't playing."

Andy ran a hand through his goatee. "Fuck yourself, Makavoy. I'm here to get you through the season."

"A consultant of sorts," Rafe added with a clap on my back. Pride stood in the way of me being fully happy with Andy's arrival.

I studied Rafe. "Think I can't call the balls anymore, Hembrey?"

Rafe shook his head. "No, man, not at all. But what could it hurt?"

There was something I couldn't put my finger on, but I let it go because, honestly, nothing was sweeter than having them both in my corner. If management didn't have a problem with it, I sure as shit didn't. Andy was an expert strategist, and though I prided myself on being the same, I put that pride in the backseat when it came to the logistics of baseball. Masterminded shit went into planning every game, and Andy was a welcome ally.

"Glad you're here, man," I said honestly and clapped his back.

"Beautiful fucking reunion, guys," Rafe taunted, "but I'm warmed up. So, let's do our jobs."

He was full of fire and feeling himself, so Andy and I indulged. And for that short time on the field, just the three of us, I felt a swell in my chest. I might never have had a real family in the sense that everyone else did, but I did have brothers in baseball.

And maybe Erica was right. Maybe it wouldn't hurt to give that to someone else.

Chapter Seven

Erica

"How's it going?" Rowe asked as I stood on the foul line and watched the commotion on the field. The catchers were getting pummeled. It was grueling for them the first few days of training. Every sharp arm in the Cactus League was firing at them. Ren seemed to be holding his own, but I knew he'd be exhausted by the end of the day.

"It's going," I said, gripping my phone as I watched Andy Pracht and Ren exchange brief words. Rafe's call to bring Andy to Arizona was a good one. I knew Andy was the perfect man to have in Ren's corner if the season got sticky.

"Tell me more, woman! Was he surprised to see you?"

"Yeah, that was clear," I said, remembering his searing ice gaze across the conference table the day before and the way he studied me at breakfast that morning. "Rowe, I can't even lie. I don't want to. The minute I saw him, I wanted to fly across the table and . . . I don't know . . . *Help me.*"

"Just remember all the reasons why you left."

"One. One reason," I said as I bundled up against the morning chill while emotion fought its way up my throat. "Well, one reason that sticks out."

"Which was?" she prompted.

"Break the cycle."

"You weren't talking like that here," she reminded. "You're already disintegrating."

"Yeah, well, with the distance between us, I got stronger. And when I saw him splashed all over the web with a new piece of ass every day, it was easier not to like him."

"Remember, he's probably bedded women who don't know how to spell syphilis."

I cracked a smile. "How do you spell it?"

A short pause.

I couldn't help my laugh. "You're Googling it aren't you?"

"Shut up, bitch. I'm trying to help here." We both chuckled as I stared at my Nikes because the alternative was too painful.

"But looking at him, Rowe. Talking to him. It's hard. I'm already letting it get the best of me."

"This isn't good," she said with a sympathetic tone. "Not this soon."

"I know, trust me. It's like the minute I saw him, I uncorked, and I can't seem to get my shit together."

Rowe sighed. "You still love him."

"Of course I do, and I hate him just as much. It's a fine line I'm walking, and every two minutes one emotion or the other rears its ugly head. I'm flailing here."

"Jesus," she whispered. "Listen, I know this is hard, but there has to be some common ground. Is he being civil?"

"I don't know if you could call it that. I'm getting whiplash; hot one minute, cold and indifferent the next. I think he hates me. I need to get the hell out of here."

"Figures." The voice was a low rumble behind me. "You didn't even make it twenty-four hours."

"Is that him?" Rowe asked, her voice in a panic for me.

"Rowe, I'll call you back."

"RESIST! RESIST!" she urged as I cut her off, slid my phone into my pocket, and turned to face Ren.

As his stunning eyes pierced me, I felt myself falter even more. I cursed my stupidity in thinking I could brush our past away and still be professional. But I wasn't going down without a fight.

"It's rude to listen in on other people's conversations."

"It's rude to quit a job without notice," he retorted. "What are you doing here?"

"I'm not quitting. I was complaining. And you're my only client at the moment. I just thought I'd come and check in."

"We had breakfast three hours ago, nothing to see," he said crossly. "But I bet you can book a flight out right now, sweetheart. And if your phone doesn't have enough signal, you can use mine."

In an attempt to ignore the sting of his words, I gave as good as I got. "You know it's not a prerequisite to be an asshole because you're good looking and talented."

"So, do you need my credit card? You can consider the price of the ticket severance pay."

"Are we back here again?" I asked. "So soon?"

"Aren't you the one who just said you wanted to leave? Look," he said as he walked toward me and began to button my windbreaker, "I appreciate your effort, but this won't work. I only have three words I need to hear this season, 'strike' and 'don't stop.' So, unless you plan on moaning those last two anytime soon, you should make yourself scarce."

I let him fasten the buttons as he spoke and stared at his full lips. His jaw had filled out and so had he since the last time I saw him. He was beautiful at twenty-four and a god at twenty-seven. I had no doubt he would age to perfection.

"I've got everything I need this season. You being here isn't going to make a difference. I have no interest in anything but baseball. This isn't necessary. *You* aren't necessary. I'll let my work speak for itself."

"Not necessary," I muttered as his cold eyes kept the focus on his task of packaging me up and sending me away. His words hurt, but his actions disagreed with what he was saying.

His fingers seemed to linger as he kept his eyes down.

"I mean no offense," he drew out.

"Offense taken," I snapped. "You can't fire me; you didn't hire me."

"I can, Erica," he said, working through the buttons and tugging my body gently toward his. "The club isn't going to pay for my reputation. You're sorely mistaken if you think they will. It was good to see you, though."

Letting me go abruptly, he turned without glancing my way, thoroughly dismissing me. Guilt began to swallow me as I did all I could to stay planted where he left me.

"I have to keep this job, Ren. Okay? If I go back to New York, I lose it."

He looked over his shoulder, ready for war, but froze when he saw my face. "Erica—"

"This job is my life, just like baseball is yours. It's all I've got."

Ren cursed as he changed his direction and moved back toward me with clenched fists.

Suddenly aware of the tears streaming down my cheeks, I wiped at them furiously. "Sorry, I don't know where that came from."

"You're still doing it," he said as another line of tears took the place of the ones I'd wiped away. It was too much too soon. No matter how hard I tried, I couldn't stop the ambush of feelings that circulated when he was close to me. I couldn't deny the ache of wanting him, the pain of losing him, the guilt of leaving him. The man who haunted my dreams and stunted any relationship I'd attempted in the last two years. I knew my mistake, and I thought I had paid for it. But his indifference to me, his cruelty, hurt like hell. My heart was hemorrhaging simultaneously with old memories and new hurts.

"I'll stop," I said as my voice shook and my lips trembled.

"Uh, you're crying even harder now," he said with an anger-laced voice.

"I'm stopping."

"No, actually you aren't," he said, taking a step forward and gripping my collar. "If it means that much to you, stay."

"I'm sorry," I said, swallowing. "I'm . . . tired I guess."

"Okay, damn it, stop," he said as he shook me gently like a Neanderthal with a broken remote. I could feel the anger, the frustration rolling off him. His hands clenched and unclenched repeatedly.

"Ren," I said brokenly. "I'm sorry."

"I heard you the first time," he whispered, refusing to meet my eyes.

"Not about crying," I sniffed.

"I know," he said through gritted teeth. "Just go back to the hotel."

I was a fucking mess, and I had only been in Arizona a day. I was humiliated.

"Okay."

"This isn't a good idea," he said, finally bringing the bluest eyes imaginable to meet mine. "You being here."

"I know."

"I don't hate you," he clipped out.

"Yeah," I huffed out a humorless laugh, "but, I hate you, I hate what you did. I hated seeing you with all those women. I didn't deserve to see how fast you moved on, Ren."

"You didn't leave me much of a fucking choice," he hissed. "Go."

"Tell me how you did it," I implored in a whisper. "Tell me how you moved on like that."

He cradled my face, wiping the blinding tears from my eyes. I'd lost the battle that day, and he knew it. He had the advantage of my regret, and I let him have it. I was sure he wouldn't answer me as my eyes flooded with an apology two years too late.

"Who says I did?" I tried to lower my head, but he kept us locked together. "But it was a long time ago, Erica. I got your message. I think it's past time we closed this door."

I swallowed back a sob as he shut down the ridiculous notion that he may ever look at me the way he once did, extinguishing the hope that had sparked inside me the minute I saw him again. It was over for him, in his mind, in his heart. And I had thought the same for me. Coming to Arizona had been a colossal mistake.

"I can't do this," Ren snapped, gesturing between us.

"Of course you can't. It's the most crucial time in your career," I said bitterly.

Ren's eyes flicked to mine. "You're goddamned right it is."

"I get it, I truly do," I said softly. "I've always understood. But you never did." I hooked the last tear away from my eye with my finger.

"What are you saying?" he snapped defensively. I let the rip spread while my heart lay bruised and bare for him to see. As embarrassed as I was, it was all out there: my regret, his anger, and the hidden animosity that ended us. All of it spilled onto the field. I wanted to explain to him I knew his passion, that I understood it more than he could ever know. But it wasn't the time, and I may not ever get it again. If his heart was out of it, there was no point.

"I'm going to go get myself together. Just forget this ever happened, and I promise you it won't happen again."

"Forgotten," he whispered, looking over his shoulder, holding up his hand to Rafe, gesturing for another minute.

He brought his eyes back to mine and opened his mouth to speak, but no words came. I know something cruel was on the edge of his tongue, so I turned and left him there on the field, my heart beating wildly and my hair flying around me. Just like my emotions.

THAT NIGHT I made my way toward the hotel bar and stopped short when I saw that Rafe, Andy, and Ren were laughing next to a cozy fire. Ren was everywhere I dared to tread. His laugh was like the sting of a thousand needles in my chest. He seemed carefree, while I felt like the earth was shaking beneath me. He had his team, he had support. Maybe he did have exactly what he needed. I could call Zellner, tell him he'd found other representation. It's not like he could fault me for it. But in a way, helping Ren through the season might prove my apology to be sincere. I wanted him to understand my reasons for leaving him. Even if the effort was futile.

And if we didn't have a future, at least I could mend a part of the past. Our break up was due to my hang up.

He might have what he needed to lock the door on us, but as it turned out, I didn't. And if I was going to get through a season, I might need my own backup.

Chapter Eight

Ren

"You could have invited her to join us," Rafe said as he looked in the direction Erica left. It was a miracle he caught sight of her because she'd stopped short directly behind him. Rafe had eagle eyes, which were a great advantage on the field.

"I didn't want her to join us," I said as I tossed back the last of my beer.

"What's the deal with her, Ren?" Andy scrutinized me as Rafe sat back, watching the TV above my head, or pretending to.

"We dated and broke up. Nothing more."

"Seems like more," Andy said.

"It may be more for her, but I shut that shit down today. Nothing will distract me this season, nothing and no one," I fired off adamantly. I was talking a good game, but the truth was, my chest had been burning since I saw her cry openly in front of me. She was trying to apologize, but I was still too angry, even after the years between us. And I wanted her as far away as possible because it burned. I wanted nothing more than to grip her to me and comfort her. But she wasn't mine to comfort. She took that away from both of us. I shook my head to ward off any thoughts as I looked up to see them both staring at me. "I've got it."

"You don't have shit. She's already screwing with your head," Andy pointed out.

Rafe came to her defense. "She's here to do a job, no more, so let it be."

I looked over at Rafe, who was staring red-faced at Andy. They were having a mental debate, and it looked like Rafe won that round before he turned to me.

"She's by herself in a hotel in the middle of Arizona with a quarter of the League. She's probably miserable."

"If there's anything that can make her miserable, it's baseball," I agreed. "But it's not my problem."

But it was, and I was hellbent on trying to figure out how to solve it. The best solution I could come up with was distance. I'd caught myself flirting with her at breakfast, and that had quickly escalated to lusting.

My line of thinking was fucked. She left me. I lashed out. We were done. End of story. I couldn't take any more chances with her. I wouldn't. She had ruined me once, and I'd let her. She wouldn't get another chance to do it again.

I PACED her floor with my head spinning. I drank too much. I needed first-aid and fast, or I would be shit for training in the morning. With my frustration circulating like the whiskey, I couldn't help but tread the carpet outside her hotel door. I needed . . . something and it was tearing me apart.

She had bared herself to me that morning. I saw it all, her regret, her apology. Erica was raw with the loss of us, and it should have brought me comfort, but all it brought was restlessness. Leave it to the brown liquor to make me forget about the promises that I'd made to myself.

My head spun as my strides got quicker. I was like an angry lion ready to rip the floor apart to get to her. And then what? More tears, more apologies? And who would that help?

Still, I was hungry for more. I wanted to taste her tears on my tongue, to silence her apology with my cock. I wanted her to suffer while I buried my misery inside her. She was sorry. Fine, but did she regret it? Did she want more with me? Slamming my palm against the elevator button, I braced my hands on either side of the door and hung my head.

Two years, and with every day, every hour, every second, I knew I still loved her. I knew I wouldn't forget her and didn't want to. She was the one woman who knew me. Aside from my high school sweetheart, she was the only one I'd let in, only to be surprised by her.

She was it. I had a one-woman heart. I'd always been a faithful man. I had no problem with monogamy, and it wasn't a choice, it was the way I was built. It'd always been assumed I was a heartbreaker and a playboy because of the way I looked, but my insides didn't match that fucked-up persona.

At the heart of me lay a man who would bleed openly for the right woman. And that woman was Erica Wild. But my faithful heart was a fucking curse, especially at that moment. Because it refused to let me acknowledge I was wrong about her, about us.

Even as I settled into the role I was expected to play, I didn't play it well. I tried everything, and no part of me wanted to forget. Loving her was torture. And the realization that I was still so much in love with her, well, that was the cruelest punishment.

Guilt I shouldn't have felt washed over me at that moment. I regretted everything I'd done with any other woman. I'd hurt her back, and she made it known today. I had no reason to feel guilty.

Damn her.

"Ren?"

"Don't," I warned as she stood behind me. Never in my life had I been so angry. "Go back to your room."

She didn't move. I could smell vanilla and mint. It drifted through my nose, and my chest burned at the memory of her taste. Throat constricting, I slammed my palm against the button.

"Go," I threatened, my voice a warning.

"No."

I whirled on her then, her eyes bulging as I closed in. She was in a T-shirt and pajama pants, without a stitch of makeup, and looked so innocent at that moment. I hated her for it because I knew she wasn't.

In an instant, I had her pinned against the wall, my lips capturing hers in a deep kiss, my tongue tasting every inch of her mouth. She was gasping as she gripped me tightly to her, her moan vibrating through us both as our tongues dueled hungrily.

And I'd never felt so fucking alive. I lifted her to wrap her legs around me, and she squeezed my hips with her thighs while I ground my rock-hard cock right where she needed it.

"Ren," she gasped, eyes closed as we shared breath. Again, I devoured her, leaving her limp before I ripped my lips away and glared down at her.

"I'm so fucking mad at you."

"I know," she countered with swollen lips.

"Damn you," I cursed as I rubbed myself against her and sank my teeth into her neck.

"Ren, please," she begged, working her hips and clawing at my shoulders.

Her heavy breath tickled my ear as I touched where I wanted to touch and began to use her to stifle the pain. But *she* was the source of it.

It was then that I stopped myself and slowly lowered her to her feet. I had to break unhealthy patterns, starting with her. I'd promised myself, and that was the most crucial promise for me to keep. She hadn't allowed me to keep the promises I'd made to her.

"I shouldn't have done that," I said, stepping away from her. Chest heaving, she gaped up at me in a daze. "I guess some things don't change. We were always good at fucking."

"Don't say that," she said, taking a step toward me. "We were more than that."

"Were we? I thought so too. Except you left me, and then you wouldn't talk to me."

"I couldn't. You wouldn't listen to me."

"I'm listening," I snapped, shoving my hands in my jeans and staring at the floor.

She was quick to speak. "It was selfish. I know that now. I knew it then. But I didn't want to be that woman. My whole life couldn't revolve around you and baseball, Ren."

"I needed you," I said thickly.

She crossed her arms defensively. "But for how long?"

My eyes snapped to hers. "How about my whole goddamn life? I was going to ask you to marry me."

"I know." She swallowed. "I saw the ring."

She hung her head when she saw the surprise in my eyes. "Ren, I was terrified."

"You saw the ring?"

"Yes," she said as her eyes clouded with more tears. "I didn't want to be a club wife. I never wanted that. But there are things you should know. Things I didn't tell you. Things that I should have told you."

The doors finally opened as I took a step back into them. My heart crushed under the weight of her words; my voice was gravel. I couldn't look at her another minute.

"I promise you, as far as I'm concerned, you'll get what you want."

Her face crumbled as the doors closed between us.

Chapter Nine

Erica

THE SUN HAD GONE DOWN, AND I SHIVERED IN MY WINDBREAKER AS I watched Ren in the batting cage. I'd walked the entirety of the Salt River Fields complex to find him. The park lights were still on, and there were a few lingering players talking shop.

After a week of watching games and radio silence from Ren, I knew I had to somehow bridge the gap between us. Though he executed the schedule I sent via text, he wasn't speaking to me at all. No reply text, not a word.

I watched Ren's body twist with each connection of bat to ball. He was thorough with his powerful swing and had one of the best averages of a catcher in the League. A huge improvement from his first year as a rookie.

"Your eye has improved, tenfold," I said, loud enough for him to hear and impossible for him to ignore. He ignored me anyway and kept his gaze on his mechanical batter.

"Ren, I know things are weird, but I want to try to get along with you."

Bat hoisted and ready, he swung and cracked the ball, sending it flying to the top of the net, before he moved back into position.

"Rafe's on fire," I said, as if my conversation wasn't one-sided. "His pitching is remarkable."

Silence.

"I met his wife at the last game. Alice. She's a spitfire. I really like her. She's no bullshit. She asked if I wanted to go skydiving over the desert," I chuckled. "She's a little daredevil. I love that about her. She reminds me of my roommate, Rowe. You would like her."

Ren's chest rose and fell, the only sign of life, his poise perfect before he swung at another ball as if I wasn't there.

"I met Andy's wife, too. April, oh God, her accent is hilarious. I didn't know Andy brewed beer, that's pretty cool. They said you used to go to Charleston and hang out once in a while. It sounds like a great place. I'd like to go there someday."

Silence. And the next crack of the bat filtered through me like the growing crack in my chest. I took a deep breath and tried again.

"We're all going out this week. Alice, April, and me. I think Rafe and Andy arranged that we meet. They're great guys."

"Is there anyone who isn't fucking great?" Ren finally grunted out as he overcompensated his footing and the ball nailed him in the wrist. I glanced at the radar. The ball had hit him at 86 miles per hour.

"GODDAMMIT!" Ren roared as he dropped the bat and clutched his arm.

I rushed toward him as he let out a heavy string of curses while he exited the cage.

"Let me see it!" I said as I chased him around in a circle. "Ren!"

"It's fine," he bit out before he stopped his feet and looked up at me with ice-blue eyes.

I lifted my hands. "Don't blame this on me. You know damn well you stepped into that. Now let me see."

Reluctantly, he gave me his arm and my jaw dropped. "It's already purple."

"It's fine," he snapped as he pulled his arm back.

"It's not fine, you need to have it looked at."

"Leave it, Erica."

"What is it with you men? If your dick were that color, you would fly in a specialist."

"My dick's just fine. If you want to drop to your knees, I'm more than happy to let you inspect it."

The slap I gave him was instant and almost playful, but my eyes told him I meant it.

"I will not *ever* be talked to like that. Unless I'm in the mood, and you know damn well I'm not in the mood."

I turned to walk away and heard his chuckle and his curse. "Erica, wait."

"Enough already, Ren. I'm done making nice. You want to keep this animosity going, you can go at it alone. I'm done fighting with you. God, just once I would like to have a conversation with you where we aren't aiming for each other's jugulars."

"Well, it's good to see some fight left in you. You've been walking around like a corpse since you got here," he yelled at my retreating back.

"That's only because I've had *you* to deal with."

"We don't have to be best friends, Erica. It's not necessary. Your small talk, *unnecessary*."

"Got it, asshole. I'll be sure to avoid it at all costs. Jesus, we sure are making up now for the fighting we didn't do as a couple."

"You have to admit we're pretty spectacular at it," he snapped sarcastically as he strode toward the parking lot.

"Go to hell, Makavoy!"

"I'm already there, Wild!"

Chapter Ten

Erica

A MIRAGE IN THE SHAPE OF MY ROOMMATE AND BEST FRIEND STOOD AT THE bar when I got back to the hotel from the field. I knew it could only be wishful thinking when I saw the sleek bob and spiked heels. But when I saw the side of her profile, I barreled toward her. She caught sight of me just as I tackled her, spilling her wine and hugging the life out of her.

"Damn it, that was a fresh glass," she chuckled as she hugged me back.

"Thank God you're here," I said with a shaky voice.

"Oh, babe, is the world kicking your ass?" she asked softly as she held me to her.

"You have no idea. The kids won't play with me," I whined.

"I had a feeling last time we talked. I'm at your disposal for the night. I have to fly back out tomorrow."

I pulled back. "Really?"

"Yeah, it's a fly-through." She wrinkled her nose. "I'm sorry. But it's the best I could do with your SOS."

"It's cool," I said, smiling. "I've got you now. And I could use some fun. Hey, I've got an idea. Are you up for some company?"

"Sure," she said, motioning to the bartender for another glass of wine.

I pulled out my phone and shot a quick text off to Alice and April.

"I have a feeling it's going to be one of those nights," I said as I ordered my first beer.

TWO HOURS LATER, the four of us were primping in my hotel room. Alice and April had found a last-minute sitter, and the four of us planned on wrecking whatever available scene Scottsdale had to offer. Seeing Alice and Rowe in the same room only confirmed my suspicions. They were personality doppelgangers and had made quick work of becoming friends. April and I watched them go back and forth like a bunch of rabid squirrels while we took our time painting ourselves up.

"I'm too old for this shit," April sighed.

"No, you aren't. You don't look your age, either."

"Still, there's got to be some rule for going to the club in your mid-thirties," she said as she straightened her boobs in her dress. "I can't even get these bastards to cooperate, let alone look perky."

"There will be none of that tonight," Alice said sharply as she glossed her lips. "We are *not* old. We are respectable married women with families who still have the ability to go and shake our asses on a whim. Don't forget you're the inventor of the booty opera."

"The booty opera?" I asked with a smile.

"Yeah," April said as Alice began to belt out "Bump N' Grind" as if she were singing at the opera. Rowe cracked up and looked back at me. "I'm so glad you called these two."

"Right?" I said with a giggle. "Okay, tell me how this booty opera works."

"You just mix a little R&B, preferably the dirty kind, and sing it as if it was an opera. I do it to get myself out of a bad mood. It's impossible to do it without smiling."

In the elevator, twenty minutes later, we were singing Keith Sweat's "Nobody" in horrible soprano, dressed to the nines, and laughing our asses off. As we walked out to the lobby, the girls caught sight of Rafe, Andy, and Ren at the bar. I braved a glance their way to see Ren's eyes cover me in slow sweep as Rafe and Andy stopped their wives for a quick kiss and a warning to behave themselves.

Alice walked away with half her lipstick, her eyes in a fog as Ren and I stared each other down. He looked pissed . . . and hot in a simple T-shirt and jeans, his hat forever backward, as he sipped his beer.

Rowe leaned over with a "He's so fucking the hell out of you right now in his head," before she grabbed my hand and tugged me forward with further instructions. "Let him see that ass before you go."

We walked through the hotel lobby arm-in-arm, hellbent on reclaiming some of our youth without distractions or talk of "mummying"—Alice's rule—or anything else that brought the weight of our everyday.

"We've still got it," April said as she sashayed out the door.

"We're not old yet," Alice chimed in agreement.

Rowe and I gave each other knowing smiles as we joined them outside. We were getting a lot of attention from the passersby, mostly ball players, as Alice spoke up.

"I'll drive."

"Nobody's driving," I said as our SUV arrived. "In fact," I pulled out Ren's credit card, the one I'd commissioned from him for PR related expenses. "Tonight's drinks are on Ren Makavoy."

NINE HOURS LATER . . .

"Oh, God," April gasped out next to me in bed, her southern drawl intact even though it came out as a croak. "I have to be a mom today," she sobbed into her pillow next to me. "To twins. And not just any twins, twins who bite. Little shits!"

I chuckled and held my head as the onset of a headache hit.

Rowe chose that moment to rise from the floor, like a corpse next to the bed, and turned to me with raccoon eyes. Her lips peeled away from her teeth as she spoke.

"I'm so phukin dersty!" Her mouth was foaming as she stared at me with glassy-eyed desperation.

Scared for my safety, I quickly grabbed the hotel's ten-dollar bottle of water from the nightstand and handed it to her. I heard every ounce hit her throat as she downed it with exaggerated gulps. Once it was empty, she handed it back to me and slowly sank back down out of sight on the floor.

From the other side of the bed, I heard Alice pipe up.

"If you guys are up, *please help*. I've been down here and awake for an hour, but I can't get up. I think I threw my back out twerking. And I really, really need to pee."

April chuckled as she ripped herself away from the bed. "Come on, girl, I've got you."

"Oh, God," Alice groaned as she was hoisted from the floor. "This is bad, so bad."

April groaned in response. "Look the other way, Alice. You could gag a maggot. Your breath reeks of Fireball. I can't handle it."

I chuckled as I realized I was in the best shape of the four of us and may be able to handle looking at myself in the mirror that day. Usually, after a night of drinking like that, I had done something stupid enough to bury my head in the sand for a solid week. I didn't remember twerking or doing unsolicited body shots like Rowe.

I was feeling pretty confident until I grabbed my phone from the nightstand and looked down and saw a text from Ren.

12:00 A.M.

Ren: I'm sitting in front of your room. We need to talk.

1:00 A.M.

Ren: Pick up the phone.

3:15 A.M.

Ren: Damn it, Erica!

I SCROLLED up to see the whole conversation. Bile rose in my throat as I saw that it had all started with me.

10:01 P.M.

Me: Unnecessary? I'm unnecessary. Isn't that what you said? When we were together, you didn't find these unnecessary.

AND WHAT FOLLOWED WAS a perfect shot of my tits in a bathroom stall.

"OH GOD, NO!" I yelled as Rowe shot up from beside me.

"What, what's wrong?"

I just groaned as I read Ren's answering texts.

10:03 P.M.

Ren: What in the hell are you doing? I'm in a meeting!

10:06 P.M.

Ren: Jesus Christ, Erica, are you drunk?

10:08 P.M.

Ren: Where are you?!

10:16 P.M.

Ren: What are you trying to do to me?

"WHAT TIME IS IT," Rowe croaked from the floor."

"Six thirty," I said, horrified as I stared at the picture.

"I'm going to miss my flight!" Rowe shot up from the floor and quickly began packing. I got out of bed to help her as she started to shove her things into her carry on.

"I sent Ren a picture," I said, mortified. "Of my *tits*."

Rowe paused and then looked at me blankly before she threw her head back and laughed. "That explains why you were in the bathroom for half an hour. You must have been looking for the right lighting."

"Got any room in that bag for me?" I asked.

"You've got beautiful boobs, girl. Own that shit."

I hung my head in shame as a firm knock landed on the door. Rowe and I looked at each other with wide eyes.

"Oh, God. I can't face him."

"Oh, but you must," she said with a chuckle as she started packing her purse. "Don't back down."

"Shut the door!" Alice screamed to April in the bathroom, seconds before I heard it close.

We were all scrambling as I gathered myself together as much as possible, pushing everything back into my dress, and then opened the door. Three very pissed off and very beautiful baseball players stood on the other side.

Ren's eyes seared into me as I took a step back and opened it for them to walk in.

"Where in the hell have you been?" Ren snapped first. "We've been calling you for hours!"

"Alice." Rafe knocked on the bathroom door with Andy on his heels, who barked out a curt "April, open up." Both men looked ready for war, as the door slowly opened.

"Hi," April said in a shitty attempt to hide her misery. "I was just about to call you two."

Rafe charged past her, and I heard Alice yelp. Seconds later, she was walked out of the hotel room in a fireman's hold over Rafe's shoulder. "My shoes, baby, my shoes!"

"Fuck your shoes," he growled.

Alice groaned before she caught sight of me and waved. "I had fun. Love you, guys! Thanks for the drinks, Ren!"

I winced at her parting words. *I was a dead woman.*

Rafe's hand landed firmly on her ass as she yelped out again. "Hey, that's sore, Hembrey!"

"It's about to get a hell of a lot worse," he promised as the door clicked shut behind them.

Andy stood in the doorway of the bathroom as his wife washed her face.

"Don't even start," she said as I caught the side of her glare in the mirror. "I don't say shit when you make a new brew and invite the team over for half the night."

"I'm not saying a word. But I did want to tell you that your son just cut another tooth," he said with a smirk.

"Get out," April ordered as Andy stepped into the bathroom and closed the door behind him. I heard a shriek and then light laughter. I smiled at the door and then connected eyes with a man who looked like he was planning my burial.

Rowe chose that moment to speak up. "I'm all set. I've got to go." I stood and gave her a hug. "Call me when you get back. Love you," I said as she moved toward the door.

"Sorry we didn't get a chance to meet, Ren, maybe some other time. Take care of my girl, okay?"

"Sure," Ren said dryly as the door shut behind her.

I rolled my eyes. "Nice."

"What is Alice thanking me for?" he asked with an icy tone.

I clamped my lips together and glanced at his credit card on the nightstand.

"Are you fucking serious?"

Throat parched, I put together a decent sentence. "I'm sorry. It's not enough but it's the truth. That was highly unprofessional, not to mention . . . that picture. Look, clearly this isn't going to work out. I get it. I'll call Zellner, and I'll be gone by noon."

Ren's eyes drifted from my foot up the length of my legs to my skirt.

"You're not going anywhere."

"Ren," I treaded carefully. "I don't want to fight. I know you don't think I'm capable of being sincere but—"

"Shut up, Erica. I need you to shut up."

Livid. That was all I could see in his posture.

"I'm so goddamn tempted to brave your breath, lift that skirt, and fuck you until you cry, even with those two in the bathroom. So, I need you to stop talking."

"We're out of here," Andy announced as they stepped out of the bathroom and saw Ren and me in a stand-off. April grabbed her bag and gave me a wink, which I returned with a smile. And then we were alone again.

Ren stood. "You're staying because you said you would, and for once, when it comes to *me*, you're going to keep your word."

"Is that all?" I asked sourly as I stood and walked toward the bathroom to grab my toothbrush.

"What exactly were you hoping for, Erica, when you sent me that picture?"

I closed my eyes, and when I opened them, he was at the door of the bathroom. "Erase it."

"Not a fucking chance."

"Fine, whatever," I said, shoving a brush full of paste in my mouth before I spoke around it. "Probaby haven't seeb a weal paiw in yebs anyway."

"What?"

I spit out the toothpaste without washing it down the drain. I could see Ren cringe at the sight of it. I held in my laughter.

"I said, you probably haven't seen a real pair of tits in years anyway. That picture was educational." I shoved the toothbrush back in my mouth while rinsing the sink to put him out of his misery.

Ren studied me as I brushed, his eyes blazing.

I gave him wide eyes of my own. "What?"

"What is going on with you? You aren't this irresponsible."

I rolled my eyes. "I got drunk. Made a bad decision. It happens, and I can honestly say, at twenty-five, that was my worst. You know anyone else around here who might do stupid shit when they've had too much to drink? POT!"

I winced at the ache in my head as the kettle pressed his lips together.

"And don't give me that double standard crap, Ren. I needed to have some fun. You're quite the moody diva to deal with. By the way, we've got an appearance at the ball camp today, and you look like you could use a few hours of sleep."

"I've got shit to do," he said as he stared at the slit in my dress that revealed the side of my breast.

I gave him a seedy smile through a mouthful of foam before he turned on his heel and slammed the door.

Chapter Eleven

Erica

I pounded on Ren's hotel door for five minutes before he opened it, a fresh towel wrapped around his glistening body, his angry blue gaze darkened by wet lashes. He was etched perfection, and my mouth went dry as I averted my eyes.

"I've been messaging you for two hours. We need to be there in twenty minutes!"

"I told you I had shit to do," he barked, leaving the door open for me.

I walked in, and my heart leaped to my throat.

"Davis!"

I ran to the English Bulldog perched in the corner and knelt down beside him. "Oh my God, you got so fat!"

"He's healthy," Ren said over his shoulder.

I glanced his way just as he covered his abs with a T-shirt.

"He's fat," I said as I hugged him to me. "God, do you remember the day I brought him home to you? I'd never seen you so excited."

"Best Christmas present I ever got," Ren said with a small, lopsided smile as he stared on at the two of us. It was the first smile we'd shared since I got to Arizona.

I scratched Davis's sides and belly. "How you doing, boy? Have you missed me?"

"He probably doesn't remember you," Ren muttered, closing the bathroom door behind him.

I looked around Ren's room. It was immaculate. Not a single thing out of place. His suitcase was still packed, and everything was folded as if he'd just arrived. I walked over to the nightstand and took a whiff of his cologne: Dolce and Gabbana Light Blue—*heavenly*.

Then I made my way to his closet. I bit my lip and glanced at the bathroom door before I rearranged a few of his hangers, ruining his carefully crafted rainbow of color. I heard the fan shut off and rushed over to pet Davis as Ren emerged from the bathroom, grabbing his keys and wallet from his dresser.

I paused my hands in Davis's thick rolled fur and pressed my nose to his wet one. "You remember me, don't you? How could you not? I was the one stuck potty training you."

"Some job you did. He took a shit in my glove an hour ago," Ren said as he leaned down and clipped a leash on him.

"Let's go, boy." He all but jerked the dog out of my arms, and I stood.

"So, this camp is exactly the type of thing that would be good for your image."

"I've been doing this for two years now with Rafe, so there's no need for you to go. I can handle this myself," Ren said, opening the door in an attempt to usher me out.

Blood boiled through my veins as Ren gave me a smug smirk.

"I'm still coming, Ren. Hate to ruin your plans, but this is my job."

"Suit yourself," he said as he closed the door behind us.

Chapter Twelve

REN

We rode the elevator to the parking garage in silence as the memory of the day I got Davis flashed through my head. Like I could ever forget it.

We had spent every moment since the season ended together, mostly in my shitty one-bedroom apartment in Atlanta. I'd come home that Christmas Eve to find her wearing nothing but a thin tee that barely covered her midriff, panties that were decorated with large, old-school Christmas bulbs, and the Ugg boots I had ordered for her that she'd opened early.

She was perched on my stepstool, decorating a small tree that she'd paid for and dragged home herself. Christmas music was playing, and the smell of burned sugar cookies lingered in the air.

When she turned to me, so proud of her handiwork on that little Charlie Brown tree, I damn near hit my knees right that moment and asked her to be my wife. I didn't, but that was the moment I'd decided to marry her. To make *her* my home. The home I never had.

After giving my neighbors the twelve-foot tree I had brought home, and washing down the burned cookies with egg nog, she insisted we watch a marathon of Transformer movies. We only made it through the first fifteen minutes of the first one before I had her coming with my name on her lips.

When the doorbell rang on Christmas morning—and she shot out of bed like her ass was on fire, her hair a tangled mess while she shoved her feet into her Uggs—I was determined to seal the deal.

And a minute after that, when she walked into my bedroom with our puppy, she made my dreams come true and gave me the family I never had.

Two months later, she took it all away.

Erica

It was only when we got to the parking garage that I realized I was at his mercy.

"I, uh . . . haven't had time to get a rental."

Ren kept walking, and I heard the chirp of the cherry red Aston Martin directly ahead of us.

"Really, Ren?"

"Figures you'd have something to say," Ren said, ushering Davis in and closing his driver's side door.

My heels clicked along the garage floor as I briefly admired the view of Ren in the driver's seat. I had to admit it was a hot car.

As soon as I clicked my seatbelt, I had a forty-pound English Bulldog placed in my lap. Ren looked over to me and lifted a perfectly arched brow.

"Technically, that's his seat, so you're going to have to get over it."

"God, you're enjoying this," I snapped.

"To the fullest," he replied, flashing his teeth.

My retort was muffled by the roar of the engine, and then we were off like a shot. I clutched Davis to me for dear life as Ren expertly navigated the streets of Scottsdale.

"I bet you bought yourself a house full of toys," I said, sliding my fingers along the leather. "I'm so happy for you, Ren. You deserve it."

Ren's jaw ticked as he waited for the light to change.

"I remember you kept your beat-up pickup truck because you were too afraid to spend any money that first year."

"It's not remarkable you remember the details from only a few years ago," he said as he raced through the streets until we were stopped by another light.

Still, I refused to let his asshole-ish remarks deter me.

"You took me to eat Italian the first night and then it was McDonald's every night after. I thought you were the cheapest bastard alive for the first month we dated."

"Well, you didn't know how to cook. One of us had to take charge."

"I had no issue eating McNuggets while you sat on a small fortune, that should be easy for you to remember."

"I was saving it in case my knees wore out, or I got injured," he said defensively.

"I can see that fear has subsided a bit." My head flew back as he floored the car and clutched the steering wheel.

I smiled as I looked around the sleek, luxurious sports car and back at Ren. "It's kind of surreal seeing you like this. And, God, I prayed you'd get here. I hope you know that."

Ren took a sudden turn, so I pulled up my phone for directions, assuming he'd forgotten them.

"Ren, you're about to pass the park. REN!"

He drove on like a bat out of hell as I watched Scottsdale pass by in a blur. Within a few minutes, we were in no-man's-land.

"Ren, what the hell are you doing?"

He skidded the car to a stop and Davis barked at him, feeling the aggression coming from him. Ren got out of the car, and I followed, leaving Davis securely inside and away from his insane master.

"What in the hell are you doing?"

"What am *I* doing? What in the hell are *you* doing?" Ren turned to me, his eyes furious. "I'm trying to keep my shit together, and you're talking about us like you didn't rip my goddamn heart out."

"I didn't—"

"Save it," he said, walking toward me, pinning the back of my knees to his hood. "You want us to get along? Then don't remind me of what a goddamn idiot I was."

"Idiot? I don't know about then, but I sure as hell know you're acting like one now."

"I don't want to hear how happy you are for me, Erica."

We were shouting at this point. Davis barked inside the car, unhappy with our behavior.

"You did exactly what you set out to do. Hey, Ren, I'm happy for you!"

Our breath mingled as the sun beat down on both of us.

"I don't need you to be *happy* for me. I don't need a stroll down memory lane with you. I don't need your approval on my car or the way I feed my dog."

"Davis is fat! This is a hot car. It's sure to draw penis envy, and that's a good thing because it's owner is a DICK!"

"You're some piece of work, you know that? The queen of mixed signals. I have no idea how I navigated my way with you in the first fucking place."

"Oh, yeah!? Here's a signal for you!" I stuck my middle finger in the inch between our faces, directly on his nose. "You can kiss my ass, Makavoy!"

Glacier eyes blazed as I scanned his face and watched a drop of sweat slide down his neck, past his pulse point. That was all I saw before I was flipped on my stomach.

"Your wish is my command, baby."

Before I had a chance to speak, my skirt was lifted, my panties were snapped away, and Ren's face was buried between my legs.

"Ren!"

My whole body seized at the intrusion until his tongue swept a path from top to bottom and remained there with lightning-fast licks of his tongue. I had nothing to hold onto as he gripped me firmly. I gasped and attempted to draw more air as he slid his fingers in and twisted them, so I was clawing at the hood. I was soaked, and he was starving.

The noises coming from us both spurred him on as I started to coil. He fucked me roughly with his tongue, pushing as far in as he could before replacing it with his fingers and sucking on my clit. I was almost there when he flipped me back over, his mouth crashing into mine.

Our tongues tangled and dueled angrily as we both gave way into the sensation. I was lost in his kiss, his hold, his absolute power over my body. I wanted him with every inch of me.

When he pulled away, I could see in his eyes the request for permission. Frantic for more, I gripped his erection firmly in my hand and got a groan.

"You're coming on my cock," he ordered as he hastily slid the strap of my dress down, freeing my breast and sucking my nipple until I was putty in his hands. My whole body trembled as I held his head in my hands, his beautiful dark brows twisted in concentration, while groans of need rumbled out of his throat.

"Ren, please," I begged as he let go of my nipple with a pop.

I unzipped his slacks, freeing him while he lifted me back on the hood, spread me wide, stuck the fat tip of his dick at my entrance, and slammed into me until we fully connected.

My back bowed at the intrusion, filling me to the brink and beyond. I was sliding down the hood with nothing to hold onto but the feel of him. Opening my eyes, I found his trained on me, filled with longing, with lust, need, and something I'd missed for far too long.

He reached for me, but I was already halfway to him when our mouths met, and our bodies began to move in sync. And then it was nothing but pure bliss as we ground into each other, watching one another until it was too much to resist. Foreheads touching, we watched ourselves connect. I was stretched tight by his thickness, and that sight alone did us both in. We licked and sucked until we were both frantically climbing.

"Oh, fuck, baby. Give it to me."

"Ren!" I screamed while I clenched around him and heard his breath hitch before he let out a growl.

He gripped my lower half, spreading me wide, and went deeper with total abandon as I exploded around him. My heart hammered as I gasped and scratched at his shoulders.

"Jesus Christ, you're drenched," he ground out as his hips picked up pace and he rocked into me so possessively that another orgasm followed.

I was consumed and spent as I watched him throw his head back and his body tense.

"Fuck, oh fuck," he grunted as he filled me full, pushing in deep and holding himself there as his eyes met mine before they fluttered closed. "I'm still an idiot."

I kissed his jaw as we clung to each other like there wasn't any amount of space or time between us. Ren cradled me with one hand and traced his thumb along my cheek before he leaned in and kissed me like I was his entire world.

I felt relieved and tried to stifle the hope of what that could mean. Because that kiss was different, and we both knew it.

When he pulled away, he set me on my feet and walked to the passenger side of his car. He unwrapped a fresh dash towel, and I tried my best to clean myself up while he walked Davis. Once inside the car, he looked over at me, and I could see so much confusion in his eyes, but I was thankful I didn't see regret.

"I don't want to pretend that didn't happen, Ren. I don't want to make more out of it than what it is, either. But please, please, let's leave it for the moment. I think you're right. I want to be here for you this season. I want to keep my word to you. I'm who you need to turn this around, and I've been letting my feelings get in the way. So, before we start analyzing this, let's just get you through the next couple of weeks. Okay?"

Ren nodded before he ripped his gaze away and started the car. Halfway to the camp, he gripped the inside of my knee and left his hand there. And I let him.

CAMP WAS A ZOO. It took the better part of an hour to get the older kids to let Ren start to give out pointers instead of autographs.

As I watched on, I felt myself heat as I remembered the way he dominated me on that hood. And every time his beautiful blues drifted over to me, and he bit his lower lip, I knew I wasn't the only one reminiscing. We'd always been good at sex. Ren hadn't been the only man, but he'd been the only that had ever mattered.

The need to go to him and quickly bandage everything that kept us apart was overwhelming. But I wanted to do this for him. I wanted to prove to him that I could keep my word. Suddenly, it was the only thing that mattered. And if I could come through for him, maybe I could forgive myself a little for being so selfish.

My smile turned sour in an instant when a mother approached him, her body language far too friendly to be innocent.

I closed my eyes. *We didn't use a condom.*

Ren's eyes shot to mine. He read my expression and then my thoughts. I moved to walk away, to swallow the panic and the burn that threatened, but Ren beat me to my retreat, breaking through the crowd around him and getting to me in seconds.

"I'm okay. I swear to Christ I'm safe," he said, gripping my arm. "I'll prove it."

"You were always careful with me," I said honestly. The first month we had sex, Ren used a condom every single time, even though I'd been on the pill for years.

"Are you . . . still protected?" he asked gently.

"If I wasn't?"

"Erica," he warned.

"Of course I am," I said, looking around to make sure no one was listening. We'd been way too stunned in the car to have the conversation, but a busy baseball camp for kids wasn't the place or the time, either.

"Good, then we should probably do that again tonight."

"Ren," I said with the slow shake of my head.

"Don't worry, we don't have to discuss it after." He winked. "Not even when I eat that beautiful ass of yours again. In fact, it would be my pleasure to make sure the only words you say are my favorite."

"Strike?" I asked playfully.

"Erica," he whispered, his voice hoarse as a ball landed at our feet. I reached for it and looked to see whose it was. A kid was waving frantically, and I moved to throw it.

"NO! NOT YOU!" the kid said as his mother scolded him to play nice.

I handed the ball to Ren, and he took it, his focus still on me. "I'm surrounded by kids, and all I can think about is touching you again."

"I won't let you reduce me to being a booty call. Not after . . ."

His thick, dark brows drew together. "Is that what you think?"

I sighed.

"We're discussing it, and we just agreed we wouldn't. The focus needs to be on you and the season. Go teach."

"This conversation isn't over," he warned. "Not by a long shot. I don't regret it, and I won't let you, either." He reached out and brushed the hair away from my shoulder.

"I don't regret it," I whispered hoarsely as my cheek heated at thoughts of watching us connect on that hood.

His mouth lifted at the corners. "Still a lady in the street and a freak in the sheets, huh?"

"Guess so," I shrugged.

"Dinner?" he asked, walking toward a line of little men dressed in his number.

"Maybe," I said thoughtfully. "We'll talk about strategy. But no card tricks, okay?"

"I haven't played with a full deck since the day I met you," he said with so much sincerity that my throat knotted before he turned to the eager faces clamoring for his attention.

Ren took charge of the group with military precision, and he was a natural. Within minutes he had their adoration and they were eating out of the palm of his hand.

My heart galloped as I watched him crouch down with a tiny catcher who couldn't be more than six years old. His gear was heavier than he was, and he kept falling over as he tried to imitate Ren's movements.

Malcolm showed up a few minutes later, and Ren made it a point to highlight his new Little Brother's strong points to the rest of his troop. I saw Malcom's reserved pride surface as Ren playfully took off his cap and knuckle-rubbed his hair.

It was refreshing to see Ren so immersed in something useful to his image but at the same time effortless for him. Ren loved kids, and I knew he had a special place in his heart for little princesses due to his affection for my niece. After they met, he'd been smitten, and I knew he wanted a daughter of his own someday. He always said little girls were the most honest humans and had the sweetest laughs.

"You're staring awful hard at your client," Andy said, standing next to me. I was still in a daze.

"I love him."

"You don't say," Andy mused as I realized what I'd just said.

"I mean I love the way . . ." I shook my head. "Please don't tell anyone."

"I would say your secret is safe, but I'm pretty sure everyone who's looking at you right now can see it. And he hasn't gone thirty seconds since you got here without looking your way."

I palmed my forehead. "Have you ever done something so incredibly life-changing that you can't make it right?"

"Kind of. I fell in love with a woman who was in love with my best friend and almost lost my wife because I was too much of a bitter ass to handle it."

"You were with April and in love with this woman?" I felt defensive for my new friend as Andy glanced over at me.

"Hell no," April piped up behind me. "I wasn't that desperate."

I paused. "Wait, she was in love with Rafe?"

Alice and Rafe walked up to us. "Who was in love with me?"

"Kristina," April said as Rafe looked at Alice. "Yeah, that was a fucking mess."

Andy turned to me. "See, it's not as hopeless as you think." All eyes were on me. My face was flaming, and to make matters worse, Rafe caught Ren looking at me.

"You two totally just had sex."

"Rafe!" Alice scorned.

"What?" He shrugged. "It needed to happen. *Had* to happen, and that new grimace on Ren's resting bitch face could actually pass for a smile."

There wasn't a hole big enough for me to climb in.

April chuckled at my discomfort. "Welcome to the family, love, and if it's any comfort we're all behind you."

While I stayed mute so as not to confirm or deny what had happened between Ren and me, a dull throb began to beat behind my eye. I hadn't had a chance to hydrate properly after our night out, and with all my frustration and stress, I knew it was just a matter of time before it caught up with me.

I willed the migraine away as they spoke around me. I had no idea how much time passed as I stood there praying it would stop, but the pain continued to set in. My vision began to blur as I looked over at Ren.

Surrounded by kids, his blinding smile vanished as he glanced over to me. In a heartbeat, he was at my side talking to Andy and Rafe while Alice and April whispered words of concern. I barely heard them as I was whisked away.

"Hold on, baby, I've got you," Ren whispered as he cradled me to his hip. "Just hang on."

"Ren," I said helplessly as he closed his passenger door and sped out of the parking lot.

"Hold my hand," he said, and I placed my palm in his. I was already sweating.

"How bad?"

I flipped down the visor to try and shield myself from the sun. "It's bad," I croaked, closing my eyes.

Within minutes, we were in the hotel garage, and I realized we were a dog short.

"Where's Davis?" I asked as Ren opened my door and leaned down to help me.

"Alice took him. Can you walk?"

"Yeah, it's not that bad yet."

"Come on. Hold onto me." My heart melted at the sight of his concerned eyes.

The next thing I knew, I was standing in the middle of my room in my panties and he was setting the pillows up on the bed, just the way I had to have them. We were right back where we were two years ago.

"Ren, you don't have to do this."

"In here?" he asked, ignoring me and lifting my purse.

I nodded. He pulled out the prescription bottle, handed me a pill, and grabbed a bottle of water out of the fridge.

"Thank you."

I took the pill, praying for quick relief.

"Come on," he said as he reached for my hand and laid me down gently before he darkened out the sun by closing the shades. A second later, the bed dipped behind me, and I felt the warmth of his chest as he wrapped his arms around me. Just like he used to do.

My heart in my throat, I felt a tear escape as he leaned down and softly kissed my neck. "Better?"

"Yes, thank you."

"Stop being so formal with me, Erica."

"I'm sorry. Ren, it hurts so bad."

"Hang on, baby. Forty-five minutes until the pill kicks in, okay? Just breathe. Follow my breathing."

And I did, just like I had done a dozen times before with him. When he took a breath, I took one. We were silent, with me in his hold, warm in his arms until I finally drifted to sleep.

Ren

I woke up a few hours later and reluctantly let go of the beautiful woman in my arms. My heart ached with the need to know exactly what we were. Or what I could expect. A part of me didn't want to have the conversation, because if it led to another dead end, I didn't think I could handle it a second time.

I fumbled around in the dark and opened my phone to check my schedule. I was free and clear for the night. I was starving and knew sooner or later when she opened her eyes she would be, too.

I made quick work of getting dressed and grabbed her cell from her purse. I set it down next to her and sent her a quick text. A few seconds later, I heard music and raced back over to the bed.

The phone was lit up with my text, and she'd put my handle as Tin Man. Erica stirred as I picked up the phone to silence it and heard the first few lyrics of the song.

I crept into the bathroom and grabbed her ear buds off the counter. I typed in the lyrics in Google search to bring up the song. Ironically it was called "Tin Man."

I sat on the edge of the tub and listened to it a few times, my heart cracking under the weight of the words. Spent inside, I unplugged my phone and crept back into bed, pressing my lips to her hair and neck as she sighed contently.

When we were together, Erica's migraines could last for a day or two. I knew she needed sleep, but she'd been on her game and doing her best to tolerate me and keep up with my hectic schedule.

All I wanted to do was wake her up and see her smile, talk to her like we used to, bury myself inside her so she could heal me, and maybe I could do the same for her.

It was all there, all of the love I thought we had lost. We were made for each other, and there was no denying it. I would try my best to make her believe it again.

I knew I had missed an important detail along the way, something that I couldn't wrap my head around. Something that she'd been pleading with me to see.

I'd been so damn stubborn and avoided her explanation for leaving me, but now it was time to listen. I didn't want any more secrets between us, and if hearing her out was how I got her back, it was time.

Erica

In a daze, I woke up to a knock on my door. I quickly looked at my phone to see five missed texts from Ren that had started a few hours after he'd brought me back from camp with a migraine. I glanced at the clock. I'd slept through the night.

Ren: I went out to get some food. I'll be back.

Ren: Something came up. I'll explain later.

Ren: We need to talk. It's important.

Ren: Call me back, I need to talk to you.

Ren: Damn it, Erica, I'm about to take the field. Call me.

I opened the door to my room, expecting to see Ren, but saw Alice instead.

"Surprise!"

I smiled because, with Alice, I had no choice. Thankful the worst of my headache was gone, I opened the door to let her in.

"What are you doing here?" I asked as I braved a look at my laptop. I had a day's worth of work to catch up on.

"I'm here to take you to the spa. No objections. You've been working your ass off and I need a girlfriend to go with, so get your shoes on."

I could have cried at the sincerity in her eyes, and I damn near hugged her. A day of pampering was just what I needed to hit the refresh button. I had let myself go while living on Ren's tight schedule. I needed to decompress and take a little time for myself.

"I could hug you right now," I said as I moved toward the bathroom. "Just let me freshen up."

AN HOUR and a half later I'd had a facial and a bikini wax, and now was in the midst of a massage beside Alice.

"I can't thank you enough for this, woman. I owe you big."

"Well, I figured while I was here I could get in a little time with you. How are things going?"

"Good, so good." I moaned into the feeling of hands working lavender oil into my back. "We're getting along. No expectations. We haven't talked about much in the way of us."

Alice turned to me with warm brown eyes. "But?"

I smiled in return. "But I feel good about us for the first time in a long time. I feel like we might have a chance. Like maybe he can forgive me for leaving. And maybe I can be there for him, *with* him despite everything. Which reminds me, with our rush to get here I forgot to text him back. He's playing this morning, and he has an interview with a local news station after."

"I'll get you there in time. No work now," she ordered firmly.

I sighed. "Right."

Walking out of that spa, I felt like a million dollars. I was eager to get back to Ren, fully relaxed and rested. I was hellbent on making whatever relationship I had with Ren work.

I felt the weight of the world had left my shoulders as I climbed into Alice's Jeep, ready to embrace the idea of a new us.

I looked over to Alice, who was glowing in her own right, freshly pampered and just as anxious to get to her husband.

"I think I'll try to start that talk today, after his interview. I love him, Alice."

She beamed at me. "I know. I'm excited for you."

I smiled down at my phone as I shot off a text to Ren.

Me: I want to talk to you too. I'm sorry I missed the game. I'm on my way.

Breaking the no work rule, I decided to check my emails and scrolled through my phone. Rowe had sent one this morning and marked it urgent. Plus, I had missed two texts from her.

Rowe: Are you okay?

Rowe: Please call me.

"Something's wrong," I voiced to Alice as the engine roared between us in the open cabin of her Jeep.

Alice pulled over as I opened the email. My heart plummeted as I studied the picture and my phone fell from my hands into my lap.

Alice picked it up and studied the picture. "He wouldn't."

"He did."

Chapter Thirteen

REN

FRESH OUT OF THE SHOWER AND INTO JEANS AND A T-SHIRT, I COULDN'T hide my smile when Erica charged into the locker room with Alice hot on her heels. It was only when Erica's blazing eyes met mine that my smile faded.

I knew I was in for a shit storm.

Samson and Griffith covered their dicks with towels as Alice strutted past me to get to Rafe.

"Woman, you are testing my patience today," Rafe growled as he gripped Alice to him and covered her eyes.

Erica made a beeline for me, her cellphone in hand.

"Get them out of here. Hembrey!" Griffith called out as he did his best to dress hastily.

Though in the wrong, Rafe came to his wife's defense. "What's the matter, Griffith? Afraid she'll see your two-inch excuse for a dick?"

"Fuck you. Get them out!"

Alice peeked over Rafe's shoulder, and he swatted her ass as she squealed in his arms.

He looked down at her with pure adoration. "How in the hell did you get in here?"

She eyed Erica with a wink. "My girl here has an interview to prep Ren for. And I've never been back here," she said as she looked back up at him with just as much love.

"Yeah, well, get out of here, babe, before I get shit from the elders."

Erica was in front of me now, her brown eyes full of hurt and anger as she confronted me.

"You had dinner with her last night?"

I nodded.

"Ren, why didn't you tell me?" She gripped the phone in her hand as if it physically hurt to hold it.

But as I studied her, my pulse picked up, and all I could see was the length of her toned legs, the cinch of her waist, the deep crease of cleavage that led up to the thin gold chain around her delicate throat. She looked gorgeous in a crimson sundress and fuck-me heels.

She was glowing, and it was only diminished slightly by the hurt in her eyes. I wanted to grab her then to wipe the worry from between her brows and quiet her thoughts with my kiss. I was burning and had been since the night she told me she never wanted to be my wife.

"I tried calling you," I said as I packed my duffle. "Her PR thought it would be good publicity for both of us if we looked like we were dating . . . instead of . . ."

"Instead of fucking," she said coldly as she again looked down at the picture.

I had to admit it did look incriminating, but that was the whole point.

"I didn't think it was a bad idea," I said, though it was a nightmare after that dinner to keep her clothed and away from my dick.

I could see the jealousy and the hurt, but much to my disappointment, she swallowed them both before she spoke.

"It's a smart move, but you should have run it by me."

"My nights are my own, remember," I gritted out, not because I didn't feel like I owed her an explanation after what happened between us the day before, but because I still couldn't claim her as my own.

We still hadn't decided anything between the two of us, and I had no idea what we were. If we were anything.

She looked up at me with venom in her gaze. "Nothing public is yours, *nothing* until this season ends."

"I tried to call you."

"I was still down with the headache."

"Natasha's rep said he's been trying to get in touch with you."

I saw it then; she was guilty. She'd purposefully avoided Natasha's reps. I couldn't help my smile as she narrowed her eyes.

"You should have tried harder, Ren."

"You are the one who put me on this bullshit schedule," I reminded her.

"I'm the one saving your reputation," she hissed. "Not *her*."

I glanced around the locker room and saw that it was mostly empty. I was getting pissed, and though I wanted to respect her decision to keep our past under the radar, her berating me in the locker room told me she was itching for a fight.

"Don't keep anything from me, Ren. Okay? Even if you think—" she looked around us and lowered her voice "—even if you think it will hurt my feelings," she said through glossy, berry colored lips. "I mean it, Ren. Don't."

"That was our first and *last* dinner, now we're supposed to let it fizzle out," I assured her.

"Good. It's all good. It shows consistency at least," Erica scolded. "We both know you haven't done anything close to that with any other woman."

"Except you, and look where that got me," I retorted.

"Makavoy," Rafe called from the entrance of the locker room as a reporter came in with a video set up behind him. "You're up."

All-Business-Erica showed up at that moment and pulled a jacket and hat from my locker.

"Here," Erica said, shoving the cap down on my head. "Remember what we talked about and what topics to stay away from, okay?"

"I can dress myself," I snapped, adjusting the hat before I pulled on the jacket. "I look like a fucking mascot."

Erica couldn't hide her smirk. "You look like a baseball player who's proud to wear his lettering. Act the part. Stay away from the personal questions and talk about your love for the ball. Your teammates. Your plans."

Ren eyed me, his jaw tightening. "I can handle an interview."

"We are rebranding you," she warned. "Ren, please, this is important to our campaign."

Before I could say another word, a teenager with a mic introduced himself. He was sickly white and sweating profusely.

"Hi, Ren, I'm Nick from WBSC," he said carefully, as if he were afraid to approach me.

"Sup," I said as Erica's eyes flared. "I mean, nice to meet you," I corrected, playing along to placate her.

Erica seemed satisfied and took a step back as Nick dug in.

"I'm a big fan, and I can say just as much for the rest of the station."

"Thank you, it's appreciated," I said with a dry tongue.

I was still looking at Erica, who was watching my every move like a hawk. I wasn't feeling it. The clothes, the interview, any of it because all I wanted at that moment was to figure out just what in the fuck was going on *out* of the spotlight.

I'd been a good boy. I'd played along with her best-laid plans, but inside I'd been fighting for weeks with my feelings after two years of waiting, and I was at my breaking point.

Nick looked between Erica and me and spoke up in an attempt to break the tension which was thick in the air between us.

"We're live in about a minute. I'm not going to delve too far in, just the usual—" He broke off on a gag, his face going pale. "Sorry, excuse me, I haven't been feeling well—"

Nick chose that moment to rear back and empty his stomach on the floor beneath me.

Chapter Fourteen

Erica

"Oh, Jesus Christ, man," Ren said as he jumped back in time to dodge the puke spewing out of our sickly reporter.

It was Ren's worst nightmare, and I could see the terror in his eyes as he watched Nick toss his cookies on the floor. It would have been comical had Nick not been so pitiful.

"I'm so sorr—" Nick began to apologize but was cut short by another wave of nausea.

The smell was repugnant as he panicked, wiping his mouth and working out another apology before he retched again. Unable to contain my surprise, I covered my mouth to hide my laugh as Ren's furious eyes found mine.

"Are we done here?" he snapped, as if to insinuate that the situation was somehow my fault.

I walked toward Nick, who was turning green. "Nick, I'm so sorry you're sick. We can reschedule for another day, okay?"

Nick nodded, his humiliation apparent as he left the locker room and the cameraman followed. I turned back to face Ren.

"What an asshole you've turned into," I scolded. "Are you such a miserable bastard now you can't even find any concern for the poor man or at least find a little humor in the situation?"

"Yep, we're done," Ren said as he slammed his locker.

"Actually, we're not," the cameraman spoke up as he rejoined us with a cell phone to his ear. "Not enough time to divert. We're live in thirty-seconds."

Ren froze as the guy lifted the camera toward him and held out the mic to me.

"Think you can swing it? You're his rep, right?"

I nodded.

"It's a three-minute segment," he instructed. "Just the usual questions. We're at fifteen seconds."

I hesitated briefly before I grabbed the microphone and lunged over the mess on the floor toward Ren, who caught me just in time.

Composing myself the best I could, a nervous laugh threatened to bubble up as Ren's eyes watered with disgust. I braved looking into the camera with a smile as the man behind it cued that we were live.

"I'm Erica Wild, filling in for Nick today in Paradise Valley. I'm standing with Ren Makavoy, an asset to Denver since he was signed two years ago."

Ren stood stiffly next to me, and I saw the surprise in his eyes when I rattled off a few of his highlight plays over the last two seasons. I turned to see his warm eyes on me.

"Ren, how are you feeling about the team this year?" Temporarily stunned with my recap of the last two years of his career—footage I'd watched on my downtime at the field—he studied my face as I gave him wide eyes to let him know he was stunting the interview.

"I'm feeling confident," Ren spoke evenly, his eyes darting from me to the camera.

He was visibly shaking, which I found hilarious, all the typical smugness wiped away by a sickly reporter and his ex-girlfriend grilling him on camera. It was all I could do to keep from laughing. I began to go over our rehearsed questions.

"Tell us, Ren, what do you see happening for Denver this season?"

"Collectively, I see us winning games, breaking records, and going all the way. Denver deserves a winning team, and we plan to give them one."

After a few more questions, I went rogue. Ren was still on edge, and I wanted to use it to my advantage.

"I'm curious, as I'm sure other fans are, to know if you have any superstitious habits?"

His jaw tick was the only sign of his irritation. "None to speak of," he said, and I had to fight the urge to roll my eyes.

"No pre-game rituals?" I pressed, feigning innocence.

Ren gave me a murderous glance before he relented. "I guess you can say I have a little ritual. I like to fool around with a deck of cards before the game. It keeps me sharp, focused."

"Care to demonstrate?"

Ren stiffened as I looked pointedly at his pocket. I knew his card tricks would wow his fans. It was something he only shared with me, but to get the point across to the rest of the world that he was a man with a little more substance and not just a pretty playboy with a bad temperament, they needed to see it for themselves.

"I think I can manage one trick," he said with a hint of ice in his voice before he gave me a half-assed wink that told me I was in deep shit.

He pulled the deck from his pocket and split it in half, shuffling the divided cards with skilled fingers. I saw a few lingering guys in the locker room pause to look on.

Ren didn't pull simple card tricks. He was an expert at it. He'd got a magic set for Christmas one year at one of his foster homes and had only been interested in the cards.

I could never get enough of seeing his face light up when he performed them. It was a peek of Ren in his best form, relaxed, confident, and smiling.

And while we were together and in bed one night, after hours of memorizing each other's bodies, I'd laid with my head on his shoulder while he performed trick after trick for an audience of one. It was one of the best nights of my life.

In that locker room, inches away from Nick's lunch and feet away from a few of his teammates, I watched him slowly come into himself on live television. And he wowed us all. Even the cameraman moved his head from behind the lens to get a better view. It was magic. A glimpse of the genuine Ren Makavoy.

"That's really something," I said, as if I wasn't the woman he'd manipulated into a first date with those cards.

The woman he hadn't ravaged on that very deck seconds after I told him I loved him.

As if he hadn't pushed into me with our hands clasped and our chests together, our mouths molded, and our hearts on fire.

I stared at the deck with longing as Ren packed them away and put them back in his pocket. His confidence returned as he looked over at me with a smug smirk.

In an instant, I was devastated and furious as I pictured him with Natasha the night before. Once again, I'd been blindsided with too much of who he was *after* us.

I white-knuckled the mic as I commanded the interview.

"So, tell us, Ren, we're all interested to know. Will there be anyone special in the seats for you this year?" I thrust the mic toward him, smacking him in the mouth and tapping his teeth, *hard*. Ren jerked back in surprise before he composed himself enough to answer.

"The fans," he said carefully, looking me over as if to ask what in the hell I was doing.

"Any special lady in your life?"

Ren blocked the mic midway to his mouth to spare his reddening lip and teeth from another blow.

Somehow, he read me and worked the camera like a pro. "Every lady with Denver gear on to show their support."

I was on dangerous ground and found relief when the cameraman gestured for us to wrap it up.

"Well, we wish you the best of luck this year, Ren."

"Thank you," he sneered as the camera cut off and he touched his finger to his swelling lip.

"What the fuck was that?"

The locker room was empty now save for the camera guy packing up his equipment, who chose that moment to compliment me.

"You did a great job," he said, giving me a wink.

Ren looked between us and his eyes dulled. "I beg to fucking differ."

"I'm Lewis." He held out his hand to me, completely ignoring Ren's tantrum, to take mine and I gave it to him. "You really should consider doing something in media."

"Thanks," I said as a sickly Nick reappeared, spitting out more apologies before Lewis began to whisk him out the door, but not without extending an invitation to me first. "Can I call you sometime?"

"Are you fucking serious?" Ren scoffed, looking between us.

Lewis wasn't half bad looking. In fact, in all the chaos I hadn't noticed just how good looking he was.

"I'm pretty fucking serious," Lewis retorted as Ren shot him daggers.

"Nice to meet you too, Makavoy."

Ren's voice was a full-on threat. "Fuck yourself."

"I knew you were full of shit, and that was all just for show," Lewis sounded off snidely as a vein in Ren's neck popped out.

"What the fuck did you just say?"

I grabbed Ren's arm and he shook me off as he took a threatening step toward Lewis.

"Ren, chill out," I said pointedly before I pleaded with Lewis, who was still holding Nick up, waiting on my answer. "Please, just take him and go."

Lewis looked between Ren and me. "Sure, but just so you know, you can do way better than this asshole."

Ren's body coiled as his eyes went to ice.

"Jesus Christ, man, do you have any intention of keeping your fucking teeth today?" He was about to snap, and I braced myself for it when Lewis finally disappeared out of sight.

"You can't engage in that crap, Ren," I said calmly.

He turned on me then, cold fury in his eyes.

"Don't engage? Says the woman who asked every question I'm supposed to be avoiding?"

"That was the first of several thousand inquiries this year of who you're sticking your dick in, boss. I'm just prepping you." I shrugged and began to head for the door as a janitor walked past us to mop up the mess between us.

"No, that wasn't prep. That was jealousy, pure and simple," he whisper-yelled, closing the space between us. I glanced around us as he closed in.

"Stop it," I hissed, on edge with anger threatening to get the best of me. I moved to get around him, and he caught my wrist.

"I don't think I will," Ren said, his voice ice. "You don't get to pull that shit on camera."

"You did," I reminded. "And I was blessed to witness it all!" Disgusted, I shook my wrist loose as he followed me toward the door of the locker room.

"I didn't fuck her. I had dinner with her. I was trying to do right by her, which she deserved. I'm trying to do the right thing by *everyone*."

I turned to him then and let my anger feed. I might have walked out on him, but he made damn sure I felt his wrath.

"You didn't even give me a chance to regret walking out on us, Ren, because a *minute* later you became exactly what I feared you would. I hated the sight of you. I resented us." I saw him flinch, and I took a step forward, gaining ground. "I resented everything that happened between us."

"You don't mean that."

"You think that back there was jealousy? That wasn't jealousy." I said as I crossed my arms.

"I'm sure of it," he snapped. "But why don't you lie to me and tell me what it was."

"That was *assumption* because that's all you ever grace us with, your adoring fans, those of us who want to see the best in you. But now we can only assume the worst. You put a sick taste in our mouths by becoming the epitome of the cliché. I had a grudge against baseball when I left you, but you made sure I was finished with it."

Ren stood, eyes widening as I let my anger reign. "You made it a joke, a disgusting ego sport on and off the field. And I pity anyone who idolized you for the man you were the last two years."

I saw the visible rip in his chest but refused to let up.

"You want a reason for why I left you? Here's a good one. This fucking sport. It destroys things; it destroys relationships and people."

"No, that was you," Ren accused as he stared down at me.

"Was it me? Or did I get out just in time, before you turned into this self-important asshole who thinks he's the only one with talent? Look at what you've become! There was no way I could watch it change you or what we had. And you are so much like him, Ren. So much."

"What in the hell are you talking about? I'm so much like who?" Ren demanded, his eyes full of hurt.

"I hate this fucking sport! That's what I'm talking about. How could I ever be the woman for you when I *hate* baseball, Ren? It ruined my family, my mother. It ruined everything!"

"ERICA!"

I stood there, stunned, as my father's voice snapped me back into the room full of watchful eyes. I had the attention of every person in the room, but I kept my eyes on Alice, who had just walked in with the purse I had left in her Jeep.

She nodded in encouragement as she watched me cower at the sound of authority behind me.

I turned to face the great Lucas Wild. A Hall of Fame inductee and career sportsman. A man who put baseball above everything, especially his wife, his sons, and his daughter.

My mother was a martyr to the sport I loathed.

She'd sacrificed her life to it, for only stolen moments when my dad felt like throwing her a bone and treating her like a stray dog afterward.

Full of contempt, I stared into the eyes of my father while his jaw ticked. I was the first to speak.

"What are you doing here?"

"I was invited," he said sternly as he eyed Ren behind me. "Good to see you, Ren."

"I invited him," Ren said behind me.

"Hey, Lucas."

I laughed without humor and looked back to Ren. "Of course you invited him. You two were thicker than thieves when we dated. I'm guessing the end of *us* wasn't the end of *everything*," I said, looking between them.

"You two have a lot in common," I said with a shaky voice, the exhaustion taking over. "So much more now, don't you think, Ren?" I asked as the first tears fell down my cheeks.

"I mean you idolized him for being a ball player *and* a family man. You couldn't wait to live a life like the *great* Lucas Wild." I shook my head and swallowed a threatening sob. "Little did you know, the life you've lived the last two years are more his style."

"Erica," my father said with bite as he glared at me with contempt.

"Sorry, Dad. Not this time. I won't keep quiet."

Ren looked stunned as he took a step forward. "What the fuck is going on?"

"Erica, you need to go collect yourself," my father snapped as I stared on at the love of my life.

Ren's eyes were filled with confusion, and I was done being the source of it.

"I couldn't make you choose," I confessed with a broken voice. "I loved you too much. But I couldn't get over it, Ren. I couldn't make peace with the game. Not even for you. I was terrified of becoming like her, like my mother. I tried so hard to get over it. But I watched it go on for years and years. I watched him *use* her and *discard* her like she was nothing. And she loved him just as much as I loved you."

"Damn it, Erica!" My father finally lost his composure, his tall frame going taught in his dressed to impress Armani suit.

He looked around the room, fuming and humiliated, his olive complexion turning beet red. I'd never been so satisfied as I was at that moment, seeing the look on his face. We had a small audience, but the audience we had was enough.

Ren's opinion of him mattered. It mattered a lot. When I introduced Ren to my father, I could see it in his eyes. My dad was excited about having another player to mentor, and I quickly realized that Ren idolized my dad.

I never had the heart to tell Ren that the man he looked up to was a completely different man off the field and out of the press. He wasn't the family man he portrayed himself to be. At all.

When it came to having a father, I was a baseball orphan. And I shared that burden with my brothers.

Lucas Wild was drunk when he was home and verbally abusive to my mother. Baseball had consumed him, body, mind, and soul. Even his precious induction into the Hall of Fame hadn't satiated anything for him. His unhealthy obsession with the sport had cost him everything, including the admiration of his sons and the respect of his daughter.

I looked at Ren, who was lost to me. Not because I had left, but because I never showed him my fear. I'd named it. I told him countless times I didn't want to have to compete with the sport for his affection, and though he gave me assurances, he never quite *got* it. I'd spent years playing along with my father's charade that we look like the perfect family, and it cost me the confidence I needed to be with Ren. I didn't believe in happily ever after *with* baseball. My father's example was far too prominent to pay attention to other examples like Rafe and Alice or Andy and April. And to be honest, I had never seen that growing up. I had always seen my father's teammates behaving like idiots among other things no kid should ever see. I'd been surrounded by good-looking liars all my life. My father included.

And when he left for another season, it was me who had to deal with my mother when she withdrew. He ruined her with his absence and half-assed love. I wouldn't, *couldn't* let myself deal with the same fate.

I was just another girl with daddy issues. But those issues were enough to make me run away from a life with Ren.

And though I knew deep down Ren was different, I still couldn't subject myself to a life filled with baseball, dedicated to a sport I felt had robbed me. At least that's what I thought when I walked out.

Ren deserved a cheerleader. Someone who could be a decent club wife and give him all the support he needed.

"I could never make you choose," I said as one tear traced another down my cheeks. "So, I chose for you."

Ren swallowed as I turned to face my fear.

"Don't worry, Dad," I sniffed as I glared at him. "I *wasn't* invited, and I'm not staying."

I looked over to Alice and gave her a pleading look. "Please get me the hell out of here."

Chapter Fifteen

REN

"I don't even have to ask if it's all true," I spoke to his back before he had a chance to get to her hotel door.

Lucas Wild turned to me, and I cringed at the way I'd put him on a pedestal for so many years. A legend, a player I'd looked up to since I was a child.

The woman I loved had his eyes and his skin tone, but that was where it ended. I'd credited him for far too much. It all made sense and began to click as I watched him sink into his guilt.

He was the reason why Erica didn't want to date a ballplayer. Lucas was the reason Erica never wanted to go home for the holidays when we were together, despite her mother's desperate invitations.

Even when I'd managed to talk her into going home, she'd been reserved around everyone, especially her father. I'd let my excitement in my budding friendship with Lucas dull the intuition that something was off.

But it had always been there, and it didn't help that Erica's mother had done just as good of a job of covering up the truth. Erica had been raised to lie, to cover for him to keep his reputation.

Lucas Wild was not who he made himself out to be. Had never been.

The man was a living *lie*. And she'd swallowed her pride and loved me enough to clean up my mistakes and do the same for me.

It was like a punch in the gut, and suddenly I was furious at my inability to look past my own dreams to see her fears. I'd been so goddamned blind.

"Ren, this is personal," Lucas said with a quick excuse.

"Goddamn right, it is," I said, stepping in front of him and blocking the door.

"You're going to have to excuse us, I need a word with her," he said, as he attempted to push past me.

"I don't think so," I said adamantly as anger radiated from me.

"She's my daughter."

"She's my *future*."

"You're overstepping, Makavoy."

"No, I'm protecting her. A job you never did."

"You don't know what you're talking about. She's exaggerating," he said nonchalantly.

"Oh?" I said, taking another step forward. "So, tell me about your daughter."

His mouth clamped shut.

"Come on, give me anything. Tell me one thing about her."

"You need to step back from that door," he said in warning.

"You don't know anything about her, do you? God, I can't believe I looked up to you. Treated you as a friend, and she was hiding it from me, to protect you."

"Again, you don't know what you're talking about," he snapped.

Even as he tried to defend himself, his eyes were full of guilt and regret. That was something, but not nearly fucking enough.

"No, I believe I do know what I've been talking about. You see, I've been listening, something I wasn't good at before. I know that now, and I'm working on it." I took a menacing step forward. "What I *know* is there's a beautiful woman on the other side of that door capable of more than she knows, who thinks she'll never be more loved than a damn game of baseball. That's on you, asshole."

I pointed to the door behind me. "I lost her once because of it. I'm not losing her again. So, you need to do whatever you have to do to get the hell out of here. Because you're no longer invited. It was *your* fucked-up priorities, your choices that came between us. It's not happening again."

Lucas's eyes sharpened as he ground out his words. "And you think you're the man she deserves? You're so fucking perfect, Ren? You think I haven't seen your tornado of shit in the media the last few years?"

"I've fucked up, too, but there's a difference between you and me."

"And what's that?" he asked crossly.

"She hasn't given up on me."

Chapter Sixteen

ERICA

A KNOCK ON MY HOTEL DOOR BROUGHT ME OUT OF MY HAZE. I HAD ALICE take me back to the hotel so I could pack. I needed to get away from everything before the season began.

I wouldn't break my word to Ren to be there, but with training ending in a few days, I could get back to New York and try to get my head on straight. My emotions were putting everything in jeopardy.

I took a deep breath and opened the door to see Ren with his hands in his jeans, his eyes burning a hole through me.

"Can I come in?"

"Yeah," I said, leaving the door open for him and doing quick work of resuming my packing.

"I know this looks bad, okay. But I'll be back for opening day. I'm not quitting on you, Ren. I just need to take a break." I brought my eyes to his.

"I'm not leaving you. Not professionally."

"What about personally?"

"I'm just full of so much shit I've never dealt with. I'm just dragging you down, and you don't need this. Not at the height of your career. I didn't mean those awful things I said. I'm so sorry. I never regretted us. Never. And I was jealous and hurt, and I can't seem to stop being *anything* but jealous and hurt."

I sat on the edge of my bed and looked up at the ceiling.

"I've lost my shit one too many times since I've been here, Ren, and in public, this isn't good for you or for me."

"I'll decide what's good for me. Last time you made that decision you tore me apart."

I tamped down the tears that threatened. "I'll always regret it. You didn't deserve it."

"Well, you didn't deserve to see what a mess I made of myself, either."

"Did you . . ." I swallowed, afraid to ask. "Did you make a spectacle of yourself so I would see?"

He wiped his hand down his face. "I would never intentionally hurt you. But after the first headline broke, I think I was too numb to care. You cut me so deep, I bled everywhere." He lifted his cap and ran a hand through his hair.

"Once you wrecked my heart, I couldn't stop trying to wreck everything else. I thank God daily for Andy and Rafe, or I might have succeeded. I never thought I would be that guy, to lose so much control over a woman. But you—" he sighed "—you were everything to me."

I folded a pair of jeans and stuffed them in my suitcase. "I wanted to come back, but after I saw those pictures, I couldn't. I didn't know if you would take me."

"I would have taken anything you gave me."

I nodded as I zipped my suitcase. "I wish I would have handled it differently." I let out an ironic tear-filled laugh.

"That's an understatement."

"Why didn't you tell me about him?" he asked, stepping in front of me and stilling my hands.

"I didn't want you to look at him the way I did. You were so animated around him, just so happy to know him. And all that talk you did about family. I knew how important it was to you."

He pushed the hair away from my forehead. "Tell me now."

"He was a total bastard at home. Demanding, judgmental, as if we couldn't do enough to please him. It was disgusting. My mother worshiped him, and he was all too happy to offer his feet to her. I honestly thought that was just the way things were until I got old enough to figure it out. He was undeserving."

"And you thought I was undeserving, too?" he asked in a thick voice.

"You know that's not true. I loved you with everything in me, but I didn't want to. Ren, the day we met, I was divorcing baseball and washing my hands of my dad. He demanded I pick my last tuition check from the ballpark, I guess to keep up appearances or boast he had raised a college graduate. Who the hell knows what his agenda was, but I was there to collect my paycheck from being that bastard's daughter. And I was done."

"You never loved ball?"

"God, yes, I did. I loved it more than anything until I was old enough to know what it was doing to my family. I mean, I know it was *him*, but I guess it was just easier to say I hate baseball than to say I hate my father. I wanted no part of the life for myself. I saw what misery it could bring, and then you blew my plans all to shit."

"But you kept them," he reminded as he stood towering over me, his eyes inquisitive as his gentle hands cupped the sides of my face.

"I would have married you in a heartbeat if it didn't chain me to baseball."

"You think marrying some lawyer who works eighty-hour weeks would make you happier?"

"It was the game, Ren, and your devotion to it. It reminded me so much of him. And, Jesus Christ, look at you."

"That doesn't matter, I was always faithful."

"I know you were. But I felt like I was up against too much. So, what I think is that I was twenty-two years old and out of my mind in love and too afraid to make the same mistake, become and do exactly like my mother no matter *how* you treated me." I paused my next words as the fear set in they would only divide us further. Looking at him, loving him, there was no way I could hold back the truth any longer.

"Because while baseball is *your* life, in a sense it took both my parents away. And if it changed us, you and me, I knew it would break me just as much as it broke her. That's the mindset of the twenty-two-year-old me."

Heart heavy with the memory of walking out of our apartment two years ago, I pressed on. "I couldn't look at you without folding, Ren. I was so far gone, there was no way I could walk away with you there. I took the coward's way out because I saw it as the only way."

"I believe that you believe that," he said in a whisper. "But do you remember what I said to you the day we met?"

I closed my eyes and nodded.

"What did I say, Erica?"

"So, this is where you come in," I said as a tear trailed down my cheek before he caught it with his thumb.

"And I meant it. I knew it was you the moment I met you. If I can love you for the last three years and only had you for one of them, don't you think I could love you for three more? And the three after that?"

"You still love me?" I asked, searching his eyes as he stared down at me.

"You know I do."

"I love you, too."

"I know."

"Is there anything you don't know?" I asked with a slight eye roll.

"I don't know how this plays out. And I'm fucking terrified you'll walk away again, but I don't have a choice because I can't stop loving you no matter what happens."

"I couldn't move on. I missed you too much. Even though . . ." I swallowed, "Even though I saw you with all those women, I couldn't stop wanting you. And I never will."

Ren traced my lips with his thumb before he leaned in on a whisper.

"Don't go."

"I don't want to. If you don't want me to, this time I won't."

"I missed you so fucking much."

"I love you, Ren. I'm so sorry. I don't expect you to forgive me."

"I'll forgive you for anything," he said, brushing his thumb over my lips again and again as he held me in his hands. "But we have two years to makeup for."

The butterflies churned in my stomach as he leaned in and brushed our lips together. My clit pulsed as the jolt of our electricity hit me.

"Ren," I whispered as he closed his eyes and brought his forehead to mine.

His voice was gravel. "I need to know right now what you want."

"I want you to let me back in."

He brushed his lips against mine again. "Saying yes to me means saying yes to baseball. You get that, right?"

"I do. I want whatever life that is. Just please don't—"

"You will never have to worry about your place with me. *Ever.* You come first, always."

He paused a moment before his lips met mine. "How's your head?"

"Better," I said. "I'm fine."

"Good, because we're about to have the best fucking make-up sex in history." He gave me a smirk, and I returned it.

I raised a brow and trailed my hand down to his rock-hard cock. "What are you waiting for?"

"Fuuuck," he hissed as he captured my lips with his and then darted his tongue out before sweeping my mouth before he dove in deep. I gasped at the feeling as my body lit up and my flesh burned.

"Oh, God," I murmured as he pulled back and we shared breath. "Please don't stop."

He eyed the bed behind me and gripped my hair in his fist. His mouth came down hard as he pushed us onto the mattress, his arm stretching behind me to clear off my suitcase. In seconds, my dress was on the floor. He pulled off his hat and tossed it. His dark hair spilled in a wave across his forehead as he bent to take my taut nipple into his mouth.

Sighing, I drank him in, hungry, needy, his neon blue gaze full of lust and longing, and the love I'd missed for so long. I swam in it, relished in the feel of it.

He fisted his T-shirt at his back and pulled it off. His body was a piece of paradise, and I mapped it with my fingers, exploring the divots cut in his stomach following the hair that trailed down his naval.

Unbuttoning his jeans, I freed his perfect cock, the plump head beaded with arousal. I held him firmly in my hand and brushed the tip with my thumb. I heard his breath leave him as I began to pump him with my fist.

I sank into the bed as he swept a hot tongue over every inch of my exposed flesh, and I whimpered at the attention he lavished everywhere but where I needed him most. A hot trail of desire blazed its way through us as his gaze commanded mine as he hooked my black lace panties with his fingers.

"I love you," I whispered.

He paused his fingers and closed his eyes. His hurt was written in his every feature. I lifted myself and wrapped my arms around his neck before I got to my knees and let his scent fill my nose.

I brought us chest to chest as I whispered in his ear, "I'm sorry I forgot about us and let my fear ruin everything."

I pulled back to look into his eyes. Ren never treated me like a woman in his bed, he treated me like the woman of his life. And I let my own hurt show as he stared at me wordlessly.

We'd both been punished enough.

"Tell me what you want. I'll give you everything," I whispered.

"I want my life back, the one you took with you," he murmured as he kissed my lips softly and gripped me firmer in his hold. "Damn, baby, I thought I lost you." He pushed me so that I fell on the mattress and followed with his lips before he spread my thighs and slipped two fingers inside. I arched my back as he cursed under his breath.

"Christ, you're wet," he said as he twisted them and pressed his thumb to my clit. I bucked under his touch as he pinned the rest of me with his gaze.

"Ren," I cried out in breathless praise while I rocked into his hand.

"Fuck," he grunted out, his breath hitting my neck before he took a bite.

I gasped as the wave hit, clutching his hair and pulling it hard while I shuddered beneath him. His name echoed off my tongue as he milked my center and the orgasm lasted for a blissful eternity.

I was still coming when he pulled back to watch my reaction.

"You look so perfect when you come," he said in a murmur as he spread my thighs wider and made his way down my body in praise before he dipped his head to lick my center.

Moaning at the feel of him, I watched him consume me. His breathtaking blue eyes were trained on me as he gripped my thighs, pushing them further apart while I rode his tongue, eagerly chasing another release. He stopped me at the brink and sucked my clit, teasing me with the promise of more.

High from the feeling of his mouth alone, I shuddered when he slipped his fingers in, playing with the wetness and sliding it over my sensitive flesh. Over and over he coated me with my arousal while he flicked out his tongue and slowly fucked me with his fingers.

Watching my reaction, he dipped in again, his licks low as his nose grazed my clit. I nearly jumped out of my skin. Skilled fingers twisted and teased while his repeating tongue brought me to the edge and pushed me over. I skyrocketed as I burst, my back bowing off the bed as my body shook in ecstasy.

"So fucking beautiful," he murmured against my skin before he lined his thick cock at my entrance and pushed in.

My breath caught at the feeling of fullness, and I closed my eyes, tightening around him.

"Oh my God," I said as I scratched the skin on his back.

He hadn't let up since we got on the bed and I was overwhelmed with pleasure, at his mercy and loving every minute.

"Jesus Christ," he hissed as he filled me, his breath ragged.

With one hand tangled in my hair, he began to thrust like a madman, our eyes connected as he swiveled his hips, hitting me deep and where I needed him.

He hadn't forgotten a single inch of me and made sure I knew it.

Bursting around him, I screamed his name until it came out in a desperate rasp. I flew over the edge while he rolled through his own release, pushing in deeper to make sure I took every drop.

Seconds later, he lay on top of me as I ran my nails along his skin.

"I haven't come that fast since I discovered my first hard on."

I chuckled as he buried his face in my breasts. "I should be embarrassed, but I'm not," he said with a sly grin as he propped his chin on my chest.

I would never see anything more beautiful than Ren when he was at ease with me. His smile, the tenderness in his eyes, despite the life he'd lived, was my eighth wonder of the world, and I was done denying it.

"I missed you," I said carefully, afraid to see any more hurt in his face.

"You didn't have to," he said, absently sucking on my nipple.

"That's kind of part of the job of loving you," I said, reminding him of the life he led.

"I'm not an idiot, you know, I know what a toll this job takes on a relationship. I just thought, well, I was sure we were stronger than that. Turns out we're going to have to work twice as hard as everyone else."

"That's all I need you to say. And that you think my ass is hotter than Natasha's." I gave a soft chuckle as he planted tender kisses below my breast.

"Isn't the better compliment that I want you forever, and I never wanted her at all."

"I will settle for better earlobes," I said pathetically.

"You have a better everything," he said as he ran a trail of tongue-laced kisses across my belly.

"I haven't been with anyone else, Ren. Not since you."

He paused at that and looked down at me. "No one?"

"No," I confessed easily.

His face was filled with shock. "Not even . . . no one?"

"Oh, I tried," I said as I looked up at him and he stole my breath. "How I tried. Like a whore on her first night on the corner, I tried."

"Little too much information, baby," Ren said as he stared down at me with adoration.

"I tried like the only bottle of lube on a porn set."

"Erica," he grated as he pinched my nipple. I ignored the pain.

"I tried like a one-legged woman at an ass-kicking contest."

He let out a sharp laugh as he turned me on my side and pulled me to him.

"I tried like a—"

"Erica?"

"Yeah?"

"I'm not letting you go this time."

"You won't have to."

His soft lips pressed against my shoulder as I pulled the covers over us. We were in for the night even though it was early. But I knew what this night would lead to. Two years of catch up. And I was finally ready to play ball.

"I tried like a Democrat on election day," I said with a chuckle as his arms snaked around me in a familiar way.

"Erica," Ren whispered. I turned back to look at him, firm in his hold, his features etched with worry. "We'll get through this season. I won't let you forget how good we feel."

"I never forgot. I'm not leaving again, Ren. I promise."

"I need you, trust me," he said before he planted the softest of kisses on my lips.

"I do."

"No lies. Don't hold back. We can do this."

"I know."

"About the women—"

"Oh, Jesus, one mountain at a time," I said as I kissed him silent.

Opening Day

"Play ball!"

I hadn't attended an opening game for years. Despite my best attempts to stay away from the sport I swore I loathed, I could feel the excitement race through me. From the first pitch, I was in the zone.

I sat next to April and Alice, who had made it a point to be with me at this game. They had turned into friends I couldn't do without. A support system that I never imagined possible.

When Rafe walked toward the dugout after a solid ending of pitches, I couldn't help my observation.

"Why does Rafe look like a raccoon? What happened to him?"

April chuckled next to me and addressed Alice who stiffened in her seat. "You have to tell her."

Alice cut her eyes to April. "I hate you."

"Come on, it's hilarious," she said as she gave me a shit-eating grin.

"Maybe to you," Alice snapped.

"Okay," I said with prodding eyes in Alice's direction. "Now I *have* to know."

"It's nothing," Alice dismissed, looking toward the field.

"You broke your husband's nose. I would say that's *something*," April mused.

"You really suck, you know that, April Pracht? Like I don't even know why

I deal with you," Alice said with a menacing smile before she took a breath and turned to me. "Okay, well, Rafe's been a little tense lately, to say the least."

"So, you broke his nose?" I asked, lost.

Alice bit her lip and slunk in her seat on a whisper. "I was trying to get him good and relaxed for the start of the season. And, well . . ."

"Go on," April said with a chuckle.

"So, we haven't had a chance to . . . ya know, do it. And well I wanted to spice things up a bit. He came home one day from meetings, and let's just say I was ready for him."

"Oh, you were ready all right," April taunted.

"You want to tell it?" Alice scolded her.

"Oh, no, honey, this one is alllll you!" April replied, her drawl making her tease that much more adorable.

"Anyway," Alice continued, "I had on some skimpy lingerie, and I put on some . . . porn. You know, on my phone, not like on TV. We don't have a subscription or anything."

"*Okay*," I said with a chuckle.

"It started out great, he came in and, well, we started you know . . ."

Her animated face was too much, and I nodded, trying to hide my smile.

"I was bent over the bed with Rafe behind me. It was getting heavy . . ."

April's body began to tremble with silent laughter.

"So, we're watching this couple go at it while we're, ya know, and it's so hot. Rafe was totally into it, and all of a sudden . . ."

I leaned in, on the edge of my seat.

"The screen flashed saying 'Congratulations, you have just published this video on your Facebook newsfeed!'"

"Oh my God!" I exclaimed, terrified for her.

"Exactly!" Alice continued, "I was so freaked out, I reared back, and head-butted him in the nose."

April was howling in her seat, tears pouring from her eyes. Alice's eyes pleaded with mine for understanding.

"Rafe was cursing and bleeding, but I couldn't even help him because I was too busy fumbling with the phone to delete it!"

"Did it post?!" I asked, horrified.

"No!" Alice said with angry, twisted features. "A few seconds later, the screen flashed again with 'Happy April Fool's Day from all of us at Porn Central!'"

April was still hysterical as Alice looked at me with wide, incredulous eyes. As much as I wanted to sympathize, the picture she painted was far too much. I doubled over with laughter as April wiped her eyes and threw her arm around Alice.

"Those bastards," Alice fumed. "I wonder how many orgasms they ruined that day. I'd sue, but then everyone would know we were watching porn."

April looked at her with sympathy-filled eyes.

"Alice, almost everyone watches porn at some point in their life. And it's okay, girl. I'm positive this is an opening day he'll never forget."

Alice winced.

"My poor man. He looks so awful. Our daughter calls him Daddy Walrus now because he had tampons up his nose for two days."

"Andy does the same thing with Kleenex when he's sick," April said. "He's just not bloody from experimental monkey fucking. But kudos on your efforts, girl. We gotta keep them happy, right?"

"Right," Alice said, biting her lip to hide her smile before she finally let herself laugh. "God, I can't believe he puts up with me sometimes."

"It's because he knows your worth it," April said with a grin.

I turned to them both with genuine interest.

"Do they make you happy?"

Both women looked at me with concern. They knew the whole story, including the truth about my father. Regardless, I knew they would give it to me straight.

"Oh yeah," April said. "I mean, Andy's retired so I'm kind of lucky, but then he gets a wild hair like he did this season and takes us with him. He's a family man through and through. I'm more a fan of his than I am of baseball. Sometimes I get sick of it, but then I do my own thing. He gets wrapped up, but I never sleep alone. And if I do, it's with my phone next to my pillow."

"Same here," Alice chimed in. "Sometimes ball consumes him, and we have little tiffs here and there, but he's never missed anything *really* important. He's present for Clover and for me even if it's just a few minutes of FaceTime. It's a tough balance, but we handle it. I'm lucky, though, since I can travel with him or I can fly anytime I want to see him."

They seemed truly happy and it gave me hope. I looked back to the field just as Ren took his position behind the plate. God, how I loved him. And he still loved me, despite the fact that we'd hurt each other so much. The anger was dissolving along with the fear as each day passed and I ended each night in his arms. It was then, sitting in those stands with those two women, that I realized how lucky I was. I was a woman who had thrown away true and unconditional love only to be swept back into it by the one thing I was afraid would ruin it.

Baseball.

I was a veteran fan by the time I could walk and talk. And for Ren, because of who he was and what he meant to me, I could be his forever fan. If any woman out there was made to love him and respect his passion and devotion for ball, it was me. But that's not what he saw when he looked at me. The sport wasn't our whole relationship. *I* was the one who put baseball between us. And his love was the tool used to tear down the divide.

And so, for the next seven months, I watched my love play his heart out, keeping his devotion to ball on the field and his promise to put me first once the glove came off. In the future I saw for myself, I'd never wanted to be devoted to baseball or one of its disciples.

But I ended up falling in love all over again, with *both*.

Ren- World Series Game 3

"Hembrey's taken out twenty-six batters," I warned Valdez who looked uneasy on his feet as he stepped up to the plate. "You're so fucked."

He glared back at me before assuming the position and lifting his bat.

"Might want to stick that ass out a little more," I said as I threw two fingers down between my thighs. Rafe offered me a slight nod from the mound.

Valdez kept his eyes on Rafe as he wound up and fired a dinger into my glove. Valdez caught nothing but air with his swing.

"Ouch," I muttered just loud enough for him to hear.

We were 2-0 and just a batter away from winning the third game. And Rafe was one out away from being the third in history to pitch a perfect game at the World Series.

Rafe shook out his arms and then resumed his spot on the mound. I quickly looked to the dugout and got the signal. We were all lined up in thought as I turned back to Rafe and threw some more fingers.

Seconds later, a perfect heater came toward us and Valdez popped it toward left field. Our third baseman, Howard, scooped it up and fired it to Hamill on first. He stomped on the bag, causing an eruption in the stands behind me.

As soon as the umpire yelled "out," I ditched my mask, running for the mound where Rafe waited with his hat over his heart and his eyes closed.

I pummeled him when I reached him. "You son of a bitch, you did it!"

He opened his eyes and clapped my back before he gave me the biggest shit-eating grin. "Eat it up, Makavoy, this was you, too," he yelled across the players joining us in the huddle.

The stands started spilling into the fields, and Rafe and I were eaten up in man hugs and back slaps. Rafe had just made history and we were about to sweep the World Series, though we were celebrating like we'd already won.

Andy shoved himself inside the huddle and gripped Rafe and me by our jerseys.

"You two, that was fucking epic," he said with pure pride.

"I can't believe it," Rafe yelled as the three of us clasped each other's shoulders.

"That was unbelievable," I agreed.

"Fuckin' A," Andy said with a watery smile.

On the field, I had a moment in time that no one could ever take away from me. Something special I would never forget, but off the field I had everything. I knew without a doubt there was a woman in those stands who had tear-filled eyes, who was just as anxious to get to me as I was to her. I knew that my future was waiting for me with a new fire in her soul that existed for only the two of us. So, while I celebrated with my family on the field. I knew for certain that woman and I were going to be celebrating again later as a new family with each other, filling in the pieces we'd both been missing our whole lives. Because I was her Tin Man and she had my heart.

Epilogue

SIX MONTHS LATER . . .

Ren

Ding. Ding.

"Baby, can you get the door? I ordered a pizza. There's some cash in my wallet."

I was sitting in my recliner with an ice pack on both knees *and* my balls, watching the highlights of other games played that day. I'd got clipped with way too many flyaway balls.

"It's really not a good time, baby," I spoke up from the living room. "My Rocky Mountain oysters are on ice."

"I just got out of the shower, I'm naked!" she yelped from the bedroom. "Fine. I'll just throw on one of your dress shirts."

"No!" I cursed and winced as I scooped the ice packs off my knees and lap and stood to feel the throb of the game I just played. I glared in the direction of our bedroom as I made my way toward the door. "Don't you dare touch my clothes. You got them all jacked up when we moved in."

I heard her laugh from behind the door.

"What did I do, baby? Did the dark blues get mixed up with light?" She teased.

"I swear to God, when I don't feel like I'm at death's door, I'm going to red your ass."

"You'll have to catch me first, Tin Man!"

The doorbell sounded again, and I made a beeline for it realizing I didn't have my wallet. I opened it as the guy stood there with a huge grin on his face, which I returned.

"Wow, I'm a huge fan, man."

"Thanks," I said sincerely. I grabbed a ball off the counter that I'd signed for the camp I was sponsoring and handed it to him as he passed me the pizza. "If you want it," I added as he stared down at it like it was the golden ticket.

"Holy shit, man. Thank you!"

"Just give me a second," I said as I spotted Erica's wallet on the counter and opened it.

There were a hundred compartments and I had searched two before I pulled out the card. My heart thudded wildly in my chest as I stared down at the queen of hearts.

Her card.

The card that kept me from having a full deck for years.

I choked on emotion as I studied it. It was worn to a frazzle and bent at the edges, like she'd pulled it out plenty of times in the years we were apart.

I cleared my throat and unzipped the right part of her wallet, pulling out the cash. I turned and paid the guy, who spoke up as if he were waiting for the chance.

"I was sad I missed the game today, but I have to say this is pretty awesome. I think you guys will take it all again this season. That series was something to watch. Congratulations."

"Thanks, man," I said with a grin, my heart still thudding from the sight of that card as I handed him the cash. "Here you go."

"Thank you, Ren. You made my day."

A thought occurred to me, and I turned and stopped him. "You want to help make mine?"

"Sure, man, whatever you need."

"Can you stick around a bit?" I asked with my heart thudding a mile a minute in my chest. "Stay right here, okay? I'll be right back."

"Sure."

Erica

"Ren, did you find the money?" I asked as I walked out of the bedroom and rounded the corner to get to the living room. The house wasn't massive, but it was perfect for the two of us. I didn't want to live in the museum Ren bought on his own. If we were starting a life together, it had to be something new. I left New York with a good résumé and was now PR for three Denver players, excluding my boyfriend. He had fired me as soon as he won the World Series. I wasn't insulted in the least, because in truth, it wasn't a good idea for us in the long haul. But I had managed to put a small dent in his bad boy reputation. We went public with our relationship a few months after his last game. It had all worked out for the best. I'd spent the last week unpacking our house and making room for Malcolm. He was coming to spend his spring break with us at Ren's insistence. Ren refused to leave his Little Brother behind in Arizona and made every effort to remain a part of his life, despite his schedule. I was proud of the man he was. Proud to be by his side when he realized his dreams. My heart was full despite the fact that I still refused to have anything to do with my father. I spoke to my mother often, though she chose to stay with him, and on occasion my brothers would visit, and it was enough for me. I had everything I needed, and most of it was held in the love in Ren's eyes when he looked at me. It was a far cry from my life in New York, a life I couldn't miss because of the new one I shared with Ren, though I missed Rowe. She had taken my position in the firm and was thriving. Though we weren't a part of each other's every day, we were lifer's, she and I. Alice had made my transition to Denver easy, making me feel right at home. And when April visited from Charleston, we always managed to venture out of the house, pissing our men off and making new memories. It was an adventure with those two to say the least.

I smiled as I passed the wall of pictures I'd just hung in the last year. Ren and I dressed as the Tin Man and Dorothy at a Halloween party. A picture of us in front of our new house with Davis. A picture of Ren and the guys the night they won the series. I straightened one of the frames as I moved toward the kitchen, the smell of pizza making my mouth water, and froze when I saw Ren down on one knee with the delivery driver behind him, a phone in his hand pointed directly at me. I let out a nervous laugh before I spoke. "What are you doing?" I saw the card in one of Ren's hands and the small black box I'd found all those years ago in the other. My eyes instantly filled with tears.

"Ren?"

"No tricks," he promised hoarsely. "And I'm showing you the only card that matters."

I lost it then, my heart in my throat, my tears falling freely with his as he spoke. "You're a ball of fire and the only woman alive who can make me feel so much without saying a word. I don't want to go another minute of this life without knowing I'm going to spend the rest of it with you. Be mine, be my wife, stay my everything. Be my family and my best friend. Will you marry me?"

I nodded before I spoke. "Yes."

Ren opened the box and slid the rock on my finger before he swept me into his arms. He kissed me deep before he swung me around our entryway. It was a spontaneous proposal, and I knew it because it was so very *us*. We both got swept up in the moment until we heard a throat clear. Ren broke from me reluctantly, and we both turned to the man smiling at our front door.

"Congratulations," he said sweetly as he held out Ren's phone. He couldn't have been more than twenty years old and was the only witness to the happiest moment of our lives. Ren thanked him again before he shut the door and gathered me back in his arms.

"I guess I'll have to order pizza more often," I murmured before placing a soft kiss on his lips. "I wonder what I'll get next."

"Anything you want," he murmured back. "Because you just gave me everything."

"Ren, let's do it today. Let's just go and do it right now."

He raised his brows. "What?"

"You don't have a game for two days."

"Here?"

"I was thinking more along the lines of a place with a full deck."

Ren's slow-building smile told me all I needed to know.

That night, in a little white chapel off the Vegas strip, I married a baseball player.

And the next day we made a little slugger.

THE END

IF YOU ENJOYED Ren and Erica's story, get to know the rest of the gang of the *Balls in Play* Series.

Rafe and Alice
Anything but Minor

Andy and April
Major Love

Acknowledgments

THANK YOU

A huge shout of appreciation to those bloggers and readers who took the time to read this novella. I can't thank you enough for your support.

Thank you to my ROCKSTARS, Bex Kettner, Donna Cooksley Sanderson, and Amy Mastin for working so hard on polishing this novella. I couldn't have done it without you.

Thank you, Christy Baldwin, for catching all the fly balls that come your way. You make my crazy look good!

Thank you to my best friend, Erica, for keeping our memories safe and reminding me of why I call you the best of friends. I love you.

Thank you to my amazing group the Asskickers. I have had so much fun with you this year and your support and friendships are priceless.

Finally, a huge thank you to the amazing ladies I had the privilege of writing this anthology with Mandi Beck, Sarah Ney, Meghan Quinn, L. J. Shen, Ella Fox, Kennedy Ryan, Emma Scott, Charleigh Rose, Adriana Locke and Rochelle Paige, I had a blast! And I'm so happy to call you friends!

About The Author

Kate Stewart lives in Charleston, S.C. with her husband, Nick, and her naughty beagle, Sadie. A native of Dallas, Kate moved to Charleston three weeks after her first visit, dropping her career of 8 years, and declaring it her creative muse. Kate pens messy, sexy, angst-filled contemporary romance as well as romantic comedy and erotic suspense because it's what she loves as a reader. A lover of all things '80s and '90s, especially John Hughes films and rap, she dabbles a little in photography, can knit a simple stitch scarf for necessity only and does a horrible job of playing the ukulele. Aside from running a mile without collapsing, traveling is the only other must on her bucket list. On occasion, she does very well at vodka.

Other titles available now by Kate

Room 212

Never Me

Loving the White Liar

The Fall

The Mind

The Heart

The Brave Line

Drive

Erotic Suspense

Sexual Awakenings

Excess

Predator and Prey
Camouflage
Crosshairs

Let's stay in touch!
Facebook | Newsletter | Twitter | Instagram | Book Group | Spotify

Sign up for the newsletter now and get a free eBook from Kate's Library!
Newsletter signup

FULL COURT PRESS

MacKenzie Decker was a question Avery never got to ask, much less answer. They met when she was a young reporter fueled by ambition, and the ink on Deck's first NBA contract was barely dry. Years later, they've climbed so high and lost so much, but one thing hasn't changed. The attraction that simmered between them in a locker room before is still there. With success like theirs, everything has been possible . . . except *them.*
But that was then.
The only question is...what about now?

Chapter One

DECKER

I'M DRIPPING WET AND ALMOST NAKED THE FIRST TIME I MEET AVERY Hughes.

It's my second season in the NBA, and I'm used to conducting interviews at my locker wearing only a towel, a ring of microphones, recorders, and demanding reporters crowded around me. But *this* reporter, *this* night, from the first look, blindsides me.

We played a shit game.

Correction. For forty-five minutes of regulation, we played a stellar game. That last three minutes—that was some shit, and as the idiot who turned the ball over repeatedly in the closing plays, most of that shit rests squarely on my shoulders.

Post-game and post-shower, I lean against my locker, eyes stuck to the floor while I duck and dodge the flurry of questions flying around my head. I should have taken the fine for not making myself available to the press. That would have cost me less. This costs me my pride and the dregs of my patience.

"Can you walk us through that fourth quarter implosion, Deck?" a husky voice raises above the fray tightly encircling me. "Those last few minutes of the game were pretty brutal."

My brows snap together at the rudeness, the audacity of this reporter. Sure, I've fielded tougher questions, but after this kind of game, a win that slipped through our fingers, and me responsible, I'm too raw and not in the mood for it.

"What kind of question . . ."

The half-formed demand withers on my lips when I meet the eyes behind the recorder thrust at me. They are the softest thing about her face. Her chin draws to a point, and her cheekbones flare out like a cat's, rounding into sharp feline femininity. She looks down her keen little nose at me with a touch of disdain and condescension. Her lips are set in a flat, determined line, but that doesn't make them less lush, less kissable. But still . . . the eyes are the softest thing in that face, darkest sable, surrounded by a fan of long, minky lashes. Those eyes lock with mine while she waits. They never lower to scrape over the bare brawn of my shoulders and chest. Don't dip to my waist or the barely knotted towel hanging onto my hip. And definitely don't slide over my legs, still dripping from my shower. Nope, she looks me right in *and only in* my eyes while she waits.

"Well, um . . ." I search for her name on the laminated media credential lanyard resting between a set of perky breasts. "Avery, we made some mistakes there at the end."

She tilts her head and lifts her brows to the angle of "obviously" before scooting her mic an inch closer. Her scent, something fresh and wild, like the dark, textured curls rioting around her face, is a high note piercing through all the testosterone rife in the locker room.

"Great night overall. Bad few minutes," I finally answer, crooking my mouth in a smile possible now that I've seen her. "Happens to the best of us on any given night."

I shrug, watching her eyes finally drop to the flexing movement, before snapping back to my face.

Ahhh, made you look, pretty lady.

The dark eyes narrow and those kissable lips part like she already has the next question cocked and loaded, but another reporter butts in with something else. I answer a few more questions, getting impatient to dress and talk to Avery without the watchful eye of every major network. When our media rep shuts down the post-game press, reporters start filing out of the locker room. I consider letting it go. Letting *her* go. I've seen prettier girls, right? I can fuck a different chick in a different city every night. Matter of fact, it's practically my civic duty on behalf of all my brethren who will never have the NBA all-access ass pass. Real talk, I'm already over that. Gorgeous, grasping and vapid. That pretty much describes every woman hanging out in the tunnel after a game. This girl—one look and one question tells me I can't have my way with her. I never could resist a challenge, and when Avery turns to leave, giving me an uninterrupted view of a firm, round ass outlined in her tailored slacks, I know I won't resist her either.

"Avery," I call, holding onto my slipping towel with one hand and gently grabbing her elbow with the other. "Hold up a sec."

She looks pointedly at my hand, so large against her slim arm, like it offends her, before looking back to my face. Some half naked, wet jock a foot taller and grabbing her probably isn't making the best first impression.

"Sorry about that." I drop her arm and flick my head toward my locker. "Could I talk to you for a minute?"

Reluctant curiosity settles on her face, and she takes the few steps back to my corner in the chaos of the locker room.

"I wanted to ask you—" I cut off my words when she thrusts her recorder in the space just above my mouth and below my nose. I push it away with a finger. "Uh . . . off the record."

She lowers the recorder to her side, suppressing what I strongly suspect is a smirk.

"You want to tell me the real reason behind your collapse tonight?" The dark brows take flight over curious eyes and she leans one silk-clad shoulder into the locker door.

"No, I mean . . . I could, yeah. Maybe over a drink or dinner. Our flight doesn't leave until the morning."

Horrified realization unfurls on her face.

"Are you asking me out?" Her incredulous words ring through the room, and I look around a little self-consciously. It just isn't done, approaching a reporter like this. In my defense, most reporters don't have an ass like Avery's.

"Yeah, for a drink or something," I whisper, modeling the appropriate and discrete tone for this kind of conversation, hoping she'll catch on. She seems like a bright girl, after all.

"Or something?" A full-blown frown materializes on her face. "I don't do *'or something'* with basketball players. I don't do anything with athletes on my beat."

"I'm on your beat?" I lean into the locker door, too, crossing my arms over my chest. "I haven't seen you before."

"Well you'll be seeing me from now on because I was just assigned." Her gaze drops to my chest and I make my pectoral muscles jump. She rolls her eyes. "And I won't compromise my professional objectivity with the 'or something' you probably have in mind."

"One drink," I urge, shifting against the door.

"My answer is still—" Her gasp chokes out the rest of her sentence when the precariously knotted towel slides right down my hip and plops at my feet. The sight of my dick, slightly erect and on the loose for all the world to see, leaches the air from the room for just a moment, the total quiet before a storm of laughter and good-natured cat calls.

"Oh, shit." Ignoring my teammates' snickers, I scramble to grab the towel from the floor, jerking it back around my waist to cover up my junk. I've been sharing showers and locker rooms since my dick was half this size, so I'm unfazed. Avery, though, looks like she swallowed her little recorder and it's about to come back up with her dinner. Over the wolf whistles, a leftover reporter adds his misplaced mockery to the mix.

"Getting an *exclusive*, are you, Hughes, your first night on the job?" he asks with a leer. "An exposé? Deck would give me the scoop, too, if I had an ass like yours."

What the hell? I'd heard comments like that all my life. Hell, maybe I've even thought them myself. This sport, this industry, is male-dominated, and we're basically overpaid, overgrown adolescents, most of us, until we've been around for a while. Some of us longer than others. Hearing that shit with her standing right here, though, seeing the hurt and irritation spark in her eyes before she quells it, makes me want to knock the bitch-ass reporter's glasses off his face. Laughter from a few others at his rude comment overtakes any hope I have of convincing her. I glare at the idiot already on his way out the door.

"Thanks a lot, asshole," she mutters, jerkily adjusting the bag on her shoulder.

"Yeah," I agree, shaking my head. "He's a piece of work."

"I meant *you*," she says, exasperation evident in her tone "You're the asshole."

"Me?" I thrust my thumb into my naked chest. "What'd I do?"

"Could you just . . ." she sputters, and gestures in the general area of my groin. "Hold onto your little towel? Those are my colleagues. Do you have any idea how hard it is for a woman in this field? To earn their respect as an equal?"

My mouth opens to commiserate, but I never get the chance.

"The answer is no," she barrels over my would-be response. "You have no idea because you've been catered to and coddled since you made your first triple-double in high school. Those other reporters don't have to worry about being pinched or grabbed on the sly. It doesn't bother them conducting interviews with half-naked men, which I don't mind either until one of them pulls me into a corner and asks for a drink *'or something.'*"

I let those words sink into the quiet that collects around us after her diatribe. By any reasonable measure, this would be considered a rough start, but I've never met a woman who could resist my charm, my smile, my good humor. My tanned half-naked body. If I'm a betting man, I don't think Avery can either.

"Soooooo . . . you've been following me since high school?" I break out my fail-proof grin. "That's really flattering. I didn't realize you were a fan."

"I'm not a fan," she snaps. "And if I were I'd be pretty disappointed with your sorry performance on the floor tonight."

"Hey now." My grin slips. "You don't have to get personal. That's my career we're talking about."

She turns to leave, tossing the last words over her shoulder. "And this is mine."

I stand there like an idiot, thinking of all the ways I could arrange to meet her. I'm sure I'll see her on the regular from now on if she's assigned to this beat. I dry the last of the water from my aching body and pull on my T-shirt and sweats before I head to the hotel alone. I'm not worried that it didn't happen for Avery and me tonight.

Maybe I'm being cocky, but I'm sure it won't take long.

It never does.

Chapter Two

AVERY- TEN. YEARS. LATER

"I'M CONVINCED THE FUNDAMENTAL PROBLEM OF SOCIETY IS TECHNOLOGY evolves much faster than the male brain."

I aim the words at my producer and best friend Sadie, meeting her eyes over my iPad.

"How else do you explain dick pic scandals? Something as simple as *not* sending pictures of your dick because it could cost you an election, a career, a marriage—men just cannot grasp. It's like this ancient urge to prove to a pride of lions you have a bigger dick. Only instead of pissing on things, they send images of their penis out into the ether."

I point to yet another post about my co-host's Junk Gate. "I thought Gary was smarter than this."

Sadie walks to the desk and peers over my shoulder at the screen.

"I thought Gary was *bigger* than this," she says.

Our inelegant snorts meet in the quiet of my office.

"I had my suspicions." I set the iPad down and whirl my seat around a few times. "He's got that look small-dick men always have."

"What look do men with small dicks have?"

"Girl, if you've never seen it," I say, stopping my spinning chair long enough to offer a wry grin. "Count yourself lucky."

"As much as I'm enjoying all this girl talk at Gary's expense," Sadie says, dark eyes sobering in her pretty face. "We need to discuss what this means for *Twofer*."

"They're not firing him from the show, are they?" I stop grinning and grip the edge of my desk. "I mean, yeah. It's bad and indiscrete and embarrassing, but surely not a fire-able offense."

"No, not firing, but it does violate the conduct clause in his contract, and it's not his first time." Sadie leans back in the seat across from me, linking her hands over her stomach. "And it's definitely a distraction the show doesn't need, so they're suspending him for three weeks."

"I figured as much. I hope, for his sake, it was worth it." A rueful grin pulls one corner of my mouth back into humor briefly before uncertainty drags it back down. "So how will we handle his absence? Rotating guest hosts? Me solo?"

"Not solo. *Twofer's* popularity is built on the back and forth of opposing perspectives. We need a guest host, just while Gary's gone." Sadie shakes her head and leans forward to grab and munch some of the salted seaweed I was snacking on before she arrived. "This stuff tastes like literal shit. You're aware?"

"Focus. You can't just say I'm getting some guest host and not tell me who, like right away. Who is it?"

"Someone the audience will love tuning in to see."

"Who?"

"Someone credible."

"Who, Sadie?"

"Someone handsome."

"What's handsome got to do with journalism?"

Sadie slants me a knowing look. It's not just journalism. It's *television*, and looks mean a lot too often even in sports. I have enough firsthand experience with producers' requests and standards to understand the look she's giving me. When we first started the show two years ago, SportsCo executives asked me to "consider" pressing my hair for a more "polished" look and said they "loved my weight" just where it was. I doubt very seriously they had those conversations with my male co-host.

"Okay. You're right. Looks count," I concede. "So he's handsome. Who?"

"Retired. He's a future Hall of Famer," Sadie mumbles around a mouthful of the seaweed she insists is vile.

"Which sport?" I ask cautiously. Some retired athlete coming on my show who doesn't know jack shit about not just *playing* sports, but analyzing them, debating them, covering them is not what I need on my set.

"We're playing ba-sket-baaaaaall," Sadie sings the famous Kurtis Blow refrain

and seesaws her shoulders.

Hmmm. Credible. Handsome. Basketball. Retired. Future Hall of Famer.

"No!" The word cannons from my mouth with fire power. "Not—"

"Mack Decker," Sadie finishes, her smile satisfied. "We got Mack Decker."

"Then un-get Mack Decker." I stand and pace, my go-to when something bothers me intensely, as the worn path in front of my desk attests. "He's arrogant, conceited, self-important—"

"Is this about that towel incident?" Sadie's evil grin hopes it is.

"That was ten years ago. Of course not."

Sadie's steady stare bores holes into my face.

"Okay, maybe a very little," I admit, rushing on over her laughter. "What professional athlete wearing a towel hits on a journalist in the locker room? Like, who does that?"

"You said yourself it was ten years ago."

"It was humiliating, and the guys on the beat teased me about it mercilessly. It took a long time for me to live that down." I stop pacing to face Sadie, digging in my heels literally and figuratively. "Besides, he may have been a professional athlete, but he's a novice commentator. No damn way I'm working with him."

"Okay, for real, *mami*?" Sadie tips her head, setting a shiny dark curtain of hair in motion. "You are all caps right now and I need you lower case."

"Isn't there someone else?" I perch on the end of the desk and kick my foot out to tap her knee. "Work with me here."

"No, there isn't." Sadie glares at the seaweed like it's compelling her to pop another strand of it in her mouth. "And I couldn't do anything to change this if I wanted to, which I don't."

"You're the producer. Of course, you have a say."

"Not in this one. Came from the very top." Sadie catches the heel of the shoe I'm banging against my desk. "Hey. It's a coup to have Deck co-hosting. He's been doing guest spots all season, and killing it. In addition to being a basketball genius, he's articulate and willing to learn. He may be new to commentating, but he's a natural."

"I know," I admit grudgingly. "I've seen him."

"So what's the problem? I never heard much about the towel thing after the initial hoopla."

"No, they ended up reassigning me, and after the initial round of teasing, it died down." I extract my shoe from her grip and walk over to the window, no less impressed by the New York City view today than when I first landed this job and this office.

"Then I don't see the problem," Sadie says from behind me.

I don't face her and maybe I don't want to face myself.

There's always been a huge question mark over MacKenzie Decker. What would have happened if I had gone against my better judgment and taken him up on his offer of "or something"? What if I hadn't been reassigned from his team's beat? All I know of him has been through the news and by reputation over the years, but every time I hear his name . . . I don't know. Something stirs in me, and I'm not sure I'm quite ready for stirring. So much has happened for us both, I know that encounter at his locker should be water long under the bridge. Deck won an MVP, two championships, and every award that counts. He got married. Divorced. Injured. Retired. I'm helming my own show on SportsCo, one of the biggest sports networks around. I was engaged. My brain short circuits before I go any further because I can't deal with all the *feelings* today. Not about my fiancé.

"You seem on edge. Is it . . ." Sadie's voice is careful in the way I've come to hate.

"Is it Will?"

She can be irritatingly clairvoyant at times.

"I'm fine." My mouth autopilots the words, a knee-jerk response to the question people have asked me a thousand times in a thousand different ways over the last year.

"If you need to—"

"I said I'm fine, Sade." I swivel a look over my shoulder that tells her not to push. For once she listens.

"Okay. Just saying I'm here. I know things have been—" Her mother's ring tone, Ricky Martin's "Living La Vida Loca," interrupts. "Hold on."

Thank God for Mama and Ricky Martin. This is the last thing I want to discuss.

"What, Ma?" Sadie asks, phone pressed to her ear.

That's the last English word from her mouth for the next five minutes since Sadie unleashes a torrent of Spanish to the woman on the other line. The only words I understand are "burrito" and "Atlanta Housewives."

I'm grateful for this brief reprieve from our conversation. Bad enough I have to work with Mack Decker. Now the feelings and memories that come with Will rise up and try to steal any peace, any confidence I've found.

"Yeah, yeah," Sadie says, easing back into English. "I'll tell her."

"Tell me what?" I demand, leaning my back against the cool glass of my window.

"How do you know she meant you?" Sadie lifts one perfectly threaded brow.

"She always means me. She loves me." I shrug. "What'd Ma say?"

"She wants you to meet my cousin Geraldo."

I chortle. That's the best way to describe the amused sound I make. I cover my mouth when Sadie glares at me.

"Sorry, Sade."

"Don't hate on my cousin, Avery."

"I'm sorry." A helpless laugh belies my apology. "As a journalist, how do you expect me to take a man named Geraldo seriously? Besides, you know I have no desire to date anyone."

"I know it's hard, and maybe it's too soon for an actual relationship," Sadie says, sympathy and determination all over her face. "But just meeting someone? That's not so bad. I just . . . you have to move on. And you never talk about it."

I swallow past the guilt clogging my throat and nod quickly, dismissively. I only talk about Will to my therapist. If you aren't charging me two hundred dollars an hour, these lips are sealed.

"You know I'm here if you need me," Sadie finally speaks softly and stands, nodding when my only response is a quick auto-smile. "Wanna grab something to eat?"

"Nah." I gesture to the open laptop planted in the spill of papers on my desk. "I got another couple hours of prep for tomorrow's show."

"Speaking of which, can you come in a little early to go over things with Decker?"

"He's starting *tomorrow*?" My mouth falls open and my heart starts running like a motor. "I can go one day without a co-host. Give me a day at least to get ready."

"You've had day-of host changes before," Sadie reminds me while she sways her hips to the door. "You're a professional. What's there to get ready for?"

Even after a decade, I still recall with perfect clarity the golden-brown hair, darkened and damp from his shower, curling at the nape of his strong neck. The chiseled landscape of chest and abs. The long legs, sculpted and bronzed extending beyond the small protective square of white terry cloth. I've only seen Mack Decker a handful of times over the years at awards shows, events, and the like. Usually he was with his wife and I was with Will. We were always cordial and polite, but somewhere deep in the secret corners of my heart, I allowed myself the tiniest bit of disappointment that he remained a question all these years. Sure, for a few weeks after the towel incident I was humiliated and offended and pissed off.

And flattered.

And intrigued.

And . . . turned on.

Three things I don't have time or space in my life for right now.

"It was ten years ago, Avery," I mumble, sitting in my chair to examine analytics for tomorrow's show.

Decker has always been an unanswered question. Bottom line under all my excuses, now that the opportunity may re-present itself, maybe I'm not ready for the answer.

Chapter Three

AVERY

MacKenzie Decker's arrogance is tailor-made, draped over him like one of his Armani suits. Fitted to his shoulders by years of fawning fans. Tapered to the broad, muscular back through myriad accolades, trophies, titles and championship rings. Perfectly fit to slide along the muscled length of his legs when he strides into SportsCo like he owns the place.

He *could* own the place. His net worth is no secret thanks to year after year on *Forbes* Highest Paid Athletes list. Most of his money comes from endorsements, not the lucrative NBA contracts he netted for twelve seasons. That smile. Those eyes. That body. His charm. Fifth Avenue served him up and Main Street feasted, making him a household name practically from the moment he was drafted.

He definitely doesn't need this job. Maybe that's what bothers me most.

He doesn't need this job. I do.

He didn't have to work to get here. I did.

Graduating at the top of my journalism class from Howard University, paying my dues on crowded sidelines, discarding modesty in locker rooms of naked men—I did whatever it took to get my own show. He just walks right in fresh from retirement like the party should start now that he's here. My show is just a pit stop between his storied career and the Hall of Fame. It grinds my teeth that he sits in the seat across from me like it's a throne. Like this is all his due and his kingdom. Like I'm his subject.

Yeah. That's what bothers me.

It better not be the way his presence sizzles in the air like hot oil tossed into a frying pan. It better not be his scent, clean and male with an undercurrent of lust. Or his amber-colored eyes surrounded by a wedge of thick lashes. It better not be any of those things because I had a talk with my body this morning, and we decided by mutual agreement that I would not respond physically to this man.

"Decker, welcome!" Sadie says, her smile unusually bright and her eyes slightly dazzled. "We're so glad to have you."

That slow-building smile starts behind his eyes, quirks his sinfully full lips and creases at the corners. We're roughly the same age, so he must be thirty-four, thirty-five by now, and the years have been oh so kind. If it hadn't been for a career-ending injury last year, he'd still be balling.

"I'm glad to be here." The voice, modulated and slightly southern, is that graveled rasp typically only earned by a few packs a day, except Decker is famously fastidious about what goes into his body, temple that it is. Nature just granted him that voice. I remind myself not to inspect all the other things nature awarded this man.

"You know Avery of course." The look Sadie turns on me holds a subtle threat in case I'm feeling froggy this morning. Lucky for her I had my cold brew coffee. That stuff keeps me out of jail. I'd hate to meet me without it.

I extend my hand, which he immediately enfolds in his. It's warm and huge. You forget how big these guys are when you watch them on television, but standing here in the well-toned flesh, Decker towers over me by at least a foot. He makes me feel small and delicate. I *love* feeling small and delicate . . . said no self-respecting sports reporter ever. Add that to the ever-growing list of things he makes me feel that I don't like.

"Good to see you again, Avery." He looks down at our hands still clasped.

"Yeah, you, too." I wiggle my fingers for him to let go, and for a moment mischief breaks through his neutral expression, before he releases me and sits at the conference room table.

"Thanks for stepping in, Deck," Sadie says. "How's the penthouse suite?"

SportsCo has a great relationship with the luxury hotel across the street, often holding events and putting up guests there. I'm assuming Deck is staying in the penthouse while he's with the show.

"It's great," Deck says. "Glad I don't have to commute from Connecticut every day."

"Well we wanted to make it easy for you. Let us know if you need anything." Sadie hands us both folders. "Now did you guys get my email with the rundown of today's show?"

When we both nod, Sadie dives into the details. I was prepared to be unimpressed. So many athletes assume because they played their sport, they know *all* sports and can just hop in front of a camera and it'll be fine. Deck obviously didn't make that assumption. He's prepared. And I've seen him commentate since he retired. He's good.

There's a studied ease to him, a carefully cloaked intensity. People can't always handle the passion it takes to do great things. I'm allergic to average and abhor mediocrity. That leaks into every aspect of my life. Type A. Driven. I'm not sure what you'd call it, but it's all over Mack Decker, too. He was renowned for it on the court, the alpha dog leading his pack to victory by any means necessary. As we review the elements of today's show, I look up more than once to find all of that intensity fixed on me. The dark gold stare pins me to my ergonomic leather seat. I make sure not to squirm, though it feels like, with nothing more than sex appeal and quiet tenacity, he's holding me hostage.

"All good?" Sadie looks between the two of us once we're done, but her query targets me. I know this because I know Sadie. I didn't want Decker stepping in, but even I can't deny his professionalism and competence. And obviously he'll be catnip for our viewers. Every excuse to *not* want him here keeps melting away. Eventually I'll have to deal with the real reason I've resisted him as a guest host.

But not yet.

"Yeah." I scribble nonsense on the pad in front of me, one of the many ways I exert my abundant nervous energy. "All sounds good to me."

Decker glances at the papers in front of him. "I'll try not to lose my shit in the last segment when Magic Johnson comes on set."

"What?" The word rides a laugh past my lips. "Are you serious?"

"I'm not allowed to lose my shit over the greatest point guard to ever lace up?" He leans back, lips twitching and arms crossed over the expanse of chest hidden beneath his crisp shirt.

"I'm glad you qualified *point* guard, not shooting guard, because we'd have a problem if you don't acknowledge Jordan as Almighty Guard."

Decker's deep-timbered chuckle moves the muscles of his throat and slides over me like a lasso, roping me in and tugging me closer.

"I'm not having the Greatest of All Time debate with you, Avery."

"Good because there's no debate about who the GOAT is." I toss my pen on the table like a gauntlet. "You tell me anyone other than Jordan, we got a problem."

He expels a disdainful puff of air.

"Then we got a problem." He holds up three fingers. "I got this many ahead of him."

"Heresy." I lean forward, salivating for a good debate with a worthy opponent. "Who you got?"

"Wilt, Kareem and Russell."

"Three!" Outrage propels the word from me. "You got three dudes ahead of Jordan? Him at number four is just . . . I . . . I . . . just . . ."

"While she tries to gather her thoughts," Sadie interjects with a grin and a glance at her phone. "I gotta take this. Thanks again, Decker. Let's have a great first show."

When Sadie leaves, there's no buffer between me and the wall of fine assness that is MacKenzie Decker. It's the first time we've been alone since he faced me naked in a roomful of laughing men a decade ago. I clear my throat needlessly since I have nothing to say. I felt safe with Sadie as our chaperone.

Now that it's just the two of us, I can't remember what we were talking about with so much ease.

"You were saying?" Decker watches me expectantly.

"Huh?" I stall and blank-face him. "What was I saying?"

"Greatest of all time?" he prompts, anticipation brewing in his eyes.

"I'll have to school you later." I force a smile, gathering the papers in front of me, tucking them into a neat stack and pressing them to my chest. "I need to review some tape from last night's games before the show. See you on set."

I walk to the door and wave over my shoulder.

"I never got to apologize properly for the towel."

His words, injected seamlessly into our conversation, stunt my steps. We were doing just fine until he had to go *there*.

"What?" I turn to consider him warily, half-hoping he'll let it go, but there's no going back now. The polite façade has fallen away, baring his curiosity, his determined frankness.

"I said," he pauses deliberately to make sure I'm hearing him clearly this time, "I never got to apologize properly for the towel. I know there was some teasing on the circuit afterwards."

"It was a long time ago," I reply stiffly. "It's fine."

"I reached out, but I wasn't sure if—"

"I got the messages you left at the station." I keep my tone neutral and project confidence. "Thank you."

"But you never . . ." There's a trail of silence after his incomplete thought.

"I was reassigned." I shift my feet and glance into the hall beyond the conference room, signaling that I'm ready to be done with this conversation. "I knew we wouldn't see each other much, so . . ."

I leave a trail of my own, shrugging and hoping we can conclude this.

"Your hair used to be curly." A grin accompanies yet another abrupt shifting of gears. "We haven't had a one-on-one conversation in a long time, but the last time we talked your hair was curly."

"Yes, well—"

"I liked it," he cuts in, stuttering my heartbeat and drifting a glance over my hair. "It's still beautiful this way."

He locks his whisky-tinted eyes with mine.

"You're still beautiful."

"Um, well, I—"

"We should grab a drink," he says, further disconcerting me. "*Or something.*"

He drops his words from that night on me, when he wore nothing but a tiny towel and super-size bravado.

Humor and irritation war inside me at the shared memory before I get them both under control.

"Look, Deck . . ." I shake my head and trap my bottom lip in my teeth before going on. "It's still a no."

He opens his mouth as if he has more to say, but my rigid expression must convince him he really shouldn't.

"Well, glad that's all behind us." The sorcerer smile, the one he must use to put people at ease, reappears. "I'll let you go prepare. See you on set."

I nod and turn on my heel, making sure to keep my steps steady and measured, even though I want to run back to my office before he decides to press the advantage I don't want him to know he has.

Chapter Four

DECKER

THERE'S SOMETHING ABOUT AVERY HUGHES THAT RUBS ME THE right way.

She gets me worked up. It starts, as with most men, in my pants, but in no time it reaches my *other* head, the one with the brain, and it's her wit and sharp intelligence, her drive that keeps me wanting more. Even if there hadn't been all the ribbing after the towel incident, I still would have thought about her for days after we met. She's the kind of woman who makes an impression and lingers in your memory.

I last saw her two years ago at a *Sports Illustrated* party. I'd been injured that season, and was pretty sure my NBA career was over. Even though my wife Tara stood at my side, glittering and clinging possessively, we both knew our marriage was over, too. It had been on life support for a while. We were scheduled to present a check from my charitable foundation that night, so we had to attend together, but we'd already filed the papers. Still, when I spotted Avery across the room with her fiancé, guilt chewed through my gut because I wanted to walk away from my soon-to-be-ex, snatch Avery from that dude and take her to some corner; pick up where we'd left off in that locker room.

It feels like I've lived a dozen lives since then. Seasons in the NBA should be measured like dog years. Not just the wear and tear on your body, but the wear and tear on your soul. Greedy people, shattered hopes, broken marriages.

Missed chances.

Avery feels like the biggest missed chance of all. Maybe she retained that mystery because I never got to know her. Never got to taste her. That night at the *SI* party, when our glances collided across eight years and a crowded room, I had to accept that I never would. I had only seen her a handful of times and from a distance since our first meeting, but in a moment, before she had time to disguise it, her unguarded expression told me she hadn't forgotten. That I was still . . . something, even if it was just an annoying, awkward memory. Avery, being the consummate professional, contorted her lips into a plastic smile and turned back to the man at her side.

Only that man hasn't been at her side the last few months. Lately, the few times I watched her show, the ring she wore that night was gone. I'm not sure what's happened, but the ring's not there now, and I'm assuming . . . okay, *hoping* . . . the man is gone, too.

When SportsCo called about subbing as Avery's co-host on *Twofer*, I cancelled whatever my team had lined up to make it happen. This could get interesting . . . if Avery would let it.

If she would let *me*.

We're a week in, and on camera, Avery and I have a natural connection that viewers are loving, but she's kept me at a polite distance otherwise. When the lights go down, her guard goes up, and she presents that phony, careful neutrality she thinks will keep me out. But every day, I see a new crack in that wall she hides behind, and it only stokes my curiosity to see what's in there. It's time to chip away at the wall. Time to be the hammer.

I study her during our production meeting. She's making a point to the team about a camera angle. An image of her pinned against the conference room door highjacks my imagination; my tongue plunged so deeply down her throat she'd have to beg for breath. Of me sliding to my knees and pushing that skirt past her thighs, pulling her legs onto my shoulders and roughly shoving her panties aside. Of my mouth open and worshiping between her legs. Of my face wet from her passion gushing onto me.

Puppies. Ice cream. Old people fucking.

I mentally run through the list that usually keeps a hard-on at bay, but it's not working this time, and my dick is a pipe in my pants. I would handle this woman. I would pick her up when I kiss her. Literally sweep her off her feet and hold her by the ass. Show her what it feels like to be kissed suspended in the air. I'd press her against me so she felt how much I wanted her. Until she felt my erection and had to deal with it. Until she had to deal with *me*. I scoot my chair another inch under the table, struggling to rein in this fantasy.

Puppies. Ice cream. Old people fucking.

If this woman is indifferent to me, I'll eat both my championship rings. I made my living reading plays and picking apart defenses. From my experience, people and relationships aren't much different, and there's no way I misread the attraction between us that badly. She's not a woman you can rush, but I only have two weeks left on my guest stint before good ol' dick pic returns. With so little time left on the clock, I think this calls for the full-court press. End-to-end coverage. Man-to-man defense . . . or in this case, man-to-woman. No letting up until the opponent is worn down. I live for this shit. No one can beat me at this game.

"Does that sound good?" Avery interrupts my inner pep talk, long-lashed eyes blinking at me over the cup of cold brew I've been bringing her every day.

What the hell are we talking about?

I glance around the conference room, packed with the crew for the production meeting. Everyone's watching me expectantly.

"Deck?" Avery asks with a tiny frown. "I said does that sound good?"

"Hmmmm . . ." I scrunch my face like I'm pondering the subject really hard, hoping she'll elaborate.

"I mean, if you want to do the Holiday predictions last instead," she continues. "We totally can."

"Nah." *Ah! The Holiday predictions. Right.* "We can leave it at the top."

She tilts her head and narrows her eyes. "You mean in the middle?"

"Middle, yeah." I nod sagely. "Perfect place for it."

"Well if we're all agreed," Sadie says, closing her laptop. "That's a wrap."

Everyone starts dispersing. I'll find some reason to linger until Avery finishes the discussion she's having with one of the show's writers.

"Don't worry," Sadie whispers to me while she finishes packing her things. "She's coming, too."

If I take my eyes off Avery for even a second, she might dart off. That woman has become really good at avoiding me. I spare Sadie a quick glance to figure out what she's even talking about.

"Coming where?" I ask. "Who?"

"You really *were* checked out." She laughs, shaking her head and shoving her phone into her purse. "Sorry if we bore you with the details of planning the show."

"It's not personal." I do an Avery check—still chatting—before looking back to Sadie. "I hate meetings. Always have, and my mind tends to drift. So, who's going where and what's up?"

"We're all going to grab drinks and dinner."

No thanks.

"I don't think I'll—"

"And Avery's coming with us," Sadie cuts in with a knowing look.

Oh, well in that case.

"Man's gotta eat." She and I share a conspiratorial grin. "What gave me away?"

"Um, what *didn't*?" Sadie leans against the conference room table. "Bringing her coffee every day. Not leaving any room until she does. The way you—"

"All right, all right." I glance around self-consciously to see if anyone heard her spouting how whipped I've been behaving. "So, what do I do about it, since you know so much?"

"*Do* about it?" Her smile is just relishing the novel positon I'm in having to chase a woman.

"I didn't think I'd ever have a shot. She was wearing some other guy's ring the last time I saw her. I don't want to waste my chance this time."

The humor on Sadie's face fades, her eyes go sober.

"Oh, Deck. You don't know."

"Don't know what?"

Before she can enlighten me, Avery walks up and Sadie's mouth snaps shut and her eyes stretch with some silent warning I'm clueless about.

"What's with all the lollygagging?" Avery asks, playfully bumping Sadie's shoulder, her mouth stretched into a wide grin. "We eating or what?"

I wish she'd be that easygoing with me. Despite our chemistry onscreen, I can barely get her alone long enough to have a decent conversation.

"I was just telling our friend here he should come with us." Sadie smiles up at me. "Right, Deck?"

Avery's grin slips, but she recovers quickly enough to offer me a polite, if stiff, smile.

"You should," she tells me. "This place does a great dirty martini, and I love their steak."

I rarely drink and gave up red meat years ago.

"Two of my favorite things," I lie. "What are we waiting for?"

The prospect of a few extra hours to crack her tough outer shell has my blood humming through my veins like it's pre-game and I'm facing an especially challenging opponent.

We're all crowded in the elevator on our way down, and I meet the guarded interest in Avery's eyes I've become accustomed to over the last week. Not an opponent. I think we're on the same team. I think we want the same thing. She just doesn't know it yet.

Chapter Five

AVERY

Two of his favorite things, my ass.

Decker ignored the steaks, went straight for the pan roasted sea bass, and has been drinking water all night.

I take a long, grateful sip of my second martini, thanking God for whomever had the foresight to invent them. It's a massage, a hot bath and an orgasm all shaken and stirred into one delightfully numbing concoction. And the closer we get to Christmas, the more numb I need to be.

"You look like you're enjoying that," Decker says, pushing his plate away.

"And it looks like you *didn't* enjoy that." I nod toward his half-eaten fish.

"No, it was delicious. I just wasn't as hungry as I thought I was."

"And you decided to forego the alcohol, too? Even though martinis and steak are your faves?" I shouldn't toy with him, but it's kind of fun watching a man so notoriously pursued by women making excuses to spend time with *me*, even though I'm not exactly sure what he wants.

Scratch that.

The barely concealed lust steaming in his eyes tells me what he wants. Problem is, I think I might want it, too, but I can't. If my vagina was the only thing I had to worry about, this would be a no-brainer. Six feet and seven inches of tanned, beautiful *man*. What's there to think about? But even just in our first week working together, I've seen a depth to him I didn't expect. The same determination and commitment to excellence that has him Hall of Fame-bound, he's applied to guest hosting. TV's a steep learning curve, and I gotta give it to him. He's doing a great job. He's funny, sharp, thinks on his feet, and can talk any other sport almost as easily as he can basketball. For most women that wouldn't be a turn on, but for me? Yeah, very much so. With a man like

Decker, the vajayjay isn't the only body part to consider. He could endanger my heart, and that troubled organ still hasn't recovered from Will.

"So, seems like we have pretty much opposite picks for every prediction," Decker says, leaning back in his seat.

"Prediction?" I snap out of my own thoughts and tune into our conversation. "What do you mean?"

"For the Holiday Picks segment." Decker lifts his brows, waiting for me to catch up. "For next week's show."

"Oh, yes," I deadpan, warming to a subject I'm comfortable discussing. "Shocking that we're at odds."

"I know, right?" He leans forward to rest his elbows on the table and turns his body toward me, effectively blocking out the rest of the table. "We both have the Wolves and the Sabers going to the NCAA Championship, but I have the Wolves winning. You picked the Sabers."

"Yeah, because Caleb Bradley and the Sabers took it last year," I remind him. "What makes you think they won't do it again?"

"August West makes me think they won't do it again. If West hadn't sprained his ankle last year, he could have taken it then. He's got that killer instinct."

"If we're both right and they both advance, it'll be one helluva final no matter who comes out on top."

"It'll be West. Mark my words. I recognize a champ in the making when I see one. Caleb Bradley may be the All-American Golden Boy, but August is the one to watch."

His smile is smug, but I can't help smiling in return. It's basketball. I know my shit, but he's *lived* it and has two championships to show for the years he put into the League.

"Who am I to disagree? You *are* the future Hall of Famer." My sarcasm delivers the compliment backhanded.

"Don't you forget it," he replies with a chuckle.

"Did you always know you wanted to play ball?" I shock myself by asking. I don't do lengthy conversations with this man. Or at least I haven't over the last week. This martini must be dirtier than I thought it was. It's going to my head. As long as it doesn't start heading south, we should be okay.

"Always." He shrugs. "Honestly it could have gone either way. Basketball or football. I had looks for both."

"You were scouted for both sports? College?"

"Yeah, I played both even through high school, but it came to the point I had to choose."

"What position did you play? Football, I mean, obviously." Everyone knows he's one of the greatest point guards to ever play basketball.

"What do you think I played?" He props his chin in his hand, the bourbon-flavored eyes brimming with curiosity. About me.

"Hmmm." I tip my head and squint one eye, assessing. "Your leadership skills are off the chart."

"Well thank you." He dips his head and smiles to acknowledge the compliment.

"You don't follow others well."

His smile falters, and he glares at me, even though there's still humor in his eyes.

"You always think you know best," I continue, enjoying this more by the second. "And you love ordering people around."

"Okay, maybe I should just tell you before you really hurt my feelings."

"Like I could," I scoff.

He doesn't answer, but looks down at the table, a smile curling the corners of his wide, sensual mouth.

"Quarterback," I say triumphantly. "Am I right?"

His laugh is richer than the chocolate ganache I ordered, but shouldn't eat.

"God, I wish I could say you're wrong," he admits with a grin. "Yeah, quarterback."

"I knew it." I brush my shoulders off.

"Uh huh," he teases. "Now who's the know it all?"

"Oh, I don't deny it." I take a sip of my neglected drink. "I always assume I have the right answer."

"I have observed that over the last week." He shoots me a speculative glance before continuing. "There's a lot I haven't learned, though."

The vodka seems to pause midway down my throat. I cough a little and wait for him to start the questions I've seen in his eyes for days.

"Like did you play any sports yourself?" he asks.

I breathe a little easier. This is comfortable territory.

"Track and field," I answer without hesitation.

"Ahhh." He nods as if answering himself. "That explains it."

"Explains what?" I ask, taking another sip.

His eyes burn a trail over my neck and breasts until the table interrupts his view.

"Your body."

I cough again, reaching for a napkin to wipe my mouth.

"My-my body?" I hate how breathy I sound all of a sudden. With a few well-placed words and a look, he has me sputtering and simmering.

"I'm sure you know women who run track and field often develop a certain body type," he says, leaning forward until I can't see much of anything beyond the width of his shoulders. "Lean arms."

Even though my arms are hidden beneath my blouse, my skin heats up when he runs his eyes over them.

"Muscular legs," he continues, locking his eyes with mine. "A tight, round—"

"I'm aware," I cut in, "of what my body looks like. I see it every day."

"Wish I could say the same."

My face heats up. I know a blush doesn't show through my complexion, but judging by the way his grin goes wider and wickeder, it doesn't take color in my cheeks to tell him I'm heating up.

"So, you chose basketball." I shift the conversation back to safer ground that won't burn under my feet like hot coals.

"Yes." His grin lingers, but he indulges my redirection. "All through college."

"And then the NBA," I add.

"Yeah, if you work hard as hell and sacrifice just about everything else in your life, dreams really do come true." He grimaces. "At least some of them do."

I heard about his divorce, but don't want to assume that's what he means. He glances up, a wry twist to his lips.

"You wear your questions all over your face, Avery."

I huff a short laugh. "Do I?"

"I did have a dream other than basketball, if you're curious." His shoulders lift and fall, but they seem to be lifting more weight than he lets on. "I wanted a wife, kids, the whole package."

"And you got them, right?" I ask softly.

I want to ask what went wrong. I wonder if that question is on my face, too, because he answers without me voicing it.

"Tara, my ex, and I didn't as much grow apart," he says. "As we never should have been together."

I've thought that of Will and me many times. Wondered if things would have ended differently if he'd never met me. Sometimes it keeps me up at night. Sometimes it's the first thing I think about when I wake up.

"Statistically, half of all married couples would say the same thing." I smile my sympathy. "And kids? I heard you had a daughter."

"Yeah, my little girl Kiera." The rugged lines of his face noticeably soften. "You wanna see?"

I nod, surprisingly eager to see how his DNA played out on a little female face.

"Oh, she's so pretty, Deck," I whisper, my eyes glued to his phone screen. She's blonde and looks uncannily like the woman I saw Decker with at a *Sports Illustrated* party a couple of years ago. Her eyes, though, are golden brown, just like her father's. I glance up from the phone.

"She has your eyes."

"That's about it." He chuckles, accepting his phone and glancing affectionately at the picture before setting it on the table. "I can't take much credit for how beautiful she is."

I look away, afraid my eyes would betray my thoughts as clearly as he said he could see them. Afraid he'll see that I think he's the most beautiful specimen I've ever encountered. That sometimes during the show, I almost lose my train of thought wondering how his tawny hair would feel wrapped around my fingers. That in just a week, I've memorized the curve of his mouth and how he smells. Not his cologne, but that rawer scent made from nothing but skin and bone and him that rests just below the veneer of civilization we all wear.

"Tara just moved to LA," Decker continues, a rueful set to his lips. "And took Kiera with her."

"I'm sorry." I frown. "It must be harder to see her now with you still on the East Coast, I guess?"

"Yeah. Takes a little more work, but she's worth it. I've accomplished a lot, but she's the best thing I've ever done." He shrugs and then turns an inquisitive look on me. "What about you?"

"What about me?" My fingers tighten around the fragile stem of my martini glass. My heart tightens in my chest, braced for questions I'll have to evade.

"Well, I know you were engaged," he says with a careful look at my bare ring finger. "And I don't think you are anymore."

He doesn't know.

I savor that tiny slice of time while I can where he doesn't know. For the last year of my life, everyone has known what happened. And I often feel smothered under the weight of their speculation, their awkward sympathy, their damn good intentions because they know everything. Well, they *think* they know everything. I have my secrets; secrets kept alive only by me because only Will knew.

And now Will is gone.

"He died." I clear my throat, my lips trembling in the most vexing way. I steady them like I've learned to steady my emotions. "Will, my fiancé, died last year around this time actually."

When I say *everyone* knows, it's not like when "everyone" knows Deck got a divorce or the details of a multimillion-dollar contract he inked. When "everyone" knows what's going on in his life, it's the world. His fame is much broader than mine. I'm a sportscaster, and I'm on television, but my life isn't national news, much less international. With Deck, the whole world could know his business. The whole world doesn't know my fiancé died last December. Only everyone who knows me and everyone who knew Will. Everyone in my life knows. And now so does Decker.

For the last few minutes, it was easy to forget that just beyond the barrier of Deck's torso and shoulders, our colleagues are drinking and talking. Laughing and blowing off steam after a long day. I didn't realize how completely Deck had managed to isolate us; to monopolize me until it gets so quiet in our little corner.

"Avery, I'm so sorry." His voice is a soft rumble of compassion. "God, I had no idea. I hadn't heard."

I nod, panicking as a familiar knot ignites inside my throat, threatening to choke me. Out of habit and necessity, I start blinking rapidly against ill-timed tears.

"Yeah, it wasn't . . . something we broadcast." Dark humor taunts the corner of my mouth. "Will would have hated that; to be a part of some media circus. He wasn't . . . he was the last one to draw attention to himself."

A door cracks open that I keep closed and locked; that I try to forget exists. The one with all my memories of Will. His smile, which had become so rare at the end. It was the first thing I liked about him; that his smile was kind and genuine. I can't do this. Not here. Not now. Not with Decker watching my face for signs of distress. If he keeps looking, he'll find it. It's not as deeply buried as I manage to convince most people. Decker isn't most people, and I instinctively know he won't be fooled.

"It's getting late." My smile is a cold, waxy curve trying its best to look alive. "I think I'll go."

"Avery," he says softly. Just that. Just my name, but there's so much more there, and I can't do this shit right now.

I ignore him and reach down to grab my purse, using those few seconds to compose myself and swipe at the corners of my eyes. When I stand, so does he. Our eyes clash for a moment, mine watery and his concerned. I step around him, snapping the thread strung taut between us, and address my coworkers.

"Okay, guys." I spread a bright smile around to everyone. "I'm heading out. Have a good weekend."

Blindly, I make my way to the door, longing for the fresh air, at least as fresh as New York City has to offer.

"Hey, Ave," Sadie calls from behind me when I'm just a few feet away from the exit. "Wait up."

I stop and turn, smoothing my expression into patient inquiry, hoping the churning waves in my gut aren't washing up on my face.

"You okay?" Sadie sees more than most. She knows more than most, too, but even she doesn't know everything.

"I'm fine." I roll my eyes when she gives me the look that says *it's me you're talking to*. "Okay. I'm not exactly fine, but I will be."

"Do you need—"

"I just need to go home, Sade." There's a pleading note in my voice that I can't suppress much longer. "Please. Just let me get out of here."

Sadie nods, hooks her arm around my neck and whispers into my ear.

"It's gonna get better, babe."

Some things don't. Some things never get better because they can never be undone. I had to learn that for myself the hardest way. I won't try to teach Sadie at the hostess stand of this nice restaurant.

"Night," I settle for saying before walking swiftly to the door.

I draw in great lungfuls of the cold night air and start walking. With every step, my heart decelerates and my breath evens and my tears dry up. That's all I needed. Some time to myself.

"Avery!" a deep voice calls from behind me.

So much for time to myself.

I turn to find Decker almost caught up to me, his long legs making quick work of the few feet separating us. I wanted to be alone, and he's ruining that. Yet my heart lifts a little at the sight of hm. I knew it! If my vagina and my heart ever get on the same page, they'll be my downfall.

"Can you not take a hint?" My voice lacks the irritation it should hold.

"Only the ones I want to take," he replies easily, hunching into his dark coat and squinting against the cold. "You walking?"

"Obviously since you're walking to catch me."

"Ahhh." He grins, slanting me an amused look. "The smartass is back."

My answering smile dims as I remember what chased me out of the restaurant in the first place.

"I meant are you walking all the way home?" he asks.

"It's not far." I glance up at him. "And I don't need an escort."

"Well you got one, lady."

I roll my eyes, which only makes him laugh. We're silent for the next few steps, and I focus on the bustling anonymity of the city. You can get lost in this hectic, harried press of humanity. I have over the last year. I've hidden myself in its crevices and I've hurt in my solitude. I thought it was what I deserved—to hurt alone. With Decker here, the sounds of the city swallowing up the yawning silence inside of me, I wonder if maybe I've been wrong. It feels good to have someone . . . here. Just here. Not demanding answers, or hovering for fear I'll self-destruct. But someone who just wants my company, and wants to offer theirs. It dents my loneliness.

"Here I am." I stop in front of my apartment building and turn to Deck, prepared to say good-bye.

Of course, he walks ahead to the entrance. My doorman recognizes him instantly, rushing over to hold the glass doors wider for him.

"Deck, we sure miss seeing you on the court," he says, an eager grin splitting his face.

"Can't say I miss being out there as much as I thought I would," Decker replies, signing the slip of whatever paper the doorman found for his autograph. "I like not aching and creaking half the year. Eighty-two games for twelve years will kick your ass."

"Not to mention playoffs in the post-season," the doorman reminds him with an admiring grin.

"Yeah, there were a few of those, too, huh?" Decker laughs and turns when the elevator arrives. "Nice meeting you."

"Great meeting you, too. Thanks for the autograph. My son'll love this. Good night, Ms. Hughes," the doorman adds, finally acknowledging me. I return his smile, not minding being ignored. It's not every day you see a living sports legend. I remember feeling that way the first night I met Decker, even though I still had to ask him tough questions. He'd won rookie of the year the season before and was already one of the brightest stars in the League. Remembering the towel incident makes me smile as we get off the elevator.

"What are you grinning about?" Deck asks, narrowing his eyes in false suspicion. "I don't trust you when you grin like that."

Feeling a little lighter, I turn to face him, walking backward toward my door.

"I was thinking about the first night we met."

"Ugh." He shakes his head and closes his eyes briefly. "I was such an immature asshole."

"I think I told you that then." I laugh when he glowers at me. "You just admitted it. I'm agreeing with you. Be happy."

"You know it's funny. That was ten years ago." His smile as we keep walking borders on wistful, if such firm lips could be described that way. "So it feels like I've known you forever, but before I started the show last week, we'd never had a real conversation. I mean, unless you count the one at my locker."

"I don't." I lean against the door to my apartment. "You were wearing a towel, and not even that at one point."

"Nice." He stops in front of me. "I'll never live that down with you, will I?"

"Do you really want to?"

"Nope," he admits with a shameless, cocksure grin. "At least I knew you would never forget me."

As if I could.

I don't say the words, but something on my face must confess that I never forgot him. That sometimes in quiet moments alone, he was always an unanswered question. Or maybe I was afraid to ask. His humor evaporates, and his eyes take on that fierce focus I'd always noted when I watched him play. The camera would catch this exact look on his face; like the prize is in sight, and it was only a matter of four quarters before his opponent would yield. I wonder which quarter we're in.

"So, like I was saying." He picks up where he left off, that intense stare like steam hovering over my skin. "I feel like I've learned a lot about you since I started with the show."

"Is that right?" I press my shoulders into the door for support because that look is melting my bones, and I need to stand my ground.

"I know that as soon as you walk into a room, you charge the air," he says softly. "Everything comes to attention around you."

My breath stutters and I lick dry lips.

"I know that people enjoy following you so much they don't even realize you're leading them," he continues, taking a step closer and stealing another ounce of air from my lungs. "And that you're usually the smartest person in the room, but you know when to let other people think they are."

I thought butterflies in your stomach were some urban myth from Harlequin romance novels, but sure enough, something is fluttering in my belly at his words.

Aw, crap. I don't do butter fucking flies.

"And I know that as much as you light up onscreen, there's something sad in your eyes, and I hate it." He steps as close as he can, cups my cheek, locking our eyes. "I saw it tonight and I hate it, Avery."

He flattens his other hand against the door, his arms making an intimate alcove I couldn't escape if I wanted to.

I don't want to.

He pulls back just enough to search my face. Surely he sees my bottom lip trapped between my teeth because I must resist yielding to the warm comfort of him.

"I want to make it better, Ave," he whispers, the cool mint of his breath breezing over my lips. "I just want to . . ."

He scans my face, waiting for some sign from me that it's okay. That the desire to kiss me so clearly telegraphed in his eyes is okay. I can't find words to articulate that in this maelstrom of grief and desire and confusion, the only thing clear, the only thing that makes any sense right now, is for him to kiss me. So I don't say a word. I just lean forward until our lips meet.

Chapter Six

DECKER

Soft and fresh like petals.

I'm a jock. Not a dumb one, but a jock nonetheless. I don't describe a woman's lips as soft and fresh or compare a kiss to flowers. Besides the few years I was married to Tara, if it opened its legs and said yes or please, I fucked it. I always rushed it. A man's got needs, but I got in and I got out. This woman, this kiss, I have to savor. I'd be a fool not to. It's a first kiss. I understand the difference now between the first time you kiss someone, and a *first kiss*. This is a discovery of tongues and lips and heat. An introduction of our souls, if that doesn't sound too pussy-ish. It's how I feel, though. Like as our lips brush back and forth, as our tongues tangle, as I taste her, mouthful by delicious mouthful, I'm learning her secrets. I'm telling her mine. My hands slide from the door to flatten into the warmth of her back through the silk blouse, bringing her incrementally closer. The air shifts and takes the shape of lust; assumes the form of want. The sound of her moaning, the slight lift and fall of her breasts against my chest, testifies that she feels it, too.

The elevator dings, and our bodies go still even as we keep exchanging breaths and heartbeats through our clothes; even though my mouth is still poised above hers. I have her against the door, and every curve of her body is impressing itself on me, making sure I'll never forget how right we fit together. I look over my shoulder toward the elevator. The doors open, but no one gets off. That interruption was enough to bring her back to her senses, though. God knows I can't find mine.

"Um . . . you should go," she whispers, a muscle rippling along the smooth line of her jaw.

I bend to breathe over her mouth, so she can taste our kisses lingering on my lips. "Or you could invite me in."

Her scent and the warmth of her body take my senses hostage. I smell her and want to kiss her again so badly it stings my taste buds.

"You don't want to come in, Deck." Her eyes already regret the last few moments I thought were so perfect. I can't calm my emotions or my body that quickly.

"I assure you I do," I tell her.

A short laugh, deceptively light, breezes past her lips. She glances down to the floor and shakes her head.

"I'd make the worst one-night stand ever," she says.

"One-night stand?" I take her chin in hand and lift, forcing her to look at me. "I've waited a long time for this path to be clear. No conflict of interest. No other people standing in our way. I don't know exactly what I want, Avery, but it's damn sure more than one night."

If anything, my assurance that it's more than just physical, more than just a night to me, lights panic in her eyes.

"Oh, that's worse." She frowns even as she sends a sad smile up at me. "I'm not anywhere near ready for something like that, Deck."

She's not a tall woman, though the strength of her personality makes you forget that. I've easily got a foot or more and a hundred pounds on her. She tucks a shiny chunk of dark hair behind her shoulder, exposing the intricate whorl of her ear, the fine angle of her jaw. She acts tough. Hell, she *is* tough, but her fiancé died only a year ago. That would leave anyone kind of fragile. Of course, she's not ready. Up this close, invading her space, past the outer wall, I see the vulnerability; the desolation and pain. It stabs me in the chest.

"I get that," I say, my voice rough. "I'm so sorry about him, Ave. About your fiancé."

She nods, the tumult churning inside her evident on her face. The need to comfort her has my hand up, palming her cheek and my other hand at her waist, pulling her into me. After a hesitation, she surrenders to it. Her forehead drops to my chest, and a ragged breath shudders through her slim body. The air thickens with lingering grief. She doesn't cry, but the dip of her shoulders, the tension of her body, broadcasts how difficult this still is. My hand traces a soothing path from between her shoulders to the small of her back, and I don't say anything, but leave her to take any comfort she can from the human contact. After a few moments, she shifts in the high heels that still barely bring her to my shoulder.

"Thanks, Deck," she says softly, pulling back. My hand tightens at her waist, anchoring her to me, despite the gap between our bodies. She feels so good, I'm not ready to relinquish her.

"I need to go." She stares at the button on my shirt instead of at me.

I'm about to refuse; to press the issue of the connection I know she feels, too, but there is just enough shadow in her dark eyes; trace amounts of the grief that brought us into each other's arms in the first place, to change my mind. My hand drops, and she turns to unlock her apartment door.

"I'll see you on set Monday." Her eyes meet mine cautiously like she thinks I might grab her.

That could happen.

"Sure." I step back. "Should be a great show."

Once she's safely inside, I board the elevator. She's right. Tonight wasn't the night. Based on what I learned about her fiancé, I can respect that. But after tasting her, not just her sweetness, but her tears, I know this is just clemency. She wants time. I can give her space, but I'm not giving up.

Chapter Seven

AVERY

Have yourself a merry little Christmas

Let your heart be light

From now on your troubles will be out of sight

I wake up with Will's favorite Christmas song in my head and my hand between my legs.

Sad and horny. That's what I am. I literally cannot remember the last time I had sex. I know it was with Will because I never cheated on him in the years we were together, but our sex life was so sporadic at the end, I can't recall the last time we made love. I need to get drunk and I need to get laid. I'm hoping at least one of those will happen tonight at the SportsCo Christmas party, but it probably won't be the latter. I told Decker the truth. I'd be an awful one-night stand, and if I were in the market for one, it wouldn't be at my office Christmas party. I've never dated colleagues or athletes, and that's pretty much the extent of tonight's guest list. Will was into advertising. He could barely tell a touchdown from a homerun. I liked that he had nothing to do with sports or my career. I needed something separate from the frenetic pace of television and the crazy news cycle I'm always enslaved to.

"God, Will." I stare up at the ceiling, fresh, hot tears rolling into my ears and soaking my hairline. "Why did you do it? *How* could you do it?"

I told Decker last night that Will died, but I didn't tell him it was at his own hand.

I've been through grief counseling. I see my therapist every week. I've read about suicide and depression and know all the statistics. Seventy-five percent of suicides are men. Statistically they follow through on their attempts at higher rates. Those stats spike during the holidays. All the signs were there, but I missed them. Ignored them? Denied them? I don't know how I lived with this man and wore his ring for two years, but never knew this morbid wish was growing inside of him, a dark bud I didn't even know had taken root.

And every morning for the last year, I woke up with one question on my lips.

Why?

"The last year," I repeat, my voice an early morning croak. "Oh, my God."

He's been gone a year today. I can't believe it, and in many ways, I feel as lost as I did the night he died.

There's a call I need to make. One I dread, but know I cannot avoid.

When it rings and rolls into voice mail, I hesitate. I could call back later, but I'm not sure I can handle it today, hearing the pain in his mother's voice. I'm ashamed to feel relief that Mrs. Hattfield doesn't answer. Even more ashamed that I take the coward's way out and leave a message.

"Hi, Mrs. H," I say after the beep. "It's me, Avery."

I pause, the right words eluding me while I squeeze the cell phone like it's the only thing anchoring me.

"I . . . um . . . I know today is difficult for you." I shove the words that feel so trite out of my mouth. "It's difficult for me, too. I can't imagine . . . I just . . ."

My voice evaporates for a moment.

"I miss him," I whisper, biting my lips against a sob and pressing my eyes closed to hold onto the last image I have of him. The deathly peace he'd taken for himself.

And it's true. I miss the guy I knew before; the one who went down on one knee at dinner and promised me forever. I even miss the sullen man who lived in the shadows the last part of his life. I'd take Will any way I could get him just to look in his eyes, grab his hands and beg him not to do it. For me. For his mother. For *himself*, to reconsider living.

"I hope you're not alone today." I take a second to compose myself before going on. "I know the next few weeks will be hard, Christmas will be hard without him."

I run one hand through my hair, frustrated that I don't have the right words and have nothing more to say.

"Okay, well, call me when you get this message," I say into the mechanical silence. "Talk to you soon."

Losing a child, it's the worst thing. When a child chooses to forfeit the very life you gave him, the pain must weigh even more. I wonder if she stares up at the ceiling some mornings asking *why* the way I do. Do her pain and grief cohabitate with a stewing rage? Does she want to drag him from the grave and shake him and call him a coward? I hate even thinking these things, but not acknowledging them to myself and at least to my therapist was ruining me. I don't know if these thoughts make me a bad person, but I know they make me sad. And frustrated. And helpless.

In my closet, I consider the row of beautiful dresses I could wear tonight. The last thing I want to do is go to a Christmas party, much less one Mack

Decker is attending. Those moments at my door two weeks ago have been a source of torture. It wasn't just a reminder to my body what it's been missing, but to my emotions. That just beyond my comfort zone there may be solace for, not just my body, but for my soul.

What was I thinking? Letting him hold me? Letting him see my vulnerability? Those moments of letting go, resting against the solidity of him; being comforted by his heart beating just beyond the wall of his chest, were some of the sweetest I've had in a year. It was intoxicating, and I have no intention of getting drunk on him. He'd go straight to my head. Straight to my heart and between my legs, and I'm not ready for any of that.

I press my thighs together against a tide of want when I recall the moments that simmered between us. Waking up thinking about Will, and getting wet knowing I'll see Deck in a few hours—it feels so wrong, but at least I'm feeling. I haven't allowed myself to want a man since Will died. Maybe no one appealed to me the way Decker does, but he's the first one to punch holes in the fence around me.

I return to my selections for the party. I've worn the black dress to several office functions. It's flattering and conservative. It's the classic "little black dress" that goes everywhere and can serve many purposes. I touch the silky material of my other option. It's a dress made of sunsets, a glorious blend of gold and red, and it still bears the tags. I've never worn it. The deep V neckline is outdone by the deeper V that bares my back. The bottom is narrow and tight and will be a testament of all the squats I've done, though my ass is mostly genetics and years of track and field. My mother and aunts have never done squats a day in their lives, and you could bounce a quarter off their butts. As good as I know the dress will look, I'm still not sure I'll wear it. It's a statement dress, and knowing Decker will be there tonight, I'm not quite sure what I want to say.

Chapter Eight

DECKER

"So what's next?"

The question catches me a little off guard. With a Jack and Coke halfway to my mouth, I pause to study Mike Dunlov, one of SportsCo's most popular anchors.

"I mean now that your co-hosting gig's up," he clarifies.

"Little bit of this," I answer flatly because I'm giving this guy nothing. "Little bit of that."

I toss back a portion of the much-needed drink. Playing pro ball allowed me to indulge many vices. I've had more pussy than any man has a right to in one lifetime, for example. I'm practically abstemious, though, when it comes to alcohol and what I eat. Always have been. This body was my lottery ticket, and I took care of it. But tonight, this liquor is a lifeline. It's been a bitch of a day. Mainly because my ex is being a bitch. Bad enough she moved my daughter across the country. Now she's making it harder for me to see her this Christmas. Changing my holiday plans because she's still playing the same bullshit games she did when we were married had me almost skipping this party tonight. Except . . . I watch the main entrance to see if Avery has arrived yet.

"Guy like you can write your own ticket," Mike continues. "I mean look at how you scored this hosting gig. How'd you enjoy working with Avery, by the way?"

His eyebrows waggle suggestively. "She's something else, huh?"

I stiffen, not much liking him or the look in his eyes.

"What do you mean?" I take my time sipping a little more of my drink, watching him over the glass.

"I mean, did you get any? We've all tried." He offers a careless shrug. "Who wouldn't try with a rack like that, but she was devoted to her fiancé. With him gone, she's been shut down. I just thought if anyone could finally tap that, it'd be you."

My teeth clench around an expletive. I know for a fact *Twofer* blows this douche's ratings out of the water. The respect of her colleagues is so important to Avery. Hearing him demean her this way sets me on edge.

"You're an asshole, you know that?" I ask, my tone deceptively calm, though my hand clamps around the glass while I imagine his little windpipe crushing under my fingers.

"So I've been told." He flashes his very-white veneers in that fake smile unsuspecting viewers fall for. "But there's no disrespect. It *has* been a year, and you know what the final stage of grief is, right?"

"Acceptance?"

"Nope." He leers over his scotch. "Horny. Somebody's gotta offer her a dick to cry on."

I'm two seconds from smashing my glass into his skull when his eyes latch onto something over my shoulder and light up.

"Damn," he mutters. "I really hope we've reached the final stage."

He's walking off before I process what he means, but it doesn't take long to figure out. Across the room, he and several other anchors and network executives are buzzing around Avery like she's a honeycomb. And I can't blame them. Her hair is pulled up, tendrils of it licking around her neck and ears. Simple gold earrings dangle and frame the curve of her cheekbones. Her makeup is dramatic, but simple, letting her sharply-drawn features speak for themselves. The slick of gold on her lips glimmers against the light copper of her skin.

And that dress.

This dress has to be inspiring erections all over the room. I can only speak for mine with any confidence, but it's pushing painfully against the flap of my suit pants.

The color, like saffron sprinkled over her firm curves, sets off her dusky complexion perfectly. Sleeveless, the dress showcases the feminine sculpture of her arms, and the neckline dips almost to her waist, the cut of it serving her breasts up beautifully. The bodice flows into a narrow skirt that paints the dress onto the flare of her hips and the tight line of her thighs. When she turns around and walks to the bar, many eyes zero in on her departure. The dress has no back, displaying a stretch of unblemished skin from neck to waist. The skirt strains across the high arc of her ass, and my fingers itch to squeeze it while I piston in and out, anchoring us together with nothing but my hands and my dick.

I take another measured sip, checking myself and allowing the smooth liquid to cool me off. I sound as bad as the other lechers in here. Mike may joke about her grief, but I've seen it up close. Even while the air sizzled with lust around us at her front door, I couldn't ignore the sadness in Avery's eyes. I won't take advantage of that. If I can help it, none of these horny sons of bitches will either.

"We do have hors d'oeuvres, you know," Sadie says from beside me. "You don't have to eat Avery."

I smile to acknowledge Sadie's comment and her presence, but I don't take my eyes off the only woman I'm interested in.

"I've seen the food." I glance down at Avery's best friend. "Far less appetizing than she is."

"You do always look at her like she's dessert." Sadie giggles. She's not usually a giggling kind of woman, so I attribute that tinkly sound to the glass of champagne. Probably not her first.

"I don't look at Avery like she's dessert." I drop the smile so she knows my intentions aren't of the short-lived, guilty pleasure variety. "I look at her like she's the main course."

That penetrates her tipsy bubble enough to widen her eyes with surprise.

"Hmmm." She takes another sip, brows up. "Tread carefully, if that's the case. You'd be better off settling for dessert, Deck. Short and sweet."

"Do I seem like a man who settles to you?" My laugh is humorless because I'm afraid this time I might have to.

"Avery's been through a lot this year." Sadie's eyes appear suddenly slightly sober. "And she doesn't need some player making things more complicated than they already are for her."

"*Former* player," I say. "In every sense of the word."

"Would your ex-wife agree on the former?"

"What the hell does that mean?" We trade glares over her presumption.

"Meaning I know they don't take the trash out of those tunnels every night, and ballers like you scoop it up, take it home, fuck it, and don't let a wedding ring stop you."

"I never cheated on my wife." I check the anger and frustration her assumptions are burning under my collar. "If you're asking if I got ass when I was single, then let me assure you, I got ass. If you're asking if I *still* get ass, then yeah. I *still* get ass, but if I'm in a monogamous relationship, I play one-on-one. Not that it's any of your damn business."

"Avery is my damn business." She mutters under her breath what sounds like "*carbon*."

"If you're gonna call me a motherfucker, you can do it in English." Humor relaxes my shoulders a little after the last few tense moments.

"You speak Spanish?" She doesn't look chagrined at getting caught.

"Only enough to realize I'm being insulted from time to time."

Her mouth loosens into a slight grin before she looks up at me frankly.

"Look, Ave may seem like she's having a great time." She waves her hand at the dance floor where Avery is dancing her ass off while managing to hold a Cosmopolitan. "But like the song says, blame it on the alcohol. The last thing she needs is some one-night stand holiday cheer."

"I know that." I hate the defensive note in my voice, but I resent her thinking I'm like Mike Dunlov, looking to capitalize on Avery's vulnerability.

"But do you know that today is the day?" Sadie asks softly. "That her fiancé died a year ago today?"

"Shit." I swipe a hand over my face. "I didn't know that."

I return the assessing look Sadie's giving me, and then some. Can I trust her? Can she trust me?

"What can you tell me about him?" I finally ask. "About his death?"

"Nothing." Sadie's mouth tips in a wry grin. "If you're serious about Avery being the . . . how'd you put it? Main course? Then that's a story she needs to tell you herself."

"Sadie!" Jerry, a cameraman I've seen on set, calls from a few feet away. "Get out here and shake what your mama gave you."

"This may take a while." Sadie laughs and hands me her glass. "'Cause Mama gave me a lot!"

She shuffles off toward the dance floor. As soon as a server passes by, I set her glass and my barely-touched Jack and Coke on the tray. The party is in full swing, but I'm already thinking about the bed upstairs in my borrowed penthouse suite. Knowing how hard today has to be for Avery, there's no way I'm leaving her at the mercy of these wolves.

Some Mariah Carey Christmas song comes on. The one from *Love Actually*. Everyone starts singing along and dancing even harder. I hate dancing. I was that guy sitting in VIP balancing a girl on each leg since I didn't really drink and definitely didn't dance. Just posted up, which is all I plan to do tonight, too. Besides, the wall gives me a great vantage point to keep an eye on Avery. If the final stage of grief is horny, I may have to protect her from herself. With Sadie off shaking what her mama gave her, it's up to me to keep Avery's virtue intact. Ironic since I've wanted in those pants for a very long time.

Another Mariah Carey Christmas song comes on.

What is *up* with Mariah Carey and the holidays?

Some other guy steps in to dance with Avery. She's good, her body moving gracefully, that dress hanging on to her curves by a literal thread. If she pops it one more inch, I think we'll have a wardrobe malfunction on our hands. Her expression is open and free like I've never seen it, but that could be because of the drink in her hand every time she dances by.

A slower song comes on, and the guy pulls Avery close, his hands slipping to her hips and his palms drifting lower. She laughs up at him and steps back, shaking her empty glass and heading to the bar.

My turn.

"Merry Christmas." I lean against the bar and block Avery's view of the rest of the room.

The smile she's been wearing since she walked through the door wavers. Her lashes drop before she looks back up at me, that fraudulent grin firmly back in place. We've seen each other on set and in meetings, but since that kiss, I've given her the space she requested.

"Not quite Christmas." She sips the drink the bartender just handed her. "Another few days."

I glance from the alcohol to her dark, glassy eyes that, up this close, are rimmed with sorrow. "What you drinking?"

"A lot." Her laugh comes loud and hollow. "I'm drinking a lot."

"I can see that." I clear my throat and lean a little closer. "You might want to ease up. Some of these guys are on the prowl tonight."

"*They're* on the prowl?" The hazy eyes turn defiant. "Maybe *I'm* on the prowl, Deck. Maybe I'm not the prey, but the hunter."

"Huntress, I think you mean."

"Hunter, huntress, whatever. I just might be prowling, so don't worry about me." She straightens from the bar and starts past me back to the dance floor. "Just stay out of my way."

I watch the steady sway of her hips as she resumes her place on the dance floor, immediately joined by Mike Dunlov. The asshole.

"Hey, homey." I proffer a hundred-dollar bill to the bartender between two fingers. "This is yours if you can water down her drinks when she comes back for more."

His eyes widen and then crinkle with a smile while he pockets the cash.

"Sure thing." He pours vodka into a cocktail shaker. "I feel for her. I do all SportsCo's parties, and she and her fiancé were great together. It's only been a year since he passed. Gotta be hard."

"Yeah," I say without offering more.

I hate discussing her like this. I've found myself in three conversations about how she's handling her grief, and none of them with her. I know she's not ready for what I'm ready for. Hell, I'm not even sure I'm ready for what I think things could be with Avery. I don't have to be in her bed tonight, but I'd love to be in her head; to know what's behind that hollow laugh and that out-of-body look. Like she's here, dancing, drinking, flirting; going through all the motions, but she's somewhere else, alone and miserable. Not really here at all.

The deejay gears the tempo down again, and Sam Smith's cover of "Have Yourself A Merry Little Christmas" comes on. Avery freezes in the middle of the dance floor, but Mike Dunlov keeps rocking, talking incessantly, barely noticing that Avery stands rigid in front of him. He misses the look of absolute devastation that twists her expression and floods her eyes. She walks off, leaving him alone wearing his confusion all over himself. I follow her path past Mike and around the corner. A few feet ahead of me, she grabs a bottle of champagne from one of the servers and steps out of sight onto the balcony.

Cold wind slaps me in the face when I join her at the rail. Noticing goose-flesh prickling the skin of her arms and back, I slip my jacket off and drape it over her shoulders. She jumps, spilling champagne down the front of her dress.

"Shit." She holds the glass and the bottle away from her body, assessing the damage.

"Sorry." I pull a cocktail napkin from my pocket and pat the wet spot on the front of her dress. "Didn't mean to startle you."

With a half-hearted grin, she watches my hands moving over the scarce material of her bodice and skirt.

"If this is some elaborate scheme to get to second base," she says. "It might actually work tonight."

My hands pause just under her breasts, and I glance from the stain on her dress to the stain on her face. The stain of sadness with a shade of inebriation.

"As much as I'd like to take you up on your offer," I say, crooking one side of my mouth even though I don't feel like smiling, and it looks like she doesn't either. "I'll take a rain check."

She narrows her eyes for a second before shrugging, setting her glass on the balcony ledge and tipping the bottle to her lips, eyes never leaving mine.

"Some other guy's lucky night then," she drawls.

I grab her wrist before she can take another sip, and the rim of the bottle is poised at her lips.

"No."

It's one word, but it covers a lot. No, she doesn't need to drink anymore. No, it's not some other motherfucker's lucky night if I have anything to say about it. And no, I won't let her drown her sorrows in champagne and meaningless sex tonight.

"No? I'm a grown-ass woman, Deck," she snaps, a shadow flitting across her face. "Grown and fancy-free."

A lone tear streaks through her flawless makeup. "God, I hate this song."

I tune into the music drifting out to us from inside.

"Have Yourself A Merry Little Christmas"? I ask.

"It was his favorite Christmas song," she whispers and clunks the champagne bottle down on the balcony ledge. "It's awful."

She squeezes her eyes closed, but more tears slip over her cheeks. I want to put my arms around her again like I did at her apartment, but she's been so unpredictable tonight, I don't know how she'll respond. I hesitate, not sure what to say. I hate it when people say stupid shit to a grieving person. I don't want to be that guy, and I'm not known for my sensitivity.

"I know this is a hard time for you."

She stares at me, sadness and uncertainty suspended between us like a rope bridge, before bringing the bottle to her lips and chugging without answering.

"Hey, hey." I urge the bottle down and away from her mouth. "That won't solve anything."

"Oh, you're so acquainted with grief, are you? That you know just what to do in these situations, huh? I'm so damn tired of being a situation. Of knowing everyone's wondering how I'm holding up, and wondering if I'm ready to date again. Wondering if I'm still . . ."

"Still what, Ave?"

She draws a deep breath and clutches the bottle to the smooth skin between her breasts displayed by the dipping neckline.

"You still on the top floor?" she demands. "Or has the network kicked you out already?"

"Nah." I draw the word out a little, buying a nanosecond to figure out where she's going with this. "I've got the penthouse for few more days."

She nods, draws her brows together like she's processing what I've told her; like she's working out some problem. And then she says the words I would have given my first-year salary to hear the night we met, but now have no idea what to do about.

"Let's get out of here," she says. "Take me to your place."

Chapter Nine

AVERY

I KNOW THIS IS A MISTAKE. I'M HUDDLED IN THE CORNER OF THE ELEVATOR, my eyes fixed on the illuminated ascending numbers taking us inevitably to the top floor where Deck has been living the past few weeks. If I knew what was good for me, I would push the red emergency button; alert maintenance that there's an accident in progress right inside this elevator car. But I can't. I woke up with this numbness spreading over my body like a plague. It's even frozen over my heart. I knew today would be painful; that it might hurt like a fresh wound, but nothing hurts and nothing feels good. Not the deceptively innocuous champagne bubbles zipping through my bloodstream. Not the many guys I danced with tonight or the secret touches they stole while we moved to the music. Nothing has made me feel all day.

Except him.

Call it lust. Animal attraction. Whatever it is, I felt it like a shot of adrenaline as soon as I saw Decker tonight. I study him from under surreptitious lashes, roving my eyes over silky hair the color of nutmeg brushed with honey. The slightest curl of it at his nape softens the hard line of his neck. His brandy-flavored eyes watch the climbing numbers, the bold nose and thick brows and wide, mobile mouth harmonizing his features into handsome. I study the impressive width of his shoulders and the bulge of his arms straining against the dress shirt. His jacket around my shoulders douses me in his scent and his warmth. I discretely snuggle deeper into its embrace, even though the arms hang limp and empty at my sides.

Yes, he makes me feel something. I want it to be as simple as lust; as the sad, horny girl who woke up with her dead fiancé on her mind and her hand between her legs, but it's not that simple. I've always known with Decker it wouldn't be.

"I don't think . . ." I struggle to wrangle my thoughts set on a wild goose chase by the alcohol I've consumed. "I'm not sure this is a good idea."

He looks at me sharply just as the doors open to his floor. We consider each other, neither making a move. The doors start closing and he catches them with one long arm.

"Come on." He tilts his head toward the landing beyond the elevator doors. "At least let me get some coffee in you. Sober you up and save you from bad decisions you'll regret tomorrow."

He thinks the bad decisions are back at the party with idiots like Mike Dunlov. No, the bad decisions are behind his closed doors, but I find myself half-stumbling after him to the penthouse. As soon as we're inside, I lean my palm onto the wall for balance and take off my stilettos. I lose another four inches, and now have to tip my head farther back to see his face.

"You're tall." I want to retract the obvious statement to a basketball player as soon as it trips past my liquor-loosened lips. Humor flits through his eyes briefly before concern swipes it away.

"Comes with the territory." He walks toward the small, neat kitchen. "Come on. Coffee."

I very carefully climb onto the leather stool at the counter, looping my bare feet on the slats. Decker makes even a simple task like making coffee look tantalizing. The play of muscles under his thin white shirt when he reaches for a mug. The efficiency of his big hands, quick and deft in the mundane preparations. There's a rugged grace to him; like rough metal that's been polished and chiseled until it gleams.

"You're beautiful," I blurt, causing him to stop what he's doing and stare at me.

I really *am* drunk. I'd never say that sober.

"Wow, you really *are* drunk." He echoes my thoughts, laughs and shakes his head, sliding the coffee across the marble counter top. "Drink this and I'm sure I'll be less beautiful soon."

I hope so because if he keeps looking like that, I can't be held responsible.

And isn't that what I want? For one night not to feel responsible? Not to feel guilty or condemned? Ashamed of my part in Will's irreversible decision? All night I've wanted to feel something, and in this moment, I feel everything. Like a wall dropped and every painful thought and emotion rushed in before I could get my guard back up.

"It's today," I speak into the quiet filled with only the hum of appliances.

"What's today?" Decker leans his elbows on the counter, gathering both huge fists under his chin and watching me closely, waiting for more.

I think he already knows. I feel like all night everyone knew that I was desperate to forget the significance of this day.

"Um . . . a year ago today, Will died." I run a fingernail over the silky material stretching across my thighs.

"I'm sorry, Avery." Sincerity lays heavy in the dark eyes, unlit by his usual good humor.

"Did you know it was suicide?" The words cut my tongue like a razor. "That he took his own life? Right in our apartment."

"I didn't know. Did you . . ." His compassion reshapes to horror. "Did you find him, Avery?"

The horrible tableau plays out across my mind again like it has countless times before.

"Yeah." My whisper breaks. "I found him, but I was too late."

Despite the warmth of his jacket around me, I shiver like I'm back there; like the premonition that slid over me when I entered our apartment that night is revisiting my skin and reminiscing with my bones.

"Shit, Ave." Decker crosses around the counter to me, his taut stomach hitting my bent knees while I sit on the stool. "I'm so sorry."

"He was . . . he was . . ." My teeth rattle, shock shaking me like I'm standing in that bathroom again. "In the water. In our bathtub with so much blood."

Deck pulls me closer by the shoulders while tears course over my cheeks and dampen the fine cotton of his shirt. I can't catch my breath. Weeping quakes my body with the stupid tears I promised myself I wouldn't shed today. I was so determined to forget all of this tonight, and here I am a sloppy mess all over Mack Decker. His wide, warm palms roll over my arms when his jacket falls from my shoulders and hits the thick pile carpet. He rests his hands at the curve of my neck and shoulder when my tears finally subside, his thumbs under my chin, lifting, forcing my eyes to meet his.

"Hey, you okay?" he asks softly.

I concentrate all my senses, all my focus on where his hands have been. My arms are warm from his touch. The sensitive skin of my neck tingles where his thumbs caress. The faint smell of alcohol and his expensive cologne, flares my nostrils. My heart slams into my ribs like I've run and leapt and landed. Wordlessly, I scoot forward on the stool, widening my legs until he's between them, bracketed by my knees. The bold action forces the dress up to the juncture of my thighs, offering a glimpse of my black panties. His eyes drop between my legs and snap up to my face. He tries to step back, hands falling away and jaw ticking, but I latch onto one leanly muscled arm.

"Don't." I scoot forward more until I'm barely on the stool. "Please don't leave me like this, Deck."

"I'm not leaving you, Avery. I . . ." He gives a decisive shake of his head. "You're not in a good place tonight and I won't take advantage of that. I want to help you, not . . ."

His words trail away and his eyes are distracted, following a path along my collarbone, between my breasts, over my stomach and between my legs. I spread my thighs another inch, showing him what he's wanted for a long time and inviting him to take it tonight.

He licks his bottom lip, a fascinating swipe of his tongue that I lean forward and mimic with my own. His pleasured groan vibrates against my mouth, but he pulls back, drawing in a deep breath and shaking his head again.

"Ave, I—"

I grip him by the neck and lick the seam of his lips. His jaw drops on a gasp, and I push my tongue in, exploring the warm, silky interior of his mouth. My hands venture between us, finding him lengthened, hardened. When I squeeze, he growls into our kiss. His hands, which have remained in deliberate discipline at his sides, encompass my waist. They're so big his fingers almost meet at my back and his thumbs rest under my breasts. My nipples tauten in proximity to his touch.

"You're playing with fire here." His voice emerges rough as Brillo.

"I know exactly," I say, my voice husky while my hand pushes up and down over his dick. "what I'm playing with."

"Avery, we should—"

"Make me feel," I cut in, steadily pumping him through his pants. "You want to help, then make me feel."

Tears gather at the edges of my eyes, trickling unchecked over my face and into the corners of my mouth.

"Make me feel something other than pain, Deck." I meet his eyes, and they reflect my sorrow back to me. He groans when my hand persists.

"Promise me," he finally says, searching my face. "Promise me you won't regret this tomorrow."

A dissonant laugh flows out of me, misplaced in the grief and lust permeating the room around us.

"I can't promise you I won't regret this tomorrow." I stare back at him, not hiding my pain or my passion or my confusion or my need. "I can only promise that I want it like hell tonight."

Chapter Ten

DECKER

AVERY'S WORDS, EVEN MORE THAN HER HAND, GRAB ME BY THE BALLS. THE sight of her arrests my heart in my chest. I've wanted this woman for a long time, but knew it would probably never happen. Here she is offering herself to me on a very unexpected platter, and I'm not sure I can do anything about it. Because after all this time, I'll be damned if I'm settling for one night with her; some drunken memory she relegates to the back of a closet and never considers repeating.

"Deck, I just want to feel good." Her lips tremble when she presses them to mine again. "Make me feel. Make me come."

"Shit," I hiss at her brazen request. "Avery, I can't. Any night but tonight. I can't."

Surprise and hurt mingle in her dark eyes, calcifying into determination. She hops off the stool and stands, allowing no space between us so I feel the heavy heave of her breasts against my chest.

"Okay." She looks up at me, her mouth a stiff line set in delicate bones. "Maybe Mike can—"

"The hell Mike."

My hands clamp around her waist, stopping her from walking to the door. I swallow the last of my hesitation. She doesn't know if she'll regret this tomorrow. I'm almost certain I will, but I lose the fight with my will, with hers, and lift her back onto the stool. She wants to feel? She wants to come? Never looking away from her face, I drop to my knees and press her open. She doesn't resist. Her legs relax, stopping where I want them. I rub my stubbled chin and cheek along the sensitive skin inside her thighs, rewarded by the gasps above my head. The closer I get to my goal, the harder it is to breathe. The smell of her reaches my nose, unhinging my restraint. I tighten my hands around her thighs, forcing myself to go slow; to be gentle. I lift her legs over my shoulders, dragging her ass to the very edge of the stool to mouth her through the black panties. They're already damp, and her flavor seeps onto my tongue, so sweet I can't help but remember Sadie saying Avery could be my dessert.

"Oh, my God, Deck." Her words are needy and breathless.

I don't look up, too absorbed in the taste of her, even through silk. So potent. I nudge the panties aside with my nose, licking up her seam. She's wet and hot and tangy on my lips. I delve into her slickness, seeking out the crown jewel tucked inside, that cluster of nerves. I suck hard, and she bucks into my mouth. The steady interplay of tongue, lips and teeth at the intersection of her body and my mouth has her hips jerking and her hand clawing my hair.

"Ahh. Ahhh. Ahhh." Her hips roll in tandem with me, and I glance up long enough to watch her inhibitions fall away. Her head drops back, the satin skin of her throat stretched and taut with pleasure. "Deck, I'm gonna . . . oh God."

I slip two fingers inside, still sucking and licking while both her hands grip my head; while she commands me like a queen in her inner court. Her legs quake against me and her body tightens around my fingers convulsively as she comes. She rides it out over my mouth, taking anything I might not be giving her. Except I'm giving her everything, and she doesn't even know it.

When her body goes still, and the only sound in the room is our labored breathing, I slide away from her. That's as far as I'll allow myself to go. She wanted to feel. She wanted to come. I've done that for her, but I have to get her out of here.

"Don't, Deck." Her lipstick is smeared and her lips are swollen from our kiss. "Don't stop."

Her hips start rocking again like her pussy is remembering what I feel like; like she's seeking something. Seeking me. The panties still pushed aside, showing me how needy and creamy she is between her thighs. I'm shaking my head, a definite denial, but when she slides the shoulders of her dress away, her breasts are naked and perfect. Most nipples are small tight buds, but Avery's are lengthened and plump and plum-colored, resting at the tips of her breasts like heavy fruit on a vine. I want to drink. I'm already dizzy with the taste of her, but the sight of her unravels my convictions until they are shredded into ribbons at our feet. She stands, pushing at the skirt, sliding it over her hips and legs, a puddle of silk at her bare feet. She's only in the black panties, but even those she persuades down her body until she's naked for me.

She traces the tip of her finger over my eyebrows, down my nose, skims my lips, cups my jaw.

"You really are beautiful," she whispers, her eyes following the path her finger took. "Give me tonight, Deck."

I got nothing left. Any resistance melts under the awe in her eyes as she runs them over my face, as her look probes beneath my clothes. I want to show her. I want her to be as enamored with my body as I am with hers. I stand up, towering over her. I pull her bare back to my chest and walk us to the bedroom, all the way, cupping her breasts, pinching her nipples, caressing her stomach, pressing my hard-on into her ass, so that by the time we reach my bedroom, her breaths are ragged, her fingers trembling when she unbuttons my shirt. I stand perfectly still, watching her eyes glaze over with every portion of me she reveals. She fumbles with my belt, but I don't intervene, enjoying the clumsy brush of her fingers against my stomach. She opens my zipper, deliberately skimming a knuckle over me through my briefs, making my breath catch and cut in my chest. A little grin quirks one corner of her mouth when she sees my reaction. She pushes the shirt off my shoulders, leaning forward to suck my nipples.

"God, Ave." My fingers lace into the hair neatly gathered up, dislodging pins so it spills around her shoulders.

She shoves my pants down, following their path to my feet, settling onto her knees. Her velvety brown eyes peer up at me, hot and hungry, as she tugs my underwear over my legs, her hands tracing the muscles of my thighs and calves.

"Oh, my God." She stares at my dick, elongated and thick, bobbing at the entrance of her lips. "I'm not sure I can take it all."

"Won't know till you try." I line up with her mouth. "Open."

Obediently, her full lips part, and I push in, groaning every inch of the way.

"Mmmmmm." She clumps her eyebrows together, and for a moment I think it's too much; that it's discomfort tightening her expression. Then she lowers her jaw, taking me deeper into the tight channel of her throat.

"Mmmmmm," she spreads her hands over my ass, gripping as much of me as she can. She presses in closer, rubbing her breasts over my legs in sync with her mouth, sharpening her nipples against me, using me. It's turning me on even more.

"Shit, you give good head," I mumble, barely able to form coherent words. I bite my bottom lip until it throbs, a counter to the bliss happening below my waist.

She adds her hand to the equation, cupping my balls, pulling her mouth from the root all the way to the tip and insinuating her tongue into the tiny opening.

"Sweet mother of . . ." I grip her jaw, holding her at just the perfect angle, and fuck her mouth relentlessly, my hips a merciless cadence while tears streak over her face. I don't know if the tears are sadness, or if she's choking on my dick, but she won't let me go. Her fingers lock so tight on my ass, her nails dig into the muscles.

I will burst soon, and it will be inside of her. I carefully pull back, watching her mouth still moving for a second until she realizes I'm gone. I skim my palms over the fragile framework of her collarbone and shoulders, and then spread my hands open, just whispering the palms over her nipples again and again. Her mouth drops open, lashes fall to kiss her cheeks and she leans back onto her heels, pressing her arms behind her, the muscles in her legs strained, palms to the floor so she's offering herself to me. I keep working in tight circles over her breasts, and her hips jerk in time with my pace.

I lift her gently onto the bed behind us and spread her out, taking myself in my hand and pumping, making her wait. Making her watch. She moves her legs restlessly, looking for relief.

"Come on, Deck." She licks her lips, eyes fixed on my dick.

I straddle her hips with my knees, letting my cock rub between her legs in tantalizing swipes.

"Give it to me." She reaches for it, trying to line us up.

"You'll get it when I'm ready, Ave." My voice is hoarse and scratchy, and I want to be buried inside her, but draw it out for us both.

I take one nipple between my lips, varying the suction from gentle and barely there, to rough and aggressive. All the while pinching the other and rolling the nipple between my fingers. I transfer my mouth to the other breast and slide my hand, palm flat against her belly, between her legs.

She jerks when I peel back the lips and rub my fingertip over her clit in a swift rhythm. It plumps and tightens.

"Damn, you're wet," I groan, seduced by the sloppy sounds her pussy makes when I finger fuck her.

"I need it to be now, Deck," she pants, stretching her legs wide and tugging at my hips. Positioning me.

"Okay. Just one more taste." I want her juices on my tongue when I enter her for the first time.

"No," she growls, her eyes narrow and her face tight with passion. "Now."

I can't help but chuckle because she looks so fierce; so much like the girl who put me in my place at my locker. So much like the driven, ambitious, commanding woman I've come to admire from a distance over the last few years, even more up close the last few weeks.

"Now, you said?" With no more warning, I thrust inside, and we share a gasp at the perfect fit. I know I'm big and she's tight as hell, but it feels perfect to me.

"You all right?" I crush the urge to slam into her, waiting for her to indicate it's okay to move. "Are you—"

"If you don't come on and fuck me, Mack Decker," she rasps, eyes half-mast and hands clenched around my ass.

My dick twitches inside of her at the coarse words, and she grins, locking her ankles behind my back. She better lock 'em. She has no idea how hard she's about to get fucked. I hitch an arm under her knee and grind in so deep my balls get wet.

Her eyes go wide, and her body moves up the bed with the first few thrusts. I pump into her at full force, rocking the headboard into the wall, making the mattress moan.

"Oh my God." One of her hands leaves my ass and grips the sheet at her side. "This is . . . oh my God."

I push her knees to her shoulders, folding her back, appreciating how pliable her body is under my hands. I glance down to watch myself enter and withdraw, watch the evidence of how much she wants me on my dick.

On my dick. Fuck.

"Condom." I pull out, and her face crumples.

"No, don't stop."

"Let me get this on." I reach into the bedside table, wrap it up in record speed, and get back in there, pulling her legs over my shoulders.

"Oh, yes." She links her fingers behind my neck and tosses her head on the pillow. She clenches around me, stiffens with wave after wave of her orgasm.

"I feel so much." She stretches her neck back, lifting slightly off the pillow. Tears slide over her cheeks. "Oh, my God. It feels amazing."

Her eyes meet mine in the dim light, and she shows me everything. The things she hasn't told me, the secrets that torture her. I may not have the words yet, but the feeling, the hurt shadows her pleasure and she tells me everything. The intimacy of it pushes me over, and I'm exploding, throwing my head back, gripping her hips, my body reduced to urges and instincts and thrusts and moans until I finish, sinking my teeth into the tender curve of her neck.

I roll onto my back, keeping her connected to me, staying inside of her, our bellies kissing. Her legs fall limply on either side of my hips. She pushes up onto her elbows to study me, tears spilling unapologetically down her face. Her mouth trembles, works around sounds for a few seconds before she speaks.

"You made me feel," she whispers. "Damn you."

And then she collapses onto my chest and weeps.

Chapter Eleven

AVERY

"He left a note."

The confession slips seamlessly into the intimacy our bodies, maybe even our hearts, made in this bed. In the darkness of this room only brightened by the skyline twinkling beyond the window.

"What?" Deck adjusts me in the crook of his shoulder, kissing my temple and pushing my hair aside to nuzzle into my neck, too. "What'd you say, Ave?"

He sounds sleepy. We just finished round two, and I must say I've never been fucked like that in my life. It was . . . possession and dominance and tenderness and ferocity taking turns, all sides of him sharing me. I love the way he arranges me exactly how he wants, pushes my legs back just so. Tips my ass up to the desired angle. Spreads me to his specifications. And then fucks me like a train.

The man fucks like a train.

And I've been railroaded; possibly ruined for everyone else. If I had known there were men out there, fucking like that, I'd have a lot more notches on my bedpost in my quest to find them.

"Ave?" he asks again, reminding me of what I want to tell him, as much as I would love to stay distracted thinking of what we just did . . . twice. For the first time, I want to tell someone other than my therapist the secret I've been wearing like an albatross around my neck for the last year.

"He, um . . . Will, my fiancé. He left a note."

Deck shifts, carefully pulling his shoulder from under my head so he can lie on his side. So he can see my face while he waits for me to go on. I punish my lip trapped between my teeth.

"It was in the bathroom with my ring."

In the sliver of silence following my last words, I know he's mentally assembling the pieces of this puzzle before he asks his next question.

"You weren't wearing your ring?"

The question comes low and soft, a sympathetic query. Not a threat or an accusation or any of the things I've told myself I deserve.

"No, I had taken it off a few days before." I try to swallow, but can't past the scalding, swollen walls of my throat. "I . . . I . . . God, I . . ."

My breaths come in choppy heaves. I clutch the sheet to my naked breasts to keep my hands from shaking.

"Hey, hey." Decker cups my jaw in one big hand, brushing his thumb over the tears trickling down my cheek. "Baby, it's okay. Take your time."

It's been so long since a man called me "baby." Since I shared any intimacy with another person. Long before Will and I ended, our sex life dried up. The casual affection of intimate touches, naked skin, bared souls and endearments had long departed.

"I broke our engagement off a few days before he killed himself." The admission storms past my lips as if the words know this is their last chance; know that if they don't escape now I won't ever let them out.

Decker scoots down until his forehead lines up with mine, the height difference so great my feet stop at his knees under the cover.

"I'm so sorry." He dusts kisses over my wet cheeks, spearing his long fingers into my hair. "I can't even imagine. Tell me."

I stare through the dim light, searching his face for judgment, but it's not there; just a patient, waiting compassion. It gives me courage to go on.

"We had been over for a long time, I think." I squeeze my eyes tightly closed. "He suffered from depression. His medication made it so much better, but he didn't like to take it. Sometimes he wouldn't take it, and he wouldn't take care of himself. He'd lose friends. His work would go bad."

I lick at the bitter smile festering on my lips.

"We would go bad."

I shrug and shiver, pulling the sheet tighter around me. "I would say he wasn't trying hard enough. He would say I didn't understand. We'd . . . fight. We stopped . . ."

My voice dies in the dark. I dip my head to hide my face, ashamed to hear my part in this tragedy spoken aloud.

"You stopped what, Ave?" Deck probes gently, kissing my forehead and encouraging me to go on. "You can tell me."

"We stopped . . ." I glance up at him through a dampened veil of eyelashes. "We stopped making love. We were like roommates, miserable more often than not, but determined to keep trying. I loved him. I did, but I'm not sure for the last year or so that I was *in* love with him."

My harsh laugh puffs across our lips, just inches apart.

"Hell, he probably wasn't in love with me either there at the end," I say. "He went on a business trip and he cheated."

Deck's hard body goes still, and his thumb caresses under my chin, urging my eyes up to meet his.

"He was a fool," Deck says. "Not to speak ill of the dead, but anyone who isn't satisfied with you is a fool."

"No, I was a shrew." I wince, replaying some of our arguments. "We both wanted it to work so badly. We loved who we were in the beginning, but we weren't those people anymore. At least not to each other."

I always knew Will had . . . spells. Seasons when he would withdraw because life felt too hard, and nothing, not even our closeness, could pull him out. I didn't realize how bad it was until last year, and even then, I never imagined he'd harm himself. He stopped going to work. Stopped eating and showering regularly. Stopped making love to me. Stopped everything that made him happy. Stopped everything that made him . . . Will. He stopped everything that made us . . . us, and it broke my heart. Long before anonymous out-of-town hook up ho, my heart had been broken in minutes and hours and over days. We drifted out of love, into heartbreak, and settled into a terrible indifference. We were unrecognizable, and I didn't know if it would have happened eventually anyway, or if his depression, the wall it erected between us, forced us to it.

"So, what happened?" Decker prompts.

"When he told me he'd cheated, I. . ." I want to cover my ears against the memory of our raised voices; of our hurtful words. "I gave him his ring back. I told him it was over and went to a hotel."

Guilt assails me, fresh and wrenching. My heartbeat accelerates and my pulse pounds in my ears.

"That was the last time I saw him alive." I struggle to get the words out. "How could I do that, Deck? I knew he was depressed, was struggling, but I never thought he'd do something like that."

"Not your fault, Ave." He squeezes my chin between his fingers firmly. "Don't do that to yourself."

Doing that to myself has become a habit I'm not sure I can break. Blaming myself for what happened.

"When I broke it off, he thought I would reconsider, and asked that we not tell our friends and family yet so no one knew that just days before, I'd . . ."

Abandoned him. Left him on his own. Left him to die.

The details of that night overtake what I see, what I hear, hurling me back into that cold bathroom. All the sounds and images and horrors flood my memory. I'd gone to the apartment to tell him I was sure; that we should go ahead and tell everyone it was over. Not just because of him cheating, but because we weren't working anymore and hadn't for a long time. As soon as I let myself into the apartment, I'd heard the music drifting from the back to the entrance.

Have yourself a merry little Christmas
Let your heart be light
From now on your troubles will be out of sight

The closer I'd gotten to the bathroom, the louder the music became and the more I was sure something was wrong. The air trembled with it. Each lyric ached with the pain I'd seen in Will for years, ebbing, flowing, sometimes less, sometimes more—always there, but finally too much.

"He was in the tub," I whisper, my eyes unfocused on the room I'm in now, but seeing that other room; seeing Will in water turned scarlet with his blood. Seeing the deep lines sliced in his wrists, perpendicular to his pain; intersecting with the misery I'd seen in his eyes for months, but been helpless to soothe. I hadn't known his despair went that deep.

I still see that note, my name scrawled in Will's loopy penmanship. I still see the ring I had returned to him there on the counter.

"Avery, I tried," I say, my mouth trembling, an unsteady messenger for Will's last words. "That's all the note said. That he tried."

Was it an apology? For cheating? For giving up? Was it a condemnation of me, for underestimating his despair? For pushing too hard? For wanting too much? Always more from him, or for him? The questions make well-worn laps in my mind, round and round, dizzying me with the finality of Will's one-sided farewell.

The song. The tub. The blood. The ring. The note.

Second after painful second, I manage to drag myself out, like I've had to do so many times since that night. I focus on Decker, pleading for him to understand, or maybe to help me understand.

"Sometimes I'd say he wasn't trying because that's all I know how to do," I say. "I've spent my whole life *trying*. Achieving. Making things happen for myself, and on some level, I didn't understand that it wasn't that easy for him. That it wasn't about trying. It was deeper than that. For him it was harder than that. Maybe he was trying until he just couldn't try anymore. And I saw that too late, Deck, and now he's gone."

My shoulders shake with the emotion I've been hiding from for a year.

"When I saw the note, it had my name on it. No one else's." I shrug helplessly. "There was no message for anyone else, so I kept it to myself."

My laugh comes out hollow, barely a laugh at all.

"And if I'm honest, I didn't want anyone to know. To blame me like I blamed myself." I swipe trembling fingers over my wet cheeks. "God, I didn't want his mother to blame me like I blame myself. For her to think he did that because of me."

The words slip-slide on my tears, barely discernible, but Deck understands. He pulls me close, one hand stroking at the small of my back and one hand cupping my face as he kisses the wetness on my cheeks.

"Listen to me." His voice falls soft and firm over my hiccupping. "I don't know what you could have done differently in your relationship. When a relationship fails, we look backward with much more perspective than when we're in it. Believe me. I learned that after my divorce."

I sniff and nod against his chest for him to go on.

"And replaying our arguments and rehearsing our mistakes won't change how we handled things," he says. "But in a situation like that, you aren't responsible for someone making that decision. Our lives are just that."

He dips his head to catch and hold my eyes with his.

"Ours." He frowns, pressing his lips together over a sigh. "You remember that *Sports Illustrated* party a couple years ago?"

"Yeah."

We hadn't spoken, but I remember that lightning strike of seeing Deck again after so long. How my palms went sweaty and my heart went haywire and my stomach went all fluttery. I had seen him from time to time over the years from a distance, but that night, he'd been so close. Closer than he had been for a long time, and as much as I made sure nobody knew, it affected me. *He* affected me.

"I wanted your fiancé out of the way." His voice is gruff, prompting me to pull back just enough to see his face. "And I didn't care that I was there with Tara. I didn't care that you were with him. I'd wanted you for years, since the first time I saw you, and I resented him touching you. Resented his ring on your finger. I resented him having you when I never got my chance."

He pauses, a deep swallow bobbing his Adam's apple.

"I thought about that when I heard he had died," Decker says. "I felt guilty for even wishing him out of the way."

"But you didn't . . ." I pause to sort my thoughts and find the right words. "You had nothing to feel guilty about. Your desire for me didn't kill Will. He did that."

"Exactly, Avery." He brushes my hair back from my face. "Exactly."

His words sink in and I try to put myself in that place where I'm absolved of guilt. I can't quite do it yet. I know he's right theoretically, but that night I found Will wasn't theoretical. It *happened* to me, and I haven't gone a day without seeing him that way. Without asking if he was there because of me.

"I can't imagine how much pain Will was in to do something like that," Decker continues. "I assume it's something he wrestled with at other points in his life."

"All through college." I pause, before sharing another thing I haven't even told Sadie yet. "His mother actually told me his first attempt was in high school, and then again in college. I had no idea."

I shake my head, overwhelmed with how much I missed. "How did I live with him, share my life with him, wear his ring, plan our future and not know he'd tried to take his own life? Twice?"

"How would you have known if he didn't tell you?" Decker asks. "We hide in the open. We cover our scars so we can move on. Sometimes we hide because we're ashamed. Because we're afraid people won't accept us or love us or understand. No matter the reason, you didn't know. But even if you did, would you have stayed in a broken relationship for the rest of your life from fear that he would do something like this? These were demons he'd wrestled with before he even knew you, Avery. You can't take responsibility for his life, for his decision. You couldn't do it while he was alive, and you can't do it now that he's gone."

My therapist has said these things to me. I've replayed them to myself on days when I thought the guilt, the weight of his death would drive me mad. But there's a ring of truth when Decker says it that I haven't allowed myself to hear before. Maybe I thought I was letting myself off easy. In situations like this, you need someone to blame, and it feels wrong to blame Will. If I allow myself to place the responsibility with him for even a second, I become furious. I get livid with him for leaving me and his mother and his friends who care about him. Who love him and miss him and will live the rest of their lives asking the same questions I do.

Why?

How could you?

What didn't I do?

Could I have been enough to keep you here?

I want to throw things at the wall and I want to punch him in the face. More than anything, I want to rewind to an illuminating moment when I could have made a difference. I replay our years together over and over, watching from an objective distance, searching for that second when I could have looked in his eyes, seen how truly miserable he was with this life, and fixed it.

And maybe that's the problem. I've accomplished all my goals and created the destiny I envisioned for myself. A woman accomplishing what I have in sports and television is rare, much less a woman of color. I rose above expectations and limitations at every turn. I defied the odds. Every hurdle, I've jumped. Every problem, I've fixed. But I could never solve Will.

If you can't come through when it's life or death, when it counts, then what good are you?

I finally drift off to sleep in the rare comfort of someone else's arms and realize that is the question that's been haunting me. I may find no peace until I have an answer.

Chapter Twelve

DECKER

I'm making French toast when she enters the kitchen the next morning.

She's not exactly shy, but she has trouble meeting my eyes. I hope it's just morning-after awkwardness, not regret. Last night was the best sex of my life. One of the best nights of my life period, even though there were tears and pain and it was hard.

It was *her*.

It was my chance to unwind the labyrinth that has been Avery all these years. To understand her and get a glimpse of what's beneath all that control. It's beautiful. So beautiful that now I'm addicted to her honesty and her vulnerability and her boldness and her brand of brokenness. If last night was my only hit, she's a high I might chase the rest of my life.

"Morning." I glance up from the toast sizzling in the pan.

"Morning." She toys with the belt of my silk robe she's wearing. The hem trails the floor behind her because there's more material than her much shorter body knows what to do with. It still looks really good on her, gaping in front, hinting at two high, perfectly round breasts and copper-toned skin stretched over a taut plane of feminine muscle in her stomach. Her hair, tousled around her shoulders, rests dark against the maroon-colored silk. She runs a self-conscious hand over the tangled strands, combing her fingers through and pushing them behind her ear.

"You look beautiful," I reassure her.

Her fingers freeze in the process of setting her hair to whatever rights she's attempting. She climbs up onto the high stool, leaning her elbows on the counter.

"Breakfast?" she asks unnecessarily.

I turn the toast with a laugh. "Looks that way."

She grimaces over my answer before surrendering a grateful smile when I pass her a cup of coffee.

"Sorry it's not your cold brew."

"It's fine." She takes a long sip. "Oh, God. Thank you."

She clears her throat, shifting a little uneasily on the stool.

"And thanks for the ibuprofen you left." She rims the lip of the mug with her finger, not looking up. "That was very thoughtful."

"You had a good bit to drink last night." I turn off the toast and start scrambling eggs in a second pan. "Thought you might be a little hungover."

A wicked smile starts in her eyes and then creeps its way to her lips.

"It's not my head that's sore."

I pause in the preparations, processing what she is saying. My laugh bounces off the kitchen walls and I walk over to her, notching my hips between her knees. My hands stroke her back through the silk. She's soft and warm and smells fresh.

"You showered?" I whisper kisses behind her ear.

"Yeah." Her answer is breathy. "Hope that's okay."

"I only hate that I missed it," I rasp at the fragrant, silky skin of her neck where my teeth marked her. "Sorry about this."

"My neck isn't sore either." She laughs, a liberated sound I want her to keep making.

"Oh." My hand wanders over her nipple and it beads under the silk. "Here?"

The slightest hitch of her breath is the only indication she's feeling this.

"No, not there."

"Hmmm." I pucker my eyebrows into a frown. "I'm running out of options."

I step deeper into the vee of her thighs until the robe splits and falls away, baring the toned length of her legs.

"Maybe it's here." I run one exploring finger from her calf, over her knee and inside her thigh, just shy of her pussy.

"You are getting so close," she says, eyes not leaving my face.

I slide a finger along either side of her clit, trapping it between the digits and then stroking it with my thumb.

"Shit," she mutters, her hips moving in the rhythm my fingers set. "That's it. Right there. Not a hangover. A fuckover."

I chuckle and stop my fingers, move my hand away.

"Oh, I'm sorry. If you're sore, maybe I shouldn't—"

"You should," she cuts in, returning my hand to her center. "Believe me you should."

And while our breakfast gets cold, I do.

STRETCHED out naked on my pillows, Avery licks sticky vestiges of syrup from her fingers, an empty plate in her lap and a sheet haphazardly covering her.

"That was good," she says, purring like a contented cat.

"Breakfast or . . ." I let my words trail off and I glance at the well-used bed where she writhed under me not too long ago.

"Both. Breakfast. Last night. This morning. All of it." She bites into the grin that graces her kiss-swollen lips until it fades with the careful look she angles up at me. "Thank you for everything. It was perfect."

We spent last night together, and half of today since breakfast became brunch the more we kissed and touched. And fucked.

Man, did we fuck.

And after just a day having her, it has been more intimate and more perfect than anything I experienced in years of marriage to Tara.

So the finality in Avery's voice wears on my nerves.

"You sound really grateful." I leave the bed, pulling on a pair of gray sweats from the floor and tying them at the waist. "What? You gonna send me a fruit basket or some shit?"

I meet her eyes head on, silently challenging her to tell me she regrets last night, this morning. That we won't pursue more. That it . . . *that we* . . .won't happen again.

"Decker," she starts softly, staring at her fingers toying with the sheets bunched at her waist. "We talked about this, about—"

"That was before," I butt in. "Before everything happened. Before we made love and we talked and we . . ."

I claw frustrated fingers through my hair. "Dammit, Ave, that was before and you know it."

"Nothing's changed." She scoots up to sit straighter against the headboard, gathering the sheet around her like forgotten armor. "I'm still as emotionally unavailable as I was at that party last night."

"Liar." The one word blasts into the chilling air separating us. "You were more available to me last night than any woman I've ever been with."

"I'm not talking about sexually, Deck."

"Neither the hell am I, Avery."

We glare at one another, our breath coming quicker with our mutual frustration. It's not totally unexpected, her withdrawal, but I thought I would have a little more time to convince her that we should try.

"I'm moving to California," I say abruptly. Her eyes widen before she catches the reaction and controls it.

"Oh, I thought . . ." She stops the nervous tugging of the sheets. "Oh."

"I told you my ex moved there. She keeps making it harder for me to see Kiera." I sigh wearily and scrub a hand over my face. "She's just pissed because she didn't get more out of the divorce."

"They say it's cheaper to keep her," Avery says with a cynical twist of her lips.

"Then 'they' don't have my lawyer or my pre-nup." We share a smile that comes a little easier to us both. "At the last minute, she pulled some crap so I have to go to LA to see my baby girl for Christmas, when she was supposed to come here for two weeks."

"I'm sorry, Deck."

"Yeah. So am I. It'll just be simpler for me to live out there." I hesitate for a moment before sitting on the edge of the bed, within touching distance if she decides to touch me. "I've been offered a front office position with that new expansion team the San Diego Waves. President of Basketball Operations, with the possibility of partial ownership eventually."

Ever the journalist, curiosity and questions stack up in Avery's wide eyes.

"And we *are* off the record, by the way," I remind her. "This isn't public yet."

"All right, all right. I get it." She pulls her legs up to her chest, resting her chin on sheet-covered knees. "Congratulations."

"Thanks. It works for me personally, so I can be closer to my daughter, and professionally because it's the kind of opportunity I've wanted, but didn't think I'd get for at least another five years."

"That's great, Deck." Her face has become the mask she showed me when we first started hosting her show together three weeks ago. "I'm happy for you."

"I don't want you to be happy for me, Avery. I want you to tell me that what we had the last twenty-four hours is enough to build on. That when I go away, we can try to build more."

"You saw me last night." Her mouth is the only thing wavering in her obstinate expression. "You know I'm a mess."

"We're all a mess." I scoot closer, palm her jaw and press my forehead to hers. "We'll figure it out."

She shakes her head against mine, not breaking the contact between our skin.

"There are some things I need to figure out on my own. Questions not just about Will, but about myself that I need to answer." She mirrors my touch, her hand cupping my jaw. "As much as I enjoyed last night, as much as I . . ."

She swallows, shutting her eyes.

"Deck, deep down you know I'm not ready."

I glance up to find her cheeks wet again, tears leaking from under her closed eyelids. I want to deny it. As much as I want to convince her that she is ready; that I'll make her ready, or be ready enough for both of us, I know it doesn't work that way. I still hear her sobs and feel her shaking in my arms, recounting the horror of finding Will in their apartment. I still hear her agony over his last words to her.

"Okay. I accept that you're not ready. I have to go to California, and I know you have to stay here in New York."

I dip my head to kiss her, coaxing her lips open for a languorous dueling of tongues that quickly ignites fire in me. In Avery, too, if her nails digging into my back are any indication.

I give her hair a gentle tug until she's looking directly into my eyes.

"The time may not be right, but we *feel* right, Ave. Tell me you see how right we feel together."

Her nod is the only answer she offers, sniffing at the fresh tears I know aren't all for Will. Aren't all for her. I know that some of them are for me. I bend to kiss her cheeks, darting my tongue out to gather the salt of her tears.

"Hey, look at me." I gently angle her face up so we have no choice but to see one another. "Promise me that when you have the answers you're looking for, that when you're ready, you'll find me."

She leans deeper into me, uncaring that the sheet drops, baring her stubble-burned breasts. She takes my mouth in a kiss that is part consolation, part declaration. She eases away, licking her lips like she can taste me there.

"That's a promise I plan to keep."

Chapter Thirteen

AVERY

"Are you sure about this, Avery?"

I ease into my cashmere coat and turn to face my mother.

"Yes, definitely." I pull my hair free of the collar. "Mrs. Hattfield only lives fifteen minutes away. I'll be back in time for dinner. Promise."

"It's not getting back I'm concerned about." My own brown eyes stare back at me from my mother's face, inlaid with concern.

"I know you lost Will, and he was your future. You loved him," Mom says. "But Will was her son. It may not feel like it now, but you'll find someone else. Marry. Have a family. You will move on. She only had one son. The pain of losing a child, you can't imagine it."

I finish tying the belt of my coat with slowed hands and a rapid heartbeat. Will wasn't my future. I wasn't in love with him, and it's a different man I already can't get out of my mind. The one who kissed my tears and rocked my world just days ago. I felt lighter after telling Deck the truth, and right now I want to tell someone else.

"Mom, there's something I haven't told you." A self-deprecating laugh escapes me. "Hadn't told anyone really until a few days ago."

I get my nose for news from my mother. A journalism professor at Georgetown, it kind of broke her heart when I chose to attend Howard. She may have chosen the classroom, and I chose the field, but she still has the inquisitive mind of a journalist, and the questions gather in her eyes and between her brows as a frown.

"Okay." She leans against the stairway bannister in our foyer. "What is it?"

Considering how closely I've guarded this secret, you'd think I'd reveal it with some ceremony. Not on my way out the door with the car already running and warming up.

"Will and I, well . . ." I drop my gaze to the hardwood floor and tug at the fingertips of my leather gloves. "We weren't happy at the end."

I glance up after a few moments of quiet. It's not a stunned silence. It's a knowing one. My mother doesn't look surprised, merely curious, waiting for more.

"I suspected as much," she finally says. "I could tell as soon as I met him that Will was a sad man, but you made him happy. As happy as one person can make another, but ultimately our happiness doesn't hang on other people. We have to first be happy with ourselves, and I don't know that Will ever was."

Now *I'm* stunned. We haven't talked much about Will's suicide. Mom knows I found him in our apartment, but not much else.

"I was getting my things from the apartment because I'd broken off our engagement." The soft admission reverberates through the foyer. "I had agreed to wait to tell everyone. He wanted that, for us to be sure, but I was sure."

Rarely have I seen my mother truly off kilter, but I do now. Her mouth forms a little O of astonishment, before she covers it with her hand. She crosses the few feet from the stairs to reach me.

"Oh, baby." She takes my face between her hands. "I had no idea. You've been blaming yourself, haven't you?"

"Mama, he left a note." I lean into the soft comfort of her hand. "For me. It was just to me, and I never told anyone. I kept it. I didn't show the police or . . ."

A sob breaks free from my chest, and tears leak into her palm.

"What did I do?" I moan. "Did I . . . should I . . . I don't . . ."

"Shhhh." She pulls me close, the Chanel perfume she's worn for decades a reassurance that breaks whatever tendrils of control I have. My tears pour out, an unrelenting, inconvenient storm. "It's okay, baby. Let it out."

She rocks me in an ancient maternal rhythm that no one teaches; the same one she used when I fell and scraped my knee. When I experienced my first heartbreak. When I buried Will a year ago. After a few moments, she pulls away, hands on my arms so she can look into my face. I sniff and pass my coat sleeve self-consciously under my runny nose.

"No, honey. That's not how it works." She gives a sad shake of her head. "Will was obviously a troubled man, and I know it feels like cause and effect. Like you broke it off and he ended his life. We experience life, all of us, in the bad and the good times and the good people and the ones who hurt us. Everyone does. There are some people life is just harder for than others. Will was one of those, but you told me before how he struggled and didn't always take his medication."

"I don't want to make this about how he failed as a person. I don't want to blame him," I rush to say. "I'm not trying to ease my guilt."

"Well I am." My mother's eyebrows elevate. "Because you have nothing to feel guilty about. Will hurt in a way that we will probably never understand, and for that there is no one to blame. But there's a difference between blame and responsibility. We are each responsible for ourselves. And what Will did, he was responsible for."

That's a distinction I've tried to make to myself more than once, but I always seem to come back to my part in it, and anything I could have done differently. I nod, leaning forward to kiss her cheek before fastening the buttons left undone on my coat.

"I hear you, Mama." I walk to the door and give her one last look over my shoulder. "I'll be back."

"Hey, you aren't planning to tell Mrs. Hattfield that, are you?"

Was I? On some level, I feel like I need to get it off my chest; like I owe her an explanation.

"You told me," my mother says, gripping my hand. "I'm glad you did, because I think you needed that, but that situation is already complicated enough for her. Knowing you and Will broke up only makes it more complicated. May just make it harder, and right now she feels you are the only one in the world close to understanding her pain."

I think of our conversations over the last year. Not many, but each one, a release, a relief for us both.

"Don't take that away from her with information that makes no difference," Mama says. "That does no good. It might make you feel better, but it does nothing for her, and she's your first concern now. That note was to you and you alone. Private. I just want her to be able to move on and accept your comfort. It wasn't your fault. She'll know that, but knowing this would only raise more questions, and she already has enough of those."

I'm playing Mama's words in my head when I pull up to Mrs. Hattfield's. I park my father's Tahoe in the driveway, noting the dying rose bush in front of the house. The grass is longer than the last time I was here, even though it's winter. Her house, always neat and perfectly kept, appears slightly disheveled. I ring the doorbell, waiting. When there is no answer after a few moments, I walk over to the garage, peering in and finding the Cadillac Will used to tease his mother about.

"Are you a pimp, Ma?" he'd ask laughingly. "Rolling around in your Cadillac."

I mouth the words, smiling at the image of Will seated in the living room just beyond the doors of this house. One year we helped Mrs. Hattfield trim her tree. Will roasted marshmallows in the fireplace. His mother and I had hot chocolate, and Will had cider. My life with him rushes back to me in vivid detail; the colors, the scents, the touches, the laughs, the tears, the good and the bad. All of it inundates my mind and blurs my vision.

And I miss him.

Not all the hurt we caused each other at the end. I miss the boy I met at a public library, who crushed on me for years without letting me know. Who took me trick or treating with his twelve-year-old cousin for our first date. I laughed with my friends about it, but we all thought it was sweet.

"God, Will." I shake my head, blinking at the tears freezing before they fall. I turn to leave, my steps dragging toward Dad's SUV.

"Avery?"

I turn at the sound of my name, and Mrs. Hattfield stands at the front door, her chin wobbling and her face already streaked with tears. I run, avoiding little patches of ice, needing to get to her. As soon as I'm close, her arms stretch out and she pulls me into her. Her sobs vibrate into my chest.

"I miss him." Mrs. Hattfield weeps unashamedly, her head buried in the collar of my coat. "God, I miss him so much."

"I know," I whisper, my pain communing with hers. "So do I."

And it doesn't matter if I was wearing his ring. If we were lovers or friends at the end. If he cheated or how we injured each other. All that matters is that I loved him, and so did she. That besides the woman I'm holding, I was closer to him than anyone else on the planet. She and I knew his strengths and his weaknesses like no one else ever did, and can console one another uniquely.

We stand like that for I'm not sure how long. Long enough for the winter cold to bite through my gloves and whip beneath my coat. I pull back and look through the open front door. It's dark in there. No sign of life. No savory smells of food cooking or the pine scent of a live Christmas tree.

"Get your coat, Mrs. H," I command gently. "You're coming home with me."

I didn't get to tell my mom I was bringing someone home for Christmas dinner, but when I arrive, Mrs. Hattfield in tow, she doesn't look surprised and already has an extra plate at the table.

"How'd you know?" I ask her quietly while we set out side dishes.

"I know you." She smiles, pride in her eyes that has nothing to do with anything I've achieved or a goal I've crushed. She's proud of me for who I am, not for what I've done. Mrs. Hattfield and I share a tearful smile at dinner before we say grace. Still sorting through the tangle of guilt and shame and pain and fury, I hope one day soon I'll know me, too.

Chapter Fourteen

DECKER

"Who's next?" Seated on the couch of the San Diego hotel suite, I stretch my arms above my head.

"It's the last of the day." My assistant Marla looks up from my schedule on her iPad.

"Thank God for that." I crook a grin at her. "Is it too early to start drinking?"

"You drinking?" she scoffs. "What? One of your protein shakes?"

"That *would* be nice." My smile beseeches. "Could you?"

She rolls her eyes, but her smile is good-natured and longsuffering, two things anyone working with me needs to be.

"Let me get you set up for this last interview," she says. "And I'll run up the street to grab one."

"From that place I like, right?" I push my luck.

"Yes, from the place you like." She shakes her head and swipes across the iPad screen. "Gimme a sec and I'll brief you on this last one."

I've lost count of how many reporters I've talked to today for the San Diego Waves' media blitz. I, along with other front office executives, have made ourselves available to the press for questions about the new NBA expansion team, our draft prospects, and the upcoming first season. My canned responses have started losing their shine. The more tired I get, the more I feel like the jock still wet from the shower, no compunction giving half-naked interviews, and less like the guy in the suit scoping talent and making multimillion-dollar decisions. Thank God this is the last of the day.

"It's your old network," Marla says with a smile. "SportsCo."

I stare at her, my heart banging against my rib cage. I'm holding my breath like some lovesick chick waiting to hear Avery's name. She texted me congratulations when my position was announced, but didn't really engage much beyond that, even when I tired. Not that I've tried much. She asked for space, and I've given it to her. Though I'm not sure how much longer I can hold out. We only worked in close proximity for three weeks, and we only had one night, but I miss everything about her. I lick my lips before I ask the next question.

"Oh yeah? And uh . . . who'd they send for the interview?"

"Huh? Oh. Lemme see." Marla trails her finger down the screen until she reaches the bottom. "Mike Dunlov is the reporter from SportsCo. Ring a bell?"

"Sheesh." I suck my teeth. "A bell? No, more like a gong. I can't stand that guy."

Disappointment settles on my shoulders, but I square them, refusing to droop. When she's ready she'll come. Avery's too strong-willed for me to force the issue. We had our night. She knows how good we are together. She needs time to heal, and I'm giving it to her. That's the thing with a full-court press. You have to know when to apply it, and when to let up, or it's useless.

When there's a faint knock at the suite door, Marla disappears from the sitting room to answer. I look up, grinning at Jerry, the cameraman who danced with Sadie that night.

"How you doing?" I stand and wait for him to shift enough of his equipment to shake my hand.

"Good, Deck," Jerry replies with a smile. "Congratulations on all of this."

"Thanks, man. I . . ."

The words disintegrate from my lips and from my mind when Avery, not Mike Dunlov, walks into the sitting room with Marla. She looks beautiful as usual, but her hair is different. It's curly, the way I told her I like it. The way it was the day we met in the locker room. She gives me her professional smile, but there's a glint in her eyes that says she knows what I look like under this suit. We are intimately acquainted, and the closer she gets, the thicker the air becomes with our knowledge of each other. Unspoken, the memory of our moans, our rough fucking, our tenderness charges the air, and even though we're having a silent conversation, it becomes obvious that Marla and Jerry sense something.

"Uh . . ." Jerry's eyes move between Avery and me staring at each another. "Where should I set up the camera and lighting kit?"

His question jars Avery, setting her into motion. She assesses the room and directs Jerry. She doesn't look at me again until everything is set up and we're ready to begin. We maintain a friendly formality, just starched enough to be professional, but with the ease of former colleagues. I answer her questions patiently, forcing myself not to stare at her breasts, or the way her waist cinches, or the length of her legs. I don't stare at those things, but I know they're there. I remember what she looks like and I'm hard as a motherfucker by the end of the interview. To avoid the awkwardness of my hard-on, I stay seated when we're done and Jerry walks over to shake my hand.

"Good to see you again, Deck." He glances at Avery. "You ready?"

She better not go with him. I've been good, controlled myself and given her this interview, even gave her a scoop on things I told no one else. If she tries to leave this room, I'm tying her to the bed.

"Uh, actually . . ." She glances at me, a knowing grin spreading her full lips. "You go on ahead. We're done for the day. I'm gonna catch up with Deck for a little bit."

Or all night long.

Once the door closes behind Jerry, I just stare at her for a few moments, and she stares back at me. It's not awkward. It's anticipation, like we're not sure where to start first, but I just want to begin.

"I like your hair like that," I finally say.

"I know." She tugs at one springy dark curl. "I wore it like this for you."

"For me?" I lean back deeper into the couch, relaxing my legs so she can see the hard-on I worked so hard to hide from Jerry. Her dark eyes go hot, glancing from my lap to my lips. She takes a step in my direction.

"Stop." I release the word as a command. "There's something you should know before you come any closer."

She links her hands behind her back, pushing her breasts up a little in the silk top she paired with fitted slacks.

"What should I know?" She cocks one brow, waiting.

"Don't come if you're not ready." As much as I want her, as much as I've missed her, I mean every word. "If you're not ready to be with me, to *really* be with me, then don't come because I'm not used to settling, and I'm not starting with you."

She blinks rapidly over the surprise in her eyes, and takes one step in my direction.

"Anything else?" she asks. "Before I come to you?"

"Yeah, I'm not letting you go." I haul my hand through my hair, freshly cut for today's dancing bear media blitz. "Shit, Ave. I've been in relationships before. I've been married before, but I've never . . ."

I'm about to sound like a chick. I know it, but I can't stop the words.

"I've never felt like this about anyone else, and I'm not giving you up once I have you. You better get used to that."

Another step, and now she's close enough for me to see tears brightening her dark eyes.

"Is that all?" she asks, her voice rich with emotion.

I nod tersely, not sure she's taking me seriously, but wanting to touch her too much to press the issue. Taking the last few steps and stopping at my knees, she nods to my lap.

"May I?" she asks.

I scoot down another inch, making room for her body to settle over mine. She scoots up until her knees rest on either side of me. She leans forward, pressing her breasts into my chest and her elbows on my shoulder.

"Now let me tell you some things that you should know." She brushes a finger over my lips. "You should know that I have missed you every day we've been apart."

I try to ignore what her scent and her warmth and the force of who she is does to me; how holding her is the best thing I've felt since I left New York at Christmas.

"Have you really?" I ask, my tone casual, my heartbeat anything but.

She leans down until her lips hover over mine.

"I did," she breathes over me before going on. "You should also know that I've done a lot of thinking. My relationship with Will taught me a lot. I don't want another relationship . . ."

She doesn't want another relationship? Pain stabs me like a physical cut. Am I willing to be her fuck buddy? The itch she scratches whenever she needs it too badly to ignore?

No, the hell I am not.

"If this is just some elaborate bicoastal booty call," I say, starting to sit up and pushing her away from me, "Then you can just—"

"Shut up, Deck." She pushes my chest so that I fall back onto the sofa. "And let me finish."

I make my eyes flinty for our stare off so she won't know she just hurt me more than any woman ever has.

"As I was saying before I was so rudely interrupted." She pauses to lift one brow. "I don't want another relationship *like I had with Will.*"

Her eyes soften, the brown darkening with emotion.

"I want a relationship where I don't hide and neither do you," she says. "Where we trust each other even with the hard things; the things that break our hearts and cause us pain."

"Avery—"

"Where I never have to worry about you cheating on me and you never have to worry about me cheating on you," she continues over me. "Where even if we're three thousand miles apart, we're as close as two people can be."

Hope climbs up my chest. After all these months apart, I was afraid to let myself hope, but she's here and she's ready, and I can't keep my hands off her even for another second. I grab handfuls of her ass and press her down onto me.

"That all sounds doable." We both pant at the first grind of her body into mine.

"'Doable?" she asks breathlessly. "I'm risking a lot here. I'm gonna need something more definitive."

"Really?" My hand moves between us until I can get down her pants, past the barrier of her underwear. She's wet and slick under my stroking fingers. Her hips rock into me, and her head drops back. With my free hand, I loosen the buttons on her blouse. It falls back to reveal a flesh-colored bra of such thin lace I clearly see her nipples.

"I love how big your nipples are." I suck them through the lace, my mouth an eager suction. She moans and slides urgently over me, seeking friction.

"Dammit, Avery, don't make me fuck you like this," I mutter, eyes clenched closed. "I wanted there to be flowers and candles and all kinds of romantic shit when we did this again."

"Fuck flowers." She deals with my belt and slides my pants down, barely waiting for me to lift my hips to help her. "There will be plenty of time for that. Right now, I need you."

She pauses, swallows, her eyes filled with passion, affection and . . . more. I'm afraid to name it, but there is more there.

"I need you," she says again.

"I'm right here, baby." I help slide her pants and panties down, not even all the way off, but gathered at her knees.

She takes me in hand and pushes down, her walls clinging to me.

"Oh, God." Her head drops back as she rises and falls over me. "Yes."

I slide the cups of her bra over her breasts urging her forward for my bites and licks.

"Shit," I mumble against the silky skin. "Avery, It's been a long time. Slow down or this'll be over before it starts.

She pauses, looking down at me smugly. "Exactly how long are we talking?"

"If you're asking if I've been with anyone since Christmas, since you." I thrust up, hard and sure. "The answer is no."

I grip her hip, commandeering the pace from beneath her.

"And if you've been letting anybody else in this pussy," I say with grave seriousness. "It's better you don't tell me because that motherfucker might end up dead."

Her husky laugh breathes over my lips.

"No other motherfucker's been in here."

"Shit." I grimace my frustration. "Why can't I remember a condom with you?"

"It's okay." She leans her forehead into mine. "I'm clean and safe."

I get to fuck Avery raw? I might shed a tear before this is all over.

"Yeah." I nod quickly before she changes her mind. "Clean."

A salacious smile curls her lips. "Then let's go."

She resumes the ride, her face twisting with the effort, with the grind. We fuck until the clothes we didn't bother shedding are wet and clinging to us. We kick off the last of our clothes. I flip her onto her back, and I'm fucking her so hard the couch is scooting with the vigor of it. Just inches scraping across the floor, but the sound of it turns me on even more.

She anchors her feet at the small of my back.

"Shit, shit, shit," she chants, eyes rolling back. "Harder, Deck."

"Fuck, baby," I mutter. If I go any harder, I'll break her, but I take her word for it and as soon as I thrust harder, go deeper, her screams pierce the luxurious quiet of the suite. And I'm not far behind, falling over a cliff into the hottest, wildest, longest orgasm of my life.

We lie there on the couch, hot and sweating and panting, laughing between kisses until our stomachs growl. Who would have thought that first night in the locker room all those years ago, that we'd end up like this? Feeding each other from room service trays, bathing together, making love, making plans, making promises. Sharing hurts, shedding tears, and loving. Yeah, the words aren't said, but it's there, and we have all the time in the world. For me, there's no doubt it's there. We've both had suffering mixed in with love. We've loved and lost and were never satisfied. But I'm satisfied with her, and I see in her eyes that she's satisfied with me. We both have pasts and we've both had pain, but what we've never had was each other.

But now we do. Thank God, now we do.

TBR Alert!!

Full-Length Basketball Romance * March 2018
LONG SHOT (A Standalone Hoops Story)

Add on Goodreads: http://bit.ly/

Release Alert!

Be notified by email once LONG SHOT is available: http://bit.ly/GRIPAlerts

Meet August West, NBA all-star, and Iris DuPree, the Louisiana girl who knocks him off his game.

"She's a gorgeous risk, but I like my odds."

LONG SHOT is a deeply emotional full-length romance set in the exciting world of professional basketball. This evocative story will make you FEEL and THINK. It's an unexpected journey that takes sports romance out of bounds!

Books By Kennedy Ryan

THE SOUL SERIES (Rhyson + Kai) – FREE in KU!

My Soul to Keep (Soul 1)

Down to My Soul (Soul 2)

Refrain (Soul 3)

Soul Series Audiobooks

GRIP Series (Grip & Bristol) - FREE in KU

Get FLOW (**FREE**)
E-Book: amzn.to/2xyGtNo
Audio Book: bit.ly/FLOWAudiobook

Get GRIP:
E-Book: amzn.to/2wJN6ib
Audio Book: bit.ly/GRIPAudiobook

Get STILL
E-Book: http://amzn.to/2kAjijx

The Bennett Series

WHEN YOU ARE MINE (BENNETT 1)

Loving You Always (Bennett 2)
Be Mine Forever (Bennett 3)
Until I'm Yours (Bennett 4)

Order Kennedy's Signed Paperbacks

Connect With Kennedy!

MAILING LIST

Never miss sales, new releases, and get a free book every month!

Follow on Bookbub
Follow on Amazon
Reader Group
Book+Main
Facebook
Instagram
Twitter

About the Author

Kennedy Ryan is a Southern girl gone Southern California. A Top 100 Amazon Bestseller, Kennedy writes romance about remarkable women who thrive even in tough times, the love they find, and the men who cherish them.

She is a wife to her lifetime lover and mother to an extraordinary son. She has always leveraged her journalism background to write for charity and non-profit organizations, but enjoys writing to raise Autism awareness most. A contributor for *Modern Mom Magazine*, Kennedy's writings have appeared in *Chicken Soup for the Soul*, *USA Today* and many others. The founder and executive director of a foundation serving Georgia families living with Autism, she has appeared on *Headline News*, *Montel Williams*, *NPR* and other media outlets as a voice for families living with autism.

SWITCH HITTER

I knew something was wrong the second she walked in the door tonight; I just couldn't put my finger on what it was.

Same hair color.
Same legs.
Same face.

Except...I look harder.
At the small dimple beneath her lip that wasn't there the last time we went out.
And her laugh—that laugh isn't as loud.

This isn't the girl I've gone out with the past few weeks.
It's her twin sister, and they've switched places on me.

Only I'm not quite ready to let them switch back.

Chapter One

AMELIA

"I NEED YOU TO PRETEND TO BE ME NEXT WEEKEND."

I stop eating, fork poised above my plate. "Why?"

"I have two dates on the same night—oops." My twin sister says it in a *duh* tone of voice, like it should have been obvious.

"No."

"Please? Come on! It'll be fun."

"No." I ignore the whining tone in her voice, the one that rises a few decibels every time she speaks. "Pretending to be someone else isn't fun for me—it's stressful."

"You're no fun."

I laugh. "Exactly my point. If I had to spend an entire night faking it, I would pass out from exhaustion."

"Maybe, but Dash is so hot, you won't even care."

"Is that supposed to be a selling point? This guy you're dating is hot?" I shove lettuce in my mouth and chew. Swallow. "Lucy, we look *nothing* alike."

Okay, so that's not *exactly* true. We're almost identical, I just hate admitting it.

"He doesn't know I'm a twin. Trust me, he won't notice."

This gives me pause. "How does he not know you're a twin?"

"I mean, it's not like we sit and *talk* about you," she quips.

"Right, but don't you tell him about yourself? Normally you love to talk, and the twin thing is kind of a fun fact." And a huge part of *who you are as a human being*, I want to add, but instead, I clamp my lips shut.

"Of course I tell him about myself. I tell him my favorite foods so if he ever decides to take me to dinner he'll know what I like, and I tell him my favorite movies so he's prepared in the event that we go to one. I also show him my best side when I'm taking selfies."

How are we related?

She twirls her hair. "But we've only gone out like, twice—I don't count seeing him at house parties and stuff. He's kind of annoying though, always trying to have deep, meaningful discussions."

My face contorts. "Why would you have a problem with that?"

"Oh my God, Amelia, it's not like we can have a serious talk in the middle of a party."

"What did you say his name was?"

"Dash Amado."

I chuckle into my espresso. "Luce, I hate sounding like an ass, but how deep a discussion could a guy named *Dash* possibly want to have?"

"That's kind of a bitchy thing to say. You don't even know him." She blows out a puff of air. "Besides, I don't think that's his real name."

I slurp my water to annoy her.

It works.

"How about you try harder to get to know him?"

"I'm trying, but you won't help me!"

"Far be it from me to judge, but methinks you're not trying hard *enough*. Stop trying to make me your stand-in."

"For the tenth time, he won't even know it's you."

"I am *not* going on this date for you! It was cute trading places in high school, but it's not cute now." Not to mention, it's immature.

"You used to think it was fun."

"Remember the time we both ran for student council? It was exhausting and embarrassing and the whole mess was completely your fault."

"What are you even talking about? The whole thing was not a mess—everything turned out great! We both got elected."

When we were freshmen in high school, Lucy and I were both running for class officer—president for her, vice president for me. The election speeches were during an assembly during the school day, but rather than showing up, Lucy spent the entire period making out with some football player in a supply closet they'd found unlocked en route to the gymnasium.

In a panic—because I was always so freaking *responsible*—I tried covering for her. Pulled a speech out of my ass, gave it in front of the entire student body, then borrowed a shirt from our friend Clarissa, changed, came back as me to give a speech for myself.

It was exhausting, and the entire time, she was shut in a closet kissing some boy.

My sister gives me a dull look over the rim of her glass, waving her hand in the air dismissively.

"Amelia, that happened five years ago, or whatever the math is. Why do you keep bringing it up? We were in high school."

"I keep bringing it up because I was terrified we were going to get caught! Just like I am now!"

"You're so dramatic. We both won, so I don't know what your problem is."

"The problem is, you're always doing this. Remember that time I dressed up as you to meet Kevin Richards at the movies so you could go do *God knows what* with Dusty Sanders? The entire movie Kevin kept trying to put his hand on my thigh because you'd let him get to third base the night before."

"And you whacked him in the balls," she deadpans dryly. "Yeah, who could forget that?"

"Whatever," I mumble. "He had it coming."

"Can we focus on Dash here, please?"

"We are twenty-one years old—don't you think we're a little old to be pulling tricks on people?"

"Um, no? There's a *reason* God gave us the same face."

That makes me laugh. "You're ridiculous."

"But you love me, don't you?" She bats her sooty lashes. "You're totally going to help me out—I can tell by the look on your face."

"What look?" I pretend I don't know what she's talking about. "I have a look?"

My sister claps her hands, excited. "Yes, you totally do, and you're totally doing this for me!" She lifts her brows and quirks the corner of her mouth into a cocky grin that mirrors the one I have on my face right now.

Shit. She's right.

My twin leans in, hands folded on the table like she's just entered negotiations in a business meeting.

"What's it going to take for you to help me out?"

I mimic her pose. "I don't know, Lucy. You tell me—what's my time worth to you?"

She stares for a few long moments, lost in thought, trying to measure my sincerity through narrowed eyes. She's trying to gauge if I'm being flippant or sincere about helping her. The thing about my sister is that everything always come so easy for her. She's beautiful and relies heavily on her looks, uses them to her advantage. She's outgoing and uses that, too.

Not that I'm not—I'm all of those things, but I'm not a *user*.

My sister is.

She doesn't do it on purpose; she just...wants what she wants, when she wants it.

Lucy isn't mean or malicious, goodness no, nor has she ever stood in the way of me being happy. She's never pulled any deviant twin crap or made me feel bad about our differences.

She's just...Lucy.

When I continue eating my salad and ignoring her hard stares, she sighs loudly, resigned. Pushes a carrot around its plastic container and sighs again.

Drama is my twin sister's middle name.

Her hair is too big, her lips are too red, and her personality is too wild.

Around campus, in certain circles, we're called the Barbie twins. It's not because we have blonde hair—which we don't—but because of Lucy's bombshell appearance. We're tall and slender with thick, wavy hair. My sister has hers shorter by a few inches, layered around her face, and it's a rich chestnut color. Mine is longer and darker.

"What's your time worth to me? I'll buy you an extra gift at Christmas—"

"Which Mom and Dad will pay for."

She sighs at me a third time, this one ending with a little drawn-out groan.

I throw her a bone, rolling my eyes. "So what's up with this guy—what does a *Dash* person do?"

This opening perks her up considerably, and she immediately sits up in her seat, enthusiastic. "He's on the baseball team—the *catcher*."

"The catcher, ooh la la! Exciting." I'm such a sarcastic jerk sometimes. "And why are you saying the word catcher like that, all whispery?" My head gives a shake. "Am I supposed to be impressed?"

I bet he's the captain or something cliché. Lucy only dates the most handsome, popular guys she can sink her long, manicured claws into. These days, those claws are painted hot pink, and when she's impatient, she taps them on the laminate tabletop to irritate me—like she's doing now.

"Let me guess"—I smirk—"they call him Dash because he's soooo so super fast."

Her smile fades. "You're a smartass, do you know that? But also, you're correct."

"What else does he do quickly?" I joke.

"I don't know." She chomps down on her vegetables. "We've only made out once, but I'm hoping to find out soon. He's giving me blue balls."

"What do you mean you've only made out once? He's a flipping *baseball* player. Forgive me for sounding confused or for buying into stereotypes, but aren't most athletes major horn dogs?"

"Dash isn't like all those guys, Amelia. He's a gentleman, and honestly, it's kind of getting annoying."

I thought the point of her dating these guys was to be seen with them, not to form emotional attachments and actually spend quality time with them.

"It's just frustrating. I'm trying to change his mind about the whole not sleeping with me yet bullshit. He's all weird because we're not committed, doesn't want to get any girls pregnant or whatever."

My brows shoot up, straight into my hairline. "What the hell does *that* mean?"

"It means he doesn't want to risk sleeping with any gold diggers who might trap him. You'd be surprised by all the baby mama drama surrounding athletes."

I stare, shocked. No, I did not know that happened. "He told you that?"

"Yeah, when he was drunk once at a party." She stops chewing, shaking a limp carrot stick in my direction. "Why are you looking at me like that?"

"Have you ever dated a guy because you genuinely liked him, or do you just date them for their status?"

Her hesitation is a brief flicker. "Both?"

At least she's being honest.

I roll my eyes. They're a touch darker than hers, the left one with a fleck of amber in the corner. Our eyes are one of the few things that set us apart—a fact that she hates—and I also have a dimple in the corner of my lip.

"Name *one* guy you *really* liked."

She bites down on her bottom lip. It's pouty and pink. "This isn't a fair question, and why is it your business if I've never really liked anyone I've dated?"

"You're making it my business—hello, you want me to switch places with you and go on a date with some stranger." Who, quite frankly, I'm beginning to feel bad for. "If you liked him so much, you wouldn't be—"

"Dating someone else at the same time," we both say at the same time.

There is a hamburger on a plate in front of me getting cold, so I take a bite, chewing thoughtfully. "I didn't even know you were dating anyone, let alone *two* someones. In fact, I've never been introduced to any of your boyfriends since we've been in Iowa."

"It never gets to the point where we're serious," she counters. "And before you say anything, it's not my fault I get bored easily."

"Um, yeah, it kind of is." I'm talking with my mouth full. "Stop *using* guys and find one you *like*. Get to know one of them and maybe you won't get bored. Stop going out with athletes. Try dating someone with substance."

"Ew. That sounds like such a mind-numbing idea."

"Try it once, for me." I bat my lashes. "Pretty please."

"No. It's easy to sit here and judge me, isn't it?"

"What's that supposed to mean?"

"You've never dated a jock so you have no idea what you're missing. Oh my gawd, the orgasms—they are so worth the headache."

True, I have never dated a jock, but the orgasms I've had with other guys have been just fine, *thank you very much*, even if a bit ordinary.

"So will you do it?"

"What? No!" *Maybe.*

"Ugh, why are you like this?" my twin sister huffs, throwing her napkin on the table in a mini tantrum. "Help me! Please. You're the sweet one—maybe if you go out with him, he'll change his mind about me."

"Is that what this is about? Do you even have two dates on the same night?"

"Yes! I swear I have two dates next Friday night."

"Then how about you do the right thing and cancel one of them?"

Lucy glares across the table. "You're the worst freaking twin."

I laugh into my burger, taking a huge chunk off.

"We used to have so much fun, didn't we?" she tries again while my mouth is too occupied to argue.

I quickly chew and swallow. "Yes, it was fun—when we were *twelve*."

"Whatever, spoilsport."

I laugh. "Eat your lunch, I have class in ten minutes."

"For old time's sake? Please? Dash is harmless—really smart and level-headed. You'll love him." Her smile curves innocently.

For the first time tonight, I pause, considering it. Set down my food, fiddle with a napkin, not meeting her eyes. "I'm listening."

"He's taking me to a battle of the bands, which you know is something I *hate*, but you *love* that kind of thing. My other date, Hudson, is taking me clubbing, which you know I love. I'm wearing that new silver dress I bought for New Year's Eve."

Hudson—*what a dumb name.*

"What if you end up having a date with Hudson for New Year's and he's already seen you in the silver dress?"

I smirk at the sight of her crestfallen expression.

"Shit. I hadn't thought of that."

"Yeah, well..." I shrug through her scowl. "That's what you have me for."

"Look, I'll make it easy: I'll drop off the outfit I'd planned to wear, and you won't have to worry about any details. Just get dressed and he'll show up."

"Where?" I'll admit to being a teensy weensy bit curious about where this date she doesn't want to go on is happening.

"The bar district, to listen to some local band."

"What kind of band?"

"I don't know Amelia! Some garage band or whatever. I was only half listening."

"Hmm." That sounds kind of fun. "What time?"

"Eight on Friday."

"And you don't think he'd notice that I'm not you?"

"No way, not a chance. He's a guy." Lucy leans in again. "Does this mean you'll do it?"

"I don't want to, but..."

She gets up from the table, comes around to my side, and puts me in a struggle cuddle from behind. "Yes! You are the best! I owe you big time."

"I know you do."

She pokes a finger in my direction. "You can't tell Mom or Dad."

"Wouldn't dream of it." Pause. "I guess...have Dash pick me up on campus?"

"Can't you come to my house and have him pick you up there?"

"You're seriously going to push your luck? Have him pick me up on campus. I'll be in front of the field house."

"Amelia, he's going to think that's so weird."

"Ugh! Fine, fine. I'll be at your house at quarter to eight." I poke a finger back at her. "You better hope he's not early."

Chapter Two

AMELIA

He's early.

FIFTEEN MINUTES EARLY, to be exact, strolling up the sidewalk to my sister's house at the same exact time I am. My house is only a few short blocks away, so I hoofed it over, heels clicking on the cement below my feet.

AS IF THIS evening wasn't already extremely awkward for me, I'm approaching Lucy's at a snail's pace when I see a guy I assume is Dash already on her doorstep, poised to knock.

I STOP SHORT, halting on the pavement to watch him, the dark shrouding me as I hover under a tall maple tree like a total creep, considering my options while teetering on these heels Lucy brought over.

STEALING A FEW MOMENTS TO OBSERVE, I have a mere second or two before he rings the doorbell or pounds on the door.

He's tall, with wide-set athlete's shoulders. I can see the planes of his muscles flexing beneath his t-shirt, highlighted by the dim porch lights on either side of Lucy's front door. Jet-black hair gleams when he shifts on his heels, raising his fist, knuckles ready to rap against the storm door.

"DASH?" I softly call out, testing the nickname on my lips, not wanting him to knock but not quire sure if this is Dash, or Hudson, or whoever my sister's date is for tonight.

I WALK CLOSER, clutching my purse, moving forward into the light.

"LUCY?"

"YEAH, it's me. I'm over here." I walk closer still, pasting on a smile, a knot forming in my stomach.

"HEY." He backtracks down the steps of the porch, jogging toward me. "What are you doing out here?"

HE'S close enough that I can see him better, nothing but strength and swagger. One look at his face and I begin stumbling over my words.

"UM, I was, uh...I had to...oh! I know!" *Jesus, Amelia, you've seen a cute guy before.* "I forgot I'd left my wallet at a friend's house? And I ran to get it. Didn't want to forget my ID, nope I did not!" I push out a laugh so fake I want to gag.

HE COCKS his head to the side, studying me, all high cheekbones and thick slashes of eyebrows. Beautiful dark skin, brawny...*God he's cute.* My sister wasn't kidding when she said he was good-looking.

WHAT SHE DIDN'T mention was that Dash Amado is Latino.

MUY CALIENTE—VERY freaking hot.

"YOU NEED to run inside or anything?"

"NAH, I'm good. We can get going." So I can get this night over with, come home, get into my pajamas—preferably by ten o'clock at the latest—and forget this whole evening took place.

HE CLICKS a remote hidden in his back pocket, unlocking the doors of his black car. Pulls the passenger side open, waits until I'm buckled in before closing the door with a dull thud. Jogs around the front to the driver's side.

I DO a quick visual scan of the car's interior. It's clean, no garbage in the back seat, and smells like masculine aftershave and gym equipment. I peel my eyes off the bat bag in the back seat as Dash folds his big body inside.

"SORRY I'M A LITTLE EARLY, but the band starts at eight fifteen and I wanted to get a spot in the front. Ready?"

READY AS I'LL ever be, considering I haven't done the old switcheroo since I was a teenager.

"YAY! SO READY," I reply in my best impression of Lucy.

HE STARTS THE ENGINE, throwing on his blinker to enter traffic, overly cautious given there's virtually no traffic on this street. It is completely deserted.

"THANKS FOR GOING ALONG WITH THIS." He glances over, large hands gripping the wheel. "When you asked me out, this was the best I could do on such short notice."

"EXCUSE ME?"

WAIT, did he just say '*when you asked me out*'?

I CLEAR MY THROAT AND, as casually as I can, ask, "I asked you out?"

HE GLANCES sidelong across his shoulder, dark eyebrows raised. "You must have been drunker than I thought if you don't even remember asking me on a date." He chuckles. It's one of those low, sexy laughs you see played out in the movies, the ones that send a shiver down your spine while watching the romance unfold.

I WANT to shake that inconvenient shiver out through my shoulders, give my face a small slap.

"MUST HAVE BEEN. You know me—fun, fun, fun! Always drunk on the weekends." *Shut up Amelia! Do you want him to think your sister is a lush?*

HE SHOOTS ME ANOTHER GLANCE, this one slightly less enthusiastic, slightly more unamused. "Right."

I SHIFT IN MY SEAT, the belt across my chest and lap constrictive, Lucy's tight denim jeans squishing my gut. I give them a tug at the waistband, looping my finger inside the fabric, pulling in an attempt to loosen the already stretchy material.

MY SHIRT—ONE of her favorites—is off the shoulder, blue with thin white pinstripes and feminine bell sleeves. My collarbone has been dusted with gold, lips a beckoning dark burgundy (her words, not mine).

ON MY FEET? Four-inch cork wedges.

I LOOK SEXY ENOUGH, I guess.

I'M TERRIBLY UNCOMFORTABLE.

"YOU HAVE to wear this shirt Amelia," my sister insisted, shoving the hanger into my hands. *"Unless we want him noticing how much bigger my boobs have miraculously gotten in the course of four days."* She dug through her closet like a stylist on a mission. *"Your boobs are bigger than mine—I don't want Dash to think I stuff my bra."*

"LUCY, no one stuffs their bra anymore."

WHEN WE'RE TOGETHER, it's like an eye-rolling competition that has no victor.

"YOU KNOW WHAT I MEAN. Just put this on and act happy, okay? Smile and make sure you touch him a lot, or he'll think I'm acting funny."

I REACH across the center console and tap his forearm flirtatiously.

"I REMEMBER ASKING YOU OUT, it just took me a second," I say in self-defense, trying to repair any damage I might have done to my sister's reputation by word-vomiting all over Dash's car. "And I do other things besides drink on the weekends."

HIS BLACK BROWS RISE AGAIN. "Like what?"

"LIKE...SPENDING a lot of time with my sister. She goes here, too," I inform him, laying the ground work for Lucy to eventually break the news that she doesn't just have a sister—she has a twin.

"NO SHIT?"

"WE'RE *REAL* CLOSE."

"THAT'S COOL." His eyes are trained on the road, and he sounds bored. "What do the two of you do when you hang out?"

"UM..." We do *her* homework, talk. "Call our parents—we're from Illinois—and when the weather is nice, we ride bikes or go down by the lake."

"I CAN PICTURE THAT." He smiles, turning left at a stop sign, heading to the tiny downtown district where all the bars are.

"WHAT'S the name of the band again?" I squeak out, sounding so unpolished and un-Lucy-like, it's positively *absurd.*

"SCOTTY'S TONE DEAF."

"OH. That...has a nice ring to it."

DASH LAUGHS, pitching his head back, filling the interior of the car with his delicious baritone voice. "That's one way of putting it. We're basically going to listen to a garage band. There's a kid named Scotty who lives at the end of Jock Row with his parents," he offers by way of explanation as he pulls into the parking lot of The Warehouse, the city's only concert venue. "He's in high school and has a rock band, has this idol worship of the guys in the house."

"INCLUDING YOU?"

HE BOWS HIS HEAD, EMBARRASSED. "*SÍ.*" *Yes.*

"THAT'S SWEET." Pause. "Did you already tell me this?"

JESUS, I sound like a complete idiot; if Lucy finds out, she's going to kill me. Seriously, I need to stop talking before I make the whole thing worse.

I RUN down the facts Lucy gave me about Dash:

TWENTY-TWO.
Six foot one.
Catcher on the baseball team.
Reserved.
Polite.
Lives on Jock Row in the baseball house.

THAT'S IT, the entire catalog of seven things I know about him, and most likely the only seven things my *sister* will *ever* know.

"YOU SURE you're okay with listening to Scotty's band? I figured you'd be cool with it." He shoots me a perfect smile, his white teeth set off by his beautiful olive skin. "I wouldn't call this a concert, I'd call it a set. They're letting Scotty's band play a few songs before the battle begins, nothing major. He's the opening act before an opening act."

"I *LOVE* THAT."

"SCOTT'S IN HIGH SCHOOL," he goes on. "I have no idea how he conned the manager of this place into letting him play, but I'm the only one from the house who promised to come listen."

"THAT IS SO nice of you. I'm looking forward to it."

I REALIZE that I actually am. Dash has been a real gentleman so far, and I'm gradually beginning to ease up and enjoy his company.

HE PULLS INTO A PARKING SPACE, puts the car in park, cuts the engine.

"I'D FEEL like a dick not showing up—the kid is only seventeen—but just so you know, there's a chance his band is going to seriously suck."

I GRIN AT HIM, unable to stop myself. "*Or* he might surprise us?"

HE'S NOT CONVINCED, yanking the keys from the ignition. "Maybe, but I doubt it."

STILL.

HE BROUGHT me to watch his kid neighbor's band play—how sweet is that? My heart dips, and not because of the guilt I feel about deceiving this guy. Quite the opposite.

DASH AMADO IS NOT ONLY AMAZINGLY hot.

HE'S AMAZING.

Chapter Three

DANTE

I PUT MY HAND ON THE SMALL OF LUCY'S BACK, GUIDING HER THROUGH the front entry of The Warehouse after standing in line and buying two tickets. I lead her toward the stage; there's plenty of room near the front.

Or there are a few tables near the back.

I point to one as we pass it. "Should we go up front, or do you want a table?"

"We should definitely stand up front so he can see you." Lucy gives me a nudge with her elbow. "You want him to know you're here, don't you?"

I nod.

Steering her forward, my hand still lingering on the small of her spine, my restless fingers find that sweet spot on the curving slope down to her ass. The fabric of her shirt is soft; I allow myself the luxury of letting it run liquid along my palm before pulling my entire arm away.

She glances at me over her shoulder, long hair swinging.

It's definitely darker than the last time I saw her, and thicker?

When she smiles at me, I notice a small divot at the corner of her mouth I hadn't noticed before, a tiny indentation near her full bottom lip.

I want to put the tip of my finger there and press it.

She catches me gaping at the dimple and touches it—covering it—offering me a wary, shy smile. Lucy, shy? No, that can't be right; this chick is a man-eater. She's the one who asked me out. She's the one who's always hanging all over me and my teammates at house parties, not the other way around.

She's aggressive.

Way more aggressive than I'm attracted to.

I don't know if I'm hallucinating, but the Lucy Ryan that showed up tonight? She's been acting uncharacteristically reserved since I found her loitering outside her house.

Once more, my eyes roam to the tiny indent near her mouth, lingering there.

Nope. That definitely *wasn't* there before.

Was it?

It's adorable—I'd definitely remember.

Wouldn't I?

Jesus Christ, *estoy perdiendo la cabeza. I'm losing my damn mind.*

We weave our way to position ourselves near the stage, early enough to score a great spot—dead center, right in the middle. Far enough up that Scotty will see me, far enough back that we can leave when the other bands play.

Unfortunately, we have to stand around for fifteen fucking more minutes waiting for this battle to begin, and Lucy doesn't strike me as the type who can engage in conversation stimulating enough to keep me interested for long, let alone a whole quarter of an hour.

I can suffer through small talk until the band starts.

It's our third date.

And our last.

After tonight, I doubt I'll ever take her out again. Girls like Lucy lack the refinement I want in a girlfriend—she's good for a quick fuck, maybe a few casual dates, but she won't *conocer a mi familia—meet my family.*

Mi madre would be fucking pissed if I brought a girl like her home.

Estaría muerto. I'd be dead.

Still...there's something about her tonight that has me second-guessing my first impressions, something I can't put my finger on.

Tonight she seems aloof. Conservative.

Pretty and polite.

Classy.

It's weird.

A *good* weird.

My lips curl into a smile as I look down at the crown of her head, the light hitting her hair, emphasizing the rich, chocolate brown color. Was it this color over the weekend? She must have gotten it dyed or whatever.

"Want anything to drink from the bar?" I lean into her, dipping my shoulders to get close, though she's tall enough with those high heels on.

"Hmm." She hesitates, worrying her lower lip. "Do I?"

I chuckle so low she couldn't possibly hear me over the noise. "I don't know, do you?"

"Are *you* drinking?"

What kind of a question is that? It's a weekend—of course I was planning on drinking. Unless...does she not *want* me to drink?

"I was gonna do a beer."

A firm nod. "Okay, that's what I'll have."

"Beer?" I feel my mouth twitch. "What kind?"

"Whatever kind you're having?"

"Are you sure?" She had white wine the last time we went out—four glasses of it, to be exact—and got shit-faced drunk. "I'm sure they have wine if you want it."

Her mouth moves, forming the words, "Shit, that's right. I drink wine, don't I?" The venue is loud and echoes, but her words are clear, perfectly formed on her lips. Lucy pauses indecisively. "I guess I'll have wine if they have it."

She looks less than thrilled, pouty even.

"Tell me what you want, and I'll grab it."

"Let's do wine." A curt nod. "I'm a wine drinker that happens to also love beer, but tonight I'll do wine, please."

My face, of its own free will, twists into a *would you make up your damn mind* expression, and I fight off an impatient groan and an irritable sigh. "You want to hold our spots while I head to the bar or come with me?"

"No, no, you go! I mean, sure—yes, I'll hold our spots," she enthuses, practically shooing me toward the bar, but not physically touching me. "Yup, you go. I'll wait here, right here in this spot. I won't go anywhere."

She flashes me a smile that's just a little too cheerful; if I didn't know any better, I'd think she was trying to get rid of me.

"All right," I say slowly. "Give me a minute. Be right back."

It takes me a solid five minutes to ease my way through the congested crowd to the bar, another five to hit the front of the line, and several more to get service.

One bottle of beer for me and one plastic cup of cheap white for her and I'm back at her side. When I sidle up, my date is furiously texting someone, head snapping up when she catches sight of me out of her periph. Shoves the phone in the back pocket of her jeans.

"Hey! I missed you!"

Plucking the cup of wine out of my hand, Lucy peers into it, squinting with one eye squeezed shut.

"Thanks." When she sips it, her lips pucker. "Bottoms up!"

I don't know why the hell she'd order it if she so obviously hates it, but I gave up trying to figure women out years ago.

"Good stuff?" I want to fucking laugh.

"Really good. Thank you." Lucy takes another labored sip, demonstrating just how tasty she finds it. "Mmm."

"If you don't want it, don't drink it."

"No! It's good. See?" Another gulp, another set of sour lips she's terrible at hiding.

"Lucy, why the hell would you order wine if you don't like it?" I pause, hold out my cup. "Do you want to chase it with some beer?"

She hesitates, glances behind us at the bar, which is now completely swarming with people. If I go back for another beer, it'll take another half hour and I'll miss Scotty's entire gig.

"Don't worry about it. This is fine."

I take a chug of my bottle of amber, offer it to her. "Want a drink of mine?"

Her hand goes up, waving in protest. "No, no, that's okay—don't worry about it."

"I'm not *worried* about it, but if you want a beer, I can share. It's not like we haven't swapped spit before."

The lighting in here is shit, but I swear to God, Lucy is blushing. Has to be by the way her head dips, unable to meet my eyes.

On stage, Scotty's band begins to saunter out, taking their places, running a sound check. The drummer inspects his kit; guitarists tune their strings. Lead singer taps the mic, raising and lowering it, tightening the screw to hold it at his preferred height.

As he's doing that, my neighbor kid looks up, catches sight of me, throws a peace sign at the same time he swings his black bass guitar strap around his neck like he's done it hundreds of times.

He probably has.

Well practiced, moving with ease, Scotty doesn't look nervous at all. In fact, the teenage shit gives me a cocky wink when they begin a warm-up, exercising their fretting hands.

Wearing the well-worn t-shirt of another popular band and torn jeans, Scott bends his knees, strumming, hair gelled into tiny spikes.

Their first cords are upbeat.

First words, in tune.

Fluid.

Soon, I find my head bobbing to the beat. Lucy and I pass the beer back and forth between us, tipping it back. It goes down cold and smooth, but it's not enough for two.

I grasp for it again, prepared to take another swig.

"Wait! Does this not taste so damn good? God I love it when they're cold."

Her eyes close when she swallows.

Her hips sway when the music begins.

It's pretty fucking great.

AMELIA

I'M NOT EXPECTING the next song to be slow, just like I'm not expecting my body to sway, hips gently rocking to the music.

I haven't had much to drink, but it's enough to loosen me up and forget myself, if only for a few moments. Enough for me to enjoy the company and the big, warm palms that slide around my waist.

It's a full house tonight, stuffy.

"*¿Está bien?*" *Is this okay?* "Sorry I keep bumping into you, but the dickhead behind us keeps knocking into me." His smooth voice speaks into my ear, the rich sound of his Spanish hitting all the nerves in my spine. "*Te sientes diferente—una diferencia buena.*"

You feel different, he says, rolling his tongue. *A good different.*

Since I'm pretending to be my twin sister—who doesn't know a lick of Spanish—I don't acknowledge the words, giving a feeble little nod without betraying myself.

In reality? My entire body is in complete and utter chaos.

I can understand him—*perfectly*.

I don't want Dash speaking Spanish in my ear, whispering words meant for someone else. I don't want Dash touching me—not because he repulses me.

But because he doesn't.

He's the antithesis of everything I thought he'd be. For the sake of my sanity, and to get me through this farce of a fake date, I desperately hoped the guy walking through my sister's door would be a jerk.

A jockhole.

I prayed he'd be a stereotype, a caricature of what I perceive the average student athlete on our college campus to be. My sister is the jersey chaser, not me.

Pompous.

Boorish.

Egotistical asshole.

Dante Amado is none of those things.

He's easygoing. Kind. Personable.

Every gentlemanly gesture out of Dash Amado has been sincere. His nice-guy routine is not an act; it's who he is.

His mama raised him right.

And I'm so confused by it.

I wasn't prepared for him to be like this.

Dammit! I'm not supposed to be attracted to my sister's boyfriend— the guy my sister is *dating*—no matter how serious it isn't, no matter how good-looking he is.

Honestly? I kind of hate myself right now.

A knot of guilt twists inside my stomach at the same time Dash's hands ease around my waist, sliding over my rib cage, giving me a little squeeze. If I had to speak, there's no way I'd be able to form a cohesive sentence.

The knot gets heavier, tighter, weighing me down. I'm the world's worst twin.

The world's worst *sister*.

"Having fun?" His baritone vocals hit my cerebellum, shockwaves finding their way down to all my best girly parts. "I really thought they were going to sound like complete shit—thank God they don't."

My throat is tight, and I have to clear it before I can speak. "I'm really impressed—I can't believe they're in high school."

As many times as I've told myself I would try to fill Lucy's high-heeled shoes on this date, I'm failing—*so miserably*. I want so desperately to be myself. I want my damn body to stop responding to Dash Amado. I want my damn heart to stop beating so wildly it feels like it's about to burst out of my chest.

If only my cheeks weren't so flushed, my palms so sweaty.

I'm a complete mess.

Dash's giant catcher's paws grip my body, loosely resting on my hips, thumbs hooking inside the front pockets of Lucy's jeans.

He lowers his head, gently resting his chin on my shoulder, lips intermittently brushing against the exposed skin of my jawline as he stares straight ahead, watching Scotty.

I let my lids flutter closed, allowing my lashes to rest on my cheekbones for the briefest of seconds, giving myself this one moment.

This is how it would feel if we were a couple.

It feels too good.

He feels good.

So good. "Tan bueno," I say, forgetting myself, muttering out loud. *"Tan bueno."*

Dash goes still.

"*¿Que es tan bueno?*" His mouth is right there, lips grazing my neck. *What's so good?* he wants to know.

Jesus, it's driving me absolutely freaking crazy—the Spanish, his cologne and his breath and the heat from his body. Even the hair on his arms is giving me goose bumps, the baby fine strands tickling the skin of my forearms as his thumbs dig gently into my hips.

"Huh?" I ask in a daze.

"You said *so good*."

"Mmm, nope. Don't think so."

"Yes you did." His lips skim the shell of my ear, speaking in a foreign language I spent years mastering. "I heard you, and you said it in Spanish."

"I did?"

"*¿Hablas español, Lucy?*" *Do you speak Spanish?*

What the hell am I supposed to say to that? My sister doesn't speak a word of it. "Um...?"

"*¿Qué más no me estás diciendo?*" *What else aren't you telling me?* "Be honest."

"Nothing." Shit, I just answered him again.

He pulls back, turns me to face him, lightly setting those massive palms on my bare shoulders, fingers spreading over my skin, guaranteed to leave scorch marks in their wake.

His fingers brush the hair off my collarbone.

"*¿Puedes entenderme?*" *You can understand me?*

Crappers.

"Sí." I cast my eyes away, chastised.

His are too intense.

Something changes in his expression then; he studies me under the lights of the stage, the red, blue, and green flickering strobes casting a glow across his skin.

Across mine.

Dash can't quite figure me out, and I don't blame him; I'm acting like I have multiple personalities. How could I let that Spanish slip out? Lucy is guaranteed to be pissed about that once she finds out.

Lucy, who could barely do her own English papers in high school.

I'm not my sister.

Not even close.

And call me crazy, but for a fleeting moment while Dash stands watching me—learning my tells—his brows lower and rise, concentrating on my face, reading every line imprinted there, eyes traveling over my chest, hair, and face.

The corner of my mouth.

In an instant, he knows.

He just doesn't *know* that he knows.

And he's confused.

"Come on." He bends now, talking loud. "We need to talk. Let's go grab another beer."

"Where?" I shout back.

Those mammoth shoulders shrug. "What about the bar? At the back of the room? We'll be able to hear each other better."

"Okay. Sure." I think I'd follow him anywhere.

Dash takes my hand without hesitating, without asking for permission, weaving us through the crowd, and I follow, fingers wrapped around his tightly.

My lifeline.

He gives them a squeeze, lacing them together, glancing back at me over his broad shoulders. It's then that I realize: I'm not paying attention to where I'm walking; I'm just watching *him.*

The muscles in his strong back contract as he works his way through the crush. His thick neck corded, sexy. I've always liked that part of a guy's body, always found it attractive.

Masculine.

My hungry eyes rake down his backside, down his tapered waist, over his firm ass, and I allow myself the luxury of *every* part of him, pretending the large hands and imposing form tugging me along belong to me.

Pretending he's mine for the taking.

We reach the bar, where the crowd has thinned out considerably since the music started, the sound of Scotty's band blasting through the subwoofers and speakers drowning out any laughter and loud chatter.

Dash orders us beer, ice water.

Faces me while we wait, one arm resting on the bar top.

I wonder how long it's going to take for him to bring up the fact that I speak Spanish.

For now, he seems content to stand here surrounded by the concertgoers, the loud music, and my quiet company. If he thinks it's strange that I, as Lucy, finally have nothing to say, he would be right. My sister is always chattering away, and she'd be talking non-stop right now, too.

The only things *I* can think of to ask Dash are personal; I want to know more about him, want to know things that are none of my business.

Does he have brothers or sisters?

Where is he from?

What's his major? What does he want to be if he doesn't play baseball after he graduates?

Are these things he and my sister have already talked about?

We stand at the bar, regarding each other, his cool black gaze caressing my exposed shoulders. I respond to it by coolly lifting the beer bottle to my lips and taking another drink of liquid courage, hoping to avoid his disconcerting scrutiny.

I don't know what it is, but Dash is someone I want to get to know more, someone I'd want to know if the circumstances were different.

I sigh.

The fact is that tonight, I am not supposed to be myself.

And I'm doing a really crappy job being my sister.

"So, you wanna tell me what's going on with you?"

"What do you want to know?"

Chapter Four

DANTE

LUCY SPEAKS SPANISH.

And not just the *I was required to take two years of it in high school* version. She actually knows how to fucking speak it, fluently.

I don't know what to do with this strange new information. It's certainly a game changer; I've never dated anyone who could have a conversation with me in any language other than English, and it's really fucking sexy.

We're sidled up to the bar, my arm draped on the lacquered wooden top, elbow propping me up as I study her.

Study her in a new light, riveted.

This Lucy isn't just a pretty face.

This Lucy isn't just a grasping jock chaser.

This Lucy has *layers*.

This version fascinates me more than the two versions that came before her.

Her striped baby blue shirt is understated but sexy, hair still falling in loose waves despite the growing humidity from all the warm bodies inside this packed concert hall.

Wavering unsteadily on high heels, she leans against the counter, mimicking my stance, mimicking the way I let my gaze trail over her, returning the favor.

She peruses me up and down, expression unreadable.

It's so fucking unsettling.

Lo amo. I love it.

"So, you wanna tell me what's going on with you?"

"What do you want to know?"

"I think you know what I'm talking about. I've never met a single person on this campus who speaks Spanish as well as you seem to, besides other Latinos."

"I spent a semester in Mexico teaching English at an immersion school."

That makes no fucking sense. Lucy is a fashion major—why would she be teaching classes in Mexico?

"Why do you keep staring at me like that?"

The beer bottle hits my bottom lip and I tip it. Chug. "I'm trying to figure you out."

"I know," she returns unhappily. "Please don't."

"Are you intentionally trying to be evasive?"

"I'm not playing games with you, I promise, but it's complicated."

The bartender finally gets to us, setting two new bottles on the counter. Lucy reaches for one, taking a dainty sip, delicate fingers wrapped around the long neck of the bottle. Nails painted baby blue, the second to last one a glittery silver.

"You know Luce, I'm really fucking busy with school and baseball, so I don't date a lot, and this right here is why: I can't stand drama."

"Neither can I," she volleys back. "Maybe I'm just not good at this, did you ever think of that?"

"Not good at what?"

"Relationships. I've never dated a single guy for more than two weeks."

"Well that's good to know."

Her eyes roll toward the ceiling dramatically. "This is only your third date —I can't even believe we're discussing this."

This is only *your* third date? That's an odd way to put it.

"Besides," she continues, "aren't you ballplayers all just looking for a little fun between seasons?"

"I'm not a stereotype, but thanks."

Her expression falls. "I didn't mean it like that. I'm just...I'm not comfortable having this conversation with you right now."

"Why?"

"Because I...it's..." She's reluctant to finish her sentence. "It's personal."

"You know, Lucy, relationships don't usually work when one person is hiding something." Jesus, why am I trying so damn hard with this girl? I couldn't stand her the last time we went out, and I'm only here with her tonight so I didn't have to come alone.

"*Hiding* something?" Her eyes are wide. "What would make you say that?"

"You're either really good at faking who you are, or you have no fucking clue what you want." I can't describe the look on her face right now, couldn't if I tried, not for a million fucking bucks. It's a cross between crestfallen and oddly captivated...stricken but expectant?

Like she wants to cry and laugh all at the same time.

So bizarre. "Why are you staring at me like that?"

Lucy swallows a lump in her throat, eyes shining. "I literally just asked you that same thing, so how am I staring at *you*?"

"Like you're dying to say something."

Her chin tips up, that little dimple by her bottom lip drawing attention to itself, imprinted in her skin.

My eyes fixate on it, narrowing. "I'm not fucking stupid. Something weird is going on with you, and I want to know what it is."

"Nothing *weird* is going on." Her nostrils flare, eyes get bright. "I have *no* idea what you're talking about."

"So it's going to be like that, huh?"

Her arms cross. "What do you think is weird?"

"To avoid the risk of feeling like a fucking dumbass, I'd rather not bring it up, okay?"

She's in my space now, fingers splayed on my forearm. "*Tell* me."

"Your hair is different," I blurt out.

"How?"

Jesus Christ, this is going to sound so stupid. "It's longer...and darker." I go for broke. "And I swear you didn't have this the last time I saw you."

I extend my arm, placing my finger on that perfect spot by her mouth. Her dark lips part.

Lucy's breath catches. Something in her eyes...

"What else?" she whispers.

"Your—" My eyes drop to her breasts then rise again. I'm such a fucking hornball. "Never mind."

Behind us, Scotty's band interrupts, striking another chord, his adolescent voice croaking into the microphone. "This is going to be it for us tonight, Bettys and gents. One last lullaby before the big show. Enjoy, and have a great fucking night."

The slow rifts of guitars still the crowd.

Still Lucy.

Her lips are curved smugly. "Were you going to say my boobs look bigger?"

There's no getting out of this one; she totally caught me checking out her tits, which I can barely see beneath her blousy top. "Maybe."

"What if you were right?" The words fall out of her mouth before her lips clamp shut. "Please forget I said that."

Yeah...not happening.

Lucy clears her throat. "So should we—"

"Dance? Sure." Why the hell not? Everyone else is.

Neither of us smile, but she lets me take her beer bottle and set it on the bar, lead her to the edge of the ballroom floor where the concert crowd is gathered, couples dancing to little Scotty's kickass garage band.

My hands catch skin when they slide around Lucy's waist, accidentally skimming above the waistband of her jeans. I let my fingers stroke the skin of her ribcage before they behave, dragging back down to the swell of her denim-clad hips.

Tentatively, her hands run up the front of my black t-shirt; it's the second time she's touched me tonight, and her warm palms, with their pretty blue nails, are doing some seriously fucked up shit to my libido as they settle on my chest.

Her chin tips up so she can look in my eyes. "You realize you finished my sentence before, and I finished yours?"

"We did?"

"Yes. No one ever does that with me except my sister."

I have nothing to add to that.

"Scott is great." She breaks the silence, fingers toying with the cotton of my shirt. "Does he come around your house often?"

"Yeah, just about every week. He plays ball, and he's mildly obsessed with our pitcher, Rowdy Wade."

"Rowdy, Dash—do you all have nicknames?"

"We call some guys by their last names."

"And you get yours because you're fast?" Affirmative. "But you're a catcher...how does that work?"

Does she not know anything about baseball?

"Everyone on the team has a turn at bat, and when my bat connects with the ball, I run like hell."

The song Scotty's band plays is actually really fucking haunting. Beautiful.

Just like Lucy.

My arms move from her hips to her waist, pulling her in so we're flush, her palms sliding down from my pecs, smoothing themselves across my shoulders, brushing imaginary lint away. I want to kiss her and we both fucking know it; I've been dying to put my mouth on that dimple of hers.

I home in on it.

"Where did this suddenly come from?" I tease, bringing my hand up to float my thumb over the tiny indent, back and forth, unintentionally brushing the satiny flesh of her bottom lip. "I swear this wasn't here last time."

"I-I don't think we should do this," she protests against my finger, lids fluttering shut when my thumb caresses her cheek. "Maybe we should go back to the bar and finish our beer."

"Hey, it's all right." My brows rise. "We're just dancing."

My fingers trace her jaw, slipping to the back of her neck, raking through her soft hair. Her eyes meet mine, a thousand words I know she wants to say shining up at me, but it's nothing I'll hear out loud. This girl has secrets she doesn't want me finding out, and I want to know what they are.

I lower my head, intending to—

"I don't think you should kiss me."

I pull back, eyebrows drawn together, perplexed. "Why?"

"Because I want you to," the whisper slides out, a confession.

"That makes no sense."

"I know," she moans miserably.

"You want to kiss me, but you don't—got it." I'm tenderly stroking her skin with the palm of my hand, the calloused pads learning the contours of her face. "You don't care if I do this in the meantime, do you? Until you change your mind?"

"I'm not going to change my mind."

Lowering my face to the crook of her neck, I trail my nose up the pillar of sweet skin, letting my mouth tag along for the ride. My wet tongue meets her flesh and I want to gently suck, but don't. I nip instead. "Is this okay? No kissing on the lips," I whisper into her ear. "Just like in *Pretty Woman*."

"F-F..." she stutters. "Fine. Sure, whatever. Just not on the lips."

What a little weirdo.

My laughing mouth finds the pulse in the slim column of her neck, and I'm satisfied when she tilts her head to one side, hair falling like a waterfall over her shoulder, giving me all the access I want and need.

Grasping her hand, my fingers flutter lightly along the length of her arm before I raise it, kiss the inside of her wrist, the pale skin a stark contrast to my own.

Dragging my mouth along the smooth flesh of her forearm, up and down the inside of her elbow. Lucy holds perfectly still.

"¿Todavía no quieres que te bese en los labios?" Still don't want me to kiss your lips?

One jerky shake of her head.

"No?"

Another shake. *No.*

"Jesus, Luce, you're killing me here," I murmur against her mouth, our lips an inch apart, so close our breaths mingle. I wish our tongues were, too.

"It's killing me too. I'm sorry."

That's the second time she's apologized, so I kiss the tip of her nose, leaning in to whisper, "Don't be."

"God Dash, don't do that," she whispers back, stroking the back of my head, wrapping my black hair around her finger.

Chest heaving, her hands unhurriedly flutter up and down the bulk of my biceps, breasts pressed against my chest as she moves closer.

This non-kissing, sexual tension-filled bullshit is better than any fucking kiss I've ever had on the mouth, that's for damn sure. It's giving me a raging boner, body hard as a rock when she arches her back.

"Don't do what?" My murmured question makes her shiver. Goose bumps form across her skin.

"Don't be so..." Lucy deliberates, choosing her words.

"Irresistible?"

"Sure, we'll go with that."

We take the moment to stare at each other, and I swear to fucking God, it's like we're seeing each other for the first damn time. My hands embrace her jawline as her fingers clench my wrists.

"Lucy."

The air between is pulled taut, intensely so.

Buzzing.

Sizzling.

"Dash, please don't." I can't hear her words, but I can see them, and it's enough to stop myself from doing something really fucking dumb, like kissing her senseless, which is taking some superhero-level self-restraint on my part.

She moves first, burying her head in my chest as the music comes to an end, the crowd around us going wild, chanting and cheering for the band, for Scotty, the kid who practices in his parents' garage and tries to hang out with guys too old for him.

"We should go," comes her muffled mumble. "I need to go."

Need to go.

We pull apart, reluctantly. I could eat her up—and out—all fucking night long.

Instead, I release her.

"All right. Let's get you home."

Chapter Five

AMELIA

Dzzt. Dzzt.

Dzzt.

It's barely six thirty in the morning when my phone begins buzzing, vibrating against my bedside table, an entire hour before I have to be up to get to my study group.

I reach for it, finger blindly searching for the *end* button but accidentally hitting *accept*. Dammit all, what's my sister doing calling so freaking early?

The last time she woke me at this hour was two Christmases ago when she and our brother, Dexter, were up at the butt-crack of dawn—like children—so they could open their presents.

My siblings, bless their hearts, are early risers.

I, however, am not.

"Luce?" My voice is raspy, sounding eerily similar to someone gasping for a last breath. "Is everything okay?"

"No, everything is not okay. Are you still in bed?" It's an accusing tone, one I simply don't have the patience for at this hour of the damn day.

I blink into the sunlight just beginning to pour through my bedroom window, rising to sit, propped against my headboard. Worried, I squint toward the clock. "What's wrong? Why are you calling so ungodly early? Did something happen to Mom or Dad?"

"Oh jeez, don't be so dramatic." I hear the sound of the wind hitting the mouthpiece of her phone, an indication that she's outside, probably getting ready for a run or something equally horrifying.

Mollified that there's no emergency, I flop back onto my side, hunkering down. Grumble, "What do you want?"

"How did it go last night?"

"Fine?"

"And?"

"And nothing. It went fine."

"My dates don't ever go 'fine'. They're either fantastic or awful. So which was it?"

"I can't even function right now. How are you this chipper?"

"Why aren't you answering the question?" I swear I can hear her stop dead in her tracks. "Is there something you're not telling me?"

My body goes still. "Why would you ask me that?"

"Twintuition." She sniffs into the phone. "I *felt* it last night while I was with Hudson."

Hudson. I still cannot get over that name.

"Oh Lord."

"You had fun, didn't you? You never texted me last night, so I was worried." Through the line, she worries her bottom lip, a trait that always gave us away; Lucy would always chew her bottom lip while we were getting yelled at, like she's doing now. "He wasn't being a jerk, was he?"

Despite how groggy I am, my brows rise. "Is he normally a jerk?"

"No?"

"Why are you saying it like it's a question? Don't you know?"

"I've only been out with him twice, Amelia. I guess he can be kind of an asshole when he's with his friends?" I imagine her bending down to re-tie her shoes. "So was he one with you?"

"No." Not at all. He was perfect.

"Yeah, I know. I just wanted to see what you'd say." She sounds satisfied. "I *felt* it."

"Honest to God, would you please stop saying that?" She is so annoying sometimes, especially before seven AM. "You're making me mental."

She ignores me. "How long were you out?"

"I don't know, I think I got home around one?"

"Really, that late?" Her air of approval is palpable. "What else?"

"Well, I mean, after he dropped me off at your place, I had to walk home." I sound begrudged. "In the dark."

"Yeah, yeah. Did he try to kiss us?"

Jesus. "Kind of."

"Did we let him?"

"No, but it was a pretty hardcore dodge and weave." *And I wanted him too, so badly.* We're both dead silent, waiting for my answer. "There's something I should probably tell you." I take a deep breath and confess, "I accidentally spoke Spanish with him last night."

Ten bucks says Lucy is wrinkling her nose at me. "He speaks Spanish?"

"Are you kidding me right now? Yes he speaks Spanish—he's Latino. Do you pay attention to anyone but yourself?"

"Sue me for not knowing, jeez. Tell me what was said and how it pertains to me, and do it quickly—I haven't started my run yet and I'm freezing my ass off out here."

"I had a *conversation* with him in *Spanish*, Luce." And the whole thing was so freaking sexy. The Rs rolling off his tongue...the deep timbre of his accent...

"Wait a minute." My twin inhales a breath, catching on. "Did you forget the small fact that I don't speak any Spanish! God Amelia, why would you do that to me?" my sister shouts through the phone. I pull it away from my ear, tapping down on the volume button.

"It just slipped out! I'm sorry, I got caught up in the moment."

"Caught up in the moment? What the hell were you guys doing? I thought you went to a concert—no one talks at concerts!"

"We did go to a concert! But he was saying stuff and it was so sweet, it just felt natural to reply in Spanish, and then one thing led to another and we were having a conversation."

"I don't understand how it just slipped out," she intones sarcastically.

I roll my eyes. "I doubt I have to explain how *alluring* he is, Lucy. You've been out with him twice—do you blame me?" Crap, that was totally inappropriate. "Sorry, I didn't mean to say that."

"Uh...if you like this guy, just tell me, Amelia."

"What would make you think I like him?" I want to face-palm myself with an anvil.

"You just said he was *alluring*. Who uses words like that?"

"I do."

"Hmm."

"You woke me up—what do you want me to say?"

The thing about my sister—no matter how flighty or vain or selfish she can be—is that she always wants what's best for me. I know I'm not going back to sleep until we talk this out.

"The entire time I was out with Hudson last night, I kept getting these niggling vibes," she begins slowly, enunciating every word. "Like, the whole damn time. I could barely concentrate on my date."

I hate when she does this.

I hate when she's right.

It's creepy.

"Your twintuition is wrong."

I'm lying and we both know it.

"Do you know," she begins thoughtfully, "he's been texting me since late last night, then again this morning, and now I know why half of them were in Spanish. I couldn't freaking understand most of them, and I'm not about to Google translate a text conversation."

"Oh? He texted you? That's good." I'm dying inside, doing my best to sound nonchalant despite this frantically beating heart.

The line goes quiet.

"Luce? What did he say?"

"The usual."

She's going to make me work for it.

"Which is what? I have no idea what the usual is."

"Well, for *one* thing—and please don't ever repeat this—Dash has never texted me before. Normally I'm the one sending him texts, which is so annoying. I hate when guys are like that. I hate having to message them first. I'm only admitting that to you because you're my sister and I forced you to go out with him."

I hate myself for asking, but, "Like...what else was he saying?" *About me.*

A loud sigh from the other end of the line. "I don't remember, Amelia. *Stuff.* The point *is*, he must have thought I was acting like a complete freak, 'cause he asked if I was feeling better and said maybe it was a mistake taking me to a concert, said he regrets how it was impossible to talk, blah blah blah. So annoying, don't you think? Anyway," she continues without letting me answer, "thanks for doing such a crap job as my stand-in that he thought I was sick. You could have made out with him to be a little more convincing. He's so hot."

"I was doing you a favor!" My mouth gapes open. "You should've thought about that when you *begged* me to be *you* for the night so you could go out with some guy name Hudson. *Hudson*—seriously, what kind of a name is that?"

"He—"

I don't let her get two words in before interrupting. "What did you *think* was gonna happen last night Lucy? With a guy like that, who has feelings—yeah, real feelings. He might be crazy good-looking, but he was really great, so yeah, the

Spanish just came flying out because I hardly get to practice anymore, and you're just going to have to deal with it."

"What the heck am I supposed to do? He's going to say all this shit I'm not going to understand."

Not to sound callous, but, "You don't even like the guy!"

"How do you know?"

"If you liked Dash, you would have gone out with him and not *Hudson*." I can barely get the guy's name out.

There's a long stretch of silence on the other end of the line, and I wonder what's going through her mind right now as she formulates a reply. It's either that or she's stretching, prepping for her run.

"You're right. You are totally, one hundred percent right." I can hear the revelation taking over her speech and brace myself. "I should break it off. I like Hudson way better. He gave me two orgasms last night, Amelia—two, *with his mouth.*"

My mouth falls open, at a loss for words. "Lucy, how can you do that? That's cheating!"

"Calm down, Miss Priss. It's not like I knew I liked Hudson better before I double-booked myself. I had to sample the goods first." She laughs cheerfully.

"And thanks to you, I know how I feel! So no, it's not like cheating. I'll text Dash as soon as we hang up and dump him."

My mouth falls open. "You're going to break up with him over *text*?"

I can hear my sister studying her nails, bored with our conversation, maybe even picking at the split ends of her long hair as she stands out on the sidewalk. "Well it's not like I'm going to *see* him any time soon, and I don't feel like going on another date with him."

Why doesn't she like him? Why would she do this? This superficial young woman is not the sister I know. It's those damn sorority girls she's hanging out with.

She's being callous and insensitive, and I don't like it.

Stay out of it Amelia, my inner voice shouts. *This is none of your business. Stay out of it before you say something you'll regret, like how Dash is a great guy who smells amazing, is sweet in an unassuming way, and is too handsome for his own good.*

And yet I can't help but add, "He's a nice guy—don't you think he deserves to be told in person? Isn't that what you would want if someone was breaking up with you?"

There's a long pause, then the loud sigh my sister is famous for in our family. "Honestly? No, not really. If someone was breaking up with me, why would I want to see their *face*?"

"Because—"

Whatever I'm about to say gets cut off when Lucy interrupts me. "Look, I have to start my run if I'm going to finish on time and keep my day on track."

"Fine," I huff.

"But if this is so damn important to you, why don't *you* break up with him for me? That saves me the trouble of doing it."

"Going on a date with him was bad enough. I did a terrible job pretending to be you, and there is no way I'll be able to look him in the eye and dump him for you."

She pauses. "Hold on, someone just texted me."

"Lucy! We're in the middle of a conversation!"

The phone is silent as she pulls it away from her ear to check it. "That was Dash—again. I just texted him back and told him I'd meet him at Zin downtown tomorrow night at seven. You can break up with him then."

"Lucy!" I shout, beyond exasperated. "I'm not breaking up with him for you!"

"Suit yourself." Her voice is flippant. "I have no problem texting him."

My stomach drops, a lead weight of guilt burdening me. "Don't hang up! Okay, okay, I'll do it. I'll break up with him for you."

She smiles on the other end of the line; I can hear it from here. "Thank you sissy. You won't regret this."

But she's wrong.

I already do.

Chapter Six

AMELIA

I CAN'T DECIDE: WHAT DOES A PERSON WEAR TO BREAK UP WITH THEIR sister's boyfriend? A sweatshirt and jeans? A flirty top? Something dressier, because technically this could be considered a business meeting?

Khakis?

I stand in front of my closet, mid-panic, discarding one unsuitable shirt after another onto my bed, when what I should have done was force Lucy to choose a breakup outfit for me, like how she dressed me for the concert, since theoretically, I'm posing as her again.

Floral blouse? Way too fun.

Hot pink sweater? No—I'd die from heat stroke before I died from mortification.

No, no, and no—three more shirts join the others then out of the corner of my eye, I spot a dressy black turtleneck and impulsively yank it off its hanger.

Hold it up, inspecting it.

Prim. Proper.

Black.

Serious.

The perfect shit to wear if I was attending a funeral.

I slide it over my frame. It's fitted, hugging all my curves, and yet, the perfect metaphor: my attendance at the death of my sister's relationship with Dash Amado.

Don't get me wrong, I might be on my way to give the guy his marching orders, but I don't want to look like a complete frump.

Still.

I need to look and feel businesslike, and this onyx turtleneck is textbook professional. I'll appear efficient, organized, and...

Now I sound like a lunatic.

With a sigh befitting my twin, I shimmy and stumble into a pair of dark wash jeans, feet sliding into black half boots, give my hair a quick tussle, swipe on some gloss, and—*oh my God, I'm primping*. I'm trying to look nice.

Which is so not the point!

"Stop it, Amelia, this is not a date," I chastise myself, glaring into the mirror, angry. Rest my hands on either side of my dresser, looking my reflection in the eye. "Why are you doing this? You *like* him. You cannot pull this off."

I rise to my full height, puffing out my chest. "Yes you can. You can do this. You've broken up with guys before. Hell, you've broken up with *Lucy's* boyfriends before."

Twice, in high school.

I felt braver back then than I do now.

What's done is done; Lucy is out with Hudson tonight, and I'm on my way to meet Dash. There's no turning back.

I can only move forward.

HE'S LATE.

At seven o'clock sharp, I watch, engrossed as a large figure emerges through the door of Zin. I'm waiting with baited breath, watching when he tosses his head to get the hair out of his eyes.

Everything about Dash Amado is dark: his black quilted jacket, his jet-black hair, his complexion.

He flashes a friendly grin to the bartenders when he walks past, toward me, his pearly whites a stark contrast against his skin. Dark. Smooth. Handsome.

Through the dim lighting in the wine bar, I watch him peel off his jacket, sauntering his way over, surveying the crowd. There aren't many people here tonight so it's not long before our gazes connect.

In a few strides he's at my side, sliding onto the barstool next to mine, kissing the top of my head. "Hey. Sorry I'm late. I had to see the trainer—he was showing me a new way to wrap my wrists."

I can't stop my eyes from glancing down. I raise my brows, curious.

"They're not wrapped right now, just for practice." He cuffs his wrist with one hand, rubbing it. "Have you been here long?"

"I walked in just a few minutes early, so no. It's no big deal, the bartenders were keeping me company." Totally something Lucy would say, only she'd add a flirtatious smile, maybe touch his sleeve.

"Speaking of which, I'm thirsty." His lean torso leans across the bar, long arm snatching a drink menu before flagging down one of the bartenders. His eyes flicker to the water glass in front of me. "Do you want anything else or are you sticking with water?"

"Water is good." I'm here to do a job and need a clear mind. Drinking would be a horrible idea, though I may need a drink at the end of the night, maybe a shot or two, or three.

Dash nods down at my beverage, speaking to the guy behind the bar as he strolls over, drying a glass. "I'll have what she's having, and an iced tea if you have it? Thanks."

Whatever words I'm about to say get caught in my throat when he spins in his seat to face me, chugging down almost all of his glass of ice water, Adam's apple bobbing. Shaved neck, dark sideburns.

Dear Lord he's good-looking.

His eyes slide up and down the front of my shirt, landing briefly on my breasts. Lips quirk. "Nice turtleneck."

I can't decide if he's being sarcastic.

"I like turtlenecks. They're warm," I croak out, body blazing like an inferno, wanting to hook my index finger in the collar of my shirt and give it a tug. Yank it off, up over my head. Get it off my body, hating it.

His black brows go up. "I said I liked it. I wasn't being a dick."

"Oh. Well...thanks, I guess."

I've never been this nervous in my entire life, not even when I took my sister's college entrance exam.

He regards me over the top of his iced tea, the lemon wedge moving up and down like a jellyfish in the ocean.

"You look good though. *Muy bueno.* I think I like this shirt better than the one you wore on Friday night."

"Really?" I run a hand over my stick-straight hair, which I let air-dry after my shower. I'm hardly wearing any makeup, just some lip gloss—basically, my attempt at looking serious.

"You can't even see my neck." You can't see *anything*. This shirt is a protective layer between us; I don't want to feel sexy or attractive or pretty when I'm here to complete a task.

And yet...the goof likes it.

"*Sí.*"

I like the way he's staring, taking my measure. I love the way he talks, the sound of his voice, even if he's not really talking to *me*.

The thought is sobering, and I gaze down at the shiny bar top despondently, picking at the corner of the white cocktail napkin under my glass of water. *Zin, a wine bar in downtown Iowa City – drink old wine, date young men.*

I study the slogan, running my fingers over the burgundy embossed writing, the texture of the paper feeling coarse under my fingertips.

Over and over it, around the cursive lettering.

He's still watching me when I look up.

"Should we have them seat us somewhere? I'm starving."

Hesitantly I nod, hopping down off the barstool, aware of just how big he is, how imposing.

Chest like a wall of steel, I bump into it inadvertently when I stand, apprehensively gathering my purse and coat from the stool, nerves making my palms sweaty.

I'm about to break up with my sister's boyfriend.

I already feel terrible for what I'm about to do—not because I think they'd make such a great couple, but because I like spending time with him, and once I tell him it's over between him and Lucy…

I'll probably never see him again.

Nonetheless, I trail along after him toward the hostess stand, idly waiting as he requests a table.

For two.

In the back corner.

When we're seated, Dash leans in, setting his hands on the table, moving aside his fork and knife and the rest of the utensils. "Can I be brutally honest with you?"

Please don't. "Sure."

"The first few times we went out, I wasn't feeling it at all."

"What do you mean?"

"You know I only went out with you because you're the one who asked, right? I never would have asked you out."

This surprises me, and I rear back in my seat, slightly affronted—and embarrassed—on my sister's behalf.

What do I even say to that?

"Before you get offended, let me finish what I was going to say."

Because I have nothing to say, I nod. "Okay."

"I haven't dated much. Since you're familiar with the Latino culture, you've probably guessed I come from a really traditional family. *Mis padres* raised me to be in a monogamous relationship, not sleep around, *¿sabes lo que digo?*" *Know what I mean?* he asks, tan, masculine hands picking apart a napkin, the tiny white pieces like snow on the black tabletop. "Anyway, I figured we'd go out a few times and that would be it."

"But?" I prod, shifting uncomfortably in my seat.

"Listen, you don't exactly scream 'relationship type'." His use of air quotes makes me blush, though I shouldn't take it personally since he's not actually speaking about me. "But I had a really great fucking time with you on Friday, Lucy. I thought about you all weekend."

At the use of my twin's name, I manage a wobbly smile. "Me too."

It's the truth; I did. I had such a great time with my sister's boyfriend, I actually lay in bed after that date, unable to sleep, seeing Dash's dark eyes every time I closed my eyes.

"Don't you want to see where this goes?"

Oh my God, he's asking if I want a relationship. He wants to date me—I mean, he wants to date Lucy.

This is my chance to break up with him. I won't have a better opportunity.

I swallow, gathering my courage.

"Date me exclusively?"

"*Sí.*" *Yes.* He laughs, my eyes drawn to his throat. "Figured I might as well bring it up now before we waste any more of our time."

Shit. He must really like my sister or he wouldn't have brought up the relationship talk before there was an actual relationship.

I've never met a guy like this before. Never.

And I'm not likely to again.

He tips his head back and laughs, the column of his thick, masculine throat contracting with the effort. I peel my eyes away, swallowing hard, squirming in the wooden chair.

God his throat is sexy.

"You want to talk about dating me? *Now?*"

I'm fascinated.

"Can you think of a better time?" His wide shoulders lift into a shrug. "I have no idea what normal guys do in these situations, but I think playing games is a waste of time. I also have no problem telling you what I want."

"Uh huh." I scan the perimeter, searching for the closest exit. A bathroom. A place where I can covertly text my sister.

He leans in farther, large body half across the table, only inches from my face. "*Te ves preciosa cuando estás nerviosa*, do you know that?"

He thinks I'm cute when I'm nervous?

"Am I?" I'm practically whispering.

"So fucking cute."

He is too sweet. "*Gracias.*"

Suddenly, breaking up with him feels terribly wrong; all I want right now is to get up from the table and climb into his big lap and kiss his gorgeous face. That beautiful nose.

Those full, sculpted lips.

What the hell is wrong with my sister?

What the hell is wrong with *me*?

I want him for myself, that's what's wrong with me! I might not believe in Insta-love or fairy tales or sparks flying when you first meet someone, but if I did, I'm adult enough to admit that I'm feeling them now.

That I felt them as soon as I laid eyes on him standing on my twin sister's porch.

"You need some time to think about it?"

"Huh?"

"About what you want to eat, and whether we're going to keep seeing each other. Be honest." He shrugs again. Shoots me a gorgeous, brilliant smile.

"Honest...right, for sure."

"Are you worried I won't have enough time for you?" He reaches across the table for my hand, but I pull mine back, resting it in my lap, where it's safe.

"My friends fight with their girlfriends about that all the time. I'd say it's a huge problem for most of them. What are you afraid of, Lucy?"

For one, he can stop calling me Lucy. It's making my skin crawl, makes me feel guilty. Makes me jealous. Resentful.

Depressed.

What if I'd seen him at the party first? What if I was the type of girl who had the courage to ask someone like Dash Amado on a date? Would things be different? Would it be *me* he's looking at the way he's looking at Lucy?

Lucy.

She's not just my friend; she's my sister. We're blood, and she will always come first.

Always.

DANTE

SOMETHING ISN'T RIGHT with Lucy.

I can fucking feel it.

Since our date on Friday, nothing is making any freaking sense.

For one, she's wearing a goddamn turtleneck.

Why is this strange? Because her boobs are always on full display. She's one of those girls who's constantly at the baseball house, desperate for attention, letting it all hang out.

I'm a *guy*, one with a fully functioning set of eyes, and from what Lucy has shown me, she has a fantastic rack—which is why it's so fucking odd that tonight she's buried in black cotton up to her chin.

Tonight, her long hair seems longer, windblown and natural. Messy, like she rolled out of bed to come meet me and didn't spend an hour in the bathroom curling it.

Her perfume, which used to smell like pure gold digger, now has traces of citrus and flowers and vanilla, hitting my nose when she flips that mass of hair over her shoulder.

She looks different tonight, conservative.

She's barely wearing makeup, just some mascara.

And—obviously—the whole turtleneck thing is confusing as shit.

The black color is stark against her pale skin. That's another thing throwing me off—the few times I've been out with Lucy, her skin has been a warm hue of...well, *orange*.

This Lucy? She looks like someone I could actually bring home to *mi madre*.

I shoot a quick glance at the front of her sweater; it might be covering the entire column of her neck, but it's tight, outlining ample curves I don't remember her having. Large silver hoops catch the light from the modern chandelier above, her one vanity.

"We can talk more after dinner," I tell her.

Her chin tips, lips say, "Okay."

A tentative smile.

We're quiet while I look at the dinner selections and steal glances at her over my menu. Lucy is staring at hers, biting down on her bottom lip, undecided.

"Need help deciding?"

"I, uh, didn't realize they had food, so I wasn't prepared for dinner."

Annnnd *there* it is. I swear to God, if she's one of those girls who eats like a fucking bird—salad with no dressing and a side of water—I'm going to seriously reconsider dating her.

"Did you already eat?"

"No."

"Are you *hungry*?"

Her head lifts. Our eyes meet. "I didn't really come here to eat, but yeah, I am hungry."

My lip curls. "Let me guess, you're going to have a salad."

"Well, let me see." She lifts the menu and disappears from sight as the waitress approaches and glances between us.

"Are you all set to order, or do you need a few more minutes?"

Lucy reappears from over the giant folded menu. "I'm ready if you are."

"Ladies first."

"Okay." Her index finger trails along the first page's entrées. "Can I get the filet please, medium rare, with a wedge salad—ranch dressing—and a baked potato with sour cream? And bacon."

She closes the menu and hands it to the waitress, clasping her hands serenely. Lifts her brows my direction.

Damn, I'm impressed.

"I'll have the same." I hand my waitress the menu, mimic Lucy's pose. "So."

"So."

My head tilts and I relax into the hard back of the wooden chair. Across the table, my date does an inventory of me that has nothing to do with physical attraction; oddly, she hasn't flirted or giggled at me once, another thing that seems...off.

Her eyes scan my broad shoulders—the width earned through hours of busting my ass on the diamond—up my thick neck, landing on my lips. My high cheekbones, the left one with a stitch holding it closed. My expressionless eyes and tired brow.

Her lips part. "Where did the bruises come from?"

"Someone's bat."

"I thought catchers wore face masks!"

"We do."

Those blue eyes go wide. "Have you ever lost a tooth?"

"Yes." I tap on my teeth. "This front one is fake."

"On a scale of one to ten, how bad does it hurt to get jacked in the face with a baseball bat?"

That's an odd way for a girl to put it, but the answer is easy: "Fifteen."

"What are your plans after college?"

I pause.

We've already discussed this, on our first date when she peppered me with questions about my odds of playing professional ball, how soon that was going to be, and if I had an agent.

"The pros." I drag the words out in a *duh* tone of voice.

She cringes. "Oh yeah, right. Sorry, I forgot." But then, "But you have a major, right? What are you falling back on, just in case? What happens if you get hurt?"

No girl has ever asked me that. "If I don't get drafted, I'll..." I shift in my chair uncomfortably. Discussing what would happen if I weren't eligible for the draft isn't something I normally talk about, not with girls like Lucy, girls who have no real investment in my future other than a meal ticket. "DNR."

"Department of Natural Resources?"

I blink. "You actually know what that is?"

She shrugs. "My dad likes to fish."

"What about you?"

"What about me?"

"What are you doing when you graduate?"

"I've never told you my major? That is so unlike me."

Did she just admit she likes talking about herself? I chuckle.

"You've told me you're a fashion major, but never said what you plan on doing with your degree. We didn't exactly do a lot of chatting on our first few dates." I shoot her a lazy smile.

"Oh. Right." Again, she tucks those long locks of hair behind her ear, causing her earrings to shine in the light. "My major is, uh, fashion design."

Now she's repeating herself. "You told me that already."

"Right, sorry." She avoids my eyes, taking a drink, suddenly fascinated by the heavy burgundy draperies covering the walls. "So, Dash, what's your real name?"

"Don't you think you should know if we're going to give this thing a shot?"

Lucy cringes. "Yes?"

"The fact that you're asking means you haven't adequately done your research. Haven't you tried looking me up at all?"

"I haven't had time?"

"It's Dante."

"*Dante*," she repeats quietly to herself with Spanish enunciation. Bites back a smile. "Dante Amado," she says, articulating my entire name. "Huh."

"What about Lucy, that short for anything?"

"She's—*I'm*, uh, named after our grandmother—*my* grandmother." Her head shakes. "Lucille. Lucy is short for Lucille."

Lucille *does* sound like someone's *abuelita*. The name is unsexy and unfuckable.

We're interrupted by the busboy refilling our water glasses. "Thank you," she says with a smile.

I recognize the dude from my environmental law class and give him a nod. "Yeah, thanks."

For a few moments, we sit in silence, and I feel Lucy sneaking glances. Then, "If you could live in any city, which one would it be?"

This one is a no-brainer. "I'd play for the Rockies."

My date rolls her eyes. "That's not what I asked."

"It's not?"

"No. I asked if you could *live* in any city, which one would it be. I didn't ask where you would *play*."

"Oh. Well..." I set down my fork. "*No lo sé.*" *I don't know.*

Lucy tilts her head and studies me, eyes softening. "That much of your future hinges on you getting drafted, huh?"

I raise my head, meeting her eyes. "Yeah."

Her clear gaze bores into me. "What's it like?"

"What's what like?"

"The *pressure*."

For a second, I want to tell her that's a strange fucking statement to make, but then I go quiet and think about it, really sit and think.

She's right.

It is a lot of pressure, especially since *mi familia* is depending on me to make something of myself.

All the money my parents sank into a lifelong baseball career that isn't even an official *career* yet, that's nothing but a goddamn hobby if I don't get drafted.

No one but *mi mamá* has ever asked me how the pressure makes me feel.

And now Lucy.

This—*this right here* is why I found myself really fucking liking her last weekend on our date. I think she might actually give a shit.

"It's heavy."

I don't mind saying it, admitting with two words that I have a world of weight crushing down on my shoulders, broad as they may be. It feels...

Whatever.

It hardly matters; my life is mapped out for me, and there's no getting off the path I'm already treading on.

"So where would you want to live?" Lucy prods again, still wanting an answer. "If you could choose."

"I don't know. I'm never thought about it."

"Well I have—I love the Midwest. I love the change of seasons. I've always wanted to live where I could ski in the winter and enjoy the sun in the summer, you know?"

"You love the Midwest? Are you nuts?" I hate everything about it—the rain, the hot, muggy summers. The cold—every damn winter I come close to freezing my balls off.

"You just said you wanted to move to Colorado to play for the Rockies!"

I laugh. "For *work*!"

Lucy shrugs. "No take-backs."

The server chooses that moment to appear with our appetizer salads: two plates of fussy lettuce, one tomato, and two cucumbers each. Rabbit food. Irritated at the small portion, I poke at the plate with the tines of my fork.

A soft chuckle has my ears twitching.

"*¿Qué es tan gracioso?*" *What's so funny?* I want to know.

Another laugh. "You. You're pouting because the salad is so small."

"So?" I grunt, stabbing some lettuce with my fork and shoving it in my gullet—and just like that, half of it is gone.

"Are you mad because there's nothing on the plate?"

My answer is a scoff.

"How about I give you whatever I don't finish?"

This perks me up considerably. "Are you planning on not finishing the salad?"

"No, but I figured the offer would cheer you up."

It does.

I'm starving, ravenous, and her offer to let me finish her plate? Fucking adorable.

"Hey Lucy?"

"Hmm?"

"Know what I'm going to do?"

"What?"

"I'm going to date the shit out of you."

Chapter Seven

AMELIA

I'M GOING TO DATE THE SHIT OUT OF YOU.

That is not good, and now my pits are sweating.

Dante isn't just eyeballing my salad like he hasn't eaten in days; he's staring at me the same way, like he's trying to figure out what's different about me all at the same time.

Lucy and I are night and day.

Most people still can't tell the difference, including our parents, so Dante's intensity is throwing me off like a curveball. It's unexpected in the best possible way.

No one has ever been able to tell us apart.

Dash is the opposite of everything I was expecting.

It's making me...

Jealous.

I'm jealous of my sister.

I knew he'd be handsome, but I didn't realize he'd be serious, or intuitive. He's direct and open, and the longer we sit here, the chattier he's becoming.

I like it.

I like him.

I'm attracted to him, too, which is *terrible*, because Lucy, Lucy, Lucy.

Because I'm here to break up with him, not charm him into another date. Jesus, I'm so bad at this.

When the server brings our entrées, I feel Dante watching me, tracking the movements when I lift my knife. Cut a small piece of steak. Pop it in my mouth and chew.

I'm afraid to look him in the eye, so I stare at the wall behind him. The curtains. The older couple at the table behind us.

Cut another piece, take another bite.

It's hard work ignoring him.

He's big and intimidating and sexy.

His gray shirtsleeves are pushed up to his elbows, muscular forearms flexing when he cuts the meat on his plate.

"So what else do you do when you're not studying fashion?" he enquires. "What do you do for fun?"

I try to channel my sister; these answers are easy. "I like listening to music."

Oh God, that sounded so lame.

"Listening to music in your free time? What do you do, lie on the bed and stare up at the ceiling?"

A laugh escapes my lips. "Something like that. Um, let me think, what else do I like to do..."

Lucy likes: traveling. Shopping. Getting her nails done. Going for coffee with her sorority sisters.

It sounds so shallow, I'm embarrassed to let the words pass my lips. Shopping and nails and coffee? *Ugh*.

"I love the stars, and I do a lot of hiking."

Lucy is going to kill me.

First I slip and start speaking Spanish, and now I've gone and told him I love astronomy. Lucy hates it outside, hates the wind and cold weather and snow.

If Dante takes her into the woods, she will throw a conniption fit.

"You know that set of bluffs you can hike to? The one past Coleman Hall?" There's a road you can take that winds around a huge hill, up and up; once you reach a certain point, you can park your car and climb the rest of the way up to a scenic point that overlooks the entire city. "I like going up there when it's overcast."

Panoramic views so far, you can see into the next state.

"Hiking?"

I avoid his intense gaze by pushing a mushroom into the steak sauce on my plate then popping it into my mouth.

"Yes. I, uh, went out west for spring break last year to Idaho and hiked a bunch of trails. Really anywhere with a view." I love it that much.

"I was in Montana for spring break."

"Doing what?"

"Snowboarding." He pauses. "Do you..." His voice trails off in a question.

"I ski." Lucy and I both do, something our parents insisted we learn. It's something I love, but my twin would rather parade around the chalet in cute ski clothes, flirting with the ski patrol and instructors that periodically come through.

"Why does that surprise me?" he asks, sitting back to study me.

"I don't know. Why does it?"

He quirks a heavy brow. "You seem more like the chalet kind of girl."

Ding ding ding! He certainly has my twin pegged better than most.

"You really shouldn't judge me by my appearance, and I'll try to do the same."

"You haven't judged me by mine?"

I give my head a little shake. "Honestly? Yes. I might have, just a little bit?" I hold out my thumb and pointer finger to illustrate the teeny tiny bit I judged him.

Physical appearances are the way Lucy chooses all her boyfriends. She spends hours on her hair and makeup to go out on the weekends, spends free time at the mall when she's not in class.

"Is that so?"

"Just a little." *Change the subject.* "Besides baseball, what is it you do for fun? What are your hobbies?"

"I work out a lot."

I crinkle my nose. "That's your hobby? Working out?"

He narrows his dark eyes. "*Sí.*"

"Anything else? Do you like to read, or watch movies, or, I don't know..." I think for a moment. "Go to the county fair in the summer?"

His expression is as blank as his tone. "The county fair."

"Rides, games, cotton candy..."

"As a matter of fact"—the corner of his mouth curls—"I did go to the state fair this summer."

"Same. I'm freakishly good at the ring toss."

This information must surprise him because he laughs. "What else are you good at?"

He's purposely laying down the groundwork for an innuendo, but I ignore it. Best not to go down that path.

"Darts," I deadpan.

"Darts?"

"Yeah, like in a smoky bar. The more beer I've had, the better I am."

"I would pay to see that."

"It's a sight. It's like"—I wave around a fork with a chunk of steak on it —"my stupid human trick."

"Wanna show me? I'll take you to Mad Dog Jacks and we'll play darts."

Mad Dog Jacks used to be a biker bar, but for whatever reason, the college kids in town have decided it's the perfect hangout on the weekends. Part dive, part...well, the place is a complete shithole no matter which way you look at it.

Nervously, I push the hair behind my ears. "I-I'll have to check my calendar."

Dash regards me quietly, eyes smiling. "You do that."

Before I know it, we've been here another hour, long after our food has been cleared away—so long I've completely forgotten myself and what I'm supposed to be doing here, ignoring all my sister's texts—the ones blowing up my purse. It's been vibrating for the past forty-five minutes.

Dante pays the bill.

Pulls out my chair and holds out my jacket so I can slide in. Guides me outside, hand at the small of my back, fingers gliding up and down my spine.

It's dark when we arrive outside, awkward when we walk to my car. The click of my heeled black boots against the concrete the only sound in the entire parking lot.

"Thank you for dinner."

"You're welcome." When he comes at me, presumably for a goodnight hug or kiss or whatever, I put my hands out to stop him.

"Dante." I take a deep breath, lean against the driver's side of my car, and look up at him. "We should probably finish the discussion we started inside."

"Which one?"

Oh Jesus. He's going to make me say it. "The relationship one?"

"Okay." His arms cross. "What about it?"

I'm definitely doing a crap job impersonating my sister. She wouldn't be having a conversation with him in a half-empty parking lot; she'd be leaning into him and running her palms up and down his hard chest. Planting her lips on his, no doubt sticking her tongue down his throat. Sucking on his neck and —*oh my God*, what am I even saying?

"I don't know if…" I clear my throat. Peel my eyes of the column of his neck.

"You saying you want to take it slow?"

"No." I can barely shake my head. "That's not what I meant."

He waits me out, silently—which is the freaking worst. If he was acting like an asshole or being demanding or pushing me into talking, I would have no problem kicking him to the curb.

Unfortunately, he's not doing any of those things. Dante is patient and willing to listen.

It's horrible.

"Want to go downtown for a drink? This was fun."

"It was," I admit reluctantly, feeling guilty for enjoying my sister's date.

Dash moves closer with purpose, and I propel myself backward until my ass hits my car door, sending me into a slight panic—he's definitely going to try to kiss me.

The problem is, I want him to—want him to so bad my lips are tingling.

Everything on my body is humming.

"But I should probably go."

I don't *have* to go; I don't *want* to go.

I *should* go.

Because he is not my date. He's my sister's, and I'm here to break up with him. I turn my back, unlocking the car to busy myself. Hand on the handle, ready to pull it open.

"You don't have a few more seconds to say goodbye?"

And by *say goodbye*, I assume he means *make out*.

"Not really—I should have been home an hour ago, sorry. Homework is calling."

"Darts then? Saturday? We can make asses of ourselves and you can show me how freakishly good you are."

"I can't."

"What about another night?"

"That probably won't work either."

"What the hell is going on here, Lucy?"

"I can't do this anymore...with you. I'm not..." I take a deep breath, blurting out, "I want to see other people."

"*Okayyy.*" He takes a step back, jamming his large hands into the pockets of his dark jeans, brown eyes scanning my face, searching. "Not that it matters, but why didn't you tell me sooner?"

"I tried."

"When?"

"Now?"

"You know, most people just do this shit over the phone. You could have saved yourself a lot of time by texting me."

"It's not my style."

"Really," he deadpans. "Breaking up with people over text isn't Lucy Ryan's style." Dante snorts sarcastically. "*¿Por qué me cuesta creerlo?" Why do I find that hard to believe?*

All in all, this breakup is going great, considering...if you don't factor in that I like the guy I'm breaking up with, he doesn't know my true identity, and once he finds out I lied, he's never going to want to speak to me again.

But at least he's not shouting. Or acting hostile. Or being a jerk.

"I was really starting to actually fucking like you."

"I'm sorry." My voice is small.

"Trust me," he scoffs. "I'll get over it."

It's not mean or rude, but it stings.

Hurts.

Still, he doesn't walk away as I climb into my car and buckle in. Doesn't walk away as I back out of the space, shooting him one more longing glance through the rear view mirror, tears threatening to blur my vision.

He stands in the parking lot, in the same spot my car was just parked in, watching me drive away.

Watching *Lucy* drive away.

He likes her.

Me.

I like him.

And I hate myself for it.

DASH

WHEN LUCY PULLS out of the parking lot, I do something I haven't done in ages.

Go on social media.

Log into Instagram.

Search: Lucy Ryan.

Scroll through her account. Scan the dumb pictures of her partying, hanging all over her friends. Frat parties. There are several of her at our house on Jock Row, another on what looks like a girls weekend. Starbucks cups. Photos of her nails. Other random stupid shit *sin sustancia. No substance.*

Then.

There, in living color, is a photo that has me seeing double. I do an actual double take, eyes practically bugging out of my fucking skull.

Holy. Shit. There are two of her—two of them.

Twins.

I fucking knew it. I knew something was off with her.

My fingers slide apart so the picture expands—the shot of them together, standing with their arms around each other's waist, long, tan legs playing peek-aboo beneath flirty dresses. Under a flower-wrapped archway, there's no denying they're both beautiful, the caption reading *Aunt Victoria's wedding #RyansTieTheKnot*

The really fucked up part of this whole thing? I can tell exactly which one I've been spending time with lately, and it sure as hell wasn't Lucy Ryan.

It was the girl on the right.

Under the dim lights of Zin's parking lot, I study that picture, zooming in on that face. Her hair. Her eyes.

They're identical, but it's their expressions that give them away: Lucy's trying to be confident and cocky while her sister is gorgeous and easygoing, letting her twin hog the camera.

I zoom again.

There's that dimple I love so goddamn much—one of them has it, the other doesn't. Lucy's hair is lighter, layered around her face, and cut a few obvious inches shorter.

And their chests? I was right about the tits.

Her twin is beautiful. *What was she doing pretending to be Lucy?*

They're nothing alike; any moron with a modicum of sense could have figured it out eventually—it only took me two dates with her to distinguish the differences.

Except I'm not fucking dating her anymore.

She dumped me.

Which is such bullshit, because after our last date together, I envisioned myself getting serious with a girl like her, doing all sorts of fun, outdoorsy shit together in the off season. Hiking and skiing and snowboarding, whatever she wanted to do.

I'd chase her anywhere.

We had a connection I'd bet money she felt, too. I would stake my ball career on it.

I'm a planner—always have been—so once the wheels get turning, there's no stopping this train.

I close Instagram, immediately tapping my phone to make a phone call.

It only rings twice.

"Uh...hello?" The reluctance in her voice makes me want to laugh.

"Lucy?"

"Hey Dash. What's up?"

I waste no time throwing down. "Why did you send your twin sister to break up with me?"

There's a long, pregnant pause on the other end. "My what? What are you talking about?"

She sounds so bewildered and confused.

"Cut the bullshit, would you? I saw a picture of you two on Instagram."

Nervous laugh. "Oh, *that* sister! I was confused for a second."

"How are you confused—just how many sisters do you *have*?"

"Um, just the one?"

"The one you had pretend to be you," I deadpan.

Lucy sighs like she's had this same conversation before, like the speech is rehearsed. "I'm sorry Dash, it just isn't working out between us. I'm already dating someone else new, so..." The sentence trails off, unfinished. I swear to God she's filing her nails and not even paying attention.

"Too chicken shit to break it off yourself?"

"Oh my God, admit it, you didn't like me that much either. Ugh, get over it."

"You're right—I didn't like you that much." *But I like your sister.*

She gasps, shocked by my bluntness. "Hey!"

"Don't act surprised—you're not my type either." I'm walking to my car now and climbing in, staring out the driver's side window while we talk. "That's not why I called, so relax."

"I'm not trying to be rude, but why are you calling? I *did* just break up with you and don't want you calling to harass me."

"Technically, you didn't break up with me."

"By proxy I did."

Is she always this fucking exhausting? *Jesus.* "Look, just tell me one thing: has your sister said anything about me?"

She's quiet a few seconds. "Like what?"

"Like..." I stare around the empty parking lot. "I don't know. After we went out, did she say anything about it?"

"Can you be more specific?" Lucy laughs, and I want to reach through the phone and strangle her. "I'm kidding, but also, no. She hasn't said anything specific—why would she? It would be breaking girl code for her to admit she had feelings for you."

The line goes quiet a second time, and then she sighs. "But if you're asking me if I got any twin vibes that she likes you, then yes. Between you and me, I think she does."

Hell yeah! I fist-pump the night air. "How do you know?"

"I know my sister, and she's been weird the past week—really defensive, short with me, and, well, I sense these things."

"Is that a genetic twin thing?"

"Yeah, except she doesn't have the gift. She doesn't feel things like I do."

Impatient, I keep this conversation moving along. "I'm going to assume you don't give a shit if I date her."

"If you can convince her to date you after I just did, you have my blessing." She laughs good-naturedly, and I remember the reason I agreed to go out with her in the first place. "I honestly do not give a shit."

"Thanks for the vote of confidence."

"All I'm saying is, my sister has a way stronger moral compass than I do. She's going to feel guilty—really guilty admitting she has feelings for you. She won't want to, you know, make me mad or whatever."

Oddly, that news makes me feel better; I don't want to date anyone who would backstab her own sister.

Lucy interrupts my musing. "Can I ask you something though?"

"Shoot."

"How did you know it wasn't me?"

"*¿Estás hablando en serio?" Are you being serious?*

"Can you not do that? I have *no* idea what you just said."

"Which would have eventually given you away." I smirk. "The first thing I noticed, though? You don't have a dimple near your lip like she does."

"That's true. I don't." She's smiling now; I can hear it. "No one can tell us apart, you know."

"Seriously?" I can't keep the scoffing inflection out of my voice. "I find that hard to believe. I can list at least five things she does that you don't."

There's another long pause before she takes in a breath. "Wow. I can't believe it."

"Believe what?"

"Well..." She pauses for dramatic affect. "There's an urban legend among twins that if you find the person who can tell you apart, that's like meeting your soul mate."

"Uhhh, let's not go *that* far."

"I'm serious!" Her excitement is palpable. "You might be her *unicorn*."

Getting called a unicorn is where I draw the line. "I'm hanging up now."

"Wait!" Now she sounds positively giddy. "Wait, don't hang up yet! I just want you to know that I won't make this awkward. You and I barely fooled around, and truly, it was like kissing my brother."

Awesome. Just what I wanted to hear. "Gee, thanks."

"For real. We had zero chemistry," she rambles on. "Like, *none.*"

"The chemistry between you and me is nothing compared to what I have with your sister."

"*Ahhh.*"

"One more thing before I let you off the hook for pulling a twin switch on me—I'm going to need you to do me a solid."

"A solid? What's that?"

"You know, a favor?"

Pause. "Yeah, okay. Let's hear it."

Chapter Eight

AMELIA

LUCY: SO HOW DID IT GO TONIGHT? DID YOU FINISH THE JOB?

Me: *Do you have to make it sound like I'm a mob hitman with a contract out on someone?*

Lucy: *Yes, because it sounds more exciting that way, don't you think? You know how I fancy the idea of being a mob princess.*

Me: *Tonight went well.*

Lucy: *WRONG ANSWER! That was a test, and you failed it. Do you know why?*

Me: *Um, no?*

Lucy: *Because Dash Amado just texted to see if I still want to play darts this weekend. DARTS, Amelia.*

Lucy: *Amelia, WHY WHY WHY is Dash texting me about another date? Let alone playing DARTS. You were supposed to DUMP HIM for me.*

Me: *I DID!!!! I did break up with him. I have no idea why he texted you, I swear.*

Lucy: *You must not have done that good of a job.*

Me: *Trust me, I did. When I drove off last night, the two of you were 100% broken up.*

Me: *I think?*

Lucy: *Don't do that.*

Me: *Do what?*

Lucy: *Don't punctuate it like it's a question. You were there—this shouldn't be a question.*

Me: *Yes, I'm sure I did. I broke up with him.*

Lucy: *Then why do I feel you hesitating?*

Me: *You really need to stop doing that. You are not telepathic.*

Lucy: *How do you know I haven't been blessed with the gift? Maybe I'm the twin gifted with that superpower, and it's finally getting powerful now that I've come of age.*

Me: *That is one of the dumbest things I've ever heard you say.*

Lucy: *But it's true.*

Me: *Fine. What's MY twin superpower?*

Lucy: *I don't know. You're good with small animals, being fake Lucy, and fake breaking up with boys?*

Me: *Haha, very funny.*

Lucy: *So just tell me this: if you for sure dumped his ass, why is he messaging me??*

Me: *Can you not say "dumped his ass"?*

Lucy: *Does it bother you when I say dump?*

Me: *Kind of.*

Lucy: *Why? Don't tell me you feel bad.*

Lucy: *How did the dumping go down?*

Me: *We were in the parking lot, talking, and I said dating him wasn't working out, and then I got in my car and he got in his car.*

Lucy: *Did you actually see him get in his car?*

Me: *No? Wait, why does that matter? The job was over so I drove away.*

Lucy: *You had ONE job Amelia, one. He wants to go out again, so...you tell me what we should do. I don't like him.*

Me: *STOP YELLING AT ME, and stop saying WE. He isn't my boyfriend.*

Lucy: *He wasn't mine either! And why are you freaking out?*

Lucy: *Amelia, tell me the truth—do you like him?*

My fingers hover over the keys, thumbs frozen.

Me: *I think he's nice.*

Lucy: *Nice, LOL. I bet he'd love hearing that. Nice is so boring. HE is boring.*

Me: *I don't think he's boring.*

Lucy: *That's because YOU'RE boring.*

Me: *Give me one more night to break up with him. I'll do a better job, I promise—although I'M POSITIVE I already did. He even said the words "breaking up". 100%*

Lucy: *Darts. Saturday night. 8:00*

Me: *Fine. I'll be there.*

Lucy: *Okay, but can I just say something? Darts are SO WEIRD.*

Chapter Nine

AMELIA

WHY DID I AGREE TO THIS?

I've broken up with this guy once already, in what were the worst five minutes of my life.

So why did I agree to meet him? Because I, Amelia Constance Ryan, am a glutton for punishment and cannot get Dante Amado out of my damn mind. Is it crazy that he's all I can think about?

I'm dying to see him.

He's got me longing for things I didn't know I wanted, and now I completely understand why my sister dates around.

It's been fun. And sexy. And a whirlwind.

Dante is great, and I like who I am when I'm with him.

It's true, we didn't spend that much time laughing, but to say there was no chemistry is a lie.

I was instantly attracted to someone my sister is dating and I hate it. I've never been jealous of her, but I'm jealous now, and I'm an idiot because I walked here, knowing he would be forced to drive me home at the end of this farce.

Does that make me a terrible human being?

Or just human?

He's easy to find when I walk in, hovering near the door, waiting—for me. Dante straightens to his full height when he sees me. I'm bundled up in my coat because it's insanely cold out, and he smiles at the sight of it.

He smiles at the sight of *me*.

I blush despite myself, beginning the process of unbuttoning the navy blue wool jacket, the toggles pulling free one by one.

It slides off like a robe, falls out of my hands and onto the floor.

Dash and I both bend to grab it at the same time but he beats me to it. We rise slowly, eyes connecting. Faces inches apart.

"Hi."

"Hi yourself."

"Thanks for meeting me here."

"Uh, sure." I tuck a stray strand of hair behind my ear, nervous about what to expect. "I didn't think I'd hear from you again after I broke up with you."

"Did you though?" His smile is pleasant, placating in an almost patronizing way.

"Are you trying to make me lose my mind? Because I remember our conversation *very* clearly, and we broke up, so I guess I'm confused about why you want to see me again."

Holy shit—what if he's some roid-rager, or a psycho who's going to start stalking my sister?

"I'm not trying to make you think you're losing your mind. I'm just questioning whether or not it was *you* that broke up with me."

I sigh. Some guys have such fragile egos. "I'm okay with you telling people you're the one who broke up with me. That's fine, however you wanna do it."

"You're totally missing my point." He winks, lips twisting into a grin—a smirk, really—eyes shining with mirth.

Something about the way he's observing me makes my stomach take a nosedive, and I actually lay my hand over my abdomen, pressing down to quell my nerves—to no avail.

Dante begins the short walk between us. Now he's standing directly in front of me, hands reaching to grasp my wrists, gently stroking with his thumbs. I glance down between our bodies, at our joined hands, then back up again.

"Dante, we broke up." I can barely choke out the words.

His dark gaze coolly assesses me. "Did we?"

He is going to make me insane.

Under the circumstances, I absolutely shouldn't be here tonight, shouldn't be seeing him again, the many reasons so numerous I can't resist tallying them up in my mind:

1. He was my sister's boyfriend
2. The boyfriend I broke up with for her
3. While pretending to be her
4. And ended up liking him
5. A lot
6. With a stupid amount of lust thrown in for good measure
7. He makes me crazy
8. I can't stop thinking about him
9. God, look at him staring at me
10. He was my sister's boyfriend

"I reserved us the dartboard in back but we're going to make this quick."

For real, he still wants to go through the motions of playing darts? Is this guy unhinged? I'm his ex-girlfriend!

"Uh, okay."

"You throw one and I'll throw one, then we can leave."

My eyes narrow doubtfully. "You brought me here to shoot one dart? Is this some kind of ploy to get back together? Because it's not going to work."

Dante busies himself by opening the container of darts, laying two on the table. "I have no intention of getting back together with Lucy."

I cross my arms, slightly irritated he's going through so much effort to win my sister back. "Do you do this with all your ex-girlfriends?"

"I don't have any." He laughs, picking up a dart from the table and handing it to me then grabbing one for himself. "And we both know you're not my ex-girlfriend."

"Uh, *okay*..."

He gestures for me to step up to throw. "Ladies first."

I'm so confused that I actually move forward without arguing, glancing back to study him before facing the board, the long heavy metal dart weighted in my fingers.

What the heck is going on?

Closing one eye to concentrate, I instinctively bite down on my tongue. The dart releases from trembling fingers, heading straight for the red outer double ring. Sticks in and hangs there proudly.

My hand is still shaking when I lower my hand, stepping off the duct tape on the floor so Dash can take his turn.

"Looks like someone isn't as calm and collected as they thought they were." His mouth isn't smiling but his eyes certainly are, palms rolling a black dart between them, eyeing the board shrewdly. He points the dart at me.

"If I get a bull's-eye with this, you spend the rest of the night with me, and I get to kiss you."

"Are you insane?"

He ignores my question, asking one of his own. "Do we have a deal?"

The odds of him actually hitting the target dead center, on the first try, without warming up, are slim, so I nod my head in acquiescence. Plus, if he makes the shot, I'll finally know what it's like to have those lips on mine, even if it's just once. I deserve it.

"Yes, we have a deal."

"Shake on it?"

I stare down at the large hand he extends, that calloused palm and the rough pads of his fingers. Glide my hand across his flesh, shivering when our skin connects.

It's positively electric.

We both shiver.

I give him a limp shake, eager to free myself from his grasp, tucking my hand away for safekeeping, the tingling sensation lingering far too long to be comfortable.

Far too long to be forgettable.

Dante steps in front of the dartboard, plucks my small silver arrow off, sets it aside, stands on the marker taped to the floor. Focuses on the target against the wall, homing in on that red, round center, leaning with one leg kicked behind him dramatically. His strong arm draws out the action of tossing the tiny missile.

My expressive eyes get wider when the dart lands the bull's-eye, heart damn near having palpitations when his heels pivot and he shrugs his shoulders as if to say, *Golly gee, look what I did!*

"Did you just hustle me?"

His shrug is easy. "Beginner's luck?"

"Liar."

Dante laughs. "You should talk."

We're staring at one another as if in a showdown, unwilling to bend.

This is getting awkward. "Maybe we should leave?"

"Thought you'd never ask. Can you hold on one second?" Removing his cell from the back pocket of his jeans, he taps open the camera. Positions it so I'm in the background of his selfie. Clicks.

"What are you doing?"

"Taking a picture so we can always remember this moment."

It's official: Dante is crazy.

He plucks his dart from the board, setting it in the box on the table. Grabs my jacket off the nearby chair then clasps my hand, tugging me through the crowded bar, past the throng, until we're shoving through the front door.

We stand under the fluorescent light on the side of the brick building. It cast an unflattering, eerie glow.

I glance around, creeped out by the stark surroundings, wanting to leave, to go anywhere but here.

"Where should we go?"

Dante stuffs his hands into his pockets, shoulders slouching. "I hate asking you this, but would you mind coming back to my place? There won't be any distractions and we need to be alone."

"You want me to come to your place...to talk."

"Unless you're more comfortable at your place? I just think wherever we go, it needs to be just us." Dante shifts on his heels, shooting me a pointed look. "Don't you have shit you want to confess?"

Confess? Why is he putting it like that?

He thinks I'm my twin, my goofy, carefree sister, who by all accounts doesn't have a care in the world, who dates two, three guys at once, letting me do her dirty work for her.

Falling for her latest conquest is *not* my idea of a good time.

I'm a fool for standing here, a damn fool for coming.

"Let me get this straight: you want me to come back to your place even though I broke up with you? What are you, a glutton for punishment?" I let the sarcasm slip.

"I know I'm an idiot. I've done some really stupid shit in my life and chasing you just might top the list, but I like you, so yeah, I guess you could say I'm a glutton for punishment."

My nostrils flare, jealously flaring up. "You don't even *know* me."

"You're right, I don't." His head tilts to the side. "Whose fault is that?"

"What's that supposed to mean?"

"You've been *lying* to me—but guess what? I like you anyway."

My mouth gapes open, and I struggle for words. "I..."

We're under the glowing neon sign of Mad Dog Jacks, still standing under the bright, fluorescent light, arguing, it would seem.

"What would m-make you think I've been lying?"

"Let's not do this here." His shoulders rise and fall casually.

"Just say what you came here to say," I press. Then add, "Please," for good measure, practically begging.

His chin goes up. "What's your name?"

"M-My *what?*"

"*¿Cuál es tu nombre?" What's your name?*

My heart—*oh my God*, my heart is beating, thumping so wildly inside my chest I actually raise my arm, resting my hand upon it like I'm about to recite the Pledge of Allegiance. I press down, breathing heavily in and out...in and out, grasping to get control of my voice before I speak.

"Wh-What do you mean?" Playing dumb: one more thing Lucy and I have in common, although she's always been better at it than I am.

"You're such a terrible actress."

I say nothing; I couldn't possibly.

Dante's hands come out of his pockets so he can throw them in the air, frustration tangible, intense. "Would you just tell me! Tell me the truth. I've been really patient here, putting up with this twin bullshit." He blows out a puff of air, trying to remain calm. "I know you're pretending to be Lucy."

I *feel* my eyes go as wide as saucers.

"Anyone with half a fucking brain can tell you're not her, and I've been going out of my fucking mind." His hands gesture around his head like his brain is exploding as he continues his rant. "Trying to figure out what to fucking do about this—pardon my French—because Jesus, I can't stop thinking about you. It's driving me crazy that you won't even say your name. Can't you understand that?"

My head nods slowly.

"Can you please just be honest about who you are and put me out of my goddamn misery? I swear, I don't even give a shit that you lied." He pauses. "Well, I *do*, but I won't be a dick about it. I'll get over it. I've done nothing but dwell on this the past few days, so can you do me a favor and just be honest?"

My breath is coming as hard and fast as his stream of words, steam rising from my mouth against the freezing pre-winter air. The tip of my nose is cold too, and probably getting red as we stand out here, gawking at each other.

Those large hands of his get stuffed back into the pockets of his jeans, and he watches me expectantly. "Now it's your turn to say something."

"I don't know *what* to say."

"Let's start with this: do you even give the slightest shit about me?"

I will not cry, I will not cry, I will not cry.

"Yes." My shoulders sag. "Yes I care."

He's closer now, arms at his side. "*¿Cuál es tu nombre?*" *What's your name?*

"*Yo me llamo,*" I begin, voice cracking. "Amelia."

My name is Amelia.

"Amelia," he repeats back, my name a revelation. "It's nice to meet you."

"How..." I swallow hard. "How long have you known?"

He falters briefly, choosing his words. "I knew something wasn't right almost from the minute I saw you. There were a few things that stuck out that I couldn't make sense of, then you smiled and I saw this." He takes his finger and touches the spot below my lip, the one he wanted to touch while we danced at the concert, only this time when his finger presses into it, I'm able to enjoy it. "And your laugh is different."

It's true. My laugh *is* different, lower and less chipper, not as flamboyant or brash as Lucy's tends to be, mostly because she likes drawing attention to herself.

"I have no idea what to say. We didn't switch places to be malicious. I was trying to help my sister, and this is a first."

"What's a first?"

"We've never been busted."

"I didn't bring you here to bust you for lying. I brought you here because I like you. I told your sister on the phone that I—"

"Wait, you talked to my sister? She knows?"

"Of course she does. I had to make sure she wasn't going to be all fucking pissed when I pursued you."

"Pursue me?"

"I said I was going to date the shit out of you, remember?"

"Yes." *How could I forget?* "What did Lucy say when you talked to her?"

"She's the one who helped me get you here." He rakes a mammoth paw through his dark, silky hair. "After you broke up with me, I stood in that goddamn parking lot staring after you, wondering what the fuck had gone wrong, adding everything up in my head. A few things you'd said didn't make sense, so I went to Lucy's Instagram feed."

My nod of understanding is slow. "And found our pictures."

He nods as well. "Yeah. That's when I called her—from the parking lot, I might add—to see if she'd care if I wanted to date *you*, not her. She basically tripped over herself trying to unload me." He laughs. "She really does not like me."

"But you don't like her."

"Not at all—I like you."

Swoon!

Nothing this romantic has ever happened to me before, ever, never in my life, and I doubt it will again.

"I'm thinking we should get out of here. I'm freezing my ass off."

"I'd like that." I close the space between us, letting my hands brush up his chest. "You know what else I'd like? Kissing you."

He dips his head a few inches so our mouths are a breath apart. "Is that so?"

"I feel like we've waited forever, don't you?"

"It's really only been a week, Amelia."

God it sounds so good hearing him say my name.

Mine.

"Only one of the best and worst weeks of my life."

"Sometimes the anticipation is the best part of playing the game, don't you think? The expectation, the tension leading up to the big play."

"Is that what you think this was? A game?" I'm trying to be flirtatious, but I don't think it's going very well; he scrunches up his nose.

"No. I don't think either of you were skilled enough to keep it going that long. You seriously suck at method acting." He grabs my hand, and I feel butterflies. He kisses my forehead.

Ugh.

"Come on, let's go."

I go, willingly.

"YOUR FRIENDS AREN'T GOING to think this is crazy, right?"

We're outside on the large front porch of the baseball house, about to go inside. Dante's left hand is poised to pull the screen door open, foot propped on the threshold, his right hand gripping mine.

I stop him from going in with a gentle tug, worrying my bottom lip.

"No, why would they?"

"You dated one sister, now you're dating the other," I explain. "You don't think your friends are going to have a problem with that?"

"*Mi cielo*, my friends aren't going to know the difference. They're a bunch of idiots."

I blush at the term of endearment. *My heaven.*

"Okay. I just don't want them to think I'm, you know...shady."

"No one is going to think you're shady." His laugh is deep, amused. "If anything, they'll think it's fucking awesome I dated twins."

I snort. "You're not Hugh Hefner—you didn't date us at the same time."

"But I *kind* of did." He turns to face me, stepping down off the stoop and pulling me into his body, hands sliding to my waist.

"But it's not like you *knew*."

I watch his mouth, engrossed by his lips. "My friends would still think I'm badass if I told them about it."

"They'd think you had a threesome." I roll my eyes. "Because most guys your age are perverts."

"I'm not."

"That's right—you haven't even tried to kiss me." My chin tilts up smugly in his direction, cocking my right brow.

"You didn't want me kissing you, remember? I've waited because I'm a nice fucking guy."

"I didn't want you kissing me because I *liked* you."

His head gives a perplexed shake. "That makes no sense."

"I didn't want you kissing me as Lucy. I wanted you kissing me as *me*."

He moves to cup my face between his palms, stroking his thumbs up and down my cheeks, giving me the tingles. "You are seriously the fucking cutest."

"No, you are." I'm trying to pucker my mouth between his hands, but just end up with fish lips.

"We're not going to be one of those disgusting PDA couples, are we?"

"You're the one with your hands all over my face." His big, rough, perfect hands. "Are you going to kiss me?"

His face inches closer. "Do you want me to?"

"Yes," I whisper. "I've waited forever for you to put those giant paws on me."

I don't know what I expected to happen when our mouths finally connected, but this wasn't it.

It's so much better.

Charged.

The slow, deliberate probing from his delicious tongue is like a dream.

Wet.

Jesus, he tastes so good, so stupid good.

Impulsively I push against his chest, backing him up against the siding of the house with a gentle shove, rubbing up on him.

Dante's palms grip my ass, squeezing. Drag me onto his firm body, into his hard-on, running those fantastic catcher's mitts up and down my backside. Tense.

His lips are full. Hard.

Soft.

I could swallow him hole.

It's not enough, not nearly.

I'm so hot right now, and horny, and *God* I hate that word but it's so true. I want to rip my clothes off so he can touch my body, so I can touch his. We've done the three-date thing; I'm ready to take it to the next level.

This kiss is ruining me—I wonder what actually having sex with him will do.

When we finally tear ourselves apart, Dante blinks. Blinks again.

Mutters, "Let's get inside."

"All right," I say breathlessly, eagerness vibrating all my nerve cells. "If you don't think your roommates are going to judge me, I'll go inside."

"I really think it's adorable that you think they'd be able to tell the difference—really goddamn adorable." He plants another heated kiss on my lips, leaving me dazed and feeling cold when he pulls back to push open the front door. "Besides, most of these guys aren't with the same girl twice, so who the fuck are they to judge."

They're sitting around the house when we walk through the door, Dash tugging me in. We pause in the entry to the living room, and I give a short wave.

"Hi."

"Guys, you remember Amelia."

They're all openly staring, friendly and interested. Curious, like a group of toddlers would be.

One guy—a huge ballplayer sprawled in the center on the couch, remote control in his hands—looks me over from head to toe, then back again, wrinkling his forehead.

"I thought you said her name was Lucy."

I grin, responding before Dante can. "Nope. It's Amelia. You must be confusing me with someone else."

The guy looked sheepish. "Shit, sorry."

Dante's index finger tickles my palm as we move toward the hall. "Anyway, we'll be in my room. Don't bother us."

When we're in his bedroom with the door closed, he turns to me and says, "That little fib slipped right off your tongue, didn't it?"

"I've had a lot of practice." I grin, slipping off my shoes, already comfortable. "Mostly with family members and a few unsuspecting teachers in grade school."

"You didn't even bat an eye when you lied to his face. Please don't ever do that to me."

"I was just teasing him." I grab Dante's thick arm, squeezing. "Which would be impossible with you since you can tell us apart."

"Lucy said I'm your unicorn." He laughs, tossing his jacket on a chair.

This gives me pause. "She did?"

"Yup. I'm a motherfucking unicorn."

DASH

THE DIFFERENCES ARE remarkable now that I know she's a completely different person; they stick out at me like red flags.

Obviously, there's the hair, and the dimple. Her brows are arched higher, eyes sharper. Amelia has an air about her that Lucy doesn't; she's deliberate and thoughtful.

Her lips? Incredible.

She sheds her jacket, sliding it down her arms, hanging it on the chair I have at the table functioning as my desk.

Truth? Now that I have her in my room, I'm not sure what to do with her.

She surveys the space, hands on her narrow hips, taking it all in. There isn't much to see, just a bed, table, chair, floor lamp. The bare minimum, not even a television.

Nothing to watch, nothing to see, no where to go but the bed.

Really it's just a beige box where I sleep, and now I seem to have acquired a girlfriend to go along with it.

I take a seat on the edge of my mattress, legs kicked apart, leaning back. Watch her preoccupying herself with my shit. The laptop on my desk and the sticky notes on my wall above it. The few books I have stacked on the table.

"This is nice, clean."

"I'm really boring." It sounds like an apology.

Amelia turns. Starts toward me, stepping in between my legs. "I don't think so."

My hands automatically slide to her waist like we've done it a million times, pulling her in for a hug. I bury my face in her flat abdomen, nuzzling her sweater.

Her deft flingers pluck tenderly at the black hair atop my head then trail down my neck, landing on my shoulders. Back and forth, fingertips kneading the muscles there.

It feels like heaven.

"I don't think you're boring at all."

I raise my head. "No?"

"*Te encuentro fascinante.*" *I find you fascinating*. "I love your big hands. They do incredible things, wouldn't you agree?"

My hands *are* fucking big. I flex them against her ass, skimming them down her denim-clad butt cheeks.

She goes on. "And you're kind."

Kind.

That's something no girl has ever called me, but I suppose it's true.

My nose finds it way between her breasts, and she laughs when I give her another nuzzle. I can't wait to see her tits, can't wait to get her naked.

"And you're as turned on as I am."

"*Sí.*" My arms encircle her, the tips of my fingers gripping her inner thighs from behind, thumb beginning to slowly massage the apex. "*Te encuentro sexy.*"

Amelia bites down on her lower lip. "Do you think we're moving too fast?"

I raise my head again. Her mouth is *right* fucking there. All I'd have to do is raise my face an inch…

"We haven't done anything."

Yet.

"No." Her lips brush mine with a moan when my fingers rub the delicate nub through her jeans. "But I want to, don't you?"

"*Sí*, but we can wait."

"I don't think I can." Her hips roll.

"Amelia," I enunciate with my accent. "I want you to know I'm all in. I'm not going to bail on you if we have sex right away."

"All in? Already, Dante, after two dates?"

"Three after tonight."

"I can live with that if you can." Her sexy voice wavers. "Do you, um, have, you know…condoms?"

"I live in a house full of baseball players—there are condoms everywhere."

"In your drawer?"

"No." *Shit.* "I'd have to go find one."

"Just in case, maybe?" She backs away. "I'm a planner, very organized."

My kind of girl.

"Be right back." Planting an electrically charged kiss on her mouth, I bolt off the bed. "Make yourself comfortable."

Shutting the door behind me, I riffle through three bathroom drawers and one cabinet before finding a brand new box of condoms, thanking Christ I didn't have to go to the living room and ask for one.

It's bad enough that I'm planning to get laid in a house full of my roommates.

I palm the bright pink box, giving my door a gentle knock before reentering. "It's me."

Nudge the door open.

Stop dead in my tracks.

Almost drop the box to the floor, almost hurl it across the room.

"Amelia…holy shit."

She's lounging on my bed in just her lingerie, breasts spilling over the cups of her bra. The material is lacy, sheer, and black. I stare at her pale flesh.

Her shoulders rise and fall apologetically. "You said to get comfortable."

Getting naked isn't exactly what I had in mind, but I'd be an idiot to argue and *mi madre no creo un tonto. My mother didn't raise a fool.*

I'm already tearing the shirt off my body when she says, "You have a shirt for me to wear later? Because I'm thinking I might spend the night."

Unbutton my jeans, slip them down past my hips. Kick them off to the side.

She's leaning against the headboard, watching me undress. "I've never met a guy so eager to be tied down."

Tied down, tied to the bed—either way, I'd be happy.

"I was bred to be with one woman, *mi cielo*."

Amelia moves first, scuttling toward me on her haunches, meeting me in the middle of the bed. "Is that so?"

She places the tip of her finger in the center of my chest, above my heart, dragging it down my body. Down my solid pecs. Down my rib cage. Over my abs, circling my belly button.

My dick is stiff when she reaches the waistband of my tight boxer briefs, hooking the material, snagging it away from my skin. I think I stop breathing when the nail of her finger brushes the head of my cock, a pleasant smile pasted on her lips, schooled expression neutral.

Neutral except for her eyes.

Those are gleaming.

Predatory.

Shining when she clasps my hard-on with all five fingers. Gently squeezes through the thin cotton of my underwear.

"I'd wondered about the size of this." Her voice is a low, seductive murmur. Her hand? Giving me another squeeze. "And now I know. Hmm, your breathing seems labored. Do you want me to stop? Let you catch your breath?"

I shake my head like a dope. Swallow hard, wanting so badly to jut my hips forward and thrust. Grip her hand so she'll tighten it around my throbbing dick.

"It's probably a good thing you're in such good shape." She releases me—*the tease*—running both palms up my abs. "I've never dated an athlete before." Plucks a nipple. "And your skin is so smooth—well, except for these goose bumps."

Still, I wait, not touching her, knowing I'll get rewarded for my patience.

"You know what I like about you Dante? Besides the fact that you're so smoking hot and look incredible with no clothes on? I love that you're so level-headed, so composed."

Amelia moves closer on her knees until her lace-covered breasts brush my chest. "I've never found anyone so sexy or attractive in my entire life."

I don't know what's making me harder—how upfront she is about what she wants or the fact that she's not wearing clothes.

When our mouths collide, one hand slides down her spine to cup her tight little ass, the other braced behind her head. Our kissing sounds fill the air, sexy moans and lapping tongues. We're messy and hurried and when Amelia starts rubbing her pussy against my dick, our pelvises grinding, it's time to get completely naked.

She beats me to it—reaches behind her back, lips still suctioned to mine, unclasping her bra in one motion. Pulls the straps down her arms, discarding the delicate black fabric on the side of the bed. Grapples for my hands, placing them on her tits.

I've never really been a boob guy, but I've just been converted into one. They're full, heavy in my hands, my thumbs brushing over her dark areolas at the same time Amelia pushes down the waistband of my boxers.

"*Eres mío*," comes her husky murmur. "*Mío*." *You're mine*.

We're whispering all sorts of sexy shit to each other in Spanish as our hands explore, limbs entwined, falling to the mattress. Amelia lazes beneath me, hair fanned out on my pillow, permitting me to explore, dreamily twirling my hair when I latch onto her nipple, sucking. Arches her back. Runs her nails down my scalp, my neck.

I rise above her, index finger idly trailing up her underwear, up the front, thumb pressing down in small, lazy circles.

Round and round and round on that little pink nub.

Her fists clench the quilt covering my bed.

"Don't," she gasps. "Or I'll come."

My finger hooks into her panties, pulling them aside, fingers stroking. "You want me to stop, *cariño*?"

"Yes. Jesus, just take off your underwear and get on top. I can't take it anymore."

"You like it on the bottom?" *Good to know*.

We're shoving down our underwear and in a group effort, I kick mine off, roll on a condom. Hover over Amelia, dragging the hard length of my cock along her thigh until we're both moaning with anticipation, both of us eager.

Willing.

Ready.

"S-Sometimes I do." Her eyes are closed, teeth biting down on her lower lip.

"I wonder something." I lean in, sucking on her earlobe as I whisper, "Do you *really* think you deserve a good fucking?"

Her eyes open, nostrils flare. "*Yes*."

I let my dick nestle between her legs. "I can't believe you fucking dumped me."

Amelia's hands pull down on my ass, urging me inside. "You are not bringing that up right now."

I reach between us, clutching my erection, running the tip up and down her slit, making her moan. "Oh, but I am."

When she pouts, turning her head and presenting me with the pale length of her neck, I lean in, sucking. "You weren't even going to tell me, were you?"

"No."

"That's really naughty of you."

"It is." She nods. "So naughty."

"You probably don't deserve this." I let the head of my cock creep in the smallest fraction.

"But you do." Amelia's face is flushed, hips beginning a slow roll, arms above her head. She looks ready to pass out.

"I do, don't I?"

"*Yes*," she hisses, panting. "God you feel good. *Ohhhh* shit..."

So fucking good, in and out.

In and out.

Just the tip, just the motherfucking tip—not even an inch—is ecstasy.

When she moans—so loud my roommates in the other room undoubtedly heard—I press a finger to her lips. "Shhh."

Her tongue darts out and flicks my finger. No sound comes out of her lips when she mouths, "*Fuck. Me.*"

We both do a lot of pleading, panting, and praying to Jesus, God, and everyone else while I'm balls deep inside her, rocking back and forth, muscles clenched.

It's gasping, desperate, breathless fucking.

My hands slide beneath her ass when I come, unloading inside, nose buried in the crook of her neck.

Mi cielo.

My heaven.

About The Author

Want to see more of Dante and Amelia? Catch glimpses of them in Jock Row, the first book in the Jock Hard series, releasing late Spring, 2018.

Do you like reading about the good guy getting the girl? Then check out this excerpt from How to Date a Douchebag: The Learning Hours, now available on Amazon and Kindle Unlimited

The learn more about Sara Ney, find her at authorsaraney.com, or subscribe to her newsletter

ONE GOOD MAN

It's spring, 1970. The Vietnam War has been raging for years with no end in sight. Janey Martin, a California college student and aspiring journalist is tired of writing puff pieces about her university men's sports teams. She wants to be taken seriously as a journalist and as a woman. With riots at their doorstep, her wealthy father sends Janey to the Sorbonne in Paris to finish her college education away from the chaos.

Janey is reluctant to leave the Big Story that is Vietnam, but vows to prove herself. Much to her dismay, her first assignment is to interview the hotshot star forward of a local soccer team. Janey is sure Adrian Rousseau is going to be like every other playboy jock she's ever dealt with, but quickly learns there is much more to Adrian than meets the eye.

The mysterious, sexy footballer just might be the biggest story of Janey's life.

Dedication

For Kate...

"Everything I know about morality and the obligations of men, I owe it to football."
— **Albert Camus**

ONE

All Along the Watchtower

ISLA VISTA, CALIFORNIA
Santa Barbara Police Department
May 8, 1970

"JANELLE MARTIN."

I jerked my head up and brushed a tangle of long blonde hair out of my eyes with my left hand. My right was handcuffed to the chair at the booking officer's desk. I'd been sitting here forever. An hour ago, a few of my fellow UCSB students marched past me, their hands cuffed. They flashed me the peace sign behind their backs as they went by. At least eight of them were booked for arson, vandalism, and resisting arrest, and then taken to jail while I sat; my ass growing numb on the hard, wooden chair.

Finally, the booking officer returned.

"Get up, Sunshine. You have visitors."

"My name isn't Sunshine," I muttered, as the officer uncuffed me from the chair.

"No?" The officer smirked. "Isn't that your hippie name?"

I wanted to tell him I wasn't a hippie. Or a flower child. I might've looked the part with the long, straight hair, peasant top and flared jeans, but hippies were about peace and love, and that wasn't my scene. I was going to graduate UCSB in a year with a double-major in journalism and French. *My scene* was following the Big Story. The biggest stories.

And Vietnam was the biggest story of them all.

I never thought the war would come to sleepy little Isla Vista, but the protests have only been escalating among my fellow students. That night, a bunch of them shoved a dumpster full of burning trash through the glass doors of the Wells Fargo Bank. My Nikon Photomic caught it all on film...and then I got caught in a cloud of police tear gas.

Tears streaming and my lungs burning, I was accosted by cops in riot gear. I tried to tell them I was a reporter, but they didn't listen. The flames of the burning bank looked like hellfire to my blurred vision, and the shadows and shouts of protestors and police created a frightening chaos. But of all the sounds tonight, the small tinkle of my camera lens breaking as the cops threw me to the ground, was the loudest.

As I walked with the booking officer, a pang of fear tightened my chest. I wondered if I've ruined my future. The officer led me to a small room that was probably used for questioning suspects. I expected to find a detective, waiting for me to rat out my fellow students.

Instead, my father was there.

A sense of nostalgia for simpler times rushed over me, like a tide. I wanted to be his little girl again instead of a twenty-year-old who'd been tear-gassed and arrested and was now in *jail*. But I had to be strong. I was tired of covering vanity pieces for the university sports teams, and this was my first real test as a journalist.

I bottled up my longing to hug my dad, and looked to the other person sitting beside him. A dark-haired woman, and for a split second, I thought it was my mother. But it was Helen Strumfield. My best friend sat beside my father, chewing nervously on her thumbnail.

Helen had been my friend since grade school. Since before the war; before any of the fires or sit-ins or marches. We used to eat ice cream sundaes and giggle over the Monkees.

A lifetime ago. Before the world went mad.

My father got to his feet as I entered, his face falling and in anguish to take in my soot-covered, bloodshot-eyed appearance.

"Janey," he said, rubbing his fingers over his mustache. Helen tugged a lock of her brown hair, her eyes darting between my father and me.

"Hi, Dad."

The urge to hug them both came back, fierce, but the idea of touching either of them with handcuffs on my wrists was too shameful. I sank into the chair opposite.

"Hi, Helen."

"Hey, Janey," she said in a small voice. But warm. My father's was cold by comparison.

"So it's come to this," Avery Louis Martin stated. "Arrested for vandalism. For *arson*. For destruction of government property."

The room was empty but for us, and yet he kept his voice low, as if the whole town of Isla Vista—or all of greater Santa Barbara—were there, listening in and snickering that the only daughter of the wealthy, upper-crust owner of Alato Winery & Vineyards wasn't the good girl everyone thought she was.

"Do you have any idea what you're done to the family these last few weeks? Never mind your poor mother. She couldn't even get out of bed when Sergeant Hollis called tonight."

"I didn't do anything but take pictures. They saw me—a college student, looking like a protester—and grabbed me too."

"They wouldn't have, if you didn't get so damn close," my father said. "Why do you have to get so close?"

"Because I'm tired of writing puff pieces on the university debate tournaments, or yet another article on the swim team's 'hopes for a good season.'" I shrugged. "I wanted to find a big story and get right to the heart of it."

"Is the heart of the story inside a jail cell?"

"It's not a locker room or out on a track," I said.

He stared me down and I did not blink.

Finally, he folded his hand on the table, and put on his deep, I-mean-business boardroom voice. "I've made a decision. You're not covering any more protests. And you're not attending college, not at UCSB."

I shot up straight. "What? Why? Where am I going to go?"

"You're going to France, to finish your education away from all this nonsense."

I gaped, honestly taken aback. And then I laughed. A dry and humorless one, but a laugh nonetheless. "France? You're pulling my leg."

"You'll withdraw from UCSB immediately," my father continued. "Your grades and your French fluency will be enough to get you into the Sorbonne, and if not, I'm prepared to pull some strings or line a few pockets if that's what it takes. You'll fly to Paris. I will arrange an apartment for you, and you'll finish out the school year, then resume your studies in September."

"So that's how it goes? You just *declare* how it's going to happen and so it does? I'm not one of your business ventures." I shook my head incredulously. "And the Sorbonne? There *is* no Sorbonne. Haven't you been paying attention? The revolution two years ago? The old buildings aren't even usable."

"The school is still operating, and you are going there to finish your degree."

I gave my head a shake. "Dad...you can't. There's no story there. Not any more. In '69, sure. But now—"

"Now, no one is getting shot," my father said, his voice heavy, his eyes heavier.

"This is ridiculous," I said. "One arrest and you totally freak out."

My father's folded hands tightened. "A month ago, a college student just like you, was shot and killed at one of these protests, Janey. And there was that terrible shooting at Kent State just last week. Four young people, dead." He shook his head. "If you keep covering the war, something might happen to you...Your mother and I are afraid."

"You don't have to worry about me—"

"Clearly, we do," my father said, loudly.

"There's nothing in Paris for me. No story..."

My father slammed his closed fist on the table, making Helen and I jump. "Your *story*, Janelle, is that you stay safe."

"Safe," I spat. "For you or me? Tell the truth, Dad. You and your fancy, rich clientele don't want to see what this war is doing to us. To the boys who are called up to go and die. You don't want to look at the photos I take, do you?" I shook my head, crossed my arms. "I'm not a helpless little girl you can ship overseas, like some kind of fragile piece of glass. Not gonna happen."

"It *is* going to happen," my father said. "To keep you out of jail. My friendship with Ted Hollis is the only reason you haven't been booked already. But I don't have to pull that string. I can set you up in a nice apartment in Paris, or you can sit in a prison cell in Chowchilla. Your choice."

My heart clanged dully in my chest. "You'd let me go to prison?"

"What else can I do?" My father's stern expression cracked to reveal the worry beneath.

Helen cleared her throat, reminding us of her presence.

"Might I have a word alone with Janey, Mr. Martin?" she asked in her timid, fluttery little voice that had never been lifted in protest.

My father gave me a final, thick look, almost pleading, and left the room. Helen waited until the door clicked shut, and then smiled at me sadly from behind her horn rims.

"Janey."

"You agree with him," I said. "That's why you're here. That's why he brought you."

"Yes."

"Why?"

She leaned over the rickety Formica table. "Because I'm worried about you, too. You kept getting closer and closer to the story, that now you've become a part of it."

I shifted in my seat, my handcuffs clanking as if to punctuate her words. Helen never said much. All through school, the kids called her Hush Puppy for her silence and her big, sad eyes. But when she did speak, when she was serious about something, you felt each word slug you in the gut.

"So what should I do?" I said. "Run to France and do what?"

"Keep reporting," Helen said, "only from a safe distance."

I snorted. "I don't want to keep at a safe distance. I'm so sick of not being taken seriously. I want the big stories."

"It's not like Paris is sleeping," Helen reminded me. "It's a mess too. And what is left for you here, anyway? You spend all your time in the journalism department's dark room. You don't talk to me... I had to hear from Karen that Bobby dumped you. He said the same thing: you're getting too involved in your work."

I rolled my eyes. "Bobby's boring and bad in bed. And you can quote me. Besides," I added, "what's wrong with hard work? I *have* to work twice as hard as a man in my field to get anywhere."

"Maybe so, but what kind of work can you do from prison?"

"My father is bluffing. He'd never let me go to jail."

"I agree, but the shootings, Janey. Those are real."

I dug my thumbnail into a crack on the table, and tried not to think about how scared I was last night. "It feels like running away."

"There will never be a shortage of stories."

"Yeah, little ones," I muttered.

Helen grinned. "I don't know. Sometimes it's the smaller stories that have the greatest impact." She reached across the table to take my hand. "Find that story, Janey. Find one that looks like nothing on the outside, but once you crack it open..." She shrugged with a smile. "...Something incredible comes out."

I pursed my lips, but my fingers curled around hers. "My dad's secret weapon: Helen Strumfeld."

"Your dad's no dummy," Helen said. "And he loves you, too."

Tears stung my eyes, but I blinked them away. I wasn't a crier. I needed my eyes to stay sharp and focused. To find the right photos to go with the best articles.

The big stories.

TWO

Subterranean Homesick Blues

MAY 15, 1970
Paris, France
Janey

MY FATHER DIDN'T KNOW how badly Vietnam had torn France apart, or how it still hadn't put itself back together. He thought the war ended for France in '54. But in the spring of '68, riots, protests, and strikes brought the country to a standstill and broke apart the very university my father was sending me to.

I tried to explain this to him during my rushed registration process, but he didn't get it. Or want to. He needed me to get away from the States, period. It didn't matter that Paris was in a state of upheaval; no one had been killed here and that's all that mattered.

As I said my goodbyes and boarded the plane, I pondered my plans for Paris. If my father thought I was going to stay out the war, he was sorely mistaken. My days of interviewing obnoxious athletes and dodging their grabby hands or ignoring their crass comments were over.

Even so, as soon as my flight lifted off, putting more distance between myself and Vietnam, I felt like a coward. Never again would I run away from a big story. There were still big stories in France; I just had to find them.

THE FLAT MY father rented for me was pretty keen, I hated to admit. I didn't want to come here as a spoiled, little rich girl; an ex-pat, living off Daddy's dime. But there I was, doing just that. The flat was in the 5th arrondissement, across the Seine River, and on the first floor of a beautiful old building. I had a small yard in the back where I could sit in the morning, in a wobbly wrought-iron chair at a tiny wrought-iron table, drinking my coffee.

I decorated the interior sparingly. No psychedelic prints or peace signs like my dorm at UCSB. The only poster was my Janis Joplin, *Live at Winterland,* and it was situated over my record player. I played a lot of Janis those first few days, and not much else. She had a reckless but melancholy feel to her singing that I loved. As if she were throwing herself at life full speed, no matter how hard it might hit her back.

All of my classes at the new Sorbonne—mostly French Literature and Journalism—were in the morning, leaving me plenty of time to myself. Too much time.

Homesickness and Loneliness were my constant companions, and I decided it was high time I ditched them in the city. Journalists had to live in strange countries all the time to chase the big stories; I needed to treat this like an assignment.

I grabbed my knapsack with my wallet and current read—*Jonathan Livingston Seagull*—and headed out.

I strolled down the Rue Cujas, past one of the old Sorbonne buildings. Shops, cafés and apartment blocks flanked me on all sides. I'd planned to sit at an outdoor café but my legs carried me past a dozen, and I couldn't make myself take a seat. I kept walking until I heard Bob Dylan floating on the warm spring air, drawing me along like a sweet scent to a hungry person.

The blue lettering on white above the door said *La Cloche.* The Bell. It had a few tables and chairs outside, but the music was coming from inside, along with many talking and laughing voices.

I followed Bob Dylan into the interior to see that La Cloche was half-café, half-club; dimly lit, with clouds of smoke hanging the air. A small stage—empty now—where a band could play, was tucked into a corner behind a tiny dance floor, also empty. The afternoon crowd was entirely young people; drinking beer, coffee, or cocktails, and clustered around rickety tables and crammed into booths. The walls were covered in posters of American and British musicians: Jimi and Janis; Led Zeppelin and the Stones; Sam Cooke and Patsy Cline.

My heart clenched at the Americana in particular, and I nearly turned around and marched back out. I scolded myself that I was tougher than that; if I didn't have the moxie to battle through homesickness, I probably wasn't cut out to be a journalist.

I sat at a small table for two. Behind me was a booth packed with young men and women; boyfriends and girlfriends, I noted after taking a peek from behind my long wall of straight blonde hair. The men had their arms slung casually over the girls' shoulders. Loud talk and laughter rolled out of the booth like waves that crashed into me over and over. The men, I deduced, were all on a soccer team—football, they called it here—and had a game coming up this Saturday.

I knew nothing about soccer except that it was a huge deal in Europe, and that the soccer players and their girlfriends in La Cloche were very loud. It was stupid to think I could read here. I started to get up to leave when another loud swell of voices lifted in greeting nearly bowled me over.

I looked around to see a young man with longish brown hair and a scruff of dark beard, join the other players. He was tall and packed in muscle; his shirt revealed the tight lines of his chest and arms, and his jeans strained to contain his thighs. He had a pretty, leggy brunette stuck to him like glue; she gazed up at him adoringly.

While the friends in the booth pulled up another table to accommodate him, the guy looked my way. A flash of his dark blue eyes met mine, sending a jolt through me, as I realized I was staring. I didn't impress easily, but this guy's blue eyes seemed to hold a depth I wasn't expecting.

At my slack-jawed stare, the guy's grin turned cocky, breaking the spell instantly. I huffed a snort and looked away.

Nope. Just another arrogant jock.

I'd dealt with enough of those back home. I'd once had to interview the UCSB men's swim team. I didn't think I'd gotten in one question of merit between crass jokes, and declining requests to go out and 'have some fun.' Not one good man among them.

Fuming, I sat and tried to read my book. I'd been about to leave La Cloche but now I was stuck. The guy would think I was leaving because of *him.* I had to kill at least five more minutes before making my escape.

With my eyes in my book, and my hair shielding my face, I eavesdropped without being noticed. My mother would've scolded me for being rude, but the group was so loud, I practically didn't have a choice.

I deduced that the girl clinging to the attractive-but-arrogant new guy wasn't his girlfriend. He introduced her as Anna, and it was clear she didn't know anyone there. She wasn't a part of the tight-knit group, and none of the other girls made much effort to get to know her. I got the impression this wasn't the first time the guy—whose name I had yet to hear—had brought a girl around.

Arrogant and a playboy. Even worse.

Minutes passed. The Rolling Stones played over the sound system. Mick sang that he couldn't get no satisfaction. Neither could I. But as loud as the soccer group was, they sounded fun, and my loneliness wouldn't let me leave them alone. When my five minutes were up, I stole a final glance.

They were all talking and laughing but for the extremely attractive guy. He sat slouched in his seat, legs spread, doodling on a cocktail napkin while his teammates talked about the big games coming up. Without the cocky grin, the guy's beauty was harder to ignore.

I stared a moment too long and the man raised his dark blue eyes to meet mine. My breath caught as he smiled again, this time softly. Warmly. A tingle of electricity danced up my arm.

I quickly looked away. "Shit," I muttered behind my wall of hair. Now I was stuck again. I couldn't let him know he flustered me.

This is ridiculous.

So was my heart that was beating a little too fast. My cheeks felt warm.

I didn't have long to wait; the team players and their girlfriends got up to go. I kept my face carefully hidden behind my hair, even as the urge to look at the guy one last time was fierce, as if he'd cast a spell over me. But I was stronger than that. I didn't turn to mush like some of the other girls at college did over a handsome man.

You also don't introduce yourself to new people. Those guys and girls could've been friends.

Loneliness leapt over Homesickness and when the group was gone and the front door of La Cloche closed behind them, I sighed. Not with relief but with disappointment.

I sat for long moments, staring at the blur of words on the page in my book, until a waiter, dressed in jeans and a black shirt—young with unruly hair—approached with a tray balanced on his hand. He held out a cocktail napkin.

"From over there," he said, jerking his head back to the booth where the soccer players had been sitting. "I think this is you."

I took the napkin. It was me, sketched in pencil. A profile. My arm was long and somewhat elegant in this rendering; my elbow propped on the table, my hand vanishing under my hair as I rested my chin on my palm. My eyes were cast down. Sad.

I stiffened and tried to hand the napkin back. "I don't want it."

The waiter only shrugged, smiled, and moved on. I pulled my hand back and stared at the sketch once more. The attractive guy made this napkin doodle. I was sure of it.

"It's probably how he reels in a new woman ever week," I muttered aloud in English. "No thanks."

But instead of leaving the napkin on the table, I tossed it into my bag, and headed out.

THREE

You Can't Always Get What You Want

JANEY

MONDAY MORNING, I dressed in a sleeveless blouse with an orange checkered print, a white skirt, and white, knee-high boots. Portfolio tucked under arm, I headed to the journalism department at the Sorbonne to plead my case.

The office door of the editor-in-chief of the university newspaper said *Antoine Heloin*. He was a tall, serious-looking guy in a black shirt and tan corduroys. His gaze lingered too long on my legs before he finally perused my portfolio from the other side of a cluttered desk. A photo of the Earth as seen from the moon hung on his wall.

"Impressive," Antoine said, flipping through Xerox copies of articles I'd written, covering the various academic activities and sports teams at UCSB. My hopes rose as he came to the end and lingered over the glossy black and white protest photos I'd taken just before leaving the States. "Very impressive. I think I have the perfect assignment for you."

I sat up straighter. "I'm ready for anything."

"The Paris Central football team is a few points away from third place in their division. If they can get into third—or higher—they will advance up to Ligue 2, a professional league. We'd already set up an interview late this afternoon with their star forward, Adrian Rousseau, but our sports writer is ill and can't do it." Antoine reached over the desk to hand me a small file folder and a piece of paper with an address on it. "The job is yours."

I took the paper slowly, my hopes deflating. "Soccer? You want me to interview a soccer player?"

"In France we say *football*, Mademoiselle," Antoine said. "I know it's not a popular sport in America, but to the rest of the world, it is everything. If you knew what an honor this assignment was, perhaps you would not look so sour now." He shrugged. "Although, I can always give it to someone else..."

And I get nothing.

I stiffened, and tucked the folder into my portfolio. "Deadline?"

"Two days."

"Is there anything I should know about Adrian Rousseau?"

Aside from the fact he's probably a giant, egotistical asshole, like every other athlete I've ever had to interview.

"He is the best center forward the sport has seen in a generation." He raised his hands as if nothing else mattered. "And a medical student. He's rich. The girls love him." He gave me an almost clinical up-and-down glance. "You're just his type, too. Try to stay focused on the job at hand. If you can."

I suppressed the urge to roll my eyes. "I'll have the interview with a photo spread in two days."

"*Fantastique.*"

I rose to my feet and flipped a lock of hair over my shoulder. "In America, monsieur, we say *groovy*."

THAT AFTERNOON, I grabbed a map to guide me to the Rousseau residence. The air was sticky with early summer humidity as I made my way to the 16th Arrondissement. The map told me the Rousseau residence was close to the major soccer stadium, Place des Princes, and a smaller stadium called the Stade Jean-Marc, where Adrian Rousseau played with his team.

On the train, I read the background info in the folder Antoine had given me. Adrian was a second year medical student at the Sorbonne, and the star center forward on Paris Central. The team was in a division called Championnat National but could advance if they had enough points.

I shut the folder with as snap. I didn't understand this soccer stuff—the European system was a mystery to me—but it looked like Championnat National was a third division league, below the real professionals.

My irritation mounted. I wanted a Big Story, not to dodge the advances of a second-rate athlete and write yet another puff piece to stroke his ego.

I spat a curse as I made my way down an elegant boulevard lined with gorgeous 19th Century buildings, one tucked tight to the next. The 16th arrondissement reminded me of the Upper West Side of Manhattan. It screamed 'old money' and I guessed the Rousseau family had their fair share. Their home was like every other here—three-stories of beige stonework, with wrought iron balconies along every window.

But as I made my way up the three steps to the front door, I noticed rust along the gate, and my knuckles scraped peeling paint when I knocked on the door.

"A moment!" came a soft, feminine voice on the other side—high-pitched and strained—as if unused to rising louder than a whisper. I heard a strange clanking of metal and then someone struggling with the door lock.

Finally, the door squeaked open on its rusted hinge, and a teenage girl—maybe sixteen or seventeen—shuffled into view. She had heavy-looking braces strapped to both legs and leaned heavily on one crutch. Her dark hair brushed her chin, and her eyes were dark blue, but bright with curiosity.

"May I help you?"

"Hi, I'm Janey Martin," I said. "I'm here to see Adrian Rousseau?"

The girl's face broke open in an unguarded smile that made her seem even younger. "Ah yes, for the newspaper? My brother is in the backyard. He knows you are coming but said it would be a man. Are you a real journalist?"

I frowned at the question and the guileless smile on the girl's face. "Yes. Or I will be once I have my degree. I'm studying at the Sorbonne."

The girl's smile brightened. "So is my Adrian."

With effort, the girl stepped aside to let me in, and my senses were bombarded with the history of the building; as if I could smell its age in the plaster peeling in places from the wall, and in the dust that danced in a shaft of light from the front window. Like the exterior, the interior had the appearance of wealth in need of upkeep.

"I am Sophie Rousseau," the girl said, closing the door behind us. "You are American, no? Your French is very good."

"Thank you," I said absently. I stared at the old-world charm of the Rousseau residence, with its oriental rugs, antique-looking lamps, and furniture that looked as if it belonged in a museum.

"A *soccer player* lives here?" I asked, incredulously.

Sophie's eyes darted away. "Yes, of course," she said, then brightened. "Adrian is a brilliant footballer, and an even better medical student."

"The Sorbonne is far from here," I said, watching Sophie struggle ahead of me, leading me through the foyer. "That's a long commute."

"It is for him to get to school," Sophie said. "But we're very close to where his team plays and practices."

We came to a curved stairway where two young women were bounding down, talking and laughing. They stopped when they saw me, and exchanged amused glances, then hurried out, toward the front door.

"Friends of yours?" I asked Sophie.

"Oh yes, of course," she said quickly, her voice high again. "Come. Adrian is through there."

I followed Sophie through the first floor of her home to a small backyard patio with green grass beyond. It reminded me of my own flat, with its wrought iron furniture, though this space was much larger.

I heard someone gasp and realized with a jolt of embarrassment that it was me. Sitting on one of the chairs, wearing jeans and a tight-fitting polo shirt, and reading a book, was the devastatingly handsome man from La Cloche.

Sophie glanced up. "You know Adrian?"

Yes, he drew me on a napkin...

"No," I said. "I thought I recognized...but no. We've never met."

I tried to master my breathing, which had suddenly become short. Adrian was even more handsome in the bright summer sunshine. It caught the gold in the dark brown hair that brushed his shoulders. His scruff of beard highlighted the strong cut of his jaw and perfect cheekbones.

I realized I was standing there like a dope, mooning over those *perfect cheekbones* and the beautiful deep blue eyes of his that were riveted to his book. Before I knew it, my hands rose to my camera around my neck. I snapped my first photo of Adrian Rousseau, the star soccer player, at rest and reading a book.

Get a hold of yourself. Be professional.

I glanced at Sophie with her crutch and braces; she'd had to struggle through the house to let in a guest Adrian *knew* was coming. A cool detachment settled over me. I thrust my chin out as Sophie showed me to the small yard.

"Adrian, this is Janey Martin," Sophie said. "From the newspaper."

Adrian's head came up and his eyes flared with recognition and surprise. For half a second, a soft smile graced his lips, but I was glaring coldly at him. His gaze cooled to match mine; his smile turned lazy.

"I was expecting someone else," Adrian said, his eyes raking me up and down. "But this works too."

His voice was velvet, with a hint of gravel. Deep. Sexy.

He's still an ass.

I crossed my arms under my camera. "So happy to hear you approve."

Sophie turned to me. "Would you like some lemonade?"

"No, I'm fine, thank you," I said quickly.

"Please. It is so warm out."

"You don't have to, really..."

"It's no trouble at all," Sophie said cheerfully. "I'm not as fast as Adrian, but I'm happy to bring you some. Let me..."

"Yes, let her," Adrian said in a low voice, meeting my gaze steadily.

I sucked in a breath. "Thank you, Sophie, lemonade would be lovely."

Sophie made her way back into the house and shut the back door. I sat in the other wrought iron chair, across from Adrian.

"Let her bring me the lemonade," I said. "Let her answer the door while you sit in the sun and read..."

"Yes? And?" Adrian returned, unruffled. "She has cerebral palsy; she's not in a coma. She's capable of answering the door to her own house or bringing a guest a drink."

I sat back in my seat. "But it seems difficult for her—"

"Sophie does what she wants. I'm not going to stand in the way of letting her take on any task she feels she can handle." His blue eyes clouded over with bitterness. "No one should."

"You're right," I said, biting each word out. "I apologize. I didn't mean any offense."

Adrian sighed and tossed his book—a French translation of *One Flew Over the Cuckoo's Nest*—face down on the table. "You're not the first to try to coddle her. She seems weak and soft, I know, but she's got more strength in her than you and I combined."

I stared at this man, and for some reason, Helen's words about finding a big story within a smaller one whispered in my ear. I bent to extract the heavy cassette recorder from my bag.

"Is this okay?" I asked, readying the recorder. "Standard procedure..."

I tried not to think about how I was about to capture Adrian's bedroom voice on tape, and inwardly scolded myself again.

His lazy smile returned. "It's fine."

"Groovy." I pressed down the play and record buttons, and the cassette wheels turned. "Interview with Adrian Rousseau—"

"I saw you at La Cloche," Adrian said. "A few days ago? You don't remember me?"

"Uh, yes. I was there," I said and stiffened. "But no, I don't remember you."

His cocky grin broadened. "I find that hard to believe."

I rolled my eyes. My fleeting sliver of a hope that this interview might not be like any of the athletes I'd done before, died a swift death.

"I don't remember you," I said, "but I know your type."

"My type? Please, tell me my type."

"Rich, arrogant, cocky. A different girl on your arm every weekend..."

"Sometimes two girls," he said with a wink.

"Of course. Using your God-given soccer talent to—"

"Score on and off the field?" he said, with brows raised. "I hope you're less clichéd in your writing."

I opened my mouth to retort but he cut me off.

"You're American, right? From New York?"

"California."

"Hollywood? You're pretty enough to be an actress."

"Speaking of huge clichés..."

Adrian shrugged, his eyes sharp again. "Annoying, isn't it?"

I opened my mouth to retort, then snapped it shut. "I'm not an actress. I'm a journalist, or will be if you'd let me get a question in."

I rummaged in my bag for a pencil and notepad to conceal how flustered he made me. My hand flailed too fast, and as I tore out my pencil and notebook, the cocktail napkin with his rough sketch of me flew out of the bag and fluttered down onto the patio. I bent to snatch it but Adrian was quicker; lightning quick.

He plucked it off the ground, an infuriating smile spreading over his lips. "I believe you dropped this."

FOUR

She's Got You

Adrian

SHE KEPT THE DRAWING.

The warmth that flooded my chest at that was unwelcome.

So she's beautiful? You've been with plenty of pretty girls.

"The waiter gave it to me," Janey said haughtily. "I meant to throw it away, actually."

"But you didn't."

She crossed her arms. "Did you draw this?"

I nodded. "Still Life with Hair and Book."

"God, you're obnoxious." She snatched the napkin and tossed it onto the table.

"But you *do* remember me," I said, sitting back and lacing my fingers behind my head. I kicked my feet up on another chair. "I thought so."

"Can we please start the interview?"

"Ask."

She huffed a breath and composed her face. "You live here with your sister?"

I nodded once, slowly. "And my mother. I help my mother take care of Sophie, and vice versa."

"And your father...?"

"He went to Vietnam in '53." I held her gaze steadily. "He didn't come back."

"I'm very sorry to hear that," she said, her voice warming. "You are the sole provider for your mother and sister, then?"

"I am."

Now her beautiful face softened and I felt another question I wasn't prepared to answer readying on her lips. I flashed her the smile that Brigitte said could disarm any woman.

"Your French is very good," I said. "For an American."

She straightened her shoulders. "*Merci*."

"How did you become fluent?"

"My nanny was French," she said. "She taught me from the time I was a baby, and I continued studying it through school."

"A nanny, eh? So you have money?"

She bristled. "That's a personal question, and not relevant to our interview."

"What does your father do?"

"He owns a vineyard, but—"

I snorted a laugh. "A vineyard? In *California*? Did he send you to France to learn the secrets of making *good* wine?"

Janey slapped her pencil on her notebook. "Our wine is perfectly good, thank you very much. Award-winning, if you must know, and our winery is quite successful, though I have no idea why I'm explaining this to you."

"Well, now we're even," I said.

"Even?"

"The rich, arrogant, footballer being interviewed by the rich, stuck-up American girl." I held my hands out. "I like a level playing field."

She clenched her teeth. "You are truly infuriating. If we could get back to the interview...?"

"I suppose."

"You don't like talking about yourself?"

"Not especially."

"Then why agree to this?"

"For the team," I said, and heaved a sigh. "Go on. Let's get it over with."

She nodded slowly. "Antoine tells me you're a medical student. Is it difficult maintaining your studies while playing soccer professionally?"

"I'm only semi-pro."

"Even so, do you have time to devote to your studies while playing a full season of soccer?"

"For now," I said. "Next year, I begin the practical training in a hospital. There won't be time for both."

"What happens to soccer then?" she asked. "Or is it med school you quit?"

I stiffened at the question. No one had ever asked me that before. Everyone—my team, my sister, my mother—they all assumed I'd quit med school if I had a shot to make it to Ligue 2 or higher. The truth rose up but I bit it back and fought for another diversion.

"Paris Central is Division 3. But we're two points from the promotion zone, which means—"

"Wait, the promotion zone? Points...?"

"Yes," I said slowly. "We get points. Two for a win, one for a draw, and none for a loss. The top three teams with the most points advance to the higher league. The four teams with the lowest are relegated down. Goal differentials decide ties..."

She scribbled furiously to get this all down.

I furrowed my brows. "You're not familiar with the EUFA tier structure of European football?"

"I don't know much about the game at all."

I sat up straighter, the perfect diversion having fallen into my lap. "Nothing?"

Janey shrugged. "I know it's a long game, and hardly anyone scores."

I had to bite back a laugh. "Why did Antoine send you to interview me?"

"The other guy was sick." She raised a brow. "Why? Not used to having someone unfamiliar with your glory and achievements? Sorry to disappoint, but I'm only here to get a little background on you, and talk about your upcoming match against...." She consulted her notes. "Consolat Marseille."

I burst out laughing. I loved her prickliness. Her refusal to flatter me like so many others—men and women—did was like a goddamn breath of fresh air after breathing in the stench of my own 'talent' for so long. I wanted to break off the cocky asshole act I kept up to keep people at a distance. I wanted to *talk* to this girl. But I couldn't talk to anyone. Not about the truth.

"Here's your article," I said, "Paris Central wins. The End."

"Thanks to you?" she asked. "The star forward?"

I let a sly grin lift one corner of my mouth. "Do you even know what a forward does?"

"Runs a lot? Tries to kick a ball into a net?"

Another laugh burst out of me. "Yes, that's true. Forwards do a lot of running. But I'm not just a forward. I'm the center forward. The striker." I leaned over the table, and dropped my voice an octave. "Strikers do all the scoring."

Janey shot me a look and then checked her watch. "Three minutes."

I blinked. "What is three minutes?"

"How long it took you to hit on me, thereby turning this interview into the same as every other interview, where I'm not taken seriously and now just want to leave as soon as possible."

My smile faltered and I sat back in my chair. She'd been burned before. Of course she had. The way men talked *about* and *to* women sometimes made me want to scream. But if it turned me into just another jock to her, so be it.

"You don't know anything about football and you clearly don't care, so why are you here at all?"

"That's a good question," she said. "I want to cover stories of *substance*..."

"Ah, I see. A bunch of guys kicking a ball up and down a pitch is beneath you."

"It's the story I have to write with the hopes of getting something better."

"Better..."

Something better than football. A long-buried longing tried to rise up in me but I quelled it with practiced ease.

"You're quite honest, aren't you?" I asked.

"Look, I'm sure soccer—"

"Football."

Her jaw clenched. "I'm sure *football* is very important to you and to France and to... all of Europe. But there are much bigger things happening in the world right now. Important, awful, history-making things that I'd rather be writing about than a ball game."

She sat back, as if bracing herself for me to kick her out, not realizing she had put that deep longing of mine into words when I never had before.

"I agree," I said, and turned my gaze from Janey to the kitchen window where Sophie was laboriously pouring a glass of lemonade from a heavy pitcher. "There are more important things in the world. More important things to do and be."

"Like a doctor?" Janey asked softly.

My gaze dropped to the tape recorder's slowly spinning wheels, ready to capture my words and make them real, let them out of this small backyard and share them beyond this American girl.

She leaned closer, into my space. "What happens to your medical studies if Paris Central moves up to Ligue 2?"

I met her gaze and held on. "They stop."

"Is that what you want?"

"Off the record?"

"Sure."

I struggled with how to answer, or whether to answer at all. This girl's honesty was like an invitation for me to do the same.

Finally, I said, "Off the record: there are more important things in this world than what I want. On the record, Janey Martin, there is nothing more important than football."

A silence fell and I realized we were both leaning over the table, less than a foot away from one another. I had a fleeting idea that Janey was diving deep into my eyes to read my thoughts.

The back door screeched open, jerking us apart. I tore my gaze from hers and smiled at my sister. "That looks good, Sophie."

She crutched down the step to the patio, a tall glass of lemonade clutched precariously in one hand.

"I poured one for you, Adrian, but I can only carry one at a time."

"I'll have it in the kitchen in a bit," I said. Her answering smile for me was sweet and adoring, instantly reminding me of my responsibilities to her and my mother.

But that doesn't mean I can't see Janey again.

I reached over and pushed 'stop' on Janey's tape recorder and turned to her. "Saturday then?"

She coughed in surprise. "What happens Saturday?"

"We conclude the interview. You need to see a football match firsthand or your article is going to sound like a bunch of amateurish gibberish. You want to be taken seriously?"

She pressed her lips together for a moment. "Yes."

"So do I. Saturday at noon at Stade Jean-Marc. We'll finish the interview after."

"Antoine wants the article in two days," she said.

"Tell Antoine I said to wait."

She took another long pull from the lemonade, her pride not letting her say yes to me so quickly.

"Saturday then," she said. "For the article."

"Right," I said, holding her gaze. "For the article."

She finished off the lemonade and set the glass down. "Thank you very much, Sophie. It was just what I needed." She gathered her belongings and turned to me. "See you."

"You have a drop of lemonade on your chin," I said.

"Where?" Her hand flew to her mouth. "No, I don't..."

I held out the cocktail napkin with my sketch of her, my brow raised.

Janey dropped her hand from her dry chin, fuming. I expected her to flounce away. But she snatched the napkin out of my hand, dropped it into her bag, and coolly walked away.

I wasn't in love with her, but in that moment, I knew someday I would be.

FIVE

Leader of the Pack

JANEY

ON SATURDAY, I got ready for my first soccer game. I was loathe to admit it, but the thought of seeing Adrian again sent a flurry of butterflies in my stomach.

But soccer? The last thing I wanted to do was spend my Saturday watching a soccer game.

This is ridiculous. He just wants to show off.

But already, I'd begun to suspect that Adrian Rousseau was much deeper than the cocky front he presented. It kept slipping off of him like a poorly-fitting mask. And I liked what I saw beneath.

I told myself this was a journalistic endeavor as I pulled on my jeans. If I wrote a fantastic article, maybe Antoine would assign me bigger stories.

Or maybe you'll get stuck with the sports beat permanently.

I paired my jeans with a pretty peasant blouse that had colorful embroidery along the collar and sleeves, and put on lip gloss. I hardly ever wore makeup. I wondered why I bothered today.

For Adrian...?

"Oh, knock it off."

I blew air out of my cheeks. Adrian Rousseau was a mass of contradictions, and that made him intriguing to me *as a journalist.* That was as much as I was willing to admit. I didn't come to Paris to get tangled up with a soccer player, no matter how *interesting* he was. I could only hope the Big Story I sensed in him was worth it in the end.

With my convictions locked firmly in place, I headed to Stade Jean-Marc to watch Paris Central—the home team—play against Consolat Marseille, the team currently holding first place in the division.

The stadium wasn't small—larger even, then the football field back at UCSB. The stands were benches, not seats, but the crowd was large. I guessed at least a thousand people had turned out in the sticky humidity to watch Division 3, semi-pro soccer teams play.

"Note to self," I muttered under my breath, "soccer is a really big deal."

I headed toward the front line near one of the goals, where other journalists were lined up taking photos and smoking cigarettes. All men. A few muttered to one another, and jerked their chins at me as I approached. A few leered at me; a few snickered at my camera hanging from my neck. I ignored them and pushed my way to the front to get a clear shot of the field where the game was already in progress.

The press pool was clustered near Consolat's goal. The Marseille team wore red and white. Paris Central was in yellow jerseys with black shorts. It took me no time at all to spot #9.

Adrian Rousseau was a streak of yellow flying between defenders, dancing with the soccer ball between his feet to dodge his opponents' attempts to steal. He passed to another PC player who nearly lost the ball; it glanced off his foot. A Marseille defender raced for it but Adrian was quicker. He beat the defender to reclaim possession and didn't pass again. With a few taps and sweeps of his feet, he got a clear shot. The goalkeeper made a valiant dive but Adrian's kick was too fast; too hard. The ball sailed between the diving goalie's gloved hands and was snagged by the net.

A swell of cheering rolled from the crowd, and around me, the journalists' cameras' clicking was like a swarm of locusts. I realized I hadn't taken a single photo, but had watched with my mouth ajar.

I lifted my camera to get a shot. Adrian's teammates crowded around him, cheering and slapping him on the back. His smile was wide but it faded almost instantly. My camera shutter clicked again and again.

I photographed him as his eyes scanned the stands, as if he were looking for something. Or someone.

Then he spotted me.

My breath caught when Adrian's smile returned. It lit up his entire face the way scoring the goal never did. He nodded his head once, and I nodded in return, ignoring how my heart was pounding. Then Adrian turned and ran back to center line to take position.

The game resumed, and all I did was take photos of Adrian Rousseau. I told myself that's what I was there for; just doing my job, but I took far more than I needed—certainly too many for a simple interview. By the second half, I managed to drop the camera to watch him play. To watch the strength in his legs as he raced—so fast—toward the ball whenever it came anywhere near him. To watch how his muscles moved under the tight-fitting jersey. To watch the power in his legs as he ran, stole, and kicked the ball with a speed and grace that almost defied reality.

He plays with a speed and grace that defies reality, I jotted on my notepad. *As if he's out of his body, moving with instinct instead of thought.*

Adrian scored twice more before the game ended, defeating Marseille 3-0.

He jogged to the end of the field where I stood, sweaty and breathing hard. Up close, I took mental photographs of him; my eyes seeking to capture every little detail. The way a lock of hair stuck to his forehead, plastered there with sweat. His jersey clung to his chest too; a streak of grime across the thick muscles of one thigh; the tuft of grass sticking out of his shin guard. He played hard and it was all over him.

Without warning, the mental photographs became a moving picture show of Adrian holding his body to mine, sweat and the scent of cut grass enveloping me as he bent to kiss me...

I jerked my head out of the reverie with a gasp to see Adrian nod his head toward a section of the stands, midfield. I followed with my gaze to Sophie sitting with an austere-looking woman—Madame Rousseau, I guessed—amid a small crowd of guys and girls I recognized from La Cloche the other day. The footballers' friends and girlfriends.

The other journalists called out to Adrian but he ignored them all—his attention was only for me. I nodded in understanding, and he grinned and ran to the locker room across the field with the rest of the players.

"Gentlemen," I said, and pushed through the cloud of smoke and lewd comments, to make my way to the stands.

Sophie saw me approach and rose shakily to her feet. "Janey!"

"Hi, Sophie," I said, and we kissed cheek to cheek. "Good to see you again."

The crowd of girls noticed my approach and I felt their attention on my back.

"I'm so happy you came to see Adrian play," Sophie said. "He's so fast, and can run with the ball like no other. Did you see him?"

"She has eyes, dear."

The middle-aged woman, her dark hair in a perfect bouffant, rose to her feet. A cloud of expensive-smelling perfume around her warred with the scents of cut grass, cigarette smoke, and the sausage sandwiches the crowd favored at half time. Her blue dress looked like a throwback to the 50's, flaring at her knees and fitted at the waist. But like her house, her clothing looked a little frayed around the edges.

"And who is your new friend, Sophie?" A tight smile touched the woman's lips as she regarded me. "Or is she one of Adrian's women? And an American, no? This is new."

One of Adrian's women.

My hackles went up, and if I hadn't just been fantasizing about him kissing me. Adrian left me confused and flustered; I'd always prided myself on never being the kind of girl who got boy crazy.

Forget it. I'm not going to let him.

"This is Janey Martin," Sophie was saying. "She's a journalist doing a story on Adrian for the university. Janey, this is my mother."

Madame Rousseau's entire expression brightened with the news that I was there to write about her son.

"How marvelous," she said. "I'm Nathalia Rousseau."

"Nice to meet you," I said.

Mme. Rousseau's handshake was tight and dry and I instantly wanted my hand back. She held on, pulled me a step closer.

"I do hope it will be a flattering article? What am I saying?" she laughed. "What could anyone say against our dear Adrian? He is a pride and a joy." She glanced at her daughter, her lips turning down in a frown. "Sophie, you must've tired yourself. You should sit."

"I'm fine, Maman..."

"Sit."

Sophie looked as if she were about to protest, but smiled tightly at me, and eased herself back down to the bench.

Mme. Rousseau's gaze flitted to the camera around my neck. "And did you take many photos of Adrian?" She laughed again, too hard—a cocktail party laugh—with her head thrown back. "He's so fast, your photos might turn out a blur."

I smiled faintly. "Yes, maybe so." I glanced over my shoulder to see some of the soccer girls watching. One—a pretty brunette with a sweet face—was biting back a smile. She shot me a commiserating look.

"I do hope your article is flattering to my Adrian," Mme. Rousseau was saying. "Scouts are constantly trying to talk to him but he keeps pushing them off until the end of the season." She smiled tightly. "Perhaps in the course of your interview, you might convince Adrian to take a meeting?"

"I'll see what I can do," I muttered.

The rest of the fans were filing out of the small stadium, and I wished I could go with them.

"Hey," said the brunette from behind me. "Hi, I'm Brigitte."

"Janey Martin."

"I heard. You're interviewing Adrian?"

"For the Sorbonne paper."

"Then we're classmates," Brigitte said, indicating her group of eight friends. Her smile was genuine and friendly, and I liked her immediately.

"Come with us to La Cloche," said a pretty blonde in a colorful beaded blouse. "It's a club we hang out in...basically all the time."

I smiled. "I think I've heard of it."

"So you'll come?"

"Um, yeah, that sounds great," I said.

Brigitte craned to speak to Sophie. "You're welcome to join us," she said. "And you too, of course, Madame Rousseau."

"No, thank you," Mme. Rousseau said, and favored her daughter a stern look. "In fact, Sophie and I must be getting back. Come."

The hopeful smile on Sophie's face died as she pulled herself back to standing. Mme. Rousseau turned to me. "I look forward to reading your article." Her cold blue eyes gave me a final once-over. "A woman journalist. Must be hard to prove oneself in such a male-dominated profession."

I started to tell her most professions were male-dominated, but I only smiled and watched, with a pang in my heart, as she prodded Sophie out of the stands.

"Tell Adrian I said he was wonderful," Sophie said to me on her way.

I nodded, then frowned. *Won't she see him when he comes home?*

Brigitte and the others moved in to surround me as soon as Adrian's mother and sister were gone.

"You're American, no?"

"From New York?"

"Your French is very good."

We chatted amicably and I learned that Brigitte was the girlfriend of Robert, the goalkeeper for Paris Central. The blonde was Lucie, and she was dating a midfielder named Thomas. Nine of the eighteen Paris Central players attended the Sorbonne and this was their group. The girls all had long hair, flared jeans, and billowy peasant blouses; the boys with longish hair and button down shirts, just like my friends back home. A tight-knit, mini-tribe of friends and girlfriends that hung out together. To be welcomed into their fold kicked my Loneliness right in the ass.

The rest of the team, Brigitte told me, were blue-collar workers, struggling at dead-end jobs.

"Most have to go straight to their work after a game," she said. Her kind face brightened. "Today's win gave them enough points to get into third place. Only the top three teams of very division advance. If Central advances to Ligue 2, they can quit their jobs and play football professionally."

"What about the players who go to the Sorbonne?" I asked casually. "What happens to their studies?"

"They quit, of course!" Lucie said with a laugh. "Who wouldn't rather play football than study all day? And some players, like Adrian, Robert, and my Thomas, have a real chance at signing with a Ligue 1 team."

"Paris Saint-Germain," Brigitte said, grazing her teeth over her lower lip. "Mmm, it's a dream."

"Is there a lot of money in Ligue 1 or 2?" I asked, while fishing my pencil and notepad out of my bag. "Enough to live off of?"

Lucie and Brigitte exchanged incredulous glances.

"Is she for real?" Lucie asked.

Brigitte smiled gently. "You have professional sports stars in America? It's like that." She leaned closer to me. "I'm very proud of my Robert, and Thomas is a great player, but only Adrian is a super star."

A strange sense of pride that I had no business feeling swelled in me. I recalled Adrian's off-the-record confession that there were more important things in life than soccer, and formulated my next question very carefully.

"Can Paris Central advance to the next division without Adrian?"

Brigitte pursed her lips. "They might advance if they can hold third place or higher. But to stay? Adrian is their top scorer by half. They need him." She cocked her head at me, a glint of suspicion in her eye. "Why do you ask? For your article?"

"Yes," I said quickly, and offered a sheepish laugh. "I know nothing about soccer."

"*Football*," Brigitte said, her warm smile returning. "And if you stick with us, you'll hear more about it than you ever wanted to in your life."

I returned her smile while my thoughts turned to the players on the team Brigitte had mentioned. Those who worked other jobs in the hopes of making it Ligue 2.

What happens to this team if Adrian quits?

I scribbled a final note on my pad to ask him this question and a dozen more. I was buzzing with them now. A bigger story, hidden behind an innocuous interview.

"See there?" Brigitte said. She nudged my elbow and nodded her head at a locker room door across the field. The stands were nearly empty now and a few players, newly showered and changed, were emerging. "Here they come."

The group headed out onto the field to meet them, and Lucie—long hair and beaded shirt flying behind her—flew across the grass and into the arms of the tall, red-haired Thomas. He picked her up and swung her around, and they kissed almost violently. All lust and dueling tongues.

I hurriedly looked away and my gaze landed on Brigitte as she slung her arms around Robert—a tall, handsome man with broad shoulders. They gazed lovingly into each other's eyes before kissing softly, as if no one else existed. In that moment, no one else did.

My heart ached inexplicably at both scenarios. I've never been so unabashedly passionate with a man, nor so in love that the rest of the world faded away in his arms. I didn't know where to look and so cast my gaze to the ground until a shadow joined mine.

"Janey."

My heart stuttered at that voice. I glanced up. Adrian wore jeans and a white polo shirt that hugged his lean muscles. The scents of his cologne and shower soap wafted to me on the humid air. His damp hair brushed his shoulders in loose waves, and he wore a thin leather headband across his brow.

"I'm glad you came," he said.

A smile spread over my lips. "Me too."

"Shall we?" Robert said, his arm slung around Brigitte, practically burying her, he was so tall. He eyed me. "Will she be joining us, Adrian?"

A blush colored my cheeks, though I didn't know if it was because I was presumed to be with Adrian as yet another one of 'his women' or because I was presumed to be with him at all. I scolded myself for being so moony, and thrust out my hand to Robert.

"Janey Martin. I'm writing an article on Adrian for the newspaper."

"She's writing about *the team*," Adrian said quickly, and flashed a winning smile. "And football itself, for that matter, since she knows nothing about the sport."

I turned to glare at him, but he had on what I now called his Soccer Mask. The bright, devil-may-care expression of a cocky star player, but his eyes were speaking a different story as they met mine.

Robert shook my hand warmly. "Excellent! We could use the exposure. But we are now in the promotion zone, my friends. Therefore first...we drink."

On the sidewalk, just outside the small stadium, we congregated at a corner to decide the best mode of transportation for our group.

"Oi! Hallooooo!"

We all turned toward the sound. A drunk vagrant staggered down the walk from a small side street, about thirty yards from us.

"Hoi, there! Did I miss it? Is it over?" He flapped his torn coat to take a swig from a whiskey bottle. A rivulet spilled over his salt-and-pepper beard, down the front of his stained shirt. "Did I miss it or is there still time to see the stars?"

He spun in a shaky circle, arms to his sides, as he approached us.

Robert and Adrian exchanged glances and a small nod.

"I'll help this old fool find his way," Adrian said. "You guys go ahead."

"Come on," Robert said. "I think we can make the next train."

He ushered us down the street, but I loitered and walked slowly, glancing over my shoulder to watch Adrian approach the bum. They spoke a few words —Adrian seemed to be calming the older man down—and then he turned the bum around to return the way he had come.

I don't know what possessed me; my insatiable curiosity maybe, but I broke from the group and jogged back toward the side street. Adrian and the bum were heading back the way the man had come, their backs to me, walking together. When the old man stumbled, Adrian's hand was there to steady him.

I lifted my camera, always around my neck, and snapped a photo just before they rounded another corner, out of sight.

SIX

Nothing But a Heartache

ADRIAN

I HURRIED BACK to La Cloche. On a Saturday afternoon it was dead; over the sound system, the Flirtations sang about the pain of loving a bad guy to mostly empty seats. Our group had taken up our usual large booth and an adjoining table. Janey, I noticed, was wedged between Brigitte and Lucie in the middle of the booth.

Fantastique.

I greeted the group and took a seat at the far end of the table, trying to hide my irritation under a bright smile.

"Who is your pretty friend, Brigitte?" Olivier was asking with a nod of his shaggy head toward Janey.

Olivier Caton was our best defender, but was constantly making lewd comments about women and racist jokes about Negroes. I hated the bastard.

"She's a journalist doing a story on Adrian for the Sorbonne rag, no?" Brigitte said.

"On Adrian, of course," Olivier snorted. He looked to me, a lazy sneer spread under his scraggily beard. "You're late. And you forgot to bring the girl with you. She's still in your bed, eh?"

I shot Janey a quick glance then took a seat at the end of the table. "*Va te faire enculer*, Olivier," I said, straining to keep my voice casual.

Olivier held up his hands, a cigarette perched between two sausage-size fingers. "Why else are you so late? But come now, you didn't even bring her here?" He snorted a laugh. "Poor girl must be thirsty—"

"Do you ever shut your mouth, Caton?" I snapped, glowering at him. "I said, fuck off."

The table went quiet and Olivier chuckled, unperturbed. "What's gotten into you, Rousseau? I'm only kidding." He gave Janey a lascivious wink. "Or are we touchy in front of our new American girl?"

Blood rushed to my face and my hands balled into fists under the table.

Lucie, who was paying more attention to her fingernails, wondered aloud, "Where *did* you go, Adrian? You were gone for ages."

I tore my gaze from Olivier and fought to come up with an excuse. "One of the reporters cornered me to talk about next season."

Everyone sat up, the cloud of tension evaporating with electric excitement.

"They did? What did they say?"

"Did they want to talk about anyone else?"

"What did *you* say?"

The weight of their hopes fell on my shoulders, pressing me into my seat. I managed my wide, bullshit smile. "I told them what I always tell them; that we have to play two more games before we start talking advancement."

Robert frowned. "I hope you weren't an ass," he said. "We don't need any bad press for the team, you know. We're depending on you."

No kidding.

"I know you are," I said. "And we won't have bad press." I looked to Janey. "That's what Janey is here for, right?"

"Yes, Janey!" Brigitte said. "This was your first football match. What did you think?"

"Were you able to understand the rules?" Olivier asked, batting his eyelashes.

My hands balled tighter but Janey ignored him.

"It was...faster than I expected," she said. "To be honest, I thought it might be rather boring but watching it up close..." Her gaze met mine. "It was breathtaking."

I sucked in a small breath as her words hit me in my head, heart and groin; all at once.

"So glad you loved it! You should come to the next one, next Saturday," Brigitte said. "I insist."

"I....sure. Thanks. Love to," Janey said. She turned to the table at large, her cheeks flushed pink. "Congratulations on the win. Only two more games in the season?"

"Yes," Robert said. "Both home games, as luck would have it. We need two more wins, IC Chambry needs to lose their match, and then we advance to Ligue 2!" He clapped his hands and rubbed them together. "And that, my friends, deserves a round."

He motioned for the waiter and a round of Pilsners were brought over a few minutes later. Robert raised his glass.

"To Chambry playing the worst game of their lives so that we may play for the rest of ours."

"Salut!"

The others raised their voices and glasses, then drank.

"We still have to win," I said into the quiet.

Robert set down his glass with a *thunk* and fixed me with a pointed stare.

I shrugged, and sat back in my seat, affecting a casual pose. "I'm just saying I think it's bad luck to toast to something that hasn't happened yet. We need to focus on us; play our best and...see what happens."

"*See what happens,*" Olivier said, and chuckled. "Such inspirational words from our fearless leader."

The table laughed and the mood remained cheerful but for Robert who gave me a final, dark look before joining the talk around the table.

I stared into the gold of my Pilsner, turning the glass around and around. The talk grew louder, the club began to fill up, and my group became noticeably more drunk.

Finally, Lucie had to use the restroom and the entire booth shuffled out to let her. When they shuffled back in, Janey ended up at the end, next to me.

On purpose?

It didn't matter. Having her closer was like basking in the sun.

"Having fun?" I asked.

"You owe me half an interview," Janey shouted over Led Zeppelin and the loud talk and laughter around us.

I laughed. "You're right. Come on. Let's go somewhere else."

Janey stiffened. "No, thanks."

My smile faltered. "Didn't you just say—?"

She leaned over the table. I could smell the wildflower scent of her perfume.

"I'm not getting up so everyone can watch me leave here with you."

I felt myself stiffen. "Of course not." I took a long pull from my beer, draining the glass, then set it down. "Meet me at the Stade Jean-Marc tomorrow afternoon, one o'clock."

She frowned. "You want to do the interview on the soccer field?"

"The *football pitch,*" I corrected. "You clearly need the lesson. One o'clock."

Janey nodded. "For the story."

"What else would it be for?"

Our gazes caught and held, and then she looked away, letting the long locks of her hair shield her blush.

"Leaving so soon?" Olivier said, watching me rise to my feet. He heaved a dramatic sigh. "So many women, so little time."

"Yes, I have to run," I said. I drained my beer and set it down. "Your mother is a very impatient woman, Caton."

Olivier bolted to his feet. Robert, sitting beside him, rose too, and put a hand on his chest. "Back off." He looked to me. "Adrian, a word?"

He walked with me to the front of the club.

At the front, he stopped and jerked his head back to our table. "What's the story with her? The American."

"The story is, she's doing a story," I said. "What's the big deal?"

Robert's eyes bored into mine. "I hope nothing. We need you to play like you've been playing. We need to win." He looked to where Janey sat. "And I don't want a single thing to change that."

I affected a winning smile, even as I clenched my teeth. "Relax, will you? She's just a girl, not the black plague."

He regarded me for a moment more and then nodded. "Just a girl. Okay, good."

Just a girl, but the first girl I'd ever wanted to know for more than a night.

SEVEN

Sunny Afternoon

JANEY

"WHAT AM I DOING?" I muttered as I took the Metro back to Stade Jean-Marc. The Sunday afternoon sun was hot and bright and I felt overdressed in a minidress and boots.

"You're interviewing a player for an article," I said in English, garnering a stare from the woman next to me. "This is not a date."

The woman sniffed and replied in thickly-accented but perfect English, "I should say not, I'm happily married."

I laughed with her and some of my tension eased...only to ratchet back up again as soon as I stepped inside the small stadium.

Adrian was there, in shorts and a V-neck T-shirt, juggling a soccer ball back and forth on his knees. I approached slowly, watching him maneuver the ball with perfect control, bouncing it in the same perfect arc, over and over. Then he popped it up high enough to hit with his head. The ball went straight up, and as it came down, he caught it at the back of his neck, let it roll down his back, and then kicked it with his heel to bring it back in front where he resumed juggling it from knee to knee.

Once again, I almost remembered my camera too late. I snapped some shots of Adrian's prowess, then crossed the grass toward him.

"That's impressive," I said. "Mildly."

He grinned and then his smile melted into a slack-jawed stare as he took in my dress.

"You look...very beautiful, Janey."

The words were like little currents of electricity, straight to my heart.

"I didn't... I mean, I wore this to be professional..." I swallowed my fumbling words, and crossed my arms. "*Merci*."

He raised his eyes to mine at my cool tone, and put on his sly smile. "You certainly didn't come dressed to play."

"I'm here to finish this interview."

"Don't you Americans have a saying? All work and no play...?"

"This article is already late," I said. "And don't think I haven't noticed that you always ask more questions about me than the other way around."

"Can I tell you something that I've noticed?"

"There you go again..."

He cocked an eyebrow, his smile widening. "You're a terrible flirt."

"That's because I'm not flirting. I don't like you."

Adrian's grin widened. "That remains to be seen. But you *are* flirting and you should smile when you flirt."

I rolled my eyes. "Here's a piece of advice, for now and into the future: don't ever tell a girl who's not smiling to smile. It's annoying."

"I'll try to remember that. So you're coming to the next game?"

"Because Brigitte invited me," I said, not meeting his eye.

"And not because you like me."

"*Oui*."

Adrian grinned that maddeningly charming grin.

"*Mon Dieu*, I can't get a handle on you," I said. "One minute you act like you don't want to be known as the team player, and the next, you're making all kinds of innuendo and teasing as if you enjoy that reputation. So which is it?"

He laughed. "Which is what?"

"The real you?"

He regarded me for a second, then resumed bouncing the ball from knee to knee.

"Are you always this prickly?" he asked.

"It's hot out and I'm...irritated."

"About?"

I don't know how to feel about you. Or why I feel anything at all.

"I...don't know what to make of you."

"I thought you had me figured out," he said with a twinge of bitterness coloring his words. "The hotshot footballer who's with a different girl every night. The casual med-school student—and that's probably just another ploy to pick up girls..."

"Is it?"

"Why does it matter to you?"

"I... It doesn't."

"Seems like it does." The ball bounced between us, back and forth, a blur of black and white. "Seems like it matters to you a lot."

"It matters to me because I'm trying to do my job and the last thing I need is to be hit on by some jock who doesn't take me seriously. I've done quite enough of those interviews, already."

His maddening grin was back. "You think I'm hitting on you?"

"Gah, there you go again. Turning everything around."

"Okay, okay," Adrian said, with a laugh. He let the ball drop to the ground. "Let's walk and you can ask all the questions you desire."

"*Merci.*"

"Though you really are quite adorable when you're mad."

I socked him in the arm.

He laughed and rubbed his bicep. "And strong." His smile softened. "You are, Janey, very strong."

I felt a blush try to creep up my cheeks. We began to stroll the length of the field, side by side.

"I have to be strong. It's tough being a woman in this field. It's exhausting, actually, trying to be professional while the person you're interviewing is trying to get a look up your skirt."

"And you presume I'm after the same thing?"

"To hear Olivier talk..."

"Olivier is an asshole," Adrian snapped. "Anyway, aren't journalists supposed to be objective?"

"Yes," I said slowly. "And they ask the tough questions." I glanced up at him. "Questions like, how do you really feel about PC advancing to Ligue 2?"

His eyes flickered to me and then to the field before us. "I'm happy, of course. It will mean great things for the players."

"And off the record?" I asked.

He stopped and looked down at me, standing so close I could smell his cologne, and feel the warmth of his skin.

Your imagination. It's hot out, that's all...

"You didn't want to interview a footballer, did you?" he asked. He held up his hand when I started to protest that he was asking the questions again. "Just hear me out. Did you?"

"No," I said. "Before I came to Paris, I'd begun covering Vietnam protests."

"Because it felt more important, *oui*?"

"*Oui.*"

"But you took this gig because you had to, otherwise your career would suffer. You did something you didn't want to do in the hopes that, someday, you'd be able to do what you really wanted."

I nodded. "Is that how you feel about football?"

He sighed. "I have to provide for my mother and sister. Two more years of med school would make that hard." He shrugged with a rueful smile and began walking again. "Therefore, on the record, I'm very excited about PC's chance at advancement."

We walked in silence for a few moments.

"You can draw," I said. "The cocktail napkin sketch you did of me was very good."

He flashed me a smile. "I had a beautiful subject." Then he held up his hands defensively. "That's a compliment, in case you were unfamiliar with the concept."

"I'm not letting you distract me from my questions, Rousseau," I stated, though his words made my cheeks warm. "You said your father was an artist. Did you get your talent from him?"

"I suppose," Adrian said. "I'm nothing compared to him. He was quite famous, actually. A Victor Rousseau painting would often fetch thousands of francs at auction. He provided quite an affluent life for my mother, sister and I. One that my mother is very, very accustomed to."

"And then Vietnam happened," I said quietly.

He nodded. "He was sent in '53, famous artist or not." He glanced at me sideways. "If I play for Ligue 2 or am picked up for Ligue 1—something the scouts have said is likely to happen—then my mother won't have to worry about money. I can save up, then go back to med school in a few years."

"But Adrian, isn't that what you really want to do?" I asked softly. "Be a doctor?"

He nodded. "Seeing my sister deal with her cerebral palsy; being so brave about it despite the pain...Seeing the death and devastation the war has wrought. It just goes on and on. I feel like the world is so much larger than a football pitch, and I want to make as big an impact on that stage as I do playing the game."

"I wish I'd had my recorder for that one," I said, offering a small smile. "Can I quote you?"

"No," Adrian said quickly, then sighed and shook his head. "I don't know. If the team knew my heart wasn't in it, they'd panic. They're counting on me. My family is counting on me." He smiled ruefully down at me. "You're counting on me to finish this interview so you can move on to bigger and better stories."

I bit my lip to keep from telling him that his story was so much bigger and better than I could have hoped. But it was one I couldn't tell.

We headed back down the pitch and Adrian picked up the ball.

"Interview Part Two," he said. "Strictly football."

"Strictly football," I agreed reluctantly, and pulled out my pen and notepad. "When did you first realize you had a talent for football?"

Adrian's smile was brilliant. "*Soccer,*" he teased. "I guess when I was a kid. My father loved the sport. He was a fanatic and took me to as many games as we had time for; any division, any league. He couldn't play himself, but he idolized the players so much. I suppose I wanted to be idolized by him too." Adrian shot me a glance. "That sounds arrogant, no?"

Gone was the cocky player most people saw, and instead was a son who'd tried to make his father proud. I reached for my camera but he looked away and the moment was lost.

"It sounds pretty normal to me," I said. "So you grew up with football, but why do you think you have such a talent for the game?"

"I don't know. Luck, I guess. But Janey..."

"Yes?"

He opened his mouth to say something and then shut it again. "I can't talk about myself anymore. Truly. It's so boring."

"It's not boring..."

"Let's do something fun," he said. "Have you ever touched a *soccer* ball before?"

I shot him a look. "I wasn't raised in a cave."

He laughed and handed me the black and white sphere. "Here. Give it a try."

"Give what a try?"

"Bouncing it on your knee."

"Why? So you can get a look up my skirt?"

"Obviously."

I crossed my arms and he laughed.

"Come on. Just try. So you can put in your article you had hands-on experience."

"I'm going to need that, since you're done answering questions."

He laughed. "Go on. The ball should hit your thigh, just above your kneecap."

I blew air out my cheeks. "Alright, but just once."

I took off my camera and set it in the grass next to my bag, then took a few steps back. I held the ball in front of me.

"Nice and easy," Adrian said.

I nodded, let the ball drop, drove my knee up...and the ball flew straight at Adrian's face. The *whack* of it hitting him stopped my heart. His hands flew to his nose and I let out a cry to see blood seep from his fingers.

"*Mon Dieu*!" I raced forward, pulling his hands away. "*Oh, putain de Dieu*, did I break it? I broke it. I broke your nose!"

"I'm fine," Adrian said, tilting his head back. "I don't think it's broken..."

Blood dripped onto the white of his shirt, bright and stark, and my heart crashed in my chest at the sight.

"No, this is bad." I bent to grab a handkerchief from my bag on the ground, and, craning on my toes, I held it gently to his nose. My other hand cradled the back of his head. "Come on. There's an infirmary near here?"

Adrian chuckled, a muffled sound beneath my handkerchief. "I'm fine, really..."

"We have to be sure," I said, walking him awkwardly toward the stadium exit. "You might have bone fragments in your brain or something..."

"I highly doubt that."

I shook my head. "I *knew* playing around was a bad idea. If you had just let me interview you like a normal person..."

"So this is my fault?" he asked with a chuckle, letting me guide him toward the street.

"*Oui*," I said. "I told you, I never touched a soccer ball in my life."

"You told me you 'weren't raised in a cave.'"

"I...No more talking," I stammered. "You'll make it worse."

He chuckled again.

We made it to the street and I wondered what to do next. This close, even with a cloth covering half his face, Adrian was beautiful. His hair was soft under my hand cradling his head. His hands came up and gently removed my handkerchief. He held my hand in his.

"I'm fine, Janey. Really." His gravelly voice lowered. "But your concern for me...It's nice."

My throat went dry. A voice in my mind wondered if it had been a long time since anyone had taken care of *him*.

The silence thickened and warmed under the sun, as Adrian gazed down at me. But a small drop of blood seeped from his nose and my panic flared all over again.

"*Merde*! We have to be sure you're okay. Come on."

We took a train back to the student infirmary at the Sorbonne, where one of Adrian's friends and a fellow medical student—a third year—examined his nose.

"Not broken," Marcel said. "Aspirin for pain, ice for swelling. You might have some bruising under your eyes, but the ruination of your exquisite face is only temporary."

"Go to hell," Adrian said with a grin. He tipped his head back and winced as he pinched his nose.

Marcel chuckled, but not one bit of this was funny to me. The thought I might have jeopardized Adrian's next soccer match made me ill.

"He has a game next week," I said, my foot tapping the floor. "Can he still play?"

"I'd advise against headers," Marcel said. "But yes, he can play."

I breathed a sigh of relief. Adrian did not.

Marcel glanced at me. "So what happened? Did he get fresh with you?"

Adrian grinned. "I keep telling her, Janey doesn't know her own strength."

I didn't know what to say to that, but didn't have to reply anyway. Marcel rummaged around his desk.

"Before I forget..." He came up with a pamphlet. "Did you see this? Dr. Max Recamiér is speaking at the Panthéon Sorbonne about his humanitarian work in Nigeria. He and another doc, Bernard Kouchner, are trying to establish something big. A global emergency-medicine foundation with doctors and journalists. They want to practice in countries that need it and help spread awareness of atrocities that are ignored by the Western world." He handed the paper to Adrian. "I immediately thought of you."

Adrian's eyes lit up as he took the brochure for the symposium. I saw it happen—a kindling of his passion at the exact moment it found its purpose.

"When...?" he asked softly, his eyes scanning the page.

"Saturday afternoon, two weeks from now," Marcel said.

"The same day as PC's final match of the season," Adrian murmured. He smiled tightly and handed the flyer back to Marcel. "Let me know how it went."

Without another word, he got up and left the clinic.

I stared after him, then hurriedly rose to my feet.

"Can I take this?" I asked. I snatched the pamphlet out of Marcel's hand and left without waiting for answer.

EIGHT

What Is and What Should Never Be

ADRIAN

"ADRIAN, WAIT!"

I stopped at the street corner, bracing myself for what I knew was coming.

Janey ran to stand before me, looking impossibly beautiful with her cheeks flushed pink and her blue eyes meeting mine with an understanding I'd never seen in anyone else before.

"You have to go to this," she said, pressing Dr. Recamier's speech pamphlet in my hand. "This is just what you want, isn't it? To help on the world's stage? This could be the start of something...big."

"I can't, Janey," I said. "The final match is that day. There will be other speeches. Other chances..."

"Adrian," she said, and I loved my name in her mouth. Loved the sound of it in her American accent.

Her French is so good; she'd make an excellent translator for Dr. Recamier's cause...

I blinked to see her staring up at me expectantly.

"Forget it," I said, bitterness clawing up my throat, making my words thick. "I can't...let anyone down."

I can't let my mother and sister starve.

"But Adrian—"

"I said, forget it, Janey. I have to play."

She pressed her lips together, likely to bite back stubborn protests. I loved that about her, too. How tough she was, and how she didn't fall at my feet like some of the other girls. She wasn't afraid to really talk to me. I'd been hiding behind my reputation for so long, I'd forgotten what it was like to really be with a girl, instead of wearing one on my arm.

But I couldn't let her get too close either. Janey came from money. A vineyard and award-winning wine. A rich father who paid her way through everything. I didn't begrudge her that, but...

If she knew the whole truth, she'd be ashamed to be seen with me.

"I understand," Janey said finally. "But I'll feel like a fraud when I finally turn in this article." She gazed up at me and her own protective shell came down to let me see the softness beneath. "There's so much more to you than football. It's a shame no one will see it."

"They can't," I said. "No one can."

Including you.

She nodded then her face morphed into shock and fear.

"Am I bleeding again...?" I touched my lip under my nose but it was dry.

"My camera," Janey said, her face going white. "I left it at the stadium. With my purse. But...my camera." Her hand clutched my arm. "We have to go back. Now."

"Of course, of course."

Instead of taking the Metro, I hailed a cab. At Stade Jean-Marc, Janey raced ahead of me to the spot where her camera and bag lay. Both were still there.

I joined her as she hugged her camera to her, her eyes shut with relief. "That was my penance," she said on a shaky breath, "for smacking you in the nose."

"That was an accident. It's forgotten."

She rose to her feet and shouldered her bag. "Not forgotten. The bruising Marcel warned of has started. I'm so sorry."

"I thought you didn't like me," I said slowly, my casual grin feeling transparent. "You're sorry for whacking me?"

"Of course I am," she said. "But I..."

"But what?" I asked, my head wanting to bend toward hers.

"Nothing. I...have to go," she said, pulling away. "This article is late. I have to give something to Antoine tomorrow."

The article, I thought. *That's why she came today. The only reason.*

"Of course," I said, taking a step back. "I'll leave you to it."

"Thanks," she said. "See you later? At La Cloche, maybe?"

I nodded.

"Okay, great. Bye."

I watched her go, her long legs striding away from me, her hair long and soft and glinting gold in the sun.

Maybe. Someday. In the future. But not now. Never now. What I wanted was just out of reach, and I was starving for the sunlight like a man locked in a dank cell.

I almost called Janey back to answer her question as to why I thought I'd had such a knack for football. Because on the pitch, eleven opposing players tried to take what was mine. The ball. The score. The match.

But I refused to let them. Only there, racing across the grass, I was in control. And when the ball sailed out of the goalkeeper's reach and into the net, and the crowd went mad; for that one brief second, I was one of the heroes my father had idolized. And I told myself that was enough.

It had to be.

NINE

Don't You Want Somebody to Love?

JANEY

THE NEXT MORNING, Monday, I went to Antoine's office at the journalism department. He noticed my empty hands first.

"Well?" he said. "The article is not ready? It was supposed to be a standard interview, mademoiselle. Perhaps a glossy photo or two of Adrian in a game. It seems as if this simple assignment is beyond you."

I bit back an angry retort. "I need another extension," I said. "The story is bigger than one interview."

He hmmph'd. "So you say. Or is this a ploy to spend more time with Monsieur Rousseau?"

I bristled even as my cheeks flushed. "It's for the sake of the story," I said. "Please. Let's see how Paris Central does against Lyon-Dejeres this weekend. Or even better, wait until the final in two weeks. If Central stays in the top three and advances up, that is a much bigger story, *oui*?"

"*Mon Dieu,* I never asked for an exposé. What's the angle?"

I bit my lip. Adrian's real story was almost entirely off the record. I wasn't about to betray his privacy, but my instincts told me if I had a little more time, something big might happen.

"Following the star center forward through his last games as a semi-pro. The finale is PC advancing, maybe even winning the championship."

Antoine frowned. "I don't care about the championship. PC winning or losing isn't the story. Adrian Rousseau is the story."

I agree completely.

"Please," I said. "One more week?"

Antoine pursed his lips. "One more week, and that is final."

BUT THAT WEEK, whatever I'd been hoping to happen with Adrian's story never came to fruition. Over the next four days. I hung out at La Cloche with the footballer group, ignoring Olivier's crude jokes and innuendo, and becoming better friends with Brigitte and Lucie.

"Olivier's a bastard, but he's one of the best defenders in the league," Brigitte had told me on Monday night as we sat gathered in their booth—our booth, now that they welcomed me as one of their own. We drank *kir* and listened to a never-ending stream of American music.

"He'll probably get called up by scouts, too," Lucie said, her lips pinched, "where he can be an ass to a whole new set of teammates."

Things were tense between Olivier and Adrian, which made Robert nervous. But Adrian ignored Olivier. Most nights, he joined the group late and left early, though he never brought another girl around like he used to. More than once, I found him watching me, his eyes heavy with something that looked like longing, but I couldn't let myself believe it was for me. On the field that Sunday, I'd asked Adrian to deny his playboy reputation and he never did.

And I refuse to be another notch on his belt.

But Antoine's snide commentary played in my mind. Was I prolonging the article just to spend time with Adrian? What did I think was going to happen all these nights at the club? That Adrian's story would miraculously break open?

So I sat, wedged between the girls every night, and not talking to Adrian. The guys ribbed him about the fast-fading bruising under his eyes, but he never told them how he got them. Every night, a different story. Once, he walked into a pole. Another, Sophie had punched him.

He joked the questions away, and never looked at me as he did.

By Friday night, I'd begun to feel like an extra in a movie, taking up the same spot in the booth, steadfastly trying not to look at Adrian. It had become painful; the sight of his beautiful face conjured a frustrating mix of emotions.

I wanted him to take me seriously as a journalist and as a woman, but some moments, a surge of heat would rush through me to remember him on the field, sweaty and fast, and better than any player there. In those moments, I had wild fantasies of him taking me home with him, of being one of his women. To lose myself in him and damn the consequences.

I felt stuck, immobile with confusion, and irritated at my girlish heart that couldn't stop thinking about him.

That Friday night, the club was playing all of Jefferson Airplane's album, *Surrealistic Pillow*. When "White Rabbit" came on, Brigitte and Lucie decided we had to dance. They tugged me to the dance floor where, under beams of white and blue light, the dozen or so dancers looked as if they were underwater.

I was self-conscious at first, but it was just what I needed. To stop thinking so damned much. I swayed to the music, losing sense of time and place. My eyes fell shut and my friends, La Cloche, all of it just fell away. Grace Slick's haunting voice took me back to America—but for the first time, I felt no pang of nostalgia. I drifted along the currents of the music.

Someone nudged my arm. "What is it about?" Lucie asked. "These words?"

"Drugs," I said, with a lazy smile, then closed my eyes again. "Escape."

The music ebbed and flowed through me, and I was sorry when it ended. I started to move off the dance floor and then Adrian was there.

"Dance?" he asked, staring down at me, his blue velvet eyes even darker in the dimness of the club. His smile was his usual cocky grin, and I hated that my heart stuttered at his sudden nearness.

I tried to push past him. "No, thank you."

Adrian caught my arm, held it gently but firmly. His grin slipped away. "Please. I want to talk to you."

"You can talk to me at the table," I said, tugging my arm free.

"Can I? Or will you barricade yourself between Lucie and Brigitte, and hardly look at me? What I have to say isn't for everyone."

I turned to where our friends sat. They were watching us as we stood in the middle of the dance floor; Brigitte raising her brows at me.

"Come on," Adrian said. "One dance."

I nodded vaguely and let him take my left hand in his, while his arm slipped around my waist. My breath caught, and I turned my face away from his, the beauty of it.

"Is this so terrible?" Adrian asked lightly. "Do you still not like me?"

"Yes," I said.

"Is that so?" Adrian laughed. "You work awfully hard to *not* like me."

"I don't know what you're talking about."

"You don't like Olivier. That's obvious. So you ignore him, and it's easy." Adrian's voice softened. "But with me, you have to put effort into avoiding me."

"I don't—"

"You do," Adrian cut me off. "I catch you, you know, looking at me. You look away but I see you try *not* to see me."

"Your imagination." My cheek was resting on his chest and I wasn't doing anything to stop it.

He lowered his voice again so that I alone could hear him. "And when I try to get close to you, you move away."

"I told you, I don't like you," I said.

He pulled back and looked down at me, and I couldn't look away. He caught and held me with his gaze, and his hand holding mine...Our fingers had somehow become entwined and he held our hands to his heart that was beating too hard.

"You keep saying that," Adrian said softly, "but right now you look as if you want me to kiss you."

"I don't..."

He leaned closer. "I want to kiss you. I've wanted to kiss you since the moment we met."

The words traveled through me like a current. Now my heart was pounding too and I couldn't catch my breath. Adrian was stealing it.

"No," I whispered.

He bent his head. "Say no again," he breathed, "and I won't."

I didn't say no.

Adrian hesitated a moment more, his eyes searching. Then he closed them, brows furrowed, and then touched his lips to mine. My eyes closed too, and a small sound escaped me, a soft little cry that turned into a breathy gasp as he deepened the kiss. My lips parted and his tongue slipped inside, softly. I gasped, utterly unprepared for how the taste of him, the feel of him touching me like this, turned my bones to sand and stole my breath. I moaned softly into his mouth and felt him react to my obvious want; I couldn't hide it. I couldn't pull away. My entire body vibrated with electricity, and Adrian felt every bit of it.

He angled his head to kiss me harder, thoroughly, his tongue no longer hesitant, but sliding against mine. God, he tasted so good. I tasted the *kir* he'd drunk: the sweetness of the black currant liqueur, and the sharper bite of wine.

All these thoughts flashed through me in the space of a heartbeat, as the La Cloche, our friends, the pulsing music...it all faded away, leaving me with Adrian's mouth on mine and nothing else.

I don't know how long we'd been kissing when Adrian finally pulled away, gasping for breath. Our bodies were pressed tightly together, his arms wrapped around me, and I was dimly aware of a hard, hot pressure through his jeans straining against me.

"Janey..." he whispered.

I slid my gaze to the group; they were all snickering and whispering; grinning at us with knowing looks I didn't like. I'd agreed to come to France to try to avoid being the silly girl who wrote about men, and men's games, and men's victories and triumphs, and here I was, falling under the charm of just one of those athletes who saw women as nothing more than another opportunity to score.

It's not true; he's different...

But if I continued with him, I wouldn't know if that were true until it was too late to protect myself. My heart, normally so guarded, was falling for him fast. Too fast.

Tears burned my eyes, and I pulled back from Adrian, from the strong, warm feel of his arms. "I'm not going to be one of your women."

His brows furrowed. "What? No...?"

Confusion flashed over his deep blue eyes, and then something I hadn't been prepared to see: pain. Not the pain of lust unfulfilled, but something stronger. My pulling away left a wound. Maybe a small one, but a wound nonetheless.

His ego is bruised. What woman turns down Adrian Rousseau?

"I have to go," I said stiffly. I left the dance floor and returned to the table.

"Janey...?" Brigitte's voice was soft with concern.

"That's what I call in-depth reporting," Olivier said. "Next, she goes *under the covers* to get at Adrian's *big* story."

"Shut up, *crétin*!" Brigitte hissed.

My cheeks burned but I managed a tight smile for Brigitte. "I have to go. Lots of studying to do."

I hurried out of La Cloche, not looking back, half-hoping Adrian would follow me. A man's voice called out for me to stop. My heart jolted but then sank when I realized it was Robert.

"Yes?" I said tightly. "It's late. I want to get home..."

"I'm going to be perfectly blunt: I want you to stay away from Adrian," Robert said, his dark eyes hard under the street lamp. "At least until the season is over."

"What? Why...?" My words burnt up in anger. "Actually, it's none of your business—"

"It is my business. Adrian is the leading scorer on our team. A striker. The best striker in the league, if not all of football. He's been different since you showed up. In his head a lot." Robert rubbed his hand over his mouth. "You're not like the other girls he's brought around."

I felt my body go stiff all over. "Exactly. I'm not one of his girls. I'm writing an article—"

"You were doing more than *writing an article* just now on the dance floor."

Humiliation inflamed my skin and I stared, unable to find a retort.

"We need him to keep playing his best," Robert said, simply. "Stay out of his head."

He turned and stepped back inside the club, leaving me alone in the dark.

TEN

Bad Moon Rising

ADRIAN

SATURDAY MORNING, I changed into my uniform with the rest of the team in the small locker room. I suppressed a yawn as I pulled my jersey over my head. I'd gotten no sleep the night before, but tossed and turned all damn night, thinking of Janey and our kiss.

The feeling in my chest when I kissed her echoed the feeling of a thousand fans cheering my name. It was tasting something sweet and good and perfect; every kind of happiness I imagined for myself, but real. She was flesh and blood in my arms; heat and wetness in my mouth.

But the fucker—Olivier—had ruined it. The whole group had ruined the moment, and made Janey feel like she was just another of my 'conquests'.

No, I fucking ruined it.

What a joke. I didn't have any conquests. All the girls I'd ever paraded in front of my friends had been for show. To keep everyone at a distance. I let them think I was out, spending the Rousseau fortune on 'my women' when in actuality, I bought them a drink somewhere, maybe kissed goodnight, and never called them again.

Easier that way, to let the group think I was too busy with my dates to have them over at my place, and getting serious with someone was out of the question.

Until Janey.

As we'd kissed, I'd felt hope rise in my chest that she wouldn't care about the reality of my situation, as shameful as it was, and that she'd see past the playboy front I kept up like a shield.

But kissing her in front of the group—especially Olivier—had been a mistake.

It's over now, whatever we might have started.

I waited for the relief that I could keep my private life private to hit me, but instead anger, frustration, and repressed lust boiled in my guts. I wanted Janey in all ways—in my bed and in my life. I wanted a different future than playing football, but the pressures of my situation were pressing me down and leaving me seething.

The rest of the guys were nervous for this match—the last one before the final—and were showing it by being extra crude and rough, shoving each other and laughing too loudly. Olivier made a lewd comment about some girl he was trying to screw and I slammed my locker shut. They all stared at me—Olivier included—with nervousness and hope in their eyes. As if I were the only one capable of giving us victory.

Such bullshit.

I wanted to shout that I wasn't the only reason we were heading toward a winning season, but I swallowed it down. My anger simmered, and I tried to channel it into my muscles and bones and blood. To play as if I were on fire and give them no reason to doubt I wanted to win, and advance, and play this fucking game for the rest of my life.

Our coach, Philippe Desjardins, rallied us just before first whistle, and then pulled me aside as the rest of the team filed out.

"You look tired," he said with his usual directness.

"I'm fine," I said.

"You sure?"

I itched to shake off his hand on my shoulder. "I'm sure. Let's go."

On the field, the stands were filled to capacity. I wondered if Janey was there, and remembered Robert's words to me last night at La Cloche after she left.

"It's better this way," he said. "No distractions."

The anger rose in me again on the field. Janey wasn't a distraction, she was...something more. Or might have been, had Vietnam not torn my entire world apart. My eyes longed to search the crowds for her, but I kept them on the pitch, staring down my opponents like a bull ready to charge.

The whistle blew, the match began.

The Lyon players, in green and yellow, were weak on defense and their best forward was called for being offsides three times in the first twenty minutes. We hadn't even scored yet and I knew we were going to win.

My blood felt like it was on fire. I ran faster and harder than I ever had, aggressively stealing the ball from a Lyon midfielder. I passed to another of our forwards, Johannes—arguably the next best player on the team, and a factory worker who desperately needed PC to advance. He was agile with the ball at his feet. We charged the Lyon net, two defenders and two wings bearing down on us.

They closed in on Johannes and instead of bolting to the side for a clear pass to me, I cut behind him. With perfectly timed precision, he danced the ball away from a Lyon defender, backwards to me. I charged and kicked, and watched as the Lyon goalkeeper made a diving try for the ball. But it hit the net, high and tight on the upper left corner, completely out of reach.

1-0.

My teammates pounced on Johannes for the perfect assist, then crowded around me. I weathered their congratulatory thumps on the back, my hands balling into fists.

"Nice shot, Rousseau," Olivier said, and gritted my teeth at as he whacked me between the shoulder blades.

"Fuck off, Caton," I muttered, and jogged back to center line.

"Someone's on his period," Olivier said as he ran past me to take up his position for the kickoff.

As striker, I stood front and center, and Olivier, some dozen meters behind me, called out, "Hey, Rousseau. I think I see your hot American piece of ass."

"Shut up, Caton!" Robert hissed.

"Why?" Olivier drawled. "I'd think he'd want to play to impress."

I couldn't help myself, but looked to where our group always sat in the stands—front rows, at midfield. Even from the center of the pitch, I could see her. Janey sat among the familiar faces of my mother, sister, and our friends. Her hair glinted long and gold in the hot sun, and my stupid heart rose with hope.

Then she lifted the camera around her neck to take a photo.

For her story...

The referee blew the whistle and Lyon player kicked off by tapping the ball behind him. To me, the sound of the whistle was like a starting gun in a race. Before the Lyon player could pass, I was on him, intercepting his ball, and corralling it in front of me.

Then I flew.

Johannes was right with me. I drove the ball forward, dancing it out of the tangling feet of Lyon defenders and passing to Johannes when they swarmed me.

Johannes took a shot. The Lyon goalkeeper got his hands on it and the ball glanced off like a bullet, flying through the air, right toward me.

The defenders were all over me, but, without thought, I leapt up in the air and headed the ball back toward the net. The goaltender scrambled to get to his feet in time but the ball sailed over his head.

2-0.

The crowd's eruption of applause reverberated in my chest the way loud music can at a concert. I felt it in my entire body and knew I'd done something extraordinary.

And it meant nothing to me.

The pain of that admission fueled my anger. *Why shouldn't I love this? What the hell is wrong with me?*

My team surrounded me again and the congratulatory thumps and shouts were like hard blows on a bruise. And then Olivier was there.

"You magnificent bastard," he laughed. "You've earned all the fucks from all the pretty girls—"

My vision clouded red. I don't remember much; no thought or conscious act, but one second I was upright, the next I was rolling in the grass, grappling with Olivier.

"What the hell...?"

He was bigger than me, but I had a second where he was baffled by shock, and I cocked back and punched him in the face. My knuckles screamed as I hit the hard bone of his jaw. His teeth tore through my skin but it was his blood that sprayed.

Breathing like a bellows, I reached back for another blow, and felt rough hands grab me under my arms and haul me off. My teammates shouted and swore, some holding Olivier back, half dragging me away from him.

"You rotten bastard," Olivier seethed, spitting blood. "What the fuck is wrong with you?"

"You talk like that about her again, and I'll fucking kill you!" I screamed. "Do you hear me? *I'll kill you.*"

A chaos of teammates shocked and angry faces surrounded me, but I tore out of their grasp just as the referee moved to stand before me.

In his hand was a red card.

"Violent conduct," he said, holding the card up for the entire stadium to see. "You're out."

A collective gasp went up, and the stands went as silent as 3,000 people can get. Robert stared at the red card, then turned to glare at me.

A vein bulged in his neck. "You stupid fuck. Do you know what you've done?"

I nodded faintly, the fire doused by a cold bucket of reality. I opened my mouth, maybe to apologize. Maybe to tell Robert I was *relieved.* That's when I heard him.

"Hallooo, hoi! There he is."

I turned toward the stands to see him there, drunk off his ass, and waving a whiskey bottle like a beacon at me. In the relative quiet of the stadium, his voice carried straight to me.

"Did you see? A goal like no other. Right off a prince's crown..."

The referees were motioning for the players to take position for Lyon's free kick, even though the foul was on my own teammate.

Not just fouled. Red carded.

The realization of what I'd done dropped into my stomach as I walked toward the sidelines. But instead of heading left toward the locker room, I walked slowly toward the stands. The fans booed and jeered at me now, many screaming *Pourquoi?* Over and over.

As I drew closer, I found my friends' group. Lucie was crying and Brigitte had her arms around her, glaring at me with pain in her eyes. Janey stared about in confusion at the crowds' reaction. She met my eye and raised her hands. I only shook my head.

My sister and mother sat in silence. My mother glared at me, a mixture of fear and anger shining in her eyes. Only Sophie, of everyone in the entire stadium, smiled for me. A small, kind smile.

"Did you see that?" the drunken man asked, pointing his whiskey bottle at me. "Did you see what he did?"

Some of the crowd was now booing him, too, and telling him to sit down or get the hell out. Sophie glanced over at him, her smile fading, her eyes full of tears.

I held up my hands to tell her I'd take care of it, and approached the man.

"Did you see that?" he asked me, his eyes glassy and bright. His breath reeked of stale booze and it dripped from his scraggly salt-and-pepper beard. "Did you see...? Do you know...what you did?"

I nodded. "Yeah, Papa, I know what I did." I put my arm around his shoulders. "Come on. Let's go home."

ELEVEN

I Fall to Pieces

JANEY

SITTING in the stands was like being caught in a storm. Swells of nervous excitement coursed through the spectators, as the teams set up for kickoff after Adrian's first goal. Lucie and Brigitte were clutching each other, their eyes locked on the field.

Not the field, the pitch, I reminded myself with a dull ache, and snapped a few shots. I had more than enough material for a puff piece interview, but I wanted more.

Adrian...

I cut the thought off before it led me down another rabbit hole of confusion and second-guessing. After Robert's cold words to me the night before, how I felt about Adrian was now tangled up with the team's chances to advance.

He's been different since you showed up.

Butterflies and nerves warred in my stomach.

And then it happened.

The whistle blew and a Lyon player nudged the ball to a player behind him. A blur of black and yellow, and Adrian was there.

"You see?" Brigitte said from beside me. "You see how he can read the field? He's three steps ahead of every defender and knows where his own teammates are. To pass without looking..."

She fell silent as the entire stadium collectively held their breath. Adrian passed to #10, a player I didn't recognize, and he took a shot. The ball glanced off the goalie's hands and—almost as if he were defying reality—Adrian leapt up and head-butted the ball into the net.

The stadium went crazy; a storm of cheering and applause and stomping feet as everyone bolted out of their seats. Lucie and Brigitte were screaming and jumping up and down together.

The crowd's thunder then hissed like a doused fire in a collective gasp as Adrian suddenly charged at Olivier, taking them both to the ground. Brigitte's hand snaked out to clutch my arm painfully, as the two men wrestled.

"What is he doing?" Lucie screeched, louder and louder. *"What is he doing?"*

When Adrian slammed his fist into Olivier's face, the crowd bellowed as if they'd felt it.

"Mon Dieu," Brigitte whispered as the teammates pulled the men apart and the ref flashed a red card in Adrian's face. "Red card. Oh *mon Dieu,* he got a red card."

Lucie burst into tears, and men in the stands around us began to curse Adrian's name.

"What is it? He got kicked out of the game?" I asked as Adrian headed towards the sidelines on our side.

"He got kicked out of the game," Brigitte said, her face pale. "They'll have to play with only ten now."

I made a face. "Okay, but PC is up two to nothing..."

Brigitte shook her head. "Adrian is kicked out of this game but a red card means he also can't play in the next game." She raised her eyes to meet mine. "Adrian can't play in the final match."

I sank back down in my seat. The bum from the last game had returned and some fans were taking their anger out on him. I watched as Adrian, still in his uniform, approached the man and put his arm around him. Together, under a hail of jeering and catcalls, they left the stadium together.

I slipped out of the stands and followed.

I caught up to them on the street corner where Adrian was trying to hail a cab. One slowed but then screeched away when the driver caught sight of the old bum, cursing and waving his bottle.

"Can I help?" I asked.

Adrian spun around. "Janey..." His glance darted to the bum and back to me. Then he slumped, defeated. "I have to get him home. He's not dangerous. Only...confused. And drunk."

I nodded. "Who is he, Adrian?"

Adrian's blue eyes held mine. "Victor. His name is Victor."

I stared, realization nearly bowling me over. "He's..."

"My father."

Victor Rousseau turned to peer at me with glassy eyes. "Eh? Brigitte Bardot right before my eyes..."

"This is Janey. She's...a friend."

Victor narrowed his eyes at Adrian, as if thinking hard. "How hard it is...to love so much? Like reaching through a fire...to pull the treasure from the flames."

"Come on, Papa," Adrian said. "Take it easy."

No taxi would stop, so we took the Metro to the 18th Arrondissement. The buildings here were as old as the grand apartments of Madame Rousseau's neighborhood, but in greater disrepair. Narrow, trash strewn streets wound like a snake between ramshackle buildings. Men huddled together outside tobacco shops, smoking and talking, and staring at me as we passed by on narrow walks buffeting narrower streets.

We came to a small, three-story pension with chipped maroon paint and a faded awning. The pension looked wedged between two other, larger buildings, like bullies muscling a little guy between them.

"I got it from here," Adrian said. "Thanks."

"I can help—"

"No, you can't," he said, his voice sounding frayed. Beside him, Victor swayed tiredly.

"You told me your father died in Vietnam," I said in a low voice.

"I said he didn't come back," Adrian said, watching his father mutter at his own hands. "That was the truth. The man who came back from Vietnam was not the same who left."

"Adrian—"

"This is all off the record, Janey," Adrian said, opening the pension's front door. "There is no story. Not anymore."

He helped his father inside and shut the door between us.

TWELVE

Stay With Me

HONEY, IT AIN'T MUCH,
It's only everything.
—"One Good Man", Janis Joplin

JANEY

I went home that afternoon, my heart and brain so at odds with each other, I could hardly think. My heart ached for what I now knew of Adrian's father. Adrian had said he wanted to be a hero for his dad, but what did it mean for him if he couldn't play the biggest game of the season? What would it mean for Paris Central?

"Hey, Antoine, how's that for an angle?" I muttered as I fit my key in the door of my flat. "The star striker gets red carded ahead of the final."

In my small place, I sank down on my couch. On the coffee table, arrayed in front of me, were the photos I'd been taking of Adrian. I'd spent hours in a darkroom at the university developing them. Dozens were of Adrian on the pitch in action. Hair flying, his face darkly handsome, smudged with sweaty grime and drawn with determination.

I fanned those photos out beside the few I'd taken of Adrian not playing. One at his home, in the backyard reading with a shaft of light falling over him. Another of him dancing the soccer ball over his knee, his expression free of worry or pressure—just him and the ball, messing around for the hell of it.

The last photo I drew toward me was of him and his father—though I hadn't known it was his father at the time I snapped it—walking down the side street. A son helping his dad make it home safely.

My eyes filled with tears.

"What do you want, Adrian?" I whispered.

I had no idea, but I knew what *I* wanted, and it had nothing to do with any article or big story. I grabbed my bag and headed out.

I TOOK the Metro to the 16th Arrondissement, to Adrian's home. The late afternoon sun cast an amber glow over the neighborhood, like an old, sepia-toned photograph. Two girls—the same two girls I'd seen bounding down the stairs the first time I'd come to interview Adrian—were coming out the front door as I stepped onto the stairs.

"Oh, hi," I said, stopping them in their tracks. They were about my age, and looked like college students dressed to go out. "You're Sophie's friends, yes?"

They both gave me a funny look.

"Not really," said one.

"We live here," said the other, and they hurried past me.

I frowned. *They live here...?*

I knocked on the door, and waited patiently for Sophie to answer. Instead, it swung open and Mme. Rousseau was there. She looked tired, her eyes red-rimmed and her bouffant hair looked a tad deflated.

"Ah, it's you," she said, tightening her housecoat tighter around her waist. "Can I help you?"

"I'm here to see Adrian," I said.

"Adrian is not here right now," Mme. Rousseau said, and while her refined manners wouldn't let her shut the door in my face, I could see she was itching to. "I will tell him you stopped by."

"Wait, please..."

"Don't you feel you've done enough damage?"

I gaped. "Me? What did I do?"

"Robert told me everything," Mme. Rousseau said. "Adrian attacked Olivier because of something crass he said about *you*."

My heart crashed against my chest, then plummeted to my feet. "Something about...me?"

"*Oui*," Mme. Rousseau snapped. "If you hadn't stuck your nose into Adrian's business, none of this would have happened. He'd still be playing in the finals, and we'd..." She bit off her last words and shook her head.

I spotted Sophie lurking in the hallway, holding to the wall for support.

"I'm sorry," I said to Mme. Rousseau. "I didn't mean—"

"They lost, young lady."

I gaped. "They...lost? But they were up two, nothing..."

"Lyon rallied and with only ten players—and without my son—PC couldn't hold. They lost and the fourth-ranked team won their match. PC is now fourth place again and out of contention for advancement. If they don't win their final game..." Mme. Rousseau's face paled and then she drew herself up. "As I said, Adrian's not here right now. Have a good day."

And then Mme. Rousseau *did* shut the door in my face. I stared at the elegant but old, peeling paint, half in a daze.

Adrian got red carded for me.

The notion gave me a little thrill that he would defend my honor like that, but it was fleeting. To think of what he might lose...How they *did* lose.

I sat down on the front steps of his house. It was possible Adrian had been delayed helping his father settle into the pension, and he was on his way back right now. Or maybe he'd gone out after. Even if it took hours, I was prepared to wait. Late into the night if I had to.

But a few minutes later, the front door opened and Sophie struggled out onto the stoop. Adrian's sister clutched the railing of the front stairs of her building with both hands; the twilight sun glinting dully off her leg braces. I rose to my feet.

"Sophie..."

"Adrian doesn't live here," she said, almost in a whisper.

I blinked. "He doesn't *live* here?"

She shook her head. "We rent his room and the guest space to two girls. University students." She brushed a lock of hair behind her ear. "We need the money."

"Where is Adrian, then?"

"He lives at 23 Rue Cassis, in the 18th arrondissement. He won't like that I told you, but he likes *you*." She smiled shyly, and looked to the ground. "And I know you won't mind."

"Mind what?"

"About our situation." Sophie glanced back at the house. "I have to go. Maman is resting but she won't be happy if she knows I told you." She turned back to me, not able to meet my eyes. "Our secret?"

"Of course."

Sophie stumbled, then caught herself.

"Can I help?" I asked.

"I can do it. I can do more than Maman thinks," Sophie said with more strength behind her words than I'd ever heard. At the door she turned. "Tell Adrian I'm sorry but...No." She shook her head and laughed softly. "I'm not sorry. I like you. For him. And I have to watch out for my brother, don't I?"

"That's right," I answered, strangely proud of her. It was odd to think of that frail woman as anyone's protector, and I know most people felt the same. Including me, up until that moment.

Sophie let go of the railing to give me a wave and then retreated back into the house, leaving me with an address and more questions. I exited the Metro and as soon as I stepped foot onto Rue Cassis, another current of shock jolted through me.

I know this street...

I recognized the street because I had just been there hours before with Adrian and his father. The address Sophie gave me was for the same ramshackle pension with a maroon awning that Adrian had helped his father into.

The front door stuck a little from too many layers of paint over the years. I opened it on a front foyer that was cramped and dim, but homey and warm. I felt comfortable immediately.

The carpet and walls were both the same maroon as the front awning, that dark color making the small space feel even smaller. Black and white photographs that looked dated from the 1940's hung on the wall, and a pall of pungent cigarette smoke.

A rotund woman with a head of short, graying curls, stepped up to the little office from a back room. She looked to be in her sixties, and wore a worn cardigan over a housedress, and rested her arms over the ledge. Behind her, a wiry, darker-skinned man with gray hair emerged to lean against the back wall, smoking the cigarette that gave the foyer its fog.

"Can I help you?" the woman asked in French, though with an accent I didn't recognize.

"I'm looking for Monsieur Rousseau?" I said.

The woman narrowed her eyes at me. "You are American?"

"*Oui.*"

The woman's heavy jowls lifted at once in a smile and she said something to the man behind her in a foreign tongue. It sounded like Arabic, but I couldn't be sure.

The wiry old man came to the desk. "New York City?"

"Uh, no. California." I glanced at the rows of numbered hooks on the wall behind the lady, most empty, some with keys dangling from them.

"This is a residence?" I asked.

The woman nodded. "You are visiting M. Rousseau, the older or younger?"

"The younger," I said. "They both live here?"

The woman's smile was kind but sad. "*Oui*, both have rooms here. The father is not well. The son, he takes care of him as best he can. We try to help, but M. Rousseau likes his drink and we can't very well lock him in."

I nodded, my heart more full that ever.

Oh, Adrian...

The wiry man spoke again.

The woman listened, nodding. "My husband reminds me of a saying we have in Algeria: no beauty shines brighter than that of a good heart. That is the young man. A good heart." She beamed at me. "You are such a pretty girl, I am happy you are here to see him."

"I am too," I said softly.

"Second floor. Number six." She indicated the small stairway to the left of the lobby—such as it was.

"*Merci.*"

At number six, I knocked on the door, my heart pounding in my chest.

"Who is it?"

Adrian sounded wary, and I suddenly felt horrible for intruding. *If living here is a secret, he wants to keep it.*

While I stood there, caught in a tangle of my emotions, the door opened.

"Janey?" Adrian immediately froze. He then closed the door tight to him, so that I couldn't see beyond him to his place. "What are you doing here?"

"I went to your home. Or what I'd thought was your home," I said gently. "Your sister told me you were here."

Adrian rubbed his eyes. He'd changed out of his uniform and wore plaid pajama pants and a white V-neck undershirt. His hair was still damp from a shower, though he looked haggard, as if he hadn't slept in days.

"So now you know the truth," he said bitterly. He pushed off the door and stepped back inside, leaving it open. "Is that why you came? To finish your story?"

"I don't know what the truth is," I said, stepping inside and closing the door behind me. "And no, I don't give a damn about my article."

I glanced around his small place that was cramped but clean. A bed next to a desk; the desk under the window, cluttered with papers and medical textbooks, still open. A little nothing of a kitchen area was on the left and beyond that, a door that I presumed was a bathroom.

Adrian leaned against the edge of his desk, facing me, his arms crossed.

"This is the truth," he said, indicating his place with a jerk of his chin. "My family is broke. My father supported us with his art until Vietnam ruined his mind. He hasn't painted since. Without his work, we've been living off my small pay from the football club and the sale of his remaining paintings. But the last was sold three months ago. There's nothing left."

I stood, my back pressed to the door. I felt he wanted to tell more, tell me everything and unburden himself. "Okay," I said slowly.

"My father lives downstairs," Adrian said. "The government-run home they put him in after he came back from the war was a nightmare, so I moved him here to keep an eye on him. My mother refuses to sell our house, so making it to Ligue 1 or 2 is how I fix everything. My dad gets the proper care he needs, and my mother and sister don't become homeless." He held up his hands. "There you go. Now you know the whole story."

"That isn't the whole story," I said quietly and swallowed hard. "What about med school? What about your dream of helping people on a grand scale?"

"It doesn't matter, Janey," he said, his voice tight, like a band ready to snap. "I have to play."

"But now you can't. Not in the final." I moved a step closer to him. "Did you red card yourself on purpose? To get out of the final? To try to get out of soccer?"

Adrian stared a moment, a thousand thoughts swimming in the dark blue of his eyes. Finally, he gave an angry, bitter laugh.

"That's the fantastic irony, isn't it? It doesn't matter that I was carded. The scouts will come for me anyway. But the team can win without me, even though they don't believe it."

"They lost today," I said in a small voice.

Adrian pressed his lips together. "*Fantastique.* Then I fucked everything up for..."

"For nothing?" I asked, my voice a whisper.

Adrian raised his eyes to meet mine. "Not for nothing."

I swallowed hard, past my pounding heart. "Your mother told me you hit Olivier because he was talking about...me."

Adrian glanced away, his hands gripping the edge of his desk. "You should go. I have nothing to offer."

"I don't want anything from you, Adrian," I said, taking another step. "Nothing that can be bought, anyway."

"No? Not an exposé on the footballer who's secretly destitute, trying to keep his family afloat? Isn't that why you're here?"

I flinched, but took another step. Adrian's harsh tone was only to protect himself and his family's reputation...and I loved him all the more for it.

I think I might love him. God help me...

"No," I said, moving closer, my lips trembling. I was right in front of him now, my body inches from his. "That's not why I'm here."

He gazed down at me, his hard defenses crumbling. His hand came up to brush a lock of hair from my face. "Then why?"

"For you." I swallowed hard, tears stinging my eyes. "I came here to be with you."

"I have nothing, Janey," he said, his eyes full of longing. "Women want to be taken care of..."

"Not all women," I said, leaning in to his space. "Not me. I want to work. I want to have a career. I want to make something of my life. And I think you do, too." I let my arms go around his neck, my fingers tangling in his hair. "You're a good man, Adrian. That's what any woman wants. What *I* want. I want you..."

Without another word, his arms wrapped around me, hauling me to him, and his mouth crashed to mine. I parted my lips to take his kiss, my knees weakening as his tongue explored my mouth, demanding and urgent. With all the heavy secrets of his life no longer hidden, I knew he was kissing me with his truest self. All of him, all of his goodness was in that kiss, even as it quickly heated into something desperate with need.

Adrian's hand slid up my back, to my hair, where he made a gentle fist that sent tingles of electricity shoot down my body. He angled my head to deepen the kiss, and held me closer, so that there was no distance between us.

I have everything.

The desperate lust I'd seen with Lucie and Thomas, and the deep emotion between Brigitte and Robert. I felt both from Adrian, and I moaned softly into his mouth.

"Janey..." Adrian broke our kiss with a gasp, like a man coming up for air. He laid kisses along my jaw, my neck, to the hollow of my collarbone. "I want you..."

"*Yes,*" I hissed in English, as he went lower, his mouth finding one hard nipple under my top. My fingers tangled in his hair as he nipped it through the material. His hand found my other breast, and I gasped as he rolled the ball of his thumb over that nipple too.

"I thought you didn't like me," he murmured against the material of my blouse.

"I do," I whispered back, my fingers raking through his hair. "I always did. I'm just bad at flirting, remember?"

Adrian laughed and then kissed me so that I felt the smile on his lips. Then he lifted my blouse off altogether. I watched his eyes flare and darken with want, as he took in my small, bra-clad breasts. I wasted no time, but found the hem of his T-shirt and hauled it off of him.

"My God," I whispered, my eyes drinking in the masculine perfection of his body. Planes of smooth skin over his pecs, the tight lines of his abs, and the narrow waist that made a perfect V. His erection strained at his pants, and I stared at that too, amazed at how badly I wanted all of him.

He pulled me to him, enveloping me in the strength of his muscles over warm skin—strength and heat and hard kisses that had the whole of his heart behind them.

"Janey," he whispered, pulling back to hold my face in his hands. "I need you... Now. But I...don't want to hurt you. I can go slow..."

"It's okay," I whispered back. "It's not my first time. I wish it were."

He held my gaze a moment longer, and I saw only myself reflected there. Then he kissed me hard, sweeping me up in the power of his want for me. My words had been the permission he'd needed, though I knew if I'd been a virgin, he would have done everything in his power to be gentle.

Our kissing began again, this time with urgency. Adrian spun me around and lifted me to set me on the edge of his desk. He kissed me harder, ravenously, pressing me back, yet holding me tight with strong arms.

I wrapped my legs around him but there was too much clothing between us. My jeans felt rough and coarse, when I wanted to feel his skin against mine. I stroked the hard length of him over his pants, as his hands went to the clasp of my bra in the back.

Still stroking him, I moaned at the touch of his hands on me, feeling their weight and bending again to put his mouth on one taut nipple. I gave him a squeeze and he answered with a groan and a bite that sent of flush of heat straight through the core of me. Finally, with a grunt of frustrated need, Adrian lifted me again and carried me to his bed.

I sank back on a clean bedspread that smelled of his cologne and green grass and *him*. Adrian lay over me, and the weight of him on my body was a new kind of ecstasy. Every muscle he had honed over the years in service to his sport was now mine; its magnificence and strength were all for me to touch and be touched. He propped himself on his elbows to kiss me, cradling my head in his hands even as our bodies below the waist strained for the other desperately.

"Janey, I have to... Now."

I nodded mutely, and he sat up, kneeling on the bed beside me. He pulled my jeans off leaving me in only my panties.

"Please," I whispered, not caring how desperate I sounded. I *was* desperate to have him, over me again and inside of me.

Adrian bent over me and trailed kisses between my breasts, down my stomach, below my navel, to the hem of my underwear.

I shook my head from side to side. "No, I can't. It's too much. It'll be too much."

"Have you ever?"

I shook my head no.

A sly grin spread over his lips. "Do you want to?"

I started to say I wasn't sure, but my head was already bobbing yes.

He laughed a little. "But Janey," his voice lowering, "I won't do anything you don't want me to."

"I know," I whispered. "But I want everything. I want all of you. Please."

"Thank God," he said, grazing teeth along my skin. "I want this so much."

He took my panties down to my knees, and tore them off. I shivered with longing and anticipation as he bent to me and licked the sensitive skin with a gentle flick of his tongue.

My hips jerked at the incredible sensation, and then lifted to offer myself to him without conscious thought.

"Oh my God, Adrian..."

"All mine, now..." he said. "I'm going to take care of you."

Then he put his mouth on me in earnest. His tongue swirled then sucked until I was writhing, grasping at the headboard as Adrian brought me to a fast-rising swell of pleasure that crashed almost immediately, and left me shuddering and wanting more.

"Come here," I moaned. "God, please..."

Adrian stripped naked and I stared at the size of him, my heart pounding. He lay over he me and my legs spread for him without me having to do a thing. I thought I'd be nervous—he was only my second—but everything about Adrian was different. Better. Perfect. I arched my back, my nails clawing into the flesh of his shoulder blades, to let him sink inside me.

"Jesus, Janey..." He growled against my neck. "So good. So perfect..."

He pressed slowly inside me until our hips were joined. I held him tight, arms and legs wrapped around him possessively. This man, this good man was mine; giving himself to me and I took all of him in every way.

He began to move slowly at first, but it was too much. The need between us was a desperate hunger that needed to be satiated immediately. We'd both been starving for each other, and now that we were here, we couldn't get enough. Not enough touches, or kisses; I couldn't get enough of him inside me—pulling back and sliding in as much as the tight knot of my legs at the small of his back would allow.

Finally, Adrian propped himself on his palms, arching himself over me, his thrusts so fast, I was delirious. English and French words fell out of my mouth: yes and more and his name. But especially *yes.* The word was a whisper, then a cry, then a scream as another swell of pleasure in me broke, this time a tidal wave. The crash was long and slow, meeting the shore of him as he ground his hips deeper into mine, shuddering hard and spilling his release inside of me.

Adrian collapsed on top of me, heavy and warm and perfect. He wrapped his arms around me and pulled me to the side so that we lay tangled up; arms and legs, and skin slick with sweat. Our breaths came hard in between kisses because we weren't done kissing. In that moment, I didn't think I would ever be done kissing Adrian. I didn't want to kiss anyone else ever again.

It was too soon to be thinking thoughts like that, but the way Adrian looked at me when we finally came up for air let me think I wasn't alone. He brushed the hair from my forehead and I traced the strong line of his jaw with one finger.

"Thank you for being here," he said to me, his gravelly, bedroom voice sounding exactly as it was meant to be heard.

I smiled and kissed him gently. "Thank you for letting me in."

THIRTEEN

Tomorrow Never Knows

Janey

NIGHT FELL OUTSIDE ADRIAN'S SMALL WINDOW. WE LAY TANGLED IN ONE another, me lying over his chest, his hand lazily sliding up and down my bare back.

"You're so warm," I murmured, nuzzling his neck. "I'm not going to leave here ever, if that's okay with you."

His chest rumbled beneath mine with his gravelly voice. "I wasn't planning on letting you go, so that works out."

I grinned and propped my chin on my hand to look at him. "You are nothing like what I expected," I said. "Nothing."

"In a good way, I hope."

"The best way."

He raised a brow at me. "Don't blow my cover."

He was teasing but I answered him seriously. "I won't. I won't write a word for the article. I don't care if Antoine fires me."

Adrian's chest rose and fell beneath me in a sigh. "I don't know, Janey. I don't know what's supposed to happen next."

"You go to that symposium with the doctors Kouchner and Recamiér," I said.

Adrian's gaze turned to the darkness outside the window. "There will be scouts at the game. Even if I don't play, I have to be there." He laughed shortly. "The team will hate me. I don't know if showing up will help them or hurt them, but I have to go."

"If they can't win without you, they don't deserve to advance, right?" I said. "A team can't survive on one player alone. That's too much pressure on you."

"It's not true anyway," Adrian said. "They have the skill to win without me but there's a mental game, too. Their confidence is obviously shaken, and they played like shit." He sighed again. "What a mess."

"You need to live your life," I said gently. "Become a doctor. Save the world. I know you can do it." I lightly grazed circles on his chest with my fingernails. "But whatever you decide, I'll support you."

Adrian smiled faintly at me. "Thank you, Janey. I feel like I can breathe again, now that someone outside the family knows what's happened. And you're still here."

"Of course I am. I'm not going anywhere. I'm pretty sure we already established that."

He bent to kiss me, and when he pulled back he regarded me a moment in silence.

"What is it?" I asked.

"I want you to write the article."

I blinked, lifted my head off my hand. "The whole story?"

He nodded. "All of it. About living here, med school, about what Vietnam did to my father..."

"But Adrian..."

"Leave out the particulars of my family's finances," he said. "For my mother's sake. She couldn't bear the humiliation. But everything else..."

My brows knit together. "Are you sure?"

"I've never been more sure. It's like confession that is long overdue."

I nodded. "I'll make sure I protect your mother, but I want to be honest about how you're providing for them. More than anything, I want to write that." I smiled. "It's the angle."

Adrian didn't return my smile. "That's not the angle. Vietnam is the angle. How war tears apart families and countries alike. It ended for France in '54, and yet we're still feeling it."

"It hasn't ended for America. It feels like it never will."

Adrian nodded. "I want to be a doctor, Janey. Helping is the only thing that makes sense to me in the chaos."

I craned forward to kiss him softly. "Go to the symposium. Promise?"

"We'll see." He took hold of my shoulders and hauled me up so that my body lay flush atop his, eliciting a squeal from me. "But that's a week away. We have a little bit of time, no?"

I kissed him long and deep. "We have all night."

THE FOLLOWING MORNING, Adrian and I woke at dawn and disentangled ourselves with effort. My body felt heavy and drowsy after a night spent bringing each other to one soaring high after another, and then sinking into each other to recover; to talk and kiss and sleep a little.

We dressed and went to an outdoor market so that Adrian could buy his father some groceries. We bought baguette, cheese, fruit, vegetables, eggs, and a hot croque monsieur ham-and-cheese sandwich for his breakfast. As we were leaving the market, I spied a stall that sold homemade jarred preserves.

"His favorite flavor?" I asked, perusing the pretty jars.

"Strawberry," Adrian said absently. His gaze flickered to the price on the sign. "You don't have to."

"I want to," I said. "And I'd like to meet him. For real, I mean."

Adrian looked at me for a long moment, then nodded. "I'd like that very much."

We went back to the pension where the Algerian man I'd met yesterday was smoking a cigarette and reading an Arabic newspaper.

"*Bonjour*, M. Hamidi," Adrian said. "How are you and Imane this morning?"

"Eh? *Bien, bien*," the man said. He peered at me through his pungent cigarette smoke. "You are the American? From New York?"

"California," I said, with a polite smile. "Why does everyone assume I'm from New York?" I asked Adrian as we made our way down the narrow hall on the first floor.

"I don't know," he said, stopping in front of #5. "When I look at you, I imagine what California must be like. I think of a beach or a tropical island under a blazing sun."

"We've turned mushy already, haven't we?" I said, laughing.

"Yes, we have." Adrian kissed me softly, then his smile faltered. "Are you ready?"

I nodded. "I am."

"My father is not violent, but he is quite unwell..."

I gave his hand not holding our groceries a squeeze. "It's going to be okay."

He smiled faintly and knocked on the door. "Papa? Are you up?"

The door flew open and I stepped back involuntarily. M. Rousseau stared at us with wild eyes, his hair askew from sleep and a loose coat hanging over his pajamas.

"You must go to Edouard," he said. "Edouard has it. *They have it*!"

I saw Adrian try to smile reassuringly through a pained expression as he gently ushered his father inside. Victor's place was the same as Adrian's, only cluttered with papers and empty bottles. I knew without having to ask that Adrian probably took great pains to see that his father didn't live in squalor.

"Who is Edouard, Papa? What does he have?" he asked calmly, as if he were accustomed to his father's incoherent talk. He set down the bag of food on a table littered with papers, half-finished sketches, and the remains of last night's dinner.

Victor rushed to his desk and began rifling frantically through the papers there.

"Vietnam. I brought it back with me and Edouard has it. I thought it was here..." He held up a wrinkled paper, inspected it, then tossed it away. "But then I remembered, they have it. Edouard. Edouard..." He smacked his own forehead. "The rest...it didn't stay."

Adrian brought his father a pill from a small bottle of medicine, and a glass of water.

"Where did you know Edouard from?" Adrian asked with practiced patience.

"The after." Victor looked at me. "They booed. They didn't want our wounded to land at Marseille. Can you imagine? We were trying to come home. That's all we wanted. To come home..."

He took the pill from his son and sank down on the chair to drink the water. Adrian turned to me.

"He means there were protests when the soldiers came back," he said.

I nodded. "It's happening in the U.S. too." I retrieved the hot sandwich for Victor, and handed it to him with a napkin. "Here you are, M. Rousseau."

The older man peered up at me, then looked to Adrian. "Edouard has it," he said, calmer now. I guessed the pill Adrian had given him was a mild sedative. "Edouard has Laos. Khmer. Vietnam. All of them. I tried to leave them behind but the shadows remained anyway." The tapped his forehead. "In here."

Victor went quiet then, and turned his attentions to his food.

"I should go," I told Adrian. "I have a story to write."

He sucked in a breath. "Yeah, I guess you do."

"It was very nice to meet you, M. Rousseau," I said, but the man was intent on his food.

Adrian walked me to the door, and glanced at his father by the window. "I know, he needs real care but he was dying at the veteran's hospital. Another reason to sign with a Premier League if they'll have me. So I can put him somewhere good."

I took Adrian's face in my hands and kissed him and hurried out before he could see my tears.

BACK IN MY FLAT, I sat at my typewriter and Adrian's story flew out of me. I wrote everything: about football and beyond. The only area where I held back was the specifics of the Rousseau's finances, though I made it clear Adrian was doing everything in his power to provide for them, even if it meant giving up his studies. It took me all of that Sunday, but by Monday morning it was done.

I stared at what I wrote and called America. My best friend.

"Hello?" Helen said.

"It's me," I said.

"Janey!" she said. "I've missed you. How is Paris?"

I told her all that happened and about Adrian.

"He sounds wonderful," Helen said wistfully.

"He is..." I bit my lip and looked at my article. "Helen, you were right."

"About what?"

"I found a big story inside a little one. The biggest story of my life."

AFTER I HUNG up with Helen, I showered, dressed, and hurried down to Antoine's office with the story and the best photos tucked under my arm.

I stood, biting my lip, as Antoine read the article. When he finished, he looked up at me, his eyes wide.

"This is true? Adrian's father is alive?"

I nodded.

"I was at the match two days ago," Antoine said. "I saw the red card..." He narrowed his eyes at me. "One could read this and feel as if Adrian doesn't want to play football, but you never clarify that at all."

"It's not an opinion piece."

"But didn't you *ask* him?"

I wasn't about to jeopardize Adrian's chances of being signed. If that's what was supposed to happen, I wouldn't interfere. But I hoped putting Adrian's story out into the universe was going help make the right things happen for him.

It has to. He deserves to be happy too.

"He will do whatever is necessary to take care of his family," I said.

Antoine regarded me a moment more, but I was unwavering. He blew air out his cheeks, shaking his head. "Very well. We'll run it tomorrow."

"Thank you."

I eased a sigh where Antoine couldn't hear it—and started to go.

"Mademoiselle Martin?" Antoine said.

"*Oui?*"

"It's very good, this article."

I waited for the pride to swell in me for the praise, but it was the story that needed to be told, and that's all that mattered. And I decided, then and there, those were the only kinds of stories I would ever tell.

I want to stand on the big stage too, right next to Adrian Rousseau.

FOURTEEN

People Get Ready

ADRIAN

JANEY'S STORY came out on Wednesday morning. I read it in my flat, knowing that my teammates and family were reading it too. I didn't expect anyone to be happy with me, so I shouldn't have been surprised when Robert pounded on my door at the pension. He was my best friend and had been the only person who knew my father was alive and torn up by the war.

He stormed into my place, a copy of the paper in his hand.

"What the fuck, Adrian?"

"Good morning to you, too," I said. "Coffee?"

He flapped the paper at me. "Why didn't you tell me?"

"Tell you what?"

"That you want to finish med school?"

I sighed, crossed my arms. "I have responsibilities to the team."

"You think we can't win without you? Is that it, you arrogant bastard?"

I was taken aback until I saw the glint of laughter in Robert's eye.

"I *know* you can't win without me," I shot back, fighting my own smile. "In fact, you should let me play forward *and* tend goal. Just be safe."

"Well, I would, except you got your ass red carded."

"I'm sorry about that. And about the team dropping back to fourth."

"Yeah, well, we've got to play the best game of our life and hope we have the points when it's done. I hate to say it, but your goals this season might save our ass." Robert raised a brow. "Tell me the truth. Did you do it to get thrown out of the game? Or did you do it for the girl?"

"Her name is Janey," I said. "And the truth is...maybe a little of both."

Robert nodded. He tossed the paper on my desk next to the anatomy textbook I had been poring over.

"I'd say I'd explain to the guys the situation, but I think this article did it for you. And I'm sorry if I added any pressure to you. All I can think about is football. I eat, sleep, live for it. It's all I want. But it's not all you want, is it?"

I shrugged. "It's what I need."

Robert nodded. "Come to La Cloche tonight. We're still your family too, no?"

"You are, but I have to study. I'm behind and have a final coming up."

We clasped hands and gave each other a half hug.

"It wouldn't be so terrible, would it?" Robert asked at the door. "To play for Ligue 2. Or 1 for that matter? To be a huge star?"

I thought a minute before answering.

"When my father was well, he used to tell me the footballers were his heroes. And I wanted to be that more than anything. To make him proud. And when he came back from the war, his mind broken by what he'd seen and done, I began to want something else. I was hardly seven years old but I wanted to be a hero for him then too. To make him well. So I played football and I went to med school. One of those things is going to help him and my family." I smiled ruefully. "That's all that matters."

ON THURSDAY MORNING, I went to visit my mother and sister. I had tried to call Maman several times, but Sophie told me she was too upset with me to talk.

Janey had class, but met me at the nearest Metro station after. She flew at me immediately, and threw her arms around my neck. Her happiness radiated through her body, and I kissed her hard, wanting her at once.

"This was a bad idea," I said, holding her tight, as people streamed past us like water around an island. "Meeting in public after so long..."

"I know," she said, breathlessly. "Two days without seeing you felt like forever."

"Fortunately, my mother is the equivalent of a long, cold shower."

Janey laughed but it faded quickly. "I'm scared she'll hate me more than she already does. She blames me for your red card."

He rolled his eyes. "Christ, the damned red card. They'll put that on my grave. 'Here lies Adrian Rousseau. Son, husband, father, punched his own teammate and blew a final.'"

She laughed and linked her arm in mine as we headed to my family's house. And having her there, on my arm as a partner, and not as a prop, was the best fucking feeling in the world. Better than an overtime goal or a cheering crowd. I glanced down at Janey as we walked.

I want this, always.

Outside my family's building, a man wearing a long coat, hat, and rumpled suit, was glancing at a paper in his hand and then up at the numbers on the front of the building.

"Can I help you?" I asked.

The man turned. He looked to be about my father's age, with a grizzled face and heavy eyes. He was clean-shaven and had some heft around the middle, and yet I could almost see him as haggard and gaunt.

He took off his hat. "*Bonjour*. I am looking for M. Rousseau."

"That's me," I said.

"You are Adrian?" the man said. "From the article?" He retrieved a torn-out copy of Janey's article from an inside pocket of his coat. "I was looking for your father, but perhaps you are who I should talk to after all. My name is Paul Lenaerts. In 1954, I worked at the Edouard Toulouse Psychiatric Hospital."

Beside me, Janey gasped just as I flinched.

"You knew my father?"

"Not very well. It is best if you come to my hotel and I will explain." He looked to Janey. "Both can come. Are you the writer of this article, miss?"

She nodded. "I am."

M. Lenaerts smiled. "I'm so glad you did. I have some items that do not belong to me, and I'm so happy to be able to return them to their rightful owner."

Janey and I exchanged looks, and the hope burning in her light blue eyes fed mine.

We took a cab to a little hotel in the 7th, and Paul Lenaerts explained that he was Belgian, but had worked for the French government as an envoy in '54 to help with the withdrawal of troops after the Viet Minh took control over northern Vietnam, essentially losing the war for France.

"I was working with the Veterans' Affairs Office—though everything was in chaos," Paul said. "I saw how many of the men were broken down by the war, and instead of going back to work for the embassy, I stayed in Marseille to tend to the wounded."

"My father was in Marseille for a year before he came home," I said, exchanging another glance with Janey. "I was too young to know the name of the hospital, or I've forgotten it."

Paul nodded. "I was an administrator at Edouard Toulouse, not a doctor, and so had very little interactions with patients." He smiled warmly. "But he was quite a character, your father. Everyone told tales about Victor."

The cab rolled to a stop at the front of a boutique hotel. Paul led us upstairs to his small, but elegantly appointed room.

"The train ride from Brussels was only an hour and twenty minutes," he said, "yet I feel as though I am sixteen years late."

He moved to the side of the bed and pulled out a flat, square bundle wrapped in a moving blanket and taped along the front. He set it down on the floor and reached for a letter opener on the hotel's small desk, speaking as he worked to cut the tape.

"My daughter attends the Sorbonne. She called me Wednesday night to tell me about the article, and how the footballer's father had fought in the war. She thought it might interest me since she knew my work in Marseille." He drew down the blankets protecting the work inside. "When she told me your father was an artist as well, I immediately thought of these."

My heart nearly stopped as Paul carefully retrieved three oil paintings from within the protective layers of blanket and leaned them against the bed, side by side. Janey gripped my hand.

I stared at the three paintings.

Laos. Khmer. Vietnam.

They were nothing like my father had ever done before, but I knew they were his. I would know his art anywhere, like his fingerprints. The paintings were of soldiers in the field—long strokes of the brush rendering tall, dry grass as helicopters droned black on the horizon. The sun felt merciless, as if it would burn my fingers to touch the canvas. The men's faces were scarred by shadow cast by their helmets, and drawn by what they had seen. As with my father's other work, they were stark in their simplicity; beautiful in their honesty.

"Please forgive me," Paul said quietly. "I left Marseille before Victor and went back to Belgium. When the hospital was cleared of veterans, many items had been left behind. One of the administrators knew I was something of an art buff and sent these to me. They're not signed; I had no way of knowing who they belonged to. I was busy with a new assignment and so put them in storage where they sat for sixteen years."

"Pieces of him," Janey whispered. "He said these were pieces of him."

"I will help you authenticate them, if necessary," Paul said. "I understand they might be of some financial help to you."

I nodded slowly, though the idea of selling these made my heart ache.

I turned to shake Paul's hand. "Thank you for this."

He smiled warmly and gestured to Janey. "Thank her. If it wasn't for her article these might have languished in my garage for another sixteen years."

WE LEFT THE HOTEL. I had two of my father's paintings tucked under each arm, and Janey held the other. Out in the street, under the sunshine, I awkwardly maneuvered my way close to her and kissed her.

"You did this," I whispered. "You did this for me."

Tears stood out in her eyes and she smiled. "Only because you let me. Because you trusted me."

I sucked in a breath to compose myself. "There's a lot happening, isn't there?" I asked. "Between us?"

She nodded quickly. "Quite a lot, I think."

"Yeah," I said, holding her gaze. "Quite a lot."

Janey blinked quickly and stood straight, tossing a lock of her long hair over her shoulder. "Stop stalling, Rousseau, we have to get these to your mother."

I laughed and kissed her again. "I guess we do." My smile faltered. "Though it's going to hurt to sell them."

"This is your future," Janey said, hefting one painting. "This is your father taking care of himself and his family, and you. So you can do what you were meant to do."

We boarded the Metro. Doing what I was meant to do was right in my grasp.

But it won't mean as much anymore, if I don't have Janey.

FIFTEEN

I'm a Believer

Janey

SOPHIE LET US INTO THE HOUSE AND HUGGED ME TIGHT EVEN BEFORE SHE saw the paintings. Adrian brought his mother down and we revealed what Paul had given us. Adrian's mother's hands flew to her mouth and she stared at the paintings.

"I never thought..." She sank into the couch, still staring. "I thought I was done missing him," she said. "I thought if enough years had gone by, I could pretend like he died over there."

Conscious of her audience, she wiped her eyes and composed herself. "You must sell them. It sounds cold and terrible to say, but we must." She turned to Adrian. "You must finish medical school. I know that is the passion that burns in you hotter than the game."

"We should keep one at least," Adrian said.

"That one," Sophie said, pointing at the lone soldier standing in the tall grass.

Mme. Rousseau nodded. "We shall keep it no matter what."

ADRIAN AND I joined the footballer group in the stands on Saturday afternoon. Adrian was nervous but Brigitte hugged Adrian with tears in her eyes.

"I'm all for you punching Olivier, but next time do it off the pitch. I won't stop you."

He laughed and the tension eased among the group. They had all read the article, and Brigitte sidled up next to me.

"You did a good thing for him," she said.

I shook my head. "I only reported what he has done and had been doing."

I eyed a bunch of scouts who had watched his arrival.

"They're dying to talk to you," I said.

Adrian nodded with a sly grin. "Which is the *other* reason why we have to skip out at half time."

The whistle blew for the half, and Robert jogged over to where we sat in the stands. Paris Central was leading, 2-0, Johannes's having scored both goals.

"Come with me," Adrian said. "Let's go say goodbye."

We joined Robert at the sidelines where he gave me a grateful look, and then clasped hands with Adrian.

"So far so good," Adrian said. "Don't screw it up."

Robert made a face. "It's going to be tight, points-wise, but your goal difference might give us the edge." He made a fist in a mock threatening gesture. "Lucky for that, Rousseau."

"Yeah, yeah, yeah," Adrian said. "Make sure you put mention of that in your Ligue 2 contract."

The two men laughed again and then Robert jogged back to finish the rest of the fifteen-minute break. The scouts we're ready to pounce on Adrian but we stayed until the whistle blew to start the second half and we snuck out while they were watching the game.

We took the Metro back to the Sorbonne where the symposium was about to begin at the Panthéon. The theater was crowded and a slideshow was set up flashing images of a war-torn country. Biafra, Nigeria, said the program that an usher handed to us as we entered.

Adrian and I sat down with three or so other doctors and journalists. We sat hand-in-hand listening to the doctors and their associates outline their plans. I thought this would be Adrian's dream but it turned out to be mine as well. The doctors wanted to not only bring medical aid to places and people who desperately needed it, but to document what was happening in the world and bring it to light in Western countries. They would need journalists and translators.

Adrian turned to me and we exchanged a look that held our entire future in it.

"*Médecins Sans Frontières,*" Adrian whispered to me. "I even love the name. What is it in English?"

I whispered back. "Doctors Without Borders."

"I love it," he said, and he leaned over in the darkened theatre to cup my cheek. "I love you, Janey."

My heart filled my entire chest, and I leaned closer to brush my lips over his. "I love you, Adrian. So much."

"So much," he whispered and kissed me softly, and I knew, in that moment, the greatest story of my life was about to begin.

Epilogue: 1975

Now, Then, and Forever

Adrian

Janey dances in the surf.

Earth, Wind, and Fire plays on the transistor radio I'd rigged up, but she's lost in her own rhythm. Her lithe body is covered only by a white bikini that makes me want to haul my tired bones off the lounger and race toward her. To touch her skin that is wet and salty with the water of Kompong Som Bay, and kiss her. Her hair is tied back while we work in the tents—me in the emergency medical unit of the refugee camp, her in the communications center. Only at night, it's down for me to tangle my hands in as she comes undone beneath me. But we have two whole vacation days—mandatory, as Dr. Kouchner insisted we take time off—and now Janey lets it free. The long gold strands catch the sun that is intense in a way I haven't quite gotten used to.

"Come join me," she says, kicking at the blue-green water.

"I can't," I say. "I haven't lain down during the day in six months, and now I can't move."

"You moved well enough last night," Janey says with a sly grin.

I once told her she reminded me of white beaches, blue water and a hot sun. California, maybe. Or Tahiti.

I never imagined Cambodia.

I glance over the white sands of the beach. It's crescent-shaped, with green grasses thickening into forest behind us. The last vestiges of an American military installation is a good kilometer and a half down; the dark green of their

Jeeps haul supplies from a small port. Their ships—one warship and the other cargo, sit on the still water, like toys from this distance.

Janey and I are alone. Or as alone as we can be with MSF's base two kilometers up the road. Other personnel, also on leave, cavort in the surf too, but there seems to be an unspoken agreement to pretend that the other doesn't exist.

I watch Janey, and as I do, no one else does exist. The Cambodian refugee crisis we've been working to help feels far away in that moment. I see only Janey and the heat drugs my exhausted mind, and drags it back to how we got here.

My father's painting "Khmer" sold for one million francs. I used the money to find a home for him that was clean, professional, where he could be given the proper care and supervision he needed. The hospital has an art therapy program, and I'm hopeful that he'll find and put back together the pieces of himself the war shattered in him.

My mother visits my father now. Every week. She writes me that it's hard, and her guilt for abandoning him when he came back broken haunts her. I imagine her sitting with him while he paints or talks or does nothing at all, and though it might not seem as if she's getting through to him, I know it matters.

Sophie, after persuading our mother, attends the Sorbonne now, studying political science. She doesn't yet know what she wants to do, but she knows she can and will do something important, and that's good enough for her.

Back in '70, Paris Central won that final match I'd been banned from, and tied for third place at 48 points. Turns out, my season goal average gave them the edge and they advanced to Ligue 2. They've maintained their position there for years, but Robert has written to they are in the promotion zone. On their way to the Ligue 1.

A part of me aches at the news, like touching an old bruise. I could be with them, on a pitch with thousands of spectators who watch with their hearts and souls on the edge of their seat as they cheer for their team. Instead, I finished med school and joined *Médecins Sans Frontières* with Janey before the ink was dry on my diploma.

We'd been stationed in Cambodia for six months, tending to the sick and wounded Cambodians as they flee the Khmer Rouge. Saigon has fallen and three million people have fled, seeking asylum in China or Thailand. We are stationed to aid them on their journey. To see that they make it somewhere safe. Many won't, but we won't abandon them as they try.

But this day, only one of two days we were willing to take away from our duties, there is just Janey and this beach and me.

She beckons again and this time I haul myself off the 'lounge chair' I'd made from a broken military stretcher. I step out from under the dried palm frond umbrella and the sun beats down on the bare skin of my back.

Janey laughs at my grimace. "The water isn't any cooler."

"That's because you're in it," I say, wrapping my arms around her waist.

"Are you trying to lay a line on me?" she laughs, reaching up to ring her arms around my neck.

"I'm trying to say you're hot," I say.

"Yeah, I get that but if you have to explain it..."

I tickle her to make her laugh, then haul her close. "I'm tired."

Her smile softens and she trails her fingers over my scruff of my beard. "I know you are. You work so hard."

"So do you."

Janey works tirelessly, writing articles and taking photos of the crisis, and seeing they get published in the *New York Times*, *Time*, and *Newsweek*; as well as French and British publications. In between, she translates bulletins and memos for MSF.

She's had bylines and photographs in some of the most prestigious publications in the world but hasn't eaten a meal in a restaurant in three months.

But today, she's mine, and if she regrets any of the work we do, it doesn't show on her beautiful face.

"I'm happy," I say. "Are you happy? It seems impossible some days, but in the quiet times, like this, it comes to the surface, how happy I am. With you."

Her smile is brilliant and soft. "I'm happy. I've never been more happy."

I kiss her gently, then harder, and when we break apart, the words fall out. "Marry me. Marry me, Janey. I have nothing to give you. No ring, no fancy proposal...I have nothing. But..."

"I told you a long time ago," she says, her lips trembling and her eyes shining. My girl was tough, but for me, she gave everything. "What I want from you can't be bought." She leans close to kiss me. "Just you, Adrian."

"Just you, Janey," I say. "Will you?"

"*Oui*," she says in my language and again in hers. "Yes, Adrian. I'm yours. Always."

I kiss her then, and her lips are salty with the sea, or her tears, or maybe my own, and it is the taste of perfect happiness.

The End

About the Author

Thank you for reading! For those who are new to me, I am an author of emotional, new adult romances, some of the ugly cry variety, such as Full Tilt and the Butterfly Project. Thanks to my amazing readers, my latest novel—a single-dad romance—Forever Right Now is an international bestseller and, like all of my novels, is FREE on KU.

Amazon: http://amzn.to/2gA9ktr

I need to thank Danielle Maurino Thomas, Robin Renee Hill, Grey Ditto, and Joy Kriebel-Sadowski, for their amazing support and help in bringing this story to light. And special thanks to Annette Chivers for schooling this American gal on the intricacies of the European football league system, though any lingering mistakes are mine. I have taken a few liberties—Paris Central is a fictional team, as is there stadium, Stade Jean-Marc.

I love being stalked by readers! You can follow me:

Facebook: https://www.facebook.com/EmmaScottwrites/

Join my reader group, Emma's Entourage. We'd love to have you: http://bit.ly/2naDnNk

Twitter: @EmmaS_writes

Instagram: @emmascottwrites

Amazon: http://amzn.to/2hikzqa

Goodreads: http://bit.ly/1Oxcuqn

Bookbub: http://bit.ly/2AJ1KYo

My super cute, non-spammy newsletter: http://bit.ly/2nTGLf6

Coming, February 2018, a new emotional romance...

In Harmony http://bit.ly/2yxJZtI

THE END ZONE

Jolie Louis is a smart girl.

She knows that her best friend, Sage Poirier, is a bad idea.

He's a walking, talking cliché. The Adonis quarterback with the bulging biceps and harem of fangirls trailing behind him on campus like a stench you can't get rid of.

Sadly, that's also the reason she can't stay away from him. Well, that and the fact that they're roommates.

Jolie is already straddling the line between friendship and more when Sage comes to her with an offer she cannot refuse: be his fake girlfriend and live for free for the rest of the semester.

She tells herself that she can handle it.

He's just the boy she saved ten years ago, right?

Wrong. So very wrong.

He is a man now, and she is his captive

Heart, body, and soul...

Prologue

Ten years ago.

ON THE EIGHTH NIGHT, SHE DECIDED TO TALK TO HIM.

Eight nights since the Poiriers had waltzed into her life, occupying the house next door.

Eight nights in which the screaming, yelling, and crying of Mrs. Poirier and the roars of her husband pierced Jolie's ears, trickled into her soul, and left her trembling under the quilt her grandmama had made for her.

Eight nights in which their kid—about her age, ten or eleven—stumbled to their squeaky porch, his dirty blond hair sticking out in every direction and his chest heaving with uneven breaths.

Cheeks stained pink.

Mouth curled in a dark scowl.

Eyes blazing hot, red rage she could see even in the pitch-black of the night.

Eight nights that he'd been climbing the oak tree which divided the land between the Poiriers' and her house. He sat there, hidden by branches and leaves. Sometimes he howled to the moon like a lonely wolf. Most times, he cried as silently as humanly possible.

Seven sleepless nights in which *she* tossed and turned and mourned for the nameless boy and his mama, before she broke down and decided to approach him. Even if he'd yell at her. Even if he'd laugh at her. Even if he'd show her no mercy like his daddy had taught him.

The girl pushed her window up with a groan, dragged an old case of books across the carpeted floor, hopped on it, and slipped through the open crack, pouring from the safety of her bedroom to the untamed, uncut meadow. The rain pounded hard on her face, the wind swooshing in her ears. It was humid, hot, muggy, and sticky. Her white cotton pajama dress clung to her skin, rain dripping from its hem to her feet. The grass was slippery, and mud coated her toes. The boy was trudging to the tree determinedly. She cautiously ambled in the same direction.

He slowed when he saw her, so she picked up the pace. Later in life, she'd learn that this was their special tango. One pulls, the other pushes. One wants, the other gives. One loves, the other hurts.

"What are you doing here?" he yelled through the rain. It was impossible to answer him. Her heart was in her throat, pounding *boom, boom, boom* like a caged animal craving freedom.

Step, another step, then another. She wondered if that's how it felt to be alive. Really alive. Not just living. Wet, uncomfortable, and shivering in the midst of a hot summer storm. Up close, he looked even angrier, his eyes a terrifying hue of midnight blue and ire.

They stopped about six feet from each other, right next to the tree. He was slightly taller, slightly wider, face slightly tenser, and a lot warier than she expected.

"Well?" he repeated, brooding. *He is far too young to brood*, she remembered thinking. And it worried her, despite all reason. "Why the hell are you here?"

"I'm sorry," she said, swallowing the pain she carried for him. Like stars in her pocket—it was huge, and she couldn't begin to understand how she'd harbored it for eight nights. He needed help, and she wanted to give it to him.

They'd start school in a couple of weeks—fifth grade—and he'd be the new kid. She decided right then and there that she was going to be his ally. She'd be his friend, whether he liked it or not.

"You're sorry?" He snorted out a bitter laugh, shaking his head. Raindrops ran from the tip of his straight nose, his full lips flattening in an angry line. "Well, don't be. I'm perfectly fine."

"You don't look fine," she insisted.

"Well, I am."

"I'm here for you." She hugged her midsection, embarrassed. Her grandmama used to say that honesty made you vulnerable, but that there was nothing stronger than the truth.

"Whatever you need, I'm here for you. I'm Jolie, by the way." She stretched her hand between them. He stared at it, contemplating, like she offered him much more than a handshake. And maybe she did. The whole thing felt bizarre. Grown-up. The oak tree beside them looked like a living thing, watching as they made this unlikely pact.

"Sage," he said, his palm connecting with hers.

She squeezed hard; he inhaled harder. He jerked her to his body, buried his head in the crook of her shoulder, and shook with tears she couldn't see.

They hugged in the rain, just like in the movies.

They hugged long, and tight, and desperately, his skin soaking into hers like a kiss.

The girl thought to herself, *this is how beautiful love stories begin.* She pressed her ear against his thrumming pulse. His body was warm, but his muscles were rigid like ice.

The girl closed her eyes and the storm disappeared. Not because it had stopped, but because beside him, she felt fearless.

And on the eighth night, the girl gave the boy more than friendship and a hug, without even meaning to—and definitely without agreeing to.

On the eighth night, the girl gave the boy her heart.

He took it silently, never offering his back.

Chapter One

Jolie

"Yo, JoJo. Your ass is on wingman duty tonight." A steaming Starbucks mug slides across the shiny chrome desk he bought for me last Christmas. I lift my head, skeptically examining him through my hazel eyes.

Sage Poirier. My best friend. Louisiana's finest college quarterback. The man who put the 'ho' in manwhore. My forever crush. The list goes on, but I'm sure you get the point. I rearrange the golden neckline of my sensible powder blue blouse, tossing my strawberry blonde tresses (heavy on the strawberry) across my shoulder.

"I have an English lit exam tomorrow." I yawn, my hand already hovering over the keyboard of my MacBook. The bribe—pumpkin spice latte with marshmallows, not technically on the menu, but the barista would throw in her own kidney to get Sage to smile at her—is appreciated, albeit pointless. With the amount of homework I have, I'm not going to budge from my seat tonight. Sage grabs the chair opposite to me and plops on a heavy sigh, his arms bracing its back. He is wearing his black New Orleans Saints cap backwards, his Wayfarers hanging under the brim of his hat from behind. It's the indisputable, international I'm-a-douchebag badge, and it occurs to me, for the hundredth time since we moved in together freshman year of college, that if I hadn't known him since age ten, I would probably find him as sexually attractive as a gassy rat.

"You're no fun." He leans forward and flicks his thumb and finger on the tip of my nose. His mischievous, dimpled smile widens when I swat his hand away.

"I have grades to keep," I retort.

"Hmm. So do I."

I snort a laugh on an eye roll. "You're one of the most sought-after quarterbacks in Louisiana. Going pro next year. At this point, you can flake your way to being a brain surgeon if you'd like. Every professor in this college would kiss the earth you walk upon if they didn't fear you'd file a restraining order against them."

Am I exaggerating here? Nope. Not even a little. Don't get me wrong—I'm thrilled for my best friend. He deserves everything he's achieved, which is *a lot*. At twenty-one, he has his own shiny, burgundy truck, a brand new apartment he rents all by himself (I pay the bills in exchange for my room), and three NFL teams courting him like he is a damsel in a Disney movie. Despite all his success, he's never once been uppity or conceited to me about it. Instead, he gives me access to his new place, new truck, and new life. He is still the good Southern mama's boy who takes off his hat whenever he visits the small farm we lived on. The only downside to being Sage's best friend is, well...

"Question is—do *you* want to kiss the ground I walk on, or better yet, *me*?" His elbows are on the desk now, his head cocked to the side attentively. "Because, Jolie, baby, you're the only person I'm looking to impress. Ideally between the sheets." He winks.

Insert an emoji of moi gagging uncontrollably at his tackiness.

This is not the first time Sage has made a move on me, and I bet it won't be the last time I shut him down.

Recap: A month ago, Sage and I accidentally bumped into each other in the hallway while I was butt naked after a shower (forgot the towel in my room). He was on his way to pee, sporting impressive morning wood through his *Orgasm Donor* boxers. I was looking down, head hanging in shame as I hurried to my room. He was looking down, rearranging his junk. That's how we ended up colliding, limbs tangling together, with me tumbling down and him reaching for my ass to make sure I didn't fall. What a gentleman, right?

From that point forward, Sage has been adamant that we need to hook up. Emphasis on the word 'need' and not 'should'.

And, Lord, forgive me. If he were any other guy, I'd be all over him like a rash after a torrid Vegas vacation. The man looks like the love child of Matthew Noszka and James Dean. The fact that he is six feet four inches of tight abs and only five percent body fat does not—I repeat, *does not*—make it easier for me to constantly reject him. But you know what makes it really easy for me to say no? The notion that Sage, whom I grew up with and know better than anyone else, is going to break my heart into a trillion pieces, smash it to dust, then skip over all the leftovers on his way to the next pink sheet-covered bed.

Because. My. Best. Friend. Is. A. Whore!

I love him, but he is a manwhore who can't keep his dick in his pants for longer than twenty-four hours. I'm pretty sure this fact could be backed up scientifically, if someone put effort into researching the subject. Anyway, I'm too attached to Sage—and to my heart—to mess with either of them so recklessly.

"It's a no from me," I say in an exaggerated English accent, folding my arms and feigning boredom, doing my best Simon Cowell impression. We've been bingeing on the British version of *X Factor* lately and Sage makes me do an impression of the British judge every commercial break. If I refuse, he tackles me to the floor and tickles the shit out of me. I thrash and try to worm my way out from between his steel arms, only to be pinned tightly onto the floor, his hard body over my soft one. He is so aggressive and dedicated, ninety percent of the time I cave simply because I'm too scared I'll accidentally come (it's been a while, please don't judge).

"I'll turn it into a 'yes' before the end of the semester." He stands up, curling his fists as he stretches and yawns. His black shirt rides up and the prominent V leading to his crotch is on full display. In a last-ditch effort to save my already-damp panties, I avert my gaze, my eyes hard on the MacBook screen, and furrow my brows as the words in my lit essay slip from my vision. I decided to major in English lit because I'm good with words, but whenever he's around, I'm nothing but a blubbery mess. Sage continues, "No girl has ever said no to me yet, and I'll be damned if the one who does is the chick I care about the most."

"But that's exactly why I'm saying no," I snap, my head shooting up from the essay. I can't fathom why he cannot see this. Sleeping together would ruin everything.

"Why?"

Why? "Why?" I look up, huffing. Yep, I'm actually huffing. And huffers are my pet peeve, but boy, does Sage make me want to huff lately. "Do you really want to throw away ten years of friendship for a quick lay?"

He smirks. "First of all, it's not going to be quick. I know what I'm doing in the sack. We're talking a minimum of twenty-five minutes, lady, and I'm being humble here, because I might be a little on the excited side when I finally roll you between my sheets." He cups his groin and winks, and I would roll my eyes if it weren't for the fact that his room is down the hall, and the thin walls confirm his statement. All the girls he brings home (roughly twenty percent of the US female population) *do* moan and scream for an average of forty minutes. "And second of all, I will not be ruining anything. You have one-night stands. I have one-night stands. We can have them together and still keep our friendship intact. We're not fucking twelve, dude."

I guess I can kill this conversation by pointing out that (A) twelve-year-olds don't usually have sexual intercourse, and (B) I'm not a dude. But there's something else I need to make clear.

"I don't engage in one-night stands." I pick up a pen and choke it to death to keep myself from punching Sage's gorgeous, cocky face. I know my fist is going to hurt more than his nose. The guy is seemingly built of steel, bronze, and copper.

"*Of* course you do. What about that Brandon dude?"

"*That* Brandon dude was my boyfriend for seven months," I deadpan. Funny he should mention it, since Brandon and I broke up last year because the latter was adamant that there was something going on between Sage and me. Which was insane, inaccurate, and incredibly irritating. But what was even more disheartening was the fact that Sage did everything he could to nurture this false assumption by constantly touching and calling me whenever I hung out with Brandon like he was trying to sabotage our relationship. I swear, Sage was only a few weeks short of pissing on my leg to claim his ownership, which was kind of rich, considering how Sage's dick has been passed around like community property. I'm surprised he's not partly funded by the government.

"That douche was never your boyfriend, JoJo," he shakes his head, sighing, like I'm an adorable puppy.

"Sorry to disappoint, but he really was."

You will not punch your best friend. You will not punch your best friend. You will no...

"Well, now I want to kick that guy's ass even more."

"What? Why?"

"Because—*sorry to disappoint*," he mimics my tone, and pretty accurately, too (the bastard), "but he was banging a Kappa Alpha Slutta whatever chick named Nadia. I saw them hanging out at parties at least twice while you were so-called 'dating', but I thought you'd never seriously dated the dickbag." He runs his huge palm over his sandy blond hair and messes it to tousled perfection. I swallow, feeling my nostrils flare. Goddamn Brandon. "So I never thought I should mention it to you. You know I always got your back."

I smile tightly, stand up, and walk to the kitchen with Sage following behind me. I want him gone, so I can cry myself to sleep, or call my bestie, Chelsea, to talk so much shit about Brandon his ears catch on fire and burn down his whole apartment block. I feel played, and stupid, and about as desirable as a bowl of stale broccoli. True, it's been months, but it still stings. What is it about me that attracts douchebags? I mean, I do occasionally wear Taylor Swift's perfume...

"Come with me," Sage coaxes again, his husky voice bleeding into my body and melting my lady parts into warm goo. I shouldn't be so turned-on by him, especially as I know him. Truly know him. All the bad and unflattering parts of him. Countless times I watched him go home with other girls, puking in national parks, and experiencing meltdowns. Crying happily when his parents got divorced, weeping sadly when his father died of liver failure after years of alcohol abuse, and roaring triumphantly when he got a full scholarship for college.

"I have an exam, remember?" I open the fridge and take out a carton of OJ. I slam the door and when I turn around, he is caging me in, bracing the counter from each side of my waist, his mouth so close to mine I can see the dimple in the center of his full lower lip. He stares me down predatorily.

My heart is in my throat.

My soul is most probably in my eyes.

And I am scared. Completely, utterly, and desperately frightened of what he can do to me if I let my guard down. If I let *him* in.

"Wasn't talking about the party, Jo. Let's go to my room. Forget about Brandon. About people. About all the bullshit. I want to make you feel good."

"Sage," I hiss, narrowing my eyes. "Please don't make this an issue. I'd hate to move to another apartment, but I will, if that's what it takes to save our friendship."

And my heart.

He throws his head back, staring at the ceiling, exasperated. Then he pushes off the counter and I'm left to stand here, watching his tight ass walking toward the hallway. What's with this dude? Did he actually not know I had lady bits before he saw me naked? I refuse to sacrifice our friendship because he suddenly sees me as the convenient booty-call-from-across-the-hall.

I swear, he's been acting so strange lately.

I watch his back, knowing the knot in my stomach—the one I'd formed when I was ten and he moved next door—is going to tighten. As if on cue, it does. Blinking, I pour myself a glass of orange juice, spilling some on the countertop, knowing the rest of my night is a bust.

Twenty minutes later, he walks through the door clad in a navy varsity jacket, dark distressed jeans, and his I-just-fucked perfect hair, looking like the perfect sin.

Forty minutes later, Chelsea appears at my door armed with Halo Top ice cream. (I liked Brandon, but not enough to waste my Pilates body on real ice cream because of him.)

An hour later, I get a stream of text messages.

Sage: Dedication doesn't have an off-season. Get ready for me, JoJo. Because I'm coming for you. And guess what? You'll COME for me, too.

Sage: Please told me you got the sexual innuendo.

*Sage: *tell. Not told. Don't give me shit. I'm not drunk. I have thick fingers.*

Sage: (that was another sexual innuendo, btw)

Sage: Also, we're out of milk, but don't worry, I'll buy some on the way home. Notice how I spared you a third sexual innuendo even though it's white and sticky...

Chapter Two

Sage

"PLEASE TELL ME YOU DIDN'T FORGET TO ASK HER THIS TIME."

Mark's elbow is propped against the kitchen island I'm leaning on. The party is a bust. Even though it's at a big-ass mansion on the outskirts of Baton Rouge, the vibe is just...*off*. Every fucker in my year seems to be here and I don't know half of these people who talk to me, but everyone knows *me*. This chains me into a string of endless, meaningless, mundane conversations about grades and football, two things I shouldn't be thinking about during my time off.

Mark snaps his fingers in front of my eyes, and I blink, realizing that he's been doing it for some time now. He is the tall, dark, handsome, nice-enough-not-to-fuck-his-secretary-in-twenty-years type. Congressman daddy. English teacher mommy. Three sisters. Perfect reputation. White picket fence and two dogs with adorably stupid names. Wholesome and nice. He is the exact opposite of *me*.

I chew on the red Solo cup that I'm holding and zone out again, letting the half-naked bodies and the heaps of alcohol melt together in my vision.

"Asked who what?" I buy time.

"Your hot roommate. Did you ask her if she's into me?" Again, I find myself wanting to punch my own balls for downplaying my relationship with Jolie. This is all my doing, and the reason I don't tell people how close we are is because I don't want any cock-blocking scenarios to get in my way of a good pussy. Well, this month it backfired in my face. Not only did I experience a life-changing moment with another girl, which pretty much served as a wake-up call to who I *really* need to be with, but now I have to deal with my smitten teammate, too.

Ever since Mark Tensely struck up a thirty-minute-long conversation with Jolie when he swung by to pick up some football gear the other day (specifically, the day before I ran into her naked in the hallway—*insert fucking fist-bite*) he's been eyeing my best friend and begging for me to hook him up with her number.

Yeah. No.

Perhaps the worst part is that Mark is smart, good-looking, well-off, and is actively seeking a steady girlfriend. Unlike Barf-worthy Brandon, he's genuine. He's the whole package. Me? The only thing I have to offer *is* my package. I'm swimming in small endorsement deals and have a scholarship, but I'm so far from well off, I can barely fucking spell the term. Plus, Jolie knows about my antics. She constantly tells me that STD stands for Sage The Douche. We joke about it, like it doesn't worry her and it doesn't insult me. But the truth is, my string of one-night stands have all ended in disaster recently. Though, even before that, I was starting to get bored with the constant hopping from one strange bed to the other.

Look, I know I'm a hypocritical bastard. I fuck around, but the minute my roommate gets a suitor, I go all Jason Momoa on his ass. But I can't control it, can I? And if it makes things slightly better, I haven't porked anyone since Mark made that comment about JoJo. Between throwing him off, dealing with my latest disastrous fling, and jerking off to memories of Jolie's naked body, sex with strangers is the last thing on my mind.

Thing is, I can't really relationship-block Mark right now. What the fuck would I say to him? "Hey, listen, man, there's nothing going on between Jolie and me, but I still don't want her to date you?" Even *I* know it's a solid ten on the Douche-O-Meter. It would be much easier to just say, 'Look, bro, I'm tapping that. Why don't you go ahead and move along to someone less awesome and, I don't know, less *Jolie*?'

"Jolie! I've been asking you to ask her about me for weeks. Forget it." Mark waves me off, grabbing a beer bottle from the fridge. There's a keg right. Freaking. Here. But I guess he's too rich for Solo cups. "I'll just ask her out. I see her around campus every Monday at three."

Over my dead body.

"Get some chill, dude. I got a lot on my plate this month. I'll ask her as soon as I get home." I clutch his shoulder and offer him the most casual smile in my arsenal. Inside, there's a green angry monster wreaking havoc in my body. If Mark takes Jolie on a date, it wouldn't be the first time she went out with someone else. JoJo had two serious boyfriends in high school and dated a string of douches ever since we started college. But they all seemed so temporary. Her mind was always elsewhere. School. Family. Even the Pilates classes that gave her that bangin' body. But this is all going to change at the end of May when we graduate. I know my best friend. Know her well.

She'll want to settle down.
Find a nice teaching job.
Get married. Have babies. Mark's babies. No way is she having Mark's babies. That fucker doesn't drink keg beer and knows how to tie a tie without looking in the mirror. He's not the type to run in the mud and rain for her. To climb on trees with her. To sit on the sidelines at school and talk shit about people in codes only she and he know.
I'm that person. I'm *her* person.
"I'll deal with it tonight," I say again, thinking, *you can say that again.*
"Yeah, okay, man," Mark mumbles, pupils dilating, and that's when I realize that I'm squeezing his shoulder hard. He shakes me off, taking a step back and bumping into two girls who are yelling the latest gossip into each other's ears over the sound of "Fetish" by Selena Gomez. They both shoot him a pissed look that softens when they notice me. "I'll text you tomorrow." Mark moves his thumbs in the air, like I don't know how texting looks like.
"Sure." I shrug, raising my cup and backing toward the landing. "See you Monday at practice."
You know shit is going downhill when you find yourself listening to a pop princess and there's no blowie to stop you from leaving. I turn around and a girl from computer science slams into my body purposely. She does the whole 90's-rom-com charade, where she laughs nervously and pretends to be embarrassed —*sweetheart, I've seen this show a thousand times*—and introduces herself. I can take her home. Hell, I can even take her upstairs. A month ago, I would have. But tonight, all I can think about is that Jolie is hella bummed about what I told her about Brandon, and I'm bummed about that goddamn tool, Mark.
"I'm Stephanie," she yells into my ear.
"And I'm not interested," I yell back, in the exact same tone.
The mask of her syrupy smile falls to the floor, almost with a thud, and her eyes narrow before she sulks and leaves. I dig out my phone and send Jolie a string of semi-coherent text messages. Then I come up with a plan to eliminate Mark Tensely from the picture.
By the time I drive back home, stone-cold sober, making a stop at a gas station to get some milk, my plan is bulletproof. Here is the end game:
Jolie is not dating anyone.
Jolie stays with me.

Chapter Three

Jolie

"WE NEED TO TALK."

Reluctantly, I crack one eye open, while still rolled between my white cotton sheets, the TV playing the same channel I fell asleep to the night before. After Chelsea left, I watched *When Harry Met Sally*. Then I opened a bottle of wine, downed three glasses, and waited for the alcohol to run through my bloodstream before I willed myself to answer my male BFF's texts.

Me: Do you think Brandon cheated on me because I'm a prude?

Me: Maybe it's because I went to see my family every other weekend when he wanted to hang out. Although, screw him, right? So I like spending time with my grandmama and parents. Ain't no shame in that.

Me: And yes to you bringing milk. I will need something to help the hangover tomorrow morning.

Me: And no to you and me sleeping together. I already told you, Sage. I care too much about you to lose you for a fling. Even if the feeling is obviously not mutual…

MY BED DIPS under the weight of my quarterback guy friend and I bury my face into my pillow, inhaling the vanilla, lilac, and lavender of my body creams and shampoo. His warm hand sneaks under the covers, cupping one of my feet and tugging me away from the pillow and toward him. With my ankle on his lap, he massages my foot. And I should really get a gold medal, or maybe a simple acknowledgement, for not spreading my legs for him right here and now and giving him exactly what he has been begging for.

Because. Sage. Poirier. Is. A. God.

That's why he's a manwhore in the first place. There is no denying his masculine appeal, raw beauty, dirty mouth, and cocky confidence.

"What do we need to talk about?" I murmur into my arm, which I've thrown over my face to block the sun seeping through the thin curtains of my window. He elevates my foot and kisses just below my kneecap. Shivers run down my spine, racing down to my tummy and making it roll with delicious anticipation.

"I need a fake girlfriend," he announces, his voice grave.

"Then go get one. Literally, you can step out of the building and every single woman with a pulse and no ring on her ring finger would gladly fill out an application," I say, hyper-aware to my morning breath. He plucks my arm from my face and throws it on the bed, leaning into me so we are nose-to-nose.

Great. Just great. Now he can smell my dead hyena breath.

"I'm serious," comes his dark whisper, and he no longer sounds like my Sage. I mean, Sage. Just Sage. He is not mine. I know that. Duh.

"So am I. Why do you need a fake girlfriend?" I speak into my cupped hand, my eyebrows crinkling.

"Want the truth?"

"No, please lie to me. But make it a spectacular lie. Something with unicorns." I widen my blurry eyes, and he chuckles, grabbing one of the pillows I kicked in my sleep and throwing it in my face.

"Rascal," he says.

"Wifebeater," I groan. He stands still, stares at me. *What?* It was a figure of speech. I didn't mean it like I was literally his wife.

"I can't tell you why, but I can tell you that you're the only girl for the job. I have a Christmas fundraising thing happening in New York next month and I need someone on my arm. You're the only girl, other than my mama, I'd like to take with me. The only one I trust not to let me down. And my mama can't get time off work, so that leaves me with you. Say yes."

I swallow, not really sure how this is different from all the other times I accompanied Sage to his football events. There's something desperate and utterly determined in the way he looks at me. Like there are so many words on the tip of his tongue that he's biting down, afraid to use.

"I don't need to be your fake girlfriend for that."

"You do. It's important. Everyone at school needs to know that we're a thing."

"But why?"

"I'd tell you, but then I'd have to kill you. Now, I'm pretty sure I'd be a top in jail, not a bottom, but still—not really into dudes. So, yes?"

Ugh with this man. "Ugh with you. What do *I* get out of this?"

Before you throw rotten tomatoes at me (understandable), accompanied by a collective 'boo' (reasonable)—let me explain why I ask: there's definitely something Sage is gaining from this, no doubt at all, and I'm trying to figure out whether it's a bet, or if he's gotten himself into some kind of woman trouble—a stage five clinger or something. Sage scans me through his signature droopy, ink blue eyes, and I swear my ovaries are singing a cappella at the sight of his jaw of steel. He should come with a book-long warning label. I'm half-tempted to Google a question about getting pregnant just by looking at him. Sage grabs the tip of my blanket, unplasters it from my body, and yanks me by the pajamas to straddle him. It happens so fast the oxygen leaves my lungs in a short *whoosh.* I'm panting now, on top of him, and his hands are on my ass, and I'm not stopping him. Why am I not stopping him? I know I should. He will break my heart and I'll have no one to blame but myself. I've seen it happen countless times before. By the time we finished high school, eighty percent of the girls broke out in hives just from hearing his name.

"You'll still get free rent, but for as long as you're my fake girlfriend, I'll also pay the bills. You'll get free access to my truck—anytime you want. Last but not least: you'll get *me.* All of me. No other women. No distractions. No games. Just you and me, JoJo. Because it's always been the two of us, and it's time we act this way, even if only for a little while."

He smells of wood and mint and a real Christmas tree. Like a sweet memory I want to cling onto. My limbs are lax and I know I'm making a huge mistake, but I'm done resisting. Believe me, I've tried. It brought me nowhere but to square one, salivating over my best friend.

I nod slowly. "Okay. What's the deadline?"

"End of May," he shoots, letting out a long sigh and placing his forehead to mine. It's intimate. So much more intimate than anything I'd ever done with the Brandons of the world, and I never stopped and debated whether I should date *them.* May is graduation month. Sage is offering me a free ride till the end of school. And let's not kid ourselves—I could use my waiting money for other things. Paying my student loan debt, saving up for life after college. That kind of stuff.

We sit like this for a long minute before he cups my ass again and squeezes. It's so playful and friendly, I don't bark at him to stop.

"Welcome to couplehood, bae. We've got this."

Chapter Four

Sage

"Hey, man, bad news."

For you, not for me, I'm refrain from adding. Actually, fucking fantastic news for me. I still can't believe she said yes. Then again, I'm not entirely sure she knew what this would entail. When I told JoJo I wanted to be her fake boyfriend, I meant it. We'll be doing things couples do. In bed, and the kitchen, and the bathroom, and even the fucking stairway, if we can't help ourselves. There is nothing fake about what I'm going to give her. Especially the orgasms part.

"What's up?" Mark lifts his head, a towel wrapped around his waist. He slams his blue locker shut and uses a second towel to rub his black hair dry. Even though he's on my team, he's been riding the bench for the last year-and-a-half. I can't help but internally curse him. Who the hell does he think he is, checking out my JoJo? *Whoa.* My JoJo? She's not mine. Only that's not entirely true. She feels a lot like something no one else can ever have, so who the hell says she's not mine?

Though, really, at this point it's just semantics. JoJo will be mine. End of story.

"So, Jolie and I are kind of together." I prop my shoulder against my own locker, looking down at him. God bless my late father. He gave me the height to tower over most motherfuckers who aren't signed with NBA teams.

Mark's eyes widen in disbelief before he schools his features and clears his throat like the good, rich boy that he is. "Oh, yeah?"

"Yep." I pop the P out with a grin.

"Let me get this straight. You slept with her this weekend, *after* I asked you for the one-hundredth time to sniff around for me?"

"Look," I say cuttingly, evading the question, "I've known this girl since we were ten." Since she promised me I'd always be a huge chunk of her world and I blossomed in her friendship, set roots in our companionship, and grew up to be someone strong. "This shit is not going away, so I suggest *you* move on."

"You're kind of a prick, you know that, Poirier?"

Oh, I know. Grew up with one. Became one. Vicious cycle, etc.

I clutch my navy football jersey and gasp loudly and comically, flattening my back against the row of lockers. "Now I'm butthurt. Which means that the only way I'll get over this is if you kiss my ass."

"Well," Mark says, his face red now, "That's not going to happen."

"In that case, you better stay the fuck away from my girlfriend *and* me, yeah?"

He doesn't answer.

Just walks away.

I watch his back, and for the first time in my life, the taste of victory bursts on my tongue outside the football field. I savor it, my throat bobbing with a swallow. I know I was being an irrational prick to Mark. I know that. But I couldn't *stop* it.

This whole thing made me crazy, and as much as it put me low on the moral scale—because let's admit it, I had zero reason to feel bitter about any of this—my temper won. It won, and I lost.

I lost my cool.

I lost my patience.

Then I lost my control.

But I gained one thing, and it was the thing that mattered—Jolie.

Jolie

So. It's official. I'm having the worst day of my life. It starts with Chelsea accidentally spilling her hot coffee on my white blouse—I don't have time to go back home and change between classes, so the stained shirt remains. It continues with my favorite professor gathering us in class and announcing her sudden departure due to a tragedy in the family, then sometime before noon, Mark Tensely, a guy I've been crushing on for six months now (silently, of course. I'm so shy I almost combusted when he came in the other day to return some of Sage's gear) came to ask Chelsea on a date, all while ignoring my existence.

By the time I get back home after a stop at the library, it's dark and Sage is waiting for me in the living room with two slices of pizza, a Caesar salad, and beers. I'm so relieved to see the food—and him—I nearly whimper at the beauty of having both of them.

This is what heaven looks like, right?

"Sit. I'll put some *X Factor* on." He pats the tangerine sofa he's slouched on. Clad only in gray running shorts, he is naked from the waist up, which is not surprising—Sage has a strict no-shirt policy around the house. I make my way over and plop down next to him with a content sigh. He hits *Play* just as I take the first bite of my pizza.

"Nice blouse." His eyes are already dead on the screen.

"Thank..." I start, but then remember it has a coffee stain the size of Mississippi and frown. "I should probably take a shower and change before dinner." I've never felt too self-conscious in front of him before, but I do now. Maybe it's because he's never acted this way to me. Quiet and attentive and...frankly, odd.

"Bullshit. I'm your boyfriend. You don't have to doll-up for me. I like the real you. The girl who snores when she is tired and smells of garlic every Sunday after her grandmama's special casserole."

"You're my fake boyfriend," I correct, trying to set some boundaries.

"Irrelevant. Everything that came out of my mouth was real."

I pat his thigh in the most platonic way possible and dig into my pizza and salad, internally admitting that my best friend will one day make a kick-ass real boyfriend, just probably not to me. Simon Cowell is slaying people in the auditions segment. Two girls cry and one guy threatens to sue him. Then the commercials come on and we both stretch out on the couch.

"Do your Simon Cowell impression for me." Sage elbows my ribs, showing off his dimples.

"Maybe later. I'm exhausted." I rub my eyes. Inhaling the pizza, salad, and beer like food is a foreign concept that's left me in a carbma (carb coma). Sage stares me down, his face intense yet unreadable.

"You know what'll happen if you refuse, right?"

I do. And I want it to happen. Shamefully, our tickle sessions are the most erotic thing in my life right now. I haven't had sex in months, and I swear there'd be cobwebs all over my vajayjay had I not purchased enough sex toys to open a store.

"I do not negotiate with terrorists," I say adamantly.

"So happy to hear, because I think I'm about done talking, anyway."

His eyes hone in on mine and his ripped body tenses before he pounces on me, tackling me to the carpeted floor. I fall with a bang, but his huge palm is covering the back of my head as it always does. He's on top of me. With me writhing beneath him. I'm pretending to fight him, throwing balled fists into his chest, waiting for the tickles to arrive, when...

"*Stop*," he breathes, and I notice that he is not moving. His pelvic bones are rubbing against mine, his erection is digging into my groin, and it is thick, and long, and tilted to the right. My mouth waters and my eyes gloss over. Jesus H, since when did my best friend become such a *man*?

"What?" I croak.

He leans forward, his mouth only inches from mine. His body heavy, his hard-on tantalizing, his scent breathtaking, he mouths into my lips, "Game change: if you want me to stop whatever it is I'm going to do as your fake boyfriend, say the name Simon Cowell."

I groan. He's giving me safe words now. I don't have to ink them onto my brain, because doubt I'll never use them. His hips start to move, and he is sliding up and down, grinding himself against my groin. I'm on fire, seeing stars, salivating at the intense friction. Every nerve in my body is buzzing with an impending orgasm, because it's been so long, *too* long, and I open my thighs for him, my denim digging into my clit.

"Say Simon Cowell, or I'll continue." His voice is heavy and rough and raw. He is the kid I fell in love with at the age of ten, and the man I would give the world to at the age of twenty. I don't even care that he is probably using me. Using me as a fake girlfriend. Using me as a sexual outlet on this carpet.

I say nothing, because I'd die if he stops. Maybe not literally, but I'm pretty sure I'll be the proud owner of the very first case of female blue balls.

He increases his speed, dry-humping me, one forearm propped near my ear and his other hand sliding to my neck. I want him to kiss me. I don't want him to kiss me. I want us to break all the rules that helped us survive our turbulent childhood, that helped us defy *When Harry Met Sally*. The rules that prove the world the men and women *can* be friends. I want to obliterate our friendship on this carpet. I want to show him that my stupid, reckless, defiant heart only beats for him.

"Fuck, you're beautiful," he growls, squeezing my neck softly. His throbbing cock is pushing between my thighs, digging deeper into my slit, even through the denim, and I know it must be painful for him. He is half-penetrating me, and my eyes roll back despite my best intentions, the darkness behind them littered with fireworks. *It's always been us...*

"Say it now, JoJo. Simon Cowell. Make me stop, or..." He leaves the sentence hanging in the air. *Or he'll take more.* But maybe I want more. He said this was going to feel real. Monogamous, even. And now that Mark Tensely is no longer an option, I might as well take him up on that offer.

If Sage thinks our friendship can survive it—or worse, that our friendship isn't worth keeping our hands to ourselves—who am I to disagree?

"Too scared to cross the line?" I hiss, my eyes widening at my own words. I've never taunted Sage about sex. About everything else? Sure. But not this. "I'm not sure what you're using me for, Sage, but if you're using me, I fully intend to use *you*."

The words barely leave my mouth before his mouth crashes down on mine, devouring me like a starved wolf. Like that boy who cried to the moon, and the moon finally answered back. It strikes me like lightning. Sage is *hungry*. And I'm his meal. His pouty lips drag against mine, seeking an opening. He captures my lower lip with his teeth and tug, tug, *tugs* until I have no choice but to part my lips and give him better access. His tongue is invading, ruling, and assaulting my own. It chases mine frantically, licks the walls of my mouth, moves across my teeth, memorizing every single spot in my mouth. My eyes roll in pleasure again when he takes my tongue between his lips and sucks on it hard, shoving his hand into my jeans. I'm not sure at what point he pulled down my zipper, but now he is rubbing my swollen, sensitive clit through my panties while he's devouring my mouth, our tongues dancing seductively with one another. My whole body shakes uncontrollably.

"Please. Oh my God. Sage."

It's too much. The unexpected, sudden gratification. Don't get me wrong—I make it a point to get myself off three times a week to keep myself sane, but I can't remember the last time my body danced on its own accord with passion and delirious need. It occurs to me that I'm about to come before he's even pulled off his running shorts, so I try to make him slow down by saying our very ridiculous safe word.

"Simo..."

His lips leave mine and he covers my mouth with his palm to keep me silent while he rises to his knees, pulling his shorts down with his free hand.

He shakes his head on a smirk. "If you want me to stop, just say no, JoJo. But from this point forward, you're not screaming anyone's name but mine. Do you want me to stop?" He takes his hand away and I grab him by the wrist and graze his knuckle with my teeth before slipping the tip of his finger between my lips and giving it a little suck.

Hell no I don't want him to stop.

His thick cock springs out of his shorts, and he presses the long, hot, velvety shaft against my bare stomach. My blouse rode up sometime during this spontaneous make-out session, and now Sage is tugging it further up to accommodate his cock, resting it on the little pink bow at the center of my bra, before reaching under me to snatch my bra, tearing it apart.

"Gonna tit-fuck you now. Been wanting to do that since your thirteenth birthday. Remember the day? Checkered baby blue dress, ham on rye in the meadow, I finally noticed the first sign of tits..." He drags his tongue across my chin, closing in on my mouth with a sloppy kiss. A kiss with too much tongue. Too much saliva. Too much *everything,* yet somehow, still not enough. My response is squeezing my breasts together around his thick cock. The pad of his thumb is rubbing my clit again, and my quivering thighs begin to jerk uncontrollably. He pinches my clit. I moan so loudly my ears ring. *Pinch, pinch, pinch.* After a dozen small pinches, I feel a tug on the invisible string of pleasure that connects us. I explode when he finally pinches harder, sending me over the edge. I writhe under my best friend, shouting his name with the kind of wild abandon I hadn't felt since the day I ran toward him in the pouring hot rain.

I barely have time to come down from my orgasm before he starts fucking my tits, the tip of his cock poking my chin every time he grinds himself on my torso. He scoots up, sitting on my stomach with his knees on either side of me. His muscular thighs harden, holding most of his weight as he goes at it like a professional porn star.

"Look at me," he growls like a wounded animal, his tone far from its usual playfulness. I raise my head. My hazels meet his blues. He smirks the most patronizing, jerk-fueled smile I've ever seen, cupping my cheeks with one hand.

"I want to come in your mouth."

I nod silently. I've never given anyone oral sex. Not that I have anything against it, but I guess I never felt super comfortable enough with any of my past boyfriends. But Sage is not just a guy I went on a few dates with. He is the boy who kicked other boys' asses when they disrespected me at school—despite my telling him that I could take care of myself—and tried (and failed) to bake me shortbread cookies every Christmas because he knew they were my favorite.

He is good enough to never mention it if I suck (no pun intended), and man enough to never say a word about it to anyone we know.

"Oh, fuck, so close. Jolie, my beautiful, gorgeous Jolie..."

He scoots up, slides his cock from between my tits, and shoves it into my mouth, cupping my head from behind and making me deep throat him. And I do. I fight my gag reflex and wrap my lips around his cock as he pumps the base, warm, thick liquid sliding down my throat in spurts. My hands are on his rear, and I'm squeezing hard, as if I'm the one who is milking him, and it feels dirty and wrong and so, magnificently right.

When he collapses next to me, his salty taste on my lips and tongue, I close my eyes and breathe, trying to rearrange the jumbled mess that is my mind. My bra is torn, my pussy throbs and burns from the friction of the denim and the pinching, and I feel like a train wreck with smeared lipstick.

A big paw reaches across my stomach, rolls me over to my side, and embraces me into a hug. Sage kisses my temple—like a loving friend, not like a quick lay—and whispers something I cannot decipher.

"What did you say?" I murmur, allowing my head to rest on his iron pecs.

He doesn't answer, and I don't probe, falling asleep in the arms of the boy I pieced back together myself with a hug.

Chapter Five

Sage

THE NEXT DAY, I TACKLE MARK TO THE GROUND IN PRACTICE. MY official reason? He's a fucker. My *real* reason? Jolie is standing across the football field with Chelsea and a few of her other girlfriends, hugging her MacBook to her chest and laughing at something one of them said. That, in itself is not a problem. But the fact that Mark just ogled her for two straight minutes? Totally is.

"What part of 'she's mine' did you not get?" I snarl in his face, nailing him to the ground. Well, this escalated quickly. Can't help it, though. The more the idea of Jolie and Mark dating assaults my mind, the more I want to punch him into unconsciousness. Luckily, Jolie and I have this kind of relationship where we don't even have to fully explain ourselves to each other, and she'd agreed to "date" me.

Just like I'd agreed to take care of her friend's pet ferret for a month junior year because her grandmama was allergic and she couldn't do it herself. We're there for each other in big ways and little ones. Always.

"I'm not looking at Jolie, dickwad! I'm looking at Chelsea. I asked her out yesterday." Mark pushes me off of him, and I roll on the hot, damp grass, laughing to the bright blue sky. It unburdens me from weight I didn't know I had on my heart. Ever since I graduated from high school, I've always had it easy—easy with girls, easy with grades, and easy with football. The rest I didn't really care about, frankly. And maybe that's why I've never had something I was in danger of losing. I do now, and hell if it's not a bitch to keep it from slipping between my fingers.

"Chelsea, huh? You move fast," I note, standing to my feet and wobbling between Michael and Elliott, who are stretching on the ground.

"Said the guy who dicked the girl I wanted to date just so I couldn't have her." Mark picks his gear up from the grass and stomps toward the dressing room behind me. He catches up to me, and I rein in the urge to steal a glance at my fake girlfriend, who really doesn't feel all that fake at all.

"Don't talk about her like that." My jaw ticks.

"Why? You talk about girls like that all the time." He snorts.

Because she's not a fucking girl; she's my best friend, I'm tempted to yell, but I'm not five, nor a pussy, so I bite my lip and change the subject.

"You inviting Chelsea to that charity thing in New York?" I jerk my chin in the girls' direction. One of my sponsors is flying me out with a plus one. I can't wait to see Jolie in a red dress—that's the dress code for the female attendees—and watching everyone's faces when this Southern belle is on my arm alone could make me shoot my load all over my tux.

"Why? Are you asking Jolie?"

"Of course, I fucking am. She's my girl. So?" I don't know why I'm pushing this. Maybe because I really want to hear that he's over JoJo.

"Fuck knows, man. We haven't even gone on one date. What's it to you?" He frowns and stops by our lockers. I shrug. I know that Mark and Jolie aren't close or anything. I'd just like to keep it that way for the remainder of our last year of college. If she finds out I cockblocked her out of this potential relationship, she is going to jerk me off with a Brillo pad.

"Just curious."

"Hey, man, don't take this the wrong way, but it looks like something's eating you," Mark says carefully, peeling his shirt off and throwing it on a bench behind us. "Is everything okay?"

Everything is not okay. I made a horrible mistake with a girl, and even though it made me realize that there's another girl I deeply want and love, I hurt someone. A lot. Of course, I don't tell him shit. Just smile my broad, shit-eating grin. "Couldn't be more perfect."

"Good." He strokes his chin. "Good."

I take my clothes off and step into the shower, letting the scorching hot water punish me for what I did.

Remember the silver lining. Remember the end game.

Jolie

The day drags.

By the time I stumble through my front door, it's already ten at night.

Between my shift at the Happy Bunny—a diner off of Bordeaux Street—and a library session with Chelsea and Penny, I'm thoroughly spent. Too exhausted to even grab myself a bite. The minute I get into the apartment, I head straight to the shower, scrub off the day's dirt, slip into my pajamas (conveniently located on a hanger in the bathroom right next to my towel to avoid any more embarrassing hallway encounters with Sage) and slide under my blanket without even turning on the lamp next to my bed. I scoot to the edge of my bed and close my eyes.

Mmm, this is nice.

So relaxing.

I can just drift and clear my mind and not think about...

Okay, something is poking my ass.

Correction: an erection is poking my ass.

Double correction: a *bare* erection is. Poking. My. Ass. *Mothertrucker!*

"Sage!" I jolt, partly pissed, but—let's admit it—mostly turned on. It's like Sage has the manual to my body and knows how to work it better than I do. Which is weird. We still haven't spoken about the sudden escalation in our relationship, but since it's already happened—what's crossing another line, right?

"Shhh, baby girl." His strong, warm palm slides down to cup my ass. "Let daddy take care of you."

"Call yourself my daddy one more time and I'm fishing your eyeballs out with a spoon."

"Fuck, my girl has some pent-up aggression in her. So glad I'm here to loosen..." He glides the sleeve of my pajama dress across my shoulder and kisses it. "Her." He lets the gown slip over my head and down my body, leaving me completely naked, save for my cotton panties. "Up." His hand slinks between my thighs, cups my pussy, and squeezes. *Hard.*

"No need, as I'm perfectly loose," I murmur, teasing him back. He slides my panties down and I wiggle my ass into his erection so that his cock is halfway between my ass cheeks, putting pressure on my tight hole. He could dream. But then again, that's exactly what I want him to do. Crave me like a fantasy.

"Nah, you're not loose. Tight as your sweet little cunt, more like." His tongue skates down my spine, leaving shivers in its wake. He is moving south. Who gave him permission to move south? This is like *Game of Thrones*. Wars should be fought to win the south. You can't just knock on the door and expect me to open it up.

Wait, you totally can if you look like Sage Poirier.

"Too tired for sex, Mr. Fake Boyfriend. I'm not in the mood to move," I protest one last time, just to tell myself that I've tried if things go wrong. Just to show myself that I really did try, I flip the lamp on for emphasis, like I'm going to be reading, or watching TV, or not thinking about having sex with my best friend (lie).

"That's okay. I skipped my carbs today, Miss *Real* Girlfriend. I think I'll just feast on you."

Real girlfriend? Don't dwell on it. He'd say anything to get into your panties right now.

"Who said it's carbs and not protein?" I blab. I should shut up. Note to self: don't try to flirt with him when he is about to go down on you. You can't think straight.

"Even better. No such thing as too much protein in an athlete's diet. Better go down there. Maybe even come back for a second serving later tonight." He cups my face with one hand and twists my head around so he can kiss me. Our tongues find each other and do a happy dance together. My nipples tighten and pucker from the heat between my legs and the chilly breeze of the room and he twists one of them between his fingers. Then he lets go and slides under my blanket, where I can't see him.

Sage throws my legs open and settles between them. He doesn't say anything at first, and my self-consciousness kicks in. I know my pussy is perfectly normal. Waxed—every part tucked in like a virgin rose right before blooming—smooth to a fault and pink. Everything is where it should be. So why is he not saying anything? Maybe he is suffocating under the blanket. I should check how he is doing. This is one obituary I wouldn't want to make.

'Died between my legs from lack of oxygen on the same day I had a tuna melt for lunch...'

Oh, God. I forgot about the tuna melt.

"Sage?" I murmur, scooting upward. He pins me down by my hipbones in one, swift movement, throwing my legs even wider.

"Shut up," he says from under the blanket, this mammoth of a man shifting beneath the soft fabric. "JoJo? I think we need to break up our fake relationship."

My eyes flare and my cheeks flush red. "Why?"

"Because I just fell in love. I'm talking love at first sight. Your pussy is just so darn pretty, I wanna marry it. Can I marry your pussy? The rest of your body can stay single, I swear."

I laugh and playfully swat what I'm guessing is his head—or his shoulder, both are super hard and round.

"If you love her so much, you should give her some TLC. Show her how you really feel," I encourage, biting my lower lip on a smile.

"Can I kiss her? Or does she not kiss on a first date?"

"She definitely does. She's a little hussy."

I feel his tongue flattening against the base of my pussy, right next to my crack, and tremble at the sudden wet and warm sensation. *Oh, God.*

"Call her a hussy one more time, and I'm kicking you out of this ménage."

"You can't do that. I'm attached to her." This is getting ridiculous. But also so much fun. Sage uses his fingers to open me wide and plunges his tongue into me, penetrating me with his tongue all the way in, and I moan loudly and clutch his head under the blanket. "Holy hell!"

"Fuck, she's an even better kisser than you," Sage says. I swat his head again as he starts working me relentlessly under the cover. Thrusting his tongue into me, in and out, all while using his thumb to rub my clit in delicious circles that make me want to shed happy tears.

"Yes, that's it. Oh, Sage. Oh, Sage. Oh..."

I'm getting close, and he knows it, because he pins my thighs to the bed, not letting me deny him access to my most sensitive part. Since his hands are now busy, he uses the tip of his straight nose to rub my clit in circles as he continues to fuck me with his tongue.

"Take back what you said." His voice is dark and serious, so far away from the best friend I know and love. And yet, this voice is no longer strange to me. This is how my lover sounds. The man I want to sleep with, and do very unfriendly, yet nice things to.

"A...about what?" I stutter on my own carnal desire.

"About your pussy being a hussy. She's not a fucking hussy. She opens up and sings, but just for me. She's a slut, but just for me. She's a fucking horny maniac—for. No. One. But. Me. Yeah?"

Jesus H, his dirty talk game is strong. I nod to myself, swallowing, feeling the hot wave of a climax washing over me, starting from the crown of my head and moving down like a wave to the rest of my body. I'm quivering, shaking like a leaf.

After I come, he glides up in one smooth movement, reappearing from under the blanket. His face is flushed pink, and his lips are glistening with my arousal. Aaaand...he looks like that boy I fell in love with again. So vulnerable and broken and unbelievably youthful. It messes with my head, and I wonder if he feels the same. Like he is treading on a tightrope between familiarity and grown-up games. Like our hearts are connected in an invisible thread, and every time one of us tugs, the other one feels.

"Tell me she is mine," he whispers. I blink. It takes me a second to realize that he is talking about my pussy. *Again.* I grin.

"Is Sage Junior mine?" I reach beneath us to cup his hard-on. He is butt naked under the covers, and I want to see and taste everything.

"He is yours. I am yours. We're both yours. If..." Pause. Beat of silence. Visible swallow. "If you'll have us."

He sounds serious. So, so serious. But I know him well enough to recognize that Sage is a total people-pleaser and cocky to a fault. I have to remind myself that he'll say whatever it is I want to hear and breeze through it without thinking about the consequences to get what he wants. Truth be told, he's never had a serious girlfriend and never brought the same girl to our apartment twice. I remind myself, therefore, that this is a game. A game that will end come May, and with it, our whole relationship will never be the same again. Sage will get drafted somewhere exotic and will become filthy rich, and I'll continue my small-town life here in Louisiana. The probability of it all slams into my chest all at once, like a cold bucket of ice.

This is all temporary.

The reality is, he wants a fake girlfriend until May, because after May, he'll be gone to Boston or California, making a career. He just wants some kind of girlfriend experience before he goes so he doesn't feel like he's missing out.

He will use me.

And will *dump* me.

He. Will. Forget. About. Me.

And every time I witness him visiting his mama across the road, on Christmas or Thanksgiving, I'll remember being a notch on his miles-long belt.

I swallow, the back of my eyeballs stinging with unshed tears.

"Simon Cowell," I croak, my voice barely audible. His eyebrows drop into a shocked frown, his lips parting in disbelief.

"JoJo?"

"*Simon Cowell*," I repeat, raising my shaky voice an octave. "Please get off," I add.

He rolls off of me, propping his head on his forearm and watching me. My heart stutters as I scurry to the edge of the bed, throw my nightgown on, suddenly forgetting about being tired and hungry and *happy*, and pad my way to the kitchen.

Don't look back, don't look back, don't look back.

In the kitchen, I open the freezer and take out the Cherry Garcia Ben and Jerry's. This is Sage we're talking about, not Brandon. He is totally worth the calories. I prop my lower body against the counter, shoving spoonfuls of ice cream down my throat, not even bothering to taste it. My back is to the hallway so I don't see him. But I *feel* him. His big steps. His commanding body. The heat rolling off his muscular frame.

"What the fuck was that all about, JoJo?" he asks behind me. He doesn't sound pissed off at all. Just sad and...disappointed. God, the idea of disappointing him after everything we've been through is nothing short of agonizing. We promised each other so much, and kept good on those promises. I don't want this to change. I don't want *us* to change.

"I can't be your fake girlfriend anymore."

"But..."

I turn around and meet his gaze, my vision slicing right through all the pain that's swimming in his blues. I don't want to see it. Facing it will undo every logical decision I need to make right now. He is wearing a tight pair of black boxers, an Adonis with a sculpted face, asking for his mortal friend to play a game only the gods can win.

"Simon Cowell," I say one last time. "Let go, Sage."

He shakes his head, turns around, and walks away, doing exactly as I tell him to.

Chapter Six

Sage

THE NEXT DAY, I DO THE UNTHINKABLE—THE UN-FUCKING-DOABLE, AND push a teammate to the ground because he stretched too close to me. Yep, I shit you not. Quarterbacks usually try to protect their hands and arms, not shove them into other footballers' personal space to start a fight.

"What the fuck is your problem?!" Michael asks, throwing his helmet to the grass and shoving my chest. I'm just looking for an excuse to rearrange some random dipshit's face, so this is all the invitation I need to get in his personal space and growl, "You've been asking for this, motherfucker!"

I'm about to throw a punch—knowing that it's going to put me in a very bad spot, knowing that scouters are roaming the training area, knowing that I could be flushing my whole future down the toilet—when I feel a big hand yanking me away from Michael. Tom and Dre are pushing Michael in the other direction while Mark is hugging my midsection and dragging me to the other end of the field. Lines of mud are forming beneath my feet. I've always been an aggressive player. Comes with the territory of being a huge-ass kid with a shit ton of issues. I was actually supposed to be an O-Liner. But it so happened that my first coach said I was too intelligent not to be a quarterback and forced me into the position. Today, I'm feeling especially confrontational. The kind of asshole that needs to be thrown inside the octagon or ring with Conor McGregor and Floyd Mayweather and can still come out of there unscathed.

"Are you trying to shit all over your future?" Mark bares his teeth, slamming me against the wall of the sports auditorium. I shrug, taking off my helmet and running my paw through my long-ish hair. I normally ask Jolie to cut it for me, but I've been too busy trying to get in her pants lately to ask her to take care of that shit.

"It's fine. He won't say a word to Coach Drescher." I wave Mark off. He puts his hands on his waist and paces in front of me like an exasperated parent. Behind him, my teammates are arguing and yelling and *I did this shit*. The realization leaves a bitter taste in my mouth.

"Doesn't matter, bro. You're still acting like King Douche of Cuntland, and you need to cut that shit before you get blacklisted. You can't afford to do that. Not when you're so close to getting drafted."

I know he's right. I also know that I've been acting like a dick all day, and that's unlike me. I need to get my head back in the game, but it's hard when I know that JoJo's a few feet away, going about her day after smashing my fucking heart on the kitchen floor yesterday.

"So, I shouldn't be a massive dick to everyone even though I have a massive dick. Gotcha." I nod, trying to lighten up the mood. Mark lifts his head and pins me with a serious look.

"What's gotten into you? Something's wrong?"

Like I'd ever tell him.

"Nothing's wrong. Everything's so dandy and fucking right I want to break into a dance." The sarcasm drips from my mouth like drool. But the truth is, I know I'm in deep trouble. With JoJo. With the mistake I've made. With everything.

"Yeah? So this has nothing to do with you and Jolie?" He lifts one lonely brow.

Her mere name on his lips makes me want to punch the wall behind me, then run a fucking marathon to spend all the pent-up aggression coursing through my body.

"Everything's great between JoJo and me. Don't say her name again, please."

Mark stares at me, dumbfounded. A smile spreads across his lips. We're not super tight, Mark and I, but I know that he is good people. I also know that he was born and raised in a nice Southern family where people hug a lot and talk about feelings and shit. That makes me uncomfortable around him sometimes. Like he can see through me. See the parts I'm only really comfortable sharing with JoJo.

"You're in love with her," he says, chuckling. "Holy shit, man. You are in love with your roommate. That's hilarious. Does she know?"

Does JoJo know? Maybe the better question is—do *I* know? Sure, yeah, I like her, but what, exactly, does it mean? Fuck, I can't even seem to read myself anymore. Why else would I act the way I do? Like the Duke of Dickwads. But admitting to myself that I'm in love—*not just love, but in love*—with my best friend is somehow like admitting defeat. Because other than a couple times recently, JoJo has never flirted with me in her entire life, and I'm pretty sure if I ever told her how I feel, she'd laugh in my face and tell me it's a phase.

It's not a phase.

It's here to stay.

I'm in love with my best friend.

With the girl who ran in the rain for me.

With the girl who did my homework all the way through elementary and high school so I could concentrate on my football, and gave me pointers and summaries when we walked to school together every day.

With the girl who believed in me before even *I* believed in myself.

And showed up at my games every weekend, her textbooks on her lap, doing homework in between cheering for me.

I'm in love with my roommate.

With the girl who cuts my hair and knows my favorite color is black and my favorite food is Cajun fried catfish.

With the proud owner of the sweetest pussy in Louisiana.

I'm in love with Jolie Louis.

And I'm going to conquer her. Consequences be damned.

Jolie

"I just had the best date of *life* yesterday. Not an exaggeration. A fact," Chelsea swoons, throwing her arms across the library desk and burying her head between them. She blows a lock of raven hair from her face. Her cheeks are pink, her eyes are bloodshot, and her huge smile is telling me that she is crushing hard, all while riding the mother of all natural highs. I sit across from her, smiling as I rearrange my sensible blouse. I've always pegged myself as a maternal chick. It's not the most feminist thing in the world to admit, but I already know my most rewarding role in life will be being a mom. But Chelsea? She's something else. She aspires to become a nanny after we graduate. Save up for a few years before becoming a mother herself. She's got a wedding and (at least) four kids on her (utterly crazy) brain twenty-four-freaking-seven.

"Where did Mark take you?" I probe, pretending to be typing on my MacBook. Really, I'm just stalling and trying to look like everything is okay. Like I'm not a mess of epic proportions. Sage and I haven't spoken a word to each other today. No texting. No stumbling together, laughing in the hallway. Even the drive to campus was silent. He tapped the wheel, I texted my mama, and liked every single thing my friends posted on Facebook. It was awkward to say the least.

"We had a picnic under the stars. Then we went to my place. Nikki is gone for the week, so we had the place to ourselves. We watched *Suicide Squad*. Then we..." She blushes, looking away. "Then we did other stuff. And, so, yeah, he's a great guy."

"I'm so happy for you." And I am. A friendship ain't worth the time you spend together unless you can wholeheartedly feel the joy and love your peer experiences when something amazing happens to them.

"Thank you, sweets. So, what about you? Still mad about that jackass, Brandon? You should really put yourself out there more, lady. Guys will be lining up as soon as you give them the signal you're interested." She wiggles her brows and closes her thick textbook. I offer her a weak smile, looking around us to make sure the library is deserted. It is. I haven't told her about the whole fake relationship with Sage yet. I kind of figured it would run its course before we even had the chance to explore it, as with many of Sage's crazy ideas. I was even partly right. True, I did most of the ruining of said fake relationship, but it doesn't matter. Not really. I don't, however, want to keep anything from Chelsea.

"I kind of hooked up with Sage this past week. Nothing too serious. We just messed around." I drum my collarbone with my fingers.

"I know," she says, straight-faced. I raise an eyebrow.

"What?"

"Dude, I know, Penny knows, every single person on campus knows," she reports nonchalantly, downing the rest of her latte and throwing the cup into the trash at the side of our desk, shrugging. "Mark and I talked about it. Sage told him. Apparently, he told the whole football team that if they as much as breathe in your direction, he'd cut their noses off. Kind of possessive, if you ask me. Never thought he was the caveman type."

I'm staring at Chelsea with my mouth agape, realizing that it's not a good look, and yet too shocked to respond coherently.

I look around me. There is only one more desk occupied in the whole library other than Chelsea's and mine. It's a bunch of sorority girls sitting across the room with their feathery pink pens and white, lush cardigans and blonde, high ponytails. They're staring at me, and I know why. If eyes could stab, I'd be bleeding to death on the floor. To them, Sage is not a real person, with a story, a personal tragedy, and complex personality traits. He's a legend. A status symbol. Like a Ferrari or a Versace item. Fierce protectiveness grips my throat. I don't know how I'd be able to live if I ever found out that he got married to this type of girl. The ones who see him for so much less than who he is.

"Earth to Jolie." Chelsea waves her little hands in front of me, smiling. I snap out of my stupor, shaking my head lightly.

"Sorry, you were saying?" I close my MacBook and grab my shoulder bag from under my chair. I admit defeat. There's just no way I'll be able to concentrate on anything other than him today.

"So things must be serious between you and Sage, if he is claiming you as his in front of the entire world." We both stand up, gather our belongings, and make our way to the door. I'm about to answer Chelsea, when...

"Slut," one of the sorority girls coughs into her curled fist, just as I pass her by.

"Social climber," the other one hisses viciously. I keep walking, ignoring them, but just as I'm about to round the corner into the hallway, I notice that Chelsea is no longer by my side. I turn my head around and see her standing in front of their desk. My eyes nearly bug out of their sockets, cartoon-style. *Oh, no.* Chelsea has some serious mama-bear-on-steroids-when-aunt-flow-is-in-town bones in her. She takes care of her own and never passes down a chance to stand up for a friend. But this bitch doesn't deserve her attention. Not one bit.

"Hey, girls." Chelsea juts one hip out, her hand on her hip and her smile Type 2 diabetes sweet as she snaps a picture of them with her phone. "Just wanted to stop by and let you know that by talking shit about the captain of the football team's girlfriend, you pretty much killed every opportunity you've ever had to date a jock in this place. Just putting it out there. So, good luck and so forth." My friend shrugs, strutting her way back to me.

"You didn't have to do that," I blurt, but still squeeze her into an embrace, my arm wrapped around her shoulder. We walk out to the orange and pink fall, toward the students' parking lot.

"I know I didn't, but I wanted to. So, are you and Sage a thing, or what?" She stops by her sensible blue Buick and fishes out the keys from her back pocket.

"Um, no. I kind of got freaked out yesterday at the possibility of him leaving the state in May and basically told him I'm calling things off. It all started with him telling me that he wanted me to be his fake girlfriend until graduation. Something about a Christmas event in New York, or something, so I think his telling people that we're an item is more because of his mysterious plan and less about a love declaration," I sullenly admit. Chelsea whips her head and gives me her best are-you-a-complete-idiot expression. It's a cross between puzzled and annoyed.

"You seriously think he's playing a game? You don't know that he likes you?"

I shake my head. I mean, I do. I know Sage likes me a lot as a friend. It's hard not to see it. We do so much for each other. But more than that? Romantically other than a lay? Nah. He had countless chances to ask me out, to blur the lines, to take a chance. Literally, a decade of opportunities ticked by. He saw me with boyfriends. On dates. At prom with Clay Jacobs. He never gave me any indication that he was even remotely jealous. No reason he caught a bad case of the feels all of a sudden.

"Jolie, he is crazy about you."

"I don't see it."

"Well, you should, because everyone else does."

I bite my lower lip and marble at her words. Maybe it's true. Maybe I'm just being a bit of a jerk. I mean, what exactly am I expecting from him right now? A declaration that he'll always be mine? A goddamn ring? Who knows what's going to happen in May? All we have is today, and today matters. Ugh.

Now I sound like an inspirational meme people post on their Facebooks on Mondays.

"Okay, I'll talk to him," I say. Chelsea nods.

"I'll give you a ride to work." She winks.

"You're the best." And for the millionth time since I met her here a couple of years ago, I thank the Lord that He gave me one best friend that I love like a drug, and another who takes care of me like a fairy.

Chapter Seven

Jolie

I TIE MY YELLOW APRON AROUND MY WAIST IN THE EMPLOYEES' ROOM OF the Happy Bunny. Trisha, my fifty-something-year-old colleague, coughs in my face, cigarette smoke drifting from her mouth.

"All I'm sayin' is, don't let a man fool ya. They're all the same, hotcakes. They will use you and leave you if you let them. Why buy the cow if you can get the milk for free? See what I mean?" She gathers phlegm and spits it into a trash can, her fire engine red curly hair littered with white cigarette ash. I pretend to fluff her mane when really, I'm just making sure she doesn't lose all her tips *and* her job by sprinkling ash into people's food like a Tinkerbell from hell.

"Yep." I smile at her, not entirely sure why we're talking about this. I haven't told her a word about Sage. I was actually trying to strike up a conversation about the weather. Trish leaves the darkened room to yell at our manager-slash-diner-owner, Travis, and I immediately fish out my phone, texting my best friend. The one I left hanging.

Me: Let's talk tonight?

He answers after less than five seconds.

Sage: Yes. Pick you up from work at eleven?

Me: Trish is giving me a ride back. She wants to talk about colleges bc her son is applying. I'll see you at home?

Sage: K. Chilling at Barnie's with the guys, but I'll be there on time. Everything good?

Me: Yeah. I just think I owe you an apology for freaking out on you yesterday like that.

Sage: Honestly, the only thing I'm worried about is how it's going to affect my relationship with your pussy, AKA my fiancée.

Me: So funny.

Sage: Also: so true.

Sage: But seriously, I don't know what happened yesterday. Whatever it was, I want to get it fixed. You're a part of my blood. I can't change my DNA, but I sure as hell can change everything else to keep you close. You know this, right?

This man. *This. Man.* Maybe Chelsea is right. Maybe I'm not seeing what's so obviously clear to everyone else. Maybe Sage does like me in the same way that I like him.

Me: I hope you mean it.

Sage: I hope you know it. Speak soon x

THE SHIFT PASSES by in a blur. I don't think I've ever made such great tips, even though I pretty much work on autopilot. I don't feel tired or stressed or anxious. I'm just excited to see Sage at the end of my shift. Or maybe I'm doing such a great job because business is slow. Five hours into my shift, Travis saunters across the checkered black and white linoleum floors, braces one forearm over a red-hot booth, and slaps Trish's ass with a loud smack. "Trish, Jol, take the rest of the night off. Split the tips in the jar. This place is deader than my old man. And he's dead, all right. Has been dead for two decades now."

Insert: awkward polite smile.

We nearly jump up and down with excitement and jog our way to Trish's piece-of-trash car (her words, not mine). She calls her old puke-green Ford Aerostar Bob after the asshole who ran away from her when she was eight months pregnant with his kid. Luckily, Bob's son is now seventeen and applying to colleges. A very different guy from his deadbeat dad.

"Where to?" Trish asks me when she gets behind the wheel, immediately lighting up a cigarette. She fluffs her hair, staring at the rearview mirror, and between us is an ashtray with enough cigarette butts to fill a bucket. I start giving her my address before realizing that Sage is not going to be there yet. So I give her the address for Barnie's, a converted barn turned into a sleazy bar all the jocks frequently hang out in.

"Aw, Barnie's. I have so many memories from that place. Most of them consisting of broken condoms and Bob, but still." Trish sighs, starts her car, and we're on a roll.

All the way to Barnie's, I'm answering questions about college when really, I'm an anxious mess. The idea that I nearly pushed the one guy I wanted more than life itself away sits heavy in the back of my head and slowly opens a well of dark thoughts. Then I remember how sweet he was when we texted and take a deep breath.

By the time Trish's car comes to a stop in front of the old red barn with the Arctic Monkey's "I Bet You Look Good on the Dancefloor" leaking from between the door and windows, I'm sweating like I jogged here.

"Go ahead. I have a phone call to make. I'll wait for you in case he's already left." She cranes her neck, as if she's trying to see Sage through the windows. I didn't text Sage because I wanted to surprise him. I haven't even mentioned I was meeting a guy here, though Trish is that kind of woman. One who can smell men from miles away.

"Thanks, Trish. You're the best." I squeeze her into a hug and hop out of the car. My knees are shaking as I make my way to the door. No one gets carded at Barnie's, because the place is in the middle of nowhere. It's almost underground. I could walk in there with a newborn and no one would bat an eye. No one would also try to rub themselves all over me, so maybe I *should* consider walking in with a baby if I ever feel like a drink but not like swatting off horny college boys.

"Jolie!" I spot Sage's teammates in the corner of the bar. Michael is the one who perks up the most, removing his arms from the counter he was plastered over and waves for me to come close. "Over here, pretty lady."

I also spot Tom, Mark, and Dre all sitting beside him, so I'm guessing the party is very much still alive and Sage should be nearby. I walk over to them, the smile on my face at odds with how I feel about wearing my orange and yellow, Happy Bunny uniform of buttoned-down mini-dress and black stockings. Tom whistles as I go, and Mark smacks the back of his neck. My smile fades as I realize Sage is nowhere to be seen. I stop by the bar, my shoulder almost brushing Mark's, and he takes two large steps back and frowns. *Weirdo.* I know he's with Chelsea. Does he really think I'm going to hit on him?

"Where's Sage?" I ask in everyone's general direction, parking my forearms on the counter. Michael raises his eyebrows silently, his lips pursed. Tom looks the other way, Dre actually whistles as he pretends to text, and Mark is the only person who clears his throat and has the decency to make eye contact with me.

"Did he know you were coming?"

"No, why would he..." I begin to ask, when a high-pitched voice pierces through the air, that's heavy with warm, stinky alcohol and men's aftershave. *A girly* voice. I swivel my head on an instinct and watch Sage standing in front of one of the sorority girls Chelsea approached earlier this afternoon at the library.

The blondest one.

The prettiest one.

The one with the whitest, silkiest cardigan.

The one who called me a slut.

I want to see him tell her that this can't happen. That it will never happen. I want him to turn his back to her and walk over to me, like in the movies. I want her to chase him, and I want him to block her. These thoughts are not kind or noble, but they're coming from my deepest, most intimate part. The part who's seen him playing around with so many girls from the sidelines, wishing he'd just give me a chance. But, to my horror, he doesn't do any of those things. *She's* the one running away toward the door, and *he's* the one chasing after her.

"Amber, no, please!" he calls.

Amber.

No.

Please.

Sage never begs. Sage never pleads. Not to me and not to anyone.

He chases after her. I stay rooted to the floor. I watch the door swinging back and forth with the force of Amber's push. He's trailing behind.

He catches her.

He's holding her.

He's *hugging* her.

Their images are blurry through the dirty, cloudy windows. I see their shapes dancing together through the dull glass and the mist of tears on my eyeballs. The way Amber pushes him away. The way he keeps on moving toward her. The sheer desperation in his body language. And that's when I feel Mark's hand on my shoulder.

"I don't know what it's about," he says, his voice quivering slightly, "but give him the benefit of the doubt."

A lonely tear escapes my right eye and runs down my cheek, free-falling into its end and splashing on the tip of my Chucks. I hear the guys shuffling and talking behind me, but can't distinguish what they're saying. My legs carry me to Amber and Sage. To the girl who called me a slut and to the guy who said I was in his blood but ran after someone else.

They're standing outside the barn. She's yelling at him. He looks miserable. The only good thing about this shitshow of a situation? Trish's car is still parked at the non-existent curb near the hay, the engine purring, as she talks on the phone, smoking a cigarette and staring at herself through the rearview mirror.

"Oh, great. Now your new girlfriend is here!" Amber shrieks, throwing her arms in the air on an eye roll. Then she huffs. I think I made my opinion about huffing clear. I narrow my eyes at the not-so-happy couple. Sage turns around instantly, his eyes growing wide.

"What are you doing here, JoJo?" The words struggle out of his mouth.

"Standing in your way, obviously. Don't worry, Sage. I'll make myself scarce so you can go back to your..." I frown at both of them, standing so close to each other, "business."

"No, wait. There's no business with Amber. No business at all. You don't understand..." He charges after me, but I take hurried steps toward Trish's car, swing the passenger door open, slide in, and nudge her to start driving. She does. She throws the lit cigarette out the window and pushes the gas pedal like we're on a police chase. I'm not sure I want to know how she mastered these escaping skills.

"Trouble with the boy?" Her voice is exceptionally cheerful, like she just proved a point. I shake my head, crossing my arms over my chest. I want to move out. I *need* to move out. I hate him. I want to kill him. I want to kiss him. I love him. I don't know what I'm feeling. Everything is wrong and twisted and final. Or maybe nothing happened at all and this has a very simple, logical explanation. I'm confused. I need to drink. I have to think about this sober.

Goddammit.

My phone starts pinging with messages as I see Sage's burgundy truck careening after us. Well, that's just dandy.

Sage: Where are you going? Who is in the car with you?

Sage: You can't just leave. I didn't know you were coming. I can explain.

Sage: I know it looks bad.

Sage: You need to answer me, JoJo.

Sage: FUCK JOJO FUCK.

"Where to?" Trish asks, lighting her four-hundredth cigarette for the day as we speed towards an intersection. She nonchalantly passes a stop sign and I'm about to pee my pants—yeah, despite all the Pilates.

"Slow down, Trish."

"Did he cheat?" She ignores me, getting all worked up. "It looks like he's been cheatin' on ya. This kinda thing doesn't fly with me. Bob cheated."

"It's complicated, but..." *I don't want to die. Not even over Sage.*

"Bastard!" She hits the accelerator so hard my head swings back. Meanwhile, the texts flow like cheap alcohol at a frat party.

Sage: Tell her to stop the goddamn vehicle or I swear I'll slam into you from the side to pull you over.

Sage: Bitch is crazy, JoJo. She'll get both of you killed.

Sage: IT'S NOT WHAT YOU THINK.

"You have to stop." I swivel my whole body toward Trish.

"Like hell I will!" she exclaims with an evil laugh. Dude. Okay. Trish might be a little on the psychotic side. Plus, she is plucking out another cigarette from her magical, never-ending pack. I grab her shoulder and squeeze lightly so she doesn't do something reckless in an attempt to gain her full attention.

"Trish, you're spinning. Stop the car or I'll take all your tips," I threaten, and the car pulls over so fast my head is swimming again. We're on the shoulder of the highway, in the pitch-black, and Trish leans over my body, throws my door open, and points outside.

"Get the hell outta my car, girl. If you're taking this cheating bastard back, I don't want to hang out with you no more."

That escalated quickly. I grab my stuff and hop out, Sage already pulling behind her with his truck. No matter what happened between him and me, I still trust him more to get me home safe. Wherever home may be. He gets out of his truck and walks toward me, chest puffed up, eyes ablaze, just when Trish hits the gas pedal again and leaves us in a thick cloud of exhaust smoke. We're standing one in front of another. I don't say a thing. Neither does he.

He pulls his phone from his pocket and texts me, his brows serious and furrowed. I stare at him like he's an absolute lunatic.

Sage: If we talk about it right now, we'll fight again. Let's go home and I'll explain everything.

I don't budge. I don't want to cry. I don't want to fight. But I don't want to be a doormat, either. He's got plenty of girls who'd be happy to play that role for him. But not me. He sighs, texting me again.

Sage: OUR home, JoJo. Don't throw away all these years for a misunderstanding. Pls?

THE DRIVE back is soul crushing, no less. The silence hangs in the air like a stench. When we get to the apartment, I kick my Chucks against the wall and walk over to my room. A big hand grabs me by the waist and spins me around. I swat it away, feeling all the humiliation, anger, and sadness I'd felt at Barnie's returning, burning in me like a red-hot wrath.

"Get off me, Sage. I mean it. All this bullshit about me being in your blood didn't feel so true when you ran after Amber, begging."

"You are in my blood!" he screams in my face, raking his fingers along his thick, lush blond hair. I look away so he won't see the tears. My cheeks are wet, and my heart is pounding loud enough to hear from across the room. "You're in my blood, in my veins, in my fucking soul. You're in my heart and in my fingertips and on my fucking lips like a prayer. You're fucking *everywhere,* Jolie Louis. Always have been, always will be." He pushes me to the wall. My back slams against it. I growl, pushing him away. He lets me. We're angry. We're desperate. We're frustrated. We're burning alive together, and we're so connected, even when we're completely torn.

"That Amber chick called me a slut today. You ran after her! Pleaded for her to stay when you thought I wasn't there. How do you think that makes me feel?"

"I don't want Amber," he says, his lips pursing and his eyes thinning into slits. "I don't want anyone else. I only want you."

"You have a funny way of showing it," I huff—oh, God, since when did I become a huffer?—turning my back to him and walking toward the hallway. He pins me against the wall again, this time bracing his arms above my head and locking me in. I can't run. I can't hide. I have to stay here and see this through. His eyes are burning. My body is heaving. There's an impending storm between us and we're both exposed.

"She *just* had a miscarriage," he snarls into my face, his breath laced with beer and cinnamon gum. "We hooked up a few months ago. The condom broke. She wanted to keep it, and I couldn't exactly tell her not to. She found out about the miscarriage last month, and she is a mess about it. That's why I was running after her. She just found out about us at the library."

I swallow a bitter lump of tears. Oh, my God. Poor Amber. Poor, poor Amber. And poor Sage. I've been so focused on how I feel, I forgot that there were other people around me.

"Sage." I cup his cheeks with my palms, my chin quivering. He holds my wrists, keeping me close.

"I've never wanted anyone but you, JoJo. Not truly. Not wholly. Not obsessively."

Sage steps closer to me, his body flush against mine, his leg between my thighs, his lips on mine as he speaks these words. "You want the truth? Here's the truth: I asked you to be my fake girlfriend because Mark wanted to make a move on you. And it occurred to me, out of fucking nowhere, that I'd rather die than see you with someone else who holds the potential to give you the things that you need. It occurred to me that I would never be able to be happy for you if you married someone else. It occurred to me that I can't even think of being with anyone but you, and when I *do* have a child, I want it to be with you. I love you, JoJo. But you already know that. I'm also *in love* with you. Crazy about you. Can't live without you."

I kiss his lips to shut him up and to give him everything he needs, my fingers running through his hair, his hands on my waist, pulling me close. We're one entity. Whole and broken. Happy and sad. Lost and so unbelievably found.

"I love you so much," I breathe, the words pouring from my mouth in a rush. "I've always loved you. From that day in the meadow, when the rain knocked so hard on our bodies I thought we were going to go back home with bruises on our skin. I loved you ever since, and I never stopped loving you. Even when I tried really hard. Even when I dated other men."

He hoists me up, my legs wrapped around his narrow waist, and carries me to his bedroom. Not mine—his. It's a statement. I very rarely wander into his bedroom, and only after I ask and only when I need to take something specific. He lowers me to the bed, ever so carefully, his mouth on mine. Never leaving mine.

He fumbles with his jeans. I fumble with my mini dress. We kiss. We bite. We mess around like the two teenagers who wanted to so bad but never dared. I'm here. All of me. Every single part of me is in the present, and it's raw and beautiful and everything I've ever dreamed about wrapped in a bow made of memories and sweet childhood moments. We strip down in silence, our eyes never leaving one another. We kick our clothes to the foot of the bed and his groin is on mine and our lips are kissing, biting, and caressing. My breasts pop free from my bra, and he takes one of my nipples into his mouth, closing his warm lips over it and circling the areola with his tongue. I arch my back.

"I love you." His breath tickles my sensitive nipple, and he works his way down my torso, peppering feathery, wet, hot kisses all over my shivering body. "I love you, I love you, I fucking love you. No matter what happens in my life, you're the constant thing I can count on. The shelter in the storm, the calm in my chaos."

He bites my inner thigh, and I roll my head onto his pillow that smells of cinnamon and aftershave and *him*. His tongue meets my sensitive flesh, licking my arousal, but this time he is not demanding and starving. He is sweet and considerate.

"Jesus, Sage. *Jesus*."

I can barely breathe. He is teasing me with his mouth to a point of tears before he slides a finger into me, curling it when he is deep enough to reach my magic spot.

"I love you." He continues kissing my pussy. "And I love you, too, JoJo," he says, and I laugh, swatting his head softly. My orgasm washes through me like an oasis. I shudder quietly before his corded, muscled body rises up and his lips meet mine again for a deep kiss.

"Love you. Have I said that lately?" He nuzzles into the crook of my neck, and I'm in heaven, I'm sure of it. I might even murder the person who wakes me up from this dream.

"Not lately." I kiss his temple. "Better tell me again."

"I love you, Jolie Louis. The kind of love that burns through the skin."

Hmm. Is it bad that I want to tattoo this on my forehead?

We kiss some more while my hand trails down the dusty line of hair arrowing from his belly button to his cock. I fist it and move my hand back and forth. I could do this all day without getting bored. Admiring his body. Learning what gives him pleasure. After a few minutes, he raises his head and looks me in the eye.

"Not to sound dramatic, but, baby, I think I'll die if I don't fuck you right this minute."

"So do it." I smile. He reaches across his bed and fumbles for a condom in his dresser's drawer. Then he rolls it down his cock as we both watch in awe, as if this is the first time for both of us—and in some weird, screwed-up way, it kind of *is*, at least for me. I'm not a virgin, but I feel like one right now, as he slides on top of me again.

"I love you." It's my turn to say. "Every part of you. The broken boy. The strong man. The lighthearted jock and the heavyhearted kid. Every piece of you is loved and cherished, Sage Poirier. Always remember that."

He enters me in one smooth stroke, and I moan at the sudden sensation of being so full, not only physically, but also mentally. My back curls against the sheet when he starts moving in and out in a rhythm I've yet to experience with a man. His movements have no start nor ending. His hips roll back and forth constantly, like an erotic dance between two bodies, and we quickly find the pace that makes us both pant harder and faster. I've never looked in a man's eyes when we had sex before. It felt too weird. Too awkward. But with Sage, I can't help not to.

His eyes are an open wound.

Mine are a bandage that wants to make it all better for him.

This is it. This is everything I wanted. He and I. Fully and completely committed to one another. His movements become jerky. I begin to quiver again. I swear I came with this man more times than I did with all my previous partners combined, which really says a lot about his dedication, but also about men in the sack in general.

"I'm about to come, baby. Please come with me."

I nod. Coming on command is the kind of thing that always made me snicker when I read it in books, but now I get it. It is doable when the person asking you to is the biggest turn-on you know.

We come in each other's arms, with him moaning my name and me whimpering when his cock drills into me one last time, and part ways on a kiss. Both our bodies are covered in sweat. We look spent, happy, and so much younger than our years.

He rolls on his back and stares at the ceiling.

I roll to my side and put a hand on his abs.

"Shit," is all he says. I throw my arm over my eyes and laugh. He's been talking sweet to me for an hour, so it only makes sense he'll be back to his old self now.

"That bad, huh?" I joke. He turns to me and pulls my arm from my face.

"That *good*. I never thought it could feel like this."

"Like what?"

He takes my wrist and presses it against his pouty, perfect lips. "Like forever."

Chapter Eight

Sage

THE DIRTY BEIGE HALLWAYS DON'T FEEL QUITE THE SAME THE DAY AFTER.

Neither does the cafeteria, which constantly smells of stale pretzels and burnt coffee.

Neither does my body. Nope. It feels lighter and much more capable.

And if I were anyone else, I'd probably say some bullshit about being a different man, but unfortunately for the world, I'm still the same douchy jock. The only difference is I now have sex with my best friend (six times in less than twenty-four hours, but who is counting?), and I don't want to read too much into this, but damn, it puts a stupid-ass smile on my face, which I can't seem to wipe off.

Enter: Amber.

I see her coming out of Sabatta Hall just as I make my way to the weight room. I stop. Last night, we left everything hanging, and as much as I felt bad about her miscarriage—the doctor told her it might've been due to the fact that she still drank heavily at parties before she'd found out about the pregnancy—I was too fucking wrapped in my own universe with JoJo. Which is shitty, I know. So I stop and clap a hand over her shoulder. She looks tired, and I feel guilty. When Amber found out that she was pregnant, I said I'd support her no matter what. She wanted to keep it, but still hadn't told her parents. Then the miscarriage happened three weeks ago and I've been trying to be there for her, but most of the time, that entails her telling me we need to try to have a baby again.

"Yo. What's up?" I squeeze her shoulder softly, giving her my most genuine smile. People pass us by, talking to each other, laughing. Amber shoots me a look, flipping her blonde, straight hair on an eye roll.

"What do you want, Poirier?" Her voice is pointed, like her expression. I look left and right, somehow still freaked out about JoJo seeing us. Even though I know she gets it. She's the kindest girl I've ever met. She felt so guilty about what happened to Amber. Like she had something to do with it somehow.

"To check how you're doing." I ignore her snark. "See if you need anything."

"I need you to stop fucking around and give me attention. That's what I need." She juts her chin out, defying me. I scratch the back of my neck, trying to figure out if this is a joke. Throughout the last month, I've been her designated bitch. Drove her places. Let her hang out with the boys and me at Barnie's. Even helped her with her studies. She tried to hit on me countless times, and I blocked it, because even though we shared a fling, I really couldn't see us doing anything more. So this is unwarranted at best and rude at worst.

"Huh?" I cock my head sideways. She slaps my chest. Hard. I take a step back, looking at her like she drank from the crazy fountain, then ate a big dish of psycho.

"You," she points at me, her eyes narrowing, "are not focused on what's important. I just lost our child, Poirier. Do you get what I'm saying? I'm mourning. I'm hurt. I don't need to see you parading your new piece all over campus, telling people she's your girlfriend. It's *so* disrespectful."

What. The. Fuck.

I straighten my back, shaking off some of my surprise.

"I really have no idea what in the good fuck you're talking about, woman. Jolie is not a piece. She's my childhood friend and we're dating now. It has nothing to do with me wanting to be there for you. When we hooked up, I said it was for fun. We had fun. The condom broke. Not so fun. Shit happened in-between. Fucking terrible, I know. Now we're dealing with this. Together. Look, I'm still here for you, yeah? But this has nothing to do with JoJo."

Her lower lip is shaking. People are starting to stop and look. Stall with their phones. Pretend to mess around with their bags. Shit. It's becoming a scene, and that's a problem. I take Amber by the elbow and usher her outside, away from the hall and toward a tree overlooking the entrance of the building. It's a gray day, and no one is out but us. I lean over her—not too close to give her the wrong idea, but close enough so that she knows that I'm serious.

"Anything you need," I say, "I'm here for you. I mean it."

"I need you to leave her." Amber's tears are now falling like a flood, and I want to stop them, I do, but I can't. Not the way she wants me to.

"Amber..."

She throws herself at me, her fists curling around the collar of my jersey. She gets into my face. "Please, Sage. Give us a chance. You're going away next year. Do you think Jolie will go with you? She's not the kind of girl to leave her family. I know her type. I'll do it for you, Sage. I'll leave this place for you."

My eyes darken, and my thoughts jumble in my head. So when Amber seeks my warmth, burrowing into me for a hug, I give it to her.

Because I gave her something else without meaning to.

And now she lost it.

Because I need to make this right for her somehow.

And because I'm afraid that she is right about JoJo.

Jolie

You know the part in the movie where the couple gets together and everything works out and everyone gets their happy ending? Well, this is *not* what happens in real life. At least not to me.

The day starts with Chelsea informing me that she and Mark are not going to the Christmas charity event in New York because she has a job interview for an au pair position in Canada. The woman is heavily pregnant and looking for a full-time nanny to assist her when the baby is born. Mark is going with her, and they'll be flying back to spend Christmas with her family right after. They're moving fast, and I'm happy for them, but at the same time, I wanted so badly to spend time with my best friend in the Big Apple.

Then, I get fired by a text message. Travis, my boss, who apparently has the diplomatic skills of a swordfish, sends me the following message:

Hi, Julie. Trish told me you had a falling out yesterday. I'm going to be completely honest. She's been with us for a decade now and this could be a problem. I think it's best for everyone if you just hand in your resignation tomorrow after your shift. Thanks for your service and stuff. – Trav.

At first, I think about firing him back my unfiltered response:

Hi, Gravis (oh? You're not Gravis? Well, guess what, I'm not Julie. It's Jolie, you prick!). No need to sugarcoat it. You want me gone because you and Trish meet at the kitchen three times a week before her shift and do some ungodly (and unsanitary) things on the counter. I am more than happy to offer my excellent services to someone who appreciates them. Have a nice life. –Jolie.

But, of course, like the good Southern girl that I am, I settle for being agreeable:

Travis, thank you for your message. I regret to hear about your firing me (because that's essentially what this is), but I'm in no way going to argue with you about it. Since your response to my altercation with Trish was immediate, I think it is only fair that my resignation will be immediate, as well. I will drop by to pick up my last check next week at a time of your convenience. Thanks. –Jolie.

After getting fired—just when I think things cannot get any possibly worse—I land my butt in a library's chair, trying to study for my next lit exam, and open up my MacBook. Five seconds into reading an essay about the history of the English language, I rub my eyes, trying to concentrate. When I feel something gooey and warm connecting with the side of my head, I freeze. It slithers down my hair and slaps my face, and my first reaction is to cover my face with both palms. After I hear the knock of whatever's been thrown at me dropping to the floor, I raise my head and look to my right, where the thing came from.

Amber.

Sitting at the desk beside me.

Smiling.

I look down. It's a Starbucks cup. I touch my hair, sniff around me, the shock still working its way to my system. It's my now-cold pumpkin latte with marshmallow. Jesus H.

Bitch.

I know her reasoning behind it, and I get it, I do—it hurts. I can't even begin to imagine how much. But it is also not my fault.

My chair scrapes the floor as I stand up and make my way to her. She is sitting with her sorority friends, their army of cardigans, pearl necklaces, and mechanically straightened hair in full attendance. I look sloppy in comparison. My Chucks are dirty, my blonde is also red, and my clothes are too casual. And still, they can't treat me this way. Ever.

"You need to stop this." I slap my hand on her desk, lifting my chin up to look down at her. She stares up at me with a conceited smile I'm dying to wipe off of her face.

"No, I don't. You have something of mine that I want back."

"And I suppose that'd be Sage?" I tilt my head sideways. She shrugs, snorting out an unattractive laugh she'd never allow herself in his presence.

"And his money. And his future. And his status. Basically, everything. The best thing about being upfront with you about it, is that you're too goody-two-shoes to even tell him I ever said it. Because you don't talk badly of people, do you, sweet girl? I know all about you and your running-to-see-mommy-every-other-weekend tactics."

Tactics?

Tactics?!

She thinks I go through life trying to impress someone? My best friend? Is she nuts? I don't even need anyone to answer this question. Of course, she's nuts. No one of sound mind would ever think in this direction. I lower my body, lean into her face, and whisper, "I know what happened to you, and I'm sorry that it did. I am. But you cannot break us up, Amber. I suggest you move on, and while you're at it, take a very long look at your behavior and priorities. Because you're not being assertive or street-smart here, girl. You're being a manipulative bitch."

The words slap her, one by one, and I see her cocky smile melting into a shocked, wide-eyed grimace. One of her friends—a brunette who is wearing a lemon yellow cardigan and a matching headband—crinkles her nose.

"Wait, how do you mean after what happened to you? What exactly happened to you?"

"I...I..."

Another girl, who sits directly in front of her, bolts up from her chair and shakes her head. Her face is so red it is completely possible she might explode.

"Jesus Christ, Amber! Tell me you didn't go through with that stupid plan! Faking a pregnancy and then a miscarriage? Like, hello, newsflash! Your life is not a bad *General Hospital* episode!"

I stagger backwards, gripping the end of my desk and staring at a very embarrassed, very angry Amber as her eyes broaden and her chest heaves up and down, the adrenaline of the lie catching up with reality.

Everything turns red.

Then black.

Then white again, because the lie is not mine. Not mine to keep, to be burdened with, nor to carry.

I turn around to collect my MacBook and my shoulder bag and dash outside the library door, making my way to the nearest bus station back home. Amber is after me. I hear her heels clacking against the floor. I don't turn around, mainly because the notion that I can do something terrible to her—slap her, yell at her, or curse her out—is strong.

She might be that kind of person, but I'm not.

Just as I round the corner of the street, Chelsea's blue Buick appears from the intersection. She stops in front of me with a screech and throws the passenger's door open.

"Need a getaway ride?"

"That seems to be the reoccurring theme in my life right now."

I hop in, then I watch Amber's disappearing figure through the side mirror as my heart finally returns to its usual rhythm.

"More coffee stains?" Chelsea chuckles, her eyes scanning my blouse. I smile, avoiding the full story.

"That's right. I'm starting to believe they're my sign for good luck."

Chapter Nine

Sage

Four days before Christmas Eve.

"YOU READY?" I ASK, STARING AT THE MIRROR AS I FASTEN MY CUFFLINKS. The crisp dress shirt is a Prada, and it's weird to wear Prada. It's weird to be able to *afford* Prada, and I constantly have to remind myself that this is a one-off. I bought this suit for the meeting I had with the Raiders in California because JoJo made me. She said I needed to dress the way I wanted to feel. Well, today I feel like I'm going to fulfill my dream and become a professional football player as of next spring.

That's one of two dreams down, one more to go.

"Just a sec!" my girl calls out from the bathroom at the fancy hotel room. Even though I've known her ever since we were kids, there is a lot I'm finding out about her, now that we're dating. Like how it takes her literally two hours to get ready to go out, even though she doesn't need more than two minutes to get ready for school when we leave for campus every morning, or that she is really (ironically) horny when she's on her period, which makes us hella creative in bed (I don't mind a little blood on my sword), but she does. Or that she is not actually that sensitive or sweet when she has a reason not to be—like that time she came back home and told me how Amber goddamn tricked me into babying her. I still haven't recovered from that shit.

Wait, that's not true. I totally did. But still. What an asshole that girl is.

"Okay! Close your eyes," she says. My tie is still loose around my neck, and

I frown, turn around, lean a hip against the dresser, and shove my hands into my pockets.

"All right. Let's see it."

"That's the whole point, Sage! You can't see it! Eyes closed, remember?" she squeaks. *Squeaks*. I make her squeak these days. I never did that when we were friends. She also does a lot of huffing, especially when I ask her if we can have sex in insane places like the plane or the beach. I think she huffs to let me know that the idea *is* insane, but we still end up doing it all the same.

"Yeah, yeah, eyes as closed as your legs this evening," I mutter, squeezing my eyelids together.

"That's right, mister. No Christmas quickie in the bathroom."

I hear her voice getting closer, and my cock jerks in appreciation. He always liked pretty things, and she is gorgeous eye candy. My girl, with the Chucks and the strawberry blonde hair who is not afraid to run in the rain for me.

"I'd like to negotiate this part." I lick my lips, my eyes still closed. I feel her closer. Her heat. Her body. The clack of her heels, which I've yet to see.

"I'm sorry. I do not negotiate with terrorists."

I smirk. "Oh, we'll see about that by the end of the night."

"Open," she says, close enough to me that I can smell her flowery perfume, but not so close that I can feel her breath on my skin. I open my eyes, and she is standing there in a long red dress with a deep slit that exposes a shapely, milky leg. The dress is all velvet, prompting me to want to touch it. To tear it. To fucking eat her out on the floor. But I still want my balls intact when we get to the gala at the Met. She's wearing minimal makeup—other than her red-hot lips—and a pair of heels where the soles are red. The expensive stuff. What I urged her to buy when I signed the deal with the Raiders, same day I got my suit. Her scarlet lips twitch into a timid smile.

"What do you think?"

"I think you look perfect, but there's one thing that's missing. Accessories. Turn around."

Her eyes widen, but she does as I ask. She turns around, and I open the drawer behind me and produce my gifts for her. I pull her hair up to put her necklace on. Nothing too fancy. A pink gold necklace with one lonely pearl. It takes me a few seconds to fasten it—this is not the movies. It's real life, and my hands are shaking like a motherfucker.

"Now back to me," I say. My voice breaks. She turns around. Slowly. So slowly. Super slowly. Why is she so slow? Is this a sign? *Shut up, asshole. Just do it.*

Very nonchalantly, like it's not a big deal, like I'm not shitting myself, I slide the ring onto her engagement finger. Like the necklace, it is simple and elegant. Thin, with one diamond sparkling in the middle. Lonely and rare, just like my girl.

I don't ask; I state.

Jolie Louis's heart belongs to me. It will always belong to me. It belonged to me the minute she decided to open her rusty window and sneak out of her room to meet me, uninvited, but all the same needed.

She looks down at the ring, and I expect her to frown, maybe ask a question, but no. She doesn't do any of those things. She looks back up, smiles, and uses her newly adorned left hand to cup my face and pull me close.

Outside, a storm is making the newspapers and trash on the streets of New York dance in circles. Inside, it's warm. We kiss. Like friends. Like lovers. Like everything in-between.

"I love you, angry boy," she says, and I answer her with the only thing that pops into my head.

"I love you, brave girl."

Epilogue

One Year Later

ON THE EIGHTH BEAT OF SILENCE, SHE FINALLY OPENED HER MOUTH.

It was dry, and numb, and painful from smiling all day, but she wanted to utter these words, even if they were the last she'd ever say.

"I, Jolie Alexandra Louis, take you, Sage Albert Poirier, to be my best friend, my faithful partner, and my one true love. You'll be my storm in the summer, my calm under the winter sky, and all the seasons in-between. To have, to hold, to cherish, and to comfort." She slid the ring with shaky fingers, their childhood tree standing in the background, wrapped in red and white sateen bows. It was a small ceremony, with only their beloved family members and college friends as witnesses. No matter how much of a superstar the boy grew up to be in his career with the Raiders, they were still the same kids from twelve years ago. Humble. Quiet. In love. *In love*. So, so in love.

"You may now kiss the bride," the priest said, his words trickling down the two lovers' souls, melting like the wedding cake behind them on that hot summer day.

On the eighth second after the girl vowed to give her all to the boy, the boy smirked and said, "Don't have to tell me twice, sir." He pulled the veil off of her face, cupped her cheeks, and kissed her so hard he stole her breath away.

People bolted up from their seats, cheering, whistling, laughing, and *living in* the moment. The girl smiled, reminiscing back to the very first time she summoned the courage to follow the broken boy, to follow her instincts, to follow her heart, and to talk to him.

Their lips moved together in a dance of love and lust. They knew the moves by heart.

On the eighth minute after the ceremony was over, the girl sauntered across the carefully cut grass to her best friend, Chelsea, putting her hand on her shoulder. Chelsea turned around, her date—Mark, whom she was now engaged to—decided to make himself scarce, muttering his congratulations as he walked away. Sage appeared by his new bride's side, his smile so big, it hit both women like a sunray.

"What's up?" Chelsea asked. She'd recently moved from Vancouver—where she lived with her fiancé—back to Louisiana, where they were both looking for jobs, eager to settle down.

"What's your schedule like in eight months?" the girl inquired, butterflies taking flight in her stomach. Chelsea lifted one eyebrow. Sage was on the verge of exploding from happiness. The girl moved her open palm across her white dress, sliding down her flat stomach.

"Pretty clear. Why?" Chelsea probed.

"Because you're hired," the girl said, as all three sets of eyes drifted down to her abdomen.

The girl got a kiss on the lips from the boy who no longer howled at the moon and cried on a tree. On the forehead. Like friends do.

Then he kissed her on the lips, like lovers do.

Then he kissed the inside of her wrists, like soulmates do.

The End (Zone)

Acknowledgments

This year has been an incredible journey for me. My readers, fellow-authors, agent, editors and friends took me places I never thought I'd reach. So much so, in fact, that I didn't want to end this year without giving my readers a treat.

The End Zone was never supposed to happen. I don't usually write novellas. I love evoking my readers' different feelings and there's nothing I enjoy more than slow-burn romances. At the same time, I felt like I needed to give you something sweet and cute for the holidays, and I hope I did just that.

I would like to thank the following people from the bottom of my heart:

My beta readers, Tijuana Turner, Mia Sparks, Lana Kart and Paige Jennifer. Thank you so much for putting up with my crazy schedule and for your attention for detail. You make my books so, so much better.

To my editors, Paige Smith and Tamara Mataya. I love our journey together. Your advice and guidance are everything an author could wish for and more. I am constantly honing my craft and you push me to my limits as I grow as an artist.

To Letitia Hasser. Please don't hate me. I know I don't know what I want half the time, but if it makes you feel any better, you have to put up with it a few times a year. My husband needs to tolerate it three-four times a week at a restaurant or when we choose furniture! Imagine that.

To my unicorn team—my amazing agent Kimberly Brower at Brower Literary, Sunny Borek, Ella Fox, Ava Harrison, my street team and my formatter Stacey Ryan Blake. Thank you for being true professionals through and through. I am so, so lucky to have you.

To the Sassy Sparrows—I love you! Thank you for brightening my day, every single day. Going through this journey with you is such a blessing.

Last but not least—dear readers, thank you so much for making me what I am today. An author, an artist, and against all odds, someone who can stay at home and write for a living. I do not take that lightly. I will not let you down. There's so much more to come, and I'm excited for all of it.

Thank you.

L.J. Shen xoxo

More Books By L.J. Shen

More Books by L.J. Shen

Tyed
Sparrow
Blood to Dust

Sinners of Saint:
Defy (#0.5)
Vicious (#1)
Ruckus (#2)
Scandalous (#3)
Bane (Coming soon)

Add Midnight Blue to your TBR (http://bit.ly/2g5k5Y2)

Stay in Touch
Join LJ's mailing list for exclusive material and free e-books ➜ Mailing List
➜ Facebook
➜Reading group
➜ Website
➜Instagram

CROSS

Cross
The Gibson Boys Series novella

USA Today Bestselling author
Adriana Locke

Dear Reader

Dear Reader,

I hope you enjoy this fun little novella.

This story is a standalone, but it does include some of the Gibson Boys. If you've read Crank, you'll see some of your favorite characters again. (This novella takes place before Crank, just as a side note.) But if you haven't—don't worry! I constructed this story so it's not necessary.

Grab a hot chocolate, kick back, and enjoy!

XO,
Adriana

Chapter One

Kallie

"Why are you smiling like that?"

Nora's question drifts through the warm summer breeze. Glancing over my shoulder, the amusement dancing on her face makes me laugh.

"What? A girl can't smile?" I ask.

"Absolutely she can, but can't her friend ask why?"

I try to shrug off her observation as I kick at a pebble lying on the sidewalk, watching it fall into the storm drain. "I don't know," I say. "Maybe it just feels good to be home."

We stop for a handful of cars along Beecher Street before we make our way onto Main. Nora takes out her phone when it chirps and whips out a few texts while I take in the town I grew up in.

Linton, Illinois is pretty much the same as it's always been. A traditional small, Midwestern town, the most noticeable changes over the last few years seem to be minor. There's a fresh coat of white paint on the post office and moss rose instead of impatiens filling the ever-present whiskey barrels lining the streets.

Closing my eyes, I breathe in the air, which is cinnamon-scented thanks to Carlson's Bakery and their famous coffee cake, a staple of my childhood. The scent brings back memories of summers with the windows down, Christmas caroling along Main Street in snow up to my knees, and the Water Festival in the fall that the entire town waits for all year. It's hard not to smile thinking about all that.

"I'm so glad you're back," Nora says, running a hand through her short blonde hair as we start across the street. My best friend since elementary school, she screamed when I showed up unannounced on her doorstep this morning. "When do you start work?"

"Next week. I'm starting over in the Merom office. Apparently, their attorneys have been sharing a paralegal and it's a mess." A hasty sigh sweeps past my lips. "I'm sure it's going to be a circus in there for a while."

"Yeah, but at least you're here. Linton hasn't been the same without you."

My laugh is light and free. "I bet."

"No, it true," she insists. "It's just me and the Gibson boys these days. Can you imagine how hard it is for me, the only girl, the only one trying to keep those boys in line?"

My smile falters, wobbling on my lips as I think about them.

"I mean, Molly McCarter tries to wiggle her way in there." She scowls. "Every time I turn around, she has her claws bared and ready to dig into one of them. You should've seen her trying to land Walker last weekend. It was disgusting."

"I forgot about Molly. What's she up to these days?" I haven't forgotten about Molly and I don't have one care in the world about what she's up to, but if I can shove off discussion about the Gibsons for a while, that's a win.

Nora snorts. "Besides whoring around? Nothing that I know of."

"What's she ever done to you?" I laugh, attempting to dissect her reaction. To hear her talk badly about anyone is strange, and there's a little more venom dripping from her words than I can just let go.

"Nothing. Nothing directly."

"Uh-huh," I tease, my curiosity more than a little piqued. "Because that's a normal reaction for someone to have to someone who hasn't ever done anything to them."

She shoves her hands in her pockets, setting her gaze on some point in the distance, broadcasting pretty clearly that it's futile for me to press the issue.

We step across chalk artwork on the sidewalk outside the library and wave to Ruby, the seventy-something-year-old librarian who used to chastise me for bringing in Goldfish crackers during story hour when I was a kid. Her silver hair is pressed to her head by a pair of glasses, and a floral-print bag is draped off her narrow shoulders. I give her a little wave.

"Well, look who it is!" Ruby calls out, her frail little hand going back and forth in front of her. "Are you in town for a while, Kallie? It's so nice to see you, sweetheart."

I pause at the base of the steps leading up to the oversized doors of the library. "It's nice to see you too. How have you been?"

"I'm heading out now to see Dr. Burns. I just have a little gout but he wants to run all these tests. The man doesn't have the sense God gave a goat." Ruby moves to come down to the sidewalk.

"Oh, Ruby." I giggle, helping her down the steps. Her hand clasps against my elbow as she steadies herself. "You should listen to him. He is a doctor, you know."

"Those fancy letters after his name don't mean he has any sense." She pats my hand and turns toward the parking lot. "Come by and see me, Kallie, and bring back that book you took out, Nora. The one about the...well, you know." She flits my friend a knowing look before unlocking her car door. "Kids these days."

"What are you checking out?" I ask Nora, curiosity piqued again.

"It's that one with grey in the title." Ruby shakes her head. "I had to order another copy because she hasn't brought it back in six weeks. Six weeks!"

"Just put my business out there, why don't you?" Nora laughs. As my laugh mixes with hers, Ruby shakes her head and climbs in her little maroon car. With a small motion of her hand as a goodbye, she pulls onto the street toward the only doctor's office in town.

"So, you love that book so much you can't bring it back?" I tease as we head down the sidewalk again. "You could've just bought your own copy instead of stealing from the library."

"Machlan has it." She sighs, rolling her eyes. "I took it to the bar one night when I figured we'd be slow and found him kicked back at a table reading it while I made drinks. He refuses to give it back to me. What am I supposed to do?"

"Machlan Gibson was reading *that*?" Eyes wide, I bite my bottom lip. The vision of one of the infamous Gibson boys—the too-hot-for-their-own-good guys I knew growing up—reading that book makes me shiver. "I don't think I can deal with that if he's even remotely as hot as he used to be."

Nora ponders this for a second. "You know how people age? Like wrinkles and beer bellies?"

"Unfortunately." Without thinking, my fingers pat at the crow's feet lining the corners of my eyes.

"Well, Machlan doesn't," she says easily. "I have no idea how he's still single with the women who throw themselves his way every night at Crave. I tell him one night I'm going to have to stage a diversion just so he can get home unscathed." Pausing to shoo away a dog yapping at the edge of a lawn, she turns to me again. "They've all aged well, Kallie."

I try to remain unaffected, to pretend like discussing our old group of friends is no big deal. It wouldn't be if we could stop with Machlan, Walker, and Lance Gibson and their cousins, Vincent and Peck, but we won't. It'll also include Cross Jacobs, and I'm not ready to do that quite yet.

"If Mach's still single, maybe you should hook up with him," I suggest. I know she'll shoot it down and she does—promptly.

"What?" she barks. "Are you kidding me?"

Laughing, I bump her with my shoulder. "It's not the craziest suggestion in the world. You've known him forever. He's freaking gorgeous. You like him."

"All of that's true, but I didn't say I was attracted to him." She makes a face like she's just bitten into a lemon. "He's like a brother to me now...sort of."

"Remember that time..." The sentence trails off as I catch myself, the rest of the words hiccupping in my throat. "Never mind."

"I know what you were going to say."

Peering up at her, I try to force the corners of my lips to turn up, but they refuse. "No, you don't."

"Yes, I do. When is the last time you talked to Cross?" The hesitation in Nora's tone only feeds the anxiety bubbling inside me, and hearing his name doesn't help either.

I've spent the last three years trying to forget Cross Jacobs. *Trying* is the operative word.

I don't have to ask if he still looks the same. I know the creases in his forehead that developed over the last year and a half like the back of my hand. I've watched through social media as he started to wear his inky black hair just a little longer than the buzz cut he used to sport, have noticed how he still gets it cut the first Monday of every month, like his father taught him to do. The playfulness I remember seeing in his jade-colored eyes has dimmed, replaced with something more stern. His shoulders are more broad, his body stockier than the man I used to curl up next to every night.

What I don't know these days is the sound of his voice at two in the morning or if he wears the same woodsy cologne, a scent that stops me in my tracks whenever I get close to someone wearing anything remotely similar. I wonder if he still favors basketball shorts to sleep in and who is there to time his boxing rounds like I used to do when he was training for a match.

My heart wrestles in my chest as I look at my friend, trying desperately to get myself in check. "When was the last time I talked to Cross?" I stop walking and glance up at the antique sign over our head that reads CRAVE. "The last time I stood here. That's the last time I talked to him."

I wait for Nora to push, but she doesn't. Instead, she tosses me a slight smile. "I need to run into the bar really quick and see if Machlan has my check ready. I don't work tonight and don't want to have to come all the way back to town later."

"Is it even open?" I ask, looking at the unlit open sign.

"It doesn't open for another two hours, but Machlan will be here. He practically lives here." The door swings free with a simple tug, the cool, salty bar air rushing out onto the sidewalk. "Come on. He'll be happy to see you."

Following her inside, my eyes adjust to the dim light. Alcohol ads glow from various positions on the walls, and strings of Christmas lights outline the mirror behind the bar and drape along a set of bulletin boards as I walk by.

All of that is hard to focus on with Machlan Gibson sitting at the bar. He leans back in the chair, dropping the remote for the television hanging in the corner onto the countertop with a flourish.

"Kallie Welch," he says, folding his arms over his chest as a smirk pulls at his lips. "What the hell are you doing here?"

"How are ya, Mach?" I grin.

He gets to his feet, a wide smile splitting his cheeks. "It's been a long time." Enveloping me in his arms, he gives me a warm hug. He's thicker, his back more muscled than the goodbye embrace he gave me before I left town in my little Honda Civic. "You home for long?"

"Yeah, actually," I say, pulling back. "The attorney I was working for in Indy got into some legal trouble of his own, and Mom's here alone now that Skylar moved to Wisconsin with her boyfriend a few months ago."

"That explains why I haven't seen her around lately," he says. "Someone said she met a guy in Chicago, but you never know what to believe."

"She did. He's a nice guy. His family is from up there so Skylar moved up to be with him, which left Mom on her own, and I feel guilty about that."

"Because you're a good girl."

Nora clears her throat. "Now that's over with, you got my check ready?"

There's something Machlan wants to say as he processes Nora's question. He watches me carefully, like he's connecting some invisible dots scattered over my face. "Yeah, I got your check. Be right back."

He moves easily through the bar with such command that I imagine if people were standing in his way, they'd move. It's amazing to see him in this light. I knew he'd bought the bar, but seeing him as a legitimate business owner and not the immature party boy I knew before is almost unbelievable.

Turning toward the bulletin boards, I sigh. A warmth I haven't felt in so long causes the stress in my shoulders to melt away. Maybe it was the friendly hug from Mach, or maybe it's being back home in Linton.

"Want to get something to eat?" I ask Nora, scanning the boards.

"Sure. We could run to Peaches. They have great fajitas."

"It's still weird that a place called Peaches serves Mexican food," I say with a laugh. Running my finger across a set of papers advertising handymen services, I chuckle at one particular set of 'services' offered on a napkin. "This is ridiculous."

Nora laughs. "We take the really bad ones down—you should see some of them after a rowdy Friday night."

"I can only imagine."

"I can imagine a lot of things." The shock of the deep, husky voice behind me causes me to jump, but as the timbre of the tone settles, the familiarity washes across my heart.

I suck in a breath, capturing a gasp, though I'm not sure if it's is mine or Nora's. Inhaling the rich, almost velvety scent from behind me doesn't help the shakiness in my hands as I bring one to my throat.

One of my unknowns is answered: Cross does wear the same cologne he used to.

Chapter Two

Cross

If Nora weren't standing beside her giving me that look, I'd swear to God I was seeing things.

The swallow I force down my throat is hot and heavy, as if it were laced with a shot of whiskey. It burns as it barrels its way to my stomach, but I don't register the drop into the pit of acid churning in my gut.

I can't do anything but stare at the back of Kallie Welch.

Her hair is pulled into a ponytail, baring the back of her neck. I used to bury my face in the crook of her neck and kiss the top of her shoulder. She loved it. She loved me.

My stomach sinks as I take her in, fighting with myself not to reach for her. It's almost impossible to keep my hands to myself as I see the woman I think about every fucking day standing in front of me.

Nora looks my way before dropping her gaze and slinking to the side. The sound of her shoes against the floor as she makes her way to the back of the bar is barely heard over the white noise coursing through my veins.

I take a half-step back as I wait for her to turn around. She sighs, lets her hand fall to her sides, but doesn't move to look at me.

"What are you doing here?" My voice is rougher than I intended.

"Nora is picking up her check." Her voice is just a whisper, quieter than I expected.

"That's not what I mean."

She brings a hand up to the side of her face, the simple diamond stud in her ear catching a ray of sun streaming through the windows. As my lungs fill with air and refuse to let it go, I drag my gaze down her slender neck, over her dainty shoulders, and down her arm until it rests on her left hand.

My jaw sets, my teeth grinding so hard I can nearly hear the squeal of enamel scraping against itself. It takes everything I have not to lurch forward and jerk her hand toward me so I can see if she's sporting a wedding band. She keeps it angled so I can't see it; whether it's on purpose or not doesn't matter. Whether it's ridiculous of me to get pissed about something like that doesn't matter either. Just when I'm ready to pounce, she moves her wrist just enough so I can see her finger is bare.

"I, um, I'm moving back—I *moved* back," she corrects, nodding her head once.

I don't say another word. I don't move a muscle. I just stand in place and listen to my heart beat so hard, like it's chanting her name so she'll turn around and look at me.

Her shoulders pull back as she pivots, turning her body so she's facing me. *Finally.*

Remaining impassive is impossible as I take in the girl I once thought I'd marry. She's more beautiful than ever with her porcelain skin, full lips, and intense brown eyes. I look ridiculous standing in front of her, not saying a word, but all I can do is tell myself to remember she's not mine.

"How are you?" I finally ask, shoving my hands in my pockets as a security measure. They've been sweating since the minute I realized she was really here.

"Good. Fancy seeing you here, of all places." She flinches as she says the words, a throwback to the fight that finally ended things between us for good. She takes a step toward me, her eyes wide. "I didn't mean it like that."

"Yeah, you did."

"Cross..."

Her eyes flood with a mix of emotions swirling so hard I can't separate them out. I could do what people do—pick out the one I want to see and roll with it—but I'm not most people, and I'm not a pussy.

"You look good, Cross," she whispers, quieter this time, studying me.

"You haven't changed a bit."

She shakes her head, running those ring-free fingers through her hair. "That's a nice thing to say. Total lie, but nice, anyway." She laughs.

"Why is that a lie?"

"Look at me."

"From where I'm standing, time couldn't have been any sweeter to you, Kallie girl." A smile tickles my lips as her cheeks flush. This is the girl I remember and, if I'm not careful, the one I'll once again be jacked up over in a heartbeat.

"Look at you being all charming."

"It's a new trick I picked up while you were gone. I figured I needed to round out my game a little."

"How's that working out for you?" She tries to play her question off like it's routine banter, but I know her too well. She's digging, prying, asking what I've been up to without having to ask.

"Win some, lose some," I say, looking her in the eye. Rocking back on my heel, I narrow my eyes. "What do you think?"

"About what?"

"Am I winning or losing right now?" My mouth fights the twitch of a smile crawling up my lips.

She takes a deep breath, steadying herself. "I'd say if we're taking into consideration the previous rounds, it's a split decision. This round doesn't look bad, but the ones before it weren't too pretty."

Trying to hide my amusement at this girl using, of all things, a boxing metaphor on me to describe our relationship, I shrug. "I don't think *all* the previous rounds were bad. I distinctly remember winning a couple of them. Hell, I thought I had the thing won a couple of rounds ago."

"You almost did," she says carefully, her voice steady now. "But that slip in the last round cost you the whole fight."

"I didn't slip," I insist, taking a step toward her. "I had a bad game plan."

"I can only score it as I see it."

There's a blip of pain in her eyes as her uncertainty fails to mask the wavering in her voice. The sound batters my heart, just like it did when she and I were together and I'd see a similar look on her face. I hate it.

We stand in the middle of Crave and don't say a word. The only sound is the shaky breaths escaping her sweet, full lips. A part of me wants to fight with her, tell her how stupid she was for walking out of my life and destroying everything I had planned for our future. Another part of me wants to toss her to the floor and fuck her so deeply, so completely that she remembers the connection and chemistry only we have together. Yet, there's another piece of me that wants to grab her and wrap my arms around her waist and hold her close if for nothing but to make sure she's all right.

"You said it's a split decision," I say, standing so close to her, our chests are almost touching. She smells of vanilla and the shampoo she always uses, the one in the red bottle. I fill my lungs with the scent of her and blow it out slowly. "Does that mean there's still a fight?"

She tucks another strand of hair behind her ear. "The bell rang on this fight a long time ago, Cross."

"Maybe the scorekeeper was wrong."

"Maybe—" She's cut off by the sound of Nora and Machlan behind me. She looks at the floor and takes a step back, like we've been caught doing something we shouldn't.

Looking over my shoulder, I shoot a glare at my best friend. "What's up, Machlan?"

"I hate to bother you two, but I gotta get this place ready to open. You can use my office, if you want."

"I think we're ready to go," Kallie says, peering around me. "You ready, Nora?"

"If you are."

"Kallie, wait." There's no denying the eagerness in my voice, but I'm too focused on not letting her out of here without some sort of commitment to worry about it.

She keeps her sights set on Nora. "What, Cross?"

"What are you doing tonight?" I ask. "Or tomorrow night?" My mind races through my calendar, trying to figure out on the fly how I'll rearrange my appointments if she takes me up on one of my offers.

"I'm pretty busy..."

"Oh, you are not." Machlan smirks, leaning against the bar.

"Stay out of this," she says, flashing him a look. "This has nothing to do with you, Mach."

"Everything that happens inside my bar has something to do with me," he teases. "So, let's cut the shit: you really have nothing to do but you're still pissed off about something that happened years ago. Sound about right?"

"Enough," I say, firing a warning shot at him.

He laughs. "Fine. Just thought I'd help you two get to the point. See you tomorrow, Nora?"

"Yup," she says before looking between Kallie and me. "I'll be outside."

My eyes lock with Kallie's as the door latches behind Nora. "Name the place and time and I'll make it happen."

"Make what happen?" She sighs.

"Coffee. Dinner. A fucking slice of watermelon from Dave's Farmstand, if that's what you want," I joke...kind of.

"Is that still open?" Her eyes sparkle, the easygoing Kallie I remember starting to come back. "How many watermelons did we eat from there over the years?"

"I think the two of us kept him busy."

"Do you remember when Peck tried to make his own watermelon moonshine?" She laughs. "He was sick for a week, and then you all were trying to find a nurse to check him out so you didn't have to tell his mom."

"I forgot about that." I chuckle. "He was sick as hell. Lance finally found a nurse somewhere."

"Leave it to Lance." She giggles, wiping a tear from her eye.

"We loaded Peck in the back of Walker's truck and met her at the Four-Way Bridge to get checked out. What a mess that was."

"Does Walker still have Daisy?" she asks, alluding to the big black pickup Walker has driven since his senior year of high school.

"I think Walker will drive Daisy until he dies. He loves that truck," I say, shaking my head. "But back to the watermelon—Dave closed it down a while back. His wife got put in a nursing home."

Kallie's face falls. "She was so sweet. That makes me sad."

"I see Dave sometimes over at Crank," I say, referring to Walker's car repair shop. "Ran into him at Goodman's gas station a couple of days ago too. He asked about you."

"Why would people ask you about me now?" She considers this for a long moment. "Doesn't that seem strange?"

"Maybe it seems perfectly normal." Unable to resist any longer, I cut the distance between us in half. With a calculated move, I raise a hand and touch the side of her face. She sucks in a breath, her skin warm and smooth under my calloused palm. "This seems perfectly normal too."

"Cross..." She pulls her cheek away, her chin dipping to her chest. "I can't with this."

"You're right," I say, stepping back. Her gaze shoots to mine, surprised etched on her pretty features. "This isn't the place. Meet me at the gym tonight at six. We'll grab something to eat and take a ride or go for a walk or sit on the mats and shoot the shit."

Before she can decline, I head for the door.

"Cross! I didn't say—"

The door shutting behind me as I walk outside cuts off the end of her sentence.

"She giving you a hard time?" Nora laughs.

"Never." I chuckle, shaking my head.

"I think she's a little shocked."

"One question," I say, turning around and walking backward toward my truck, the sun warming my face. "Did you know I was here?"

"Well, I knew Machlan wouldn't have my check until Monday, and I also know you drive the silver Dodge Ram parked right over there, so you figure out what I did and didn't know."

A laugh I haven't felt slip past my lips so easily in years bellows out. "Nora, I owe you one."

"Yes, you do."

Chapter Three

Kallie

"Do you still want to go to Peaches?" Nora asks. There's a forced easiness to her tone, like we just didn't walk all the way to the car and drive almost the entire way to my mother's house in silence.

"No."

Every step we took from the bar had me wanting to look over my shoulder in hopes of catching a glimpse of Cross. Every mile we pull away has me wanting to yell at Nora to turn around.

My head spins with the offer to see him again. My cheek sings with the memory of his touch. My heart aches as it absorbs the instructions from my brain to not forget the bad in favor of the good.

The endless partying with Machlan.

The two times I had to bail him out of jail for reckless driving and disorderly conduct.

Failure to take anything seriously or make a plan for the future.

A chill rips through me despite the warm summer sun.

"I really wanted a margarita," Nora says, turning toward my mother's house. "Are you sure you don't want to go to Peaches?"

"I'm not hungry."

"You're not hungry or you're mad at me? I'm really feeling like 'I'm not hungry' is a passive-aggressive and untrue response."

"I'm not mad at you," I say finally, watching the bright green grass roll by. "Although I know that was a setup."

"Maybe, maybe not."

"Don't lie to me." I laugh. "You totally set that up."

"What can it hurt?" She sighs, turning into the driveway. "I know it's none of my business, but..."

Her forehead is creased and her knuckles re-grip the steering wheel. Settling into the soft leather seat, I lean my head against the headrest. The adrenaline recedes, leaving me with a sluggish, almost hangover-style feeling in place of the excitement from a few minutes ago.

"He always asks about you," she says softly. "I never told you that because it felt like it didn't matter, but he does. Every time I see him, he says hello and then his features fall a little bit and he asks how you're doing." She glances at me over her shoulder. "He's not a bad guy, Kallie."

"I know he's not." I groan, closing my eyes. "He's not a bad person, he's just not someone I can be with." The words land on my own ears and my spirits fall. "And that sucks."

"Maybe he's not the guy you remember."

"Leopards don't change their spots, Nora," I say, unbuckling my seat belt and grabbing my purse. "Thanks for the ride."

"Call me tomorrow. Let's do lunch or something." She touches my shoulder. "I'm so glad you're back."

"Me too. Talk to you tomorrow."

Climbing out of the car, I shut the door. Nora honks the horn twice before pulling onto the street.

My mom's home sits in front of me, a little white square with dark green windows. There's a carport on one side that offers little protection from the wind in the winter, and my stomach twists that I've not been able to get it replaced yet.

"Someday," I mutter as I climb the stairs to the front door. It opens before I get to the top. "Hey, Mom."

"I thought I heard a car out here. I'm not used to having visitors." She smiles, letting me by. "Did you have fun with Nora, honey?"

"Yeah. We walked around town, and I talked to Ruby at the library. I can't believe she's still alive."

"Kallie Rae!" She laughs as she follows me to the kitchen. Pictures of me from various ages line the walls of the hallway. "See anyone else?"

"Machlan."

"How is he?" she presses.

"Good."

Pulling out a chair, she drops into the seat. "I saw him a few weeks ago at the post office. Good-looking boy."

"He's all right," I say, shaking my head.

"All right? Sometimes I'm not sure you're my child." She chuckles. "If I were your age, I'd have snapped up one of those men in a heartbeat."

Turning away, I look out the window over the sink. The small back yard is tidy, her trash and recycling cans in a neat line by the gate. My old brown swing set still sits by the fence in the back, and the picnic table where I had dozens of chats with my friends growing up is in need of a good dose of paint.

All of these things are better topics than dating, or Machlan, or the one I know is coming: Cross.

My mother loved him like he was her son. She made sure he had homemade macaroni and cheese when he was over for dinner and always had his favorite soda in the fridge. When we broke up, she supported me, but I know down deep, she wishes things had worked out.

Maybe I wish that too.

Maybe wishes are pointless.

"We could get some paint tomorrow and redo the picnic table," I say.

"I wouldn't be able to move for a week."

The room gets quiet. The quieter it gets, the louder I hear my heartbeat.

"I'm supposed to go to my women's club meeting this evening with Dina. Do you want to go?" she asks. "Or did you make plans with Nora?"

Glancing at the clock, I see I have an hour until Cross asked me to meet him. My chest rises and falls, my fingers tapping on the counter.

"Well, you're invited if you want to come." She groans, getting out of the chair. "I'm leaving in about an hour. Let me know if you want to join, honey."

Her steps get softer as she pads down the hallway, and I'm left standing in the kitchen with nothing but a decision to be made.

KALLIE

SLIPPING on a pair of cotton shorts and a tank top after my shower, I make my way into the living room. The hardwood floor creaks as I traverse the room and plop unceremoniously onto the plaid sofa. The remote is on the other side of the room and I don't have the energy to get it. Besides, the quiet is something I kind of love.

Living in the city made me forget what silence really is. There are no tires squealing or sirens blaring, just an occasional dog barking from the house across the street.

The room is filled with mementos of my life that could only be collected by a mother. A frame hangs to the right with every school picture I ever took. An art piece I created in fifth grade is propped up on a bookshelf, and a trinket we bought on a vacation at Lake Michigan sits next to the television. Each one of those things has a memory of Cross tied to it.

My heart sinks as I squirm on the sofa. There's a hole in my chest that seems to have reopened since I pulled back into Linton, a big, gaping crevice that I was able to fill well enough in Indiana with work and hobbies and remembering things how I chose to remember them, but now? It's not that easy.

I had to force myself to get into the bath and shave my legs so I wouldn't run to the gym to see him on a whim. I washed my hair twice and then used a conditioning mask just to kill time. By the time I got out, I knew he would be gone.

A low rumble from the other side of the wall sounds through the air. Swinging my legs to the floor, I sit up and listen. It trails to the front of the house and stops. There's a long pause, then a squeak, and then it starts again. Jumping up and heading to the front window, I peer out of the curtains.

My breathing halts, my hands shaking as they hold the lace fabric out of the way.

Cross is dragging my mother's trash can from the back of the house to the street. He lines it up next to another one and brushes his hands off. Without looking up at me, he disappears into the back yard again.

"What the hell?" I whisper, dropping the curtain.

Finding my sandals, I slip them on and scurry to the kitchen door. When I step into the yard, he's latching a cable through the handles on the doors of the shed in the back corner.

Wearing a pair of grey jogging pants and a red t-shirt, he looks tall and lean and as broad as the shed. A darkened spot between his shoulder blades flexes and pulls as he works the cable. The fabric pulls tight along his muscles, giving me an idea of their definition and making my knees weak.

He turns around abruptly, catching us both off guard.

"Hey," he says, stopping in his tracks.

"What are you doing here?"

There's a smile that flashes briefly, but it doesn't give me the warm fuzzies. "I'm not here to bother you, if that's what you're thinking."

"Cross..." A lump takes root in my throat as I step across the soft grass. Sitting on top of the picnic table, I look at him still standing by the shed, just a few feet away.

So many summers we hung out back here in a swimming pool that's since been removed. We played badminton when I went through an obsessive stage with that game and watched the fireworks from a big trampoline we sold in a yard sale the summer before I left.

Our first kiss took place back here under the oak tree, and we buried Fluffy, my poodle, together near the back fence.

All of this hits me like a flood as my gaze locks with his, and when he speaks, the tone of his voice makes me think maybe it hit him too.

"I take your mom's trash to the road every week. While I'm here, I do some odds and ends I see she needs done. It's not a big deal," he says softly.

My heart slams against my ribcage, knocking the wind out of me. "You do? Since when?"

"I've done this for a long time, Kallie. It's no big deal."

"But...why? Why would you do this?"

His shoulders rise and fall. He rocks back on his heels, twisting his lips together. "What does it matter?"

"I had no idea," I say, forcing a swallow.

"I asked her not to tell you." He heads toward the gate, taking a curved path so he doesn't get too close to me. "Believe it or not, I'm not a bad guy."

"Cross, wait," I say, jumping off the table. The words are out of my mouth before I even know I've said them, and I have no idea what to follow them up with. There are so many things in my brain competing for a chance to roll off my tongue, and I know I better weigh them all carefully before I choose a thought I don't want shared.

He turns to face me, his brows lifted toward the sky. "What?"

Sucking in a breath, I plead with my brain to use the right filter and go for it. "I know you aren't a bad guy."

He averts his jade eyes, settling his gaze somewhere in the distance. I take the opportunity to study him without the usual glare of a computer screen.

His jawline is more defined, the angle visible even under the day-old scruff. His lashes are thicker and darker, outlining the set of eyes that seem to have seen so much and, when they turn back to find mine, it causes me to jump. He tries not to notice, but his sly smile gives it away.

"Sorry," I grumble, fiddling with a strand of hair.

"Let's flip the script for a minute and you tell me why you moved back to Linton."

Clearing my throat, I pause. "Well, my old boss seems to be heading to jail for a while. Skylar moved away so Mom was alone, and it's easier to start again here than in Indy."

He doesn't blink.

"What?" I ask, furrowing a brow at his lack of a reaction.

"Just waiting for you to tell the truth."

"Um, I did." On instinct, I tilt my head at him, annoyed.

"Uh, ya didn't."

"Whatever," I huff, walking away from him. I stop at the fence and look over the top at the setting sun, feeling a little peace fall over me. The sky is painted a beautiful mosaic of pinks and purples, like a painting done by a master artist. "It's beautiful, isn't it?"

His hand touches the small of my back as he steps beside me. Suddenly, the sky isn't on my radar anymore. All I can focus on is how his hand feels on me, how every nerve is acutely aware of his presence and the pull of his body on mine.

"It is beautiful out here tonight," he says softly, "and the sky is pretty too."

My cheeks flush as I look at him. "You really can turn on that charm, huh?"

"I don't try it too often, but I'm hoping it works out for me today."

"Why are you helping my mom, Cross?"

"Well, the way I see it," he says, leaning on the rail, "she took care of me for a lot of years when I needed it. She hemmed my baseball pants every year, went to bat for me when Mr. Varian suspended me my junior year...and how many nights did she have something hot and ready for me to eat after practice?"

"A lot." I smile. "How many times did she make corn because you liked it and not green beans because you didn't? I hated you because green beans are my favorite."

We exchange a laugh that's easy and carefree, like two friends on a level most people never ascend to. Once our voices have died down, he pulls away and looks me in the eye. "For the record, I've never hated you."

I don't know what to say to that, but even if I did, it wouldn't matter. The searing gaze penetrating mine halts any words from flowing through my lips.

"I want you to know that..." His head dips, his sneaker running back and forth across the lawn. "I take responsibility for everything that happened between us."

"Cross—"

"No, it's my fault. I was the shithead who couldn't get my life together." He raises his eyes, a glimmer in the jade orbs. "I admire you."

"Me?" I snort. "Why?"

"You were smart enough to know your worth." He lays a hand over mine, his palm hot and heavy and swamping mine in size. I can't look away from them, his tanned skin sitting atop mine. "You taught me a lot, made me who I am, in a roundabout, heartbreaking kind of way." He chuckles.

"Aren't you full of surprises?" I ask, his words wrapping around my chest and squeezing it so tight I can barely breathe.

"There's a lot you don't know about me."

"Strangely, I believe that."

He twists around and leans against the fence. "Want to talk? Ask questions? Kiss me?"

"No." I laugh, taking a step back for my own good. "I just got out of a job that had federal investigators asking me a million questions, and then I packed up my things and moved home. I don't need any more complications for a minute."

"Maybe I won't complicate it." He shoots me a grin that melts me from the inside out.

Pointing a finger his way, I giggle. "You always do."

"How's that?"

"That grin—it complicates everything, every time."

It stretches across his face, reaching from ear to ear, and it pulls mine right along with it. We stand in the setting sun, grinning at each other like two kids as my mother wanders into the back yard.

"What are you kids doing out here?"

My entire body sags at the interruption as Cross snickers.

"Just taking the garbage to the road, Brenda."

"Looks to me like you were doing more than that, Mr. Jacobs."

"Oh, Mom, hush."

Her face lights up like a Christmas tree. "I just want to say seeing you two together makes this old woman's heart feel full. Reminds me of old times, my two kids happy and together."

"That sounds disgusting and illegal," I say as I laugh.

"Good thing I'm not known for my law-abiding tendencies," Cross chimes in, looking at me out of the corner of this eye.

Mom and I laugh as I punch him in the arm. He feigns injury, shaking his bicep back and forth.

"Stop it," I say, shaking my head.

"You have a terrible punch. It's embarrassing."

"What? If that's embarrassing, it's your fault."

"How do you figure?" That grin still plays on his lips.

"You're the one who taught me to punch!"

"Oh, no," he says, pressing his lips together. "I didn't teach you that. Don't blame that crap on me." He captures my gaze, his eyes sparkling. "If you want me to teach you *again*, I'm happy to."

"I don't really punch people a lot."

"Never know," he teases. "You wouldn't want to rest on those laurels."

"You're an ass."

He pretends to consider this as he circles me and heads to the gate. "Trash is out, Brenda. Fixed the latch on the shed—try not to break it again."

"I'll do my best," she promises. "Want to come in for dinner? I brought home Carlson's."

He stops at the gate and looks at me over his shoulder. My heart skips a beat as I watch him make up his mind. I wish I could ask him to stay, wish I could enjoy our banter for a little while longer, but as he looks back at my mother, I know I'm better off if he says no.

"I have a private session in fifteen minutes. I better go, but thanks for the offer." With a final look at me, he opens the gate. "See ya around, Kallie girl."

"Good night, Cross."

Chapter Four

Cross

A BEER SLIDES ACROSS THE BAR IN FRONT OF ME, STOPPING ONLY WHEN IT hits a set of hands at the end. Machlan's brother, Walker, snaps it up and shoots me a curious look.

"How's it goin'?" he asks, sitting on the stool next to me.

"It's goin'."

"That good, huh?" He takes a long, steady gulp of alcohol before letting the bottle plunk against the wooden bar top. "Peck took a last-minute job at the shop tonight and I'm just getting out of there."

"Should've left him there with it," I offer.

"Yeah, but he had to jack this piece of shit up in the air and, my luck, I leave and it falls on him or something." Giving me a frustrated glance, he takes another drink. "In retrospect, may not have been a terrible idea."

Peeling at the label of my own bottle, I feign interest in the television. It does no good.

"Not that I give a fuck, but what's wrong?" Walker asks.

"Not a damn thing you want to hear about."

"That's true, and I don't even know what it is." He grins. "But, Machlan is keeping his distance, so that means it might be interesting."

"It's not."

His chest rumbles with a silent chuckle before downing the rest of his brew. I consider getting up and heading to the pool tables in the back just to get some privacy. If I thought it would actually work, I'd try it, but it won't—not with this bunch.

Machlan and I grew up with his brothers, Walker and Lance, and their cousins, Peck and Vincent. We were all close in age and have been tight since preschool.

If I get up and head to the back, Walker will signal Machlan over and he'll tell him what's going on. Walker will rib me for a minute, and if I'm lucky, Peck and Lance won't join in. Walker will then proceed to tell me I'm a dumbass while giving me some token of advice.

The problem? I don't need advice. I need a damn smack to the side of the head.

Running my hand down my face, frustration jumps back into the driver's seat of my life. My stomach twists, sloshing the two beers I've nursed since I came in this evening.

"Okay, I won't play dumb. I know Kallie's back," Walker says, stopping for a moment to acknowledge a woman who stopped to whisper something in his ear. Once she's gone, he turns back to me, but now he's sidetracked. "That's the problem with the world right there."

My gaze trails after the girl I've seen work in the post office then I refocus it on Walker. "What? Easy pieces of ass with great legs?"

"Yup." He motions for Machlan to bring him another beer. "Those girls ruin it for everyone."

"I don't follow you."

"Good idea," Peck says, slipping onto the stool on the other side of Walker. "Don't follow him. This fucker will lead you astray."

"Seriously?" Walker looks at his cousin out of the corner of his eye. "When have I led anyone astray?"

"I think I need to join this conversation," Machlan says, handing Walker a beer. "When has Walker led anyone astray? What about the time you added a little engine to my skateboard and the thing bolted then tossed me off the ramp you built in the back yard and I broke my collarbone?"

"That was your fault." Walker laughs. "Your balance is shit. I had forgotten about that." He scratches his chin. "You know, that was really a good concept."

"I remember that day," I say, looking at Machlan. "I think my last words to you were 'This is not a good id—' I didn't even get 'idea' out before you were on your ass."

"Face," Peck inserts. "I think he was on his face, legs kicking in the air."

"Which, in a really weird way, takes us back to pieces of ass with great legs," I say, circling back to the original point. "How is that the ruination of the world?"

"Whoever said that, I agree completely," Machlan adds, shoving off the counter. "The better the ass and legs, the leerier I am of a woman. You get those chunky thighs around your face and—*boom!* The next thing you know there's a pink toothbrush next to yours in the bathroom. It's dumb as hell."

Walker laughs. "So is Kallie's toothbrush back in your bathroom, Cross?"

Peck's eyes widen, but he wisely doesn't say anything. Instead, he hops the bar and rummages through the beer cooler. Machlan lectures him on the law, that he can't be on that side of the bar without a license, but Peck doesn't listen. He never does.

"You saw her," Walker states.

"Yeah."

"And?"

I shrug. Twisting the bottle in my hands, I realize Walker may be the best person in the world to get advice from about this after all. "Fine. I saw her today. We talked for a few minutes and then I saw her again when I went by to do a few things for Brenda."

"You have plans to see her again?"

"I don't know. I'd like to. I tried to cast out some bait, but I'm not sure she took it."

He tips back the new bottle, his eyes focused on the television. A vein in his temple pops, and I wonder what he's going to say. It could be anything with this guy. Whatever it is, it'll be what he believes to be the truth. That's all you get from Walker Gibson.

"Well, in my humble opinion, I say don't," he says.

The finality in his tone irks me. "What do you mean?"

"Look, I know you liked her—hell, we all did. She was a cool girl and you spent your entire adolescence glued to her hip. Trust me," he says, staring off into space, "I get that. You have history with her like you never will with anyone else."

"It's not that..."

"It is." He turns his attention back to me. "But don't do that. She left you once. I know that makes me an asshole to say it bluntly like that, but she did it, not me. You tossed that line out there tonight and she didn't take it. That's enough for me right there. Fuck her," he says, bringing the bottle back to his lips.

My jaw sets, the pulsing almost cracking my back teeth. "Easy there."

Peck leans on the countertop and looks at Walker and then at me. "Don't listen to him unless it has an engine and weighs at least a ton."

"Just offering my opinion," Walker says, getting up. He takes his drinks and meanders toward the back of the bar.

"Listen," Peck says, looking at me with his brows tugged together, "he's wrong."

"How the hell do you know?"

"Because my balls aren't the ones that ache so bad I can't see straight." He grins.

"If I were giving myself advice, I'd say to forget it too," I admit. "I see Walker's point, but then I think about how many nights I go to bed wondering where she is and how often I miss her. Then it seems stupid to pretend I don't at least want to get to know her again."

"You've answered your own problem."

"How do you figure?"

Peck shakes his head, downing half his bottle. Wiping his mouth with the back of his hand, he sighs. "You said you could pretend, which means..."

"Yeah..."

"You have two options here," he declares. "You can either let this thing go or you can see what you can make out of it. If you pick option one, get over it. You'll have to, but because I know your ass and know you won't just get over it because you haven't since that fight outside of Crave years ago, option two should come with a lot of consideration. You feel me?"

"I feel you."

"Good. Now that's done, I'm going to see what kind of trouble I can get into tonight." He winks before disappearing into the growing crowd of bodies behind me.

I sit for a long while, returning hellos and chiming in to basic chitchat when required. All the while, my mind is replaying the interactions with Kallie from today. With every second that goes by, I feel a burn in my gut grow hotter.

Leaning forward, I grab my wallet out of my pocket and find a twenty. I put it on the counter and set my beer on top of it. "Hey, Mach! I'm out of here," I say, nodding to the money.

"Tell her I said hi." He grins.

"Fuck off. I'm not going to see her." I look down at the money and then back up at him again. "Maybe tomorrow after work."

Machlan laughs. "Make some time in that busy schedule of yours for me. I want to talk business."

"Will do. Later."

"Later."

Chapter Five

Kallie

"You shouldn't be doing this, Kallie." Rolling my eyes as I head across the parking lot, I set my sights on the building nestled between the laundromat and a secondhand store. "Now I'm talking to myself—totally losing it."

My feet stop and I stand on the edge of the curb, peering into the windows of the gym. The early morning sunlight shines through the glass. Cross is standing in the middle of a stretch of blue mats in a sleeveless shirt and a pair of basketball shorts. A short, caramel-haired woman in all spandex stands in front of him. She's facing me, her hands running through the air as she tells Cross a story. He's watching her, his arms folded in front of him, one eyebrow cocked in the air.

My skin suddenly feels too tight, too unforgiving as I try to draw air into my lungs. When her hand rests on the curve of his bicep, I squeeze my car keys so hard that the alarm goes off behind me.

"Shit!" I mumble, twisting around and shoving the keyring toward the parking lot. "Stop it. Stop it!" Pressing the button repeatedly, the frantic beeping finally stops. "Sorry," I call out to a woman and her child as they climb into the car next to mine. She gives me a look like I'm crazy before speeding off.

I take a deep breath as I feel a gaze on my back. Turning around, I see Cross and the woman in the gym are watching me. I contemplate saving some face and fleeing, but Cross is stalking toward me before I can make a break for it.

He shoves the door open, the muscles in his arms flexing as he holds it. "You all right out here?"

"Yeah." I wince, tucking my keys in my pocket. "My alarm is faulty. Probably a recall or something."

"I bet." He tries to hide his amusement, but fails. "Wanna come in? I mean, I'm assuming you weren't coming this way to do laundry."

Blushing, I walk past him and into the gym.

"Do you know Megan McCarter?" he asks.

"I don't think so. I'm Kallie Welch. Nice to meet you."

"You too," she says in a way that lets me know she doesn't think there's anything nice about meeting me at all.

"Wait, McCarter? Are you related to Molly?"

"She's my older sister," she says, eyes glued to Cross. "Want to show me that move one more time? I think I forgot it already."

"If you forgot it already, you aren't going to remember it next week either," he replies. "I think that's it for us today. Good work."

"I..." She looks at me, then back at Cross. "See you next week."

We wait as she takes her time gathering her things, including a glittery pink water bottle, and heads out. Once the room is free of her noxious perfume, Cross speaks.

"What brought you down here?"

It's the question I asked myself on the car ride here, the one I still haven't answered. All I know is I thought of him all evening and dreamed of him last night. There was no awkwardness in my dream, no feelings of anything other than happiness. I woke up wondering how much of that was just the dream and how much of that was reality. It was hard to tell the two apart.

Shrugging, I look around the room. One half is set up like a gym with treadmills and free weights, and the other has mats and a makeshift boxing ring elevated in the corner. The walls are white with posters of motivational sayings hanging here and there. It's impressive.

"Guess I just wanted to see what you were up to," I say finally. "Is this place yours?"

"Yeah. I opened it a couple of years ago. Have another one in Fairview too."

"Really?" Turning a small circle, I take in every little detail. "That's amazing. Is it just a gym?"

"Just a gym." He snorts, heading to the mats. "It's definitely not *just* a gym, thank you."

"How do I know?"

"You don't, until you ask." He winks. "It *is* a gym. People pay a membership fee to use the facilities, but I also train a couple of amateur fighters and have a boxing program for kids. That's really my favorite thing. They love it for the love of the art, you know? Not because they can whip ass in a bar or flex around town."

"You used to do both things," I point out, moseying my way toward him.

Leaning against a wall, his face sobers. "I did. I still do, if it's warranted, but that's not what I'm about anymore."

The way he speaks the words, the level of sincerity in his tone...it has my heart swelling in my chest. It's a reminder that I don't quite know this man anymore and it raises a host of questions, including how different he just may be now than he was when I left.

"What are you about these days, Cross?"

"I've settled down some, I suppose. Don't interface with the law much these days." He grins. "I work a lot, either here or over at the Fairview gym. I do some online coaching and personal training sessions."

"Like with Megan?"

He shoves off the wall, a twinkle in his eye. "Like Megan," he goads. "Did that bother you?"

"What? Megan? No," I insist, brushing it off. "Why would it?"

"Just an inkling."

"Your inkling would be wrong. How is it my place to have any feelings about what you do in your business?"

"It's not."

It's a simple statement, two little words that pack so much of a punch. *It's not.* It's not the words that irritate me so much; it's the reason for needing them. Even as I stand here inside his gym, even though I feel this link to Cross and have since I saw him yesterday inside Crave, he's nothing more to me than somebody I used to know.

"I don't train many women," he says, picking up a couple of towels along the mats. "I only agreed to three sessions with Megan because someone bought them for her birthday. She has one more next week and then it's over."

"You aren't training her any more than that?"

"Nah. She knows it. It's ridiculous, really. She doesn't want to know how to box any more than I want to know how to bake a cake."

Laughing at his analogy, I grab a few dumbbells off the floor and put them back in the rack. "I'm glad you found something to do with your life that makes you happy. I always worried you'd float around and get stuck doing something you hated."

"Come on," he teases. "You were really worried I'd end up in jail or on your couch."

"True." I giggle, turning to face him. "But I like this version of you, all grown up."

"Well..." He blows out a breath. "You can thank yourself for that. If you'd have stayed here, I don't think I ever would've realized what a punk I was."

"You weren't a punk."

"I was. I did whatever I wanted and had no plan for going anywhere. Then you left and I realized..." He looks at me and then at the floor. "I realized I'd already lost the best thing that would ever happen to me."

There isn't a reply to that. I just hold a breath and watch his beautiful eyes soften.

"So," he goes on, "one night I decided I was going to do something with myself, and if you ever came back, maybe I could show you I wasn't a loser."

"What if I never came back?"

"Honestly? I'd have been a little relieved.

"Gee, thanks."

"What?" He chuckles, motioning for me to follow him. "Is it wrong that I would've found relief in knowing I wouldn't be falling in love again?"

I stop walking. "What if I did come back?"

He pauses too and turns around. Running a hand through his thick, silky locks, his cheeks redden. "Then I'd fight like hell to get you back."

"You're just being charming again," I whisper, knowing it's a lie as soon as I say it. There's no denying the stripped-down emotion on his face, the crinkle in his forehead just between his eyes. The corners of his lips flicker, almost pulling into a smile, but not quite.

"Come on," he says, turning away. "Let's teach you how to throw a punch."

Chapter Six

Cross

It's a gamble, a big risk, one I'm not entirely sure is going to pay off, but one I feel absolutely sure about making.

Taking the steps two at a time, I press my finger on the doorbell. Footsteps fall against the hardwood floors on the other side before the door pulls open.

My chest fills like it does every time I see Kallie. I fight the stupid smile that plays on my lips, but it's no use—I'm grinning like a fucking loon.

"Hey," she says, her fingers playing at the hem of her shirt. "What are you doing here?"

"Well, I was driving by Carlson's a bit ago and saw they had Cobb salad on the sign. I thought maybe we could grab a bite to eat."

"You remember that I like Cobb salad?"

"With extra avocado and bacon, no egg, right?"

Her eyes light up as she grins. "Yeah." She laughs. "That's right."

"So, wanna go?"

She looks over her shoulder before turning her attention back to me. "Um, sure. Let me get my shoes and purse and I'll meet you outside, okay?"

"Sounds good."

In a few minutes, we're sitting in the cab of my pickup and heading down the road.

"My shoulders are sore," she says, working her arm in a circle. "How do you punch all day and still have use of your extremities?"

"You get used to it. Do it long enough and your muscles get built up."

"That explains a lot."

I look at her quickly before turning my attention back to the road. "That explains what?"

"Your arms," she gushes, wrapping a hand around my bicep. "They're ridiculous, Cross, and your back. Is that from boxing?"

"Been checking me out?" I love that she's looked hard enough to take notice.

"No. Well, yeah." She smirks. "It's kind of hard not to. You look good."

"And here I thought it was my charm drawing you in."

She smacks my arm before pulling her hand away. "Your charm is better, but it's still not your forte."

"So you only want me for my body? That's what you're saying?" I joke.

"No!"

"I mean, it's okay. I have no problem being wanted for my body—none. I'll strip right now if it'll help."

"You're too much."

Chuckling, I pull the truck into the parking lot of Carlson's. We climb out and meet at the front then, without thinking, I take her hand in mine. Her small palm is delicate and fits inside mine like it was designed for this purpose alone. I expect her to pull it away, but much to my surprise, she just looks up at me and smiles.

Once inside, we take a seat next to the front windows. Before I can get a word out, Veronica is halfway across the building. "Kallie Welch!" she squeals. "I haven't seen you in ages!"

"Hi, Veronica." Kallie gets to her feet and greets Veronica with a hug. "How are you?"

"Better now that I've seen you," she says as Kallie settles back in. "Where have you been? Are you home now?"

"Yeah, I'm home now. Cross saw you had Cobb salad on the menu for today and picked me up."

Veronica raises a brow. "I see. You and Cross back together, huh?"

"Oh, no," Kallie replies quickly, shaking her head. "No, not like that."

"And why not? Have you seen this boy lately? He's a catch, Kal. Every girl in town has tried their hand with this one."

"Should I walk away for a while? Because this is a little awkward with me sitting right here." I chuckle.

"Every girl, huh?" Kallie puts her face in her hands and watches me. "Do tell."

Shaking my head, I grab a menu out of the holder and flip my attention to the words on the plastic. "I'll have a ham and Swiss on sourdough, cheddar and sour cream chips, and a pop. Kallie?"

"Cobb salad and a water."

Veronica disappears into the back after whispering into Kallie's ear. Once she's gone, I breathe a sigh of relief. "So..."

"So..." she says, taking my menu and sliding it back in its spot. "Did you have a lot of clients today?"

"None as fun as you," I say with a wink.

"Oh, I bet. I was a barrel of fun."

"What did you do today?" I ask, watching the sun stream onto her face. It creates a halo effect around her blonde hair, which seems fitting.

"After I left you, I had lunch with Nora. Ran into Peck at Goodman's—he hasn't changed a bit."

"Nope. He's the same thirteen-year-old boy he always was."

She laughs, relaxing back in her seat. "I hope he never changes. He's so sweet and kind and handsome."

"Do I have competition?"

She doesn't answer, just rolls her eyes.

Plates of food are set down in front of us, Veronica making small talk with Kallie about her mother and once upon a time when Kallie worked at Carlson's. I don't touch my sandwich. Instead, I watch the girl in front of me act like she hasn't been gone a day. On the other hand, it seems like she's a completely different person.

Her old soul is still there; that hasn't changed. It's one of the first things I fell in love with. Her ability to think clearly and make good, solid choices was something I couldn't do, and it drew me in like a magnet. It didn't hurt that she was gorgeous, made straight As, and was the captain of the cheerleading team.

"What?" she asks, catching me staring.

"I was just thinking about you."

She stabs a chunk of avocado and pops it in her mouth. "What about me?"

"Wondering why you really came home."

She chews slowly, as if biding her time. The lines around her eyes crease as she considers her response. "I told you," she says, pausing to take a drink of water. "My job got a little crazy and Sky moved. It was the right time."

"That's not true."

"How do you know?"

Setting my fork down on the side of my plate, I rest my elbows on the table. "You don't have to tell me anything you don't want to. I don't care, as long as you're safe and you're here. That's all that really matters."

"I'm fine, Cross. Safe and here," she says, extending her arms to the side as if to say, *Look! Here we are!* "Maybe I just..." Her arms fall to her sides and she takes a gulp of air. "Maybe I got tired."

My heart twists in my chest and I reach for her hand. She allows me to take it. I turn it over, palm up, and press my thumb in the middle.

"I'm not complaining," she says quietly. "I don't want it to come across as a pity party, but I'm just *tired*. I've worked my ass off since I was fifteen years old."

"I know. No one can ever say you're a slacker."

"Not with a straight face." She sighs. "I loved my job in Indy. It was exciting and challenging and something different every day. When my boss was indicted, it shook me to the core. I had no idea he was doing anything wrong," she insists. "All of a sudden, what little time I did have was spent with investigators, telling them everything I knew so I didn't get in trouble too." She takes a napkin off the table and dots the corner of her eye. "I couldn't eat, couldn't sleep. My stomach was in knots. I remember sitting on my bed one night at three AM and just thinking, 'Why am I doing this?'"

Squeezing her hand, it takes everything I have in me not to bolt around the table and sweep her up in my arms.

Her chin dips down as she removes her hand from beneath mine. I want to snatch it back up, pull her over the table and onto my lap, and kiss the hell out of her.

As I watch her mind go elsewhere, mine goes back to the original question. "That all makes total sense," I say carefully. "But it's not enough to make you uproot your life."

She lifts a brow.

"It's not," I insist. "I know you. Something else happened. What was it?"

Leaning back in her seat, she shakes her head. "Everyone else just took the story and ran with it. Why can't you?"

"Because I know you?" I offer, suppressing a chuckle. "Because that look in your eyes wasn't put there by some boss who did something stupid and caused all these problems."

She watches me for a long moment, the internal war she fighting plain as day on her face. Finally, she rushes out a breath and leans forward. "My boyfriend cheated on me, okay?"

"Boyfriend?" I deadpan.

"Ex-boyfriend," she corrects. "Look, it's not a big deal. Yeah, it bruised my ego a little but—"

"I'd love to see the girl he cheated on you with." I laugh, not even trying to hide my amusement. "Or maybe it was a guy—that would make more sense."

"Cross!"

"I mean it. There's not a woman better than you in the entire world. Maybe there's a guy." I shrug. "I wouldn't know because I'm not looking over there."

"But you're looking at women?"

"Don't distract me," I admonish, wagging a finger in the air. "That's not what we're discussing."

"Maybe it's what I want to discuss."

"Too fucking bad." I grin. "So some asshole broke your heart?"

A shadow drifts across her face as her features soften. "That's true, but that was a few years ago."

I shouldn't want to smile at that, but I do anyway. It should incense me that I broke her heart, but I've had a few years to deal with that guilt. All I can process from that sentence is what I can read between the lines, and that shit makes me happy.

She wasn't in love with him.

"Yeah, well, you know what they say." I shrug.

"What's that?"

"If you break something, it's your responsibility to fix it."

"If you break something, you're generally not trusted with it again," she tosses back.

"Oh, come on," I scoff. "That's like telling a man he's not allowed to eat off the good china because he broke a plate when he was a baby."

She makes a face. "That's a terrible analogy."

"Whatever. You know what I mean, and I know just what you need tonight."

"I bet you do," she says, narrowing her eyes. "One track mind, Cross?"

Grinning, I lean forward. "I think we have two different things we're thinking of, but by the look in your eye, I'm more than happy to go with yours."

"What are you thinking?"

Picking up my sandwich, I take a bite. "Eat up. Then I'll show you."

Chapter Seven

Kallie

"Oh my God," I squeal, bouncing in the seat of Cross's truck. "Storybook Village! I thought they shut this place down!"

The truck slides into a spot in front of a cutout of a giant shoe. I take in the ducks waddling around and the smell of manure as the engine stops.

"They did," Cross says. "I think it was down when you left."

"It was. It hadn't been open for a few years."

"Well, this guy named Charlie bought it and opened it back up, last summer, I think. I thought maybe we could play a round of putt-putt."

Like a kid on Christmas morning, I clap my hands. "You're going down, Cross."

"We'll see, Kallie girl."

We get out of the truck and enter through the little doorway where the frame around it is painted like a pirate ship. This was where our class had our senior pictures taken because we'd all spent so much time here in the summers growing up.

Storybook Village was a small-town version of an amusement park. The only ride was a little train Paul would start up when enough people were visiting, and it took you on a tour of the entire setup.

Growing up, this was as good as going to a far-off country. There were peacocks and giraffes, a bear and a tiger. I could spend all day milling around, feeding the ducks handfuls of corn, then ending the day with a round of mini golf.

"Nice to see you, Cross," an older lady says as we enter the little check-in area.

"How are you, Maggie?"

"Good, honey. I'm good. What can I do for you?"

"Two for a round of putt-putt," he says, placing a twenty on the desk. "I'm gonna show this girl how it's done, Mags."

"Whatever," I scoff, picking out a pink ball. "He doesn't know what's about to hit him."

Maggie laughs candidly as she sorts through a bag of change. Handing Cross the difference, she tells us to grab our equipment and start through the door on the left.

The afternoon sun is warm as we step into the golfing area, and a giant plastic giraffe greets us.

"Do you remember when Peck tried to climb up the legs and get a picture taken on its back?" I laugh. "I thought old man Paul was going to have a heart attack."

"I forgot about that. Do you remember when Machlan tried to capture a peacock? And it trashed the hell out of his arm?" Cross laughs. "Apparently it was mating season and the male thought he was competition for his woman."

We exchange smiles as I set my ball on the little circle to start. One crack of the club and it misses the blade of a giant pinwheel, making it to the other side through a little tunnel. With one more putt, I'm in the cup.

"Beat that," I say, marking me down for two strokes.

He takes his green ball and sets it on the tee. The club looks so tiny in his hands, and he almost bends in half to take a swing. Once he does, the ball rips through the tunnel, runs a circle around the rim of the cup, and sinks in.

"Dammit." Narrowing my eyes, I head to the second hole. "You got lucky."

Lining up my ball, I get into position to hit it. Before I do, I feel him behind me. My heart flutters in my chest like it has the wings of a butterfly. Holding my breath, I wait as I feel his proximity grow near, my body pulled to his like there's an invisible wire connecting us, reeling me in.

"You're right," he whispers, his breath hot against the shell of my ear. "I did get lucky."

Instinctively, I sag backward, my back resting against his chest. It takes about half a second for his arms to wrap around my waist, pulling me into him. His face finds the crook of my neck and he breathes in, the air trickling over my sensitive skin and making me shiver.

The air is saturated with the scent of his cologne, infiltrating my senses and making me lightheaded. I grab his arms where they're locked at my belly to steady myself. His forearms are roped, thick with muscle, his skin coarse against my fingers.

A flood of emotions comes raring back. Suddenly, I'm reminded of the uncertainty of him staying out all night with Machlan, of being rumored to be with another girl every other Friday night, of him showing up late for everything and his failure to get a job.

Cross sweeps the hair off the back of my neck and presses a soft kiss just above my shoulder.

"Cross?"

"Yeah?"

"Can I trust you?"

He presses another kiss to the same spot before raising his face and resting his chin on the top of my head. "You can never go by what someone says to that question, Kal. You have to go with your gut."

It's the right answer, but it's no help. I don't know what in the world my gut is saying. I can hear my brain, feel my heart, experience the throb between my legs, but my gut? No clue.

He moves slightly behind me, just enough so his hardness presses into my back. I gulp, the length rock solid as he stills.

Everything picks up pace, my sensations overloading as I run my hands up his forearms and close my eyes. There's not a thing about this moment that feels wrong or out of place, not one single thing that screams at me to stop or reconsider.

"How dedicated are you to finishing this game of golf?" I ask, subtly pressing my ass against him.

"All I want is a hole in one."

Spinning around, I catch the grin on his lips. "That's a terrible line."

"Can't win 'em all." He laughs. "Ready to get out of here?"

"Depends on where we're going."

His gaze drags down my body, blazing a trail as he works his way back up to my eyes. Licking his lips, he takes the club out of my hands. "My house is closer."

"What are we waiting for?"

KALLIE

THE DOOR CREAKS as Cross twists the knob and presses it open. We enter, stepping into a little foyer that has dark hardwood floors and beige walls. He's decorated the place sparsely, with few pictures and little else.

"Live here long?" I ask, looking at the three little images framed near the doorway to the living room. There's one of him and Machlan on their high school graduation day, another of him and the Gibson boys at Bluebird Hill in the middle of winter. The last one is of himself, one hand raised in the air at a boxing match. "I remember that," I tell him, pointing to the last one. "You won by knockout."

"I did," he says, placing a hand on my hip. "You were there, two rows up."

"You were so good. I'd never seen anything like that before. So controlled, so careful."

"So not like me every other minute of my life, huh?"

Turning to see him, I cup his cheek in my hand. "That's what confused me so much. You were so talented, so cautious. Then outside the ring, you were the opposite."

"In the ring," he says, pulling his brows together, "someone cared. My trainer wouldn't let me get by with crap or acting like an idiot, but outside of the ring, no one cared."

"I cared."

"Maybe a part of me thought you shouldn't."

"Maybe...maybe I should've cared more."

"Oh, no," he says, sweeping an arm under my legs and picking me up in a bridal carry. "We're not going down that road."

He carries me with ease, a teasing grin on his face as we walk down a blank hallway and into a room at the end. There's a huge bed with silver-grey blankets and more pillows than any one person should ever need. Instead of laying me down easily, he tosses me into the center. I bounce as I hit, sending a few pillows toppling to the floor.

Everything smells like a mixture of his cologne and soap, a scent I could fall asleep and wake up to with no problem, a scent that reminds me of Cross. It's a scent that warms my heart.

His phone begins to ring and he pulls it from his pocket. After a quick glance, he holds the side until it stops and then tosses it on a dresser. A few seconds later, he's stretched out his long frame beside me.

"Was that important?" I ask as he rolls over on his side to look at me.

"Nope. Nothing is more important than you in my bed right now." One hand rests against my stomach, just below my breasts. He tenses his fingers and they press lightly into my skin. "I'm going to kiss you."

"It's about freaking time," I tease, my breath coming out in ragged heaps.

"I'm warning you, because once I start, I don't think I'll be able or willing to stop. It's a very slippery slope."

He's giving me an out. I do a quick internal inventory, looking for a reason to get up and walk out. There's nothing to warrant that, but there are a hundred reasons to reach over and wrap my hand along the back of his neck. I guide his head toward mine, and our lips touch.

Immediately, every muscle in my body relaxes, every care in the world dissolving under his touch. His lips move tenderly, but there's an undercurrent of possession that is undeniable. It's freeing to be in his hold, to know that it's him guiding me, protecting me, because if there's one thing about Cross I've never once felt unsure about, it's that he'd never let anything happen to me.

Being with other men was never like this. It was a mess of awkward touches, weird hang-ups, and a strange dance between the two of us that demonstrated how unsure, how wrong we were with one another.

I lie on his bed, his body hovering over me, his lips kissing every thought and feeling into mine. Our mouths move together, mine opening, his tongue slipping right past my lips, as if this is the way things are supposed to be.

Lifting the hem of his shirt, I drag it up and over his head. He breaks the kiss just long enough to let the fabric rush by then crashes his mouth to mine again. The silky strands of his hair glide through my fingers, the stubble on his cheeks roughing up my palms as I find every way possible to make contact with his body.

The muscles of his back flex as he moves off me, the lines in his sides stretching as he climbs off the bed and to his feet. He grins salaciously, panting as hard as I am.

"Why do you still have clothes on?" I ask, running my eyes down his tanned, taut skin.

"Why do you?"

I flinch for one brief moment, waiting for the fear I have of getting naked in front of another person to kick in. At that exact second, when I feel the niggle of embarrassment start to work its way in, Cross decides to smile—not the sexy one, the one that makes me want to take off my clothes because my libido is running wild, the other one...the shy one, the one that builds me up in a way that makes me want to be with him. They are two very different things.

Lifting my hips, I skim my shorts down my legs and kick them off. They sail through the air then he catches them with one hand.

"Best answer ever," he says, tossing them to the floor.

"I didn't think you'd mind, but you still have your pants on, and that's a problem."

His chest rumbles with a chuckle as he works his pants and boxers down his body one glorious inch at a time. "It's gonna be a big problem."

I see what he means.

He palms his cock in his hand, the tip of it almost reaching his belly button. It's swollen, ready for me, a bead of pre-cum sitting at the top as he squeezes the shaft.

"It's a good thing," I begin, twisting around on the bed so my feet aren't dangling off the end, "I'm a good problem solver."

The mattress dips with his weight, my skin burning as his swipes against it. He sits back on his knees at my feet and looks down at me. "Promise me one thing."

"What's that?" I ask, my heart pounding in my chest. The way he looks at me steals my breath, knots my stomach into a bundle of emotions I can't begin to unravel right now. It's as if he's not just seeing my body, or my anticipation of his next move. He's seeing me in a way that's bare and has nothing to do with a lack of fabric on my body.

"You'll stay with me for a while tonight."

"Why?"

He plants his hands on either side of me, leaning down just enough so his chest touches the peaks of my nipples. "Because holding you in my arms is my favorite part."

"Oh, Cross," I whisper, my heart melting on the spot.

Wrapping my legs around his waist, I press my lips to his. He nips at my bottom lip, tugging it between his teeth. I can't stop the moan that escapes my throat as I tilt my hips up to his.

His cock is at my opening, teasing me. It dips in, parting me with its girth before slipping back out again. He does this over and over, swiping at my swollen clit with each pass. His hands cup my breasts, kneading them in his coarse palms.

"I want to touch every inch of you," he whispers, sliding his hands up my chest and across my collarbone. "I need every piece of you to remember it belongs to me."

I whimper, trying to move as he slides into me.

"You've always been mine, Kallie girl, just like I've always been yours."

"Yes," I eek out. "Gah!"

He slides inside me, almost like he teased himself too long, like he couldn't wait a second longer to get inside me.

"I'm glad I didn't bother asking if you were ready," he says, closing his eyes as he sinks into me again. "So...damn...wet."

His Adam's apple bobs in his throat, a low guttural groan originating somewhere deep inside. I could almost get off just watching him enjoy me.

Dropping my knees wider, I roll my head to the side to allow him to bury his head in the crook of my neck. "You are so sexy," he whispers through gritted teeth.

"Go deeper," I pant, locking my heels around him. It puts me in a position I know he loves, an angle I know he can't resist.

"God," he groans, thrusting harder. "This feels so good."

"*So good.*"

He kisses me at every possible point, doing just as he promised—touching me in every place he can. He holds my shoulders, pinches a nipple, cups the side of my face, the outside of my thigh, making every possible connection he can between us.

Up, up, up I go, pulled into a swirling state of bliss between the friction of his cock and the sweet words he whispers in my ear. It's a heady mix, a complicated yet simple combination that is as irresistible as he is.

"Cross," I pant, my legs shaking with the impending climax. "I can't...you..."

My eyes squeeze shut with the force of the eruption that's starting to build in the bottom of my belly. Like a slow-burning fire, the heat rolls out to the tops of my thighs, into my chest before radiating into my toes and the top of my head.

"Cross!"

He pounds me into harder, his breath whispering over my skin with each push. He mutters something under his breath, but I can't make it out over my moans.

My body falls apart around him, my mind reeling with an influx of sensations. I feel him tense, his body shifting on top of me before he enters me hard and holds the position with the tip of his cock at the back of my pussy.

As he slips it back out and milks his orgasm, he flutters his eyes open. Instead of the lust I saw a few minutes ago, all I see now is something different, something soft...something I want to hold on to for a very long time.

He presses a soft kiss to my lips before pulling out and settling on the bed beside me. Pulling me into him, he nestles his face into my hair.

"I know you need to get up," he whispers, kissing a spot just above my ear. "But give me a few seconds first, okay?"

As I drift off to sleep, I keep reminding myself to get up and go to the bathroom, but I don't. This feels too good.

Chapter Eight

Kallie

"THAT GLOW SAYS EVERYTHING I NEED TO KNOW." NORA LAUGHS, SITTING down across from me at Carlson's.

"You don't know anything."

"Look me in the eye and tell me you haven't slept with Cross."

I grab a menu and hold it vertically between us in hopes of covering my blushed cheeks. It's not that there's anything to be embarrassed about, but it seems like it was so expected and I just caved.

How could I not?

I set myself up for this by going home from the golf course with him. It's absolutely what I wanted. Yet, now that I crawled out of his bed this morning after staying with him all night and got a few cups of caffeine in me, both the soreness between my legs and a hint of concern are becoming evident.

Nora laughs from the other side. "So I was right. Go on, say it."

The menu drops to the table. "Of course you're right, but that squeal"—I point a finger in her direction—"is not necessary."

"Oh, yes it is! This is almost as good as Justin and Britney getting back together. It's the natural progression of things, the way they're supposed to be. How can I not celebrate this?"

"You realize you're essentially celebrating my orgasms, right?"

"Plural?" She throws her head back. "Of course plural. Fucking asshole." While I laugh at her reaction, she takes moment to recover. "So, I'm assuming he's better than before."

"He was always my best. No matter what, he was the bar I measured everyone else up to, you know? But now...it's like that's not the same person."

Nora's eyes grow wide as she gulps for effect.

"He's patient now, almost...tender? He kisses me and—"

"No more." Nora's hands are an inch away from her ears, mock trying to block out my recant of last night.

"What?" I giggle.

"I have to see him every Friday night at Crave. I don't want to be looking at him thinking of the way he kisses you in private time and all that. It would be weird."

Veronica comes out of nowhere and leans against the table. She pretends not to have overheard us for a minute and then, like the small-town business owner she is, she gives in. "You and Cross are together now, huh?"

"No," I say as Nora says, "Yes."

Veronica laughs. "I remember the two of you dating. You were always so cute, this big tough guy and a sweet little girl."

"Yeah, well, we aren't together," I say, looking at Nora pointedly. "We're feeling things out, I guess."

"I'd say you felt it out." Nora tosses me a wink. "You're fighting the universe here, Kal. You and Cross are supposed to be together, having beautiful little babies. You can't fight it forever."

"I'd say she's right. I saw how he was looking at you yesterday," Veronica chimes in. "But I'm glad to hear you aren't together right now, not officially, anyway." She looks down at her notepad and takes an ink pen out of her pocket like she just didn't say that.

Avoiding Nora's eyes and swallowing past the lump in my throat, I try to look unaffected. There's zero doubt she's toying with me, seeing if I'll take the bait she just dropped. I wish I could ignore it and continue on with my order and my day, but I'm not strong enough for that. "Why do you say that?"

"No big deal," she says, giving me a fake laugh. "He was just through the drive-through a few minutes ago with that Megan, and we all know that girl's reputation."

"Cross was with Megan McCarter?" Nora asks. "Today?"

"Yeah. I mean, if he's not taken, how can you blame him? Men have needs," Veronica says.

"That's the biggest load of horse shit I've ever heard." Nora takes her menu and slams it into the condiments tray.

My hand visibly shakes as I try to get my menu lined up with hers. The plastic rattles as it swings back and forth, bouncing off the metal. Nora has sympathy and takes it from me then puts it away.

"I'm not with him," I say. It's aimed at Nora, my words directed across the table, but in reality, I'm saying it for me. "He is working with her at the gym."

"Look, I didn't mean to stir the pot..." Veronica looks at me with more smugness than I ever care to see on a person again.

"It's fine," I say, grabbing my purse. "Hey, Nora, can you take me to the library? I forgot I'm supposed to meet Ruby there in ten minutes."

"Sure."

Veronica watches us get to our feet, ignoring the death stare from Nora. "Want me to send someone over with delivery?"

"No, thanks though." With a final smile that I have to force, we walk out of the bakery. As soon as we're in Nora's car, I collapse into the soft leather seat. "I won't make a big deal about this."

"Don't, not until we know for sure what he was doing with her in his car."

My heart quivers in my chest. Biting down on my bottom lip, I buckle my seat belt. "Can you drive me to the gym?"

"You sure?"

"Absolutely."

CROSS

"GOOD WORKOUT TODAY, Cobble. See ya next week." I grab a towel and wipe my face off as my fourth appointment of the day gathers his things. Usually by this time of day, my ass is dragging, but not today. Today I have so much damn energy I could train an entire football team.

A few minutes will go by and I'll forget I spent the night with Kallie. I'll get caught up in teaching a jab or timing a round on the jump rope and she'll momentarily be gone from my mind.

Then I'll remember.

The image of her spread out on my bed, how soft her skin felt last night as I held her tight against me will come charging back, and I immediately have another spark in my step.

It doesn't seem real in many ways. This girl I thought I lost, the girl I knew I'd never stop thinking about is all of a sudden back and has fallen in step with me again.

Thank God.

The door chimes and I look up, expecting to see Cobble leaving. I do, but I also see Kallie walking in.

"Hey, babe..." My voice drifts off as I take in the look on her face. "What's wrong?"

"Um, nothing...not really."

"Then why do you look like you lost your puppy?"

She crosses her arms and then drops them. She crosses them again. "How has your day been?"

"Good. Getting better—I think," I add, still unsure as to what's causing her to fidget with the hem of her shirt. "How was yours?"

"Fine." She heads to the free weights and drags her finger over them. "Did you train Megan today?"

"Yup. Last session. She took it reasonably well."

She raises a brow. "Took what?"

"The fact that I'm not training her anymore," I explain. "We talked about that."

Her arms go across her middle again, this time firmly. She takes a deep breath, almost like she's counting to ten before blowing it out. It makes me take one too in an attempt to settle the little fire that starts to burn in my gut.

"So, the things you said to me last night, Cross, about how this changed things between us..."

"Yeah?"

"Exactly how did you mean that?"

"I meant it like if I see a man hitting on you, I'll break his face. Exact enough?" I'm partially teasing, but she there is no levity in her reaction. Instead, she bites the inside of her cheek.

"I was just in Carlson's with Nora. Veronica said you and Megan were in your truck—"

"Dammit!" I throw the towel at the basket near the wall. "Why is she starting trouble?"

"So you were with her today? Getting lunch?"

"No—well, yes, I took her to Carlson's and grabbed a sandwich because it was the easiest fucking way to get her out of my gym."

Her jaw clenches as she huffs. "Really, Cross?"

"Yes, fucking really," I say back. My head spins in disbelief. "She had Molly drop her off here and she didn't come to pick her up. Was that intentional? Probably. Did I want it to happen? Absolutely not."

"Explain to me again why she was in your truck getting lunch?"

Forcing a swallow, I try to be calm. "I needed to head to the school for a boxing class I was putting on for the sophomore class. Megan was still here. What was I supposed to do, Kal? Leave her on the sidewalk?"

"That's where whores usually do their work. She'd probably feel right at home."

"I know you didn't mean that, but dammit..." I laugh, leaning against the wall. "When did you get so mean?"

"When I feel messed with."

"I was just trying to move on with my day."

She turns her back to me, looking at the parking lot. "I need to move on with my day too."

There's a finality in her tone, an insinuation that she doesn't just mean her day. Panic shoots through my veins and I'm to her before she can even take a step. "Hey, don't get crazy." My hands go to her hips. I feel her body wanting to cave back into mine, but she doesn't let it. "I'll cancel my last session today if you'll go home with me."

"I..." She gulps. "I have things to do today."

"You do not."

"Yeah, I do."

"Then come over tonight."

"I'm helping Mom sort things she pulled out of the attic."

"Want me to help?" I ask, running my hands up and down her arms.

"No."

"Kallie," I groan, twisting her around. "Stop it."

"I think you're right. That's exactly what I'll do," she says, looking away from me. "At least for now."

"Oh, no. You're not doing this."

She snorts, flipping her gaze to mine. It's steeled, with an iciness to it I haven't seen since that night way back when. "What in the world am *I* doing, Cross?"

"You're not giving me the benefit of the doubt."

"No," she says with a simple shrug. "I'm not, because I've been through this with you before and I don't know why I thought it might be different this time. It's not."

"The hell it's not!" I roar, taking a step back. "I fucking love you, Kallie. I've waited on you to come back for years and you tell me it's not different? Maybe you're not different, but I fucking am!"

She blanches, stepping away from me too. The corners of her eyes wet as she takes another step back. "Maybe we both are."

My chest reverberates as I watch her take each step toward the door. With each inch of distance added between us, the air stagnates. A hollowness begins to form in my chest, and I know it will never fill this time.

"I love you," I tell her, my voice the softest this gym has ever heard.

"Do you? Do you really?"

"I had this big thing worked up to tell you but then I thought it would be better to show you, to make you believe it so much you didn't have to ask or wonder," I admit. "Guess that failed."

"I need time to think," she says, her voice seeping with unshed tears. "I forgot what it's like to date in a small town. It's so damn hard."

"It's not hard if you love someone. You take the truth for the truth and the shit for what it is—shit." My head nods as I pick up a clean towel. "I've never, ever cheated on you, Kal. Have I messed up? Sure. Should I have had Megan in my truck? Maybe not, but I've been alone for a long time and I forgot about dating in a small town too."

"I hate this," she says. "I hated the rumors then and I hate them now. Sitting there with Veronica acting like I don't know some big secret is awful, Cross, and I've spent a lot of years in that position, whether you were really cheating on me or not. It hurts. It eats away at you."

"And being accused over and over eats away at me too." I wipe my face with the towel, scrubbing a little harder than necessary. "I can't make you love me any more than you could change who I was back then. I changed because I wanted to, but I can't make you love me if you don't want to."

Her tears fall. I want to go to her and hold her and kiss them away, but I don't. I leave her to them. She's the one who wants to believe a stupid-as-shit reason enough to warrant them falling.

"See ya, Cross."

Before she can leave me again, I turn away from her and head into the back room.

Chapter Nine

Cross

"I TOLD YOU." WALKER KICKS BACK ON THE SOFA IN HIS LIVING ROOM WITH a look I'd like to knock off his face. While I'm ninety-five percent sure I could take him, the five percent isn't a risk I want to take tonight. "If they wanna go, let 'em go."

"This is such bullshit," I spit out, grabbing a beer off the coffee table. "I didn't do anything with Megan fucking McCarter. Not at any point in my life have I ever even touched her."

"I have." He grins. "But good choice not to—it's not worth it."

Every inch of my skin itches. It's uncomfortable, making me feel like I need to move, to run, to rip something to shreds.

"I'm caught between a rock and a hard place," I comment, more to the universe as a whole rather than to Walker specifically. "As pissed as I am right now, I know she's the girl I was meant to have. If I don't go after her, I'll lose her, but if I do, doesn't that make me look guilty? Or like a pussy? Or set the stage for a power vacuum in our relationship?"

"Yeah."

"Yeah? That's all you got?"

He turns off the football game and sighs. "Look, man, I'm not the best guy to go to for relationship advice...obviously."

"You're all I fucking have right now."

"Oh, so I was the last resort?"

"No, Lance was the last resort, but he's fucking some nurse he met on a dating app. You are whatever falls after that."

Walker laughs. "You're not as dumb as I thought you were."

"Here's the difference between my situation and yours," I tell him, bending forward and resting my elbows on my knees. "You don't care. I love her."

"Love is such an overrated thing, Cross. What's it really mean, anyway? How long does it last? Too many variables to make decisions based on love."

"Maybe I don't know what it is."

"Know what what is?" Peck asks as he rounds the corner. "By the way, the alternator is changed on the SUV in the shop."

"Do you knock?" Walker asks. "But good work on the SUV."

"No, and thanks. Now, what are we talking about? You look so serious."

I take a minute to fill Peck in, getting more irritated as I go. Before I'm finished, I see he's side-eyeing Walker.

"First of all, whatever that jackass has told you, ignore it—all of it," Peck says.

Walker shrugs. "He asked."

"Second of all, you need to head that way now and apologize."

"Me?" I bark. "I didn't do anything."

"And do you really want the rest of your life messed up because you were so worried about your ego that you wouldn't apologize?"

I snort. "It's not ego, it's principle."

"You can call it whatever you want, it's the same damn thing. Either you want to feel like you have some high and mighty set of principles, which we all know you don't, or you can get the girl—your pick. I'd pick her, because she's really hot."

Narrowing my eyes, I watch Peck laugh.

"Nah, not really because she's hot, because she's nice. She's sweet. She gave you a second chance," he throws in. When I don't react, he stands. "Do what you want, but don't come a-cryin' to me when she's at the bar with someone else."

"I'll kill them," I snarl.

"Then avoid prison and go apologize."

He tells Walker something about a transmission, but I can't hear it over the roar of blood over my ears. Walker turns the television back on, but I can't figure out who has the ball or what the score is because I'm mulling over Peck's advice.

The thought of going home and never having her in my kitchen, in my bed, on my sofa again twists me up so bad I don't even want to go. My phone sits in my pocket, and its failure to ring or buzz with a call or text from her hurts my heart.

I sit for a few more long minutes before I just can't sit any longer. "I'm gonna go," I tell Walker, standing. "May as well get a workout in since all I want to do is hit something."

Walker doesn't even look up. "Tell Kallie I said hi."

Chapter Ten

Kallie

THE BAGS CRUNCH AS THEY HIT THE COUNTERTOP, AND MOM STARTS sorting through the groceries. She doesn't even have to look at me to know something is wrong.

"Are you going to tell me or do you want me to guess?" she asks.

Curled up on a kitchen chair, my hair in a messy bun, I sniffle. "I don't want to talk about it."

"If you didn't want to talk about it, you would be in your bedroom or driving around a back road, not sitting in the kitchen."

Putting my feet on the floor, I straighten my shirt. I don't know how to talk about this with my mother. She loves Cross maybe as much as she loves me, and I'm not sure her opinion will be unbiased. Yet, she's my mom. I just need my mom.

"Did you date Daddy in a small town?" I ask.

Her hand stills in the air before she puts the jar of peanut butter in the cabinet. "We dated in Detroit, mostly. We were newlyweds when we moved down here. Why do you ask?"

"Nora and I went into Carlson's today and Veronica told me Cross had a woman in his car today, buying lunch."

"I see." She turns around and leans against the counter. "And that's where you were all night? At Cross's?"

"Yes."

She nods her head, her face twisted in thought. "Did you ask him if it was true?"

"Yes, and he admitted it."

"He did?"

"He said she wouldn't leave the gym and he had somewhere to be," I say, testing the words out loud for the first time since I calmed down.

"Do you believe that?"

"Megan is that way...but he shouldn't have had her in his truck."

She takes a deep breath before turning back to her groceries. "I'm a little bit in shock."

"Me too." I sigh. "I hate this, Mom. I hate the way everyone gossips and almost sets you up to be a joke."

"No one made a joke out of you." She spins on her heel. "She made a tramp out of herself, but that's the end of that."

A flood of warmth trickles through my body as I watch my mother watch me. Just knowing she has my back and is in my corner helps—a lot.

"I left here because he wouldn't grow up and I was sick of the gossip," I remind her. "Then my ex in Indiana cheated on me, and now I'm back and it's the same damn thing."

She sticks a gallon of milk in the fridge before pausing. "Maybe what you are seeing is how the world really works, Kal. I know you see pictures of perfect little houses and marriages and friendships, but it's not real. Life is a bitch."

"Don't I know it." I chuckle.

"The key to happy relationships is trust. It's the hardest thing to master, but if you can, it's the secret key that opens a world you can never know otherwise."

"But doesn't trusting someone leave you exposed? They can stick a knife in you and twist it." I wince, thinking that's exactly how I felt this afternoon.

"Yeah, it does. It leaves you wide open, but you can't get through that door without doing it. You just have to learn who you can trust and who you can't."

"So, basically, conquer Rome in a day? Got it." Wiping the fog off my glass of ice water, I think back to Cross's face. "He was mad at *me*, Mom. Can you believe that?"

"I'd be more worried if he wasn't."

"Why?"

A soft smile ghosts across her lips. "Maybe it insulted him that you would accuse him of something. Maybe he thought you knew him better than that."

"It still doesn't make this any easier."

"The world isn't black and white, Kal. It's a wonderful mixture of the two that has a lot of blurry lines, and if you care what people do and say, you have a long life ahead of you, honey." She sits across from me and folds her hands on the table. "Trust your gut, and remember what led you back to him in the first place."

She gets up, kisses me on the head, and walks down the hallway. Her words, however, stay behind.

KALLIE

THE DOG across the street barks, breaking the late-night silence. My car starts up, the lights shining into the living room as I back down the driveway.

My stomach is all twisted, an ulcer beginning to form somewhere in the pit of my bowels. No matter what I do—read, sing, or create—I can't stop thinking about Cross.

Walking five miles just got me a sore hamstring, doing the dishes left me with a sliced finger, and I've sung the hell out of my favorite playlist on my phone. Through it all, I've thought about him.

It's those nights in Indiana all over again. It's the emptiness in my soul, the craving to love and be loved...by him, only him. It's only ever been him.

As I sort through my memories, I see his face from earlier when he was telling me nothing happened. Even though I didn't want to at first, I believe him. Something in my gut tells me to, says to at least hear him out without being pissed off to start.

The car glides down the street, heading into town, the streetlights getting more frequent as I go. The clock reads almost one in the morning, and my body shivers against the cool summer night.

A set of headlights comes my way and the driver clicks them down, turning off the brights. As we pass, I glance over my shoulder and see Cross's face.

My heart leaps in my chest as his tail lights come on in the rear view, his tires squealing as he rips the truck around. Before I know what's happening, he's behind me, traveling in the same direction.

The high school is a block ahead and I turn my turn signal on in hopes he'll slow down a bit and get off my ass. My throat is constricted as I pull in, my blood pounding in my veins as I stop the car. He's out of his truck and around the front before I ever even get the door open. He does the honors for me.

His hair is wild, his shirt soaked with sweat. "You okay?"

My feet on the asphalt, I stand and breathe him in. "I was coming to look for you."

"I'm sorry."

"Nope," I say, shaking my head.

"Dammit, Kal—"

I take the words out of his mouth with my own, pressing my lips against his so quickly it shocks him. My hands go to his damp hair, urging him to kiss me harder. I need this. I need...him.

He finally pulls away, dragging in a lungful of air. "Kallie?"

"*I* am sorry," I say, resting my forehead on his.

"It was me that had her in my truck."

"And it was my insecurities that let that matter. I mean, yeah, don't do it again"—I laugh—"but you didn't exactly do something wrong."

"It was wrong if it makes you feel anything but great." He wraps me up in his arms, pulling me to his chest. "I was at the gym, working out, and all I could see was you standing there mad at me."

"I was sitting on my bed and kept thinking about how last night I was in yours, how many nights I wished to be there, and how tonight I wasn't because I was mad, like a child."

He squeezes me tighter. "I was also wrong when I said I couldn't make you love me. I damn sure am going to try for the rest of my life."

My hand stills on his back, his heartbeat picking up against my cheek. "Cross?"

"Yes, I want to marry you," he whispers under the lights of the parking lot. "But I want to ask your mother before I ask you, and I want to find the perfect ring and the perfect spot first. You deserve that."

"I don't need any of that," I say, choking back a sob. I'm so desperate for him, my chest coming undone and overflowing. "I just need you. I'm never letting you go again."

"Damn right you're not." His body shakes with his chuckle. "Do you want to ride with me back to my house or have me follow you?"

Grinning through my tears, I pull away and look into his spectacular green eyes. "Follow me."

"The view of your behind is one of my favorites."

I swat at his arm, but he pulls me in for a quick kiss instead.

"Hey, Cross?"

"Yeah?"

I grab his hand and lace our fingers together. "I love you."

"I love you too."

Epilogue

Cross

A few weeks later

"WHY DOES golf always end up with fucking? Not that I'm complaining." He grins, looking at me over his shoulder.

The streetlights create shadows in the cab of his truck as we make our way back to his house after a night of fun. We watched a chick flick that he hated, ate seafood that I hated, then capped it off with four holes of putt-putt before we turned our sticks in and parked on the first desolate back road we found so we could have sex.

"I guess you like the way I handle balls," I suggest, making him laugh. "Really? I don't know. It's weird though."

"I guess it's not that different from anything else we do. Dinner?"

"Fucking."

"Laundry?"

"Oh, I love when we do it on spin cycle," I note.

"Painting the back porch?"

"Yeah, but sex in public isn't my thing. You caught me on a bad day." I giggle.

"First of all, it's not public. Second, I was thinking it was a really, really good day."

Grinning, I blow out a breath and settle into the seat.

Being in Linton has changed everything for me—finding Cross again, reconnecting with my mother, finding a career in a firm that's a lot quieter, but more fulfilling.

When I was younger, all I wanted was to get out of my hometown. Everything here was boring, predictable, without opportunities to do anything great. It's not without its faults, that's for sure. I still deal with the whispers of women who want Cross, still hear murmurings at the soda fountain at Goodman's while I get my daily drink, but now that I'm older and maybe a little wiser, none of that matters as much.

"Crave is up ahead. Want to go in for a while?" Cross asks. "Machlan wanted to talk to me about expanding his business. I thought it might be a good investment."

"Sure, but do you think you can talk to him on a Friday night? Crave is always so busy."

"If not, at least we'll be entertained. I'm sure something is going on in there."

He pulls the truck over to the side of the street. We climb out and he grabs my hand like he always does.

"Hey," I whisper, nudging him. "Is that girl hitting Walker's truck with a bat?"

Cross looks to the left as we keep walking. "Probably someone he fucked and chucked."

"I hate, hate, hate that terminology," I mutter.

"I don't know how else to describe it."

"As long as you don't subscribe to that theory, I guess I'll survive." I sigh, squeezing his hand.

He stops and stands in front of me. His green eyes look like slices of pure jade in the hazy streetlights. "I subscribe to one theory, and one theory only."

"What's that?"

"To keep you wanting to be my girl."

"Always."

WANT to read more of the Gibson Boys? Walker's story, CRANK, is available now on Amazon and in Kindle Unlimited. Check it out!

Books by Adriana Locke

The Exception Series

The Exception

The Connection, a novella

The Perception

The Exception Series Box Set

The Landry Family Series

Sway

Swing

Switch

Swear

Swink

The Gibson Boys Series

Crank

Cross

Craft—coming January 2018

Standalone Novels

Sacrifice

Wherever It Leads

Written in the Scars

Battle of the Sexes

Lucky Number Eleven

Twelve Days Until Sunday—fall 2018

Don't miss a release! Sign up for my Amazon Live Alert.

About the Author

USA Today Bestselling author Adriana Locke lives and breathes books. After years of slightly obsessive relationships with the flawed bad boys created by other authors, Adriana created her own.

She resides in the Midwest with her husband, sons, two dogs, two cats, and a bird. She spends a large amount of time playing with her kids, drinking coffee, and cooking. You can find her outside if the weather's nice and there's always a piece of candy in her pocket.

Besides cinnamon gummy bears, boxing, and random quotes, her next favorite thing is chatting with readers. She'd love to hear from you!

www.adrianalocke.com

Facebook - www.facebook.com/authoradrianalocke
Twitter - www.twitter.com/authoralocke
Instagram - www.instagram.com/authoradrianalocke

Subscribe to the exclusive Locke List:
https://app.mailerlite.com/webforms/landing/n8q6t9